JOURNEY TO THE
END OF THE NIGHT

TO
ELISABETH CRAIG

Travel is a good thing; it stimulates the imagination. Everything else is a snare and a delusion. Our own journey is entirely imaginative. Therein lies its strength.

It leads from life to death. Men, beasts, cities, everything in it is imaginary. It's a novel, only a made-up story. The dictionary says so and it's never wrong.

Besides, every one can go and do likewise. Shut your eyes, that's all that is necessary.

There you have life seen from the other side.

Notre vie est un voyage
Dans l'Hiver et dans la Nuit,
Nous cherchons notre passage
Dans le Ciel où rien ne luit.

(Chanson des Gardes Suisses 1793)

JOURNEY TO THE
END OF THE NIGHT

BY

LOUIS-FERDINAND CELINE

Translated from the French by
JOHN H. P. MARKS

A NEW DIRECTIONS BOOK

Voyage au Bout de la Nuit first published in France November, 1932
First published in 1960 as New Directions Paperbook No. 84

Copyright 1934 by Louis-Ferdinand Céline
Library of Congress Catalog Card Number: 49-8925
(ISBN:0-8112-0019-1)

Manufactured in the United States of America

Published in Canada by George J. McLeod Ltd., Toronto

New Directions Books are published for James Laughlin
by New Directions Publishing Corporation,
80 Eighth Avenue, New York 10011

FIFTEENTH PRINTING

IT ALL BEGAN JUST LIKE THAT. I HADN'T SAID ANYTHING. I HADN'T said a word. It was Arthur Ganate who started me off. Arthur, who was studying medicine the same as me, a pal of mine. What happened was that we met on the Place Clichy. After lunch. He seemed to want to talk to me. So I listened. "Don't let's stay out here," he said. "Let's go inside." So I went along in with him. "It's grim," he said, "out here on the *terrasse*. Come this way." We noticed that there was nobody in the streets because of the heat; no traffic, nothing. And when it's very cold there's nobody about, either; why, I even remember that it was he who said to me, speaking about this, "Everybody in Paris seems to be busy but actually they only walk about all day, and the proof of it is that when the weather's bad, when it's too cold or too hot, they disappear; they're all inside cafés, drinking white coffee or bocks. Isn't that so? They talk of this being an age of rush and hurry. How d' you make that out? Everything's changing, they say. But it isn't true. Nothing has really changed. They just go on being impressed by themselves and that's all. Which isn't new, either. A few words have changed—but not many of them, even. Two or three little ones here and there . . ." And very proud at having come to these important conclusions, we sat back, feeling pleased with life, and watched the ladies of the café.

Afterwards, conversation turned on President Poincaré, who that morning was going to open a show of lapdogs, and from him to *Le Temps*, where we'd read about it. "Now there's a really great paper for you!" said Arthur, trying to get a rise out of me. "There isn't another paper like it for defending the interests of the French race."

"And I suppose the French race needs it, seeing that it doesn't exist!" said I promptly, to show that I knew what I was talking about.

"But of course it exists! And a very splendid one it is too!" he insisted. "It's the finest race in the world, and don't you believe any fool who tells you it isn't!" He had started in to harangue me for all he was worth. I held my ground, of course.

"That's not true! What you call the race is only that great heap of worm-eaten sods like me, bleary, shivering and lousy, who, coming defeated from the four corners of the earth, have ended up here, escaping from hunger, illness, pestilence and cold. They couldn't go further because of the sea. That's your France and those are your Frenchmen."

"Bardamu," he said to me then, gravely and a little sadly, "our fathers were as good as us; you mustn't speak of them in this way. . . ."

"You're right, Arthur, you're right there. Venomous yet docile, outraged, robbed, without guts and without spirit, they were as good as us all right. You certainly said it! Nothing really changes. Habits, ideas, opinions, we change them not at all, or if we do, we change them so late that it's no longer worth while. We are born loyal and we die of it. Soldiers for nothing, heroes to all the world, monkeys with a gift of speech, a gift which brings us suffering, we are its minions. We belong to suffering; when we misbehave, it tightens its hold on us. We have its fingers always round our throats, which makes it difficult to talk; you have to be careful, if you want to be able to eat. . . . The merest slip and you're strangled. . . . Life's not worth living. . . ."

"But there is still love, Bardamu!"

"Love, Arthur, is a poodle's chance of attaining the infinite, and personally I have my pride," I answered him.

"Talk about yourself, you're nothing but an anarchist!" Always the little devil, you see, and just about as advanced as possible.

"You said it, fathead; I *am* an anarchist! And to prove it, there's a sort of social prayer for vengeance I've written. You can tell me this minute what you think of it. 'Wings of Gold' it's called." And I recited it to him:

"A God who counts the minutes and the pence, a desperate God, sensual and grunting like a pig. A pig with wings of gold

which tumbles through the world, with exposed belly waiting for caresses, lo, 'tis he, behold our master! Embrace, embrace!"

"That little piece of yours doesn't make sense in actual life. Personally, I'm for the established order of things and I'm not fond of politics. Moreover, if the day should come when my country needs me, I certainly shan't hang back; it will find me ready to lay down my life for it. So there." That was his answer to me.

At that very moment War was drawing near to us without our realizing it, and I wasn't at all in a sensible mood. Our short but exciting argument had taken it out of me. On top of that too, I was a bit put out because the waiter had seemed to think I had under-tipped him. Anyway, I made it up with Arthur, so as to put a stop to all this nonsense, once and for all. We agreed about almost everything, really.

"You're right," I said, wishing to be conciliatory. "You're quite right of course, really. But after all, we *are* all in the same boat, we are all galley slaves together, rowing like the devil—you certainly can't deny that. Sitting on nails to it, too. And what do we get out of it? Not a thing. A big stick across our backs, that's all, and a great deal of misery, and a hell of a lot of stinking lies poured into our ears! 'A fellow must work,' is what they say. It's the lousiest part of the whole business, this work of theirs. You're stuck down in the hold, puffing and panting, all of a muck-sweat and stinking like polecats. . . . And up on the bridge, not giving a damn, the masters of the ship are enjoying God's fresh air with lovely pink ladies drenched in perfume sitting on their knees. They have you up on deck. Then they put on their top-hats and let fly at you as follows:

" 'See here, you set of sods!' they say. 'War's declared. You're going to board the bastards on *Country Number* 2 yonder and you're going to smash them to bits! Now get on with it. There's all the stuff you'll need aboard. All together now. Let's have it — as loud as you can make it: "God save *Country Number 1!*" You've got to make them hear you a long way off. There's a medal and a coughdrop for the man who shouts the loudest! God in Heaven! And if there's any of you who don't want to die at sea, of course, you can go and die on land, where it takes even less time than it does here.' "

"You've just about hit it," agreed Arthur, who'd certainly become very easy to convince.

Whereupon, damn me if a regiment of soldiers didn't come marching past the café where we were sitting, with the colonel in front on his horse and all, looking simply fine and as smart as you make them. I gave just one great leap of enthusiasm.

"I'll go and find out if that's what it's like!" I cried to Arthur, and off I went to join up, as fast as my legs would carry me.

"Don't be such a bloody fool, Ferdinand!" yelled Arthur after me, annoyed, I suppose by the effect my heroic gesture was having on the onlookers.

I was rather sick that that should be the attitude he took toward it, but that didn't stop me. I was striding along in step. "Here I am and I'll see it through," I said to myself.

"We'll see, you mutt, you!" I managed to get in at him, before we turned the corner, with the regiment marching along behind the colonel and the band. That's exactly, word for word, how it happened.

We went on marching for a long time. There were streets then there were still more streets, with civilians and their wives cheering us as we passed, and throwing flowers to us from the café tables, by the stations and from the steps of crowded churches. What a lot of patriots there were! And then, after a bit, there began to be fewer patriots. . . . Rain came down, and there were fewer and fewer of them, and then finally no one cheered at all, not another cheer along the road.

Were we all by ourselves then? A column of men, in fours behind each other? The music stopped. Then I said to myself, as I saw how things were going, "It's not such fun, after all. I doubt if it's worth it." And I was going to go back. But it was too late! They'd shut the gate behind us, quietly; the civilians had. We were caught, like rats in a trap.

ONCE ONE'S IN IT, ONE'S IN IT UP TO THE NECK. THEY PUT US ON horseback and then, after two months of that, they put us back on foot. Perhaps because it cost too much. Anyway, one morning the colonel was looking for his horse; his orderly had gone off with it, no one knew where, somewhere no doubt where bullets sang less merrily than in the middle of the road. Because that's exactly where we finished up, the colonel and I, plumb in the middle of the road, with me holding the forms on which he wrote out orders.

Far away up the road, as far as you could see, there were two black dots, in the middle of it, like us — only they were two Germans, very busy shooting. They'd been doing that for a good quarter of an hour.

The colonel perhaps knew why those two fellows were firing and the Germans maybe knew it too; but as for me, quite frankly, I didn't at all. However far back I remembered, the Germans had nothing against me. I had always been quite friendly and polite to them. I knew the Germans a bit, I'd even been to school with them as a kid, near Hanover. I'd talked their language. They were then a lot of noisy little idiots, with the pale and furtive eyes of wolves; we all used to go and neck the girls in the woods near by, where we'd also shoot with bows or with the little pistols you could get for four marks. We used to drink sweet beer. But that was one thing and now letting fly at each other, without even coming over to talk first, and right in the middle of the road, was another, — not the same thing at all. It was altogether too damn different.

The war, in fact, was everything that one didn't understand. It couldn't go on.

Had something extraordinary then come over these people? Something which I didn't feel at all? I must have failed to notice it.

At any rate, my feelings towards them had not changed. In spite of everything, I felt I wanted to understand their brutal behaviour; but even more I wanted, I terribly wanted, to go away, it all suddenly seemed so much the result of a tremendous mistake.

"In this sort of business there's nothing for it; the only thing to do is to shove out of it." That's what I said to myself. After all. . . .

Over our heads, an inch or half an inch away, one after the other those long tentative steel strings which bullets make when they want to kill you came twanging in the warm air of summer.

Never have I felt so futile as among all those bullets in that sunshine. A vast, a universal ramp.

I wasn't more than twenty at the time. In the distance were deserted farmhouses and open and empty churches, as if the peasants every one of them had left these hamlets for the day, to go to some gathering at the other end of the canton and had left in our keeping all they possessed, — their countryside, their carts with upturned shafts, their fields and patches, the road, the trees and even the cows, a dog on its chain, everything. So that we should not be disturbed and could do what we wanted while they were away. It seemed a kindly thought on their part. "All the same," said I to myself, "if only they hadn't gone off, if only there was still somebody about around here, we surely shouldn't be behaving so badly — so disgracefully! We wouldn't have dared with them here. Only there's no one to see us. We're by ourselves like newly married folk doing dirty things when every one's left."

And I thought too (behind a tree) that I should love to have the biggest Jingo of the lot here with me, to explain what *he* would do when a bullet hit him slap in the pan.

These Germans, squatting on the road, sniping away so obstinately, weren't shooting well but they seemed to have ammunition enough and to spare, stacks of it obviously. No, the war wasn't by any means over. Our colonel, I must say, was showing amazing coolness. He walked about, right in the middle of the road, up and down in the thick of these bullets, just as carelessly as if he were waiting for a friend on a station platform; a little impatiently, that's all.

As a matter of fact, I may as well admit that I've never liked the country, anyway; I've always found it depressing, with all its endless puddles and its houses where nobody's ever in and its roads leading nowhere. But with a war on as well, it's intolerable. The wind had come up fiercely from both sides of the embankment, the gusts in the poplar leaves mingling with the rustle that was directed against us from up the road. They were missing us all the time, these unknown soldiers of ours, yet they put a thousand deaths round about us so close that they were almost a garment. I didn't dare move.

What a monster that colonel must be, though. I was sure that, like a dog, he had no idea of death. It struck me at the same time that there must be lots like him, as gallant as he, in our army, and as many again, no doubt, on the opposite side. One wondered how many. A million — or two? Several millions in all, perhaps. From that moment, my terror became panic. With creatures like that about the place, this hellish idiocy might go on indefinitely. . . . Why should they stop? Never had I felt the way of men and things to be so implacable.

Could it be that I was the only coward on earth, I wondered. The thought was terrifying. Lost in the midst of two million madmen, all of them heroes, at large and armed to the teeth! With or without helmets, without horses, on motor bicycles, screeching, in cars, whistling, sniping, plotting, flying, kneeling, digging, taking cover, wheeling, detonating, shut in on earth as in an asylum cell; intending to wreck everything in it, Germany, France, the whole world, every breathing thing; destroying, more ferocious than a pack of mad dogs and adoring their own madness (which no dog does), a hundred, a thousand times fiercer than a thousand dogs and so infinitely more vicious! What a mess we were in! Clearly it seemed to me that I had embarked on a crusade that was nothing short of an apocalypse.

One is as innocent of Horror as one is of sex. How could I possibly have guessed this horror when I left the Place Clichy? Who could have foreseen, before getting really into the war, what was inside the foul and idle, heroic soul of man? There I was, caught up into a general rush towards murder for all, towards fire. . . . It was a thing that had come up from the depths and here it was on top of us.

All this while the colonel never faltered; I watched him receive little messages from the general, there on the embankment, where he straightway tore them up after reading them without haste, amid the bullets. Did none of them contain the order to put an immediate stop to this frightfulness? Was he not being told by H.Q. that there was some misunderstanding, some ghastly mistake? That the cards had been wrongly dealt and something was wrong? That we were meant to have engaged on manœuvres, for fun, and not in this business of killing? Not at all.

"Carry on, Colonel! Go right ahead as you are." That must be what General Des Entrayes, our Chief of Division, was telling him in these messages which were brought to him every five minutes by a runner, who each time looked greener and more liverish. He could have been my brother in fear, that boy; but there wasn't the time to fraternize, either.

What, was there nothing wrong then? This shooting at each other like this without a word, — it was all O.K. It was one of the things you can do without getting hauled over the coals good and proper. It was actually accepted, it was probably encouraged by decent folk, like drawing lots in conscription or getting engaged or beagling! There was nothing for it. I had suddenly discovered, all at once, what the war was, the whole war. I'd lost my innocence. You need to be pretty well alone with it face to face, as I was then, to see the filthy thing properly, in the round. They'd touched off the war between us and the other side, and now it was flaring! Like the current between the two carbons in an arc lamp. And it wasn't going to be put out soon, either. We would all be going through it, the colonel along with the rest, for all his fine airs, and his guts would look the same as mine when the current from opposite flashed through his middle.

There are a lot of ways of being condemned to death. What wouldn't I have given at that moment to be in gaol instead of where I was! If only, fool that I was, if only I'd gone and stolen something, looking ahead when it was still so easy, when there was still time. One thinks of nothing! You come out of gaol alive, but not out of a war. That's a fact and everything else hot air.

If only I'd still had the time, but I hadn't it any longer! There was nothing left to steal. How cosy it would be in a dear little prison cell, I told myself, where no bullets ever came. No bullets, ever. I knew of one all ready and warm, facing the sun. In my mind I could see it, the Saint-Germain it was actually, close to the woods; I knew it well; I used to pass by it often at one time. How one changes! I was a kid in those days and the prison used to frighten me. I didn't yet know what men were like. I shall never again believe what they say or what they think. It is of men, and of them only, that one should always be frightened.

How long would the delirium of these monsters need to last for them to stop in the end, exhausted? How long could a fit of frenzy like this go on? A few months? A few years? Perhaps until every one was dead, every one of these madmen. To the very last of all? Well, since things were taking this desperate turn, I decided to risk everything at one throw, to try the final, the supreme move, and on my own, alone, to try and stop the war! My small section of it, at any rate.

The colonel was walking about, two yards away. I would go and speak to him. I'd never done that before. Now was the time to dare to do it, though. Where we were, there was hardly anything further to lose. "What do you want?" I could see him saying it, very surprised, of course, by my cheek in interrupting him. Then I should explain it all to him as I saw it. We'd see what his views on the matter were. The all-important thing in life is to say what's in your mind. And two heads would be better than one.

I was about to take this decisive step when, at that very moment, hurrying along towards us came a dismounted cavalryman (as they were called in those days), limping, hobbling, with his upturned helmet in his hand like a blind beggar, and properly spattered with mud, his face even greener than the company runner's. He was muttering as if sick at heart or as if he were suffering the pains of hell, and was trying somehow to struggle up out of a grave. So here was a ghost who disliked the bullets as much as I did, eh? Perhaps he could foresee them, like I could.

"What's up?" The colonel savagely stopped him short, glaring coldly at this apparition. To see this deplorable trooper in such slovenly undress and shuddering with excitement thoroughly irritated the colonel. Fear was not to the colonel's liking in the least, one could see that. And then above all, that helmet held in his hand like a felt hat, when ours was a front-line regiment, a regiment on the attack, — that was the last straw. He looked as if he were taking off his hat to the war, this cavalryman, as he walked into it on foot.

Under this stare of disapproval, our uncertain messenger came to attention, with his little fingers along the seams of his trousers, which is the proper thing to do in such cases. He stood there on the road, stiff and swaying, with the sweat running down his throat, and his jaws were working so hard that he uttered little grunting cries like a puppy dreaming. You couldn't make out whether he wanted to say something to us or whether he was crying.

The Germans squatting at the end of the road had just changed weapons. They were now carrying on their pranks with a machine gun; it crackled like a lot of big boxes of matches, and infuriated bullets swarmed all around us, pricking the air like wasps.

All the same the man managed at last to get out something intelligible.

"Quartermaster Sergeant Barousse has been killed, sir," he said in one gasp.

"Well?"

"He was killed on his way to meet the bread waggon on the Étrapes road, sir."

"Well?"

"He's been blown up by a shell."

"Well, good God, and what then?"

"Well, that's what it is, sir."

"Is that all?"

"Yes sir, that's all, sir."

"And what about the bread?" asked the colonel.

That was the end of the conversation, because I distinctly remember that he had time to say, "And what about the bread?" Then that was all. After that there was only a flash and then the noise that came with it. But it was the sort of noise that you never would believe existed. My eyes, ears, nose and mouth were so full of it suddenly that I really believed it was all over and that I had been turned into fire and noise myself.

But no, after a while the fire had gone and the noise stayed a long time in my head, and then my arms and legs were shaking as if some one from behind me were waggling them. They seemed to be leaving me but in the end they stayed where they were. In the smoke which pricked my eyes for a long time the smell of powder and sulphur was strong enough to kill all the bugs and fleas in the whole world.

Directly after that, I thought of Quartermaster Sergeant Barousse who the other fellow had told us had been blown up. That was good news. So much the better, I thought to myself. "That's rid the regiment of one more bastard." He'd tried to have me up for a tin of jam. "Every one has his own war to wage," I said to myself. Looked at in some ways, there seemed at times to be some point in the war. I certainly knew of three or four other swine in our company whom I'd have been very willing to help find a shell, like Barousse had.

As for the colonel, I had nothing against him. Nevertheless, he was dead too. I couldn't see where he was at first. He'd been flung onto the embankment on his side and the explosion had thrown him into the arms of the despatch bearer, who was dead also. They were in each other's arms and would continue the embrace for ever, but the cavalryman hadn't his head any more, only his neck open at the top with blood bubbling in it like stew in a pot. The colonel's stomach was slit open and he was making an ugly face about that. It must have been painful when that happened. So much the worse for him. If he'd gone away when the firing began, he wouldn't have had it.

All this heap of flesh was bleeding like the deuce. Shells were still bursting to right and left of the picture.

I wasn't slow to leave the place after that. I was delighted to have such a good excuse to clear out. In fact, I sang a bit as I walked, tottering slightly as one does after a hard afternoon's rowing when one's legs are behaving rather funnily. "Just one shell; it doesn't take long for just one shell to do the trick," I told myself. "Well, I'm damned!" I kept repeating all the time. "Well, I'm damned!"

There was nobody left at the end of the road. The Germans had gone away. But just that once had taught me pretty quick to keep to the cover of the trees in future. I was in a hurry to get back to the lines to find out whether any others in our lot had been killed while out reconnoitering. Besides, I went on, there must be some pretty smart ways of getting yourself taken prisoner! . . . Here and there wisps of bitter smoke were wreathed around the earth clods. "Perhaps they're all dead by now." I wondered whether they were. "As they're such obstinate fools, that would be the best and most practical way out, that they should all have been killed without delay. . . . Then we should be through with it at once. . . . We'd go off home. We'd go through the Place Clichy again maybe, in triumph. . . . The two or three of us who had survived . . . That's what I hoped. Just a few good fine-looking fellows swinging along with the general in front. All the others would have been killed. Like the colonel — like Barousse, like Vanaille (another sod) and all the rest. . . . They'd cover us with decorations and flowers and we'd march through the Arc de Triomphe. We'd walk into a restaurant and they'd serve us free. We'd never have to pay for anything any more, never again. 'We're your heroes,' we'd say, when the bill came, 'the saviours of our country!' And that would be enough. Little French flags would do for payment. Why, the girl at the cash desk would refuse to take money from heroes; she'd even make us a present of some and kiss us as we went past her till. Life would be worth living."

As I was escaping, I noticed that my arm was bleeding, but only slightly, from a scratch, not a decent wound. It wouldn't be enough; I should have to carry on.

It began to rain again and the Flemish fields seemed to dribble dirty water. For a long time I still hadn't met anybody, only the wind and a little later on the sun. From time to time, I couldn't think from where, a bullet would come after me, gaily through the sunny air, looking for me in all this emptiness, determined to kill me. Why? Never again, even if I lived to be a hundred, would I go for a walk in the country. That I promised myself.

As I walked along, I remembered the ceremony that had taken place the day before. It had been in a meadow on the side of a hill; the colonel in his loud voice had harangued the regiment: "Up, boys, and at 'em! And long live France!"

If you've no imagination, dying doesn't matter much; if you have, it's too much. That's what I think. Never had I understood so many things at once.

The colonel never had had any imagination. All his bad luck was due to that, and ours especially. Was I then the only one in our regiment to have any idea what death meant? I preferred my own taste in death, a leisurely one. . . . To come in twenty years' time, or thirty or maybe longer. Better than the one they planned for me to have right away, swallowing a full mouthful of Flanders mud, more than a mouthful, my face split from ear to ear in one flash. One has surely the right to have an opinion about one's own death. But where could I go? Straight ahead? With my back to the enemy? If the M.P.'s were to catch me at a loose end like that, I should be in for a good time. I should be given a rough-and-ready trial that very evening in a secondary-school classroom. There were plenty of empty ones wherever we went. They would have played at justice with me as one does when the master is out of the room. The N.C.O.'s would be seated on the dais, while I stood handcuffed in front of the little desks. At dawn I should have been shot; a dozen rounds plus one. What then?

I thought again of the colonel and how fine the fellow looked, with his cuirass and his helmet and his moustaches. Put him on at a music hall, walking about among the bullets and shells as I had seen him, and the turn would have filled the Alhambra those days. He'd have wiped the floor with Fragson herself, though at the time I'm speaking of she was tremendously popular. That's what I was thinking. Down, boys, and leave 'em alone, I thought.

After hours and hours of carefully sneaking forward, at last I caught sight of our men by a group of farmhouses. It was one of our advance posts, part of a squadron billeted thereabouts. Not one of them had been killed, they told me. Everybody alive and kicking. But it was I who had the big piece of news. "The colonel's dead!" I yelled to them, as soon as I was within distance.

"There's no shortage of colonels!" Lance Corporal Pistil, who was on duty, and also on fatigue, snapped back at me.

"And while waiting for the colonel to be replaced, I'll tell you what you can do, me lad. You get on with fetching the grub, together with Empouille and Kerdoncuff here. There's a couple of sacks for each of you, and it's behind the church over there that you'll find it. . . . And you can see to it you don't get handed a bag of bloody bones, as you did yesterday. And I'll thank you to get a move on with it and not come bleedin' in here after night-fall, you stiffs. . . ."

So off we went again, all three of us.

"I sha'n't ever tell them anything in future," I said to myself. I was annoyed. There was clearly no point in telling their sort about such a thing as I'd just seen; one only got bawled at for one's pains. It was already too long past to be of any interest. And when you think that a week before I would have had four columns in the papers, along with my photograph, for announce-ing the death of a colonel like that. Just a brainless lot of sods, that's all!

It was in a cherry orchard dried up by the August sun that the meat for the whole regiment was being doled out. On sacks and on tent canvas spread out on the ground and on the grass itself were pounds and pounds of tripe and whitish-yellow fat and whole disembowelled sheep in a havoc of entrails which oozed curious little streams into the surrounding grass. The carcass of an ox had been cut in two and hung in a tree. The four butchers of the regiment were still clambering around it, swear-ing and tugging at portions of its flesh. There was any amount of brawling between sections over morsels of rich meat, and kidneys in particular, amid clouds of those flies which are only seen at such moments and are as lusty and clamorous as sparrows.

And then, too, there was blood everywhere, softly flowing through the grass in search of sloping ground. The last pig was being killed near by. Four men and one of the butchers were already squabbling over some of the bits to come.

"Damn your eyes, it was you pinched the sirloin yester-day. . . ."

I had time to glance twice at this discussion of food values, as I leant against a tree, and then I had to give way to an over-whelming desire to vomit — more than a little, until I fainted.

Well, they took me back to camp on a stretcher, but not with-out making good use of the opportunity to rummage through my two rubber-lined meat sacks.

I awoke into another of Pistil's cursing fits. The war was still in full swing.

EVERYTHING COMES TO YOU IF YOU WAIT; I WAS MADE LANCE corporal in my turn, towards the end of that same August. I often used to be sent with five men on liaison under General Des Entrayes. This "brass hat" was a slim and silent little man who didn't strike one at first as either bloodthirsty or heroic. Still, one couldn't be too sure. . . . He seemed to prefer his own comfort to anything else. He was caring about comfort the whole time, and although we had been busy retreating for more than a month, he'd curse right and left if his orderly hadn't found him a clean bed and an up-to-date kitchen every time he halted for the night.

This worry about his well-being was a very great nuisance to our brigade major. The general's domestic fussiness aggravated him. Especially because he himself was sallow, dreadfully gastritic, and constipated; his own food didn't interest him a bit. Nevertheless, he had to take his boiled eggs at the general's table and listen the while to his complaints. Either one's a military man or one isn't. But I can't say I was ever very sorry for him, because as an officer he was a first-rate swine. For instance, when we had dragged ourselves and our fodder along uphill roads all day, we would eventually pull up somewhere or other so that the general could get to bed. We'd search for a quiet sheltered village, where there were no troops billeted, and we'd find it for him, and if the men were there, they moved on quickly enough; we merely bundled them out and they slept in the open, even if they had already made up their straw.

The village was commandeered for the General Staff alone, with its horses, canteens and baggage and this damned major. This sod's name was Pinçon, Major Pinçon. I hope he's rotting by now — and not too comfortably, either. But at the time I'm speaking of, he was still bloody much alive, was Major Pinçon. He'd parade us runners every evening and bawl us out for a while, just to smarten us up and put some spirit into us. He'd curse us all to blazes, we who'd dragged around behind the general all day. Dismount! — Mount! — As you were, there; dismount again! — And off we'd have to go, carrying his orders all over the shop. You might just as well have drowned us by the time it was over. That would have been the easiest thing for every one concerned.

"Dismiss! Back to your regiments, all of you! And double to it!" he'd yell.

"Where is the regiment, sir?" we'd ask.

"At Barbagny."

"Where's that, sir?"

"It's over there."

Over there, where he was pointing, there was nothing but the darkness, which is all there was anywhere, anyway, — a black darkness eating up the road two feet in front of our face, and what you could see of the road was about the size of your tongue.

God knew where we were to find his Barbagny in this world's end! You'd have had to sacrifice at least a whole squadron to find it. And a squadron of brave men at that. Well, I wasn't a brave man and I couldn't see at all why I should be; I had less wish than anybody to find his Barbagny, about which he was entirely vague himself. It was as if by dint of shouting at me, they had tried to make me want to go away and commit suicide. You either get things that way or not.

In all this solid blackness, which you felt would never give you back your arm, if you stuck it out in front of your face, there was only one thing that was clear to me, which was — and it at least was very clear indeed — that the desire to kill was lurking within it, vast and multiform.

This brute of a brigade major busied himself when evening came sending us to our death, and often he'd get like that as soon as the sun set. We used to put up some sort of inert resistance to him; we were careful not to understand what he meant, and somehow or other we'd manage to stick close, when we could, to a comfortable bivvy; but in the end, when there were no longer any trees in sight, we'd have to give in and do a bit of facing up to death; the general's dinner would be ready.

Everything, after that moment had come, was a matter of chance. Sometimes you'd find your regiment and his damned Barbagny, and sometimes you wouldn't. It was usually by mistake that you did find it, when the sentinels of the squadron on guard fired at you as you came up. The result, of course, was that you explained who you were and nearly always you ended up the night on some sort of fatigue or other, carrying a lot of sacks of oats or pails of water and being sworn at until you were dizzy as well as dropping asleep.

Next morning off we'd go, we runners, the five of us, to report at General Des Entrayes' quarters and carry on the war.

But most often we wouldn't find the regiment, and then we'd just wait for daylight while we detoured around villages on unknown roads, skirting deserted hamlets and sinister-looking copses. These were to be avoided, because of the German patrols. Still, you had to be somewhere while you waited for the dawn; you had to be somewhere or other in the night. You couldn't avoid it all. Ever since then I've known what rabbits must feel like in a warren.

It's amusing the way a sense of pity comes to one. If one had told Major Pinçon that he was nothing but a cowardly, murderous brute, that would have given him the very greatest pleasure, the pleasure of having us shot out of hand by the Captain of the M.P.'s, who was about at his heels the whole time and whose one particular idea was just that. It wasn't the Germans this policeman was after.

So we had to risk being ambushed night after night in this idiotic way, with only the hope, each time less and less reasonable, of coming back at last — that and no other hope, except that if one ever did come back, one would never forget, absolutely *never* forget, that one had met in this world with a man made in the likeness of you and me, but far more obscene than any crocodile or any shark that hangs about ships in West Indian waters, waiting for the refuse and the rotten meat to be thrown overboard into his gaping gullet.

The greatest defeat, in anything, is to forget, and above all to forget what it is that has smashed you, and to let yourself be smashed without ever realizing how thoroughly devilish men can be. When our time is up, we people mustn't bear malice, but neither must we forget: we must tell the whole thing, without altering one word, — everything that we have seen of man's viciousness; and then it will be over and time to go. That is enough of a job for a whole lifetime.

Personally, I should have been glad to throw Major Pinçon to the sharks, and his policeman with him — just to teach them the proper way to live.

And my horse could have gone too, so that he shouldn't suffer any more. He hadn't any back left, poor brute, it was so sore; only two round open wounds where the saddle went, as wide across as my two hands, raw and running with pus, which streamed from the edges of his blanket down to his hams. But one had to ride him all the same, jogging on and on. . . . He sagged as he trotted along. But horses are much more patient than men are. He undulated as one rode and had to be left out in the open air. Inside barns, the stench that came from his wounds was so strong it was enough to stop one's breath. When one got up on his back it hurt him so that he arched himself, as gently as he could, and his belly reached to his knees. It felt like clambering onto a donkey. That made him more comfortable to ride, I must admit. We were very tired ourselves, with all that metal we carried on our heads and shoulders.

General Des Entrayes, in his private quarters, was waiting for his dinner. The table had been laid, the lamp was in its place.

"Get to hell out of here!" Pinçon yelled at us once again, swinging his lantern in front of our noses. "We're sitting down to table. I don't want to have to tell you again, d'you hear? Will you get out, you sods?" he screamed. Pushing us out to rot like this brought a little colour to his waxen cheeks.

Sometimes before we went, the general's cook would pass us out a bit of grub. The general had food enough and to spare, as the regulations allowed him forty rations for himself alone! He was no longer young, that man. In fact, he must have been about due for retirement. His knees gave way too, as he walked. Probably his moustaches were dyed.

As you went out, you could see the veins of his temples in the lamplight; they meandered about like the Seine at the outskirts of Paris. He had grown-up daughters, so they said, unmarried and, like him, badly off. Perhaps it was remembering this that made him so fussy and so full of grouses, like an old dog disturbed in its habits, looking everywhere for its basket if some one will only open the door for it.

He was fond of gardens and roses; wherever we went he never missed one. There's nobody like a general for being fond of roses. It's a well-known fact.

Well, we'd get going. What was a job was getting our hacks to trot. They were afraid to move, anyway, on account of their sores, and they were afraid of us too, and they were afraid of the darkness; they were afraid of everything. Yes, hell, and so were we! We'd go back again and again to ask the major the way once more. Each time he called us louts and good-for-nothing sons of bitches. By good use of our spurs we'd at last pass the most forward outpost and, giving the guards the word, we dived straight out into the dirty business ahead, into the darkness of No Man's Land.

After wandering a good while from shadow to shadow, one would begin to see a bit where one was going, or so it seemed. . . . As soon as one cloud was a little lighter than another, you told yourself you had seen something. . . . But in front of you there was nothing you could be sure of except the echo which came and went, the echo of the horses' trotting hooves, which made a vast noise that stifled you, you wanted it so much not to be there. They seemed to trot aloud to heaven, these horses, to be calling to everything on earth to come and kill us. And it would be so easily done, done with one hand, with the rifle propped against the trunk of a tree. I was always telling myself that the first gleam one would see would be the rifle-flash that was the end of one.

By the end of those four weeks which the war had lasted, we had grown so tired, so wretched, that through sheer fatigue I'd lost a little of my fright by the wayside. The hellishness of being bullied night and day by these N.C.O.'s, by the lesser ones particularly, who had become even more brutish, meaner and more odious than usual, was enough at last to make you a little doubtful, however obstinate you might be, about going on living.

Oh, how one longed to go away! To get away and sleep! That, first of all. And if there's really no longer any way to go off and sleep, then the wish to live just disappears. So long as you were still about there, alive, there was nothing for it but to look as if you were hunting for your regiment.

A lot of things, a lot of very cruel things, have got to happen to a fool before his mind can change its thoughts. What had made me think for the first time in my life, really think hard, and get ideas that were of some use and my very own, was assuredly that damned inquisitor of a Major Pinçon. I thought about him as hard as I could, as I bobbed along, all dressed up and loaded with junk, taking my part in this unbelievable international rumpus, which I had joined with such enthusiasm. . . . I admit that.

Every yard of darkness ahead of us was a further promise of an end to it all, a promise of death — but what sort of death? The only uncertain thing in the whole business was what uniform one's executioner would wear. Would it be one of ours? Or one from the other side?

I'd never done anything to Pinçon! No more to him than to the Germans, I hadn't. He, with a head like a rotten fish, and his four stripes glittering all over him, from his neck to his navel, with his bristling moustache and sharp, bony knees, and the field glasses hanging around his neck like a cowbell, and his army ordnance map. I'd ask myself what raving desire possessed him to get every one else killed. Every one else who hadn't an ordnance map.

We four horsemen on the road made as much noise as a couple of platoons. You must have been able to hear us coming four miles away — or perhaps no one wanted to. That was possible, of course. Perhaps the Germans were frightened of us: who knows?

On each eyelid we were carrying a month of sleep, and as much again in the back of our heads, as well as our pounds of iron and steel.

My riders weren't much good at expressing themselves. They hardly talked at all, as a matter of fact. They were lads who had come from the further end of Brittany to join up, and what they knew they'd not learnt at school but in the ranks. That particular evening I'd tried to talk a bit about this village of Barbagny with the one who was next to me, whose name was Kersuzon.

"Listen, Kersuzon," I said to him. "We're in the Ardennes country here, you know. . . . Can you see anything ahead of us? I can't see anything at all."

"It's as black as your bottom," Kersuzon told me. Nothing more.

"Say, listen, haven't you heard any one mention Barbagny during the course of to-day? Or say where it was?" I asked him. "No."

So there we were.

We never found Barbagny. We turned back at last, towards morning, towards another village where the man with the field glasses was waiting for us. His chief was taking his early morning coffee on the terrace outside the mayor's house when we arrived.

"What a fine thing Youth is, Pinçon!" the old man remarked in a loud voice to his brigade major as we went by. After which he got up and went off to pee, and then came and walked about with his hands behind his back, a little bent. The general was very tired that morning, his orderly whispered to me; he'd slept badly. There was something wrong with his bladder which bothered him, so one heard.

Kersuzon always answered me in the same way when I asked him something at night; I came to be amused by the oddity of it. He told me two or three times more that it was as black as your bottom, and then he died; killed, quite soon after that, on leaving a village which, I remember quite well, we mistook for another, by some Frenchmen who mistook us for somebody else.

It was only a few days after Kersuzon's death that we thought out a way of not getting lost at night any more. We were very pleased with this idea of ours.

They'd be chivvying us out of camp, you see. All right, we'd not say a single word. We wouldn't try to scheme off any more. "Get out of here!" he'd yell, as usual, in his rasping voice. "Very good, sir."
And off we'd go at once, the five of us, in the direction of the firing. We might have been going blackberrying. It was fine country, full of little valleys, in that direction: Meuse country with its hills, and vines on them, the grapes not yet ripe, and autumn, and villages built of wood, which had got very dry in three months of summer, so that they burned beautifully.

We'd noticed this one night when we hadn't any idea where to go. There was always a village burning where the firing was. You didn't go very close to it, not too close; you just watched it from a distance, say from six or seven miles away, as a spectator. And every evening after that, about this time, a lot of villages caught fire; one after another, all around one, like the flares of some absurd fair ground, which has the whole of the countryside, they'd burn away in front of one and on each side, with the flames rising up from them, licking the clouds.

You could see everything disappearing in the blaze, churches, farms and haystacks, which burnt with brighter and taller flames than anything else, and girders which reared straight up, flickering in the darkness, and then crashed down into the brightness of the fire.

You can see very clearly how a village burns, even a dozen miles away. A pretty sight. You've no idea what a fine effect even the most insignificant little hamlet, which you wouldn't even notice in the daytime, in the dullest country, will make at night when it's burning. You'd think it was Notre Dame! A village takes all night to burn, even a small one; it looks like a great big flower of flame, then a bud, then nothing is left. It smokes for a while, and then morning comes.

The horses we left saddled in the field close to where we were, and they never moved. We went off and dozed in the grass, except one of us, of course, who took his turn on guard. But when there's a fire to watch, the night passes much more easily;

it's no longer a wretched thing to get through, it's not so lonely any more.

Unfortunately the villages didn't last long. . . . By the end of the month there were none left in the district. The woods were shelled, too, but they didn't last out a week. Woods burn beautifully, but they're over in no time.

After that all the roads were filled by artillery columns going one way and refugees going the other. As for us, in fact, we could no longer either go or come; we had to stay where we were.

Every one queued up to go and get killed. Even the general couldn't find any place that wasn't full of soldiers. In the end we all slept out in the fields, whether we were generals or privates. Those who still had a little courage left lost even that. It was from that month on that they began to shoot troopers by squads, so as to improve their morale, and the M.P. began to be mentioned in despatches for the way in which he was waging his own little war, the really genuine war, the most desperate of all.

WE WERE GIVEN A REST AND THEN, A FEW WEEKS LATER, WE GOT ON our horses and started out north again. The cold went with us. And the guns never left us, either. Still, we never met the Germans except by chance, sometimes a hussar, sometimes a section out sniping; one ran into them here and there, wearing yellow and green, pretty colours. We looked as if we were trying to find them, but we moved on somewhere else as soon as they came in sight. Each time we met, two or three troopers were left behind, sometimes their fellows, sometimes ours. Their riderless horses would gallop free and come dashing towards us from a long way off, with stirrups clattering loose from those saddles of theirs, with their odd cantles made of leather as bright as a new pocketbook. They were coming to join our horses, whom they recognised as their friends at once. Well, they were lucky. We couldn't have done the same.

One morning, as we came in from reconnaissance, Lieutenant Sainte-Engence was protesting in the midst of a group of officers that what he had just told them was quite true. "I killed two of them!" he insisted, and he held out his sabre for them to see. There was indeed some dried blood on it, which filled the little groove made for that purpose.

"He was great. I wish you could have seen him!" Captain Ortolan bore him out. *"How* he went for them! Well done, Sainte-Engence!" It had all happened in Ortolan's squadron.

"I missed none of it. I was right behind him. Lunge forward and right! Zip! Over goes the first of them! Then the point into the other's chest—on the left this time. Cross and thrust! Why, it was good enough for Bertrand's! Well done again, Sainte-Engence! Two lancers they were — less than a mile from where we're standing. They're lying out there now, in a ploughed field. No more war for those two, eh, Sainte-Engence? What a wonderful double thrust! They went over like rabbits. . . ."

The lieutenant accepted the compliments and congratulations of his fellow officers with modesty. His mare had already galloped a long way, but now that Ortolan was bearing witness to his exploit, all was well and he rode off and circled slowly around the assembled squadron, as if he'd just finished a point-to-point, before bringing her back to be rubbed down.

"We ought to send out another reconnoitring party to the same spot right away," said Captain Ortolan in great excitement. "Those two sods must have come this way and got lost, but there are probably others behind them. . . . Hey, you, Bardamu, you go off after them with your four fellows!"

It was to me the captain was speaking.

"And when they open fire, mark them carefully and come back at once and tell me where they are. They're probably Brandenburgers, I should say. . . ."

According to the regulars, Captain Ortolan was practically never to be seen about barracks in peace time. But now, with a war on, he bobbed up all over the shop. Nothing was too much for him, certainly. The energy with which he devoted himself to duty, even with so many other crazy fools about the place, was every day more and more astonishing. He took cocaine, too, so they said. Pale, hollow-eyed and shaky, his feeble legs gave under him when he got off his horse, but he'd pull himself together at once and scramble angrily up every slope in search of some danger to defy. For two pins he'd have sent us to fetch a light from the mouths of the German guns. He aided and abetted death as much as he could. One would have sworn that Captain Ortolan and Death had entered into a contract together.

He had spent the first part of his life, so I learned, competing at horse shows and breaking a rib or two half a dozen times a year. He'd also broken his legs so often and used them so little for walking that now they had no calves left. He went about taking jerky, sharp steps, as if on stilts. Seeing him in his enormous cloak, huddled in the rain, you'd have taken him for the phantom quarters of a race horse.

It should be explained that at the outset of this horror to which we were condemned, that is to say in August, and even into September, there were still certain times, sometimes whole days, and certain corners of a road or a wood, that were bearable to us. . . . You could imagine that things were almost all right; you might be able, say, to get through a tin of fruit with your bread and not be too harassed by a presentiment that it would be your last. But by October there was an end to such little lulls, the hail got thicker and heavier, more spiced, more stuffed with bullets and shells. Soon the storm would be in full force and then the thing you were trying not to see would be plain in front of your eyes and there'd be nothing you could see besides that: your own death.

The nighttime, which one had been so frightened of at first, had now become almost sweet by comparison. We came at last to look forward to it, to long for the night. They couldn't shoot at us as easily at night as by day. And that was the only difference that mattered.

It's difficult to get at the essential truth at the bottom of anything, and even in the case of war imagination dies hard.

But a cat will eventually take to water rather than face being burnt in a fire.

Now and again at night one could snatch an odd quarter of an hour which was a little like the lovely times of peace, that now incredible time when everything was calm and pleasant, when nothing really mattered, when you could do so many things that now seemed marvellously, amazingly delightful. Peace time had been Paradise. . . .

But soon the nights too were made merciless. Almost always you had to force your weariness to work a little and suffer a little bit more, merely so as to be able to eat or to snatch forty winks in the darkness. The food supply was dragged to the front line heavily and laboriously in long limping lines of quaking waggons, full of meat and prisoners and wounded, oats, rice, M.P.'s and wine. The wine came in those great quivering, fat-bellied demijohns, which make one think at once of good times past.

Behind the smithy and the bread, men dragged themselves along on foot, prisoners of our own lot and their fellows too, handcuffed, condemned to this penalty and that penalty, tied by the wrist to the stirrup of an M.P., some of them to be shot next morning but no sadder-looking than the rest. They too ate their ration of that tunny fish which is so difficult to digest (they wouldn't have time to digest it, anyway) while they waited on the side of the road for the waggon train to get under way once more; and they ate their bread too with a civilian chained to them, who they said was a spy but who wasn't aware of it. And neither were we.

Then the horror continued in its night guise, and you felt your way along twisting little lanes in blank, pitch-dark villages, staggering under a sack heavier than a man, from one unknown barn to another, shouted at, threatened, haggard and without hope of any end to it all other than in slush amid oaths and in disgust at having been tortured and duped to death by a horde of vicious madmen, who had suddenly become incapable of doing anything else as long as they lived, but kill and be slit in half without knowing the reason why.

One would sink to the ground between two stacks of manure when they had yelled at one and kicked one enough, only soon to be heaved onto one's feet again and sent off to load up some other waggon train somewhere else.

The village would overflow with food and men in a night, oozing fat, apples, oats and sugar, which you had to cart about and distribute wherever you might find a squad of men. The supply waggons brought every mortal thing with them, except escape.

The fatigue would flop down exhausted around the cart and then along would come the commissariat officer with his lantern lighting up these corpses. He was an ape of a man with two chins, and he had to find a watering place for the horses, no matter how great the chaos was. Water for the horses! But I have seen four of them, four of the men, fall fast asleep, fainting with sleep, in the water, body and all in it, up to the neck.

After finding a watering place, you had to find the farm and the track you'd come along, where you thought you'd left your squad. If you didn't find it, you were free to sink down for an hour by the side of a wall, if there was still an hour left. In this suicide business you mustn't make difficulties, you've just got to pretend that life's going on as usual: that's the hardest part about it all, that damn lie.

Then the waggons went off back behind the lines. Before dawn they went their way, screeching on every twisted wheel, and carrying with them a prayer of mine that they'd be surprised and smashed to bits, burnt to the ground that very day, like you see in war pictures, the supply train destroyed, wiped out for ever with all its hideous policemen and horseshoes and lantern-swinging regulars and all its sacks of lentils and flour; I longed never to see any of them again. Because one may go under through unbearable fatigue or any other way, but the bloodiest way of all is to die carrying sacks into the depths of the night.

The day those swine and their waggons were smashed to splinters they'd leave us alone, I thought, even if it was only for one whole night, and then at least one would get a complete night's rest for body and soul.

This revictualling was one more added nightmare, a nagging little demon, a parasite on the greater fiend of war. Brute beasts to the fore, on each flank, to the rear: they were everywhere. And we who were condemned to a deferred death, we could not be rid of our overwhelming desire to sleep, and everything besides that had become a misery, including the effort of eating and the time it took. A stream or a wall one would seem to recognize . . . and one traced one's way back to one's squad by smell, as if one had become a dog again at night in those deserted villages in war time. The odour of excrement was the best guide of all.

The chief commissariat officer, keeper of the hatred of the whole regiment, was for the time being lord of creation. You're a rogue if you talk of the future; it's the present that counts. To invoke posterity is to declaim to an audience of maggots. At night in those war villages, the adjutant herded his human cattle in readiness for the great slaughterhouses that had just been opened. The adjutant was king! The King of Death! Adjutant Cretelle! Just so. Nobody was stronger than he — and no one was even as strong as he was, except some adjutant of theirs on the other side.

There was nothing left alive in the village, bar a few frightened cats. The furniture had been smashed and used for firewood — chairs, sofas, sideboards, large or small. And everything that could be carried on one's back, the fellows took away with them: combs, lamps, cups, worthless little knick-knacks and even bridal wreaths, — everything went the same way. As if there were years yet to live. They swiped these things for something to do, so as to feel there was lots of time left — which is always man's desire.

The guns meant nothing to them but noise. That's why wars can go on. Even those who fight in them, while they're fighting in them, can't realize what war is. With a bullet in their bellies, they would still have gone on picking up old soles on the road, which might still "come in handy." A sheep dying on its side in a field will go on browsing in its death agony. Most people don't die till the very last moment: but some start to die twenty years before their time, and sometimes earlier. They are the unhappy ones of this world.

I wasn't very wise myself but I'd grown sensible enough to be definitely a coward forever. Due no doubt to this resolve, I gave an impression of great calm. At all events, coward as I was, I inspired a strange confidence in our own Captain Ortolan, who decided to entrust me that very night with a delicate mission. He took me aside and told me that I was to trot off before daylight to Noirceur-sur-la-Lys, the weavers' town, fourteen kilometres from the village where our camp was. My job was to find out on the spot itself whether the enemy were there or not. On this point no two runners had been able to agree since morning. General des Entrayes was impatient to know for certain. I was allowed, when I set out on this reconnaissance, to choose myself a horse from among the least badly maimed in the platoon. It was ages since I'd been alone. I felt as if I were going off on a journey; but it was a false sense of relief.

As soon as I had started out, I was so tired that, try as I might, I couldn't properly imagine, precisely enough and in detail, what my death would be. I went forward from tree to tree, in the midst of my own clatter of steel. My fine sword alone was as good as a piano for noise. Maybe I was to be pitied; most certainly I was absurd.

What was General des Entrayes thinking of to send me out like this into such a silence, and me all dressed up in cymbals? For certain it wasn't me he was thinking of.

The Aztecs, so I've heard, used to disembowel eight thousand believers a week in their Temples of the Sun, as a sacrifice to the God of the Clouds so that he would send them rain. It's one of those things that must be hard to believe until you've gone to a war. But once you're there, everything is understandable and the Aztecs' unconcern for other men's bodies is the same as the said General Céladon des Entrayes must have felt for my humble insides; for he had risen in rank until he himself had become a sort of exact god, a kind of horrible, merciless little sun.

There was only one little hope I had left — that I might be taken prisoner. It was not much of a hope, a bare thread. Just a thread in the night. Because circumstances would not make polite overtures at all easy. At such moments a rifle shoots you quicker than a man can raise his hat. Besides, what should I find to say to a German soldier, an adversary anyway, and one who had come half across Europe on purpose to kill me? If he hesitated for one second (which would be all I needed) what should I say to him? What might he be himself in the first place — a shop assistant? A professional man called up again? A gravedigger, perhaps, in civil life — or a cook? Horses are lucky. They go through the war, like us, but they're not asked to approve of it or to seem to believe in it. In this business they were unfortunate but free. Enthusiasm, alas, was *our* dirty prerogative, reserved for us!

I could see the road clearly just then and by the side of it, rising out of the slush, the square masses of houses with whitewashed walls shining like the moon, like great uneven blocks of ice, silent and colourless. Was this the end of everything? How long should I stay in this wilderness before I was done for, before it was all over? And in what ditch? By which of these walls? Would they finish me off, I wondered — with a knife, perhaps? Sometimes they cut off one's hands, one's eyes, and the rest. . . . One heard of all sorts of things, far from pleasant things. God knows! One step of my horse . . . and another . . . would that be enough? These brutes trot like two men in steel boots tied together, at an absurd uneven double.

My heart behind my ribs crouched like a rabbit, warm, trembling, stupefied. That's very much what one must feel when one jumps off the Eiffel Tower — wishing one could stop oneself in space.

The village ahead kept its threat for me secret — but not entirely secret. In the middle of the square a trickle of water in the fountain babbled for me alone.

Everything was mine that evening; it all belonged only to me. I had the moon to myself and the village and a tremendous sense of fear. I was going to start to trot again. Noirceur-sur-la-Lys was still, I supposed, at least one hour's ride away, when I saw a well-muffled light above a door. I went straight towards the light and so discovered in myself a sort of bravery, a deserter's bravery it's true, but unsuspected all the same. The light went out at once, but I had seen it. I banged at the door. I went on banging and I shouted out in a very loud voice, half in German, half in French, ready for either or any emergency, calling out to these wraiths barricaded in the darkness.

The door at last opened, one of its leaves ajar.

"Who are you?" said a voice. I was saved.

"I'm a dragoon."

"A Frenchman?" I could just see the woman who was speaking.

"Yes, French."

"Only German dragoons have just passed this way. . . . They also spoke French. . . ."

"Yes, but I really am French."

"Oh."

She seemed to doubt it.

"Where are they now?" I asked.

"They went off towards Noirceur about eight o'clock." She pointed north.

A girl in a shawl and a white apron came out of the shadow, almost to the door.

"What did the Germans do to you?" I asked her.

"They burned a house near the Town Hall and here they killed my little brother . . . with a lance. He was playing on the bridge, watching them as they went by. Look," she said, pointing again, "there he is."

She wasn't crying. She relit the candle which first had attracted my attention, and there sure enough at the back, was the child's corpse on a mattress. He was dressed in a sailor suit and his face and neck showed as white as the flame of the candle above his large square blue collar. He was rolled up on himself, his arms, legs and back huddled together. The lance had passed, like an axis of death, through the middle of his stomach. His mother was crying on her knees by his side, and so was the father. Then all began to moan at the same time. But I was very thirsty.

"You haven't a bottle of wine you could sell me, have you?" I asked.

"Ask Mother. She may know if there's any left. The Germans took a lot of it just now."

The two women began to argue together about it in low tones.

"There's none left," the daughter said, turning back to me at the door. "The Germans took it all. Although we had given them a lot on our own already."

"Oh, yes, they drank a lot of it," the mother said, and stopped crying suddenly. "They love drinking. . . ."

"A hundred bottles or more, I should say," added the father, still on his knees.

"Isn't there a single bottle left then?" I went on, still hoping there might be, I was so terribly thirsty. Above all, I wanted white wine, that good bitter kind that wakes one up a little. "I'll pay for it. . . ."

"There's only the very best. It's worth five francs a bottle," the women then admitted.

"All right," I said, and I took five francs from my pocket, a large five-franc piece.

"Go and get one," she told the sister quietly.

The girl took the candle and came back a moment later with a litre bottle from the cellar.

I'd had what I wanted and I could go.

"Are they coming back?" I asked, becoming anxious once more.

"Perhaps," they all answered together. "If they do, they'll set fire to everything. They said so when they went."

"I'll go and have a look."

"You're a brave fellow. . . .That's your road." The father pointed in the direction of Noirceur. He even came out into the road to watch me go. The girl and her mother stayed timidly to watch beside the little body.

"Come back," they called out from inside. "Come in, Joseph; there's no need to go out on to the road."

"You're a brave chap," the old man said again, shaking me by the hand. I set off towards the north, at a trot.

"Don't tell them we're still here, anyway." The girl had come out again to shout that after me.

"They'll see for themselves to-morrow whether you're there or not," I answered. I was angry at having parted with my five francs. The five francs were between them and me. Five francs are enough to make one hate a person, to make one wish them all in hell. There's no love to be lost in this world as long as there are five francs left in it.

"To-morrow," they murmured doubtfully.

For them too to-morrow was a long way off; it didn't make much sense, a to-morrow like that. Really the thing for all of us was to get through another hour; one more hour, in a world in which everything has been reduced in scale by murder, is miraculous enough.

It was not very long after that. I trotted along from tree to tree, expecting to be challenged or shot any moment. And that was all. . . .

It must have been nearly two hours after midnight, not more, when I came to the crest of a little incline, at a walking pace. From there I suddenly saw below me row upon row of shining gaslights and in the foreground a railway station all lit up, with its coaches and buffet. But no sound, no noise at all, came from it. Streets and broad walks and street lamps and still further parallel rows of lights, block after block, and round and about all this nothing but the empty eager darkness circling the town, which lay stretched out before me as if it had been lost in the night, spread out full of bright light plumb in the middle of the darkness. I got down off my horse and sat on a hummock for some little time, and looked at it.

All the same, that didn't tell me whether or not the Germans had been in Noirceur. But as I knew that normally in such cases they set fire to a place, if they'd been here and hadn't burned the town at once, it must mean that they had some unusual plan in mind. No guns either. It was very odd.

My horse wanted to lie down too. He tugged at his bridle and that made me turn around. When I looked back, something had altered in the appearance of the mound in front of me — nothing much, it's true, but enough to make me call out, "Hey! Who goes there?" A few feet away the shadows had shifted. . . . There must be somebody there.

"Don't shout so loud!" A very French voice answered me, a man's voice, heavy and thick. "You on your own too?" he asked. I could see him now. He was an infantryman with the peak of his cap cracked and jauntily worn. After all these years I can still remember his silhouette perfectly clearly as he came out from the grass like a dummy target in a wood.

We went closer to each other. I had my revolver in my hand. I might have shot, any minute, without knowing why.

"Listen," he said, "have you seen them?"

"No, but I've come here to see them."

"145th Dragoons?"

"Yes, and you?"

"I'm a reservist."

"Oh," I said. I was surprised to hear that — a reservist! He was the first reservist I had met in the war. We'd always mixed with real army fellows. I couldn't see his face but his voice was different from the voices of our lot, sadder somehow and so more decent. For that reason I couldn't help having a certain confidence in him. It was something, after all.

"I've had enough," he said. "I'm going to get myself nabbed by the Boche."

That was pretty frank.

"How're you going to do it?"

I was suddenly very interested, very interested indeed, to know how he was going to carry out his plan and get taken prisoner.

"Dunno yet."

"How did you get this far, anyway? It's not easy to get yourself pinched."

"I don't give a damn, I'll go and give myself up."

"Aren't you frightened?"

"I'm frightened, all right. But I think it's all bloody stupid, if you ask me; I don't care a curse about the Germans, anyway. They never did anything to me. . . ."

"Shut up," I told him; "maybe they can hear us. . . ."

I felt somehow I ought to be polite to the Germans. I should have liked this reservist to tell me, while he was about it, why I too was too frightened to be in this war with every one else. But he didn't tell me anything at all; he simply said he was through.

Then he told me about how his regiment had been scattered the night before, towards dawn. Our dismounted cavalry pickets had fired on his company by mistake, across country. They hadn't been expected just then. They'd arrived three hours before time. So the other fellows, who were tired and taken by surprise, had shot them up. I knew that turn well enough myself; I'd met with it before now.

"And I took advantage of it, I can tell you," he went on. " 'Robinson,' I said to myself — Robinson's my name. Léon Robinson. — 'It's now or never,' I said to myself. Wasn't I right? So I went off along by a copse and there, suddenly, I came across the captain. . . . He was leaning against a tree, smashed to bits. . . . Dying he was. . . . He was holding himself and spitting. . . . There was blood all over him and his eyes rolled. . . . No one about. He'd certainly got his. 'Mother, Mother!' he whimpered and he was pissing blood. 'Stop that!' I said to him. 'Mother! what the hell!' Just like that, as I passed him, out of the corner of my mouth. That must have bucked him up, the sod. Eh? One can't often say what one thinks to a captain. Take the chance when it comes. It's not often. . . . And so as to get out quicker, I dropped my haversack and rifle and everything. . . . Threw them into a duck pond that was near. . . . You see, myself, as I stand here, I don't want to kill any one; I've never learnt. . . . I never liked a row, even in peace time. I used to go away. . . . So you can imagine . . . As a civvy I used to try to go to work regularly. . . . I was an engraver for a time, but I didn't like that because there were always quarrels. . . . I preferred selling papers in the evening in a quiet quarter where I was known, near the Bank of France. . . . Place des Victoires, as a matter of fact. . . . Rue des Petits-Champs — that was my pitch. I never went beyond the Rue du Louvre and the Palais-Royal on one side, if you know where I mean. . . . In the morning I'd do an errand or two for the tradespeople. . . . A delivery in the afternoon from time to time. I did every sort of job . . . a handy man. I've been a mechanic. . . . But I don't want a rifle! What if the Germans see you with a rifle? It's all up with you. But if you're in fancy things like I am now—with nothing in your hands and nothing in your pockets. . . . They feel they won't have so much trouble taking you prisoner, don't they? They know what it's all about. . . . If one could get over to the Germans without anything on, now, that would be better still. Like a horse can! Then they wouldn't know what army you belonged to, would they?"

"That's true," I said.

I realized that being older in years helps when it comes to thinking. It makes you practical.

"Is that where they are, eh?" We discussed and estimated our chances together and gazed at the great lighted expanse of the silent town as if into a crystal, trying to discover what the future held in store for us.

"Shall we go?"

First we had to cross the railway lines. If there were sentries, we'd be seen. Or perhaps we mightn't. We'd have to find out. And go over or underneath through the tunnel.

"We've got to hurry," said this Robinson.

"You've got to do this sort of thing at night: in the daytime people are less friendly; everybody plays to the gallery more. The daytime, even in war, is not so honest. You taking your horse with you?" I took the horse. So as to be able to bolt quicker, if we weren't well received. We came to the level crossing, with its raised red-and-white arms. I'd never seen one like it before. They were different round about Paris.

"D'you think they're in the town already?"

"Sure," he said. "Come on!"

And now we had to be as brave as truly brave men, because of the horse which followed us calmly, as if it were pushing us before it with the noise it was making. You could hear nothing else — clatter! clash! went its hooves. It crashed and echoed heavily, as if nothing was wrong.

Did this Robinson think the darkness would get us out of this? We walked in the middle of the empty street, the two of us, openly, striding along as if it were a parade ground.

Robinson was right. The daytime was without pity, from earth to sky. Walking along as we were on the road, we must have looked pretty harmless and simple, both of us, as if we were returning to barracks after leave. "Have you heard that the 1st Hussars were taken prisoner, the whole lot of them, at Lille? They marched in, I've heard, suspecting nothing, with the colonel in front and all. In a main street, my boy! And it shut up on them. Huns in front and behind — everywhere! At the windows, all over the shop. That was that. Like rats in a trap, just like rats! What a bit of luck."

"Damn them."

"God, yes, I should say so." We couldn't get over the beautiful finality, the neatness of that capture. . . . It made our mouths water. The shops all had their shutters down, all the houses were shut too, with their little gardens in front, all neat and nice. But past the post office there was one house, whiter than the others, shining with lights burning in every window, upstairs as well as on the ground floor. We rang the bell, taking our horse with us. A thick, bearded man opened the door. "I'm the Mayor of Noirceur," he announced at once, though no one had asked him, "and I'm expecting the Germans." And he came out into the moonlight to have a look at us. When he saw that we weren't Germans but still French, he wasn't so solemn — merely friendly. But he was rather annoyed too. Obviously he wasn't expecting to see us; we rather upset his arrangements, muddling his plan. The Germans were to have arrived in Noirceur that night and he'd arranged everything with the Prefect of Police; their colonel to be put there, their Red Cross here, and so on. What if they didn't come now? With us there? That would surely mean a lot of trouble! There'd be complications, for certain. He did not say so in so many words, but you could see he was thinking it.

So he began to talk to us of the common good, standing there in the night, lost in the silence as we were. The common good, that's what. . . . The material interests of the community. . . . The artistic patrimony of Noirceur, which was his trust, a sacred trust if ever there was one. . . . He told us particularly about the fifteenth-century church. What if they burnt the fifteenth-century church, eh? As they had the church of Condé-sur-Yser near by? Just because they were annoyed . . . because it put them out to find us there. He made us realize what a great responsibilty we were shouldering. . . . Unthinking young poilus, that's what we were. . . . The Germans weren't at all fond of tiresome towns with enemy soldiers still hanging about. . . . Any one could tell you as much.

While he talked to us like this, *sotto voce*, his wife and daughters, two buxom delectable blondes, agreed heartily with what he said, chipping in from time to time. . . . We were being turned away, in fact. All about us floated the sentimental and archeological values of Noirceur, become suddenly very powerful, since there was no longer any one in Noirceur to oppose them. . . . Patriotic, ethical ghosts they were, wafted this way and that by his words; the mayor tried to tie them down but they vanished, dispersed by our fear and our selfishness — and by plain and simple facts.

It was touching to see him trying his level best to make us see that duty called us away quick as hell from his town of Noirceur. He was less brutal, of course, but just as determined in his way as our own Major Pinçon.

Certainly there was nothing we could put against all this show of strength except our own puny little wish not to die and not to burn. It was little enough, especially as such things cannot be said in war time. So we turned back to our empty streets. Every one I had met that night had opened his heart to me.

"Just my luck!" said Robinson, as we went off. "Why, if only you'd been a German, you're a decent fellow and you'd have taken me prisoner, and it would have been all over and done with. It's a hard job trying to get rid of oneself in a war!"

"What about you?" I said to him. "If you'd been a German, wouldn't you have taken me prisoner just as much? You might have had their military medal for it. I wonder what they call their medal. It must have a devil of a name in German."

As we couldn't find any one on our way who would have anything to do with taking us prisoners, eventually we went and sat down on a bench in a little square and there we ate the tin of tunny fish which Private Robinson had been carrying about and warming in his pocket all day. Far away you could hear the guns now — but they were really very far away. If only the two sides could have stayed where they were, leaving us alone where we were!

After that, we wandered along a wharf and there, near the half-unloaded barges, we pissed long into the water. We led the horse all the time by the bridle, following behind us like an enormous dog, but near the bridge, in the pastor's single-roomed house there was a dead man stretched out on a mattress, — a Frenchman. As a matter of fact, he looked rather like Robinson.

"Isn't he ugly?" said Robinson. "I don't like dead men. . . ."

"The odd thing about it," I said, "is that he's a bit like you. He's got a long nose like yours and you're not much older than he is."

"It's because one's so tired; of course, we all look rather alike. But you should have seen me in the old days. . . . When I used to go for long rides on my bike every Sunday. I wasn't a bad-looking chap. Fine calf muscles I had, I can tell you. . . . Sport's the thing, you know. And it develops your thighs too. . . ."

We went outside. The match we'd lit to see him by had gone out.

"Look, it's too late; you see, it's too late!"

Far away, a long grey and green streak showed already along the crest of the hill outside the town in the darkness. Dawn! One more dawn. One less. We'd have to try to get through it and through all the others which ringed us round more and more narrowly, like circles of falling and bursting shells.

"Listen, will you be coming along this way again to-morrow night?" he asked me as we parted.

"There's no to-morrow night, man. D'you think you're a general?"

"I don't think anything at all, I tell you," he said, turning away. "Nothing at all, d'you hear me? I only think of not dying, that's all. And it's enough. What I say to myself is that every day gained is one more day."

"You're right. Good-bye, fellow, and good luck."

"Good luck to you too. Maybe we'll be meeting again some-time!"

Each of us returned to his own war. And things happened, a whole host of things went on happening, which it isn't easy to talk about now, because nowadays people wouldn't understand them any more.

IF ONE WANTED TO BE RESPECTED AND DECENTLY TREATED, THERE was no time to be lost in hitting it off with the civilians, because as the war went on they became rapidly more unpleasant. As soon as I got back to Paris, I realized this. The women were in heat and the old men had greed written all over them; nothing was safe from their rummaging fingers, either persons or pockets.

Back at home they'd been pretty quick to pick up honour and glory from the boys at the front, and had learnt how to resign themselves to it all bravely and without flinching.

The mothers, all nurses or martyrs, were never without their sombre livery and the little diplomas so promptly presented to them by the War Office. The machine was getting smoothly to work, in fact.

It's just the same at a nicely run funeral. One's very sad there too, but one thinks of the will, and of next holidays, of the attractive widow (who's good value, so they say) and, by contrast, of going on living oneself quite a time yet, of never dying at all perhaps . . . who knows?

As you follow the bier everybody solemnly takes his hat off to you. That's nice. It's the time to behave very properly, and look respectable, and not to make jokes out loud, to be only inwardly happy. That's allowed. Everything's allowed inside oneself.

In war time, instead of dancing upstairs, one danced in the cellar. The men on leave put up with that; they even liked it. In fact, they insisted on it as soon as they came back and nobody thought it unseemly. The only thing that's really unseemly is bravado. Would you be physically brave? Then ask the maggot to be brave too; he's as pink and pale and soft as you are.

There was nothing for me to complain of. I was winning my freedom with the military medal I'd been given, and my wound and all. They'd brought the medal to me in hospital, when

I was convalescing. The same day I left the hospital and went to a theatre, to show it off to the civvies in the interval. It was a great success. Medals were a novelty in Paris at the time. There was quite a to-do.

It was on this same occasion in the foyer of the Opéra Comique that I met my little American Lola, and it was due to her that I had my eyes opened completely.

There are certain days which count in that way, after months and months which don't mean a thing. That day of the medal at the Opéra Comique was for me all-important.

It was due to Lola that I became curious about the United States. I immediately asked her a lot of questions about that country, which she hardly answered. When you start out on journeys in this way, you come back as and when you can. . . .

At the time I'm speaking of, every one in Paris wanted a nice uniform. Only neutrals and spies hadn't got one, and there wasn't much to choose between *them*. Lola had hers and a pretty little thing it was too, all decked out with little red crosses on the sleeves and on the diminutive cap, which she always wore at a tilt on her head of wavy hair. She had come to help us save France, as she told the manager at the hotel, and though she couldn't hope to do much, she was ready to do what she could with all her heart. There was understanding between us at once, but it was not quite complete because I'd come to dislike the feelings of the heart very much. I really much preferred the feelings of the body. One should distrust the heart — the war had taught me that, very clearly; and I wasn't likely to forget it.

Lola's heart was tender, weak and enthusiastic. Her body was charming, very attractive, and the only thing to do was to accept her as she was. She was a sweet girl really but the war was between us, that vast and bloody madness which, whether they wanted it or not, was making one half of humanity drive the other half into the knacker's yard. And of course a thing like that was disturbing to our relationship. To me, who was making my convalescence last as long as possible, and who didn't in the least want to take my turn again in the blazing graveyards of the front line, the absurdity of our massacre was startlingly ob-

vious at every step I took in the city. A horrible chicanery
pervaded everything.

However, I had little chance of getting out of it. I knew none
of the sort of people you need to know in order to get out of it.
The only friends I had were poor people, that is to say, people
whose death was of no interest to any one. As for Lola, it was no
good counting on her to help me out of it. In spite of the fact that
she was a nurse, you couldn't imagine a more bellicose creature
than that dear child — except perhaps Ortolan. Before I ever went
into the muddy hash of heroism myself, her little Joan-of-Arc manner might perhaps have thrilled and converted me, but now, after
joining up in the Place Clichy, I was violently ready to reject
all forms of patriotism, either verbal or real. I was cured, thoroughly cured.

For the convenience of the ladies of the American Expedi-
tionary Force the group of nurses to which Lola belonged was
lodged at the Paritz Hotel, and to make things pleasanter for
her in particular, because she had certain connections, she was
given the supervision of a special service of apple fritters, which
were delivered from the hotel itself to the hospitals of Paris.
Every morning tens of thousands of them were sent out. Lola
performed this charitable duty with a devotion which, as a
matter of fact, was later to have the very worst effects.

The truth is that Lola had never cooked an apple fritter in her
life. So she engaged a number of professional cooks and soon the
fritters were produced up to time, beautifully juicy, golden and
sweet. All Lola had to do was to taste them before they were
sent out to the different hospitals. Every morning she'd get up
at ten and after her bath go down to the kitchens, which were
below ground near the cellars. Every morning she did that,
dressed only in a black and yellow kimono which a friend from
San Francisco had given her the day before she left.

Everything was going splendidly, in fact, and we were well on
the way to winning the war, when one fine day, at lunch time,
I found Lola in a state of prostration and refusing to eat any
food. I was seized by anxiety lest some misfortune or sudden illness
had overtaken her. I begged her to rely on my loving care.

Thanks to punctiliously tasting confectionery every day for a month, Lola had put on two full pounds. Her little waist bulged in evidence of this disaster. She burst into tears. Wishing to console her as best I could, I took her in a taxi — in the stress of the emotion — to a number of drug stores in various parts of the town. All the weighing machines, chosen at random, implacably agreed that the two extra pounds had been well and truly added; they were undeniable. I suggested that she should hand over her job to a colleague who, on the contrary, was eager to gain weight. Lola would not hear of such a compromise, which seemed to her shameful, amounting to a desertion of duty. It was then that she told me of a great-great-great-uncle of hers who had sailed in the glorious and never to be forgotten *Mayflower* and had landed in Plymouth in 1620. In respect to his memory she couldn't dream of neglecting her culinary duties, which were a humble, ah yes, but sacred trust.

Anyway, from that day onwards, she only delicately nibbled her apple fritters, with very even, delightful little teeth. This horror of putting on fat took all the pleasure out of life for her. She languished. Soon she was as afraid of the fritters as I was of shells. We began to go for long healthy walks on the boulevards and by the river because of them, and we stopped going to the Napolitain because ice creams are so bad for ladies' figures.

I had never dreamed of any place as comfortable to live in as her room, which was all pale blue and had its own bathroom next door. There were signed pictures of her friends all over it, not many women but a great many men, good-looking boys, dark and with curly hair, which was her type. She used to tell me the colour of their eyes and talk about those loving and solemn dedications, every one of them final. At first making love among all these effigies used to worry me, but after a while one gets accustomed to it.

As soon as I finished kissing her, she'd go on again about the war and the apple fritters; I couldn't stop her. France came a good deal into our conversations. In Lola's mind France was a sort of chivalrous entity, not very clearly defined either in space or time, but at present grievously wounded and for that very reason extremely exciting. But when people talked to me about France, I thought at once of my guts, so that of course I was rather reserved and not very prone to any access of enthusiasm. Every one has his own fears. However, as she was kind to me in the matter of sex, I listened without ever contradicting her. But as far as soul was concerned, I could scarcely be said to satisfy her. She would have liked to see me keen and eager for the fray, but I for my part could not conceive why I ought to be in that exalted state, and I had on the other hand a hundred irrefutable reasons for remaining in precisely the opposite humour.

After all, Lola was only radiating happiness and optimism in the way that all folk do whose life is easy, privileged and secure; who, enjoying these things and good health, can look forward to living many more years.

She bothered me with her things of the spirit, which she never stopped talking about. The soul is the body's pride and pleasure when in health, but it is also a desire to be rid of the body when one is ill or things are going badly. You choose either the one attitude or the other, whichever suits you best at the particular moment, and that's all there is to it! While you are free to choose between both, all is well. But for me there was no choice; my course was settled. I was up to the neck in reality and could see my own death following me, so to speak, step for step. I found it very difficult to think of anything except a fate of slow assassination which the world seemed to consider the natural thing for me.

During this sort of protracted death agony, in which your brain is lucid and your body sound, it is impossible to comprehend anything but the absolute truths. You need to have undergone such an experience to have knowledge forever after of the truth or falsity of the things you say.

I came to the conclusion that even if the Germans were to arrive where we were, slaughtering, pillaging and setting fire to everything, to the hotel, the apple fritters, Lola, the Tuileries, the Cabinet and all their little friends, the Coupole, the Louvre and the big shops, even if they were to overrun the town and let hell loose in this foul fair ground, full of every sordidness on earth, still I should have nothing to lose by it and everything to gain.

You don't lose anything much when your landlord's house is burnt down. Another landlord always comes along, if it isn't always the same one — a German or a Frenchman or an Englishman or a Chinaman — and you get your bill just the same. . . . Whether you pay in marks or francs, it doesn't much matter.

Morals, in fact, were a dirty business. If I had told Lola what I thought of the war, she would only have taken me for a depraved freak and she'd deny me all intimate pleasures. So I took good care not to confess these things to her. Besides which, I still had other difficulties and rivalries to contend with. More than one officer was trying to take her from me. Their competition was dangerous, armed as they were with the attraction of their Legions of Honour. And there was beginning to be a lot about this damn Legion of Honour in the American papers. In fact, I think that after she had deceived me two or three times, our relationship would have been seriously threatened if just then the minx had not suddenly discovered something more to be said in my favour, which was that I could be used every morning as a substitute taster of fritters.

This last-minute specialization saved me. She could accept *me* as her deputy. Was I not myself a gallant fighting man and therefore worthy of this confidential post? From then onwards we were partners as well as lovers. A new era had begun.

Her body was an endless source of joy to me. I never tired of caressing its American contours. To tell the truth, I was an appalling lecher — and I went on being one.

Indeed, I came to the very delightful and comforting conclusion that a country capable of producing anatomies of such startling loveliness, and so full of spiritual grace, must have many other revelations of primary importance to offer — biologically speaking, of course.

My little games with Lola led me to decide that I would sooner or later make a journey, or rather a pilgrimage, to the United States; and certainly just as soon as I could manage it. Nor did I ever find respite and quiet (throughout a life fated in

any case to be difficult and restless) until I was able to bring off
this supremely mystical adventure in anatomical research.

Thus it was in the neighbourhood of Lola's backside that a
message from a new world came to me. And she hadn't only a fine
body, my Lola, — let us get that quite clear at once; she was
graced also with a piquant little face and grey-blue eyes, which
gave her a slightly cruel look, because they were set a wee bit on
the upward slant, like those of a wildcat.

Just to look into her face made my mouth water like a sip of
dry wine, of silex, will. Her eyes were hard and lacking the animation of that charming trademark vivacity reminiscent of the
Orient and of Fragonard, which one finds in almost all the eyes
over here.

We usually met in a café around the corner. Wounded men in
increasing numbers hobbled along the streets, in rags as often
as not. Collections were made on their behalf. There was a "Day"
for these, a "Day" for those, Days above all for the people who
organized them. Lie, copulate and die. One wasn't allowed to do
anything else. People lied fiercely and beyond belief, ridiculously,
beyond the limits of absurdity: lies in the papers, lies on the
hoardings, lies on foot, on horseback and on wheels. Everybody
was doing it, trying to see who could produce a more fantastic lie
than his neighbour. There was soon no truth left in town.

And what truth there was one was ashamed of, in 1914. Everything you touched was faked in some way — the sugar, the æroplanes, shoe leather, jam, photographs; everything you read,
swallowed, sucked, admired, proclaimed, refuted or upheld —
it was all an evil myth and masquerade. Even traitors weren't real
traitors. A mania for lying and believing lies is as catching as
the itch. Little Lola knew only a few phrases in French but
they were all jingo phrases: *"On les aura," "Madelon, viens!"*. . .
It was enough to make you weep.

She hovered over the death which was confronting us, per-
sistently, obscenely — as indeed did all the women, now that it
had become the fashion to be courageous at other people's expense.

And there was I at that time discovering in myself such a fondness for all the things which kept me apart from the war! I asked her again and again to tell me about America but she only answered with vague, silly and obviously inaccurate descriptions, which were meant to make a dazzling impression on me.

But I distrusted impressions just then. I'd been had that way once before; I wasn't going to be caught so easily again. Not by anybody.

I believed in her body, I didn't believe in her mind and heart. I considered her to be charming and cushily placed in this war, cushily placed in life.

Her attitude towards an existence which for me was horrible, was merely that of the patriotic press: *Pompon, Fanfare, ma Lorraine et gants blancs. . . .* Meanwhile I made love to her more and more often, having assured her that it would make her slim. But she relied more on our long walks to do that. I hated these long walks myself. But she was adamant.

So for several hours in the afternoon we would stride along in the Bois de Boulogne, around the lakes. Nature is a terrifying thing and even when well domesticated as in the Bois she still inspires a sort of uneasiness in real town dwellers. They are pretty apt in such surroundings to take you into their confidence. Nothing like the Bois de Boulogne, wet, railed-in, sleek and shorn as it is, for calling up a flock of stubborn memories in the minds of city folk strolling amid trees. Lola was a prey to this mood of melancholy, confidential unease. As we walked along, she'd tell me, more or less truthfully, a hundred and one things about her life in New York and her little friends there.

I couldn't quite disentangle what was convincing from what was doubtful in all this complicated rigmarole of dollars, engagements, dresses and jewelry, which seems to have made up her life in America.

That day we were going towards the race course. At that time one still came across children on donkeys there, and horse-cabs, and more children kicking up the dust, and cars full of men on leave, hunting all the time in the little paths, as fast as possible, between two trains, for women with nothing to do; they raised even more dust, in their hurry to go off and have dinner and make love, agitated and oily, with roving eyes, worried by the passage of time and the wish to live. They sweated with desire as well as with the heat.

The Bois was less well-kept than usual, temporarily neglected by the authorities.

"This place must have been very pretty before the war," Lola remarked. "It must have been awfully smart, wasn't it, Ferdinand? Tell me. Were the races like those in New York?"

To tell the truth, I'd never been to the races before the war myself, but I at once made up a colourful description of them for her benefit, basing myself on what I'd often heard about them from other people. Beautiful dresses . . . smart society women . . . splendid four-in-hands. . . . They're off! The gay trumpets . . . the water jump. . . . The President of the Republic. . . . The excitement of changing odds. . . . And so on.

She was so delighted with these idealized vignettes of mine that my remarks brought us closer together. From that moment on Lola felt she had discovered a taste which we had in common, a taste, for my part well dissimulated, for the gay social round. She even kissed me there and then in her excitement, a thing which seldom happened with her, I must confess. And then the sadness of fashions dead and gone overcame her. We all mourn the passage of time in our own particular way. For Lola it was the passing of fashion which made her perceive the flight of years.

"Ferdinand," she asked, "do you think there will ever be races held here again?"

"I suppose there will, when the war is over, Lola."

"It's not certain, though, is it?"

"No, it's not certain."

The possibility of there never being any more races at Longchamps upset her. The sadness of life takes hold of people as best it may, but it seems almost always to manage to take hold of them somehow.

"Suppose the war goes on for a long time, Ferdinand, for years perhaps. Then for me it will be too late . . . to come back here. . . . Don't you understand, Ferdinand? You see, I'm so fond of lovely places like this . . . that are so smart . . . and attractive. It will be too late, I expect. I shall be old then, Ferdinand, when the meetings begin again. I shall be already too old. . . . You'll see, Ferdinand, how it'll be too late. I feel it will be too late."

And then once again she was filled with despair, as she had been before about the two pounds' added weight. I said everything I could think of to reassure her and give her hope. After all, she was only twenty-three, I told her. . . . And the war would be over very soon. Good times would come again. As good as before, better times than before. . . . For her, at least, an attractive girl like her. . . . Lost time was nothing: she'd make it up as easily as anything. . . . There'd be people to admire her, to make a fuss over her, for a long time yet. She put on a less unhappy face, to please me.

"Must we go on walking?" she asked.

"But you want to get slim?"

"Oh, I'd forgotten that. . . ."

We left Longchamps, the children had gone away. Only the dust was left. The fellows on leave were still looking for Happiness, but out in the open now. Happiness was to be tracked down among the café tables around the Porte Maillot.

We walked towards Saint-Cloud along the river banks hazy with autumn mist. Near the bridge several lighters pressed their bows against the arches, lying deep in the water, loaded with coal to the bulwarks.

The park foliage spread itself like an enormous fan above the railings. These trees are as detached, magnificent and impressive as one's dreams. But I was afraid of trees too, since I had known them to conceal an enemy. Every tree meant a dead man. The avenue led uphill towards the fountains flanked by roses. Near the kiosk the old lady who sold refreshments seemed slowly to be gathering all the shadows of evening about her skirts. Further away in the side alleys great squares and rectangles of dark-coloured canvas were flapping; the canvas of the tents of a fair which the war had taken by surprise and filled with silence.

"They've been away a whole year now," the old lady reminded us. "Nowadays only a couple of people will come along here in all the day. I come still, out of habit. . . . There used to be such a crowd. . . ."

The old lady had understood nothing else of what had happened: that was all she knew. Lola had a curious desire to walk past the empty marquees, because she was feeling sad.

We counted about twenty of them, big ones full of mirrors, and a greater number of small ones, sweet stalls, lotteries, and a small theatre even, full of draughts. There was one to every tree; they were all round us. One in particular near the main avenue had lost its canvas walls altogether and stood empty as an explained mystery.

They leaned over towards the mud and fallen leaves, these tents. We stopped close to the last one, which was further aslant than the rest, its posts pitching in the rising wind like the masts of a ship with wildly tugging sails about to snap the last of its ropes. The whole tent swayed, its inner canvas flapping towards heaven, flapping above the roof. Its ancient name was written in green and red on a board over the door. It was a shooting alley. "The Stand of All Nations" it was called.

There was no one to look after it, either. He himself was away shooting along with the rest perhaps, the proprietor shooting shoulder to shoulder with his clients.

What a lot of shot had struck the targets of the booth! They were all spotted with little white pellet marks. There was a funny wedding scene, in zinc: in front the bride with her bouquet, the best man, a soldier, the bridegroom with a big red face, and in the background more guests — they must all have been killed again and again when the fair was on.

"I'm sure you're a good shot, aren't you, Ferdinand? If the fair was still here, I'd take you on. . . . You shoot well, don't you, Ferdinand?"

"No, I'm not a very good shot."

Further back, beyond the wedding, was another roughly painted target — the Town Hall with its flag flying. You shot at the Town Hall, when it was working, into the windows, and they opened and a bell rang, and you even shot at the little zinc flag.

And you shot too at the regiment of soldiers marching up a hill near by, like mine in the Place Clichy; amid all these discs and uprights, all there to be shot at as much as possible, now it was I who was to be shot at — who had been shot at yesterday and would be shot at to-morrow —

"They shoot at me too, Lola!" I cried out. I couldn't help it.

"Come on," she said. "You're being silly, Ferdinand — and we shall catch cold."

We went on towards Saint-Cloud down the Royal Avenue, avoiding the mud. She held my hand in hers, such a small hand, but I could think of nothing else but the zinc wedding of the "Stand of All Nations" which we had left behind us in the gathering darkness. I even forgot to kiss her; it was all too much for me. I felt very strange.

In fact, I think it must have been from that moment that my head began to be so full of ideas and so difficult to calm.

When we got to the bridge at Saint-Cloud it was quite dark. "Would you like to eat at Duval's, Ferdinand? You like Duval's. . . . It would cheer you up. . . . There's always a lot of people there. Unless you'd rather have supper in my room?" She was being very attentive that evening, in fact.

We finally decided on Duval's. But we'd hardly got our table than the place struck me as ludicrous and horrible. All these people sitting in rows all around us seemed to me to be sitting there waiting, they too, to be shot at from all sides as they ate.

"Run, all of you!" I shouted to them. "Get out! They're going to fire! They'll kill you. They'll kill us all."

I was hurried back to Lola's hotel. Everywhere I could see the same thing happening. All the people in the Paritz seemed to be going to get themselves shot and so did the hotel clerks at the reception desk. There they were, simply asking for it, and the porter man down by the door of the Paritz in his uniform of sky blue and his braid as golden as the sun, and the soldiers too, the officers who were wandering about, and those generals — not so grand as he, of course, but in uniforms nevertheless — it was all one vast shooting alley from which none of them, not one of them, could possibly escape.

"They're going to shoot!" I shouted to them at the top of my voice, in the middle of the main hall. "They're going to shoot! Clear out, all of you, run away!" Then I went and shouted it from the window too. I couldn't help myself. There was a terrible scene. "Poor boy," people said.

The porter took me along, very gently, to the bar. With great kindness he made me drink, and I drank a lot and then finally the gendarmes came to fetch me; they were rougher about it. In the "Stand of All Nations" there'd been gendarmes too. I remembered having seen them. Lola kissed me and helped them to handcuff me and lead me away.

After that I was feverish and fell ill; driven insane, they said in hospital, by fear. They may have been right. When one's in this world, surely the best thing one can do, isn't it, is to get out of it? Whether one's mad or not, frightened or not.

THERE WAS QUITE A TO-DO ABOUT IT. SOME SAID: "THE CHAP'S AN anarchist, and they'll shoot him, of course. Better do it at once, right away. Can't have any shilly-shallying in war time!" But there were others, more patient, who held that I was simply syphilitic and quite genuinely mad and should therefore be shut up until peace came, or anyhow for several months, because they, the not-mad, who were in full possession of their faculties, they said, wanted to take care of me while they carried on with the war on their own. Which just shows that there's nothing like infernal nerve for making people believe you're sane. If you've got plenty of cheek, that's enough; pretty nearly anything is allowed then, any damn thing. You've got the majority on your side, and it's the majority which decides what is mad and what isn't.

But they were still very uncertain about my diagnosis, so the authorities decided to have me kept under observation for a time. My dear little Lola was allowed to come and see me sometimes, and so was my mother. But that's all.

They housed us, the wounded and mentally deranged, in a school at Issy-les-Moulineaux which was specially organized to receive cases like myself, whose patriotic ideals had either been slightly shaken or else entirely warped. The idea was, all in good time, either gently or forcibly, according to circumstances, to extract a confession from us. We weren't treated downright badly, but one did feel all the time that one was being watched by the staff of silent male nurses, all of whom had enormous ears.

After undergoing this surveillance for some time, one was sent away quietly to the lunatic asylum, or to the front, or even, pretty frequently, to face a firing squad.

I always wondered which of all the chaps in that sinister

place, as he muttered to himself at table, was next to become a ghost. . . .

The concierge, who lived in a lodge by the entrance gate, used to sell us barley sugar and oranges and the materials we needed for sewing on buttons. She also sold us our pleasure. The price of pleasure, for N.C.O.'s, was ten francs. It could be had by any one. But you had to beware of confiding too easily in her at these moments. Such unburdenings could prove very costly. She scrupulously repeated all one had told her to the Chief Medical Officer, and it went into your dossier for a court-martial. It was pretty well certain that a series of confidences of this sort had led to the shooting of a lance corporal in the Spahis, not yet twenty years of age, together with a sapper from the Reserves, who had swallowed nails to give himself stomach ache, and also another man, suffering from hysteria, the chap who told how he had brought on his paralytic fits at the front. . . . One night, by way of sounding me, she offered to let me have the papers of a father of six children who had died, so she said, of a disease of the anus; she suggested I might find them useful. In fact, she was a thorough bitch. Of course, in bed, she was marvellous value, one always came back for more and she gave us the hell of a time. As far as that was concerned, she certainly had it all taped. You need to, anyway, if you're going to have a real good time. After all, between the sheets a certain salacious ingenuity is as essential as pepper is to a good sauce; it makes a finished job of it.

The school buildings were flanked by a broad terrace, golden in summer among the trees, from which one could see Paris grandly unfolding itself in perspective. It was there that visitors waited to see us on Thursdays, Lola among them, punctually bringing me cakes, advice and cigarettes.

We saw our doctors every morning. They questioned us kindly but one never quite knew what they were thinking. They went among us, and in the most charming way in the world dangled our death warrants in front of our noses.

A good many of the patients under observation, more nervous than their fellows, were reduced by this torturing atmosphere to such a state of exasperation that at night, instead of going to sleep, they got up and paced up and down the dormitory, protesting aloud against the agony within them, huddled between hope and despair as in a dangerous mountain crevice. They suffered like this for many days and then suddenly one night they'd collapse completely and go and tell the chief doctor everything. One never saw them again after that. I wasn't easy in my mind myself. But when one's weak, the thing that gives one strength is stripping those one fears of the slightest prestige that one may still tend to accord them. One must teach oneself to see them as they are, as worse than they are, that is; one should look at them from all points of view. This detaches you, sets you free and is much more of a protection than you can possibly imagine. It gives you another self, so that there are two of you together.

Their actions no longer have that foul mysterious power over you, weakening you and wasting your time, and their foolishness is no more pleasing to you or useful to your own intimate development than that of the lowest swine.

In the bed next to mine slept a corporal, a volunteer like me. Previous to the month of August, he told me, he'd been a teacher of history and geography at a school in the Touraine. After a month or two at the front this professor proved himself to be an absolute prince of thieves. They couldn't stop him stealing canned food from the regimental supply waggons, from the commissariat and company ration dumps, or anywhere else he could find it.

With the rest of us he had been cast up here, an uncertain figure on the "case-list" of the Army Council. However, as his family was trying hard to prove that shellfire had stupefied and demoralized him, judgment on his case was deferred from month to month. He didn't talk to me much. He used to spend hours combing his beard, but when he did speak, it was almost always on the same subject, — the method he had discovered to avoid getting his wife with child. Was he really mad? When the world is all upside down and it is mad to ask why one is being assassinated, obviously it is very easy to be considered insane. You have, of course, to give an impression of madness, but when it's a question of avoiding wholesale slaughter, some minds are capable of magnificent imaginative efforts.

Truly everything that is really interesting goes on in the dark. One knows nothing of the inner history of people.

Princhard was this schoolmaster's name. What plan can he possibly have hit upon to keep his arteries, his lungs and his eyes intact? That's the essential question which we men ought to have asked each other in order to remain strictly human and sensible. But we did nothing of the sort; hemmed in by insane martial trivialities tottering along after an absurd ideal, like rats already stupid with smoke, we tried to escape from the burning ship, but without any plan of action or any confidence in each other. Bewildered by the war, we had become mad in another way; mad with fear. There you have war seen both ways.

All the same, this Princhard chap seemed to show a certain liking for me in the midst of our general delirium, though naturally he was very cautious about it.

Where we were, in our predicament, no friendship, no trust, could possibly exist. No one expressed aloud anything except what he thought might help to save his skin, since everything, or nearly everything, would be repeated by eager sneaks.

From time to time one of us disappeared: that meant that his case was settled, and would come to an end before the Army Council, at Biribi, in the front line or, for the more fortunate, at the asylum at Clamart.

More and more soldiers suffering from doubt kept on arriving from all sections of the army, some very young and others almost old, either in an awful funk or else swaggering and crazy. Their wives and relations and their wide-eyed children visited them on Thursdays.

Everybody cried copiously in the waiting room, especially in the evening. The unfit of the wartime world came and wept there when the wives and children, their visits over, left dragging their feet along the dim gas-lit corridor. Nothing but a bunch of disgusting snivelers, that's all they were.

It was still an adventure for Lola to come and see me in this kind of prison. We two did not cry. We had nothing to cry about.

"Have you really gone mad, Ferdinand?" she asked me one Thursday.

"Yes," I confessed, "I have."

"Then are they going to cure you here?"

"Fear can't be cured, Lola."

"Are you as frightened as all that, then?"

"More than that even. Listen, Lola, I'm so frightened that if, later on, I were to die a natural death, I wouldn't want them to burn my body. I want to be left in the ground to rot in the cemetery, peacefully, ready to start living again maybe. . . . One can't ever tell! . . . But if I was burnt to ashes, Lola, it would be all over, quite over. A skeleton, after all, is something like a man. It is nearer to living again than ashes are. . . . With ashes it's finished. . . . What do you think? You see, the war — "

"Oh, then you're an utter coward, Ferdinand! You're as repulsive to me as a rat . . ."

"Yes, an utter coward, Lola. I refuse to accept war and all that it entails. I don't want it or desire it. I won't resign myself to it. I will not let myself be overcome with self-pity because of it. I simply reject it, absolutely refuse to have anything to do with it and all its soldiers. If they were nine hundred and ninety-five million and I were only one alone, they would still be wrong, Lola, and I right, because I am the only one who knows what I want. I want not to die."

"But you *can't* refuse to fight, Ferdinand! Only cowards and madmen refuse to fight when their country is in danger. . . ."

"Then long live all cowards and madmen! Or rather, may it be the cowards and madmen who survive! Look, Lola, can you remember the name of any one of the soldiers who were killed in the Hundred Years' War? Have you ever tried to find out one single name among them all? No, you can't; you've never tried, have you? To you they're all anonymous, unknown and less important than the least atom in this paper weight on the table in front of you, less important than the food your bowels digested yesterday. You can see that they died for nothing. For nothing at all, the idiots! I swear that's true; you can see that it is. Only life itself is of any importance. Ten thousand years hence I bet you that this war, all-important as it seems to us now, will be completely forgotten. Possibly a dozen or so learned men may wrangle about it occasionally, and about the dates of the chief hecatombs for which it was famous. Up to the present time that is all that Humanity has ever succeeded in finding memorable about itself, after a few centuries have gone by, or a few years, or even after a few hours. . . . I don't believe in the future, Lola."

When she saw how shamelessly I proclaimed my deplorable lack of courage, she ceased to find me in the least worthy of pity. She considered me definitely despicable.

She made up her mind to leave at once. It was too much. When I accompanied her back to the gate of the hospital that evening, she did not kiss me.

Obviously it was impossible for her to admit that a man condemned to death might still not want to die. And when I asked after our apple fritters she did not even answer me.

When I got back to our room I found Princhard standing before the window in the middle of a circle of the men, trying out a pair of spectacles against the gaslight. He had had this idea, he told us, on a holiday by the seaside, and now that summer had come, he intended to wear them during the daytime in the park. This park was an enormous place, well guarded, of course, by squads of vigilant warders. The next day Princhard insisted that I should go with him as far as the terrace, because he was going to try his lovely glasses. The afternoon sun shone down brilliantly on Princhard protected by his dark glasses. I noticed that his nostrils were almost transparent and that he breathed very quickly.

"My friend," he confided in me, "time slips by and sides against me. . . . My conscience is inaccessible to remorse; I have freed myself, thank God, from such worries. It's not wrong-doing which matters in this world. They gave up that a long time ago. It's blunders. And I think I have been guilty of a blunder . . . an absolutely irreparable one."

"What, stealing canned food?"

"Yes, I thought that was cunning, just imagine! I thought by that means to get myself taken away from the gunfire, ashamed of myself but still alive, and to come back to peace as one comes up to the surface again, exhausted after a long dive. I almost succeeded. But really the war is lasting too long. . . . As it goes on longer and longer, it becomes harder to conceive of individuals sufficiently disgusting to disgust their country. The Motherland has now taken to accepting all sacrifices, wherever they come from, all the available butcher's meat. She has become infinitely indulgent as to her choice of martyrs. Nowadays there are no soldiers unworthy of bearing arms and, above all, of dying under them and being killed by them. They now say they're going to make a hero of me! The massacring mania must be extraordinarily strong that they should have begun to overlook the theft of a tin of jam! 'Overlook,' did I say? They'll forget it entirely. True, we've been accustomed day by day to admire colossal bandits, whose opulence the whole world venerates as we do, and whose life shows itself to be, when examined closely, one long crime renewed each day; but these people enjoy glory, honour and power; their crimes are consecrated by the law, while as far back as we can go in history — and there I *am* in a position to talk — everything shows us that a petty theft, especially of some trivial foodstuff such as a loaf, a ham or a cheese, inevitably draws upon the man who commits it the formal opprobrium and categorical repudiation of the community, with heavy punishment, automatic dishonour, inexpiable shame; and that for two reasons, first because the author of such a crime is generally a poor man, which state in itself implies a fundamental unworthiness, and secondly because his act contains a sort of tacit reproach to the community. The poor man's theft becomes a spiteful reprisal by an individual, you understand. Where does this lead us? You will notice that the repression of petty larceny is vigorously pursued in all countries, not only as a means of social defence but also and chiefly as a stern recommendation to all unfortunates to remember their place and their caste, — that of wretches submitting joyfully through the centuries and for ever to a death of misery and hunger. Up till now, however, under the Republic there's been one advantage left to these petty thieves, that of being deprived of the honour of bearing their country's arms. But to-morrow this state of affairs is to change; I, a thief, am going back to-morrow to my place in the army. Those are the orders. It has been decided in high places to sponge out what is described as my 'temporary lapse', and this, mark you, in consideration of what they term 'the good name of my family.' What benevolence on their part! I ask you, Comrade, is it my family that is going to serve as a strainer and a sieve to a mixture of French and German bullets? It will be just me alone, won't it? And when I am dead, will the honour of my family resurrect me? Listen, I can see my family now, the war and everything over — for there is always an end to all things — here and now I see my family joyously disporting themselves on fine Sundays on the lawns of returning summer. While three feet below ground I, their father, will be streaming with maggots, stinking more horribly than a heap of bank-holiday dung, all my disillusioned flesh absurdly rotting. To manure the furrows of an unknown labourer, that is the true future of the true soldier. Ah, my friend, this world is nothing but a vast attempt to catch you with your trousers down. . . . You are young. These moments full of wisdom should be worth years to you. Listen to what I am telling you, Comrade; note the danger signal which marks all the murderous hypocrisies of our society, and never again let it pass you by without fully grasping its importance. 'Commiseration of the fate and the condition of the down-at-heel.' I tell you, worthy little people, life's riffraff, forever beaten, fleeced, and sweating, I warn you that when the great people of this world start loving you, it means that they are going to make sausage meat of you. That is the sign, it is infallible. And it starts with affection. Louis XIV, he at least, remember, did not care a damn about the people. The same applies to Louis XV. He didn't even bother to kick them in the pants. Life was not easy in those days, certainly; for the poor, life has never been easy. But they weren't set upon and gutted quite as rabidly and ruthlessly as they are by their tyrants of to-day. There is no rest for the humble except in despising the great, whose only thought of the people is inspired by self-interest or sadism. You must know, as we are on this subject, that it was the philosophers who first started telling the poor people stories. The poor man knew nothing but his catechism. They were out, they said, to educate him. They had various truths to reveal to him! Fine truths! Not worn-out truths either, bright shining new ones! They dazzled him completely. 'That's right, that's right,' the poor devils started in to say. 'That's absolutely true. We must die for it.' The people have never asked for anything except to die. It's always the way. 'Long live Diderot!' they shouted, and then, 'Bravo, Voltaire!' Those are your real philosophers. And long live Carnot, who's so good at organizing victories, and long live everybody! Those fellows, at any rate, won't let the people die in ignorance and superstition. They show them the way to liberty. They emancipate them. It doesn't take long! First every one must learn to read the papers. That is salvation. And quickly too, by God! No more illiterates, We will have none of them. Nothing but soldiers and citizens who vote, read, fight, march and blow kisses. The people were soon done to a turn under this régime. An enthusiasm for freedom must serve some useful purpose, after all, mustn't it? Danton wasn't eloquent for fun. A few hoarse roars, loud enough for one to be able to hear them still, and he had the people under arms in an instant. And then came the first departure of the first battalion of the emancipated and frenzied. Of the first voting and flag-wagging sods led by Dumouriez to Flanders to get holes drilled in themselves. As for Dumouriez himself, come too late to this little game of ideals, entirely unlettered, preferring good clinking coin on the whole, he deserted. He was our last mercenary. Being a soldier for nothing was a new idea. So new that Goethe, in spite of his being Goethe, when he came to Valmy, got a shock at the sight of it. In the presence of those ragged, impassioned troops, who had come there of their own free will to be ripped to pieces by the King of Prussia in defence of this brand-new fiction of patriotism, Goethe felt that he still had a great deal to learn. 'From that day,' he proclaimed magnificently, in his own inimitable style, 'a new epoch commences.' I should damn well think it does! After that, as the idea worked so well, they started to turn out heroes in series, and they cost less and less as the system became more and more perfect. Every one's done the same. Bismarck, the two Napoleons, Barrès, as well as the bold Elsa. Flag worship promptly replaced divine worship, an old cloud already punctured by the Reformation and condensed a long time ago into Episcopal coffers. In the old days the fanatic fashion was 'Jesus for ever!' and 'Burn the heretics!' Still, the heretics after all were rare and of their own choosing. But now, in our time, immense hordes are roused by the cry: 'To the stake with all gutless sissies, fibreless hacks and innocent bookworms. Millions, face right!' Those who do not want to spitcher or assassinate anybody, the stinking pacifists, take, seize and quarter them. Then truss them up in thirteen different dirty ways. To teach them how to live, just tear their bowels from their bodies, their eyes from their sockets, and the years from their nasty dribbling lives. Let them die, legion after legion of them, die, turn hollow and hum, bleed, and corrode in acid — all in order that their country should become more loved, more joyous and more sweet. And if there are any wretches so low as to refuse to understand the sublimity of all this, they can straightway go and bury themselves with the others — but no, not with them, but at the far end of the cemetery, under the shameful epitaph of cowards without ideals: because, infamous wretches, they will have forfeited their glorious right to any particle of the shadow cast by the monument which the community has raised in the central alley to commemorate the decent dead, and also their right to the least echo of a Cabinet Minister's words when he comes one fine Sunday to have lunch and urinate at the prefect's house, before yawping emotionally above the graves."

But they were calling Princhard from the bottom of the garden. The head doctor had sent the warder on duty to fetch him immediately.

"I'm coming," said Princhard, and he just had time to hand me the notes of the speech he had been trying out on me. A comic thing to do.

I never saw Princhard again. He had the intellectual's vice; he was futile. The fellow knew too much and it confused him. He had to resort to a lot of tricks to kindle his own enthusiasm, to make up his mind.

It's already a long time ago, that evening that he went away, when I think of it. The houses on the edge of the park stood out once more clearly, for a moment, as do all things before the night captures them. The trees grew bigger in the dusk and rose into the sky to meet the night.

I have never made any attempt to find out what happened to him, or if he really "disappeared", this Princhard, as was said. But it is better that he should have disappeared.

THE SEEDS OF OUR MALIGNANT PEACE WERE BEING SOWN ALREADY IN the war time.

You could guess what it would be like — an hysterical vacuum — when you saw it stirring in the Olympia den. Down on the dance floor in the basement, amid a hundred glinting mirrors, it was prancing in the dust and the despair of negroid-Hebrew-Saxon strains. Britishers and blacks were there together. Levantines and Russians were everywhere, smoking, loud-voiced, melancholy and military, sitting in rows along the crimson sofas. Those uniforms which one can now only just call to mind were the seeds of the present day, that ugly thing which is growing still and which will not for some time yet have finally become manure.

With lusts well roused by a few hours spent at the Olympia every week, we'd all go along to call on Madame Herote, who kept a lingerie-*cum*-glove-*cum*-bookshop behind the Folies-Bergère, in the Impasse des Bérésinas, which to-day no longer exists, where little dogs on leashes were brought by little girls to do their business.

We ourselves were there fumbling for our happiness, which was threatened savagely from all sides. We were ashamed of wanting it as we did, but it couldn't be helped; one went to it just the same. It's harder to lose the wish to love than the wish to live. One spends one's time in this world killing and adoring, and one does both together. "I hate you! I adore you!" You defend yourself and have a good time and pass on life to some biped in the next century, frantically, at all costs, as if to be continued were a tremendously pleasant thing, as if, after all, that could make one live forever. Whatever happens, one has to make love, as one has to scratch.

My mental condition was improving but my military situation was still pretty doubtful. I was allowed to go into town from time to time. The name of our lingerie lady was, as I say, Madame Herote. Her forehead was low and so narrow that at first one felt embarrassed in her presence, but her lips had such a way of smiling, and were so full, that one soon found it impossible to escape from her. Under cover of an astonishing volubility and an unforgettable temperament she harboured a number of simple, rapacious, earnestly mercantile intentions.

She began to make a fortune in a few months, thanks to the Allies and, particularly, to her own person. The fact is that she had undergone an operation the year before, and her ovaries had been removed. This castration, which gave her freedom, made her fortune. Certain feminine ailments of this sort turn out to be providential. A woman who is always dreading a possible pregnancy is as good as impotent: she will never go far on the road to success.

Old and young thought, and so did I, that there was an easy way of making love, not too expensively, in the back premises of certain lingerie-bookshops. That was still true some twenty years ago, but since then a number of things have changed, and this custom has gone out along with others less delightful. Anglo-Saxon puritanism is drying us up more and more every month; it has already reduced these impromptu backstair gayeties to negligible proportions. Marriage and respectability are the fashion entirely.

Madame Herote put to a good use our last available freedom to copulate cheaply and standing up. An out-of-work auctioneer passed by her shop one Sunday, went in and is there still. He was then just a bit "gaga", and he stayed that way, but that's all. Their joy was their own affair; no one spoke of it. While the papers were raving with appeals for every possible patriotic sacrifice, life went on, carefully rationed and full of foresight, more cunningly than ever. Such are, like light and shade, the two sides of the same medal.

Madame Herote's auctioneer used to invest money in Holland for his better-informed friends and when they got to know each other well, he did the same for Madame Herote. Her stock of scarves, brassières, and almost-chemises attracted a regular clientele of both sexes and above all incited them to frequent visits.

Parisians and foreigners continually met behind those short pink curtains amid the ceaseless babble of the proprietress, whose solid, voluble and sickeningly perfumed bulk would have made the most liverish customer frisky. Far from losing control of these gatherings, Madame Herote got her reward, first in money, by taking her tithe of these sentimental transactions, and secondly because a lot of loving went on all around her. She took at least an equal pleasure in joining couples and separating them, with her naggings, insinuations and trickery.

Never for a moment did she stop devising delights and alarums. She encouraged a passionate view of life. And her business went all the better for it.

Proust, who was half a ghost himself, with extraordinary determination became immersed in the Infinite, in the misty futility of the functions and formalities which twine about the people of society, that vacuum full of phantom desires, of uncertain fools always awaiting their Watteau, irresolute, smut-fingering seekers after unlikely isles of amorous enchantment. But Madame Herote, who came of sound, popular stock, was held firmly to earth by stupid, healthy, definite desires.

People are so bad perhaps only because they suffer; but it takes a long time after they have ceased suffering for them to become a little better. Madame Herote had had a fine success, both material and emotional, but it had not yet had time to soften her domineering disposition.

She was no more malicious than most of the little shopkeepers round about, but she took a great deal of trouble to show she was, which is why one remembers her chiefly. Her shop was not only a rendezvous, but a sort of backdoor to a world of luxury and wealth, into which, much as I had wanted to, I had never yet entered, and from which I was anyway promptly and painfully ejected after one furtive intrusion, my first and my last.

The rich in Paris live all together. Their homes form a wedge, a slice of urban cake whose point touches the Louvre and whose rounded end meets the trees between the Pont d'Auteuil and the

Porte des Ternes. There it is, the best part of the town. All the rest is wretchedness and rubble.

When one enters the wealthy quarter one does not at first notice any great difference from other parts of the town, unless it is that the streets are a little cleaner and that's all. In order actually to make one's way into the life of the people in this place, one has to trust to luck or to some intimate relationship.

Through Madame Herote's shop one was able to penetrate this reserve a little, thanks to the Argentines who used to come down there from the privileged quarters of the town to buy knickers and chemises and also to fool about with her bevy of ambitious young friends from the world of music and the theatre, well-formed little creatures whom Madame Herote took care to gather around her.

One of these girls, although I had nothing to offer her but my youth, as the saying goes, began to interest me a great deal too much. She was called Musyne by the rest of the set.

In Bérésinas alley every one knew every one else in each of the little shops. It was really like a little province of its own, which had been sandwiched for years on end between two streets in Paris; in other words, every one spied on and maligned his neighbour as much as was humanly possible.

On the material side, before the war, what these shopkeepers talked about was a niggling and desperately thrifty way of life. Among other trials was the chronic misery of being forced, in their gloomy interiors, to light the gas as early as four o'clock in the afternoon, so that the wares in their windows could be seen. But this, on the other hand, provided suitable lighting for delicate propositions inside their shops.

Owing to the war, many businesses, despite all efforts, were going to have to close down; but Madame Herote's, thanks to her young Argentines, to officers on extra pay and to the counsels of her friend the auctioneer, was booming in a way which, as can well be imagined, gave rise to the most scabrous comment.

It was at this time, for instance, that the famous confectioner at Number 112 suddenly lost his beautiful clients, owing to the mobilization. The lovely ladies who had come regularly in long gloves to taste his sweets, now that horses were being requisitioned and they had to come on foot, came no longer. They were never to return. As for Sambanet, the music binder, he suddenly failed to resist the desire he had always had to intrigue with some soldier boy. An indiscretion of this sort one unfortunate evening was enough to wreck his reputation with certain patriotic gentlemen who straightway accused him of being a spy. He had to shut down.

On the other hand Mademoiselle Mermance, at Number 26, might have managed very well, things being what they were. Her specialty had up till then been a certain rubber article which it may or may not be proper to mention. But she had the greatest bad luck in that she found it appallingly difficult to get her stock through from Germany, which is where her goods came from.

It was only Madame Herote, in fact, at this dawn of a new age of flimsy democratic underclothes, who slid easily into prosperity.

People used to write anonymous letters to each other in the different shops, pretty spicy ones. Madame Herote found more amusement in writing them to important personages; this in itself was evidence of the strong ambition which was the very foundation of her character. She wrote, for instance, to the Prime Minister with the sole object of telling him he was a cuckold; and to Marshal Pétain she wrote in English, with the aid of the dictionary, just to annoy him. But what did it matter? Anonymous letters were water off a duck's back. Madame Herote used to get her little bundle of them every day, and very smelly ones they were, too. They used to flabbergast her and make her thoughtful for ten minutes or so, but she would invariably quite quickly get over it somehow, on any pretext that came to hand, because in her inner life there was no room at all for doubts and still less for truth.

Among her clients and protegées there were quite a few girls who came to her with more debts than clothes. Madame Herote gave all of them sound advice and they made good, Musyne among them, who seemed to me the most attractive of the lot. An angelically musical little creature she was, an absolute pet of a violinist, but a very unconcerned pet, as she soon showed me. She was quite determined to be a success in this world and not in the next, and when I met her she was managing very well in an utterly charming and very Parisian little act, long since forgotten, at the Variétés. She used to come on with her violin in a sort of rhyming and musical prelude; a complicated and delightful type of entertainment.

Infatuated with her as I was, I had a frantic time of it, dashing from the hospital to her stage door. I was, of course, not the only one to wait for her there. She would be whisked away on the arm of a territorial or more easily still on that of an aviator. But the palm of seduction went to the Argentines. As fresh contingents swarmed into being, their frozen-meat industry had practically become one of the forces of nature. Little Musyne did as well as she could out of that boom period. She was quite right; the Argentines are now no more.

I couldn't make it out. I was a cuckold in everything — in women, in money, in ideas. I was being deceived and I was unhappy. Even in these days I sometimes come across Musyne by chance, about once in every two years, as one does meet people that one has known very well in the past. Two years is just the interval that is needed to make you aware at one glance, irrefutably and as if instinctively, of the ugliness that has come over a face, even one which was delicious in its day.

For a moment one hesitates before it and then finally one accepts this face as it now is, with all its awful, increasing lack of beauty. You have to acquiesce in this careful caricature which two years have slowly etched. You have to admit the passage of time, accept its portraiture of yourself. Then you can say that you really have recognized each other (as at first one hesitates to take a foreign bank note), and that you weren't on the wrong road, that you have been going along in the right direction all this time, without ever having come together; two more years along the unavoidable highroad, the road to rottenness. And that's all there is to it.

Whenever she met me casually like this, Musyne was so shocked by the sight of me that she seemed to want to run right away, to run off and avoid me somehow. . . . She didn't like the look of me, that was obvious; I reminded her of a whole past life. But I know her age, I've known it too many years; there's nothing she can do, she can't escape me any more. So she stands there, looking annoyed to see that I exist, as if she were face to face with some monster. She, who is so sensitive, seems to think she has to ask me idiotic and thick-headed questions, like a housemaid caught out by her mistress in some misdemeanour. Women are all housemaids at heart. But perhaps she imagines this repulsion rather than feels it; that is my remaining consolation. Perhaps all that I suggest to her is that I am horrible to look at. Perhaps I am an artist in that line. After all, why should there not be as much possible artistry in ugliness as in beauty? It's one line to take up, that's all.

I had for a long time thought little Musyne stupid, but that was only because I was vain and had been jilted by her. Before the war, you know, we were all of us much more ignorant and fatuous than we are to-day. We knew practically nothing about the world in general: a lot of oafs we were, in fact. Little people like myself were much more liable to mistake cheese for chalk in those days than they are to-day. Because I was in love with Musyne, I imagined that that was going to give me added strength in everything, above all, that it would give me the courage I lacked, all because she was so pretty, so musical and sweet, the little darling! Love is like alcohol; the more intoxicated and incapable you are, the stronger and quicker-witted you think yourself, and the surer you are of your rights.

Madame Herote, several of whose cousins had been killed at the front, never left home except in deep mourning; actually she didn't go into town often, as her auctioneer friend was rather jealous. We used to meet in the dining room at the back of the shop, which with this new-found prosperity had blossomed into quite a salon. We gathered there and talked and passed the time, very properly and prettily, in the gas-light. At the piano little Musyne would charm us with classical music, classics being the only suitable thing to play in those sad times. We would sit there right through the afternoon, side by side, with the auctioneer in the middle, nursing all together our secrets, fears and hopes.

The servant whom Madame Herote had recently engaged was very keen to know when each of us was finally going to decide to marry somebody else in the group. Where she came from in the country, love without wedlock was inconceivable. All these Argentines, officers and ferreting clients filled her with almost animal apprehension.

Musyne was more and more often being taken up by South American customers. The result was that I came to know the servants' quarters of these gentlemen very well, because I used to wait there for my beloved. Their valets used of course to take me for a pimp. After a while every one used to take me for a pimp, including Musyne herself and, I believe, all the habitués of Madame Herote's shop. There was nothing I could do about it. It was bound to happen sooner or later, anyway; people have to classify you in some way or other.

I got the military authorities to allow me another two months' sick leave and there was even some talk of invaliding me. Musyne and I decided to go and live together at Billancourt. She did it really so as to be able to trick me all the more easily; she used to come home less and less often, on account of our living such a long distance out of town. She was always finding new excuses for staying in Paris.

Our nights at Billancourt were sweet; sometimes they would be disturbed by silly air-raid alarms which provided the inhabitants with a chance to feel frightened and justified. While I waited for my mistress, I used to walk, when night had fallen, as far as the Pont de Grenelle, where the shadows of the river rise as far as the platform of the overhead Métro, with its necklace of lights high in the darkness and a mass of metal rails roaring straight into the side of the great apartment houses on the Quai de Passy.

There are certain corners like that in big towns which are so offensively hideous that one is almost always alone in them.

Musyne ended up by only returning to what I may call our hearth and home once a week. She was more and more frequently being engaged to accompany singers at the Argentines' houses. She could have made her living playing at cinemas and it would have been much easier for me to go and fetch her from there, but the Argentines were amusing and paid well, whereas the cinemas were depressing and paid badly. Life is made up of such choices.

The last straw for me was the foundation of the Théâtre aux Armées. Musyne immediately got to know people at the War Office and was continually going off to entertain our brave lads at the front — for weeks at a time. She expounded sonatas and adagios to the troops, with the General Staff, nicely placed in the stalls, admiring her legs; the rank and file on the benches behind their superior officers could enjoy only audible harmonies. Naturally, too, she had to spend eventful nights in hotels in the war zone. One day she came back to me from the line full of high spirits and boasting a certificate for bravery, signed, if you please, by one of our great generals. This diploma was the starting point of a definitely successful career.

In the Argentine colony she made herself extremely popular at once. She was endlessly fêted. Every one was mad about my Musyne, such a dear little active-service violinist! So sweet and curly-headed, and a heroine into the bargain. These Argentines knew a good thing when they saw one; they professed a limitless admiration for our leaders, and when my Musyne was returned to them with her impressive document, her cute face, and her lively, heroic little fingers, they began to make love as fast as they could, outbidding each other, one might say, in competition for her. The poetry of heroism appeals irresistibly to those who don't go to a war, and even more to those whom the war is making enormously wealthy. It's always so.

Oh, this gallant, rebellious patriotism, it's enough to make one sick! The Rio shipowners offered themselves and their shares in marriage to the sweet little thing who was so prettily typifying for their benefit the valiant French nation at arms. I must admit that Musyne had thought out for herself a very attractive little repertoire of war stories, which suited her to perfection, like a saucy little hat. She often astonished even me with her finesse, and, hearing her talk, I had to acknowledge that in the matter of drawing long bows I was clumsiness itself compared to her. She had a gift for placing her flights of fancy in distant, dramatic settings which somehow lent them precision and credibility. As for us combatants, we, I suddenly realized, merely existed in the realm of these conceits as temporary, cloddish adjuncts. Things eternal were the stuff my pretty one worked in. One must believe Claude Lorrain when he says that the foreground in a picture is always unattractive and that Art demands that the interest of the canvas should be placed in the far distance, where lies take refuge, those dreams which blossom out of fact and are man's only love. A woman who can take account of the wretchedness of our natures easily becomes our darling, our vital and supreme inspiration. We expect of her that she shall preserve our lying *raison d'être*, but all the while she can, in exercising this magic function, to a large extent earn her own living. Musyne, by instinct, did not fail to do so.

The Argentines lived in the Ternes direction, chiefly around the Bois in smart, aloof little villas, so cosy and warm inside that when you came in from the street these winter days your thoughts all of a sudden took an optimistic turn, in spite of yourself.

So distressed and nervous was I that, as I have said, I used to go as often as possible, making a complete fool of myself, to wait for my lady-love below stairs. I hung around patiently, sometimes until morning came; I was sleepy, but jealousy, and a lot of white wine which the servants gave me, kept me well awake. As for the Argentine masters of the house, I very seldom saw them; I heard the songs they sang, their rumbling Spanish and the piano which never stopped playing. But mostly it was played by other hands than Musyne's. What was she doing with her hands all this time, the little tart?

When in the morning we used to meet on the doorstep, she pulled a face at seeing me again. I was still as natural as an animal in those days; I wouldn't give her up, as a dog won't leave a bone. And that's all there was to it.

A great part of one's youth is lost in trial and error. It was obvious that the girl I loved was going to throw me over, and that before very long. I hadn't yet learnt that there are two human races on this earth, the rich and the poor, and that they aren't at all the same. It's taken me, as it's taken so many people, twenty years and the war to learn to stick to my own group and to ask the price of things and people before laying hands on them, and especially before setting any store by them.

And so it was that, while I warmed myself in the kitchen with my servant companions, I failed to understand that above my head the Argentine gods were dancing. They might have been German, French or Chinese, that didn't matter in the least — but they were gods; they were the Rich, that's what it was important to understand. They were upstairs, with Musyne; I was downstairs, without anything. Musyne was thinking seriously of her future; naturally she preferred to plan it with a god. I too, of course, thought of my future, but rather wildly, because all the time, secretly, I had the fear of being killed in the war and also the dread of dying of hunger in peace time. I was in constant terror of death and I was in love. It was an absolute nightmare. Not far away, less than sixty miles away, millions of brave, well-armed, well-trained men were waiting for me to kill me, and there were Frenchmen too, waiting to have the skin off my bones if I didn't want to have it flayed to bleeding ribbons by the other lot opposite.

The poor man has two fine ways of dying in this world, either through the complete indifference of his fellow men in time of peace or by the homicidal fury of these same fellow men when war comes. If people start to think about you at all, then it's how to torture you they think of at once; and nothing else but that. You're of no interest to them, the swine, except when you're bleeding. Princhard was quite right on that point. When the slaughterhouse is near, you don't bother very much about anything to do with your future, you only think of loving in the days that are left to you, because that is the only way to forget for a moment about your body, which you'll soon be having slit for you from top to toe.

I considered myself an idealist, because Musyne was running away from me. That's the way one clothes one's little private instincts in big words. My leave was coming to an end. The papers urged the recall of all available combatants, those who had no relatives first of all, of course. It was official that there was to be no more thought of anything except of winning the war.

Musyne too was very keen, just like Lola, that I should go back to the front at once, or sooner, and stay there. But as I seemed to be rather slow in starting, she made up her mind to hustle things, which wasn't, as a matter of fact, at all like her.

One evening, when for a change we were actually going home to Billancourt together, fire-brigade buglers came out to give the alarm, and all the people in our house scuttled down into the cellars in honour of some Zeppelin or other.

These little scares, during which the inhabitants of a whole neighbourhood, to escape from an almost entirely imaginary danger, would disappear underground in pyjamas, grasping candles and clucking, were a measure of the distressing absurdity of these creatures, who behave at one moment like a lot of frightened hens, at the next like fatuous, docile sheep. It is monstrous incongruities like this which are so well calculated to revolt the most patient, the most obstinate believer in society, for good and all.

As soon as the first bugle call sounded, Musyne forgot all about the heroism she'd been taught at the Théâtre des Armées. She begged me to rush down with her into a subway, the Métro or a coal hole — anywhere, as long as we lost no time about reaching safety in the depths of the earth. Seeing them all scurrying like this, our fellow tenants, large and small, silly or sedate, four by four, into any hole which seemed safe, gave me in the end a feeling of indifference. There's not much to choose between being brave and being cowardly. The same man will be a rabbit on one occasion and a hero on the next, and equally unconscious of what he's doing on both. Everything that is not making money is miles beyond him. What life and death really are does not enter his mind. Even his own death he envisages unclearly and all wrong. Money and footlights are all he understands.

Musyne began to snivel when I refused to go. Other tenants pressed us to join them and finally I allowed myself to be persuaded. A lot of different suggestions were made as to which cellar we should choose. The butcher's eventually gained the majority of votes, as it was supposed to be deeper than any of the others in the block. Across its threshold came whiffs of a pungent smell with which I was very familiar and which I suddenly found intolerable.

"Are you going down there, Musyne, with all that meat hanging on hooks?" I asked her.

"Why ever not?" she asked in great surprise.

"Well, personally," I said, "there are certain things I don't forget, and I'd rather go back upstairs. . . ."

"Are you leaving me then?"

"Yes, you can come and find me again when it's all over."

"But it may go on for a long time."

"I'd rather wait for you upstairs," I said. "I don't like dead meat, and it will be over soon."

While the raid lasted, these refugees, intrenched and safe, exchanged compliments and banter. Ladies in dressing gowns, the last to arrive, swept swiftly and majestically towards this malodourous den and were received with ceremony by the butcher and his wife, who apologized continually for the artificial cold necessary to the proper preservation of their meat.

Musyne disappeared with the rest. I waited for her upstairs in our apartment that night, all next day, a whole year. . . . She never came back to me.

From that time onwards, I found it harder and harder to be contented and there were only two ideas in my head: to save my hide and to go to America. But to escape the war was enough of a job, to start off with, to keep me breathless for months on end.

"Guns! Men! Munitions!" — The patriots seemed never to tire of clamouring for them. Apparently no one would be able to sleep until poor little Belgium and innocent Alsace had been snatched from under the German yoke. One gathered that our choicest spirits were so troubled about it all that it prevented them from breathing, eating and copulating. Yet it didn't seem to stop any one who was still alive from doing business. Morale back of the lines was certainly excellent.

Gaps in the ranks had to be filled right away. But as soon as they examined me, I was found to be still too far below normal, and only fit to be sent on to another hospital, this time one given over to fractures and nervous cases. One morning six of us left the Depot, three dragoons and three artillerymen, ill or wounded, looking for this place where they could cure loss of spirit, disordered reflexes and broken arms. Like all the wounded at that time, we were sent first of all to be looked over at Val-de-Grâce, that portly, noble, tree-girt citadel, whose corridors smelt so like a third-class railway carriage, with that strong blending stench of feet, straw and oil lamps. Our sojourn at the Val was not a long one; they took one look at us, then two twitching, overworked officers gave us the devil of a talking to and threatened us with court-martial, and we were shot out into the street again by other members of the staff. They'd no room for us there, they said, telling us vaguely where to go — to some bastion, somewhere on the outskirts of the town.

Stopping for an absinthe here and a coffee there, and continually misdirected on our way, we blundered along, all six of us, looking for this new home where, apparently, a specialty was made of the care of incapable heroes like ourselves.

Only one among the six of us had any scrap of personal property, and actually that was all contained in a tin labelled "Pernot Biscuits", a brand which was well known at the time though now one no longer hears of it. This chap had some cigarettes and a toothbrush in the tin; we all pulled his leg about the care he took of his teeth, which wasn't at all a usual habit in those days, and called him a pansy for being so outlandishly refined.

At last, about midnight, after a great deal of uncertainty, we came to the dark and bulging buttresses of this Bastion de Bicêtre, "No. 43", as it was called. It looked all right to us.

It had just been restored to house the old and lame. The garden wasn't even finished. When we arrived, there was no one living there, in the military part of the building, except the concierge. It was raining hard. The concierge was frightened of us when she first heard us, but we made her laugh by slapping her at once on the right spot.

"I thought it must be the Germans!" she said.

"They're a long way off," we told her.

"Where are you wounded?" she asked us anxiously.

"Everywhere — but not where it matters!" one of the artillery blokes answered her. Well, that of course was a terribly funny thing to say and the concierge certainly appreciated how funny it was.

We lived in future in this same bastion with some old men lodged there by the Poor Relief. New buildings full of miles and miles of glass had been quickly run up for them, and they were kept there for the duration of the war, like insects. On the slopes round about a mass of attenuated little allotments struggled for possession of a sea of mud, which lapped up to the doors of several rows of precarious cabins. Sheltered by them, from time to time a lettuce and three radishes grew there; and, for some obscure reason of their own, the disgusted slugs would leave them to the owner of that particular allotment.

Our hospital was beautifully clean, as they are for several weeks if you're quick and have a look at them directly after they've been started, because as a nation we take no care for the upkeep of things; in fact, on this sort of point we're plumb lazy. We went to bed joyfully, as I say, on metal bedsteads and by the light of the moon; the whole place was so new that electricity hadn't reached it yet.

Early next morning our new doctor came and introduced himself to us. He was all cordiality on the surface, seeming very pleased to see us. He himself had good reason to be in a good humour, he had just been made a major. Besides which, he had a pair of very beautiful eyes, velvety and deep, which he used freely to make havoc among the four charming and sympathetic nurses, who were always out to please him with captivating little ways, and never missed his smallest gesture. As soon as he met us, he took control of our dilapidated morale without more ado. He told us so himself, taking one of us familiarly by the shoulders and shaking him in a fatherly way. In comforting tones he outlined for us the regulations as well as the shortest and quickest route for us to go back like good fellows and get ourselves shot up again.

Wherever they came from, they definitely could think of nothing else. One would have thought it did them good to think that way. It was a new form of vice.

"France has put her trust in you, my friends — like a woman, like the most beautiful of women!" he chanted. "France relies on your gallantry! She has been made a victim of the most cowardly, the most abominable aggression! She has a right to demand from her sons the utmost vengeance. She must have every inch of French territory restored to her, cost what sacrifice it may! We shall, for our part, all do our duty here — my friends, see that you do yours! Our skill belongs to you: use it! All its resources will be devoted to healing you. Help us in your turn with willing coöperation. I know we can count on that, on your good will. And soon you will be able to take your place once more, your rightful place, beside those other brave lads in the trenches, defending our beloved soil. *Vive la France!* Onward, my boys, to victory!" He knew how to talk to soldiers.

We stood at attention listening to him, each at the foot of his own bed. Behind him one of the group of pretty nurses, a brunette, could hardly control her feelings and was crying a little. The others were doing their best to comfort her: "It'll be all right, dearie. . . . He'll come back, you'll see. . . ."

Her cousin, the rather plump blonde, was consoling her best. She told me, as she passed us with her arms round her, that her pretty cousin had been overcome in this way because her fiancé had just joined up in the navy. Our ardent lecturer was disconcerted and tried to mitigate the beautiful and tragic impression made by his short and glowing harangue. He stood before her, confused and very worried. He had roused too painful an anxiety in so tender and sensitive a breast, capable obviously of the deepest feeling. "If only we had known, Doctor," whispered the blonde cousin, "we could have warned you. . . . You see, they're so much in love with each other!" The nurses, together with the doctor, went off noisily down the passage, chattering hard. No one bothered about us.

I tried to remember and understand the sense of the speech we had just had from this man with the beautiful eyes, but, personally, when I thought them over, these words, far from making me sad, seemed to me extraordinarily well calculated to put me off dying. The other fellows thought so too, but they did not see in them as well a sort of insulting defiance, as I did. They didn't in the least try to understand what was happening around us in life; they only barely realized that the ordinary madness of the world had swollen during the last months to such proportions that truly there was no longer anything stable on which to prop one's existence.

Here in hospital, as in those nights in Flanders, death harried us — only that here we were not so closely threatened by it, though it was just as inexorable as it had been out there, once the vigilant care of the authorities had aimed it at you.

We weren't yelled at here, it's true; we were even spoken to with kindness; they spoke to us always on any subject except death — yet every form we were asked to sign was our death warrant; we were sentenced in every precaution they took on our behalf. Medals. . . . Identity disks. . . . The least leave we were given, the smallest piece of advice. . . . We felt that we were counted, supervised, numbered in the great reserve of those who would be going off to-morrow. And so, naturally, all these civilians and doctors who surrounded us seemed lighter-hearted than us by comparison. The nurses, little bitches, did not share our destiny; their only thought was to live long, and go on living and, of course, fall in love, and wander around, and make love not once but again and again. Every one of these sweeties nursed a little plan in her insides, like a convict, — a plan for later on, for making love, when we should have died in the mud somewhere, God knows how.

Then they would sigh for you with extra-special tenderness, which would make them even more attractive than they were already, and in silence, deeply moved, they would call to mind the tragic days of the war, the ghosts of time gone by. . . . "Do you remember little Bardamu?" They would say, thinking of me, as the evening shadows lengthened. "The boy who coughed so, and we could never stop him coughing? Poor lad. I wonder what became of him?"

A little sentimental regret at the right time and place becomes a woman as well as wisps of fine-spun hair in the moonlight.

Behind everything they said, behind all their solicitude, what one had to be able to read was this: "You're going to die, soldier boy, you're going to die. There's a different life for each of us — a different part for each of us to play — a different death for each of us to face. We seem to be sharing the wretchedness of your lot — but death cannot be shared with any one. . . . Everything should be a matter of enjoyment for healthy souls and bodies, no more or less, and we are fine young women, beautiful, respected, healthy and well brought up. . . . For us everything becomes, by instinctive biological law, a joyous spectacle and a source of happiness! Our health demands that it should be so; we must not allow the ugliness of sorrow to encroach upon us. . . . What we need is something stimulating, nothing but stimulants. . . . We shall soon forget all about you, soldier boy. . . . Be kind, and hurry up and die . . . and let the war stop soon, and then we can marry one of your charming officers. A dark and handsome one, if possible. . . . Hurrah for our country, as Father always says! Mustn't love be wonderful when your beau comes back from the war! The man we shall marry will be a very distinguished soldier. . . . He'll have a lot of medals. . . . And you may polish his lovely boots on our happy wedding day, if you're still alive when that day comes, soldier boy. . . . Then won't you be glad to see us so happy, soldier boy?"

Every morning we saw our doctor, we kept on seeing him, with his nurses always in attendance. He was a very clever man, we were told. The old men from the almshouse near by used to come hobbling past our part of the building, unevenly and fatuously. They wandered from room to room, carrying with them their tainted breath and a store of wheezing, raggle-taggle gossip and jabbering, contemptible chitchat. Cloistered here in their official poverty, as in a moat of slime, these old workmen lived on the filth which accumulates about the human soul after long years of servitude — impotent hatreds rotted by the piddling idleness of communal living rooms. They devoted their last trembling energies to doing a bit of harm and destroying what little life and joy was left to them.

That was their supreme pleasure. There was no longer a single particle of their dried-up bodies that was not entirely cruel.

As soon as it was arranged that we soldiers should share the relative comforts of the bastion with these old men, they began to hate us in unison, though they gathered around all the same to beg through the windows for odds and ends of tobacco and bits of stale bread from under the benches. Their parchment faces were pressed at mealtimes against the panes of our refectory windows. They peered at us with screwed-up, bleary eyes, like greedy rats. One of these old wrecks seemed to be more cunning and quicker witted than the rest; he came and sang the popular ditties of his day to us for our amusement. Papa Birouette they called him. He was perfectly willing to do any mortal thing for you as long as you gave him tobacco — any mortal thing, that is, except walk past the morgue in the bastion, which was never empty. One of the usual jokes was to take him along in the direction of the morgue, as if for a stroll. "Won't you come on in?" you'd say to him, just as you got level with the door. Then he'd rush away, wheezing, as fast and as far as his legs would carry him and you saw nothing more of Papa Birouette for a couple of days at least. He had caught sight of death.

For the purpose of putting some spirit into us, our medical officer, Doctor Bestombes, of the beautiful eyes, had had installed a lot of very complicated paraphernalia in the way of shining electrical apparatus with which he gave us shocks every so often. He claimed these currents had a tonic effect; one had to put up with them or be thrown out. It seems that he was a very rich man, Bestombes; he must have been, to be able to afford all these costly electrocuting gadgets. His father-in-law, a figure in the political world, had wangled things well in buying land for the Government and so could afford to allow him these extravagances.

One had to take advantage of it. Everything works out all right, — crimes and punishments. Such as he was, we did not hate him too much. He examined our nervous systems extraordinarily carefully and asked us questions with polite familiarity. This nicely regulated kindliness of his was the great delight of the nurses under him, who were all well-bred; dear little things, they looked forward each morning to the moment for enjoying his display of charming manners, like kiddies expecting a lump of candy. We were all acting in a play in which he, Bestombes, had chosen the part of the understanding philanthropist, the wise and kindly man of science. You had to know what you were at, then it was all right.

In this new hospital I shared a room with a Sergeant Branledore, who had served once and been called up again. Branledore was a hospital guest of long standing. For months and months he'd trailed his perforated guts from clinic to clinic, having run through four of them.

In the course of this progression he had learned how to attract and to hold the active sympathy of nurses. He brought up, and pissed, blood, and he bled internally pretty often, did Branledore, and he had very great difficulty in breathing; but these things would not have sufficed to win him the quite special good graces of the nursing staff, which had seen them frequently enough. So, if a doctor or a nurse was passing, between two fits of choking, Branledore would cry out, "Victory! Victory! It shall be ours!" —or he muttered it with as much or as little of the breath in his lungs as he could, according to the circumstances. Having fallen into line in this way with the right enthusiastically warlike ideals, thanks to an opportune piece of play-acting, he enjoyed the highest prestige. He'd got it taped all right.

The whole thing was pure theatre; you had to play a part, and Branledore was absolutely right. Nothing looks so silly and is more irritating, after all, than a dumb member of the audience who has strayed onto the stage by mistake. When you are there, dash it, you've got to enter into the spirit of the thing, you've got to wake up and act, make up your mind or clear out. The women, above all, wanted to see something going on and they were without pity for the amateur who dried up. There's no question about it, war goes straight to their tummies. They wanted heroes and those who weren't heroes either had to look as if they were or be prepared to undergo the utmost ignominy.

After we had spent a week in this joint, we realized how urgently necessary it was to pull a different sort of face, and thanks to Branledore (a lace merchant in private life), these same fear-struck men, obsessed by shameful memories of slaughter, shunning the light — and that is what we had been when we first arrived — were now transformed into a bloody band of fire eaters, determined on victory and, I assure you, all out for slaughter and bristling with the most terrifying intentions. Ours had become a terse speech, so tough, in fact, that sometimes these ladies blushed to hear it, although of course they never complained because, as every one knows, a soldier is as brave as he is thoughtless, and coarse more often than he need be; and the fouler-mouthed he is the braver he is.

At first, though we did our best to copy Branledore faithfully, our little patriotic gestures did not strike quite the right note; they weren't truly convincing. A full week and more of intensive rehearsing was needed before we reached a really high standard.

As soon as our Doctor Bestombes noticed, in his wisdom, the brilliant improvement of our mental and moral state, he decided, by way of encouraging us further, to let us have visitors come and see us, our relations first of all.

Some soldiers who are really good at their job, so I had heard, experienced in the thick of battle a sort of intoxication and sometimes even acute sensual pleasure. For my part, no sooner did I try to imagine a sensual pleasure of this very remarkable kind than I went sick for at least a week. I felt so incapable of killing anybody that it was definitely better for me to give it all up right away and not to think of trying. Not that I hadn't had the necessary practice — they had indeed done everything they could to give me a taste for it — but the gift itself was lacking. Perhaps I ought to have been initiated rather more slowly.

One day I decided to tell Doctor Bestombes about the difficulty I had in being as brave, body and soul, as I should have liked to be and ought, in the present sublime circumstances, to have been. I was rather afraid that he would consider me impertinent, forward and too talkative. But not at all. Quite the reverse. The good doctor expressed himself as altogether delighted that I should have come to him in this frank way to lay bare the troubles of my soul.

"You're better, Bardamu, my friend! You know, you're much better, that's what it is," was the conclusion he came to. "Your coming to me like this, quite spontaneously, to confide in me, — you know, Bardamu, I consider that a very encouraging indication of a distinct improvement in your state of mind. . . . Vaudesquin, that humble yet how wise observer of cases of faltering morale among the soldiers of the Empire, once indeed summed up his conclusions in a monograph which, although unjustly overlooked by present-day students of such things, has now become a classic. In it he described very clearly and precisely crises of confession, as they are called, which, when they occur, are the surest of all signs of a moral convalescence. Our great Dupré, almost half a century later, established in connection with the same symptom his definition, since become famous, of this very crisis, which he calls a crisis of 'reassembled memories', and goes on to state that it should, if the cure be well conducted, shortly precede a general collapse of the fear complexes and a definite clearance of the conscious area of the mind, thereby constituting the second stage in the course of psychic rehabilitation. Elsewhere Dupré, in that brilliantly metaphorical terminology of which he alone seems to have had the secret, gives the name of 'thought-flux of relief' to that condition of the patient which is manifested by a very active sensation of harmony, a most noticeable release of the activity of reflexes including, among other phenomena, a marked increase in sleep, which will suddenly continue for twenty-four hours at a time; and finally a further stage, to wit, superactivity of the genital functions, to such a degree that it is not unusual to observe crises of veritable erotic frenzy in patients previously frigid. Hence the formula: 'The sick man does not struggle through to health; he rushes headlong at it.' Such is the, I think you will agree, magnificently descriptive phrase for these triumphant recuperations which another of our great French psychiatrists of the last century, Philibert Margeton, applies to the truly marvellous reawakening of all normal activities in patients recovering from fear neuroses. . . . As for you yourself, Bardamu, I consider you therefore already on the road to recovery. . . . Would it interest you to know, Bardamu, since we have now reached this satisfactory conclusion that as a matter of fact I am to-morrow reading a paper to the Society for Research into Military Psychology on the essential qualities of the human spirit? It is not, I flatter myself, entirely without weight. . . ."

"Indeed, sir, these matters are of the keenest interest to me. . . ."

"Well then, Bardamu, let me explain to you, in a word, the theory I am putting forward in this paper. I hold that, before the war, Man was a closed book to the psychiatrist and the resources of his mind an enigma . . ."

"That is exactly my own most humble opinion too, sir."

"You see, Bardamu, the war, affording as it does various incomparable means of testing nervous systems, acts as a wonderful revealer of the human spirit. We have been given recently enough material in the way of pathological discoveries to last us a century of careful meditation and absorbing study. . . . Up till now we had done no more than suspect the treasures of Man's emotional and spiritual make-up. But now, thanks to the war, we have won through! We have broken into the innermost precincts of Man's mind, painfully, it is true, but as far as science is concerned, providentially, decisively. . . . As soon as the first revelations were to hand, for me personally the duty of the modern psychologist and moralist was no longer the least in doubt. We need to overhaul completely all our psychological ideas."

That is just what I, Bardamu, thought too.

"I think, sir, that what ought to be done — "

"Ah, yes, you think so too, Bardamu; you don't need me to tell you! The good and the bad, you see, are balanced in Man's mind, selfishness on the one hand, altruism on the other. . . . In the finer spirits you'll find altruism outweighing egoism. Is it not so? Is it not as I say?"

"It's true, sir; it's perfectly true. . . ."

"And what, I ask you, Bardamu, what is the highest known ideal that can excite the altruistic impulses of the more sensitive spirit and reveal its unselfishness in such a way that it cannot be denied?"

"Oh, sir, it's patriotism!"

"Ah, there you are, you see; it is not I who put the words into your mouth! You understand me perfectly. . . . Bardamu, it's patriotism. Patriotism and glory, which goes with it — glory which is its emblem and its proof!"

"How true, how very true!"

"Ah, yes, our brave lads on their first experience of being under fire immediately and spontaneously shed all secondary concepts and false notions, particularly the sentiment of self-preservation. Instinctively and unhesitatingly they merge with the cause of their country, that real justification of all our existences. For the acceptance of this truth not only is intelligence unnecessary, Bardamu, it's a hindrance! Like all essential truths, the truth of our duty to our country is comprehended in the heart — your man in the street makes no mistake about that! Yet that is just where the wicked wise man errs. . . ."

"Lovely words, Doctor! Almost too lovely. . . . No Greek philosopher could have put it more perfectly."

Almost affectionately Bestombes seized my two hands in his. In tones which had become fatherly he was kind enough to add for my benefit: "That is how I endeavour to cure my patients, Bardamu, by electrical treatment of the body and strenuous doses of the ethics of patriotism for the soul, by absolute injections of revitalizing morale!"

"I understand, Doctor."

In fact, I was beginning to understand better and better. When I had left him, I hurried away to join my revitalized companions at Mass in the brand-new chapel, where I saw Branledore giving proof of his moral health by treating the concierge's little daughter to a lesson in animation behind the big door. I joined him at once on his invitation.

That afternoon our relations came down from Paris, for the

first time since we'd been there; and after that they came each week.

I had at last written to my mother. She was happy to have found me again and whimpered like a bitch whose puppy has been returned to her. No doubt she thought too she was helping me a lot by kissing me, but she remained a good deal short of the dog's level because she believed what they told her when they took me away. The dog at least believes only what it knows by sense of smell. My mother and I went for a long walk one afternoon through the streets around the hospital, trailing along the half-finished thoroughfares of those parts, where the lamp-posts were still unpainted and long rows of sweating houses showed in barred windows a hundred ragged little hangings, the shirts of the poor; and you could hear the small noise of frying midday grease, a storm of cheap and crackling fat. In the great hazy desert around a town, where its luxury, ending in rottenness and slime, is proved to be a lie, the town presents its posterior among the dustbins to all who wish to see. There are some factories one avoids walking past; they give out every sort of smell, some of them almost unbelievable, and the surrounding air can stink no more. Close by, a little travelling fair moulders between two tall chimneys of unequal height, its wooden horses too costly for the rachitic little urchins, picking their noses, who sometimes for weeks on end long to ride them, attracted, repelled and fascinated all at once by their abandoned air, poverty, and the music.

All life is spent in efforts to hold at bay the reality of these places, but it returns in its universal sadness; nothing does any good, drinking does no good, not even red wine, as thick as ink; the sky remains the same there, shutting you down, a huge reservoir of soot from the suburbs.

Beneath your feet the mud drags you to fatigue, while you are shut out from where life is by houses and factories, whose walls are already the sides of a coffin. Now that Lola had gone completely, and Musyne too, I had nobody left. That's why in the end I had written to my mother, so as to see some one I knew. I was twenty years old and already had nothing but the past.

We walked through miles and miles of Sunday streets, my mother and I. She told me the little details of her business, and what she had heard people say about the war, what they were saying about it in town: that the war was a sad business, "frightful" even, but with a great deal of courage we should all get through it. For her the dead were only victims of an accident, like at the races — if you looked out, you didn't fall. As far as she herself was concerned, she only regarded the war as a new sorrow, which she tried not to think about too much. It was as if she was afraid of this cause for sadness; it was full of sinister things which she did not understand. She believed really that small fry like herself were meant to suffer all the time, that that was their rôle on earth, and if things had of late been going so badly, it must surely still be due, for the most part, to their having committed a lot of faults, which had been adding up. They must have done a lot of foolish things, without realizing it, of course; but they were to blame nevertheless and it was really very kind that they should be allowed to expiate their transgressions by suffering in this way. She was an "untouchable."

This tragic and resigned optimism was her faith and formed the basis of her character.

We both of us went along streets of empty lots in the rain; the pavements there dip and disappear; in winter the little rows of ash trees keep the drops of rain on their boughs, a tiny fairyland which trembles in the wind. The road to the hospital led past many newly built houses, some of which had names. Others were still happily without them. "To let" was all they were called. The war had emptied them of all their planks and workmen. Their tenants would not even come back to them to die.

My mother cried a little as she took me back to the hospital. She accepted the accident of my death, she not only consented to it but wondered whether I was as resigned as she was. She believed in Fate as implicitly as in the standard metre at the Conservatoire National, about which she had always spoken to me with respect, because as a girl she had learnt that the one she used in her mercer's shop was an exact copy of this beautiful official rule.

Among the holdings of this broken tract of land, a few fields here and there were still under cultivation and a peasant or two, wedged between the new buildings, still clung to these shreds. When there was time enough before I had to be back, Mother and I used to go and watch them, these funny old peasants, earnestly picking with a hoe at that soft, sacred thing which is the earth, where the dead are put to rot but from which nevertheless we get our daily bread. "The ground must be very hard!" said my mother with a very puzzled air each time as she watched them. She had no conception of any other sorts of hardship except the one she herself endured, the hardship of life in towns; she tried to imagine what the hardship of life in the country must be like. That was the only curiosity I have ever known my mother show — and it was enough to entertain her for a whole Sunday. When she returned to town, that is what she took back with her.

I got no more news at all of Lola, or of Musyne either, the bitches! They kept to the safe side of all this, from which we, cattle marked down for slaughter, were barred by a smiling but implacable password. I had twice been sent back in this way to the places where hostages were penned. It was only a question of time and of waiting. The die had been cast.

BRANLEDORE, THE SERGEANT, MY NEXT-DOOR NEIGHBOUR, ENJOYED, as I have said, a persistent popularity with the nurses. He was covered with bandages and exuded optimism. Everybody in the wards envied him and copied his behaviour. Now that we had become presentable and not in the least morally disgusting, we in our turn began to be visited by distinguished society people and representatives of officialdom in Paris. It was continually being said in drawing-rooms that Doctor Bestombes' home for neurotic cases was becoming a centre of intense patriotic fervour, a rallying point, one might say. After that, our visiting days were patronized not only by bishops but by an Italian duchess, a great munition manufacturer, and soon by the Opéra itself and stars from the Théâtre Français. People came to admire us in our own haunts. A beautiful young lady from the Comédie, who recited verses marvellously, even came to my bedside and declaimed some particularly heroic ones for my special benefit. Her wild auburn hair (she had the complexion which goes with it) tossed astonishingly the while in a way which I found intensely disturbing to my morals if not to my morale. When this divine creature asked me to tell her my war experiences, I provided her with so many and such vivid and highly coloured details, that from that moment she never took her eyes off me. Deeply moved, she asked if she might have the most exciting of the incidents I had told her put into rhyme by a poet friend and admirer of hers. I acceded at once to her request.

Doctor Bestombes, on being informed of the scheme, declared himself emphatically in favour of it. He even granted an interview on the subject, that very day, to a reporter and photographer from the great *Illustrated National Magazine* and a picture was taken of us all standing together, with the lovely *diseuse*, on the steps of the hospital. "In these tragic days through which we are living," declared Doctor Bestombes, who never missed a golden opportunity, "it is the poet's highest duty to rekindle in us a taste for the Epic. Puny compositions no longer suit the times we live in — let us have an end to literary trifling! A new spirit has blossomed for us in the midst of the vast and stirring din of battle! A great patriotic renascence requires the highest flights of literary grandeur to chronicle its feats! We must demand the glorious thunders of an Epic Muse! For myself, I think it admirable that here in this hospital, which is my charge, there should have taken place under our very eyes, unforgettably, a sublime creative collaboration of this sort between the Poet and one of our heroes!"

Branledore, my stable companion, whose imagination, compared with mine, had lagged a little in this matter, and who hadn't appeared in the photograph, was keenly and obstinately jealous. From then on he began to compete with me savagely for the palm of heroism. He made up new stories, he surpassed himself, no one could stop him, his exploits became deliriously wonderful.

I found it hard to think of anything still more fanciful to add to the outrageous things I'd already said. Yet no one at the hospital gave up; they all vied with each other to see who could invent further glorious records of the war, in which to figure personally. We were living a tremendous saga in the skin of fantastic characters, deep down within which we ourselves derisively trembled in every corner of our heart and soul. How they would have gaped with astonishment if they had seen us as we really were! The war was very odd indeed.

Our great Doctor Bestombes was visited by many distinguished foreigners, scientific gentlemen who were neutral, sceptical and curious. Inspectors from the Ministry of War pranced through our halls, clanking swords; their soldierly lives were always being prolonged by fresh indemnities, they felt continually rejuvenated. They therefore weren't at all niggardly with their praises and commendations. Everything was going splendidly; Bestombes and his wounded heroes were a credit to the Medical Corps.

My beautiful patroness from the Comédie came back in person

to see me on one further occasion, while her pet poet was putting the finishing touches to the recital of my exploits in rhyme. I came across this pale and anxious young man at last, around some corner in the corridor. The delicacy of the mechanism of his heart, he confided in me, was, according to the doctors themselves, well-nigh miraculous. So they kept him far away from the army, these doctors who take such care of fragile beings. In return, our little bard had undertaken, at the risk of his very health, with all his remaining spiritual energy, to forge an Aria of Victory for our benefit — a useful instrument in verse, unforgettable of course, like all the rest of it.

I wasn't going to complain, when he had chosen me among so many other undeniably gallant men to be his hero. And he did me proud, I must say. It certainly was magnificent. The recital took place at the Comédie Française itself, one afternoon of so-called poetry reading. The whole hospital had been invited. When, magnificently gesticulating, my red-head appeared on the stage for her tremulous recital, her waist swathed in the long, at last voluptuous folds of the tricolour, the whole audience sprang avidly to its feet and burst into an endless ovation. I was prepared, it's true, but none the less I was really surprised; I could not hide my stupefaction from those who sat next to me when I heard my superb friend holding forth in this way, and even groaning, so that we should not miss an iota of the dramatic value of the episode I had made up for her. Her poet could certainly give me points in this matter of imagination; he'd monstrously enlarged upon mine with the help of fine-sounding rhymes and tremendous adjectives which rolled out solemnly in the vast, admiring silence. On coming to the climax of a period, the most fervid passage in the piece, my actress, turning towards the box where Branledore and I, with a few other wounded men were sitting, held out her splendid arms and seemed to offer herself to the most heroic one amongst us. The poet at that point was faithfully depicting a fantastic act of gallantry which I had attributed to myself. I don't quite remember what was supposed to be happening, but I had certainly not stopped at half measures. Fortunately, nothing in the way of heroism is incredible. The audience grasped the significance of her symbolic gesture and the whole hall, stamping excitedly, howling with joy, turned towards us and clamoured for the hero.

Branledore took up the whole of the front of the box and left the rest of us nowhere; he was able, with all his bandages, to blot us out almost completely. He did it on purpose, the bounder.

But two of the chaps managed to get themselves admired by the mob over his head and shoulders, by climbing onto chairs behind him. They were greeted with thunderous applause.

"But it's me it's all about," I nearly shouted at that point. "Nobody but me!" I knew my Branledore; there'd have been a brawl in front of all these people and we should even probably have come to blows. In the end, it was he who won the day. He wouldn't budge an inch. There he was, all alone as he wanted to be, acknowledging this vast acclamation. We'd been defeated and there was nothing for it but to rush off back stage, which we did, and there they made a great fuss over us. That was something. But our actress-inspirer was not alone in her dressing room. By her side stood the poet, her poet, our poet. He was fond of soldier lads too, like herself, in a charming way. They put it to me very nicely. A bit of a party. They told me all over again, but I took no notice at all of their kindly suggestions. A pity that, because things might quite easily have turned out well. They had lots of influence. I took my leave in a hurry, foolishly annoyed. I was very young.

Let us sum up: the Air Force had snatched Lola from me, the Argentines had taken Musyne, and finally this melodious invert had just snooped my splendid actress friend. Alone in the world, I left the Comédie as the last lights were being turned out in the corridors, and by myself I returned through the night, not taking the tram, to the hospital, a mousetrap set in the all-pervading mud, on the obstinately ragged outskirts of the town.

JOKING APART, I CERTAINLY MUST ADMIT THAT I'D NEVER BEEN VERY strong in the head. But now at any little thing I had a fit of dizziness. As easily as anything I might have been under the wheels of a bus. I was all of a tremble in the war. As for pocket money, while I was in hospital I had only the few francs which my mother with great difficulty spared me each week. So soon as I could, I started to look out for a few extras here and there, wherever I could find them. First of all, a visit to one of my former employers struck me as propitious. I went to see him at once.

I remembered at the right moment that I had once in a dim period of my life, worked for this Roger Puta, who kept a jeweller's shop near the Madeleine, not long before war was declared, as extra lad. My work with this disgusting jeweller consisted in odd jobs, and polishing all the silver, of which there was a large and varied selection in his shop. At certain seasons of the year, when people bought presents, it was extremely difficult to keep clean.

As soon as school was over (I studied hard and, because I always failed the examinations, interminably) I would tear back to the rear of Monsieur Puta's shop and spend two or three hours until supper time battling with silver polish his coffeepots.

In return for my work I was fed, and well fed, in the kitchen. Another part of my job was, before lecture hours, to take out the dogs which guarded the shop. For all this I was paid forty francs a month. Monsieur Puta's shop windows sparkled with a thousand diamonds at the corner of the Rue Vignon, and each of these diamonds cost as much as my salary for several decades. And they are there still. When mobilization came, Puta's services were put at the disposal of a particular Cabinet Minister, whose automobile he drove from time to time. Besides which — and this he did in a thoroughly efficient way — Puta made himself exceptionally useful in providing the Minister with jewelry. High officials speculated very successfully on the closed and closing markets. As the war went on, more and more jewels were needed. Monsieur Puta sometimes even had difficulty in meeting all the orders for jewelry he received.

When overworked, Monsieur Puta's face took on a certain little look of intelligence, because he was so tired and harassed, and that's the only time it did. In repose his face, in spite of the undeniable fineness of his features, formed so harmonious a portrait of placid stupidity that it is difficult not always to remember it and be aggravated by it.

His wife, Madame Puta, was one flesh with the till in the shop, which she practically never left. She had been brought up to be a jeweller's wife. It had been her parents' ambition. She knew her duty, every bit of it. The happiness of the family depended on the fullness of the till. It's not that she was ugly, Madame Puta; she wasn't, she would even have been fairly pretty, like so many other women, if she hadn't been so careful, so distrustful, that she stopped short of good looks, as she stopped short of life, with her too neat head of hair, her rather too ready and sudden smile, and gestures a little too quick or a little too furtive. One worried one's head trying to decide what there was that was too calculating about this person and why one couldn't help feeling irritated when she came up to one. This instinctive repulsion which tradespeople inspire in men of sensitive feeling is one of the very rare consolations for being so impoverished which are given to those of us who don't sell anything to anybody.

Niggling business cares, then, were the whole of Madame Puta's life, as they were of Madame Herote's, but in a different way. She belonged to them as nuns belong to the Almighty, body and soul.

From time to time, however, my employer's wife was slightly troubled by what was going on. She would sometimes think, for instance, of those who had sons at the front. "How sad the war must be, though, for people with grown-up children!"

"Think before you speak!" her husband would at once reprimand her. Sentimentalities of this sort found him resolute and prepared. "Would you have France undefended?"

Thus, good people, but good patriots above all else, these stoics went to sleep every night of the war over the millions in their shop, a French fortune.

In the brothels which Monsieur Puta occasionally visited, he was exciting and determined to show that he knew the value of money. "I'm not an Englishman, girlie," he used to say straight off. "I know what earning the stuff means. I'm a little French soldier with lots of time on his hands!" That was his opening remark. The women thought highly of him because of this sensible way he had of taking his pleasure. Fond of the game, but no fool — a real man. He turned his knowledge of the world to account by transacting a little regular business with the second in command of the brothel. This good woman believed in jewelry and not in the stock markets. Monsieur Puta was making great strides from the military point of view, from temporary successes to positive gains. Quite soon he was set completely free, after I don't know how many medical examinations. One of the keenest joys of his existence was to contemplate and, if possible, to fondle a pretty calf. That at least was a pleasure which put him ahead of his wife, who lacked an interest in anything outside her business. Given equal temperaments, there always seems to be a little more restlessness in a man than in a woman, however limited and hidebound he may be. Let us say that this fellow Puta had the small beginnings of an artist. Many men, as far as art goes, like him never get beyond a particular fondness for pretty calves. Madame Puta was very happy not to have any children. She so often expressed her satisfaction at this state of affairs that eventually her husband came to mention this source of joy of theirs to the under brothel keeper.

"But after all, somebody's children have got to go," she answered him. "It's a duty." True enough, the war did mean duties to be fulfilled.

The Cabinet Minister, whose car Puta drove, had no children either; Cabinet Ministers don't.

Another extra hand did small jobs for the shop when I was there, sometime in 1913: Jean Voireuse his name was. At night he'd sometimes have a walking-on part at one of the smaller theatres and in the afternoon he delivered for Puta. He too put up with a very small salary. But he got along all right, thanks to the Métro. He could travel almost as fast on foot as in the Métro, to deliver his parcels. So he pocketed the price of his ticket. The whole lot to the good. It's true his feet smelt a bit, not to say a lot, but he knew that and used to ask me to tell him when there were no customers in the shop, so that he could do his accounts quietly with Madame Puta. As soon as the money was safely in the till, he was sent away at once to join me in the back of the shop. His feet also stood him in good stead during the war. He was supposed to be the fastest company runner in his battalion. He was wounded and while convalescing came to see me at the Bicêtre bastion and it was then that we both decided to go and "touch" our old employer. No sooner said than done. When we got to the Boulevard de la Madeleine, they had just finished dressing the window. . . .

"Well, well, look who's here!" Monsieur Puta was pretty surprised to see us. "I'm so glad, though. Come in, come in. You look well, Voireuse. That's good. But you, Bardamu, you look seedy. You're young, though. You'll get over it. You fellows are lucky, you know, all things considered. When all's said and done, you're living a great life out there, aren't you? Out in the open too. You're making history, my friends, that's what I always say! A stirring life. . . ."

We didn't answer Monsieur Puta at all, we let him run on as he pleased before touching him for the money. And he went on: "Oh, yes, the trenches aren't exactly a picnic, I'll admit that. That's perfectly true. But it isn't a picnic here, either, you know. You've been wounded, have you, you two? I'm worn out, quite worn out. For two years I've been in town on night duty. D' you know what that means? Think of it, worn out, dead beat. God, the streets of Paris at night! Unlit, my young friends — and having to drive a car; with the Minister in it, as often as not! And fast too. You've no idea what it's like! One's liable to kill oneself ten times over every night."

"Yes," broke in Madame Puta, "and sometimes he drives the Minister's wife about, too."

"Yes, indeed — and that's not all . . ."

"Terrible," we said, both together.

"And how are the dogs?" asked Voireuse politely. "What's happened to them? Are they still taken out for exercise in the Tuileries?"

"I've had them put away. They weren't doing me any good — German sheepdogs! A bad thing for the shop."

"It's a great pity," said his wife. "But the new dogs we've got now are very nice; they're Scotch terriers. . . . They smell, rather. Whereas our sheepdogs — you remember them, Voireuse? —they didn't smell at all hardly. They could be shut up in the shop even when it had been raining. . . ."

"Yes, indeed," said M. Puta. "Not like Voireuse here, the old scoundrel, with his feet! Do they still smell, eh, Jean? You young scamp, you!"

"I think they do, a bit," Voireuse said.

Just at that moment some people came into the shop. "Well, I won't keep you any longer, my friends," said Puta, anxious to get Jean out of the shop as quickly as possible. "Get well soon, that's the main thing. I won't ask you where you've come from. No, National Safety before everything else, that's what I say!"

At the words National Safety, he put on a very serious look, like he did when he paid out money. . . . We were being dismissed. Madame Puta handed us each twenty francs as we went out. The shop was as spick and shining as a yacht, we didn't dare cross it because of our shoes, which looked monstrous on the fine carpet.

"Oh, look at the two of them, Roger! Aren't they funny? They've got out of the habit — you'd think they'd walked in something!" cried Madame Puta.

"They'll get over it," said Puta, in a cheerful and friendly way, delighted to have got rid of us so quickly and inexpensively.

Back in the street we reflected that we shouldn't get very far with twenty francs each. But Voireuse had another idea.

"Come with me," he said. "We'll go and call on the mother of a chap I knew who was killed in the Meuse. I go once a week to see his parents and tell them how their kid was killed. . . . They're well off. . . . His mother gives me about a hundred francs a time. They're glad to do that, they say. . . . So, of course I — "

"What should I be doing at their house? There's nothing I can say to his mother."

"Why, you can say that you saw him too. . . . She'll give you a hundred francs as well. They're very nice people, I tell you. Not like that bastard Puta. They don't mind . . ."

"All right, but are you sure she won't ask me for details? After all, I never saw the fellow. I'd be sunk if she asked me about him."

"No, no, it doesn't matter, you say just the same as me. . . . You just say 'yes' all the time. Don't worry about that. The woman's unhappy, don't you see, and as soon as you talk to her about her son, she's pleased. . . . That's all she asks. . . . Doesn't matter what you say. . . . There's no difficulty about it."

I found it hard to make up my mind to go, but I very much wanted a hundred francs and these seemed to me very easy to come by, and a godsend.

"Right you are," I agreed at last. "But I mustn't have to make anything up, see, I warn you of that. . . . Promise? I'll just say what you say and that's all. How did the chap get killed anyway?"

"A shell hit him slap in the face, quite a big shell too, at a place called Garance, in the Meuse country, on a river bank. . . . There wasn't that much of him left to pick up, laddie. . . . Just a memory, that's what he was after that. . . . And he was a big feller, you know, squarely built and all that, and an athletic sort of lad, but of course not much use against a shell. You can't stand up to a shell!"

"That's right," I said.

"Thoroughly cleaned up, he was, I tell you. His mother, you know, still can't believe it, even now! It's no use my saying so and going on and on saying so. . . . She will have it that he may just be missing. . . . It's a damn silly idea . . . missing! But it's not her fault; she's never seen a shell, she hasn't, can't understand how you can pass out into thin air like that, like a fart, and that's that — especially since it's her own son. . . ."

"Obviously."

"Anyway, I haven't been to see them for a fortnight. . . . But you'll see when I come along she receives me at once, in the drawing-room, and you know it's a fine place they've got, like the theatre, all full of curtains and carpets and mirrors everywhere. . . . A hundred francs isn't much to them. . . . It's like that number of sous is to me, I should say, more or less. . . . To-day she ought to be good for two hundred. She hasn't seen me for a couple of weeks. . . . The servants have gold buttons on them, you'll see . . ."

We turned up the Avenue Henri-Martin and then off to the left and after going on a little way came to a pair of iron gates in the middle of some trees forming a private approach.

"See?" said Voireuse, when we got there. "It's like a sort of *château* . . . told you so. The father's somebody of importance in railways, so I've heard. . . . He's a big bug."

"Not a stationmaster is he, by any chance?" I asked, trying to be funny.

"Don't be a fool. There he is over there, coming along towards us." But the elderly gentleman he pointed out to me didn't come to us straight away; he walked around on the lawn, bent double, talking to a soldier. We went over towards them. I recognized the soldier. He was the same reservist chap I'd met that night at Noirceur-sur-la-Lys, when I was out on reconnaissance. I even remembered at once what he'd said his name was: Léon Robinson.

"D' you know that infantry bloke?" Voireuse asked me.

"Yes, I know him."

"Perhaps he's a friend of theirs. They're talking about the mother, I expect. I hope they don't stop us going to see her. . . . Because she's the one who hands out the dough. . . ."

The old gentleman came up to us, tottering.

"My dear friend," said he to Voireuse, "it is extremely painful for me to have to tell you that since you last came to see us, my poor wife has succumbed to our terrible sorrow. . . . On Thursday we left her alone for a moment. . . . She asked us to. She was crying . . ."

He couldn't finish what he was saying. He turned hurriedly and left us.

"I recognised you," I said to Robinson at that point, when the old man was out of earshot.

"And I recognise you, too. . . ."

"What's happened to the old lady then?" I asked him.

"Oh, she hanged herself the day before yesterday, that's all," he answered. "What a blow!" he added. "She was my military godmother, used to send me things at the front. . . . Just my luck, dammit! Think of it! The first leave I get too! I'd been looking forward to to-day for six months."

We couldn't help being amused, Voireuse and I, at this misfortune which had overtaken old Robinson. It certainly was a bit of an ugly blow for him all right, but her being dead didn't give us our two hundred francs either, and we'd come all this way ready to spin a good yarn. At one fell swoop all parties had been done in the eye.

"You were all set with the soft soap, eh, Robinson, you dirty dog?" We were trying to get a rise out of him and make him mad. "You thought you were going to squeeze them, didn't you? You had an idea you'd get a few square meals out of them, eh? And maybe snaffle his wife from him too, what, didn't you? But it didn't turn out so good, did it?"

But anyway, as one couldn't stand there staring at the grass and pulling his leg, we went off, the three of us, towards Grenelle. We counted up all the money we had between us; it didn't come to much. We had to get back in the evening to our respective hospitals and depots, and there was just enough for supper for the three of us at an estaminet, with a wee bit left over, but not enough for galleries at a show or anything. We went along all the same and joined the claque, but only just to have a little drink at the bar downstairs.

"Well, I'm glad to have seen you again," Robinson told me. "But can you beat that fellow's mother going and doing a thing like that? And I'm damned if she doesn't go and hang herself the very day I get back, strike me pink if she doesn't! Can't get the woman out of my mind. . . . I don't go and hang myself, do I, because I'm bloody miserable? I'd be hanging myself every other minute, if I did. What about you?"

"People with money," said Voireuse, "are more sensitive than the rest of us."

He was a good-hearted chap, Voireuse. And he went on, "If I had six francs, I'd go up to bed with that dark girl over there by the slot machine. . . ."

"Go ahead," we said to him. "You can tell us later on whether she knows her job or not. . . ."

However, search as we would, we hadn't got enough, including the tip, for him to go with her. We could just pay for a coffee all round and two *cassis*. Once we'd wetted our gullets, we went out again for another walk.

Eventually we separated on the Place Vendôme. Each went his own way. None of us could see the others, and we talked low, everything echoed so. No lights either; they weren't allowed.

Jean Voireuse I never saw again. Robinson I've often run across since. Jean Voireuse was accounted for by poison gas on the Somme. He went off and died by the sea in Brittany two years later, at a naval sanitarium. He wrote to me twice when he first went there, then he didn't write any more. He'd never seen the sea before.

"You've no idea how beautiful it is," he wrote. "I do a little bathing, it's good for my feet, but I think my voice has been done in once and for all." That worried him a lot because his real ambition was to be able to get back some day into the chorus at a theatre.

Chorus work is much better paid and more artistic than plain walking-on parts.

I WAS DROPPED BY THE QUACKS IN THE END AND WAS ABLE TO KEEP my hide intact, but I'd been branded now for good. There was nothing to be done about it. "Get out," they said. "You're no longer any good at all."

"I'll go to Africa," I said to myself. "The further away I go, the better." It was a Corsair Line boat which took me on board. It was headed for the tropics, like all the company's other boats, with a cargo of cotton goods, officers and colonial administrators.

So old was the boat that they'd taken away the brass plate on the upper deck which had the date of its birth on it; that had been so very long ago it would have given rise to apprehension, as well as jokes, among the passengers.

They put me on this boat, then, for me to go and try to make a new man of myself in the colonies. They wished me well and were determined that I should make my fortune. Personally I only wanted to get away, but as one ought always to look useful if one isn't rich and as, anyway, my studies didn't seem to be getting me anywhere, it couldn't very well last. I hadn't enough money to go to the States, though. So "Africa has it," I said, and I let myself be hounded towards the tropics where I was told you only had not to drink too much and to behave fairly well to make your way at once.

These prognostications made me think. There weren't many things to be said in my favour, but it was true that I bore myself decently and quite well. I was deferential, and always frightened of not being in time, and careful never to get ahead of any one in life; in fact, I was polite.

When one's been able to escape alive from a mad international shambles, it says something after all for one's tact and discretion. But about this voyage. While we stayed in European waters, things didn't seem likely to go too badly. The passengers squatted about the lower decks, the lavatories and the smoking room in suspicious, drawling little groups. The whole lot of them were soaked in *amer picons* and gossip from morning till night. They belched, snoozed and shouted by turns and never seemed to regret having left Europe at all.

Our ship was called the *Admiral Bragueton*. She could only have floated on these steamy seas thanks to the paint on her hull. So many coats of paint had been laid one on top of the other on her hull that the *Admiral Bragueton* had a sort of second skin, like an onion. We were cruising towards Africa; the real, vast Africa of limitless forests, dangerous swamps, unbroken solitudes, where negro kings squatted amid a network of unending rivers. For a packet of Pilett blades they were going to barter fine long pieces of ivory with me, and birds of bright plumage and slaves under age. That's what I'd been promised. I was going to really live, so they told me. I'd have nothing in common with this Africa, innocent of all agencies, public monuments, railways and tins of toffee. There'd be nothing of that sort. Oh, no! We were going to see Africa in the raw, the real Dark Continent, we bibulous passengers on board the *Admiral Bragueton*.

But when we were past the coast of Portugal, things began to go wrong. One morning we woke up to find ourselves overcome by a breathless sort of stove atmosphere, disquieting and frightful. The drinking water, the sea, the air, the sheets, our own sweat, everything was warm, sticky. From then onwards it was impossible, by day or by night, to feel anything cool in one's hand, under one's bottom, down one's throat, but the ice in the whiskey served at the ship's bar. An ugly despair settled on the passengers on board the *Admiral Bragueton*; they were condemned never to leave the bar, dripping, clinging to the ventilators, grasping little bits of ice, threatening each other after bridge and incoherently apologizing.

It didn't take long. In this maddeningly unchanging temperature the whole human freight of the ship clotted together in one vast tipsiness. People walked wanly about the deck, like jellyfish at the bottom of a pool of stagnant water. It was then that one saw the whole of the white man's revolting nature displayed in freedom from all constraint, under provocation and untrammelled; his real self as you saw it in war. This tropic stove brought out human instincts in the same way as the heat of August induces toads and vipers to come out and flatten themselves against the fissured walls of prison buildings. In the cold of Europe, under prudish northern fogs, except when slaughter is afoot, you only glimpse the crawling cruelty of your fellow men. But their rottenness rises to the surface as soon as they are tickled by the hideous fevers of the tropics. It's then that the wild unbuttoning process begins, and degradation triumphs, taking hold of us entirely. A biological confession of weakness. As soon as work and the cold restrain us no longer, as soon as their stranglehold is loosened, you catch sight in the white race of what you see on a pretty beach when the tide goes out; reality, heavy-smelling pools of slime, the crabs, the carcasses and scum.

And so when Portugal was passed, every one on the boat began, ferociously, to give vent to their instincts: they were helped in this by alcohol and that comfortable feeling, best known to soldiers and officials in service, which comes of not having to pay one's fare. To feel that for a month on end one is being given food, drink and one's bed free and for nothing is enough in itself, you'll agree, to make one rave with delight at such economy. I, the only paying fare on board, was considered, as soon as the fact became known, extraordinarily bad-mannered, a quite intolerable bounder.

If, when we left Marseilles, I had had any experience of colonial society, I should have gone on bended knee, in my unworthiness, to ask pardon and mercy of that colonial infantry-officer, the highest in rank on board, whom I was continually meeting everywhere about the ship. And perhaps I should have prostrated myself also, to make assurance doubly sure, at the feet of the oldest civil servant. Then do you think these fantastic travellers would have tolerated my presence among them without unpleasantness? But, in my ignorance, my unthinking claim to be allowed to breathe the same air as they very nearly cost me my life.

One is never fearful enough. As it was, thanks to a certain

skillfulness on my part, I lost nothing but what was left of my self-respect.

And this is the way things happened.

Some time after passing the Canary Islands, I learnt from a steward that I was generally looked upon as a *poseur*, not to say an insolent fellow. That I was suspected of pimping, not to mention pederasty . . . of taking cocaine as well, a bit. . . . But that only as a side line. . . . Then the notion got about that I'd had to make my escape from France following certain very grave offences against the law. Even so, I was only at the beginning of my trials. It was then that I found out about the practice usual on this line of never taking paying passengers except with extreme circumspection, and of subjecting to as much ragging as a new boy gets at school all passengers who did not travel free, either on a military pass or thanks to some bureau-cratic arrangement, since French colonies actually belong, as is well known, to the élite of the government departments.

After all, there aren't many valid motives which might induce an unknown citizen to venture in this direction. . . . I was a spy, a suspect; a thousand reasons were found for cold-shouldering me, the officers averting their eyes, the women with a meaning smile. Soon the stewards themselves were encouraged by this to exchange heavily caustic remarks behind my back. In the end no one doubted at all that I was really the nastiest and most intolerable dirty dog on board—the only one, in fact. It was a fine lookout.

At table, I sat next to four toothless, liverish, postal officials from the Cameroons. At the beginning of the voyage they had been familiar and friendly; now they didn't address a single word to me. By tacit accord I was being sent to Coventry and closely watched by every one. I no longer left my cabin, except with extreme caution. The boiling atmosphere weighed down on us as if it were solid. Naked, behind my locked door, I lay quite still and tried to imagine what plan these devilish people might have devised to be rid of me. I knew no one on board, yet every one seemed to know me. My description must have become well-known, photographed in their minds, like that of a famous criminal published in the Press.

Without wishing it, I had begun to take the part of the necessary "infamous unworthy wretch," the scorn of humanity, pointed at through the centuries, familiar to every one, like God and the Devil, but assuming always a different shape, so fugitive on earth and in life as to be actually indefinable. To pick out this wretch, to seize on him and identify him, exceptional conditions had been needed, such as only existed on our restricted hulk.

A general moral rejoicing was imminent aboard the *Admiral Bragueton*. This time the evil-eyed one wasn't going to get away with it. And that meant me. The event in itself was enough to make the voyage worth while. Surrounded by these people who chose to be my enemies, I tried as best I might to identify them without their knowing it. To this end I spied on them with impunity, especially in the morning, through the porthole of my cabin. Before breakfast, in pyjamas transparent against the light, covered with hair from their eyebrows to their navels and from the small of their backs to their ankles, my enemies came out to enjoy the morning coolness or sprawled against the side and roasted, glass in hand, threatening to vomit at any minute — especially the captain with his bulging, bloodshot eyes, whose liver troubled him from dawn. Regularly every morning he asked after me from the other buffoons, wanting to know if I'd been "flung overboard" yet. "Like a lump of dirty phlegm!" To add point to his remarks, he spat into the viscous sea. A hell of a joke.

The *Admiral Bragueton* made hardly any headway: she seemed to drag herself along, grunting between each roll. It was an illness now, a voyage no longer. The members of this morning council of war, as I examined them from my coign of vantage, all seemed to me pretty seriously stricken with some disease or other — malaria, alcoholism, syphilis probably. Their decay, which I could see at ten yards' range, consoled me somewhat for my own personal worries. After all, they were beaten men, like me, these fire eaters! They were arrogant still; that was the only difference! The mosquitoes had already started in to suck their blood and fill their veins with poisons which cannot be got rid of. . . . Gonococci by this time were filing away their arteries. . . . Alcohol was eating up their livers. . . . The sun was cracking their kidneys. . . . Crabs had fastened in their hair and eczema covered their stomachs. . . .The blazing light would eventually dim their retinas. . . . In a little while what would they have left? A few scraps of brain. . . . What could they do with that? I ask you . . . where they were bound for. Commit suicide? It wouldn't be of any use to them where they were going except to help them commit suicide, in the places they were headed for. Whatever you may say, it's no fun growing old in countries where there are no distractions. . . . Where one has to look at oneself in a glass which is itself decaying, filming over. . . . You rot quick enough in green places, especially when it's hideously hot.

The North will at least preserve your flesh for you; Northerners are pale for good and all. There's very little difference between a dead Swede and a young man who's had a bad night. But the Colonial is full of maggots the day after he gets off the boat. That's just what these infinitely industrious larvæ have been waiting for, and they won't let him go till long after life is over. A crawling carcass, that's all he is.

We'd eight more days at sea before touching at Bragamance, our first taste of the promised land. I felt as if I were living in a case of high explosives. I hardly ate at all, so as not to have to meet these people in the saloon, or cross their decks in daylight. I didn't open my mouth. I was never seen walking about. It was difficult to be as small as I was and still remain on the boat.

My cabin steward, who was a family man, kindly informed me that our fine upstanding colonial officers had sworn, with glasses raised, to slap my face at the first opportunity and then to throw me overboard. When I asked him why, he said he hadn't any idea and himself asked me what I had done for things to come to such a pitch. We were left in doubt on this point. . . . It might go on a long time. I was a cad, that's all there was to it.

They'd never again get me to travel in the company of people who were so hard to please. They had so little to do, what's more, shut up alone with themselves for a whole month, that it needed very little to make them angry. If it comes to that, one may as well realize that in everyday life at least a hundred people thirst for your miserable life in the course of a single ordinary day — all those people, for instance, whom you annoy by being ahead of them in the Underground queue; all the people who pass by your apartment and haven't one of their own; all those who would like you to hurry up and come out of the lavatory so that they can go in there themselves; your children too, and a host of others. It goes on all the time. One gets accustomed to it. On board ship this friction is more easily noticeable, so it's more annoying.

In this bubbling stewpot, the grease exuded by these human ingredients becomes concentrated; a presentiment of the frightful loneliness which in the colony is going soon to engulf them and their hopes for the future, makes them groan already like dying men. They clutch, bite, scratch, ooze. My importance on board increased prodigiously from one day to the next. My rare appearances in the saloon, however furtive and silent I strove to make them, had now become events of real significance. As soon as I came in, a hundred passengers gave a single start and began whispering.

The colonial officers at the captain's table, primed with *apéritifs*, the tax collectors, and the governesses from the Congo (of which we had a fine selection on board the *Admiral Bragueton*) had endowed me with an infernal importance by jumping from malicious suppositions to slanderous conclusions. When we'd embarked at Marseilles, I was little more than an insignificant dreamer: now, owing to the venomous concentration of these alcoholic males and unsatisfied females, I had been brought unrecognisably and unpleasantly into the limelight.

The captain, a shady fellow, cunning and covered with warts, who when the voyage began had gladly enough shaken me by the hand, now when we met seemed no longer to recognise me; he avoided me as one avoids a wanted man actually guilty of some crime. . . . Guilty of what? When there's no risk attached to hating people, stupidity quickly discovers conviction; motives spring up ready-made.

As far as I could make out in the serried ranks of antagonism pitted against me, there was one young governess who led the feminine element of the cabal. She was going back to the Congo to die — at least, I hope so. She was hardly ever separated from the colonial officers, resplendent in their gorgeous tunics and armed with the oath they had sworn that they would annihilate me, as if I were some infectious insect, long before our next port of call. It was widely debated whether I should be more unpleasant flattened out than I was alive and kicking. In fact, I was a source of entertainment. This young lady spurred them on, invoked the wrath of Heaven on my head, wouldn't rest till I had been picked up in pieces, until I'd paid the penalty for my imaginary offence in full, been punished indeed for existing and, thoroughly beaten, bruised and bleeding, had begged for mercy under a rain of blows and kicks from the fine fellows whose pluck and muscular development she was aching to admire. Deep down in her wasted insides, she was stirred at the thought of some magnificently blood-bespattered scene. The idea of it was as exciting to her as that of being raped by a gorilla. Time was slipping by and it is unwise to keep the arena crowd waiting. I was the victim. The whole ship clamoured for my blood, seemed to tremble from keel to rigging in expectation.

The sea kept us fast in this floating circus. Even the stokers knew what was afoot. And as there were only three days more before we berthed — three decisive days — several executioners volunteered their services. And the more I avoided the fracas, the more aggressive and threatening towards me every one became. Those about to perform the sacrifice were getting their hand in. My cabin was sandwiched between two other cabins at the end of a cul-de-sac. I had escaped hitherto by the skin of my teeth, but it was becoming downright dangerous for me to go along to the lavatories. So now that there were only three more days, I decided definitely to renounce all Nature's needs. The porthole was enough for me. A weight of hatred and boredom bore down on everything around me. It certainly is an unbelievable boredom on board a ship — a cosmic boredom. It covers the whole sea, the boat and the sky. Even reasonable people might be driven to wild excesses by it, let alone these unreal savages.

A sacrifice! A sacrifice! I wasn't going to be allowed to escape it. Things came to a head one evening after supper, when I'd felt too hungry to resist going to the saloon. I'd kept my nose down over my plate, not daring even to bring out a handkerchief to mop the sweat from my face. Nobody has ever eaten more unobtrusively than I did. A small regular throb came up under one's seat from the engines as one ate. My neighbours at the table must have known what had been decided about me, because they began, to my surprise, to talk to me about duels and sword-play, pleasantly and at length, and to ask me questions. At that moment too, the Congo governess — the one whose breath smelt so strongly — entered the lounge. I had time to notice that she was wearing a spectacular lace evening gown; with nervous haste she went over to the piano and played, if one can call it playing, a number of airs, all of which she left unfinished. The atmosphere had become extremely sinister and tense.

Like a shot, I bolted back towards the refuge of my cabin. I'd almost reached it when one of the officers, the greatest swaggerer and the toughest of them all, barred my way resolutely, but with-out violence. "Let's go up on deck," he enjoined me. We were there in no time. He was wearing for the occasion his most gold-braided képi, and had buttoned up his tunic from top to bottom, which he hadn't ever done since the voyage began. So we were to have full dramatic ceremonial, evidently. I didn't amount to much; my heart was thumping somewhere about the level of my navel.

Such unusually formal preliminaries suggested a slow and painful execution of sentence. The man seemed to me like a further fragment of the war confronting me again, purposeful, murderous, inescapable.

At the same time, drawn up behind him, very much on the alert, four junior officers blocked the companionway, forming an escort to Fate.

There was no way out. The harangue which followed must have been meticulously thought out. "Sir, you are in the presence of Captain Frémizon of the Colonial Service. In the name of my fellow officers and of the passengers on this ship, all of whom are

justly indignant at your outrageous behaviour, I have the honour
to demand an explanation from you. We consider intolerable
certain remarks which you have made about us since you came
aboard at Marseilles. Now is the time for you, sir, to air your
grievances aloud, to repeat openly the shameful things you have
been whispering these past three weeks — to say, in fact, whatever
you may have to say for yourself!"

I was immensely relieved when I heard these words. I had feared
a summary execution of some sort, but they offered me, in that
the captain was talking to me, a means of escape. I seized this
ray of hope. Any chance of cowardice is a wonderful possibility
of salvation if you know what you're up to. That's what I thought.
Never quibble about how to escape being gutted, nor lose time
in puzzling out the reasons for a persecution directed against
oneself. Escape in itself is enough, if one is wise.

"Captain!" I said to him in as confident a voice as I could
just then muster. "You are making an extraordinary mistake!
Me of all people! And you, Captain! How *can* such disloyal
feelings be attributed to me? Really, it is too unfair! The very
thought of it dumbfounds me. . . . How *can* they? I, who but
the other day was fighting for our country! I, whose blood with
your own has flowed in so many unforgettable battles! What
an injustice you are heaping upon me, Captain!"

Then, addressing myself to the whole group, I went on: "Gentlemen, what is this appalling slander which has deceived you
all? How can you have dreamt that I, your brother in arms,
could ever descend to spreading monstrous rumours about gallant
officers of the army! It is too much; really it is too much. . . .
And that I should choose to do so at just such a time when, brave
men one and all, they're going out again to guard, loyally to
guard, our immortal Colonial Empire! That Empire in whose
service the foremost soldiers of our race have covered themselves
with eternal glory — the Mangins, the Faidherbes, the Galliénis!
Oh, Captain, that such things should be said of man!"

I broke off and waited. I hoped to have impressed them. Fortunately I had, for one short moment. With no loss of time,
therefore, I took advantage of this truce and their confusion and,

going right up to him, seized both his hands with a fine show of emotion.

I felt better with his hands firmly clasped in mine. Never letting go of them, I went on volubly explaining my position, and while I assured him that he'd been entirely in the right, I said that we must make a fresh start, he and I, this time getting things quite straight between us. That my understandable if foolish timidity was alone responsible for this fantastic dislike that had been taken to me. That my behaviour might indeed very well have been considered extraordinary and arrogant by this group of ladies and gentlemen, "my gallant and charming fellow travellers. . . . Luckily they were people of character and understanding. . . . And many of the ladies were marvellously musical, an ornament to the society on board!" I made an honourable and profuse apology and wound up by begging them to admit me without the least suspicion or reserve into the heart of their happy company of patriots and brothers. . . . I wished them to like me henceforth and always. . . . I didn't let go of his hands, of course, but I redoubled my eloquence.

When not actually busy killing, your soldier's a child. He's easily amused. Unaccustomed to thought, as soon as you talk to him he has to make terrific efforts in order to understand what you're saying. Captain Frémizon wasn't engaged in murdering me, he wasn't drinking either, he wasn't doing anything with his hands, or with his feet: he was merely endeavouring to think. It was vastly too much for him. Actually I had him mentally overcome.

Bit by bit, while this humiliating trial lasted, I felt my self-respect, which was about to leave me anyway, slipping still further from me, then going completely and at last definitely gone, as if officially removed. Say what you like, it's a very pleasant sensation. After this incident I've always felt infinitely free and light; morally, I mean, of course. Perhaps fear is what you need most often in life to get you out of a hole. Personally, since that day I've never myself wanted any other weapon, or any other virtues.

The captain was at a loss, and his fellow officers, who had

come there for the purpose of smashing me and scattering my
teeth about the deck, now had to put up with mere words scattered
in the air instead. The civilians, who'd also come rushing at the
news of an execution, glowered unpleasantly. As I wasn't quite
certain of what I was saying (except that I stuck for all I was
worth to the lyric note) I gazed straight ahead at a given spot
in the soft fog, through which the *Admiral Bragueton* was wend-
ing her way, wheezing and slobbering at every stroke of her
propeller. At last, to conclude my speech, I risked waving one
arm above my head, and letting go of one of the captain's hands
to do so, only one, I came to an impressive close:

"Among soldiers and gentlemen, should any misunderstanding
be allowed to exist? Long live France, then, in God's name! *Vive
la France!*" It was Sergeant Branledore's gambit. And it worked on
this occasion too. That was the only time my country saved my
life; till then, it had been quite the reverse. I noticed my audience
hesitate for a second; but after all, it's very difficult for an officer
to strike a civilian in public, however ill-disposed towards him
he may feel, just when the other is shouting *"Vive la France!"*
as loudly as I had then. Their hesitation saved me.

I grasped two arms at random in the group of officers and invited everybody to come along to the bar and drink to my
health and our reconciliation. The gallant fellows hung back
only for a moment; then we drank for two hours. But the females
on board watched us silently and in slowly growing disappointment. Through the portholes I watched the piano-playing governess
obstinately prowling up and down, with several lady passengers,
like a hyena. They guessed, the bitches, that I'd slipped out of the
ambush by a ruse, and they meant to catch me again on the re-
bound. All this while, we men went on drinking under the useless
and maddening electric fan which, since we left the Canaries, had
feebly churned an air like warm cotton. But I had to keep in
form, I had to start the ball rolling again, so as to please my new
friends, making things easy and pleasant for them. I never ran
dry of patriotic admiration, wary of slipping; I went on and on
asking these heroes one after another for more and more stories
of colonial feats of arms. War stories are like the dirty variety;

they never fail to please all soldiers of all nationalities. What you really need to make a sort of peace with these men, whether they're officers or privates — a fragile armistice it's true, but nevertheless very valuable — is, whatever happens, to let them expand and bask in idiotic self-glorification. Intelligent vanity does not exist. It's merely an instinct. Yet there is no man who is not vain before all else. One human being can only tolerate another human being and rather like him, if he plays the part of an admiring doormat. I didn't have to do any mental hard work with these military gentlemen. It was enough never to stop seeming amazed and delighted. And it's easy to ask for more and more war stories. My young friends simply bristled with them. I could have imagined myself back in the good old hospital days. At the end of each of their anecdotes I did not forget to show my appreciation, in the way I'd learned from Branledore, with a fine phrase. "That's something that deserves to go down to History!" As a formula, it's as good as they make them. The circle I had so stealthily squeezed my way into began bit by bit to consider me an interesting fellow. They began to say many things about the war as wildly absurd as those I had heard in the old days and later invented myself, when competing imaginatively with my mates in hospital. Of course, their setting was different; their fantasies wandered at large in the forests of the Congo instead of in the Vosges or in Flanders.

My good Captain Frémizon, the one who earlier had assumed the task of purifying the boat of my disgusting presence, began, now that he had noticed my habit of listening more attentively than any one else, to show me the more charming side of his character. His arteries seemed to be softened by my novel expressions of admiration, his vision cleared, those bulging, bloodshot eyes that betrayed the confirmed toper finally even sparkled, despite his brutishness, and the few little doubts as to his own worth which may have assailed him still whenever he was very depressed, were now adorably dispersed for a time by my marvellously intelligent and pertinent comments.

By Gad, I was the fellow to make a party go! They slapped their thighs in approbation. No one else could make life so enjoyable in spite of the moist horror of these latitudes. The point is that I was listening beautifully.

While we were carrying on in this way, the *Admiral Bragueton* began to go slower still; she slowed down in her own juice. Not a breath of air stirred about us; we were hugging the coast and doing it so slowly that we seemed to be shifting through molasses.

Syrupy too was the sky above the decks, nothing but a black, deep paste which I gazed at hungrily. To get back into the night was what I wanted most of all, to get back there, sweating and groaning or any way, it didn't matter how. Frémizon never stopped talking. Land seemed quite close but my plan of escape filled me with deep anxiety. . . . Little by little our talk ceased to be military and became jaunty, then frankly smutty, and at last so downright dirty that it was hard to know how to keep it going. One after another my guests gave up the attempt and fell asleep, and were shaken by snores, unpleasant slumber grating in their noses. Now or never was the time to get away. It's no good wasting these intervals of kindness which nature somehow manages to impose on even the most vicious and aggressive of earthly creatures.

We were at anchor just then, not far from land. All you could see of it were a few lanterns waving along the shore.

Very quickly a hundred swaying canoes full of chattering black men came alongside. These natives swarmed all over the ship, offering their services. In no time I was at the gangway with the few bundles into which I had furtively made up my things, and streaked off behind one of the boatmen, whose face and movements in the darkness I could hardly see. At the bottom, down by the water slapping the ship's side, I wondered where we were going.

"Where are we?" I asked him.

"At Bambola-Fort-Gono," the shadow answered.

We pushed off into the open, paddling hard. I helped him, so as to increase our speed.

In my flight I caught one more glimpse of my dangerous companions on board. Under the lights between decks I could see them, overcome, comatose and gastric, still twitching and grunting in their sleep. Bloatedly sprawling, they all looked the same now, all these officers, civil servants, engineers and traders, mingling, swarthy, spotted, guzzling. A dog looks like a wolf when he's asleep.

In a few minutes I had reached land once more and had found the night as well. It was thickest under the trees and there for me too, beyond the night itself, was all the complicity of silence.

OVERTOPPING THE WHOLE OF THIS COLONY OF BAMBOLA BRAGAMANCE and everybody in it, was the governor. The soldiers and civil servants under him hardly dared to breathe when he deigned to cast his eye upon them.

Far beneath these notables the resident traders seemed to thieve and prosper more easily than in Europe. Not a coconut or a groundnut throughout the whole territory escaped their depredations. The civil servants realized, as they grew more tired and ill, that they'd been done in the eye when they were sent out here and weren't getting anything after all except braid, and forms to fill up, and practically no salary for it all. So they glowered at the traders. The military group, which had fallen even lower than the other two, merely existed on a diet of imperial prestige, helped down with a lot of quinine and miles and miles of regulations.

Understandably enough, from continually waiting for the barometer to drop, everybody was becoming more and more obtuse. And so endless petty quarrels, both personal and between groups, were always in progress between the military and the civil servants, between these latter and the traders, and between both of them joined in temporary alliance against the former, and then between all three against the black man and finally between the black men themselves. Such vital energy as was not sapped by malaria, thirst and the heat of the sun was consumed by hatreds so bitter and insistent that many of the residents used to die in their tracks, poisoned by themselves, like scorpions.

This state of virulent chaos, however, was encircled by a serried cordon of police, like crabs in a bucket. It was in vain that the officials whined; the governor could always recruit as many shabby levies as he needed to keep his colony in order, as many as there were defaulting Negroes driven by penury in their

thousands towards the coast, bankrupted by the traders and searching for a crust to eat. These recruits were taught the law and how
to admire the governor. As for the governor, he seemed to parade
all the gold of his income on his uniform; with the sun shining on
it, it was incredible, and that not counting the plumes on his
helmet.

The governor had a supply of Vichy sent out to him every
year and read nothing but the *Official Gazette*. A great number of
the Civil Service servants had lived in hopes that one day he'd
go to bed with their wives, but the governor had no liking for
women. He had no liking for anything. Through each succeeding
yellow-fever epidemic the governor lived on as if by magic, while
many of the people who longed to help bury him died like flies
at the first wave of infection.

It was recalled that one fourteenth of July, when he was
reviewing his troops at the Residency, curvetting about at the
head of his guard of Spahis, alone before a devilish great flag, a
certain sergeant, no doubt driven out of his right mind by fever,
sprang out in front of his horse and shouted, "Get back, you
dirty bastard!" It appears that the governor was much affected
by this sort of attempt on his person, which anyway was never
satisfactorily cleared up.

It is hard to take a reasonable view of people and things in
the tropics because of the aura of colour which envelops them.
Things and colours are in a haze. A little sardine tin lying open
at noon in the middle of the road throws off so many different
reflections that in one's eyes it takes on the importance of an
accident. You've got to be careful. It's not only the human
beings who are hysterical down in those parts; things get involved in it too. Life doesn't become even barely tolerable until
nightfall and even then the darkness is seized almost at once by
swarms of mosquitoes, — not one or two or several score, but
billions of them. To pull through under such conditions becomes
a veritable feat of self-preservation. A carnival by day, a caul-
dron at night, it's the war again *in petto*.

When the bungalow one sleeps in has at last become silent, and
the air indoors is almost fit to breathe, the ants set to on its

foundations, busily engaged night after night, the little brutes, in eating away your supports from under you. Then let a gale sweep down on this treacherous fretwork and whole streets will be puffed away.

This place I had come to, Fort-Gono, the flimsy capital of Bragamance Territory, was perched between the sea and the jungle, but could boast nevertheless of a whole array of banks, brothels, cafés and sidewalks, not to mention Faidherbe Square and the Boulevard Bugeaud, where one could take a stroll, and, just to make it quite the little metropolis, even a recruiting station; in all, a group of glaring buildings set in the midst of rough cliffs of larva which generations of energetic whites had scaled.

The military element round about five o'clock used to growl over its *apéritifs*, which as a matter of fact when I arrived had just been put up in price. A consumers' delegation was going to the governor to ask for an injunction to restrain this profiteering by the liquor merchants in the *cassis* and absinthe markets. According to certain old stagers, colonizing was becoming more and more arduous on account of ice being available. The introduction of ice into our colonies was, to be sure, a signal for a loss of vitality among the colonizers. Thenceforward, accustomed never to be without his iced drinks, the colonial administrator must needs give up attempting to overcome the climate by his own stoicism alone. Let us remember that the Faidherbes, the Stanleys and the Marchands allowed their thoughts to dwell on nothing more appetizing than lukewarm, muddy beer, wine or water, which they drank year after year without complaining. There you have it — that's the way you lose your colonies.

Lots of other things I learnt too beneath the palms, which for their part flourished — irritatingly enough thanks to their own sap — along those streets of fragile houses. It was only this startling note of crude green which prevented the place from looking like the gloomier outskirts of Paris.

When night had fallen the native hubbub got well under way amid clouds of busy mosquitoes primed with yellow fever. Sudanese ladies offered the passer-by whatever joys their skirts concealed. For a very reasonable sum whole families were at your disposal for an hour or two. I should have liked to flit from sex to sex in this way, but I simply had no time to lose in making up my mind to look somewhere for a job.

The general manager of the Pordurière Company of Little Togo was looking, they told me, for some newcomer to take charge of one of his trading posts in the interior. Without losing another moment I went and offered him my own incompetent but eager services. It wasn't a particularly charming reception that the general manager gave me. He was a maniac, as a matter of fact, living not far from the Government House in a very large bungalow, built on piles and thatched. Before even so much as looking at me he asked, quite savagely, a few questions about my past and then, slightly mollified by my very naïve answers, became moderately indulgent in his scorn for me. But he still didn't think it worth while to offer me a seat.

"It seems from your papers that you know a little about medicine?" he remarked.

I answered that I had as a matter of fact studied medicine a little.

"You'll find it useful," he said. "Have a whiskey?"

I didn't drink.

"Will you smoke?"

I again said no. Such abstinence surprised him. He made a face.

"I don't at all like my men not smoking or drinking. . . . Are you a bugger, by any chance? No? That's a pity. That sort don't steal as much as the others. It's a thing I've noticed from experience. They get attached . . . Anyway," he had the goodness to amend, "generally speaking, I seem to have noticed that particular characteristic of homosexuals, a point in their favour. . . . Well, perhaps you'll prove just the reverse!" Then, changing the subject, "You're feeling the heat, are you? You'll get used to it! You'll have to, anyway. How was the journey out?"

"Unpleasant," I told him.

"Well, my friend, you haven't seen anything yet: you'll have plenty more to say about this country when you've spent a year at Bikomimbo, where I'm sending you to take the place of that other rogue."

His negress, squatting by the table, was fiddling with her toenails, picking at them with a little piece of wood.

"Get out, you lump!" her master shouted. "Go and call my boy. And get me some ice at the same time!"

The boy who'd been sent for took a long time to arrive. When he did come, the manager, furious because he'd been kept waiting, sprang to his feet and greeted his servant with a couple of terrific slaps in the face and two kicks in the pit of the stomach which could be heard for miles.

"They'll drive me crazy, that's what'll happen," the manager groaned. And he fell back into his armchair, which was covered with some dirty, shapeless yellow material.

"I say, old man," he turned to me, suddenly kindly and familiar, as if relieved by the brutality he had just shown, "pass me my quinine and the water jug, will you? There on the table. . . . I oughtn't to let myself get worked up. . . . It's stupid to give way to one's temper like that."

From his house we overlooked the river harbour, shimmering below us through dust so thick and solid that one could hear the sounds of its chaotic activity more clearly than one could make out the details of it. On the shore, strings of Negroes were unloading, bale after bale, the never-emptied holds, clambering up flimsy, swaying gangplanks with great, full baskets balanced on their heads, amid curses, like some sort of upright ants.

They came and went, jogging in single files through a red haze. Among these forms at work some bore an extra little black dot on their backs: they were the mothers who had also come to carry sacks of dates, with their children as an added burden. I wonder whether ants can do as much.

"It's like Sunday all the time here, don't you think?" the manager continued humourously. "It's gay! And bright. The females always naked, you'll have noticed. And not bad-looking females either, eh? It seems quite odd when one first gets here from Paris, doesn't it? And what about us? Wearing white drill all the time! As if we were at the seaside on holiday. . . . Pretty we look, don't you think? All dressed up for First Communion. . . . It's one long holiday here you know — a real swelter-

ing Empire Day! And it's like that all the way to the Sahara!
Think of it . . ."

Then he stopped talking, sighed, groaned, said a filthy word two
or three times, mopped his face and again picked up the conversation.

"Out there where the company's sending you, it's the thick of
the bush, and damp. . . . It's a ten days' journey from here. . . .
First by sea. Then up the river. It's a bright red river, you'll
find. . . . On the other side are the Spaniards. . . . Between
ourselves, the chap you're replacing at this dump's an absolute
bastard. . . . I mean to say, we simply can't make the damn
man send in his accounts. Can't do it. Note after note I send
him, but it's no good. . . . A man's not honest long when he's
alone by himself. . . . You'll see. . . . You'll find that out
too. . . . He's ill, he says. . . . Fancy that! Ill! Dammit, I'm ill
myself. What's he mean — *ill?* We're all ill. You too, you'll get
ill before very long. That's no excuse! We don't give a damn if
he's ill or not. What does the company mind about that? As soon
as you get there, be sure to make an inventory of what he's got
left. . . . He has enough food at that store to last three months,
and enough trade stock for at least a year. . . . You won't be
short! Above all, don't start out at night. Be careful. He'll send
his blacks to meet you on the coast and they'll tip you overboard,
maybe. . . . He'll have been at them, probably. . . . They're as
shifty as he is. By God yes. . . . He'll have slipped them a word or
two about you all right. . . . That sort of thing happens, you
know, out here. . . . And don't forget to take your quinine with
you, your own quinine; get it before you go! He's quite capable
of having put something into his for you. . . ."

The general manager was through giving me advice; he got
up to say good-bye. The ceiling above us, made of canvas, seemed
to weigh a couple of hundred tons at least, it kept the heat down
on us so. Both our faces expressed our irritation at the heat. It
was enough to kill you there and then. He added:

"It probably isn't worth while meeting again before you go,
Bardamu. Everything's so tiring out here. Oh, I don't know, I'll
go down and see you're O.K., before you start, all the same. . . .

We'll write to you when you're out there. There's a mail once a month. . . . The runner starts from here. Well, good luck!"

He disappeared into the shadow between his sun helmet and his vest. You could see the tendons in his neck quite distinctly, knotted like two fingers sticking out against the back of his head. He turned back once more.

"Don't forget to tell the other bloke to come down here at once. . . . Tell him I've a word or two to say to him — and not to waste time on the way. Bah! The blighter! Hope at least he doesn't die en route. . . . That would be a pity. A great pity! The dirty swine."

One of his blacks walked before me with a large lantern, taking me to the place I was to stop at, before setting out for this lovely Bikomimbo of my dreams.

We went along streets in which every one seemed to have come out for a stroll after dusk. The night, hammered by gongs, was everywhere pierced by dry incoherent voices singing, like hiccups — that great black night of hot countries with its brutal pulse beating, like a tom-tom, always too fast.

My young guide slid nimbly along on naked feet. There must have been Europeans in the thickets; one could hear them snooping around, white men's voices recognizable at once, impatient and aggressive. The bats all the time came flapping and swerving through the swarms of insects which our light attracted around us as we passed. Each leaf of every tree must have hidden a cricket, judging by the deafening din they were all of them making.

We were stopped at a cross-roads halfway up a slope by a group of native soldiers arguing around a coffin which lay on the ground covered by the large folds of a tricolour flag.

A man had died in hospital and they weren't at all certain where to bury him. Orders had been vague. One or two of them wanted to bury him in a field somewhere down the hill, others were in favour of a patch right up at the top of the incline. A decision had to be made. So the boy and I said our say in the matter.

Finally they picked on the lower burial ground in preference to the higher, because it meant going downhill. Further along our road we met three of those little white youngsters of the sort that in Europe spends its free afternoons watching rugby matches, excitable, keen and pasty-faced lookers-on. Out here they belonged, as I did, to the Pordurière Company; they very kindly showed me the way to the unfinished house where, for the moment, I was to find my camp bed.

We went. It was an absolutely empty building except for one or two cooking utensils and my so-called bed. As soon as I had stretched myself out on this quivering, netlike contraption, a score of bats came out of the corners and swooped noisily back and forth, like so many swishing fans, over my uneasy rest.

My little black guide came back once more to offer me the delights of his person. He was disappointed when I explained that I really wasn't feeling up to it that evening and immediately suggested introducing his sister to me. I would have been curious to know how, on such a night, he would have set about finding his sister.

Quite close by, the village tom-tom with little strokes chipped one's patience into tiny fragments. A horde of diligent mosquitoes at once took possession of my thighs and I didn't dare set foot to the ground again because of the scorpions and poisonous reptiles which I was sure were out on their abominable hunt for victims. Certainly they had their choice of rats. I could hear them gnawing away at everything that can be gnawed; I could hear them in the walls, under the floor, about to flop from the ceiling.

At last the moon came out and things were a little more calm in the hut. It wasn't, in fact, much fun being out in the colonies.

Next morning came eventually, a baking horror. An utter longing to return to Europe filled me, body and soul. Only lack of money prevented my escape. But that was enough. And I only had one more week to spend in Fort-Gono before taking over my post at Bikomimbo, of which I'd heard so much.

The largest building in Fort-Gono, after the Governor's Palace, was the hospital. I came across it everywhere I went: I couldn't walk a hundred yards through the town without coming up against one or other of its wards, smelling distantly of carbolic.

Sometimes I wandered down to the quay-side and stood there watching my unhealthy little colleagues at work; the Pordurière Company used to bring them over from France in droves. An aggressive haste seemed to possess them to keep up the loading and unloading of one cargo after another without pause. "Harbour duties cost such a devil of a lot," they kept repeating, as sincerely put out as if it were their own money which was being spent.

They harassed the black dock hands quite frantically. They were full of zeal, no one could dream of denying that, and they were just as vacant and bloody-minded as they were zealous. Employees worth their weight in gold, in fact, carefully picked men, as enthusiastic and unreasoning as one could wish. Sons such as my mother would have liked to bear, dead keen on their jobs. What would she not have given to have had just one such son, of whom she could be truly proud before all the world, a really *legitimate* son!

Gutless little creatures, they had come out to the West Coast to offer up to their employers their selves, their blood, their lives, their youth, suffering martyrdoms for twenty-two francs a day (minus board and lodging), and pleased, yes, quite pleased to carry on until the ten millionth mosquito had sucked from them their last red corpuscle.

The colony makes little clerks fat or it makes them thin, but it doesn't let them go. There are only two ways to die under the sun, — the fat way and the lean. There is no other. One could choose which one preferred if it didn't simply depend on one's make-up whether one dies fat or with only skin on one's bones.

The general manager up there on his red cliff top, now writhing diabolically with his black woman under that canvas roof, with its hundred thousand pounds' weight of sunshine, he too would not escape disaster. His was the thin type. He was putting up a show against it, that's all. He seemed to be able to cope with the climate. But that was a vain illusion. In reality, he was burning away to nothing even more rapidly than every one else.

It was said that he had a magnificent embezzlement scheme which would make his fortune in a couple of years. But he would never have time to make his plan come true — even if he set himself to defraud the company all day and all night. Twenty-two general managers of the company before him had all tried to make their fortunes, each with his own pet system, like at roulette. All that was as clear as daylight to the shareholders, who were keeping their eye on him down there, and to others who watched from further afield, from the Rue Moncey, in Paris, and it only made them smile. The whole thing was childish. The shareholders were themselves greater bandits than any one. They were aware too that their general manager was syphilitic and terribly hard pressed by the heat of the tropics, and that he swallowed enough quinine and bismuth to burst his eardrums and enough arsenic to make all his teeth drop out. In the company's books the general manager's salaried months were numbered, numbered like the days of a fattening pig.

My little fellow clerks exchanged no ideas between themselves — only fixed formulas, baked hard and rebaked like little turds of thought. "Pack up your troubles," they'd say. Or, "Keep the ball rolling." "The manager's a bastard." "Kicking niggers is the White Man's Burden."

In the evening, after work was finally over, we met again over *apéritifs* with the Assistant Inspector of Works, M. Tandernot, from La Rochelle. Tandernot only mixed with the traders so as to be stood drinks. He had to bow to this defeat; he was entirely broke. His position was as low as it well could be in the colonial hierarchy, his job being to oversee the making of roads through the thick of the forest. The natives worked on these roads; under the lash of his levies, of course. But as no white man ever used the new roads which Tandernot built, and as for their part the natives preferred their own forest tracks, so as to make themselves as small as possible and avoid taxation, and as in any case Tandernot's roads didn't really lead anywhere, they used to get overgrown and vanish very rapidly; from one month to the next, as a matter of fact.

"Believe me or not, last year I lost one hundred and twenty-two kilometres!" this fantastic pioneer would vouchsafe, quite readily, about his roads.

I discovered one solitary conceit in Tandernot while I was

there, a humble boast: which was that he was the only European who could catch cold in Bragamance when it was 107° F. in the shade. This odd talent consoled him for many things. "I've gone and caught cold again, like a dam' fool," he'd say over his *apéritif*. "It doesn't happen to any one but me." The rest of our silly little group would exclaim, "What an extraordinary chap old Tandernot is!"

And that was better than nothing; there was a certain satisfaction to be got out of it. In this matter of vanity, anything is better than nothing.

Another form of amusement in this group of the Pordurière Company's little employees was to organize fever competitions. It wasn't difficult, but you could keep the contest going for days on end, so it whiled away the time all right. When evening came the fever almost every day came with it, and one took one's temperature. "Hey, look, mine's up to 101!" — "What the hell, I can get up to 102 as easy as anything."

These recordings were entirely accurate and usual, as a matter of fact. By the light of the hurricane lamps we compared our thermometers. The winner triumphed all of a tremble. "I can't piss now I'm sweating so," the most emaciated of our number truthfully remarked. He was a slim little fellow from the Pyrenees. The champion at this feverish game, who had come out there, he told me, to escape from a seminary where he'd "not had enough liberty."

But time went by and not one of my companions could tell me what sort of an odd person the man I was going to replace at Bikomimbo was. "He's an extraordinary chap," they informed me, and that's all I could get out of them.

"When you start life in this country," the feverish little Pyrenean warned me, "you've got to make the devil of an impression. It's all entirely one way or the other. You'll either be the apple of the manager's eye or absolute anathema to him. And you're summed up right away, mark you." Personally, I was terrified of being placed in a class with the anathemas, or even worse.

My young slaver friends took me to call on another of our

colleagues in the company, who deserves special mention in this story. He kept a shop counter in the middle of the European quarter. Rotting with fatigue, oily, on the verge of collapse, he dreaded the light because of his eyes, which two years of uninterrupted scorching under a corrugated iron roof had dried up appallingly. He spent half an hour of a morning opening them, so he said, and even then it was another half-hour before he could see at all clearly. Every bright ray of light hurt him. A vast mangy mole.

To stifle and suffer had become almost second nature to him and to steal had too. Any one who could have made him healthy and scrupulous at one stroke would have done him a very bad turn. His hatred for the general manager still seems to me to this day, so long since, one of the fiercest passions that it has been my lot to come across in a man. At the thought of the general manager, an astonishing fury would transcend his aches, shaking him and making him rave tremendously on the slightest provocation, while he went on scratching himself uninterruptedly from top to toe.

He never stopped scratching all round himself, in circles, so to speak, from the base of his spine to the top of his neck. He furrowed layer after layer of his skin with bloody finger nails, never on that account forgetting to serve his customers, of whom there were many, most of them more or less naked Negroes.

With his free hand he would dip busily into different receptacles to right and left in the darkness of his shop and, without ever making a mistake, with marvellous efficiency and quickness would produce exactly what the purchaser needed in the way of strong-smelling shreds of tobacco, damp matches, tins of sardines and great ladlefuls of molasses, or over-proof beer in faked cannisters which he would instantly drop again if seized by a frantic need to scratch somewhere, let's say, in the vast profundities of his trousers. When that happened, he'd plunge his whole arm down them, and after a while it would appear again from the front, which he had the precaution to keep always open.

He gave this malady which was consuming his skin its local name of "Corocoro." "This infernal Corocoro! When I think that swine of a manager hasn't caught it yet," he'd burst out, "it turns my stomach sourer than ever. The Corocoro can't get a hold on him. He's a damn sight too rotten already. That bastard — he's not a man, he's a disease. He's an absolute lump of filth."

Every one at once burst out laughing, and the negro customers copied them and laughed too. He frightened us a bit, this chap. But he had a friend all the same, an asthmatic little creature with greying hair, who drove one of the company's lorries. He always used to bring us ice, which of course had been stolen from the ships in port whenever he could lay hands on it.

We used to drink his health on the counter amid the tremendously envious black clients. His clients were Negroes who were sufficiently sharp not to be afraid of mingling with the whites, only a certain set among them, in fact. The other Negroes were less uninhibited and preferred instinctively to keep their distance. But the boldest of them, the most contaminated, became assistants at the shop. You could recognize which were the negro assistants about the place by the way they cursed and swore at the other blacks. Our Corocoro friend trafficked in crude rubber which was brought from the bush and sold to him, in the form of moist balls, by the sackfull.

As we stood there, never tired of listening to him, a family of rubber tappers came timidly up and hovered about his doorstep. The father was at their head, a wrinkled old man wearing a little orange-coloured loin cloth and dangling his long cutlass in his hand.

The poor savage didn't dare come in. So one of the native assistants called out to him, "Come on, nigger! Come along in! We no eat black man!" Thus addressed, they managed to make up their minds. They trooped into the glittering store at the back of which our Corocoro patient was raving.

The black, it seemed, had never seen a shop before, or any whites either, maybe. One of his wives followed him, with lowered eyes, carrying balanced on the top of her head a great pannier full of raw rubber.

The assistants brusquely snatched at her pannier to weigh its contents on the scales. Poppa native didn't understand the business of the scales any more than the rest of it. His wife didn't dare raise her head. The other members of the black family waited outside, with very goggling eyes. They were made to come in, all the children and everybody, so that they shouldn't miss anything of the show.

It was the first time they'd come all together like that from the bush towards the white men and their town. They must have all been working away for a very long time to collect all that rubber. So that the result of the deal was naturally of great interest to the whole family. It takes a long time to sweat rubber into the little containers you hang on the trunks of the trees. It often takes over two months to get a small cupful.

When the weighing had been done, our scratching friend took the gaping Negro behind the counter and worked out in chalk what was due to him and stuffed a few pieces of silver into the hollow of his hand. Then, "Get out," he said to him, just like that. "There's your money!"

All his little white friends squealed with laughter, he'd put the deal over so well. The Negro stood there unhappily before the counter, with his little orange covering round his loins.

"Don't understand money, do you, bo? Don't know nuthin, eh?" the most irrepressible clerk, who was anyway probably accustomed to these peremptory transactions, shouted at him to wake him up. "You don't parly French, do you? Still a gorilla are you? What do you savvy then, tell me? Kouskous? Mabillia? You're a clod, ain't you? A bush ape — a damn great clod."

But the Negro stood before us, holding the coins in his fist. He'd have bolted if he'd dared. But he didn't dare.

"What you buy with your dough then, nigger?" put in the scratcher at just the right moment. "I haven't seen quite such a mug as this for a long time, I must say," he observed. "It must have come from way back. What d'you want? Give me that stuff!"

He snatched the money away from him and in its place shoved into the palm of his hand a large bright-green handkerchief which he nimbly extracted from a drawer in the counter.

The Negro hesitated to leave with his handkerchief. Then the scratcher went one better. He certainly knew all the tricks of a roaring trade all right. Waving the great square of green cloth before the eyes of one of the little black kids: "Don't you think that's pretty, you little bug, you? Haven't seen a handkerchief like that before, have you, my pretty one; have you, my dungheap, my little black-belly?" And without more ado, he tied it round the kid's neck, dressing him completely.

The backwoods family now gazed at their little one adorned by this great green cotton thing. . . . There was nothing more to be done about it now that the handkerchief had come into the family. There was nothing left but to accept it, take it, and go away.

So they all began to back gradually out and through the door. Just as the father, who was last, turned to say something, the toughest of the assistants, who wore shoes, helped him out with a great kick on the behind.

The whole little tribe, in a group, stood silently on the other side of the Avenue Faidherbe, under a magnolia tree, watching us finish our drinks. You'd have said that they were trying to understand what had happened to them.

It was our "Corocoro" friend's party. He even played his gramophone for us. There wasn't anything you couldn't find in his shop. It reminded me of the supply trains in the war.

AND SO, AS I SAY, THERE WERE A WHOLE LOT OF NEGROES AND whites working away with me in the warehouses and on the plantations of the Pordurière Company of Little Togo when I was there, — little clerks like me. The natives after all have to be bludgeoned into doing their job — they've still got that much self-respect. Whereas the whites carry on on their own; they've been well schooled by the State.

The wielder of the lash gets very tired of his job in the end, but the white man's heart is brimful of the hope of power and wealth and that doesn't cost anything: not a thing. Let's hear no more about Egypt and the Tartar tyrants! In the supreme art of urging the two-legged animal really to put his back into his work, these classical exponents are the merest conceited amateurs. It never entered the heads of the antique school to give the slave a "Mister" before his name, to get him to vote now and again, to buy him his newspaper; above all, to put him in the front line so as to rid him of his baser passions! With two thousand years of Christianity behind him (I should know something about that), a man can't see a regiment of soldiers march past without going off the deep end. It starts off far too many ideas in his head.

So I decided, as far as I myself was concerned, to watch my step very carefully in the future and moreover to learn to keep my mouth well shut, not to let any one see that I was aching to clear out; in fact, if possible and in spite of everything, to get on in the service of the Pordurière Company. There wasn't a minute to lose.

Alongside our warehouses down by the slimy banks of the river a cunning line of crocodiles permanently and watchfully lingered. Metallic sort of brutes, they revelled in the delirious heat; and so, it seemed, did the Negroes.

In the middle of the day one wondered whether this activity of hustling crowds throughout the docks could all be true, this parrot house of excited squawking blacks.

With a view to learning how to check over sacks before taking to the bush myself, I had to get used to being gradually asphyxiated along with the other clerks in the company's main warehouse, standing between two great weighing scales stuck in the middle of a mass of sweating Negroes covered with sores, in rags and singing. Each of them trailed along a little cloud of dust behind him which shook to his rhythm. The dull thuds of the overseers' lashes fell on their magnificent backs without calling forth the least protest or complaint. Theirs was a cretinish passivity. They bore pain as simply as they put up with the torrid atmosphere of this dusty furnace.

The manager came along from time to time, almost always in a bad temper, to make sure that I really was getting on in the business of checking numbers and faking weights.

He cleared his way through the press of natives with great swipes of his cane. "Bardamu," he said to me one morning when he was feeling good, "you see all these niggers here, don't you? Well, when I first came out to Little Togo, nearly thirty years ago, they lived by hunting, fishing and killing each other off, tribe against tribe, the dirty scum! When I started as a mere clerk in charge of a trading station, I used to see them, just like I'm telling you, coming back to their villages after a victory, carrying upwards of a hundred baskets full of good, bleeding, human flesh, which they were going to stuff into their bellies! D'you hear, Bardamu? Bleeding human meat! All that was left of their enemies! Talk about a binge! Nowadays, they don't do any scrapping. We've come along — and there aren't any tribes now! No nonsense. No funny business. Hard work and monkeynuts, that's what. A job to be done. No more hunting! No more rifles — just monkeynuts and rubber! So that they can pay their taxes. Taxes so that they can bring us in more rubber and more monkeynuts. Life's like that, Bardamu! Monkeynuts! Monkeynuts and rubber! . . . Oh, look, here's General Tombat coming our way."

He it was indeed, coming towards us, an old man on the verge of collapse beneath the enormous weight of the sun.

The general was no longer really a soldier, and yet he wasn't simply a civilian either. He was adviser to the Pordurière Company and served as a link between the colonial authorities and Business Interests — an all-important link, since these two bodies were always in league and at war with each other. But General Tombat was a marvelous "fixer." He, and a few others, not long ago, had somehow wriggled out of a shady transaction in enemy shares which high circles had considered it beyond their power to unravel.

Soon after the war started, General Tombat's ear had been slightly split: just enough to put him honourably onto the retired list, after Charleroi. He'd immediately placed his services at the disposal of Greater France across the water. Yet Verdun, which was long since over, still worried him. He was always waving telegrams about. "They'll hold it, bless 'em — our brave lads are holding fast!" It was so infernally hot in the warehouse and it was all so far away, France and everything, that no one cared a hoot for General Tombat's prognostications. Still we all, including the general manager, said politely, in chorus, "They're wonderful!" and at these words Tombat left us.

Shortly after that the manager opened his vicious way again through tight-packed bodies and in his turn disappeared into the peppery dust.

His eyes were glowing like coals; the man was possessed by the excitement of having the whole company in his grasp; he frightened me rather, I found it difficult to get accustomed to his presence, even. I wouldn't have believed that there was one single human carcass in the world capable of such a maximum intensity of greed. He hardly ever spoke to us in a natural voice, only in muffled phrases; you'd have said that he only lived, only thought, in order passionately to plot and spy and betray. It was declared that on his own account he stole, swindled and embezzled a lot more than all the company's other servants put together — and *they* weren't wasting their time, I can tell you. But I've no difficulty in believing it.

While I remained in Fort-Gono, I still had a little time to walk about this so-called town, where only one spot struck me as desirable — the hospital.

As soon as you arrive in some place, you discover ambitions in yourself. Personally what I wanted to do was to be ill, just ill, nothing more than that. Allow a man his likes. I wandered around these hospitable and attractive buildings, distant, sad and set apart, nor ever left them and their antiseptic charms without regret. Lawns encircled this domain, which were adorned by little furtive birds and scurrying, multicoloured lizards. A sort of earthly Paradise.

As for the black men, one soon gets used to them, to their gay somnolence, to their too slow gestures and the protuberant stomachs of their women.

The black race stinks in its poverty, its endless little vanities, the obscenity of its resignation: just like our own poor, in fact, except that they have more brats about the place and less dirty washing hanging up, and less red wine.

When I'd finished sniffing at the hospital, inhaling it in this way, I went off, following the native crowd, to stand for a while outside the sort of pagoda which a trader had built near the fort for the amusement of the brighter rakes in the colony.

The well-to-do whites in Fort-Gono used to show up there of a night, and gamble wildly and drink hard, and yawn and sweat. For two hundred francs you could have the good lady who ran it. The merrymakers' trousers were the devil of a nuisance to them when they wanted to have a good scratch; their braces were always slipping.

At night a whole crowd of people came out of their huts in the native quarter and stood about in front of the pagoda, never tired of seeing the white men jogging around the mechanical piano, with its moist chords and those tuneless waltzes they'd put up with. The manageress looked cheerful and happy as if she'd rather like to dance, as she listened to the music.

After several attempts on various days I at last got into conversation with her, surreptitiously, once or twice. Her clients exhausted her, she told me. Not that they made love frequently, but because drinks at the Pagoda were rather on the expensive side, they used to try, while they were at it, to get a bit extra for their money and would pinch her bottom a lot before they left. That's really what made her so tired.

This good business lady knew all the gossip of the colony and all about the love affairs which were entered into in desperation by officers harassed with fever and the handful of commissioners' wives who, melting away in endless monthly courses, lay prostrate on verandas dotted with permanently lowered deck chairs.

The streets, the offices and shops of Fort-Gono overflowed with vain desires. To do everything that is done in Europe, despite the hideous heat and a growing, inescapable imbecility, seemed to be the chief and fiercest obsession, the joy and aim of all these sentence servers.

The bloated vegetation in the gardens could barely be kept at bay within their palisades. Untamed, fierce sprouts flared up like nightmare lettuces round each house containing, like the solid great wrinkled white of an egg, the yolk of a slowly rotting, jaundiced European. So that Fachoda Avenue, the liveliest and most crowded in Fort-Gono, became a row of as many brimming salad bowls as there were colonial administrators.

I went back every evening to my hut, which obviously no one would ever finish building, and there my skeleton of a bed awaited me, made up by my pervert of a boy. He vamped me, he was as lascivious as a cat; he wanted to become part of my family. But I was haunted by other, much more important things to think about, and particularly by the idea of escaping to the hospital for a little while, the only respite within my reach in this blistering jamboree.

In peace time as in war, I wasn't at all inclined to futile pleasures. And other offers besides, which came to me through the boss's cook, and were very genuinely and exceptionally obscene, roused none of my enthusiasm.

I went one last round of my Pordurière Company colleagues, trying to discover something about this faithless servant whom I was being ordered to find and replace, at all costs, in his forest home. Chatter was all I got. Nor could I get anything more definite out of the Café Faidherbe, at the end of Fachoda Avenue, which in the evening hours buzzed with hatred, malice and all uncharitableness. Only vague suppositions. All the dustbins of rumour were emptied in this half-light cast by many-coloured lamps. The wind, shaking the lace-like foliage of giant palms, shed clouds of mosquitoes into one's cups. The governor, because of his high position, got his fair share of the ambiguously expressed remarks that were passed. His extraordinary asininity formed the basis of the conversation over cocktails, which relieves a queasy colonial liver before dinner.

All the cars in Fort-Gono, about ten in all, passed at this hour to and fro in front of the café. They never seemed to go far, these cars. Faidherbe Square had a clearly defined personality of its own, with the forthright architectural beauties, the vegetable and verbal excess of a Midi main square gone mad. And the ten autos never left Faidherbe Square without returning to it five minutes later, having once again completed their round, bearing a cargo of prostrate, anæmic Europeans in light-coloured clothes, like so many melting ice creams.

These colonizers passed each other in the street week after week and year after year until they were so tired of hating each other that they no longer looked at anybody. Some of the officers took their families for walks, all of them on the look-out for salutes from the military and bows from the civilians: the wives swaddled in special sanitary wrappings, the children like some awful sort of pale-face maggot from a northern latitude, dissolving in the heat, suffering permanently from diarrhea.

To give orders, you need more than a képi; you need soldiers. In this hot climate white troops melted away faster than butter. A battalion at Fort-Gono behaved like sugar in a coffee cup — the longer you looked the less you saw of it. The greater part of the white contingent were always in hospital, sleeping off their malaria, crawling with a different sort of parasite to each hair and every cranny of their bodies; whole squads lying back amid cigarettes and flies, contriving an infinite number of deliberately induced, fake, shivering fits.

They lay there shirking, poor devils, a shameful group in the pleasant half light cast by the green shutters; they'd not been long in the ranks before they dropped out and rejoined little shop assistants — the hospital was both civil and military — in common flight from their bosses and the bush, tracked down by both.

So utterly apathetic and hot are these moist, unhealthy siesta hours that even the flies fall asleep. Bloodless, hairy arms hang down each side of the bed, dangling dingy novelettes; always tattered too they were, these books, lacking half their pages, because the dysentery patients never have paper enough, and also because the more disagreeable nuns have their own method of censoring all volumes that they consider "not quite nice."

Depressing as the hospital was, it was nevertheless the only place where you could feel yourself forgotten for a while, safe from the outer world, safe from your superiors. A respite from slavery, an essential relief, the only form of happiness I could hope for.

I made enquiries about the conditions of entry, about the doctors' habits and special fads. I no longer regarded my departure for the bush with anything but despair and disgust, and I was already promising myself that as soon as ever I could I would catch every infection within reach and return to Fort-Gono sick, and so emaciated, so revolting, that they'd simply have to make up their minds not only to take me in but to send me home. The tricks for getting ill I knew well enough, some of them first-class ones, and I picked up some special new ones for the colonies.

I prepared myself to overcome innumerable difficulties, since neither the heads of the Pordurière Company nor the leaders of the military were at all easy to sidetrack from their scraggy prey, tossing and twitching between stinking sheets.

They would find me ready to rot with any illness they cared to name. Besides, as a general rule, one didn't stay long at that hospital — unless one terminated one's colonial career there for good and all. The most subtle, the smartest fever patients, the ones with most force of character behind them, sometimes managed to slip on to some transport and get taken home. It was a sweet miracle if you did. Most of the hospital inmates confessed themselves at their wits' ends, no match for the rules and regulations: they went back into the jungle and faded away. If quinine entirely failed to hold them together while they were still in the hospital's care, the almoner merely closed their eyes at six o'clock in the evening and four Senegalese orderlies stumped off with the bloodless rubbish to a plot of red clay near the church at Fort-Gono, which was so hot under its corrugated iron roof, twice as tropical as the tropics, that no one ever went there more than once. If you tried to stand up in that church, you panted like a dog.

That's the way it goes with men — it's certainly very hard to accomplish all that's required of one in life, first as a butterfly when young, and then as a maggot when the end comes.

Again I tried to glean some information here and there, a few details, to give me some idea. What the general manager had told me about Bikomimbo struck me as indeed incredible. It appeared it was a tentatively established trading station, an attempt at penetration far into the interior, ten days away at least, an isolated spot in the midst of the aborigines and their jungle — which latter was described to me as a vast domain crammed with wild beasts and infectious diseases.

I wondered if they weren't quite simply envious of my luck, these little fellow employees of mine, whose mood was always alternately either acute melancholia or aggressiveness.

Their stupidity (that's all they had) depended on the quality of the alcohol they had been imbibing, and the letters they had received from home, and on the greater or smaller amount of hope they had lost during the day. As a rule the more depressed they were, the more bombastic they became. They were ghosts (like Ortolan at the front) and would have been capable of any sort of bravado.

Cocktails before supper lasted three full hours. The governor was the main pivot of all conversations, he was always talked about; the rest of the time it was anything and everything that could or couldn't be stolen; and finally sex: these three topics made up the colours of the colonial flag. The civil servants who were present frankly accused the military of contravening and abusing authority; and the military had a great deal to say in return. For their part, the traders considered the whole bunch a lot of hypocritical, dishonest bullies.

As for the governor, the rumour that he was being recalled had gone the round every morning for ten long years and still the looked-for telegram which was to depose him never arrived — in spite of the at least two anonymous letters which, week after week from time immemorial, were sped to the Minister for the Colonies back at home, bearing a careful catalogue of this local tyrant's horrible misdeeds.

The blacks are lucky with their desiccated skins: the white man, poor wretch, encased in his ærtex shirt, gets poisoned by the acid sweat of his own body. So beware of going too near him. I'd learnt my lesson on the *Admiral Bragueton*.

In a very few days I'd found out a wonderful lot about my own manager — about his past, as full of shady deals as any prison of a port of war. All sorts of things were to be unearthed in his past, including, I imagine, several marvellous miscarriages of justice. It's true that his appearance was against him with that appalling, obvious criminal's face of his; or rather, not to be too harsh on any one, that look of the headstrong man hell bent on asserting himself — which comes to the same thing.

During the siesta, if you passed that way, you caught a glimpse of an occasional white woman lying around in her shaded bungalow on the Boulevard Faidherbe, the wife of some officer or resident. Poor dears, the climate troubled them much more than the men themselves! With their whispering little voices charmingly breathless, and their tremendously indulgent smiles, they looked like women dying happily, their pallor plastered over with paint. These middle-class ladies showed less courage and bore themselves less well than the good woman at the Pagoda, who had no one but herself to depend on. Meanwhile the Porduriére Company was getting through a large number of its little white servants like me; every season it lost ten or a dozen of these sub-men in jungle trading stations near the mangrove swamps. Pioneers, they're called.

Every morning the Army and Commerce came and whined for

their missing units at the office of the hospital. Not a day passed without some captain or other thundering threats at the Chief Medical Officer, and damning his eyes for not sending back right away the three sergeants quaking with malaria and the two syphilitic corporals who were exactly what he needed to form a company. If he was told that his clodhoppers had died, he stopped bothering the damned doctors, and himself went back to have another little drink at the Pagoda.

You hardly had time to notice men, things and days as they disappeared in all this lushness, this climate, the heat and the swarms of mosquitoes. Everything went the same way — it was revolting; in bits, in words, in dwindling flesh, in regret, in beads of sweat, melting away in a torrent of blazing light and colour; time and taste went with the rest; it all passed out the same way. There was nothing in the air but a glittering death agony.

At last the little cargo boat, which was to carry me down the coast one stage nearer my destination, anchored in sight of Fort-Gono. The *Papaoutah* she was called. She was a good flat-bottomed boat, built for navigating estuaries, and she burned wood for fuel. I, as the only white on board, was allotted a nook between the ship's kitchen and the lavatory. We progressed so slowly that at first I thought we must be manœuvring our way out of the roadstead. But we never went any faster. The *Papaoutah* was incredibly weak. We travelled along like this in sight of the coast, an infinite grey strip tufted with little trees in a dancing mist of heat. What a journey! The *Papaoutah* nosed her way through the water as if she had sweated it all herself, very pain-fully. She split one wavelet after another, as if they'd been stitches in the dressing of a wound. It seemed to me from a distance that the pilot was probably a mulatto; I say "seemed" because I never found sufficient energy to go all that way up onto the bridge to find out. I stayed down below in the passageway with my negro fellow travellers until about five o'clock. If you don't want the sun to burn the eyes out of your head, you have to blink like a rat. After five you can treat yourself to a look around the horizon — what a life of luxury! That grey fringe of land, tufted down by the water's edge like some lank underarm, meant nothing much to me. The air was horrible to breathe, even at night, it was still so warm and sticky and salt. What with the smell of the engines as well, and by day waves that on one side were too yellow and on the other too blue, the staleness of it all depressed one to the heart. One was actually worse off than on the *Admiral Bragueton*, except, of course, for the absence of murderous soldiery.

At last we approached my destination. I was reminded of the place's name: Topo. After coughing, spitting and quivering on these oily dish-waters for as long a time as it took to consume three times four meals of tinned food, the *Papaoutah* finally hove to.

Three large, thatched huts stood out on the sharp, tufted edge of the land. From a distance and at first sight it was rather a pleasant-looking spot. There was the mouth of the great sandy river up which, they explained to me, I was to go in a canoe to reach my home in the heart of the forest. It had been arranged that I was to stay only a few days at this coastal trading station at Topo — just long enough to get myself finally broken in to the idea of life in the colonies.

We headed for a flimsy landing stage, but the fat-bellied *Papaoutah*, before reaching it, fouled the bar. I remember that bamboo landing stage well. It was an interesting object. It had to be rebuilt, I gathered, every month, because thousands of agile, ready molluscs gnawed it away as soon as it was mended. Its continual reconstruction was one of the maddening jobs which made life unbearable for Lieutenant Grappa, commandant at Topo station and the surrounding district. The *Papaoutah* only called once a month, but a month was all those molluscs needed to polish off the landing stage.

On my arrival Lieutenant Grappa seized my papers, verified their correctness, copied their particulars into a virgin register, and offered me a drink. I was the first traveller, he confided to me, who had come to Topo in more than two years. People didn't come to Topo. There wasn't any reason why they should. Serving under Lieutenant Grappa was Sergeant Alcide. In their isolation, no love was lost between these two men. "I have to keep my second in command in his place," Lieutenant Grappa told me on our first meeting. "He is inclined to be rather too familiar."

As in this desolate place it would have been impossible to invent happenings that were not too utterly improbable (the setting didn't lend itself) Sergeant Alcide made out a lot of "O.K." reports which Grappa signed at once, and which in due course the *Papaoutah* delivered to the governor-general.

Among the neighbouring lagoons and in the depths of the forest emaciated tribes stagnated, bemused by sleeping sickness and chronic poverty: even so, these wretched creatures produced their small tax, levied, of course, under the lash. What's more, a few of their younger men were recruited as militiamen and delegated to handle the lash themselves. A dozen men comprised this force.

I know what I am talking about; I knew them well. Lieutenant Grappa equipped these lucky ones as best he might and fed them on a regular diet provision of rice.

They were given one rifle between twelve and a little French flag apiece. No boots. But as everything in this world is relative and comparative, the original recruits at Topo thought that Grappa did things in fine style. Every day he had to turn away enthusiastic volunteers who were fed up with life in the jungle.

Game was scarce near the village, so, failing gazelle, at least one grandmother was eaten per week. Every morning at seven Alcide's troops paraded for drill. As I was living in a corner of his hut which he had given up to me, I had a front-row seat for this fantasia. Never has any army in the world had soldiers who showed greater keenness. On Alcide's word of command, these primitives spent themselves, as they tramped across the sand in fours and eights and all twelve at a time, in imagining that they had packs, boots and even bayonets of their own and, more marvellous still, in actually pretending to use them. Newly emerged from a vigourous, near-by Nature, an apology for khaki shorts was all they wore. Everything else had to be imagined — and was. At Alcide's peremptory "Attack!" these ingenious warriors of his put down their make-belief packs and dashed wildly forward, to lunge imaginary bayonets at imaginary enemies. Then, making as if to unbutton their tunics, they would stack their rifles and at another sign from Alcide become passionately absorbed in abstractions of musketry. To see them in open formation, thus assiduously gesticulating, or capering in a pattern of intricate and prodigiously futile movements, was depressing to the point of nausea. Especially as at Topo the breathless heat was acutely magnified on this strip of sand between the glittering reflections of the sea and the river. You could have sworn by your backside that you were being forced to sit on a burning chunk broken off the sun.

But these pitiless conditions did not stop Alcide from shouting. Far from it. His yells sailed out over his ridiculous squad at drill to the venerable cedars on the distant outskirts of the jungle. And even further echoed the thunders of his "Companeee— 'Shun!"

Meanwhile Lieutenant Grappa was engaged in maintaining the law. (We shall come back to that later.) And he always watched from afar, from the shade of his cabin, the fugitive reconstruction of his wretched landing stage. Each time the *Papaoutah* called at Topo, he would go down optimistically and sceptically to await the arrival of full equipments for his recruits. For the last two years he had been vainly clamouring for this equipment. Being a Corsican, Grappa felt perhaps more acutely humiliated than most at the thought of his militiamen remaining unclothed.

In our hut, I mean Alcide's, a more or less illicit trade went on in a few trifling bits and pieces. As a matter of fact, all business in Topo was in Alcide's hands, since he had a small stock, the only existing stock, of tobacco in leaf and in packets, a few litres of alcohol and some yards of cotton goods.

Yet it was obvious Topo's twelve militiamen entertained a real affection for Alcide, in spite of the fact that he bellowed at them all day long, and kicked their backsides rather unjustly. Nevertheless these military nudists discerned in him unmistakable traces of kinship with themselves— the great kinship of innate and incurable poverty. Tobacco had brought them together, as such things will, black though they were. I had a few European papers with me. Alcide looked through them, trying to bring his mind to bear on those absurd columns of print; he could not get through them. "I don't really care a damn now about what's happening," he confessed to me after these vain attempts. "I've been out here three solid years!" That didn't mean that Alcide wished to impress me by playing the hermit, but the brutal indifference with which the world in general had always treated him was forcing him in his turn to look upon the great world beyond Topo, in his simple sergeant's way, as some sort of remote planet.

But Alcide was a good sort really, willing and generous and so on. I was to understand this later — a little too late. He was being overwhelmed by his wonderful resignation to fate, the basic quality which makes poor blighters in the army as easy to kill off as to let live. They rarely, if ever, ask the why and the wherefore of what happens to them, of all they have to put up with. They merely hate the sight of each other and that's enough.

Round about our hut bright, curious little fugitive flowers pushed their way here and there through a waste of burning, merciless sand; green, pink or purple, such as one never sees in Europe except in reproduction and on certain porcelains, a primitive sort of convolvuli. They lived through the whole abominable day closed on their stems and in the evening opened to tremble prettily on the first luke-warm breeze.

One day when Alcide saw me picking some of these flowers, he warned me: "Pick them if you like, but don't water them, the little beauties. . . . It only kills them. They're terribly fragile, not like those sunflowers at Rambouillet which we used to make grow when we were kids. You could piss on them — they'd drink anything! Flowers, of course, are just like men — the bigger they are, the bloodier fools they are." This of course was meant for a hit at Lieutenant Grappa, that vast calamity of a man, with his square, appalling, purple hands. Hands which would never understand anything. But then Grappa never even tried to understand.

I stayed two weeks at Topo, during which time I not only lived and messed with Alcide and shared his fleas (both sorts: sand fleas and the other kind), but also his quinine and his water, from a well near by, which was invariably tepid and gave you diarrhea.

One day when Lieutenant Grappa was feeling particularly amiable he asked me, for a change, to come and take coffee with him. Grappa was a jealous creature and never let any one see his native woman. So to invite me he'd picked on a day when his Negress had gone to her village to visit her family. It also happened to be the day of his functions in court. He wished to make me feel impressed.

Around his hut, having been there since the morning, stood a curious group of plaintiffs and chattering witnesses, in variously coloured loin cloths. Defendants and lookers-on mixed indiscriminately, all smelling foully of garlic, sandalwood, rancid butter, saffron and sweat. Like Alcide's soldiers, everyone of these beings seemed intent above all on an agitated frenzy of make-belief. They were enveloped in a clacking haze of words like castanets and their clenched fists were being brandished above their heads in a torrent of argument.

Lieutenant Grappa, deep in his cane chair, which creaked plaintively under his weight, smiled in the face of all this incoherency gathered together. He trusted for guidance on these occasions to his native interpreter, who passed back to him in his own meaningless way, and at the top of his voice, a series of incredible requests.

The case might well concern a one-eyed sheep which the parents of a girl who had been quite legally sold in marriage but never delivered to her husband were now refusing to return, on account of a murder which her brother had seen fit to commit in the interval on the person of the sister of the man who was at present keeping the sheep. And many other and more complicated grievances. . . .

Looking up at us, in their excitement over all these problems of conflicting interest and custom, a hundred faces bared their teeth, uttering little clicking, or great gurgling, negro words.

The heat had reached its zenith. One peered through an angle of the roof at the sky, to see if something ghastly wasn't about to happen. Not even a storm.

"I'll settle all their differences once and for all, damn me if I don't!" decided Grappa at last, driven to making up his mind by the heat and all this palaver. "Where's the bride's father? Bring him in!"

"There he is!" twenty of them answered, pushing forward a feeble old Negro draped with great dignity in a yellow cloth like a Roman toga. The old duffer bore witness with his closed fist to everything that was being said around him. He didn't look at all as if he had come to lodge any complaint himself, but just to while away the time listening to a lawsuit from which he had long since given up any hope of obtaining any positive result.

"All right," said Grappa. "Twenty cuts! Let's get on with it. Twenty cuts of the lash for the old sod. That'll teach him to come and bloody well waste my time every Thursday in the last two months with all this drivel about bogus sheep. . . ."

The old man saw four hefty policemen bearing down on him. He didn't understand what was up at first, and then he began to roll eyes gone bloodshot with terror, like the eyes of some aged beast that has never before been beaten. He didn't really try to resist, but he didn't know either what position to take up so as to be hurt as little as possible by this infliction of justice.

His captors were dragging at his clothes. Two of them insisted on his kneeling, whereas the others told him to lie on his face. In the end they just had him down anyhow, removing his garment; then right away one of those flexible batons was laid across his backside and shoulders hard enough to make a hefty burro bray for days. As he writhed, the fine sand spurted up round his stomach, mixed with blood; he spat sand as he screamed. It was as if some enormous pregnant basset bitch were being wilfully tortured.

Every one round was silent while it was going on. The sounds of punishment were all one heard. Once the thing was over, the old man after his trouncing tried to get up and pull his toga about him. His mouth, his nose, and the whole of his back especially, were pouring with blood. The crowd led him away, fussing and buzzing and commenting on it all as gloomily as if it had been a funeral.

Lieutenant Grappa relit his cigar. With me there, he wished to appear detached. Not, I imagine, that he was more of a Nero than most, but simply because he didn't enjoy being forced to think. It annoyed him a great deal. What made him particularly irritable when he sat in court was that people would keep asking him questions.

We witnessed that day two other memorable inflictions of punishment, following on further perplexing acccounts of dowries returned, poisons promised, promises unfulfilled and uncertain offspring.

"Oh, if they only knew how little I care about their bloody lawsuits, they'd never leave their forest to come and bother me here with all this drivelling nonsense. . . . Dammit, I don't run to them with my little troubles, do I?" He paused. "Eventually I shall come to believe the damned fools *like* my justice," he went on. "I've been trying for two whole years to cure them of their taste for it, but they come back every Thursday just the same. Believe me or not, young man, it's almost always the same ones that come! It's a vice with them, damn me if it isn't."

After that, conversation turned towards Toulouse, where Grappa always spent his leaves and where he meant to go when he retired in six years' time. That was what he had in mind. We had come, very pleasantly, to the Calvados stage when we were again interrupted by a Negro with God knows what sorrow on his mind, who had been late in coming to be eased of it. He'd arrived on his own, two hours after everybody else, to have himself thrashed. He'd been two days and two nights on his way in from his village and had no intention of returning home, so to speak, empty-handed. But he was late and Grappa never made allowances in the matter of penal punctuality.

"That's his own damn fault! He shouldn't have gone away the last time he was here. I sentenced him to those fifty strokes last Thursday, not this, the silly bugger!"

But the fellow protested. He said he had a perfectly good excuse. He'd had to hurry back to his village to bury his mother. Four or five mothers he had apparently, all of his own. There was a lot of arguing. . . .

"It'll have to wait till next session."

But there was hardly time for this masochist to get to his village and back before next Thursday. He protested. He became obstinate. We had to kick him very hard up the backside to get him out of the camp. That pleased him a good deal, but not enough. He ended up by going round to Alcide, who seized the opportunity, quickly selling our masochistic friend a whole assortment of tobaccos, in shag, in packets and in the form of snuff.

Having been much entertained by all this, I took my leave of Lieutenant Grappa; it was time for his siesta and he went indoors. At the back of the hut his native woman was already waiting for him, having just come back from her village. She had a grand pair of teats, this Negress, and had been very nicely brought up by the nuns in French Guinea. Not only did this admirable baby speak French with a pretty lisp, but she knew how to give you your quinine properly mixed with jam, and how to hunt for jiggers deep in the soles of your feet. She could make herself pleasant to her white master in a hundred different ways without tiring him, or by tiring him, whichever he preferred.

Alcide was waiting for me. He was feeling a little aggrieved. No doubt it was this invitation I'd had the honour to receive from Lieutenant Grappa that prompted him to confide in me. And they were a lot of very ugly things he told me. Without my asking for it, he favoured me with a specially disgusting and frank word picture of Grappa. I answered that I entirely agreed with him in everything he said. Alcide's particular weakness was that in spite of military regulations, which utterly prohibited it, he did business with the natives in the neighbouring villages and also with the twelve men under his command. All these people he mercilessly supplied with tobacco. When his soldiers had been given their bit of tobacco, there wasn't any of their pay left; they'd smoked it all away. They even smoked it in advance. Grappa made out that considering the scantiness of the population in the district, this niggling practice adversely affected the tax returns.

Lieutenant Grappa was prudent enough not to wish to provoke a scandal in Topo while it was under his jurisdiction, but perhaps he was jealous; at all events, he was touchy and disagreeable about it. He would naturally enough have preferred the whole of the natives' financial resources to have remained at the disposal of the tax collector. Every one has his own way of looking at things and his own little ambitions.

At first this system of credit on their pay had seemed rather amazing, and even a bit hard, to these soldiers who were serving merely for the privilege of smoking Alcide's tobacco; but they'd had their bottoms kicked until they'd got used to it. They now didn't even attempt to go and collect their pay; they sat quietly smoking it away ahead of time, amid the little bright-coloured flowers near Alcide's cabin, between two spells of imaginative drill.

The point is that even at Topo, small as the place was, there was room for two methods of civilization: Grappa's rather Roman system, which consisted in merely bambooing your subjects to extract tribute from them (and to keep a shameful tithe of it oneself, according to Alcide), and the Alcide system proper, which was more complex and showed certain signs of a secondary social stage, since in it every native soldier has become a client: a military-commercial combination, in fact, which is much more up-to-date and hypocritical, — the system we use to-day.

As for geography, Lieutenant Grappa had to depend on a few very rough maps which he kept at the post to calculate the extent of the vast regions confided to his care. As a matter of fact, he wasn't particularly anxious to know much about them, anyway. Trees and jungle, after all, are obvious enough; you can see them perfectly well from several miles away.

Hidden away in all this flowering forest of twisted vegetables, a few decimated tribes of natives squatted amid fleas and flies, crushed by tabus and eating nothing all the time except rotten tapioca.

In absolute primitive innocence and simple cannibalism, they lived in grovelling poverty and were ravaged by every pestilence. There was no earthly point in having anything to do with them. There was nothing to justify sending some painful expedition to take them in hand, which would only leave no trace. So Grappa, when he had finished meting out justice, preferred to turn towards the sea and gaze at that horizon across which he had one day come to Topo, and beyond which he would one day go, if all went well. . . .

Familiar and finally pleasant as these parts had become for me, I had to be thinking of moving on towards the forest shop which was to be mine when I'd spent several days travelling up the river and fighting my way through the bush.

Alcide and I had come to understand each other very well. Together we used to try and catch swordfish, those sort of sharks which swarmed in the sea in front of his cabin. He was as bad at this game as I was. We never caught anything.

His cabin had nothing in it except his camp bed and mine and a few packing cases, some empty, some full. It struck me that he ought to be putting by quite a tidy bit, thanks to that little business of his.

"Where do you put it?" I asked him a number of times. "Where d' you hide your dirty little pile?" I thought I'd get a rise out of him. "You're going to make a hell of a splash when you get back, aren't you?" I'd say, trying to pull his leg. And at least twenty times while we put down that invariable meal of tinned tomato, I made up a hundred and one astonishing adventures which he would have on his triumphal return to Bordeaux. He never said a word. He only grinned as if it amused him to hear me talk this way.

Except for drill and the sessions of justice, really nothing at all ever happened at Topo — so of course I went back again and again to my same joke, because there wasn't anything else to talk about.

I had lately thought of writing to M. Puta to touch him for some more money. Alcide would see that my letter was posted by the *Papaoutah* the next time she called. All Alcide's writing materials were kept in a small biscuit tin exactly like the one Branledore used to use. Evidently all sergeants had them. But when Alcide saw me start to open the thing, I was surprised by his making a move to stop me. I was annoyed. I couldn't think why he should want to prevent my opening it, so I put it back on the table. "Oh, all right, open it," he said at last; "it doesn't matter." There, stuck on the inside of the lid, was a photograph of a little girl. Only the head, a sweet little face, though — with the long curls that were worn in those days. I took some paper and the pen and quickly shut the tin. I felt very uncomfortable because I'd been indiscreet, but all the same I wondered why he had been so put out about it.

I at once imagined that it must be a child of his that he had not told me about. I didn't ask him any more about it, but behind me I could hear him endeavouring to tell me something about the photograph, in an extraordinary tone of voice which I had never heard him use before. I didn't know how on earth to tide this over. It was going to be a very painful confidence to listen to, I felt sure. And honestly, I wasn't at all keen.

"Don't mind about that," I heard him say at last. "It's my brother's child. . . . They're both dead. . . ."

"Her parents?"

"Yes, both of them."

"Who's looking after her now then?" I asked him, just to show some interest in the story. "Your mother?"

"My mother's dead too."

"Who, then?"

"Why, me. . . ."

Alcide sniggered, scarlet in the face, as if he'd just done something very wrong. He added hastily:

"Listen, I'll explain. . . . I'm having her educated by the nuns at Bordeaux. But not by nuns for poor folk, you get me. . . . By real better-class Sisters. . . . I see to that all right, don't you bother. I want her to have the best of everything. Ginette's her name. She's a sweet little kid. Very like her mother, as a matter of fact. I get letters from her now, she's getting on. But of course that kind of school isn't cheap. . . . Especially now that she's ten years old. I'd like her to have piano lessons too. What do you think about piano lessons? The piano's a good thing for a girl to learn, isn't it? And what about English? English is very useful too, isn't it? You speak it, don't you?"

I began to take a very good look at Alcide, with his little waxed moustache, his comic eyebrows, his parched skin, while he blamed himself for not being generous enough towards his little niece. Decent little Alcide! How he must have scraped on his wretched salary, his footling little profits, his absurd little bartering business — all these months, all these years, in this infernal Topo! I didn't know what to say to him, I wasn't up to it; but he was so much better a man than I that I went very red in the face. Compared to Alcide, I was a useless ass, loutish and vain. There were no two ways about it. There it was.

I did not dare say anything; I suddenly felt terribly unworthy to speak to him. And only yesterday I hadn't taken much account of Alcide, I had even despised him a little.

"I've not had much luck," he went on, not realizing that he was embarrassing me with his confidences. "You see, two years ago she had infantile paralysis. Think of it! You know all about infantile paralysis, don't you?" He then explained to me that the child's left leg was atrophied and that she was undergoing electrical treatment from a specialist in Bordeaux.

"Does it come back, do you think?" he asked anxiously.

I assured him that one could get over it entirely, that time and electricity worked wonders.

He spoke of her mother who was dead, and of the child's infirmity, with a good deal of reticence. He was afraid, even at a distance, of hurting her.

"Have you been to see her since her illness?"

"No. I was out here."

"Will you be going soon?"

"I don't think I will be able to for another three years. . . . You see, the thing is this. . . . I am by way of doing a bit of business out here. And that's a help to her. If I went on leave now, my place would be taken, especially with that blighter Grappa about. . . ."

So Alcide was asking to stay on longer, to do six consecutive years at Topo instead of three, for the sake of his little niece from whom he only had a few letters and this portrait.

"What worries me most," he continued, when we were going to bed, "is that she has nobody for the holidays. It's hard on a little kid. . . ."

Clearly Alcide could rise to sublime heights without difficulty, could feel at home there; here was a fellow who hobnobbed with the angels and you would never have guessed it. . . . Almost without noticing he had given these years of hardship, the annihilation of his wretched life in this tropical monotony, to a little girl who was vaguely related to him, without conditions, without bargaining, with no interest except that of his own good heart. He was offering this little girl far away tenderness enough to make a world anew, and no one would have known it.

Suddenly he slept, with the candle burning. In the end I got up to study his features by its light. He slept like anybody might. He looked quite ordinary. It wouldn't be a bad idea if there were something to distinguish good men from bad.

THERE ARE TWO WAYS YOU CAN GO ABOUT PENETRATING A FOREST. One is by tunnelling your way through it, like rats through a hayrick. It is the suffocating method. I struck at that. Or you can face going up the river bundled up in the bottom of a hollow tree trunk, paddled along from bend to wooded clump, glimpsing an end of endless days, surrendering yourself entirely to the glare, without respite. And so, dazed by these squawking blacks, you get to whatever place you are going to in whatever state you can.

Your boatmen always need time, at the start, to get evenly under way. Inevitably there's a dispute. Then first comes the splash of a paddle, followed by two or three rhythmic yells, which the forest's echo answers, and you're off, gliding forward, two paddles, then three. You wonder what it's all about; waves, chantings, and if you look back over your shoulder, the expanse of sea down there slips further from you, and in front is the long, flat stretch up which you are working; and there on the landing stage, already almost lost in the river mist, a little Alcide, his enormous bell-shaped topee hiding him almost entirely, a little cheese of a face, and the rest of him below loose in his flapping tunic like an odd memory hanging up in white trousers.

That is all I have left of this place, this Topo.

How long have they still been able to defend that scorching hamlet against the sneaking encroachments of the drab-coloured river? And are those three flea-ridden huts still standing? And are new Grappas, unknown Alcides, still training recent recruits in insubstantial battles? Is simple justice still administered there? And does the water that you try to drink still taste so sour, so warm? Warm enough to make you loathe your own mouth for a whole week after each attempt. . . . No ice chest yet? Or how go those battles of sound between the flies and the ceaseless buzzing of quinine in one's ears? Sulphate? Hydrochloride? And anyhow, are there still any niggers there to parch and rot in that oven? Perhaps not.

Perhaps nothing of all that remains; perhaps the Little Congo has flipped Topo away entirely with one lick of its great muddy tongue, one stormy night, quite casually and by the way, and now it is all over, all completely gone, even the name itself wiped off the maps; maybe there's only me left to remember Alcide at all. . . . Forgotten even by his little niece. . . . Lieutenant Grappa may never have seen his Toulouse again. . . . And the forest which always, from time immemorial, had its eye on the sand dunes, when the rainy season came around again, may have obliterated everything under the shade of its giant cedars, even those tiny unexpected flowers which Alcide wouldn't let me water. . . . All of it may have gone.

As for those ten days going up the river, I shall long remember them. They were spent in the bows of the canoe looking out for muddy whirlpools, choosing one cautious passage after another between tremendous floating branches, which we nimbly avoided. Straining like convicts making a dash for it.

At sundown each day we'd make a halt on some rocky promontory. Finally one morning we left our foul canoe and struck into the forest, up a hidden track which squirmed its way into the damp green gloom, lit only by an occasional ray of sunlight which fell from the topmost vaultings of this vast cathedral of leaves. Monster fallen trees forced us frequently to detour. Where their roots had been, an entire Métro could have shunted about with ease.

All of a sudden the blazing light came back to us. We had come to the edge of a clearing, and there was further to climb, an added effort. The rise we topped dominated the measureless forest rippling with yellow, red and green summits, clothing, blotting over, hills and valleys, as terrifically abundant as the sky or sea. The man whose habitation we were looking for lived, they explained to me by signs, still a bit further on . . . in another little dip of the land. There we found him, waiting for us.

He had made himself a sort of native hut between two great rocks, sheltered, he pointed out to me, from the eastern gales, the worst, the most destructive. I was quite willing to admit that at least that was an advantage, but as to the hut itself, surely it belonged to the last, most tumble-down category of hut, a dwelling place almost in theory only, dilapidated on every side. Certainly I had been expecting something of that sort in the way of an abode, but the reality surpassed my expectations.

I must have struck the chap as very disgruntled, for he spoke to me sharply to rouse me from my reverie. "Listen here, you'd be worse off in the trenches! Here at least one can get along somehow. The grub's rotten, true enough, and as for the drink, it's absolute mud, but you can sleep as much as you like. . . . There ain't no guns here, my friend, and no bullets either. You'll find it'll do, in fact." He spoke in rather the same tone as the general manager, but his eyes were pale, like Alcide's.

He must be nearing the thirties and he had a beard. I had not looked at him at all carefully when I first arrived, I had been too overcome by the poverty of these quarters which he was going to bequeath to me, which were, for years perhaps, to be my home. . . . But then I found, on looking at him more closely, that he had a distinctly adventurous face of very clearly marked angles; in fact, one of those rebellious heads which come up against life too sharply instead of letting themselves be carried along by it, with a great round nose and the prominent cheeks which meet Destiny halfway, obstreperously. Here was an unlucky man!

"Yes, that's true," I said; "nothing could be worse than the war!"

That was all for the moment, I volunteered no further remark. However, it was he who spoke again on the same subject.

"Especially now that they make them so damned long," he added. "Anyway, all I can say, old man, is that you won't find it very lively here! There's damn little to do. . . . It's a sort of vacation. . . . Only they'd be fine vacations here, what? Well, I don't know, I guess it all depends on what a fellow's like himself, in temperament. . . ."

"What about the water?" I asked. What I could see of it in my cup, which I had filled myself, made me uneasy; it was yellowish. I drank some of it; filthy and just as warm as the water in Topo. Dishwater dregs three days old.

"Is this the water?" The water trouble was going to begin all over again.

"Yes, that's all there is around here, apart from the rain. . . . The only thing is, when the rain does come, I'm afraid the shack won't last long. You see the state it's in?" I saw.

"As for the food," he went on, "it's all tinned stuff. I've been eating it all the last year . . . and I'm not dead yet! In a way it's pretty convenient, but it doesn't do you any good; the natives, they eat rotten tapioca, that's their own lookout, they like it. . . . For the last three months I haven't been able to keep anything down. . . . Diarrhea. Maybe a touch of fever as well; I've got 'em both. . . . Around five o'clock, you know, I see things more clearly. . . . And that's why I think I must have the fever, because with the heat you can't tell, can you; one couldn't very well be hotter here than one is anyhow, just with the temperature of the place! So I imagine it's more likely to be these shivers which would let you know if you were feverish. . . . And also the fact that one's rather less bored. . . . Maybe that too is a matter of temperament; one could, of course, take spirits to buck oneself up but personally I don't like liquor . . . can't do with it. . . ."

He seemed to set great store by differences of "temperament."

Then, while he was about it, he gave me further engaging details and advice. "By day it's the heat, but at night it's the noise that's so unbearable. You wouldn't believe it was possible! Beasts of prey chasing each other to copulate or kill; I dunno, that's what they tell me. Anyway, talk about a bloody din! . . . And the noisiest of the lot are the hyenas. They come right close up to the hut; that's when you'll hear them. . . . And you can't mistake it. . . . It's not like quinine noises; you can sometimes make a mistake between birds, big flies and quinine . . . that's quite possible. But hyenas laugh like hell. It's your flesh they're sniffing out . . . and that makes them laugh! They're in a hurry for you to peg out, you know, hyenas. . . . You can even see

their eyes, so they say. . . . They're very fond of carcasses. . . .
Personally, I've never looked them in the eye. I'm sorry, in a
way . . ."

"It's pretty strange here," I said.

But that wasn't all about the pleasures of night life at
Bikomimbo.

"Then there's the village," he went on; "they're not a hundred
niggers in it, but they kick up enough shindy for ten thousand, the
dirty cows! You'll see, you'll see! Oh, and if you've come out
here for the tom-toms, you've come to the right colony. Because
here, either because there's a moon they beat them, or otherwise
because there isn't a moon . . . or else because they're waiting for
the moon. . . . In any case it's always something. You'd say they
were in league with the animals to shatter you, the skunks!
Enough to drive you crazy, I tell you. I'd smash the whole lot
of them, the whole damn shoot, if I weren't so tired. . . . But
I prefer to put cotton wool in my ears. Before, when I still had
some vaseline left in my medicine chest, I put it on it, on the
cotton wool; now I use banana oil instead. It's quite good, banana
oil. . . . Then they can gargle God's thunder, if they want to,
the dirty sods! I don't give a damn with my ears all bunged up
with cotton wool! Can't hear a thing. These niggers are all dead
and stinking; you'll soon find that out. They squat there all day;
you wouldn't believe them capable of even getting up to go and
piss against a tree, and then as soon as its night, my God! . . .
They go all hysterical, all nerves, all bloody-minded. Part of the
night itself gone crazy — that's what the niggers are, I'm telling
you. The set of dirty beggars! Degenerate scum. . . ."

"Do they often come and buy from you?"

"Buy? God, man, be serious! You've got to rob them before
they rob you; that's business, and that's all there is to it! They
don't bother about me at night, anyway — naturally not, with
me with all that cotton wool in my ears! They'd be mutts to
stand on ceremony, don't you agree? And besides, as you see,
I've no doors to my hut either, so of course what d'you think? They
go right ahead. It's a grand life for them here."

"But what about a stock list?" I asked him, quite flabbergasted by his remarks. "The manager particularly told me to make an inventory as soon as I arrived, a very careful one."

"As far as I myself am concerned," he then answered me, perfectly calmly, "the manager can go to hell. . . . And I have very great pleasure in telling you so."

"Still, you'll go to see him when you get back to Fort-Gono, won't you?"

"I shall never see Fort-Gono *or* the manager again. . . . The forest isn't small, my little friend!"

"But then, where will you go?"

"If anybody asks you, you will say you know nothing. But as you seem interested, allow me, while there is still time, to give you a bloody good piece of advice. Let the affairs of the Pordurière Company go to the devil, just as they for their part will see you in hell, and if you're as quick about it as they are, I assure you here and now that you qualify as a Derby winner! . . . You be thankful that I'm leaving you a certain amount of stock and ask no more of me. As for his stock, if he told you to take it all over . . . you can tell the dear manager that there's none of it left, and that's that. . . . If he won't believe what you say, well now, that's no great matter either. . . . We are all of us looked upon as thieves in any case. So that won't make the slightest difference to what is said and thought about you, and just for once it'll bring us in some small profit. . . . The manager in any case — don't you worry — knows what he's up to better than any one, and there's no point in going out of one's way to contradict him. That's what I think. Do you agree? It's obvious that to come out here anyway you've got to be capable of murdering your grandmother! Am I right? Well, then . . ."

I wasn't at all convinced of the truth of all this he was telling me, but in any case this predecessor of mine impressed me at once as an out-and-out rotter.

I didn't feel at all happy about it, not at all. "Another dirty break my way," I was telling myself, and felt more and more convinced of it. I stopped talking to this brigand. In a corner I discovered, haphazard, the merchandise he was being kind enough to leave me, a few insignificant bales of cotton. . . . But on the other hand native cloth and sandals in dozens, pepper in boxes, rags, an irrigator, and above all an alarming quantity of tinned stew, marked *"Cassoulet à la Bordelaise"* and finally a coloured picture postcard of "la Place Clichy."

"Near the central post in the hut you will find the rubber and ivory I bought off the niggers. . . . At first I used to take some trouble about it. . . . Oh, and here you are, take them — three hundred francs. . . . That's the lot."

I didn't know what he meant by that, but I didn't ask him.

"You may do a bit more actual bartering," he said, "because, you know, money's no earthly good to any one out here; it's only useful for doing a bunk!"

He burst out laughing. And I didn't want to annoy him just then in any way, so I followed suit, laughing with him as if I thought everything was swell.

In spite of the scantiness of his amenities here all these months, he had gathered about him a very complicated domestic staff, consisting chiefly of little boys who eagerly handed him either the only household spoon, or his unspeakable tin cup, or neatly extracted from the soles of his feet the unfailing and inevitable burrowing jigger bugs. The only labour I saw him personally undertake was that of scratching himself, which he did, like the shopkeeper at Fort-Gono, with that marvellous dexterity which is only to be seen in the colonies.

The furniture he was leaving me showed what could be done with broken soap boxes in the way of little tables, sideboards and armchairs. This queer devil also showed me how one could amuse oneself by flipping away to a great distance, with one swift movement of the toe, the heavy, scaled caterpillars which kept clambering up all the time, quivering and sweating, to besiege our jungle hut. If you are clumsy enough to crush them, look out for yourself! You are punished by a week's revolting stench which wafts up slowly from their nasty mess. He had read somewhere that these flopping horrors were the most ancient of all created animals. They dated, so he said, from the second geological period. "When we are as old as they are, my friend, what sha'n't we smell like?" Just like that.

Sunsets in this African inferno were amazing. They never failed. A tragedy each evening like a vast assassination of the sun. An incredible piece of tomfoolery. But it was too staggering for the admiration of one man alone. For a whole hour the sky preened itself in great mad streaks of scarlet from end to end, and a green light flared out in the undergrowth and swirled upwards in flickering clouds towards the first stars of the night. After that the whole horizon turned grey, then red once more, but this time a tired and short-lived red. That then was the end. The colours all fell back in strips like paper streamers at a carnival. This happened every day on the stroke of six o'clock.

Night then opened the ball with all its prowling beasts and its myriad croaking noises.

The forest is only waiting for this signal to start to shake, whistle and moan in all its depths: like some huge, lecherous, un-lighted railway station, about to burst. Whole trees bristling with squealing life, voluptuous savagery and horror. We could no longer hear ourselves speak in the hut. I had to hoot across the table myself, like an owl, for the other fellow to hear me. I was out of luck, I who do not like the country.

"What's your name? Didn't you say it was Robinson?" I asked him.

He was just telling me that the natives in these parts suffered appallingly from every conceivable illness and that they were in such a state they couldn't be expected to go in for any sort of trade. While we talked about the natives, flies and large insects in swarms came settling down all around the lamp, such clouds of them that we had to put it out.

I saw Robinson's face once more, veiled by this haze of insects, before I put the light out. That perhaps was why his features impressed themselves more subtly on my memory, when before they had reminded me of nothing very definite. He went on talking to me in the dark, while I searched through the past, using the sound of his voice as a key with which to try locked doors of many years and months, and finally days, wondering where I could possibly have met this man before. But I could find nothing. No voice answered me. You can lose yourself groping among these twirling forms of memory. It's terrifying how many people and how many things no longer stir in one's past. Living people whom one has pushed into the crypts of time sleep there so soundly with the dead that one same shadow envelops and confuses both.

As one grows older, one can't tell which to wake, the living or the dead.

I was trying to identify this Robinson when, close by in the night, a sort of hideously exaggerated peal of laughter, made me start. Then they shut up. He'd told me so, of course; hyenas presumably.

After that there was nothing but the blacks in the village with their tom-tom, that senseless beat on hollow wood, gnawing fragments on the wind, like ants.

It was particularly this name of Robinson which worried me, more and more definitely. We began to talk in our darkness about Europe and the meals you can have back there, if you've got some money; and the drink too, such marvellously cool things to drink! We didn't mention the next day when I should have to stay here alone, perhaps for years to come, here with all those tins of *cassoulet*. . . . Was the war perhaps preferable then? Surely it was worse. Oh, yes, much worse! He himself had agreed on that point. . . . He too had been to the war. . . . And yet he was leaving this place. He'd had enough of the forest, all the same. . . . I tried to get him to talk about the war again. But this time he wouldn't.

In the end, when we were going to bed each in his own corner of this conglomeration of leaves and partitions, he confessed to me quite frankly that, all things considered, he would rather come up before a civil court for theft than put up any longer with the life on a diet of *cassoulet* which he'd endured here for nearly a year. A nice lookout for me.

"Haven't you any cotton wool for your ears?" he asked me once again. "If you haven't, pull some of the fluff off your blanket and put some banana oil on that. You can make quite good little stoppings that way. Personally I hate to hear those cows wailing."

Actually there was every sort of thing in this awful place, except cows, but he stuck to this unpleasing and generic figure of speech.

It suddenly struck me that the business of the cotton wool was probably a cloak to some damnable machination of his. I couldn't help being seized by a terrible fear that he might start to murder me there, on my camp bed, before going off with what was left in the cash box. . . . The idea petrified me. But what should I do? Call out? But to whom? Those cannibals in the village? . . . Was I lost? Surely I was, already. Even in Paris, if one has no money, no debts, and no expectations of wealth, one barely exists, it's very difficult not to have already disappeared. . . . So what about disappearing in this place? Who would take the trouble to come as far as Bikomimbo even to spit a couple of times in memory of me, not more than that, even? Nobody, obviously.

Hours passed in fits and starts. He didn't snore. All these forest calls and noises made it impossible for me to hear him breathing. No need for cotton wool. In the end, however, the name Robinson went on obsessing me until it recalled to my mind a body, a walk, a voice too, which I had known. . . . Then, just when I was really going to fall asleep, the whole person appeared to me beside my bed, I grasped the image, not of this man, of course, but of that Robinson of Noirceur-sur-la-Lys, way back there in Flanders, who had been with me that night when we were both of us looking for a hole through which to escape from the war; and then later on the same man in Paris. . . . Everything came back to me. Years sped by in a single moment. I had been very ill in the head, I'd been unhappy. . . . Now that I knew, now that I had recognized him, I couldn't help being thoroughly alarmed. Had he known me? In any case, he could count on my silence, on my complicity.

"Robinson! Robinson!" I called out gaily, as if I had a piece of good news for him. "I say, Robinson! Hey there! . . ." There was no answer.

My heart beast fast; I got up, expecting an ugly jab in the face. Nothing happened. Then, greatly daring, I ventured, groping my way, to the other end of the hut where his bed was. He had gone.

I waited for the dawn, striking matches at intervals. Day came at last in a burst of light, and the negro servants arrived too, cheerfully offering me their utter uselessness, save only that they were gay. They were trying to teach me not to care! It was no good my attempting to indicate to them by carefully thought-out gestures how much Robinson's disappearance alarmed me; it made no difference, they didn't seem to give a damn. It is the height of stupidity, true enough, to concern oneself with anything except what is actually before one's eyes. In this whole business it was the cash box I minded about most. But it is unusual ever to see the person who walks off with a cash box again. That fact made me think that Robinson would hardly return just for the purpose of murdering me. That at least was something gained.

So I had the whole place to myself! But I guessed I would have plenty of time to inspect the inward and outward mysteries of this immense forest of leaves, this ocean of reds and dappled yellow, these flamboyant flowering plants, magnificent no doubt for those who love Nature. I definitely hated it. The glamorous beauty of the tropics sickened me. The sight of it, my thoughts about it all, kept returning to me with a taste of nausea. Whatever any one says, it will always be a country for mosquitoes and panthers. There's a place for everything.

I preferred to go back to my hut and straighten it up in anticipation of the tornado which could not be long in coming. But, there again, I had to abandon this attempt at consolation. The more commonplace parts of this structure would fall to pieces but could not be stood upright again. The thatched roof, infested with vermin, was being riddled away; my house would not have made even a passable latrine.

I dragged myself around a little way in the bush but was forced to come back, lie down and shut my eyes, because of the sun. The sun was always there. Everything is silent, everything is afraid of being burnt up in the middle of the day; the least thing is needed; grass, men and beasts are at fever heat. A midday apoplexy.

My chicken, my one and only chicken, dreaded this noontide too. He came indoors with me, alone in the world, Robinson's legacy. Three weeks he lived with me, sharing my walks, following me about like a dog, clucking incessantly, noticing a snake under every bush. One day, when profoundly bored, I ate him. His flesh, bleached by the sun, tasted of nothing at all; it might have been calico. Perhaps it was he that made me so ill. In any case, the fact remains that the day after this meal I could not get up from my bed. About midday, utterly helpless, I dragged myself across to the medicine chest: there was nothing there but some iodine and a map of the Nord-Sud Railway. As to customers, none came to the store, merely a few black loiterers everlastingly gesticulating and chewing kola, malarial and lubricious. Now they gathered around me in force; it seemed to me they were commenting on my ugly mug. I was ill, extremely ill — so much so that I felt I had no use for my legs at all; they hung over the edge of the bed, utterly useless and a little comic.

The mail runner from the manager, from Fort-Gono, only brought me letters stinking with abuse and absurdities — and threats. Business men, who all think themselves so devilish clever at their jobs, usually prove in practice to be complete dunderheads. My mother way back at home begged me to take care of my health, as she used to during the war. On the guillotine steps she would have scolded me for forgetting my muffler. She never missed a chance of making out that the world is a fine place and she had done well to conceive me. This supposed Providence is the subterfuge of maternal carelessness. It was of course perfectly easy to leave all this chitchat of the Boss and my mother unanswered; which I did. But that didn't improve my lot particularly, either.

Robinson had stolen practically everything this flimsy structure had contained, and who would believe me if I said so? Should I write about it? What was the use? To whom? To the Boss? Every evening regularly about five o'clock I chattered with fever, a real lively fever, and my bed creaked and shook with it like a seesaw. The blacks without ceremony had taken possession of my person and the hut: I hadn't asked them in, but to send them away was too much of an effort. They wrangled around what was left of the stock, making a hideous mess out of the barrels of tobacco, trying on the last few loin cloths, appraising them, carrying them off, adding still further, if that were possible, to the general chaos of my home. Rubber scattered all over the floor mingled its resin with bush melons and those sickly pawpaws whose taste of piddled-on pears, when I remember it now, fifteen years later, still makes me retch, I ate so many of them in the place of beans.

I tried to get some idea of how helplessly low I had sunk, but I couldn't manage it. "Everybody steals," Robinson had three times told me before he left. That's what the general manager thought too. In my fever those words tormented me. "You've got to manage somehow, look out for yourself." He'd said that too. I tried to get up. Couldn't do that, either. The water there was to drink — he was right — it was mud, worse than that, slimy dishwater dregs. My little blackamoors did indeed bring me bananas, big ones, little ones and red ones, and those inevitable pawpaws, but my stomach revolted so against these things, against all, all, all of it! I could have brought up the whole world.

As soon as I felt the least bit better, slightly less bewildered and battered, that damnable fear took hold of all of me again, — the fear of having to account to the Pordurière Company. What should I say to these hard-hearted creatures? How should they believe me? They'd certainly have me arrested. Then who should I be judged by? A special group of men armed with frightful laws deriving their authority from Heaven knows where, like a court-martial, laws whose real intentions are always kept from you, judges whose sport is to urge you bleeding along a narrow track skirting the pit of hell, a road which leads the poor to their destruction. The Law is misery's great Luna Park — when an underdog gets caught in it, you can hear him screaming forever after.

I had rather lie there chattering and sweating with a temperature of about 104° than have to foresee lucidly what was awaiting me at Fort-Gono. In the end I took no more quinine, so that the fever should hide life from me as much as possible. One drugs oneself with whatever's at hand. While I lay there frothing, days and weeks, my matches gave out. We hadn't any. Robinson had really left me nothing at all but *cassoulet à la Bordelaise*. But of that, I will say, he had left me plenty. I vomited tins and tins of the stuff. And even to get that result you had to heat it up.

My shortage of matches brought me one interest in life: I watched my cook lighting his fire with two flints in the dry grass. That's when the idea came to me, watching him. I was very feverish besides and that idea I got took shape, remarkably. Athough naturally clumsy, after a week of attempts, I too, like a native, knew how to strike my little spark between two sharp stones. In fact, I was beginning to be able to get along in the primitive state. Fire is the most important thing; then there's hunting, of course, but I had no ambitions that way. My flint fire was enough for me. I worked away at it hard. I had nothing else to do all day. I'd become much less proficient at the game of flipping "secondary age" caterpillars, I still hadn't learnt the knack of it. I squashed lots of them and got bored. I let them come in and out of the hut like friends. Two great storms came along, one after the other, the second lasting three days and above all three nights. We had rain water to drink in the can at last. Tepid, of course, but all the same . . . The stuffs in stock began to get sodden in the rain, running into each other, a ghastly jumble of goods.

The Negroes kindly brought me bundles of lianas from the forest to make the hut fast to the ground, but in vain; at the least wind the leaves the partitions were made of flapped madly above the roof, like broken wings. Nothing was any good. Quite a party, in fact.

Blacks large and small decided to share my ruin with me, living there in complete familiarity. They were enchanted. Great fun. They came and went about my place (if that's what it was), as they pleased. Liberty Hall. We made signs to show how well we understood each other. If it hadn't been for the fever, I might perhaps have tried to learn their language. I hadn't the time. As to kindling a fire, though I'd improved, I still had not learnt their best, their quickest method. The sparks still mostly flew into my eyes, which made the Negroes laugh a lot.

When I wasn't burning with fever on my camp bed or striking my primitive lighter, I thought of nothing but the company's accounts. It's odd how difficult it is to get accustomed to the idea of irregular dealings. I must have inherited this nervousness from my mother, who had contaminated me with her principles: "Little things lead to big things, and opportunity makes the thief." You learn such ideas too early in life and later on they come and terrify you, inescapably, at any crisis. What a weakness it is! Only the force of circumstances has any power to overcome it. Luckily the force of circumstances is enormous. Meanwhile we were sinking together, the store and I. We slipped further into the mud after each downpour, thicker, soupier than the last. What yesterday had looked like a rock was to-day a treacly mess. From down-hanging branches tepid rain water pursued and drenched you wherever you went; it lay about the hut and everywhere around like a dried-up river bed. Everything was melting away in a welter of trashy goods, hopes and accounts, together with the fever, itself moist too. The rain struck you so hard that it was like a warm gag in your mouth. But it didn't stop the animals chasing each other; after sunset the nightingales began to make as much noise as the jackals. Anarchy everywhere and inside the Ark myself, a broken-down Noah. The time seemed to me come to put a stop to it all.

My mother's sayings were all eminently respectable; she used to say too, I remembered at just the right moment, when she was burning old bandages at home, "Fire is the great purifier!" One's mother provides precepts for all Fate's occasions. It's a question of choosing the appropriate one.

The moment came. My flints were not very well chosen, they weren't awfully sharp, the sparks always seemed to burn my fingers. In the end, however, the first lot of stock caught fire, in spite of the damp; it was an absolutely sodden package of socks. All this took place after sundown. Flames spurted eagerly upwards at once. The natives came and gathered around the blaze, yelping with excitement. The crude rubber which Robinson had bought smouldered away in the middle, its smell reminding me invincibly of the famous Telephone Building fire on the Quai de Grenelle, which I'd gone to see with my Uncle Charles, who sang "Romance" so well. The year before the Exhibition that was, the Great Exhibition, when I was still a very little boy. Nothing entices memories out of their hiding place as well as flames and smells. My hut smelt exactly the same. In spite of being wet through, it burned to the ground, entirely, merchandise and all. All accounts were liquidated now. The forest for once was silent. There was absolute stillness. Owls, leopards, toads and parrots must have had an eyeful. A blaze is what startles and impresses them. Like war does us. Now the forest with its roaring vegetation could sweep down on the débris and take possession again. I had rescued nothing but my small personal belongings, my camp bed, the three hundred francs and, of course, alas, a few tins of *cassoulet* for the journey.

After an hour's blaze, there was very little left of my shanty. A few little flames flickering in the rain and a few gurgling Negroes jabbing about in the ashes with the points of their spears, amid puffs of that odour of disaster, that odour inseparable from all the defeats that have been in this world, the reek of smoking gunpowder.

Now was the time to beat it, quick. Should I go back to Fort-Gono, retrace my steps? And there try to explain my behaviour and what had happened? I hesitated. But not long. There is nothing you can explain. The world only knows how to kill you, turning on you and crushing you as a sleeper kills his fleas. That would surely be a very stupid sort of way to die, I thought, the way every one dies. To trust in men is itself to let oneself be killed a little. I decided, in spite of my condition, to take to the bush myself, following in the footsteps of Robinson, that most unlucky man.

ALONG OUR ROAD I WAS CONTINUALLY HEARING THE PLAINTS AND calls and tremolos of forest creatures, but I practically never saw any of them, not counting of course the little wild pig I once nearly stepped on near one of my halting places. One would have thought from those gusts of squealings, callings and yellings that all the animals were there in their hundreds and thousands, quite close to you, around the corner. Yet when you neared the place their din came from, there were none about except those great blue parrots, all dolled up in their plumage as if for a wedding, and so clumsy, coughing and hopping from branch to branch, that you'd have thought some accident had befallen them.

Nearer the ground, in the mossy undergrowth, large heavy butterflies, embroidered like antimacassars, trembled with difficulty in opening their wings, and then, lower down still, there were we paddling in the yellow mud. We got along only with the greatest difficulty, especially as the Negroes were carrying me in a litter made of sacks sown end to end. They could very easily have slung me into the water when we were crossing a small swamp. Why didn't they? I found that out later. Or otherwise couldn't they have eaten me, seeing that that was one of their customs?

Every now and then I asked the fellows a question. They invariably answered, "Yes, yes." Always eager to agree in fact. A good-hearted set of chaps. When I wasn't suffering acutely from diarrhea, the fever took hold of me again at once. You wouldn't believe how ill I got, going on at that rate. As a matter of fact, I was beginning not to see at all clearly, or rather I saw everything as green. At night all the wild animals in the world came and surrounded our camp; we lit a fire. And here and there even so a cry would pierce the great black vellum smothering us. Some stricken beast actually calling out to us, since we were near, in spite of its fear of men and the fire.

By the fourth day I didn't even try to make out what was real amid the absurd things which the fever sent coursing through my head, one thing telescoping into another and bits of people and tail-ends of good resolutions and despairs, — an endless stream.

All the same, I tell myself, when I think back on it, surely that bearded white man whom we came across one morning standing on a pebbly promontory where two rivers met, — surely he was real? And you could hear a terrific din of near-by rapids, I remember. He looked the same sort of man as Alcide, but he was a Spanish sergeant. Wandering more or less at random from one jungle track to another, we had landed up in Rio del Rio, a colony long in the possession of the Crown of Castile. My poor Spanish soldier also had a hut. I believe he laughed a good deal when I told him all about *my* horrible hut and what I'd done with it in the end. His looked a little more presentable, I admit, but not much. His own particular torment was red ants. They'd seen fit to make a pathway for their annual migrations slap across the middle of his hut, the little brutes, and for two months they hadn't stopped coming through.

They took up nearly all the room; it wasn't easy to move about and besides, if you got in their way, they stung you sharply.

He was immensely pleased when I gave him some of my tinned stew, because he himself hadn't eaten anything but tomato for three years. It was all right with me. I knew all about that. He'd already consumed more than three thousand tins of it on his own, so he told me. He was tired of serving it up in different ways and now he simply gulped down his tomato with the least possible fuss, through two little holes bored in the tin, like a raw egg.

As soon as the red ants got to know that a stock of new food had arrived, they mounted guard around the *cassoulet* stew. You couldn't have left a single tin about, open; they'd have called the entire race of red ants into the hut in no time. Nothing's more communist than a red ant. And they'd have gobbled up the Spaniard as well.

I learned from my host that the capital of Rio del Rio was called Santa Tapeta, a city and harbour well known along the whole of the coast as a supply station for ships bound for distant ports.

The track we'd been following actually led there. We were on the right road; all we had to do was to carry on along it another three days and three nights. Wanting to ease my delirium, I asked this Spaniard whether he knew of any good native medicine which might put me right. My head was in a terrible way. But he wouldn't have anything at all to do with any bugaboo of that sort. For a Spanish colonizer he was strangely Africanophobe — so much so that when he went to the lavatory, he wouldn't use banana leaves, but kept instead his own special stock of *Heraldos de Madrid*, which he cut up for this purpose. He never read a paper now, either; just like Alcide in that too.

Three years he'd been living there alone with the ants, a few little idiosyncrasies, and his old newspapers — as well as that terrible Spanish accent which is like somebody else in the room, it's so strong. So he wasn't easily roused by anything. When he yelled at his niggers, though, it sounded like a thunderstorm; Alcide was nowhere compared to him, in the matter of lung power. In the end I gave this Spaniard all my *cassoulet*, I took such a liking to him. In grateful return he made me out a very beautiful passport on handmade paper stamped with the Royal arms of Spain and one of those marvellously elaborate signatures which it took him ten careful minutes to complete.

There was no missing the road to Santa Tapeta; he was quite right, you simply followed your nose. I don't in the least remember how we got there, but I'm quite sure of one thing, which is that as soon as I arrived I was handed over to a priest, who was so meek himself that just having him about made me feel strong and capable by comparison. But not for long.

The town of Santa Tapeta was stuck on the side of a rock directly facing the sea and you've no idea how green it was. A marvellous sight it must have been, as seen from the roadstead; sumptous and grand from a distance, but when you came down to it, nothing but overworked carcasses baking and rotten, just the same as at Fort-Gono. As for the Negroes of my little safari, when once a lucid moment came to me, I packed them off home.

They'd come through a great hunk of jungle and were frightened for their lives on the return journey, so they said. They wept about it a lot, but personally I wasn't feeling strong enough to be sorry for them. I'd been too ill and sweated too much. My illness went on and on. There seemed to be no end to it.

As far as I can remember from then onwards, a lot of chattering people (the township seemed to be full of them) came bustling night and day about my sick bed, which had been rigged up in the vestry on purpose, because all forms of diversion were rare in Santa Tapeta. The priest filled me up with *tisanes,* a long gold cross waggled on his stomach, and deep down somewhere under his soutane there was a great clinking of money whenever he came near my bed. But there was no longer any question of entering into conversation with all these people; even mumbling had become an intolerable effort to me.

I really believed I was finished; I tried just to have one more look at what could be seen of this world through the curé's window. I shouldn't dare to say that I could describe that garden now without making gross and absurd mistakes. Sun there was, that's certain; always there, as if a great furnace were forever being opened right in your face; and below that more sun, and rows and rows of those fantastic trees, sort of bursting lettuces the size of oaks, and a kind of dandelion, three or four of which would make a perfectly good chestnut tree back at home. Throw in as well a toad or two, as fat as spaniels, waddling desperately from one thicket to the next. . . .

It's by smells that people, places, and things come to their end. A whiff up one's nostrils is all that remains of past experiences. I shut my eyes because I really couldn't keep them open any longer. Whereupon night after night the acrid odour of Africa faded from me. I found it harder and harder to recognize its mixed stench of decayed soil, private parts, and powdered saffron.

There was time, and the past, and still more time, and then came a moment when I underwent a number of new twists and shocks and after that a rocking more gentle and regular, as if I were in a cradle. . . .

I was on my back still. That much was certain. But now it was on something that was moving. . . . I let myself slip and then I vomited and woke up again and once more fell asleep. We were at sea. I felt so queasy that I barely had the strength to hold the new smell of tar and rigging. It was cool in the unsteady corner where I'd been put in a heap under a wide-open ventilator. They'd left me entirely alone. We were still travelling, apparently. But what voyage was this? I could hear footsteps on the wooden deck above my nose, and voices, and the sound of waves slapping and breaking against the ship's side.

It is very seldom that life returns to your bedside, wherever you may be, except in the form of some damnable cad's trick. For instance, the trick these people in Santa Tapeta had played on me! Had they not taken advantage of my condition to sell me on the quiet, just as I was, to a galley? A beautiful galley for sure, I admit, stately in build, well rowed, crowned with lovely sails of purple hue, a gallant golden craft, beautifully upholstered in the officers' quarters, with, forward, a fine portrait in cod-liver oil of the Infanta Coñita in polo costume. This princess, they told me, had given the ship the patronage of her name, her swelling breasts and her royal reputation. Flattering thought!

After all, I thought, when I considered what had befallen me, suppose I had stayed at Santa Tapeta, I was as ill as a dog, anyway, and should surely have died at that priest's where the Negroes had left me. . . . What if I'd gone back to Fort-Gono? In that case, I certainly shouldn't get off with under fifteen years on the score of those lost balance sheets. . . . Where I was at the moment, we were at any rate on the move and there was some hope even in that. . . . Come to think of it, the captain of the *Infanta Coñita* had done a bold thing in buying me, even dirt cheap, from that priest of mine when we weighed anchor. The captain had risked all his money in that transaction. He could have lost the whole lot. . . . He'd speculated on the sea air putting me right. He deserved his reward. And he'd get it too, because I was feeling much better already, and I could see that he was very pleased about it. I still raved dreadfully but there was a certain amount of logic in my delirium. . . . As soon as I opened my eyes, the captain came to see me in my lair, wearing his plumed hat. That's how he looked to me.

It amused him a lot to see me trying to lift myself on my *paillasse* in spite of the grip the fever had on me. I'd vomit. "Well, you scum, you'll soon be able to row with the others," he said to me. That was nice of him; he roared with laughter, tapping me gently with a cat-o'-nine-tails, but in a very friendly way, on the nape of the neck, not on the backside. He wanted me to be happy and to share his pleasure at the excellent bargain he'd made in acquiring me.

The food on board seemed to me to be admirable. Though I couldn't stop muttering, quite soon I was strong enough, as the captain had foretold, to go and row with the other men from time to time. But where there were only ten of them, I saw a hundred: my eyesight was weak.

One didn't get tired on this crossing because most of the time our sails carried us along easily. We were no worse off in our quarters between decks than ordinary third-class passengers in a railway carriage over the week-end, and far less dangerously placed than I had been on the *Admiral Bragueton* coming out. We were often becalmed for long stretches at a time on this journey from East to West across the Atlantic. The glass dropped. No one minded about that between decks. We only felt it was all rather slow. Personally, I had seen enough fine views of the sea and the jungle to last me through eternity.

I should have liked to ask the captain one or two questions about where we were going and why, but now that I was feeling definitely better, he'd stopped taking any interest in how I was getting on. Besides which, I still talked too wildly to indulge in serious conversation. I now only caught sight of him in the distance, — like a real boss.

I started to try and find Robinson on board among the other galley slaves, and several times in the silent hours at night, I called out his name at the top of my voice. There was no answer, except a threat and a curse or two, in that black hole of Calcutta.

Still, the more I considered the incidents and circumstances of my adventure, the more probable it seemed to me that he had had the Santa Tapeta trick played on him too. Only it must be on some other galley that Robinson was rowing at this moment. The niggers must all have had a hand in the business. One at a time, that's how it's always done. One's got to live, so the people and things you're not going to devour at once you take away and sell. The comparative kindness which those Negroes had shown me stood revealed in the nastiest possible light.

The *Infanta Coñita* sailed on for weeks and weeks across the seasick Atlantic rollers, and then one fine evening everything suddenly became calm. I was no longer delirious. We were bobbing about at anchor. Next morning when we woke up, we realized on opening the portholes that we had arrived at our destination. What an incredible sight!

TALK ABOUT A SURPRISE! WHAT WE SAW SUDDENLY THROUGH THE fog was so astonishing that at first we wouldn't believe it was true, and then, standing there bang in front of it all, galley slaves that we were, we had to laugh, seeing it jutting right up in front of us like that. . . .

Understand that it went straight up in the air, quite straight, that town of theirs. New York is a town standing up. Of course we'd seen plenty of towns in our time, fine ones at that, and famous cities and seaports and all. But at home, dammit, cities lie on their sides along the coast or on a river bank; they lie flat in the landscape, awaiting the traveller — whereas this American one, she didn't relax at all; she stood there very stiff, not languid in the least, but stiff and forbidding.

It seemed damned funny to us; we laughed and laughed. It can't help being funny, a town built straight up in the air like that. But we could only laugh above the neck, because of the cold blowing in just then from the open sea, through a great grey and pink mist, quickly and sharply attacking our pants and the chinks in this city wall in front of us. The streets of the city these were, where the clouds took refuge, too, from the wind. Our ship had its narrow berth on the edge of some jetties where a dung-coloured stream swirled about a nagging string of little rowboats and eager, hooting tugs.

For a down-and-out it's never a particularly pleasant business landing anywhere, but for a galley slave it's harder still, especially as these people in America hate galley slaves coming in from Europe. "They're all anarchists," they say. What it is, they don't let anybody in who is merely curious and unlikely to bring them in a bit of cash, because all the currencies of Europe are sons of the Dollar.

I might perhaps have tried, as others had successfully before

me, to swim across the harbour and once I was on the quay to start
shouting "Long live the Dollar! Long live the Dollar!" It's one
way of doing it. Lots of chaps have landed that way and afterwards
made their fortunes. So they say; you can't really tell. Odder
things still occur to you in dreams. Personally I had another
scheme in my head, along with the fever.

Having become very good on board at counting fleas (not
only catching them, but adding them up and subtracting them,
in the way of statistics I mean), I wanted to make use of this
intricate craft of mine, which you mightn't think amounted to
much but which does possess, when all's said and done, a technique of its own. You can say what you like about the Americans,
but in these matters of technique they win, hands down. They'd
be crazy about my way of counting fleas, I was positive of that. As
I saw it, the thing was a cinch.

I was going to offer them my services at once, but just then
our ship was ordered to its quarantine station in a little creek
near-by. It was a sheltered place within hailing distance of a
small, closed-in village in the centre of a quiet bay, two miles or
more from New York.

And there we all stayed, under observation, for weeks and weeks
— long enough to get quite accustomed to the place. And every
evening after supper, a squad pushed off from the *Infanta Coñita*
to go and fetch our water supply from the village. And I had to
be in it, so as to accomplish the end I had in view.

The other chaps knew what I was driving at, but it wasn't their
idea of fun at all. "He's mad," they said, "but harmless." We
weren't badly fed on board our tub, the lads had a bit of an eye
kept on them but only up to a certain point — in fact, it was
pretty well all right. A passable job. Besides which and best of
all, they were never discharged from service and the king had
even promised them a sort of little pension at the age of sixty-two.
This prospect kept them cheerful; it was something to dream
about, and furthermore, on Sundays, so as to feel they were free
men, they would play at having the vote.

During all the time we were in quarantine they raised the
devil of a racket between decks and fought and buggered about

in turn. And then too, what really stopped them running away along with me was chiefly that they didn't care a damn about these United States which I was so thrilled about. Every one has his own dislikes; America was their *bête noire*. They even tried to put me off it completely. It was no good my telling them that I knew people in the place — among others my little Lola, who must be very well off these days and no doubt Robinson too, who'd probably have made his way in business here by now; they wouldn't budge from their dislike of America, their disgust, their hatred for it. "You'll always be cracked," they said to me. One day I pretended I was going along to the village pump with them and then I told them; I said, "I'm not going back to the ship. So long!"

They were a decent lot of chaps at heart, a hard-working crowd, and they told me all over again that they didn't at all approve of what I was doing, but they wished me good health and good luck all the same and joy of it too — though they had their own way of putting it.

"Go ahead!" they said to me. "Go right ahead — but let us tell you once more, big boy; you're a down-and-out and you're making a big mistake! Your fever's sending you crazy. You'll come back from that America of yours a damn sight worse off than we are! It's your lousy tastes that'll be the end of you! Out to learn something new, aren't you? You know a whole heap too much already, considering what you are!"

It was no good my telling them I had friends in the place who'd be pleased to see me. They didn't understand.

"Friends?" is all they said. "Friends, eh? Your friends'll see you in hell, that's what. They forgot all about you a *long* time ago!"

"But I want to see these Americans, I tell you," I said, but it made no difference. "Why, they've got the most marvellous women in the world here. . . ."

"Aw, come back with us, man," they went on. "There's no point in going, we keep telling you. You'll only get more sick than you are already! We'll tell you right now what the Americans are like, if you want to know! They are all either millionaires or scum — nothing in between! And the way you are now, you're not going to see much of the millionaires. . . . But scum, my God, you'll get plenty of that sure enough. And right from the word 'Go'; don't you worry. . . .''

That's the way these fellows took it. They got on my nerves at last, these little rats, the poor fish, the sissies. "Go to hell, all of you!" was what I said to them. "You just babble because you're jealous, that's all. We'll see whether the Americans knock me over the head or not! Leave that to me. But there's no doubt about one thing — which is that you may look like men but you're not, you're not men between the legs at all, d' you hear? You're a lot of silly little runts, that's what!" Let them have it straight, I did. Then I felt fine.

Night was coming on so they were whistled for from the ship. They started to row back in unison, all the lot except one — me. I waited until I couldn't hear them any more, then I counted up to a hundred and after that I ran as fast as I could go to the village. The village was a charming little place with lights shining and a lot of wooden shacks, standing empty on both sides of a chapel, in complete silence; but I was shivering with malaria and also with fear. Here and there one met a sailor from the garrison who didn't seem to have anything much on his mind and there were even children about and a young girl with marvellous muscles. The U.S.A.! I had arrived. That's what it does you good to clap eyes on after wandering about so long and getting so dried up. It makes life juicy again, like a fruit. I'd dropped into the one village which wasn't any good, though. A small garrison of sailors and their families looked after it and saw to the upkeep of all these buildings, in readiness for the day when a raging plague should come along on some boat like ours and threaten the great port of New York.

It was in these buildings that as many foreigners as possible would be killed off so that the people in the town shouldn't catch anything. They even had a cemetery all ready to hand and full of flowers. They were waiting. For sixty years they'd been waiting, doing nothing but just wait.

I found a little empty hut, sneaked into it and fell asleep at once. Next morning the alleys were full of sailors wearing short jackets, as square-shouldered and well-built as anything, playing about with brooms and whirling a hose around my retreat and on all the grass plots in their theoretical village. It was no good my pretending to look detached; I was so famished that I couldn't help hovering around a place where there was the smell of cooking.

It was there that I was nabbed and run in between two sailors determined to identify me. Immediately the question arose of whether to sling me into the water and drown me or not. They rushed me into the presence of the Chief Quarantine Officer, and there, although constant adversity had taught me a certain amount of nerve, I cut a pretty sorry figure: I still felt too feverish to risk any sparkling sally. No, I beat a retreat: my heart wasn't in the game.

It was better to faint. Which I did. In that office, when later I regained consciousness, the place of the men around me had been taken by ladies in white, who put me through a vague and kindly catechism which I should have thought met the case very nicely. But kindliness in this world does not last, and next day the men began to talk to me again about prison. For my part, I took this opportunity to talk to them about fleas — just like that, quite casually. . . . I said I knew how to catch them . . . how to count them . . . that that was my job, and I could also make out accurate statistics of the various groups of parasites. I could see at once that my manner interested them, made them observe me more closely. . . . They were listening to me, but as to believing me, that was quite another kettle of fish.

Then along came the officer in charge of the whole station. He was called the "Surgeon-General" — which would make a splendid name for a fish. He was tough in his manner but showed greater decision than the others. "What's this you're telling us, my boy," he said, "about knowing how to count fleas? Come, come." He was making a great to-do about it to put me off my stroke. But I at once let him have the little harangue I had prepared. "I believe in the numbering of fleas! I believe it to be a civilizing factor, because numeration is the basis of statistical data of incalculable value! A progressive country ought to know the number of its fleas, divided according to sex, subdivided according to age, by years and seasons. . . ."

"Come, come, young man, that'll do!" the surgeon-general broke in, "We've had a lot of scallywags from Europe here before you who've spun us yarns of that sort and then turned out to be anarchists, like all the others, worse than the others. They didn't even believe in anarchy! Cut it out, see? To-morrow we'll try you out on the immigrants over on Ellis Island, in the bathhouse. Major Mischief, my second in command, will tell me if you've been lying or not. . . . For two months now, Major Mischief has been clamouring for an official flea-counter. You can go to him for a trial. Now get out! And if you've pulled our legs, you'll be shot into the sea. Go on, beat it now! And look to yourself!"

So I "beat it" from the presence of American authority, as I had beaten it before from so many other authorities; by showing him first my front view and next, with a rapid right-about turn, my backside, accompanying the whole thing with a military salute.

I figured that this statistics method would be as good as any other for landing me in New York. Next morning, Mischief, the major in question, explained to me in a few brief words what there was for me to do; he was a fat, yellow man, as short-sighted as he well could be, and he wore dark glasses. He must have taken me in as wild beasts recognize their prey, by general appearance, because to make out details would have been impossible with spectacles like the ones he had on.

We fixed up about the job without any difficulty and I even think that by the end of my stay old Mischief had taken quite a fancy to me. Not to be able to see anybody is a good reason to start with for liking people; besides which, my astonishingly facile way of catching fleas quite enchanted him. I hadn't my equal in the whole station for shutting up in boxes the most restive, the hairiest, the most impatient fleas of all. I was able to choose them according to their sex on the immigrants themselves.

It was a terrific task, I can assure you. Mischief in the end came to have an implicit trust in my dexterity.

By the evening I'd have crushed so many fleas that the nails of my forefinger and thumb were terribly bruised and even then I

wasn't through, as there was still the most important part of my
job to be done: drawing up the day's record. Polish fleas in one
column, Yugoslav fleas in another . . . Spanish fleas . . . Cri-
mean crabs . . . Peruvian lice . . . I had at the tip of my finger
nails all the crawling, biting things that thrive on broken-down
humanity. A labour obviously at once both meticulous and mon-
umental. Our figures were checked over in New York, in a special
office fitted with electrical flea-counting machines. Every day the
good little tug *Quarantine* crossed the harbour from end to end,
carrying our figures over there to be queried or filed.

And so many days went by, I began to feel stronger but as my
temperature and the delirium slipped from me in my present
comfortable state, a desire for fresh adventure and new worlds
to conquer returned to me, and soon became imperative. With a
temperature of 98.4° things became dull and banal again.

Still I could have quite well have stayed on there indefinitely
in peace, and well-fed from the station kitchen — especially as
Major Mischief's daughter (I can remember her still, superb in
her fifteen summers) used to come and play tennis at five, in extremely short skirts, before our office windows. Finer legs I've seldom seen — a bit masculine perhaps, yet even so somehow more
delicate — a vision of budding young flesh, an absolute challenge
to happiness, an exclamation of promised delight. The young
naval ensigns of the post never left her side for a moment.

They didn't have to justify themselves by useful work like I
did, the young scamps! I watched their every gesture and caper
around my little idol and paled several times a day as I watched.
In the end I told myself that perhaps I too might pass in the dark
for a sailor. I was still harbouring this hope when one Saturday,
after I'd been there twenty-three weeks, there was a sudden turn
in the tide of events. An Armenian colleague of mine, who was in
charge of the statistics sloop, was suddenly promoted to an official
flea-counting post in Alaska, to deal with the gold prospectors'
dog teams.

That was a leg up in the world for him if ever there was one.
Naturally he was overjoyed. Huskies are of course valuable animals. You can't do without them. They're awfully well looked

after. Whereas immigrants can go to the devil — there are always too many more where they came from.

As now there was nobody on hand to carry our lists to New York, it didn't take them long at the office to appoint me. My boss Mischief shook me by the hand when I left for the shore, telling me to behave well and sensibly while I was in town. It was the last piece of advice this honest man ever gave me and, just as he had never seen me to date, he never saw me again. As soon as we landed, the rain lashed fiercely down on us, soaking through my thin suit and washing away the statistics I held in my hand. Some, however, I'd kept in a good thick wallet sticking out of my pocket, so as to look as much like a business man in the city as possible, and off I dashed, full of fear and excitement, towards new adventures.

Lifting up my nose towards these bulwarks, I felt an upside-down sort of giddiness, because there were really too many windows up there and they were all so much alike everywhere you looked that one felt sickened by them.

Thinly clothed as I was, I hurried shivering towards the darkest gap I could see in all this giant façade, hoping that the passers-by would hardly notice me in their midst.

But I needn't have felt ashamed. There was nothing to bother about. The street I had chosen was easily the narrowest of all, no wider than a fair-sized stream at home would have been, heavily silted at the bottom, very damp and very dark: so many other people, both large and small, were already walking along it, that they carried me with them like a shadow. They were journeying up to town like me, going to their work, no doubt, with their noses to the ground. Here, too, they were the usual poor.

AS THOUGH I KNEW WHERE I WAS GOING, I PRETENDED TO CHOOSE again and changed my direction. I took another, better-lit turning on my right; "Broadway" it was called; I read it's name written up. High above the topmost storeys was the day, in little crumbs and particles of sky. But we went along in the twilight below, as sickly as that of the forest and so grey that the street was full of it, like so much dirty cotton waste.

Like a running sore this unending street, with all of us at the bottom of it, filling it from side to side, from one sorrow to the next, moving towards an end no one has ever seen, the end of all the streets in all the world.

There was no wheeled traffic passing along it, only people and more people.

It was the valuable district, they told me later, the home of gold: Manhattan. You only enter it on foot, like entering a church. It is the very core of the banking centre of the world to-day. Yet some men spit in it as they go along. You need a nerve.

It is a quarter filled with gold, a miracle indeed, and you can even hear this miracle through closed doors, its din of jingled dollars, the Dollar which is always too light, a veritable Holy Ghost, more precious than blood itself.

All the same, I had time to go and see them; I went in and talked with the employees who guard the bullion. They are sad and underpaid.

When the faithful enter their bank, you mustn't think they can take what they want for themselves as they please. Not at all. They communicate with Dollar, murmuring to Him through a little grille; in fact, they make their confession. Very little noise, dim light, a tiny *guichet* set between lofty columns, that is all. They do not swallow the Host. They lay it against their heart. I couldn't stay there long admiring them, I had to be following the crowds in the street between those flat, shadowy walls.

All of a sudden our street widened, like a cañon ending in an open space. You found yourself before a lake of glaucous light set in a ring of monstrous houses. And right in the middle of this clearing was a little pavilion, with a kind of rural air, surrounded by unhappy lawns.

I asked several people near me in the crowd what this building was that one could see over there, but most of them pretended not to have heard. They had no time to lose. One young passer-by, however, was good enough to inform me that it was the Town Hall, a relic of colonial days, he said, simply stiff with historical interest . . . which had been left there. The outskirts of this oasis formed a square, with benches in it, which were good enough to see the Town Hall from, if one sat down. When I arrived, there was very little else to see.

I stayed a full hour in this place and then from out this gloom, this jogging, disjointed, mournful crowd, there surged towards noon, a sudden avalanche of absolutely lovely women!

What a discovery! What an America! What delight! Oh, memory of Lola! As a type she'd not deceived me. It was *true!*

I was getting to the quick of my pilgrimage. And if I had not at the same time felt frequent pangs of hunger, I should have believed myself to have reached a moment of unearthly æsthetic inspiration. These beauties I was discovering could, with a little confidence and comfort, have ravished me from my trivial condition of humanity. Indeed, all I lacked was a sandwich to be convinced that it was all the sheerest miracle. But how I lacked that sandwich!

But still, what suppleness, what grace! What unbelievable delicacy of features! What a treasure trove of harmony! What daring tints — always, invariably successful! Every possible masterpiece of face and figure among so many blondes! And all these brunettes, these red-heads too! And the more there were of them, the more kept on arriving. . . . Is Greece reborn perhaps, I asked myself? I'd happened along at just the right moment!

They struck me as all the more divine, these apparitions, because they appeared to be entirely unaware of my presence, my existence, as I sat there close beside them on my bench, goggling in the fullness of my erotico-mystical admiration, silly with quinine and also, one must admit, with hunger. If it were possible to come out of one's skin, I should have been out of mine then and there, once and for all. There was nothing to hold me back.

They could have carried me off, these unreal office girls, could have sublimated me, with only a gesture, with but one word, and I should have sailed away at once, all of me, into the world of dreams. But no doubt they had other business to attend to.

An hour, two hours passed in this way, this stupefaction. I hoped for nothing more.

I had to be careful, come down to earth, and not blow my small reserve of money all at once. I hadn't much, I didn't even dare to count it. I couldn't have, anyway, I was seeing double. I could only feel it there, thin, shrinking notes in my pocket, along with my incomplete statistics.

Men went by too, mostly young men, with wooden, pink faces, a dry, monotonous look, and chins one couldn't get used to, they were so large and vulgar. . . . Still, no doubt that's how their women like their chins to be. The sexes seemed to keep each to itself in the street. The women looked mostly only at the shop windows, taken up by the attraction of handbags, scarves and little silken things, shown very few at a time in each window, but definitely and exactly displayed. You didn't find any old people in this crowd. Nor couples either. No one seemed to think it at all odd that I should be sitting there hour after hour, watching the people pass. But, at a given moment, the policeman standing like an ink-pot in the middle of the road began to suspect me of being up to something very odd. It was obvious.

Wherever you are, as soon as you begin to attract the attention of authority to yourself, the thing to do is to hop it, quick. Don't stop and explain. "Out of sight!" I said to myself.

Just to the right of my bench, as a matter of fact, there was a great wide hole in the middle of the pavement, rather like our Métro at home. This hole seemed to me just the thing, huge as it was, with stairs inside all of pink marble. I had already seen quite a number of people disappear down it from the street and come out again. It was in this subterranean resort that they went about

Nature's needs. I was struck dumb at once. All marble too was the hall below where these things were going on. A sort of swimming bath, but not emptied of all its water, a horrible swimming bath, filled only with a filtered, dying daylight fading on the backs of unbuttoned men, red in the face in the midst of their own stinks, as they attended to their dirty business in public, to an accompaniment of frightful noises.

Among men, that way, without fuss, and to the tune of laughter and encouragements from all around, they settled down to it as to a game of football. You take off your coat right away as you come in, as though for strenuous exercise. One dresses the part, in fact, for the thing's a rite. And so, completely at their ease, belching and worse, gesticulating like madmen, they install themselves in a closet. Fresh arrivals have a thousand dirty pleasantries addressed to them as they come downstairs from the street; yet they all appear enchanted.

The stricter, the more mournful even, the behaviour of these men out there in the street, the more the prospect of having to empty their bowels in tumultuous company appears to solace and inwardly delight them.

The closet doors, mostly smudged and dirty, swung loose, wrenched from their hinges. You wandered from one little cell to the next, to crack some joke, while those who were waiting for a vacancy smoked heavy cigars and tapped the shoulder of each occupant as he travailed, bowed head between his hands. Many groaned like wounded men or women in labour. The constipated were threatened with ingenious tortures.

When a flush of water announced the end of a session, the din redoubled around the unoccupied pan, and often it was tossed for, heads or tails. The newspapers they read, although as thick as cloth, were instantly torn asunder by this eager gang. You could hardly see their faces through the smoke. I didn't dare go near them because of their smell.

This contrast was well calculated to disconcert a foreigner. Here all this easy shamelessness, this stupendous intestinal familiarity, and then out there on the street that absolute restraint! I was utterly nonplussed. I went up the same steps into the daylight and sank back onto the same bench. Sudden vulgar, digestive debauchery and discovery of a joyous communism in filth: I disregarded each of these baffling aspects of the same question. I hadn't the strength to analyse them, to find their synthesis. Sleep was what I needed most of all. Oh, rare, delicious urge to sleep!

So I joined in the procession of passers-by up one of the adjoining streets; we went along in jerks because each shop window disturbed the flow of the crowd. There was an hotel entrance there, making an eddy on the pavement. People spurted out of its revolving doors into the crowd and I was caught up and flung the other way into a vast vestibule.

Bewildering at first. . . . You had to guess at it all, to imagine the grandeur of it, the majesty of its proportions, because everything went on beneath lights so shaded that one only grew accustomed to it after a little while. There were a great number of young women in this twilight, sunk in armchairs as in so many shells. Men, silent and attentive, passed around them to and fro, a little way off, timidly and inquisitively, just out of range of crossed legs displaying magnificent heights of silk. It seemed to me that these young women sat there awaiting events of extreme importance and costliness. Clearly their thoughts were not of me. And I in my turn passed by, most furtively, before this long and palpable temptation.

Since there were at least a hundred of these haughty, half-recumbent bodies set in a single line of chairs, I reached the reception desk in a dream, having absorbed so much too strong a dose of loveliness for the man I was that I staggered as I walked.

At the desk a pomaded clerk roughly offered me a room. I chose the smallest in the hotel. I couldn't have had more than about fifty dollars in my possesion at that moment, few thoughts left in my head and absolutely no confidence at all.

I hoped it really was the smallest room in all America the clerk was offering me, as his hotel, the Gay Calvin, was advertised on its posters as the most luxuriously appointed of all the leading hotels on the whole continent.

Above me, what an infinity of furnished suites! And near-by

in those armchairs, what rows of invitations to the rape! What pitfalls! What perils! Is there then no end to the æsthetic trials of the pauper? An agony more obstinate than hunger? But I hadn't the time to succumb to them, for the reception clerk had already given me a key, lying heavy in my hand. I didn't dare budge.

A pert little boy dressed like some very young brigadier general sprang out at me from the shadows; a commander to be implicitly obeyed. The sleek reception clerk rang his bell three times, my bell-hop started to whistle. I was being packed off. Away we went.

First along a corridor, at a great lick, we forged, determined and in darkness like an underground train. The kid was leading. Around a corner, a bit farther, then another. Going fast enough. We banked a bit. . . . Right, here's the elevator. Zup! Is this it? No, another corridor. Darker still, ebony panelling the whole way, I thought; I hadn't time to examine it. The little lad whistled away, carrying my flimsy suit case. I didn't dare ask him anything. We had to get on, I was well aware of that. In the darkness here and there, as we went along, a red or green electric light glowed an order. Long splashes of gold were the doors. We had long ago passed the 1800's and then the 3000's, yet we went on, urged ever forward by our same invisible destiny. He rushed after the unknown in the darkness, this glinting bell-hop, as if by instinct. Nothing in this labyrinth seemed to find him at a loss. His whistling modulated plaintively as we passed a Negro chambermaid. And that was all.

In my attempt to walk faster, I had lost along these similar corridors what little confidence I had left after my escape from quarantine. I was crumbling to pieces, as I had seen my hut crumble in the winds and warm rain of Africa. I was lost in a tornado of unfamiliar sensations here. There comes a moment between two civilizations when one finds oneself struggling in a vacuum.

Suddenly, without warning, the bell-hop swung around. We had arrived. I hurled myself through a door into my room, a large, ebony-panelled box. Only on the table did a lamp cast a glimmer of dim, greenish light. The manager of the Gay Calvin Hotel

wished to make known to visitors that he, the manager, took a
personal interest in their welfare and would at all times be ready
to make sure of their being continually in good spirits throughout
the length of their sojourn in New York. Reading this announce-
ment, which was put up where one couldn't miss it, added, if anything, to my confusion.

As soon as I was alone, it was much worse. All this America
was nagging at me, asking me huge questions and filling me with
horrible presentiments, even here in this room.

For a start I tried nervously from the bed to get used to the
gloom of this little pen. With rumbling regularity the walls by my
window trembled at the passing of an elevated railroad car. It
hurtled along opposite between two streets, like a shell filled with
quaking, jumbled flesh, careering from one district to another
across this lunatic city. You could see it down there, rushing
over a network of steel girders whose echo groaned on long after it
had passed at a hundred miles an hour. Dinner time slipped by
during this prostration and bedtime too.

It was above all else this frantic railway which wore me down.
On the other side of my little mine shaft of a courtyard the house
wall opposite lit up first one, and two, then dozens of its rooms.
In some I could see what was going on. Families going to bed.
These Americans seem as weary as our own people, after hours
of standing up. The women had very pale, very full thighs, at
least, those I could see properly had. Most of the men shaved,
smoking a cigar, before going to bed.

Once in bed, they take off their spectacles first, and then remove
their dentures, which they put in a glass, and then place the whole
lot on show. Just as in the streets, the sexes don't seem to speak
to each other. You'd say they were fat, very docile animals, very
used to being bored. I saw in all only two lots do, with the light
on, at any rate, what I was waiting for, and not violently at all.
The other women just ate sweets in bed, while waiting for their
husbands to finish their toilet. And then they all put out the
light.

That's what's sad about people going to bed. You can easily
see that they just let things run their course, you can see that

they don't think to wonder why they're there at all. They don't care. They sleep no matter what happens; insensitive dolts, mere oysters. Americans or not, their consciences are always easy.

But I, I'd seen too many awkward things to be easy in mine. I knew too much and yet too little about it. "I must go out," I said, "Out into the street again. Perhaps you will meet Robinson." It was an idiotic idea, of course, but I only gave it to myself to have an excuse for going out again, because, however much I tossed and turned on my little cot, not the tiniest bit of sleep could I snatch. Nothing that I could do brought me either comfort or distraction. . . . And that is to sound the utmost depths of depression.

What is worse is that one wonders how, to-morrow, one will find strength enough to go on doing what one has been doing the day before, and for so much too long before that, — strength for the whole mad business, for a thousand and one vain projects: attempts to escape crushing necessity; attempts which are always stillborn; and all just to convince oneself once more that Destiny is insurmountable, that one must fall back each evening to the bottom of the wall, under the burden of next day, each time more precarious and more sordid.

Perhaps too it is mostly Age, that traitor, who comes and threatens us as well. There's not much music left in one that Life can be made to dance to, that's what it is. All of one's youth has gone now to the end of the world, in a silence of facts to die. And where can one go, I ask you, when one is no longer sufficiently mad? Truth is a pain which will not stop. And the truth of this world is to die. You must choose: either dying or lying. Personally, I have never been able to kill myself.

The best thing then was to go out into the streets, a minor suicide. Every one has their own little remedies, their own ways of attaining sleep and food. I had to manage to get to sleep, somehow, so as to have the strength again to-morrow to earn myself a crust of bread. Energy had to be found, just enough energy to get a job next day and meanwhile, now at once, to enter the unknown of sleep. Don't imagine it's as easy as all that to fall asleep once you have begun to disbelieve everything, mostly because of all the times you have been frightened.

I dressed and somehow or other found myself at the elevator, feeling rather gaga, however. I still had to cross the vestibule past more rows of ravishing enigmas with such alluring legs, and delicate, severe little faces. They were goddesses, of course, kidnapping goddesses. One might have come to an understanding with them. But I was afraid of being arrested. All too difficult. Almost every desire a poor man has is a punishable offence. So back I went into the street. It was no longer the same crowd as before. These people strolling along the pavements showed a little more spirit, as if they came from a less arid country, one of diversion, an evening country.

The crowds rolled forward in the direction of sky signs high in the darkness, like twisting multicoloured snakes. More people flowed in from all the surrounding streets. "They're worth a good many dollars," I thought, "a crowd like that, just for their handkerchiefs alone, or their silk socks. Even for their cigarettes." And just to think that you can be in the middle of all this money yourself and it doesn't bring you in a penny more, even to go and eat with! It's maddening to realize how completely men are walled away from each other, like so many houses.

So I dragged myself along towards the lights: one movie palace, then another next door, and yet another, and so on the whole way. We lost a large section of the crowd in front of each. I chose one of these movies for myself, where the photographs outside showed women in undies — and, my, what thighs! Oh boy! Heavy! Full! Perfectly shaped! And then such sweet little heads on top, drawn, as though by contrast, so delicately, so daintily, in such easy and unerring line, perfect, without a fault, without a blemish anywhere, — perfect I tell you, fragile yet firm and concise at the same time! Every daring loveliness that life could lavish, a prodigal beauty, a rash extravagance of the most profound, the most divine harmonies possible!

It was pleasant inside the movie house, warm and comfortable. Immense organs, as gentle as those in a cathedral, but a warm cathedral, as rich as thighs. Not a moment lost. You plunge

straight into an atmosphere of warm forgiveness. You only had
to let yourself go to feel that the world had at last become indulgent. Already you almost did think that.

Then dreams waft upwards in the darkness to join the mirages
of silver light. They are not quite real, the things that happen on
the screen; they stay in some wide, troubled domain meant for
the poor, for dreams and for dead men. You have to hurry to
stuff yourself with these dreams, so as to get through the life
which is waiting for you outside, once you've left the theatre, so
as to last through a few more days of this strife with men and
things. You chose from among these dreams those that will warm
your heart the most. For me, I must admit, it was the dirty ones
that did. It's no good being proud, you've got to take from a
miracle whatever you can hold. A blonde with unforgettable neck
and nipples saw fit to break the silence of the screen with a song
about her loneliness. I could well have wept with her.

That is what's so good. What a fillip it gives you! There'd be
courage in my bones — I felt it there already — for two whole
days after that. I didn't even wait for the lights to go up in the
auditorium. I was ripe for all resolution to sleep, now that I had
absorbed some of this admirable psychological effervescence.

On returning to the Gay Calvin Hotel, although I saluted him,
the porter failed to wish me good night, as ours at home do. But
I wasn't worrying at present over any porter's misdemeanours. The
glow within me was enough in itself to soften the rebuffs of
twenty years. That's the way it is.

In my room, I had scarcely shut my eyes when the theatre
blonde came at once to sing again, for me alone, her sorrowing
song. I helped her, so to speak, to put me to sleep, and I succeeded
pretty well. . . . I wasn't quite alone any more. . . . You can't
possibly sleep quite alone.

IF YOU WANT TO EAT CHEAPLY IN THE UNITED STATES, YOU CAN GO and buy a little hot roll with a sausage inside; it's convenient, they sell them at the corner of any little street and they're not at all expensive. Eating in the poorer districts didn't worry me of course, in the least, but never to meet those lovely creatures of the rich, that was really terrible. Under those circumstances there wasn't any point in eating at all.

At the Gay Calvin, on its thick carpets I could still pretend to be looking for some one among those too exquisite women in the entrance hall, and become hardened, bit by bit, to their equivocal attitude. On thinking it over, I decided that the boys on the *Infanta Coñita* had been right to bawl me out. I was discovering, by experience, that I hadn't at all the right sort of tastes for an under dog. All the same that didn't give me back my will power. I went and took more and more doses of the movie, here, there and everywhere, but it only just provided me with the energy for a little walk or so. No more. In Africa I had indeed found a sufficiently frightful kind of loneliness but the isolation of this American ant heap was even more shattering.

I had always suspected myself of being almost purposeless, of not really having any single serious reason for existing. Now I was convinced, in the face of the facts themselves, of my personal emptiness. In surroundings so much too different from those in which I had previously had my meagre being, it was as if I had at once fallen to pieces. I discovered that now that I no longer heard mention of familiar things, there was nothing to prevent me from slipping into an irresistible condition of boredom, a sort of sickly, terrifying collapse of the mind. It was a disgusting experience.

When on the point of losing my last dollar in this venture, I was still bored. So bored that I even refused to consider my most urgent needs. We are, by nature, so futile that distraction alone can prevent us from dying altogether. I clung to the movies with a fervour born of despair.

Leaving the crazy gloom of my hotel, I again tried wandering about a bit in the principal streets of the neighbourhood, an insipid carnival of vertiginous buildings. My lassitude deepened before a row of these elongated façades, this monotonous surfeit of streets, bricks, and endless windows, and business and more business, this chancre of promiscuous and pestilential advertising. A mass of grimy, senseless lies.

Down by the river I came on other little streets, lots of them, which were more ordinary in size; I mean, for instance, that here all the windows of a single house opposite could have been broken just from where I was standing on the pavement.

The smell of endless frying pervaded this quarter of the town. The shops no longer had displays out, for fear things might be stolen. Everything reminded me of my hospital at Villejuif, even the little children with bulging bowlegs along the sidewalk, and the hand-organs too. I could well have stayed there with them but they, the poor, would not have fed me either, and I should have seen them all the time and their too wretched state frightened me. So I went back to the central part of the town. "You dirty dog," I said to myself, "You really have no goodness in you." You've got to become resigned to knowing yourself a little better each day, since you haven't the courage left to put a stop once and for all to your own snivellings.

A car ran along by the Hudson, towards the centre of the town, an ancient car shaking on every wheel and in all its pitiful body. It took a good hour to cover the distance uptown. The passengers submitted without impatience to a complicated ritual of paying their fare by means of a kind of coffee grinder for money, which there was at the entrance to the car. The conductor watched them work this thing, dressed like one of ours in a sort of "Balkan prisoner of war" uniform.

At last we arrived, exhausted, and after these proletarian excursions I again passed in front of that never-failing double row of loveliness in my tantalizing hotel lounge; again and again I went by, in a trance and filled with desire.

My penury was such that I didn't dare look in my pocket to find out for certain. As long as Lola had not chosen this of all times to be out of town! I thought. And anyway, would she be willing to receive me? Had I better touch her for fifty or for a hundred dollars to start with? I hesitated, I felt sure I shouldn't have the necessary nerve until I had eaten and slept really well for once. And then, if I succeeded in this initial enterprise, I would redouble my efforts to find Robinson, that is, as soon as I felt strong enough again. Robinson wasn't at all like me! Oh, no, not Robinson. He, at any rate, was a man of guts. A real fine fellow! He was certain to know already all the ins and outs, all the tricks of the trade over here. Maybe too he had some way of laying hold of this certainty, this peace of mind, which I so badly needed. . . .

If he too had come off a galley, as I imagined he must have, and been up and around in these parts for some time before me, he'd be certain to have settled himself into some job in America by now. *He* wouldn't ever be bothered by the ceaseless racket of this hurdy-gurdy. Perhaps if I'd thought it out clearly, I myself could have gone and looked for a job in one of these offices whose dazzling name plates I read outside. . . . But the thought of having to go into one of those buildings startled me and enfeebled my wits. My hotel was quite enough — that gigantic, odiously animated tomb.

Was it possible that all this bulk of matter, all this hive of offices, this endless crisscross of girders, didn't really have the same effect on the inhabitants as it did on me? Maybe this mighty torrent in suspense spelt security to them, whereas to me it was nothing but a ghastly system of restraints and bricks and corridors, Yale locks and *guichets*, a Gargantuan, inexplicable architectural agony.

To philosophize is only another way of being afraid and leads hardly anywhere but to cowardly make-believe.

With only three dollars to my name, I went to watch them twinkle in the palm of my hand under the light signs in Times Square, that astounding little open space where publicity flares out over the heads of a mob engaged in choosing itself a movie to go to. I was looking for a very cheap restaurant and found one of these rationalised eating places where service is reduced to a minimum and the business of feeding is simplified down to the barest level of nature's needs. At the door a tray is put into your hands and you queue up. You wait your turn. By my side extremely nice-looking candidates for supper, like me, said nothing at all. It would be pretty astonishing, I thought, to be able to address oneself to one of these pert young ladies with a neat, enchanting nose. "Mademoiselle," one would say, "I am rich, very rich . . . pray tell me what you would like for supper. . . ."

Then everything would become simple at once, utterly, divinely simple, everything which a moment before was so complicated. The whole thing would change and a horribly hostile world would roll to your feet, a sly, soft, silent, velvet ball. At the same time too, maybe you'd lose that wearing habit of dreaming about success and the happiness of wealth because now you could put out your finger and touch all that. . . . The life of penniless people is one long refusal of a long delirium, and actually one only knows, one can only be delivered from, what oneself possesses. For my part, so many dreams had I picked up and abandoned that the wind whistled through my disgustingly tattered and tumble-down conscience.

Meanwhile I dared not enter into the mildest of conversations with these young things in the restaurant. I held onto my tray in orderly silence. When my turn came to pass along in front of the counter piled with delicatessen, I took everything that was given to me. The place was so clean, so brightly lit, that you felt you were being carried along on its polished surface like a fly on milk.

The waitresses, looking like hospital nurses, stood behind the *nouilles*, the rice and stewed fruits. Each had her own specialty. I filled up from where the nicest of them stood. Alas, they didn't smile at their customers at all. As soon as you had what you wanted, you had to go quietly away and sit down, leaving room for others. You walk delicately about, balancing your tray, as if crossing an operating theatre. It was a great change from my little ebony and gilt room at that Gay Calvin Hotel of mine.

But if they showered all this light on us customers, if for a moment they lifted us from out of our accustomed darkness, it was all part of a plan. There was some idea of the proprietor's behind all this. I felt distrustful. It has a very weird effect on you after days of shadow to be bathed all of a sudden in a flood of light. Personally, it added a little extra craziness to everything for me. Not that that required much doing.

I couldn't manage to hide my feet under the spotless little glass-topped table I found myself sitting at; they spread out everywhere all around. I could have wished them somewhere else for the moment, those feet of mine, because from the other side of the shop window we were in full view of rows of people whom we had left behind us in the street. They were waiting till we had finished swallowing our meal, so that they could come and take our places. In fact, it was for this reason and so as to keep their appetites up, that we were so flooded with light, and emphasized, as a piece of living publicity. The strawberries on my *gâteau* shimmered with so many reflections that I couldn't bring myself to eat them.

There's no escaping American business method.

But in spite of everything, through all this glare and uneasiness, I was aware of a delightful waitress coming and going in our immediate vicinity, and decided not to miss a single one of her charming movements.

When my turn came to have her take away my plate, I made a careful note of the exceptional shape of her eyes, which were set at a much sharper angle, upward and outwards, than those of French women. The eyelids curled up too, very slightly, towards the eyebrow by her temples. Cruelty in fact, but just the right amount of it, a cruelty to be kissed, a sharp insidious quality like that taste of Rhine wine which one somehow can't help rather liking.

When she came near me, I started to make little knowing signs to her, as though I recognized her. She watched me entirely without any pleasure, like an animal, but with some slight curiosity, all the same. "Here," I said to myself, "is the first American woman who hasn't been able to avoid looking at me."

When I'd eaten my sparkling pie there was nothing for it but to give up my place to somebody else. Whereupon, dithering a little, instead of making straight for the very obvious exit, I had the audacity to ignore the man at the cash desk, who was waiting for us all and our money, and steered towards my blonde, detaching myself in a quite unheard-of way amid all those well-ordered waves of light.

The twenty-five waitresses in a row at their posts behind the food all signalled to me that I was going wrong, that I had made a mistake. There was a great stir on the other side of the window among the people waiting, and those about to begin hesitated to sit down. I had broken the set order of things. Every one around expressed their astonishment aloud. "Must be some foreigner, surely," they said.

But I had my own idea, for what it was worth, and I wasn't going to let the beauty who had served me slip through my fingers. She had looked at me, the little darling; so much the worse for her! I had had enough of being alone. No more nonsense. Now for some sympathy, for real contact! "You know me hardly at all, Mademoiselle, but I already love you; would you like us to get married?" That's the way I spoke to her, the most honest way possible.

Her reply never reached me, because a giant of a doorkeeper, he too dressed all in white, came along at that moment and pushed me outside, neatly, quietly, without being at all insulting or rough, into the night, like a dog that's forgotten itself.

It was all quite all right and straightforward; I had nothing to complain of.

So I went up back to the Gay Calvin.

In my room the same thunderings continued, in snatches, to shatter their own echoes; first the roar of the Elevated, which seemed to be hurling itself towards us from a very long way off, and every time it passed to be taking all its supports with it to wreck the city, and in between the incoherent hoots of vehicles below, which came up from the streets, and then as well that soft murmur of a moving crowd, always hesitant, always about to disappear, and then hesitating again and coming back. The bubbling, like jam, of people in a city.

From where I was up there, you could perfectly well shout out over their heads whatever you pleased. I tried it. They disgusted me, the whole mass of them. I hadn't the guts to tell them so to their faces during the daytime, but where I was I ran no risks. I called to them "Help! Help!" just to see if they'd take any notice. None whatever. They were pushing life and the night and the daytime before them; life hides everything from them. In the midst of their own noise they hear nothing. They don't give a damn. And the bigger the town and the higher the town, the less they bloody well care. I'm telling you. I've tried. And it's no use.

IT WAS ONLY FOR FINANCIAL REASONS, BUT EXTREMELY URGENT and pressing ones, that I began to try and find Lola. Had it not been for my piteous need of money, I should certainly have let her grow old and disappear without ever seeing my little minx of a friend again. Whatever one may say, she had treated me — and there appeared to be no doubt about that when I thought back on it — in the most scurvy and deplorable fashion.

The selfishness of people with whom one has come into contact in life, when one remembers them in later years, is apparent for what it was — hard as metal, hard as platinum, and far more durable than Time itself.

When one is still young, one manages to excuse the stoniest indifferences, the most bare-faced impositions, making allowances for them on grounds of personal idiosyncrasy and God knows what sort of callow romanticism. But later on, when life has taught you how much caution, cruelty and malice are required of you, if only you are to live through it reasonably well at a normal temperature, you realize, you're in a position to understand the dirty deals a past contains. All that you need to do, and what you always need, is to take a very careful look into your own heart and see what you yourself have sunk to. There's no mystery, no nonsense left; you've had to swallow all the poetry you ever had, since you've survived till then. Life's become a lot of pork and beans.

I found my nasty little friend eventually, after a lot of trouble, on a twenty-third floor in Seventy-seventh Street. It's incredible, when one's going to ask a favour of people, how unpleasant they seem. She had a comfortable little place, very much the sort of thing I had expected.

Having stuffed myself beforehand with large doses of Hollywood, I was pretty well mentally in readiness, and just about emerging from the state of coma I had been in since my arrival in New York; our first meeting was less unpleasant than I had imagined it would be. Lola didn't seem very surprised to see me, only somewhat displeased when she recognized me.

I embarked by way of a start on an anodyne conversation about various topics of our common past — keeping it all on as prudent a footing as possible and mentioning the war along with other things, not stressing it too much, just incidentally. There I dropped quite a bad brick. Lola wouldn't have a word said about the war, not at any price. It made her feel old. She was annoyed and retaliated at once by admitting that she would not have recognized me on the street, age had already so wrinkled, thickened, caricatured me. There we were, busily exchanging compliments. The little slut, did she think she could get my goat with that sort of flapdoodle? I didn't even deign to take up these cheap gibes.

Her taste in furnishing wasn't anything much out of the ordinary but the room was pretty nice all the same — anyway, it seemed all right to me after my Gay Calvin Hotel.

The way a quickly made fortune comes, the details of it, always gives one an impression of magic. After the "arrival" of Musyne and Mademoiselle Herote, I knew that sex is the poor person's pocket gold mine. This feminine pettishness on Lola's part delighted me, and I would certainly have given my last dollar to her concierge just to start her talking.

But there wasn't a concierge in her house. There wasn't a concierge in the whole of New York. A city devoid of concierges can't have any life, any atmosphere; it's as dull as a soup without salt or pepper, a wretched thin brew. Oh, those choice morsels! Titbits gathered in boudoirs, kitchens and attics, dripping, cascading downstairs to the concierge, who sits there in the midst of life, — what a rich infernal harvest! Some of our concierges at home succumb at their posts; laconic, coughing, adorable, bewildered, they are consumed and stupefied by so much truth, like martyrs to it.

One must admit it's a duty to try everything against the abomination of being poor — one should get tight on anything one can, on the cheapest wine, the movie, anything. One shouldn't be difficult, "particular," as they say in America. Our own concierges provide year in and year out for those who know how to take it and what to do with it, cherishing it in their hearts — hate enough and to spare and for nothing, enough to smash the world. In New York one is dreadfully lost without this vital seasoning, this mean but genuine, all-important condiment, lacking which the spirit languishes and is reduced to merely vague malignings and a babble of pale slanders. Without a concierge, you don't get anything that bites, harms, cuts, maddens or obsesses and adds something positive to the general stock of hate in the world, illuminating it with a thousand vivid details.

A loss which was all the more to be regretted, since Lola, seen in her own surroundings, was making me experience quite a new sensation of disgust. I longed to spew out my horror at her absurdly petty smugness and success — but to whom was I to turn? The effect was instantly contagious and Musyne's memory at once became hostile and repugnant for me too. A lively hatred for the two women was born in me; it's with me still, it has become an essential part of my make-up. A whole lot of corroborative details was what I needed to be delivered in time and forever from any present or future feeling of indulgence towards Lola. One can't relive one's life. Forgiveness is not what's difficult; one's always too ready to forgive. And it does no good, that's obvious.

But let me get on with my story: Lola was wandering about her room without much on, and her body struck me after all as still really very desirable. A well-cared-for body always suggests the possibility of theft, of a lovely, direct, intimate intrusion into the reality of wealth and luxury, without the fear of punishment.

Perhaps she was only waiting for a move from me to turn me out. Actually it was mostly this damned momentary lecherous impulse which made me careful. Food first. And anyway, she went on telling me all about the trivialities of her daily life. The world would surely have to be shut down for two or three generations at least, if there were no lies left to tell people. There'd be nothing to say to one another — or very little. Eventually she asked me what I thought of this America of hers. I confessed that I had reached that stage of misery and weakness where anybody and anything fills you with fear, and that her country terrified me quite definitely more than the whole sum total of threats, actual, hidden and unforeseen which I found it contained, particularly on account of the vast indifferences towards me which, as far as I was concerned, was what it stood for.

I had got to earn a daily crust, I told her, and so would have to get over all these foolish fears as soon as possible. I was already pretty far behindhand in this respect, and I assured her I would be extremely grateful if she would be kind enough to give me an introduction to some possible employer . . . some friend or relation of hers. . . . And at her very earliest convenience. A very small salary was all I wanted. . . . And a lot more pretty nonsense I spun at her. . . . She didn't take to this humble yet indiscreet petition at all well. Her manner was discouraging from the outset. She said she knew absolutely nobody who could give me a job or any sort of help. We were forced to come back to life in general and her existence in particular.

We were still sizing each other up morally and physically like this, when the bell rang. Whereupon, without pause or interval of any sort, four women came into the room: four painted, middle-aged females, well covered with muscles and jewellery, who greeted Lola effusively. I was very summarily introduced and Lola, who was clearly annoyed at their arrival, tried to lead them off somewhere else; but they obstinately took no notice and all together turned on me to tell me all they knew about Europe. An old-world garden apparently, full of antiquated, erotic, greedy madmen. They knew their Chabanais and Invalides by heart.

Personally, I'd never visited either of these places, the first being too expensive, the second too far away. But I was filled by an answering gust of automatic, weary patriotism, absurder than one usually feels on such occasions. I retorted with some heat that their town got on my nerves. A sort of wretched general store, I told them, damnably bad yet destined, one supposed, to be obstinately made to succeed. . . .

While I talked away artificially and conventionally like this,

I couldn't help seeing other reasons besides malaria for my present state of mental and physical prostration. It was a question as well of a change of habits. I would have once more to learn to recognize new faces in new surroundings, other ways of talking and of lying. One's laziness is almost as strong as life itself. The fatuity of this fresh farce you've got to play gets you down; you need, when all is said and done, more cowardice than courage to begin all over again. That's what moving about, travelling, is; it's this inexorable glimpse of existence as it really is during those few lucid hours, so exceptional in the span of human time, when you are leaving the customs of the last country behind you and the other new ones have not yet got their hold on you.

Everything at such moments adds to your wretched insufficiency, forcing you in your weakness to see things, people and the future as they are — that is to say as skeletons, nothing but ciphers, which nevertheless you will have to love, cherish, defend and encourage, as if they really existed.

A new country, other people around one behaving rather oddly, a few little vanities gone, some conceit or other now without its *raison d'être*, its lie, its familiar echo, and that is all that's needed; your head spins, doubt takes hold of you, the infinite opens for you in particular; a ridiculous little infinite it is, and you tumble into it.

Travel is the search for this nothing at all, this little moment of giddiness for fools. . . .

Lola's four friends were extremely amused to hear me making my flamboyant confession like this, quite the little Jean-Jacques, in front of her. They called me a number of names which I barely understood with their extraordinary accent, the unctuous and indecent way Americans have of speaking.

When the black servant brought in the tea things, there was silence. But one of these callers must have been more observant than the rest, for she announced in a loud voice that I was shivering with fever and must surely have a frightful thirst. What we had in the way of tea absolutely delighted me, in spite of feeling so shaky. Admittedly those sandwiches saved my life.

There followed a conversation about the comparative merits of the more spectacular Parisian brothels, but I didn't take the trouble to join in it. The pretty ladies next sampled a good number of complicated drinks, and under their warming, confidential influence got very excited on the subject of "marriage." Although I was pretty much overcome by our repast, I couldn't help noticing *en passant* that they were talking about some very special kind of marriage, apparently the mating of very young couples, of mere children, which somehow brought them in a commission.

Lola noticed that the conversation was rousing my keenest curiosity and attention. She stared at me very hard and stopped drinking. The men Lola knew, her American men, were never guilty like me of inquisitiveness. With some difficulty I behaved myself under her scrutiny. I would have loved to ask these women a whole lot of questions.

Finally our guests took their leave, moving heavily, exalted by alcohol and erotically enlivened. They squirmed as they talked with a curiously elegant and cynical sexuality. I caught a glimpse in all this of some Elizabethan thing which I myself should also have liked to feel, concentrated and deliciously vibrating, in its proper place.

But to my great grief and regret, I never got more than just this inkling of this particular biological communion, a vital exchange, which when one is travelling is an experience of such decisive importance. Sad, sad thought.

Lola, when her friends had gone, was frankly furious. The whole incident had caused her very great annoyance. I didn't say a word.

"What hags!" she exclaimed, a few minutes later.

"How did you get to know them?" I asked.

"They're old friends. . . ."

For the time being she was in no mood for further confidences.

Judging by their rather arrogant way of treating her, it had struck me that these women had a hold over Lola in certain circles — probably some definite power over her. I was never to know more.

Lola spoke of going downtown, but suggested that I stay there at her place and wait for her, eating something if I felt like it.

Having left the Gay Calvin without paying my bill and, for excellent reasons, not intending to go back there, I was very grateful to her for this permission — a few more moments of warmth before going off to face the street again — and, my godfathers, what a street!

As soon as I was alone, I went along a passage towards the place I'd seen the Negro emerge from. I met him halfway there and shook him by the hand. He accepted me at once and took me along to his pantry, a fine orderly place, much more logical and pretty than the drawing-room.

Right away he began to spit on the magnificent tiled floor in front of me — spitting as only Negroes can spit: a long way, a lot and to perfection. I spat too, out of politeness, as well as I could. Thereafter he took me into his confidence. Lola, I learnt from him, had a speed boat on the river, two cars in the garage, and a cellar full of bottles from every country in the world. Catalogues were sent to her from the smartest Paris shops. There it was. And he began to outline this same summary information over and over again. I stopped listening to him.

As I slumbered beside him, the past came before my eyes — Lola leaving me in Paris during the war — being hunted, tracked down, ambushed, the harangues, the lies, the general craftiness; Musyne, the Argentines, their ships full of frozen meat. Topo. The crowds of scum on the Place Clichy; Robinson, sea waves, poverty, Lola's glistening white kitchen, her black servant, and me inside it all like any one else might have been. Everything would go on just the same. The war had burnt up some and warmed others, as a fire can torture or comfort, according to whether one is standing in it or in front of it. You have to look out for yourself, that's all there is to it.

It was true too, what she'd said about my having changed. Life twists you and crushes your face. It had crushed hers too, but not so much, nothing like so much. The poor fade. Poverty is a giant who uses your features like a piece of cotton waste to wipe a filthy world. And still there's some left over.

All the same, I thought I noticed a change in Lola, moments of depression and sadness, gaps in her hopeful stupidity, those moments in which a human being needs to gather strength to carry a little further the acquisitions of his passing life; but they're too heavy now, do what he will, for what energy he still has left, for his dirty little remaining sense of poetry.

Her black man suddenly began to skip about. Something had started him off again. As his new-found friend, he insisted on stuffing me with cakes, loading me with cigars. He ended up by producing from a drawer, with infinite precautions, a round leaden mass.

"My bomb!" he angrily announced. I jumped back. "*Libertá! Libertá!*" he screeched delightedly.

He put it back in its place and spat again, superbly. What an ecstasy of emotion! He was terribly excited. His laughter infected me, that colic sensation of merriment. One gesture more or less, I told myself, what does it matter? When Lola at last returned, she found us together in the drawing-room, smoking and laughing hard. She pretended not to notice.

The Negro quickly disappeared; she took me back to her room. She seemed sad, she looked pale and tired. Where could she have been? It was beginning to be quite late. It was the hour when Americans are lost because around them life has begun to beat to a slower rhythm. One car out of every two is back in its garage. It's the moment for half confidences — but you've got to hustle if you're going to avail yourself of it. She led up to it with questions, but her tone of voice when she asked me about the life I'd been living in Europe irritated me considerably.

She made no bones about considering me capable of any sort of caddishness. She realized quite clearly that I'd come to see her to ask for money and that in itself set up a very natural sense of strain between us. Such feelings verge on murder. We stuck to trivialities and I did my utmost to avoid a definite misunderstanding. Among other things, she inquired after my genital lapses and wanted to know if I hadn't somewhere on my wanderings produced some little child she could adopt. It was a curious notion of hers. The idea of adopting a child was an obsession with her. She believed rather simply that a scamp like me must have founded secret dynasties more or less everywhere under the sun.

She was rich, she told me, and ached to be able to devote herself to a little child. She had read all the books about care of the child, especially the ones which go all lyrical about motherhood — books which, if you thoroughly steep yourself in them, rid you absolutely of any wish ever to copulate again. Every virtue has its own indecent literature.

As what she wanted was to sacrifice herself entirely to some "little being", I myself was out of luck. I had nothing to offer her but my own large person, which she found utterly repulsive. Only prettily presented poverties are any good in fact, poverty imaginatively dished up. Our conversation languished. . . . "Listen, Ferdinand," she suggested at last. "We've talked enough; I'll take you over to the other side of New York to see my little protégé — I like looking after him but his mother irritates me. . . ." It was an odd time to choose. On the way there in the car we talked about her amazing, fire-eating Negro.

"Did he show you his bombs?" she asked. I admitted that I had been subjected to that ordeal.

"The lunatic's not really dangerous actually, Ferdinand. He fills his bombs with my old bills. . . . There was a time long ago in Chicago when he belonged to a very powerful secret society for the emancipation of the blacks. . . . They were frightful people, apparently. The police broke it up but my Negro has had a taste for bombs ever since. . . . He never puts any gunpowder in them. The idea of the thing's enough. . . . It's really only his artistic temperament. . . . He'll always be plotting revolutions. But I keep him on, he's such an excellent servant. And taken all in all, perhaps he's more honest than other people who don't plot revolutions. . . ."

And she came back to her adoption mania.

"Really, it's a pity, Ferdinand, that you haven't a little girl somewhere. . . . Your dreamy temperament would go very well in a woman, whereas it doesn't seem at all fitting in a man. . . ."

The rain streamed down, closing the night around Lola's car as we slid along on smooth strips of asphalt. Everything was cold and hostile to me, even her hand which I was holding very tight in mine all the time. We were completely apart from each other.

We came to a house which from the outside looked very different from the one we'd just left. In an apartment on the first floor a little boy about ten years old and his mother were waiting for us. The furniture in the flat aped Louis XV and you could smell the remains of a recent meal. The little boy came and sat on Lola's knee and kissed her very prettily. The mother also seemed to me to be very sweet to Lola, and while Lola was talking to the child, I managed to take the mother into a near-by room.

When we returned, the kid was practicing for Lola's benefit a dance step which he'd just been taught at school. "He'll have to have a few more private lessons," said Lola, "and then perhaps I could introduce him to my friend Vera at the Globe. There may be quite a future for the child." His mother at these kind and encouraging words burst into gratitude and tears. She was given a little roll of green dollars which she popped into her bosom like a *billet-doux*.

"I'd quite like that kid," Lola remarked, when once we'd left the house. "But I have to support his mother too and I don't like mothers who are as sharp as all that. . . . And the kid's too vicious, anyway. . . . It's not the sort of attachment I really want. . . . I'd like to have entirely maternal feelings. Do you understand, Ferdinand?" Where food's concerned I can understand anything anybody wants me to: it's not brains any longer, it's a piece of elastic.

She would go on about her desire for purity. A few streets farther on she asked me where I was going to sleep that night and walked along with me a few yards. I answered that if I couldn't lay my hands on a few dollars right away, I shouldn't be sleeping anywhere.

"All right," she said, "come back with me and I'll give you some money at home and then you can go wherever you like."

She was all for shooting me out into the night at the earliest possible moment. Of course; it was the usual thing. If you go on being pushed out like that into the night, you end up somewhere, I supposed, all the same. That's the consolation. "Cheer up, Ferdinand," I told myself several times just to keep going. "Through being thrown out of every place, you'll surely finish up by finding out what it is that frightens all these bloody people so, and it's probably somewhere at the farther end of the night. . . . That must be why they don't go into the depths of the night themselves!"

After that, it was quite cold between us two in the car. The streets we went along seemed to threaten us with all their silent stones, armed and towering above us, a sort of suspended downpour. A watching town, a monster bituminous and rain-sodden, ready to pounce. At last we drew up. Lola went in before me.

"Come up," she said. "Follow me."

Her room again. I wondered how much she was going to give me to have done and be rid of me. She was looking for dollar bills in a little handbag on the table. I heard the tremendous rustling of scrunched notes. What moments of excitement! There was no other sound but this in all New York. But I was still so worried that I asked, I don't know why, quite unsuitably, after her mother, whom I'd forgotten.

"My mother's ill," she said, turning around and looking at me straight in the face.

"Where is she at the moment?"

"In Chicago."

"What's the matter with her?"

"Cancer of the liver. . . . I've put her in the hands of the best specialists in the place. . . . Her treatment is costing me a lot of money, but it'll save her life. They've told me so. . . ."

She rushed on to tell me a lot more details of her mother's condition in Chicago. Having suddenly become all friendly and solicitous, she couldn't prevent herself appealing to me for some intimate comfort. Now I'd got her.

"What d' you think, Ferdinand; don't you think they can cure her?"

"No," I answered, very deliberately and firmly. "Cancers of the liver are absolutely incurable."

She went as white as a sheet. It was certainly the first time I'd seen the little bitch disconcerted by something.

"But after all, Ferdinand, the specialists assure me that she'll get well! They guarantee it. They've written and told me so. . . .

You know, they're very wonderful doctors, Ferdinand. . . ."

"For a fee, Lola, there will fortunately always be very wonderful doctors. . . . I'd do the same for you myself, if I were in their place. . . . And you too, Lola, you'd do the same. . . ."

What I was saying struck her abruptly as so obvious, so undeniable, that she couldn't get away from it.

Just for once in her life, for the first time in her life maybe, her impudence was going to fail her.

"Oh, but listen, Ferdinand, you're hurting me horribly, can't you see? I'm very fond of my mother; don't you know how fond of her I am?"

That was a smart remark! God in Heaven! What the hell does the world in general care whether you love your mother or not?

Sobbing in an emptiness all of her own. Dear little Lola!

"Ferdinand, you're an absolutely loathsome cad!" she went on in a rage. "You're an unspeakable brute. . . . You revenge yourself for the beastly position you're in as shamelessly as you can, by coming here and saying frightful things to me. . . . Why, I'm sure you're actually doing Mother a lot of harm by talking like that!"

There were tag ends of the Coué method trailing about in her despair.

Her savage temper didn't frighten me half as much as that of the officers on board the *Admiral Bragueton,* who had intended to slaughter me for the titivation of a few bored lady passengers.

I watched Lola closely all the time she was calling me every name under the sun, and I felt a certain pride as I realized that the more she cursed me the greater grew my indifference — no, what am I saying — my joy. One's really quite all right inside.

"She'll have to give me at least twenty dollars to be rid of me now," I calculated. "Perhaps even more."

I took the offensive. "Lola, please lend me the money you promised me, or I shall be staying the night here, and you'll have me going on and on telling you all I know about cancer and its complications and its hereditariness — because, you know, cancer *is* hereditary, Lola, don't forget."

As I proceeded to pick out, to toy with details of her mother's case, I saw her blench, weaken, give way before my eyes. "Ah, the slut," I said to myself, "hold on to her tight, Ferdinand! Just once you've got her where you want her. . . . Don't let her go. You won't get another chance like this for a *long* time!"

"There you are, take it!" she screamed, quite beside herself. "Here are your hundred dollars, and now get out of here and never come back, d' you hear me — never! Get out! Out! *Out!* You dirty beast!"

"Give me a little kiss, though, Lola; don't let's quarrel," I suggested, just to see how far I could go. Then she got a revolver out of a drawer — and she meant it. The stairs were good enough for me; I didn't wait for the elevator.

Still, this slap-up scene gave me back a taste for work and bucked me up no end. Next day I boarded a train for Detroit, where I'd heard it was easy to get taken on at a lot of little jobs that weren't too hard and were well paid.

PEOPLE SAID TO ME IN THE STREET WHAT THE SERGEANT HAD SAID to me in the forest. "There you are," they said; "straight ahead. You can't go wrong."

And I came in fact to a group of great squat buildings full of windows, through which you could see, like a cage full of flies, men moving about, but only just moving, as if they were contending very feebly against Heaven knows what impossibility. So this was Ford's? And then all about one, and right up to the sky itself, the heavy many-sided roar of a cataract of machines, shaping, revolving, groaning, always about to break down and never breaking down.

"So here we are," said I to myself. "It's not very exciting. . . ." It was even worse than everywhere else. I went closer, to a door where it said on a slate that there were men wanted.

I wasn't the only one waiting. One of the others in the queue told me that he'd been there two days and was still in the same place. He'd come from Yugoslavia, this goat, to get a job. Another down-and-out addressed himself to me; he said he'd come to take a foreman's job just because he felt like it — a madman, a bluffer.

Hardly any one spoke English in this crowd. They gazed at one another distrustfully, like animals used to being thrashed. A urinous, sweaty smell rose from their ranks, like at the hospital. When they talked to you, you avoided their mouths, because the poor already smell of death inside.

It was raining on our little army, as we stood very close together in single file under the eaves. People looking for jobs can be packed together very tight. What he liked about Ford's, an old Russian confided in me, was that they took on anybody and anything. "Only look out," he advised me, "don't miss a day here, because if you do they'll throw you out in a jiffy and in another two two's they'll have put one of those mechanical things in your place, they're always handy; and then if you want to come back, you're out of luck." He spoke good Parisian, this Russian; he'd been a taxi-driver for years but then they'd shot him out after a cocaine affair at Bezons and in the end, playing *zanzi* with a fare at Biarritz, he'd staked his taxi and lost it.

It was true what he'd said about their taking on anybody at Ford's. He hadn't lied. I didn't believe him, though, because tramps are very apt to talk a lot of hooey. There's a point of poverty at which the spirit isn't with the body all the time. It finds the body really too unbearable. So it's almost as if you were talking to the soul itself. And a soul's not properly responsible.

They had us stripped, of course, to start with. The examination took place in a sort of laboratory. We filed slowly through. "You're in terrible shape," the assistant informed me, as I came up, "but that doesn't matter." And I'd been afraid they might refuse to give me the job because of the fevers I'd had in Africa, as soon as they noticed, if by any chance they prodded my liver. But not at all; they seemed very pleased to find invalids and wrecks in our little lot.

"In the job you'll have here, it won't matter what sort of a mess you're in," the examining doctor assured me at once.

"So much the better," I replied; "but you know, sir, I'm an educated man and I once studied medicine myself. . . ."

He at once gave me a dirty look. I realized that I'd again gone and put my foot in it, to my own disadvantage.

"Your studies won't be any use to you here, my lad. You haven't come here to think, but to go through the motions that you'll be told to make. . . . We've no use for intellectuals in this outfit. What we need is chimpanzees. Let me give you a word of advice: never say a word to us about being intelligent. We will think for you, my friend. Don't forget it."

He was right to warn me. It was better that I should understand their way of doing things and know what to expect. I'd made enough silly mistakes in the past to last me another ten years at least. I meant to be taken for a good little worker from now on. When we'd put on our clothes again, we were sent off in slow-moving single files and hesitant groups towards the places where the vast crashing sound of the machines came from. The whole building shook, and oneself from one's soles to one's ears was possessed by this shaking, which vibrated from the ground, the glass panes and all this metal, a series of shocks from floor to ceiling. One was turned by force into a machine oneself, the whole of one's carcass quivering in this vast frenzy of noise, which filled you within and all around the inside of your skull and lower down rattled your bowels, and climbed to your eyes in infinite, little, quick unending strokes. As you went along, you lost your companions. You gave them a little smile when they fell away, as if it was all the greatest fun in the world. You couldn't speak to them any longer or hear them. Each time, three or four stayed behind around a machine.

You resist, though, all the same; you find it difficult to dislike your own substance; you long to stop it all and be able to think about it and hear your heart beating clearly within you; but now it's impossible. It can't stop. Disaster is in this unfortunate steel trap, and we, we're spinning round in it with the machines, and with the earth itself. All one great whirling thing. And a thousand little wheels, and hammers never falling at one time, their thunders crowding one against the other, some of them so violent that they spread sort of silences around themselves which make you feel a little better.

The little bucking trolley car loaded with metal bits and pieces strives to make headway through the workmen. Out of the light! They jump aside to let the hysterical little thing pass along. And hop! There it goes like a mad thing, clinking on its way amid belts and flywheels, taking the men their rations of fetters.

The workmen bending solicitously over the machines, eager to keep them happy, are a depressing sight; one hands them the right-sized screws and still more screws, instead of putting a stop once and for all to all this smell of oil, and this vapour which burns your throat and your eardrums from inside.

It isn't shame which makes them hang their heads. You give in to noise as you give in to war. You let yourself drift to the ma-

chines with the three ideas you have left aflutter somewhere behind your forehead. And it's all over. . . . Everywhere you look
now, everything you touch, is hard. And everything you still
manage to remember something about has hardened like iron and
lost its savour in your thoughts.

You've become old, all of a sudden, — disgustingly old. Life outside you must put away; it must be turned into steel too, into
something useful. You weren't sufficiently fond of it as it was,
that's why. So it must be made into a thing, into something solid.
By Order.

I tried to speak to the foreman, shouting into his ear. He answered by grunting like a pig, and merely made signs to show me,
very patiently, the extremely simple job I should be engaged on
from then onwards, forever. My minutes and hours, the rest of
my time, would be spent like the rest of them here, in passing
small bolts to the blind man next to me who sorted them out in
size, sorted them out now as he had been sorting them out for
years, the same bolts. I was very bad at it from the start. No one
blamed me at all, but after three days on this first job, I was
moved on, a failure already, to trailing around with the little
trolley of nuts and oddments which went coasting along from one
machine to another. There I left three, here a dozen, yonder only
five. No one spoke to me. One only lived in a sort of suspense
between stupefaction and frenzy. Nothing mattered except the
continuous feeding of the several thousand machines which ordered all these men about.

When at six o'clock everything stops, you carry the noise away
in your head. I had a whole night's noise and smell of oil in mine,
as if I'd been fitted with a new nose, a new brain for evermore.

So by dint of renunciation, bit by bit I became a different man
— a new Ferdinand. All the same, the wish to see something of the
people outside came back to me. Certainly not any of the hands
from the factory; my mates were mere echoes and whiffs of
machinery like myself, flesh shaken up for good. What I wanted
was to touch a real body, a body rosy and alive, in real, soft,
silent life.

I knew nobody in this town, particularly no women. After a lot of trouble, I collected the vague address of a "house", a secret joint in the northern quarter of the town. I wandered about that part on several consecutive evenings after work, reconnoitering. The street looked the same as any other, though cleaner perhaps than mine.

I'd discovered the little house where these goings-on took place; it had a garden around it. You had to go in quick so that the cop on a near-by beat could not have noticed anything. It was the first place I'd been to in America where I was received without brutality, even kindly, for my five dollars. And they were good-looking young women there, plump, bursting with health, grace and strength, really almost as beautiful as the ones at the Gay Calvin Hotel.

And then too, these at least could be handled quite frankly. I couldn't help going back there regularly. All my pay was spent there. When evening came, I needed the promiscuous transports of these splendid ever-ready creatures, to fashion myself a new soul. The movie was no longer any good to me, too gentle an antidote which produced no real effect against the materialistic horror of the factory. I had to seek starker tonics to keep me going, a more radical cure. A very moderate fee was all that was charged me in this house, merely by way of a settlement between friends, because I'd brought these ladies a tricky system or two from France. No little tricks on Saturday nights, though; then trade was at its height and I had to make way for baseball teams making whoopee, magnificently lusty sods, to whom pleasure seemed to come as easily as breath itself.

While the players took their joy — which keyed me up too — I used to write short stories in the kitchen. The enthusiasm these athletes showed for the personnel of the place fell undoubtedly short of my own impotent fervour. In the autonomy of their own health, these baseballers set no great store by physical perfection. Beauty is like alcohol or comfort; one gets accustomed to it and takes it for granted.

They visited the house chiefly for fun. Often they'd end up fighting like hell. Then the police would come along and carry off the lot in little vans.

I soon felt for Molly, one of the young women in this place, an emotion of exceptional trust, which in timid people takes the place of love. I can remember, as if I'd seen her yesterday, her gentleness and her long white legs, marvellously lithe and muscular and noble. Whatever they may say, true aristocracy in a human being is shown in legs, there's no doubt about it.

We became intimate in body and companionable in our minds, and went out for long walks in town together every week. Molly was well off; she made close on a hundred dollars a day at the house. Whereas I at Ford's wasn't earning more than six. The love she performed for a living didn't tire her at all. Americans manage like birds in these matters.

In the evening, when I'd finished peddling my little truck around, I forced myself to look cheerful when I went to see her after supper. You've got to be gay with women, at any rate at the start. I was harassed by an overwhelming vague desire to talk to her about things, but hadn't the strength. Molly understood the stupor of industrial workers, she was used to the ways of factory hands.

One evening quite suddenly, apropos of nothing, she offered me fifty dollars. I looked at her at first. I didn't dare take it. I thought of what my mother would have said at such a thing. And after that I reflected that my mother, poor woman, had never offered me as much herself. To please Molly, I went at once and bought with her dollars a beautiful buff-coloured suit (four piece), which was what was being worn that spring. They'd never seen me looking so smart when I turned up that evening at the *bordello*. The good lady who ran the place put on her great big gramophone just to teach me to dance.

After that, Molly and I went off to the movies to try out my new suit. On the way there she asked me if I was jealous or anything, my clothes were making me look so sad. They made me not want to go back to the factory, either. A new suit upsets all your ideas. She kissed the stuff of my new suit with little passionate kisses, when people weren't looking. I tried to think of something else.

What a woman this Molly of mine was, though! What generosity! What a body! What fullness of youth! A feast of desires.

And I began to be all restless again. Pimp, by any chance? I wondered.

"Don't go back to the works!" Molly urged me, making it worse. 'Find some small job in an office instead. . . . Translating, for example; that's really your line . . . you like books. . . ."

She was very sweet giving me this advice; she wanted me to be happy. For the first time in my life a human being was trying to help me, my own real self, from inside, if I can say it that way, putting theirself in my place, not merely judging me from theirs, like everybody else.

Ah, if only I'd met Molly when there was still time to choose between one road and another! Before I lost my enthusiasm over that slut of a Musyne and that horrid little bitch Lola! But it was too late to be young again. I didn't believe in it any more. One gets old very quickly — and what's more, in an unalterable way. You notice that by how you've grown attached to your unhappiness, despite yourself. It's that Nature is stronger than you are, that's all. She tries us out in one mould and we can't ever escape it again. I'd started out myself in a restless direction; gradually you take your rôle and your destiny seriously, without properly realizing it, and then when you spin around, it's too late to change it. You've got all restless; it's fixed that way for always.

Molly tried very sweetly to keep me by her, to dissuade me. "Life's as enjoyable here as it is in Europe, you know, Ferdinand. We shouldn't be unhappy together. . . ." And in a sense she was right. "We'll invest what we earn. We'll buy ourselves a shop. . . . We'll be like every one else."

She said these things to calm my scruples. Plans for the future. . . . I agreed with her. I was even rather ashamed of all the trouble she took to hold me. I was very fond of her, of course, that's certainly true, but I was fonder still of my own obsession, of my longing to run away from everywhere in search of something, God knows what; prompted no doubt by stupid pride, by a conviction of some kind of superiority.

I didn't want to annoy her; she guessed it and forestalled my anxiety. She was so sweet to me that in the end I confessed to her about being harassed by this mania for beating it from every place I was at. For days on end she listened to me tiresomely spreading and explaining myself as I struggled among my phantoms and my conceits, and she didn't lose patience with me at all. On the contrary, she simply tried to help me to overcome this vain and silly agony of mind. She didn't quite understand what I was driving at with all my talk, but all the same she was ready to side with me and not my bugbears, or vice versa, whichever I preferred. She was so gentle in her persuasion that her goodness became familiar to me and almost personal. But then it seemed to me that I was beginning not to play fair with this confounded fate of mine, my *raison d'être*, as I called it, and I immediately stopped telling her what was in my thoughts. I turned back alone into myself, happy to be more miserable now than I'd been before, because I'd carried back with me into my loneliness a new kind of distress, something too which bore a resemblance to genuine feeling.

All that's very ordinary. But Molly was gifted with angelic patience, and she happened to have a fierce belief in vocations. Her youngest sister, for instance, at the University of Arizona, had caught a craze for photographing every sort of little bird in its nest and eagles in their eyries. So in order that she should be able to pursue further this fascinating pastime, Molly used to send her photographer-sister fifty dollars regularly every month. Truly a heart of infinite goodness, with something really sublime in it, which could be turned into cash, — not mere bluff, like mine and so many others. Where I was concerned, Molly wanted nothing better than to aid me financially in my greasy adventurings. Although at times I struck her as pretty crazy, my obsession seemed to her genuine and definitely worthy of not being encouraged. She only begged me to keep a sort of little account for her of an allowance for expenses which she wished to make me. I couldn't bring myself to accept this gift. A last shred of decent feeling prevented me from making more out of this really much too lofty, generous nature, from speculating further on it. Thus I deliberately fell out with Providence.

At this point I even felt shamed into making an effort or two to go back to work. Nothing, however, came of my heroic little gesture. I went as far as the gates of the factory, but on this boundary line I stood rooted and the thought of all those machines whirring away in wait for me irrevocably quashed my wish for work.

I went and stood in front of the main boiler-room window and watched that multiform monster roaring and pumping and compressing something, I don't know what from I don't know where, through a thousand shining pipes as complicated and as evil-looking as forest lianas. One morning when I was standing there, gazing fatuously in, my Russian taxi-driver came along. "Well, buddy," he remarked, "you certainly let yourself out all right. . . . You haven't been along for three weeks. . . . They've got a machine-thing in your place now. . . . After all, it's what I warned you would happen. . . ."

"That being so," I said to myself, "that's that, at any rate. . . . There's no point in going back now. . . ." And off I went back into town. On my way home I looked in at the Consulate; I thought I'd ask if they'd heard anything of a Frenchman called Robinson.

"Yes, indeed we have," the consular people told me. "He's been along here twice and he's got a false passport and all. . . . He's wanted by the police. Do you know the man?" I left it at that.

From then onwards I expected to run into Robinson any minute. I felt it bound to happen. Molly was very kind and sweet to me still. In fact, she was even kinder now that she was convinced I really did want to go away. It wasn't any good, though, being kind to me. We often went for walks together on the outskirts of the town these last farewell afternoons.

Little grassy mounds there were, and clumps of birch trees around miniature lakes, and people dotted about, reading grey-looking magazines under a sky leaden with clouds. We avoided being complicated and confidential in our talks, Molly and I. Besides, there it was: she was too sincere to have much to say when she was hurt. What went on inside was enough for her, inside her heart. We kissed. But I didn't kiss her at all well, as I should have, on my knees. I was always rather thinking about something else, about not wasting time, or tenderness, as if I wanted to keep it all for something grand, something sublime and later on, but not for Molly, and not really even for that. As if Life were going to take away from me and hide from me, while I was devoting all of myself to kissing Molly, what I wanted to know about it, about Life itself beyond all this blackness; and then I shouldn't have enough fervour left and in the end I should have lost everything through being weak, and Life, the one and only mistress of all true men, would have tricked me as she had tricked every one else.

We walked back towards the crowds and then I'd leave her at the place because at night she was kept busy by her customers until the early hours. While she was looking after them, I felt after all very unhappy and this feeling of unhappiness spoke so clearly to me of her that I felt even more with her then, than when she was actually by my side. I used to go to a movie to while away the time. Coming out of there, I'd get onto a tram somewhere and be carried around through the night. Soon after two o'clock, timid passengers would board the tram, of a sort you never meet either earlier or later than at that hour, always so pale and sleepy, in quiet groups, going out to the suburbs.

If you went all the way with them, they took you far. Well beyond the factories, towards indistinct lodgings and little streets of jumbled houses. On cobblestones glistening with dawn rain the daylight laid a tint of blue. My tram companions and their shadows disappeared together. They shut their eyes against the day. It was difficult to make them talk. Too tired. They didn't complain, these shades, no; it was they who cleaned the shops at night, all the shops and all the offices in town, after closing time. They seemed less restless than us daytime folk. Perhaps because they'd got right down to the very heel of people and things.

On one such night, when I'd got onto yet another tram and we had come to the end of the route and every one was quietly getting off, I thought I heard my name called: "Ferdinand! Hey, Ferdinand!" It sounded obstreperous, of course, in that dark place. I didn't like it at all. Above the roofs the sky was already returning, in little cheerless patches cut into by the eaves. Some one *was* calling me. Turning around, I recognized him at once: Léon! He came up whispering and we talked. He too had been cleaning an office like all the others. That's all he'd been able to get in the way of a billet. He trod along very ponderously, really majestically, as if he'd just accomplished some dangerous and, so to speak, sacred mission in the town. It's what happens to these night charmen, I'd already noticed it. Fatigue and solitude bring out God's image in man. He too had that look about his eyes, as he opened them wider than ordinary eyes, in that bluish half-light we were in. He too, even he, had also cleaned rows and endless rows of lavatories and polished a whole prairie land of silent floors.

He went on, "I recognized you at once, Ferdinand! By the way you stepped onto the tram. Fancy, just by that sad look you had when you found there wasn't a woman on it. Isn't that so? Isn't that just like you?" It was true; it was, of course, just like me. Certainly I had the morals of a stoat. So there was nothing to be surprised at in his very accurate suggestion. But what did surprise me, much more, was that he had not got on in the States, either. That wasn't at all what I should have expected.

I told him about the business of the galley and Santa Tapeta. But he didn't understand what I meant. "You're ill," he replied, quite simply. A cargo boat he'd come by. He would have tried to get in at Ford's too, but really his papers were too blatantly faked, he wouldn't have dared show them; so he didn't try. "Just about good enough to carry around in one's pocket," he explained. They didn't look into such things much when engaging you for night duty. They didn't pay well either, but there wasn't any fuss made. . . . A sort of Foreign Legion of the night.

"What about you?" he asked, "What are you doing? Are you still bitten? Haven't you had enough bad breaks and funny business yet? Do you still want to run around and see places?"

"I want to go back to France," I told him, "I've seen plenty. As you say, I've had enough."

"You're right," he said, "we're through. . . . You get old without noticing it. I know what it's like. . . . I'd like to go back myself, but it's these damn papers. . . . I'll hang around till I can get some good ones. . . . Must say it's not a bad job I've got. There are worse. But I don't seem to learn their language. . . .

There are some chaps in the cleaning line been at it thirty years and haven't got beyond 'Exit', because it's written up on the doors you clean, and 'Lavatory.' See what I mean?"

I saw what he meant. If ever Molly failed me, I too would have to go and get a job cleaning up offices at night. There's no reason why that should come to an end.

In fact, when one is in the war, one says things will be better when peace comes and you bite into that hope as if it were a lollipop, and it isn't; it tastes like filth. You don't dare say so at first, not wishing to upset any one's feelings. After all, one's really quite a nice-mannered chap. . . . And then one fine day, one spits the thing out in front of everybody. One's fed up with muck and misery. But people suddenly say you've been very badly brought up. And that's all there is to it.

We met two or three times after that, Robinson and I. He seemed depressed. A French deserter who distilled bootleg liquor for the lads of Detroit had let him in on his business to some extent. Robinson was tempted. "I'd quite like to make a little moonshine myself to pour down their dirty gullets," he confided to me. "On my own. But the thing is now I've got cold feet. . . . I'm sure the first time a cop started snooping around on me, I'd crumple up. I've seen too many of them in my time. . . . Besides, I feel so sleepy all the time. . . . Naturally; sleeping by day's no sleep at all. And that's not counting the stinking dust you fill your lungs with in those offices. See what I mean? It knocks a chap up. . . ."

We arranged to meet again another night. I went back to see Molly, and I told her all about it. She tried very hard not to show how much I hurt her, but all the same it wasn't difficult to see that I did. I kissed her more often now, but she'd been really and truly hurt; her hurt was much deeper than ours is, because what happens with us is that we're more given to making things out worse than they are. With American women, it's just the opposite. One hesitates to see it, to admit it, it may be pretty humiliating, but all the same it really is genuine sorrow; it's not pride, it's not jealousy either, nor just making a scene — it's real heartache, and you are forced to admit that inside we are lacking all that; and as for the pleasure of being really hurt, we are not capable of it. One's ashamed of not being richer in heart and in everything else, and of having after all judged humanity lower than it really is.

From time to time though, Molly would allow herself to utter some little reproach, but always very moderately, very gently.

"You're a dear, Ferdinand," she'd say to me, "and I know you try not to be as bad as the others, but I don't think you know in your heart of hearts what you really do want, Ferdinand. You'll have to find some way of earning your living when you get back to France. And anyway, you won't be able to stroll around all night dreaming, like you do here. . . . Which is what you're so fond of doing . . . while I work. Have you thought of that, Ferdinand?"

In a way she was absolutely and entirely right, but every one is made differently. I hated the idea of hurting her. Especially as she was so easily hurt.

"Molly, I promise you that I do love you . . . that I'll always love you as much as I can . . . in my own way."

My way wasn't much, though. Molly was fine, she had a fine, real body; there it was, it was tempting enough. But I had this awful liking for phantoms as well. Perhaps not entirely my own fault. Life forces you to have far too much to do with phantoms.

"You're very fond of me, Ferdinand, I know that," she said reassuringly. "Don't be upset about me. . . . You're sort of ill with this desire of yours always to be discovering something new. . . . That's all it is. It's just your particular road in life, I suppose. Going along, all on your own. . . . Well, he travels furthest who travels alone. . . . Will you be leaving soon then?"

"Yes, I'm going to finish off my studies in France and then I'll come back," I told her brazenly.

"No, Ferdinand, you won't ever come back. . . . Besides, I shan't be here." She wasn't fooled.

The time to go came. We went down to the station one evening a little before the time she usually went back to the house. I had been to say good-bye to Robinson earlier in the day. He wasn't pleased at my going, either. I seemed always to be saying good-bye to people. . . . On the platform, while we waited for the train, Molly and I, a couple of men passed. They pretended not to recognize her, but they whispered together.

"You're on your way now, Ferdinand. You really are doing exactly what you want to do, aren't you, Ferdinand? That's the important thing. Nothing else matters as much. . . ."

The train came in. I wasn't so sure what I wanted to do once I saw the engine. I kissed Molly with all the fervour I had left in my wretched carcass. I was sad for once, really sad, sad for everybody, for myself, for her, for all men.

Maybe that is what one is looking for throughout life, that and nothing more; the greatest misery there is to feel, so as to become oneself truly before death.

Years have gone by since that departure, many years. . . . I have often written to Detroit and to every address I could remember, where they might have known her and might have traced her. I have never had any answer.

The house is shut now. That's all I have been able to find out. Good, admirable Molly, I should like her, if she ever reads these lines of mine, to know for certain that I have not changed towards her, that I love her still and always shall, in my own way; that she can come to me here, whenever she may care to, and share my bread and my furtive destiny. If she is no longer beautiful, ah, well, no matter! The more's the pity, we'll manage somehow. I've kept so much of her beauty with me still, so warm, so much alive, that I've enough for both of us, and it will last another twenty years, long enough to see us through.

Surely I needed to be very mad to leave her, and mad in a cold-blooded, dirty way. All the same, I've held on to my soul till now and if tomorrow death came to take me, I know I should not be as heavy, or as ugly, or as hard, as the others are, because of all the kindness and the dreams Molly made me a present of during those few months in the United States.

TO HAVE RETURNED FROM THE OTHER WORLD ISN'T EVERYTHING! You pick up the thread of your sticky, precarious life where you left it straggling behind you. There it is waiting for you.

For weeks and months still I hung around the Place Clichy, my old starting place, and thereabouts, doing odd jobs for a living in the Batignolles quarter. What they were is of no importance. In the rain and poring over hot auto engines, when June had come, burning your throat and nose, almost like Ford's. My amusement was to watch the people pass, people going to their theatre or the Bois of an evening.

Always more or less on my own in my spare time, I spent hours looking through books and papers and all the things I had seen as well. Once I'd begun studying again, I eventually got through my examinations, somehow or other, while I earned my living at the same time. The Science of Medicine is well defended, let me tell you; the Faculty is a battlemented stronghold. Rows of pots and very little jam. Anyway, now that I had survived five or six years of academic tribulations, I'd got my degree all right, — such a swell degree. So I went and set myself up in the suburbs, the right sort of practice for me, at Garenne-Rancy, which you come to on your way out of Paris just beyond the Porte Brancion.

I hadn't any big ideas myself, nor much ambition either, just the wish to breathe a bit more freely and feed a bit better. I stuck my name plate on the door and waited.

The inhabitants of Rancy came and looked at my name plate, suspiciously. They even went and asked at the police station whether I was a real doctor or not. Yes, they were told, I was. He's registered as one, he *is* a doctor. Then every one in the district went about remarking that there was a new doctor in town, besides all the others. "He won't earn his bread and butter," was the concierge's prophecy. "There are far too many doctors round here already." And that was perfectly true.

In the suburbs it is mostly by tram that life returns in the morning. Strings of them rattle past, chock-full of vacant faces, clanking up the Boulevard Minotaure to work.

The young ones seemed almost happy to be going to work. They urged on the traffic, clinging on to running boards, the dear boys, laughing gaily. Extraordinary! But when for twenty years you've known the telephone box at the local *bistrot,* so dirty that you keep mistaking it for the lavatory, you've no wish to joke about serious matters any more, or about Rancy in particular. Not when you realize where you've been stranded. The houses obsess you, foul-smelling interiors behind secretive façades — their hearts the landlord's property. Him you never see. He wouldn't dare to show himself. Sends round his agent, the bastard. Yet they say in the quarter that the landlord's quite a good fellow when you meet him. That may mean nothing.

The sky at Rancy is same as at Detroit, a sooty light lying like dew on the common all the way from Levallois. A waste of buildings fast in a black quagmire. Chimney stacks, tall or short, looking the same from a distance as stakes in seaside mud. And we ourselves inside all that.

You've got to have the courage of a crab at Rancy too, especially when you're getting on in years and know perfectly well that you'll never get out of it again. At the other end of the tramway lines there's that grim bridge spanning the Seine, an open sewer. All along the embankment at night and on Sunday people clamber up on to the ledge to pee. The sight of the water flowing past makes men muse. They micturate with a sense of eternity, like sailors. Women don't ever stop to think, Seine or no Seine. The tram in the morning carries its crowds along to be squeezed in the Métro. You'd think, to see them all tearing in that direction, that something terrible must have happened the other way, at Argenteuil, that their homes were on fire. As each day breaks, this thing takes hold of them, they cling in bunches to every passing car. One vast rout. Yet they are only running to an employer in Paris, to the man who saves them from dying of hunger; they're in a panic they might miss him, the cowards. But he makes you sweat for your pittance. Ten years later you smell of it still, and twenty years and longer. You don't get it for nothing.

There is a good deal of chattering in the tram, just to start the day well. The women bleat faster than sheep. They'd hold up the whole line for a mislaid centime. Of course, some of them are sozzled already, mostly the ones that get down at Saint-Ouen for the market, the demi-bourgeoises. "How much are carrots?" they shout long before they get there, just to show they've got the money.

Heaped like a rubbish in a can, one crosses the whole of Rancy in that metal box, and stinks a good bit too, especially in summertime. At the town walls you quarrel and shout just once more and then are lost to view; the Métro swallows you all and all of you, faded suits, shabby dresses, silk stockings, indigestion and feet as dirty as socks, collars as impossible and stiff as a quarter's rent, abortion to come and ex-service heroes, — all of it trickles downstairs smelling of coal-tar soap and Condy's fluid, into the black hole, grasping a return ticket which itself costs as much as a couple of loaves of bread.

There's the slow anguish of the thought of instant dismissal always hovering in the brain of tardy office workers, with a curt reference from the boss, when he wants to cut down overhead expenses. Shuddering recollections of the Slump, of the last time one was out of a job, and all the advertisements one had to read, penny papers, penny papers . . . waiting in queues in search of work. Such memories strangle a man, however settled he may look in his year-round overcoat.

The city conceals its crowds of dirty feet as well as it can in its underground electric sewers. They don't come to the surface again until Sunday. Then, when they're at large, you have to stay indoors yourself. Watch them amusing themselves on Sunday and it's enough to make you never want to be gay again. Around the entrance to the Métro curls the endemic smell of drawn-out wars, of half-burnt, mangled villages, of abortive revolutions and businesses gone bankrupt. The local garbage men are busy year in and year out burning the same little heaps of damp rubbish in ditches to the lee of the wind. They go around coughing to the neighbouring drug store instead of overturning the trams into a gutter and going off to smash up the local tollgates. No guts, no nothing. When the war comes, the next one, they'll make money again selling ratskins, cocaine and gas masks.

I had found a little apartment on the outskirts of the district for my consulting room. From it I could see the workman who always seems to be standing about in the street, with his arm in a sling, a casualty from the machines, gazing into space, not knowing what to do or what to think about, without enough in his pockets to go and get a drink — and come alive again.

Molly had been right. I was beginning to understand what she meant. Studies change you, they make a man proud. Before, one was only hovering around life. You think you are a free man, but you get nowhere. Too much of your time's spent dreaming. You slither along on words. That's not the real thing at all. Only intentions and appearances. You need something else. With my medicine, though I wasn't very good at it, I had come into closer contact with men, beasts and creation. Now it was a question of pushing right ahead, foursquare, into the heart of things. Death comes chasing along after you, you've got to get a move on, and you have to find something to eat too, while you're searching, and dodge war as well. That makes an awful lot of things to do. It isn't easy.

Meanwhile, no patients came to see me — not so as you'd notice them, that is. It's always a bit slow at the start, people told me reassuringly. For the time being it was mostly I myself who was sick.

Nothing could be worse than Garenne-Rancy, I felt, when business is at a standstill. My word, yes. It's best not to have to do any thinking in a place like that — and here had I actually come there to have a quiet time to think in — from the other end of the world too! I'd gone and put my foot in it! Proud little fool! A dark, heavy cloud of depression had come my way. . . . It was no laughing matter, and there was nothing I could do about it. There's no tyrant like one's own brain.

Below me lived Bézin, the little antique dealer, who always said to me when I stopped at his door, "You can't have everything,

Doctor! Either betting or a little glass of something now and then — it's one or the other! A man's got to choose. Personally, I'm all for a drink. I'm not fond of studying form."

The stuff he liked best of all was *gentiane-cassis*. Not a bad little man normally, and then after a few drinks not half so nice to know. . . . When he went to buy junk on the second-hand market, he'd stay out three days at a time "on a trip", as he put it. They'd bring him back home. And he'd say:

"I know what the future's going to be like. . . . One long petting party. With films showing most of the time. . . . Why, it's pretty much like that already. . . ."

He could see still further into the future when he was in that state. "I know there won't be any more boozing. . . . I'm the last of the drinkers. I have to hurry. . . . I know just where I go wrong."

Everybody coughed in my street. It was mostly all there was to do. You've got to go up to the Sacré-Cœur to get a sight of the sun. because of all the smoke.

It's a fine view you get from up there: you can see perfectly well where we are, where all those houses we live in are, right away in the distance. But when you look for them in detail, you can't make them out, not even your own house, everything you can see is so ugly and all so equally ugly.

Farther away still there's the Seine, winding in dirty, glaring zigzags from one bridge to the next.

When you live in Rancy, you don't even realize how sad you have become. You just don't want to be doing anything much. Chiefly because you have to economize on everything all the time, you come not to have any wants.

For several months I borrowed money here and there. Every one was so poor and so suspicious in my district that only at nighttime could they make up their minds to come and see me, and yet I was an inexpensive doctor. I spent nights and nights chasing after ten and fifteen francs in little courtyards with no moon.

In the morning the street sounded like a drum with the beating of carpets. One morning I met Bébert, the concierge's nephew, raising a cloud on the pavement with a broom; his aunt was out shopping and he was keeping the lodge for her.

At Rancy whoever failed to raise his own little whirlpool of dust around seven o'clock was looked upon in his own street as a pretty dirty sort of skunk. You flapped your mat out of doors, a sign of cleanliness, and that meant that you kept your house in decent order. That was enough. Your breath might be foul, but after that you were O.K. Bébert was swallowing all the dust he raised as well as what was beating out over him from the upper windows. A few streaks of sunlight did reach the ground, but it was like the inside of a church, pale, soft, mystical beams of sunlight.

Bébert saw me coming. I was the doctor who lived on the corner, where the busses stop. Too green he looked, Bébert, an apple that would never ripen properly. He was scratching himself and it made me want to scratch too. I had my fleas as well, it's true, caught off sick people at night. They hop into your overcoat eagerly enough; it's the warmest, dampest place they can find. You're taught all about that at the Faculty.

Bébert stopped sweeping to wish me good-day. They watched us talking from every window.

If it's a question of loving something, it's less of a risk to love children than grown men; you always have the excuse of at least hoping that they'll be more decent than you are yourself, later on. You can't be sure.

A smile of pure affection which I have never been able to forget danced on his glistening little face. A gay thing for the world to see.

Few people have any particle of that left, after twenty years, any of ready animal affection. The world is not what one thought. That's all. So one has altered the expression on one's face. God, yes — and not just a little, either. One was wrong. . . . And damnably tough one's become in no time at all! That is what shows on your face twenty years later. There's been a mistake made. One's face is just a mistake.

"Hey, Doctor!" Bébert said to me, "Didn't they pick up a chap on the Place des Fêtes last night with his throat slit across by a razor? Weren't you on duty? It's true, isn't it?"

"No, I wasn't on duty, Bébert. It wasn't me, it was Doctor Frolichon."

"Oh, that's too bad. My aunt said she hoped it would have been you and that you could have told her all about it."

"It'll have to wait till the next time, Bébert, I'm afraid."

"They often kill guys around here, don't they?" Bébert remarked. I crossed his puddle of dust but the municipal sweeper rumbled past at that moment and a great typhoon swirled up from the gutters, filling the whole street with even thicker and more peppery clouds of dust. You couldn't see a thing. Bébert skipped about with joy, sneezing and yelping. His haggard little face, his mop of greasy hair, his legs like an emaciated monkey's, all bobbed about convulsively at the end of his broom.

Bébert's aunt came back from shopping. She'd already had her little tot of something and she smelt slightly too of ether; that was a habit she'd picked up once when she worked for a doctor and had had such aches in her wisdom-teeth. She only had two teeth left in the front of her mouth but these she brushed assiduously. "When you have worked for a doctor, like I have, you know what hygiene means." She gave medical consultations in the neighbourhood, and further afield, as far as Bezons.

I should have liked to know whether Bébert's aunt ever thought about anything. No, she didn't think at all. She talked a hell of a lot without thinking at all. When we were alone, with no possible eavesdroppers about, she would try to get free medical advice out of me. It was flattering, in a sort of way.

"Bébert, Doctor — I can tell you because you're a medical man — is a nasty, dirty little boy! He abuses himself. I've noticed it going on for two months now and I can't think who can have taught him such a loathsome habit. I've always brought him up well. . . . I tell him he mustn't. But he won't listen to me."

"Tell him he'll go mad," I said: classical advice.

Bébert, who was listening, wasn't a bit pleased. "I don't; it's not true. It was the Gagat kid who suggested I — "

"There you are, you see; I thought so," said his aunt. "You know the Gagats, the people on the fifth floor? They are a vicious family. It seems that the grandfather used to go in for flagellation. . . .

Ugh, I ask you, flagellation! Look, Doctor, while we're on the subject, couldn't you make him out a syrup of some kind that would stop him playing with himself?"

I followed her into the lodge to prescribe an anti-vice tonic for little Bébert. Of course I was too kind to every one, I realize that. No one ever paid me. I gave consultations on sight, chiefly out of curiosity. It's a mistake. People revenge themselves for the kindnesses you do them. Bébert's aunt, like all the rest, took advantage of my being so disinterested and proud, the most unfair advantage. I did nothing about it. I let myself be fooled. These sick people had me in their power, they snivelled more and more each day, they led me by the nose. And at the same time they showed me, one after another, all the horrible deformities hidden away in their hearts which they revealed to no one but me. Such hideousness cannot be adequately paid for. It slips through your fingers like a slimy snake.

I'll spill it all one day, if I can live long enough to tell everything. "Listen, you swine! Let me be nice to you for a few more years; don't kill me yet. Just look humble and helpless and I'll tell you everything. I promise you that. And you'll suddenly turn tail like those sticky caterpillars that used to crawl around my hut in Africa, and I will make you more cunningly cowardly and obscene than ever, so much so that at the last maybe you'll die of it."

"Is it sweet?" asked Bébert, meaning the syrup.

"For heaven's sake, don't make it sweet," the aunt said; "dirty little beast! He doesn't deserve it should be sweet, and anyway, he steals enough sugar from me as it is. He is thoroughly naughty, thoroughly depraved! He'll end up by murdering his mother!"

"I haven't got a mother," Bébert flatly retorted, knowing exactly what he was about.

"Hell!" said his aunt. "I'll lay across you with the broom handle, if you answer me back." She went and seized the broom, but Bébert had slipped out into the street. "You vicious old thing!" he shouted at her from the doorway. His aunt blushed and came back into the lodge. There was a silence. We changed the conversation.

"Doctor, perhaps you ought to go and see the lady at Number 4, Rue des Mineures. The husband used to work at the notary's office; he's been told about you. I said you were the kindest doctor in the world with ill people."

I knew at once that Bébert's aunt was going to lie to me. Frolichon is her favourite doctor. She always recommends him when she can, and me she invariably runs down if she gets the chance. My humanitarianism makes her hate me in a thoroughly animal way. After all, she is an animal, one mustn't forget that. Only Frolichon, whom she admires, makes her pay on the nail, so she consults me on the quiet. It must be an absolutely gratuitous visit for her to have recommended me, or else some extremely shady affair. But as I left, I remembered Bébert.

"You ought to take him for walks," I said; "the kid doesn't get out enough."

"Where could the two of us go? I can't stray far from my lodge."

"Well, take him to the Park on Sundays then."

"But the Park's even more full of people and dust than this place is! You're all on top of one another."

She's quite right in what she says. I think of somewhere else to suggest.

Timidly, I suggest the cemetery. The cemetery at Garenne-Rancy is the only place of any size in the whole neighbourhood where there are a few trees.

"Why, that's true, I hadn't thought of that; we could go there, of course!" At that moment Bébert reappeared.

"Listen, Bébert, would you like to go for walks in the cemetery? I have to ask him, Doctor, because he's as obstinate as a mule about walks, you know. . . ."

As a matter of fact, Bébert has no opinion on the subject. But the aunt is pleased with the idea, and that is enough. She has a weakness for cemeteries, like all Parisians. You'd say that on this point she was really about to do some thinking. She considers all the pros and cons. The town walls are *infra dig.* . . . The Park is too dusty. . . . But the cemetery now, the cemetery's all right. And the people who go there on Sundays are on the whole respectable people who behave themselves properly. And, besides, it's very convenient, because you can do your shopping in the Boulevard de la Liberté on the way back; some of the shops are kept open there on Sundays.

Yes, that was it. "Bébert," she concluded, "take the Doctor round to Madame Henrouille's in the Rue des Mineures. You know where Madame Henrouille lives, don't you, Bébert?"

Bébert knows where every place is, as long as it's an excuse for a stroll.

Between the Rue Ventru and the Place Lénine there is nothing now but tenement houses. Contractors have taken over everything that was left of the country there, Les Garennes, as it was called. There is just a wee bit of it left, on the outskirts, a few vague strips of land beyond the last gas lamp.

A detached house or two survives and moulders away, sandwiched between the larger buildings: four rooms with a large stove in the passage downstairs. For the sake of economy, the stove is kept barely alight. It smokes in the damp atmosphere. These are the detached dwellings, such as remain, of people with a certain amount of invested capital. They are not rich people who have stayed on here; certainly the Henrouilles weren't, whom I'd been sent to see. But all the same, they were folks with a certain little something put by.

The Henrouilles' house, when you went into it, smelt, besides the smoke, of lavatories and stew. The place had just been paid for. That had meant fifty long years of scraping for the Henrouilles. As soon as you went in there and saw them, you wondered what was the matter with them both. Well, the matter with the Henrouilles, what was all wrong about them, was never in fifty years having spent a penny, either of them, without regretting it. They had a house fashioned as it were out of their own flesh and personal endeavour, like a snail. But a snail manages to do that without fussing about it.

The Henrouilles, on the other hand, couldn't get over having gone through life merely so as to have a house, and that gave them a very strange look, like people who have just been dug out of some place alive. People must pull very odd faces when they are taken out of an *oubliette*.

Before they were married the Henrouilles had already thought of buying a house. First each thought of it on his own, then they both thought of it together. They had refused to think of anything else for half a century, and when life had forced them to think of something else, of the war, for instance, and above all of their son, it had made them quite ill.

When, as a newly married couple, they had moved into their little house, each with ten years' savings in hand, it wasn't quite finished. It still stood in the middle of the fields. In winter you needed your *sabots* to get to it; you left them at the fruiterer's at the corner of the Rue Révolte in the morning, when you went to work, at six o'clock, by horse tram to Paris, three kilometres away, for a penny.

You need to have very good health to get through a whole lifetime doing that. There was a photograph of them over the bed, on the first floor, taken on their wedding day. Their bedroom, all their bedroom furniture, had been paid for a long time ago. All the bills that have been paid these ten, twenty, forty years are lying pinned together in the top drawer of the chest of drawers, and the book in which the accounts are kept, right up to date, is downstairs in the dining room, where no one ever eats. Henrouille will show you all these things if you ask him. On Saturdays he balances the accounts in the dining room. They themselves have always eaten in the kitchen.

I learned all that, bit by bit, from them and then from other people and finally from Bébert's aunt. When I got to know them better, they themselves told me their great fear, the worry of their whole lives, that their son, their one and only son, who was in business, might do badly. For thirty years that awful thought had pretty well spoiled their sleep at night. In the pen business, that boy of theirs. Just think what ups and downs there have been in the pen trade these last thirty years! There probably hasn't been a worse, a more uncertain business than the pen trade.

Of course, there are some businesses that are so bad you do not even think of borrowing money to put them on their feet again, but there are others which entail borrowing almost all the time. When they thought of a loan like that, even now with the house paid for and all, the Henrouilles would get up from their chairs and look at each other and blush. What would they do in a case like that? They would refuse.

They had decided from the first to refuse to lend any sum however small, ever. . . . For the sake of their principles and so as to keep something for their son, a legacy, the house, his patrimony. That's the way they had thought it out. He was a sensible lad, it's true, their son, but it's so easy in business to be led astray. . . .

When they asked me, I thought exactly as they did.

My mother too had had a business. And her business had never brought us in anything but sorrow, a little bread and a lot of trouble. So I had no love of business, either. I could understand at once the danger this boy was in, the possibility of his having to consider borrowing money to get out of some tight corner. There was no need to explain these things to me. Papa Henrouille himself had worked for fifty years as a small clerk in a notary's office on the Boulevard Sébastopol. So he knew any amount of cases of ruined fortunes. He told me one or two, hair-raising ones. His own father's in the first place; it was because of his father going bankrupt that Henrouille hadn't been able to go in for teaching but had had to start right away and become a clerk. You don't easily forget that sort of thing.

Then at last their house was really their own, properly paid for and all, not a penny owing, and they had nothing more to worry about, either of them, with regard to their financial security. That was in their sixty-sixth year.

Just then he began to feel somewhat unwell; or rather he had really had this thing a long time now, but he hadn't thought about it, because there was still the house to be paid for. When that was all arranged and settled and signed, he began to think about his curious malady. It was a kind of dizziness that came over him and a whistling in both his ears like steam.

It was about that time too that he began to buy a daily paper, as they could afford it now. There was a bit in the paper, as a matter of fact, telling all about what Henrouille felt in his ears. So he bought the medicine which the advertisement recommended, but it didn't make any difference to how he felt; quite the reverse; the whistling seemed to get louder than ever. Louder perhaps because he thought more about it? Anyway, the two of them went and saw the doctor at the hospital. "It's heightened blood pressure," he told them.

The phrase made a big impression on him. But really this new worry came to him at just the right time. He had worried himself so sick for such a number of years over the house and his son's reverses that now there was a sort of sudden gap in the fabric of continual anxiety which through year after year of liabilities had hemmed him in and kept him in a state of craven agitation. Now that the doctor had spoken to him of the pressure of blood in his arteries, he listened to its throbbing deep in his ear, against his pillow. He even got out of bed to feel his pulse and then he would stand there in the darkness a long time beside his bed, feeling his body shake in little soft throbs as his heart beat. It was going to kill him, that throbbing, he told himself; he had always been frightened of life; now there was something else he feared — his death, his own blood pressure — just as for forty years he had feared not being able to finish the payments on his house.

He had always been unhappy, as unhappy as he was now, but all the same he had to set to and find a good new reason for being miserable. It isn't quite as easy as it looks. It is not merely a question of saying: "I'm unhappy." You've got to prove it to yourself, convince yourself definitely. That was all he wanted: to be able to find a good, solid reason for the fear he felt, a reason that really counted. The doctor had said he had a pressure of twenty-two. Twenty-two is a good deal. The doctor had taught him how to find his own way towards Death.

Their son, the pen manufacturer, practically never put in an appearance. Once or twice around Christmas time he came to see them. And that was all. But really he could often have come to see them now. Papa and Mamma had nothing left to lend. Anyway, he had practically given up coming.

It took me longer to get to know Madame Henrouille; she had no fear on her mind, not even the fear of her own death, which did not enter her thoughts. She only complained of getting old, but it didn't really bother her; it was just that everybody else did the same; and she complained that life was "getting dearer." Their life's work had been accomplished. The house was paid for. So, to settle the last bills a bit sooner, she had started to sew buttons onto waistcoats for one of the great stores. "It's unbelievable how many you've got to sew on to earn five francs!" And then to go and deliver her work, there was always the business of taking a second-class ticket on the bus; and one evening too she'd been roughly handled. A foreign woman had done it, the first and the only foreigner she had ever spoken to in her life; and then only to shout insults at her.

The walls of their house had been dry in the old days, when air circulated freely all round it, but now that tall houses closed it in on all sides, everything was damp in the house; even the curtains were stained with moisture.

When the house had become theirs, Madame Henrouille's face was a happy and smiling one for a whole month afterwards; she was as delighted as a nun after communion. She it was who had said to Henrouille: "You know, Jules, from now on we can take the paper every day, we can afford it. . . ." Just like that she said it. She had thought of her husband, she had taken a look at him, and then after that she had taken a look round and she had thought of his mother, Mother-in-law Henrouille. And then she grew serious again all of a sudden, as she had been before the house was entirely paid for. And that is how it all began all over again, when that thought came to her, because there was further saving to be done because of that old mother of her husband, whom they seldom mentioned among themselves or to any one outside the family.

She lived down at the bottom of the garden amid an accumulation of old brooms and chicken crates and all the shadows of the neighbouring buildings. She lived in a low shed, which she practically never came out of. And it was a tremendous business just to get her her food. She would not let any one into her shelter, not even her son. She was afraid of being murdered, she said.

When the idea came to the daughter-in-law of saving a bit more, she tried just hinting at the subject in a few words at first to her husband, feeling her way, to see if, for instance, they couldn't send the old lady to St. Vincent's Convent, where the nuns looked after poor old things of that sort. The son did not say yes and he didn't say no. Something else was on his mind at the moment, those noises in his ears which never stopped. He worried about them and listened to them until he told himself that these awful sounds would stop him getting to sleep. And indeed he did listen to them instead of falling asleep, whistlings, drummings, rumblings . . . It was a new torment. He fretted about it all day and all night. He was carrying every sort of noise inside his head.

Bit by bit, though, as months of this sort of thing went by, his worry began to wear out and there wasn't enough of it left to take up all his time. So then he went to market with his wife at Saint-Ouen. The market of Saint-Ouen was the cheapest in the neighbourhood, it was said. They started out in the morning for the whole day, which they spent adding up and commenting on the prices of different articles, and calculating what they could have saved if instead of doing one thing they had done something else. . . . At about eleven in the evening at home they would begin to be afraid once more of being murdered. It was quite a regular fear with them. He felt it less than she did. It was mostly those noises in his ears which he would cling to desperately at that hour of the evening when it was very quiet outside in the street. "I'll never be able to sleep if this goes on!" he'd say to himself out loud, so as to upset himself still more. "You've no idea what it's like!"

But she had never tried to understand what he meant, nor to imagine what chafed him so about the buzzing in his ears. "You can hear me all right, can't you?" she'd ask him.

"Yes," he told her.

"Well, that's all right then. You would do better to think about your mother, who costs us such a lot, and about the way prices are going up every day. . . . And her quarters, which have become so poisonously dirty. . . ."

The charwoman who came to them three hours each week to do the washing was the only visitor they had had for many years. She also helped Madame Henrouille to make her bed, and so that the charwoman should be certain of repeating it about the neighbourhood, every time in ten years that they turned the mattress together, Madame Henrouille would announce in as loud a tone as possible: "We never keep any money in the house." This was meant as a hint and a warning, so as to discourage burglars and possible murderers.

Before they went up to their room, they went the rounds together, shutting all the doors and windows, one of them supervising the other. Then they went along to the shed at the bottom of the garden, to see if Mother-in-law's lamp was still alight. That showed that she was still alive. She burned an awful lot of oil. That lamp was never put out. She too was frightened of murderers, and frightened of her son and daughter at the same time. She had lived there for twenty years and she had never opened her windows, winter or summer, and she had never put out the lamp.

Her son kept his mother's money for her, her little income. He looked after it carefully. Her meals were left on her doorstep for her. And they kept her money. It was the proper way to do things. But she complained about this arrangement, and not only about that; she complained about everything. Through her closed door she shouted abuse at any one who came near her hut. "It's not my fault if you are growing old, Grandma," the daughter-in-law would try to reason with her. "You have your ailments like all old people have. . . ."

"Old yourself, you little slut! You're a bad lot, you are! You'll be killing me yourself one of these days with your foul trickeries!"

She denied her age ferociously, old Mother-in-law Henrouille. . . . Inside her redoubt, she battled irreconcilably against the buffetings of the whole wide world. She stuck out against the contact, the fates, the resignation of the outside world like a dirty imposture. She wouldn't hear a word about all that. "Lies and trickery!" she'd shout. "You made it all up yourself!"

She defended herself with terrific stubbornness against everything that went on outside her broken-down abode and against all enticements towards a good understanding or any form of reconciliation. She was quite certain that if she opened her door the enemy forces would rush in on her and seize hold of her, and that then the game would really be up.

"They're very cunning nowadays," she'd shout. "They've got eyes all round their heads and they're full of gaping mouths all over them, and all they do is lie . . . That is what they are like . . ."

She talked in a harsh voice, as she had learned to talk in Paris at the Temple Market as a little girl, a peddler there with her mother. She came of a time when the young people had not yet learnt to hear themselves grow old.

"I shall have to get some work to do if you won't give me my money," she would shout to her daughter-in-law. "Do you hear me, you hussy? I want work!"

"But you're not strong enough, Grandma!"

"Oh, I'm not strong enough, aren't I? Try coming into my kennel — I'll soon show you whether I'm strong enough or not!"

So they left her to look after herself for a while in her hut. All the same, they insisted on showing me the old lady, by hook or by crook; that's what I had come for, and all sorts of subterfuges were necessary before she'd receive us. But I couldn't really make out what was wanted of me. Bébert's aunt, the concierge, had told them I was a nice doctor, a very kind and easy-going man. . . . They wanted to know if I could make the old woman keep quiet just by giving her some medicines to take. . . . But what they really wanted more, at bottom (particularly the daughter-in-law) was that I should get her shut up for them once and for all. . . . After we had knocked at her door for a good half hour, she finally flung it open suddenly, and popped out there in front of me, with her watery red eyes. . . . But a bright expression danced in them above her flaccid, grey cheeks, a lively glance which you noticed at once and which made you forget all the rest, because it was light and youthful and gave you a feeling of pleasure, in spite of yourself, and instinctively you found yourself trying to remember and retain something of it afterwards.

This gay glance of hers enlivened everything in the shadows round with something young and blithe about it, a minute but sparkling enthusiasm of a kind we no longer possess. Her voice, which was hoarse when she shouted, sounded sprightly and charming when she talked normally; then she made her words and her sentences frisk about and skip and come bouncing merrily back, as people could with their voices and everything in the days when not to be able to tell a story well or sing a song when necessary was considered feeble, deplorable and stupid.

Age had covered her, like an old, swaying tree, with jaunty branches.

She was a gay old Henrouille; discontented and grimy, yet gay. The bleakness she had lived in for more than twenty years had affected her spirit not at all. On the contrary, it was from the outside world that she had shrunk in self-defence, as if the growing cold and all the frightfulness and death itself were to come to her from there, not from inside. From inside herself she seemed to fear nothing. She seemed certain of her own head as of something definite and solid and understood, understood once and for all.

And there was I, always chasing after mine, chasing it all over the world.

Mad, they said she was, "mad"; it's easily said. She hadn't come out of her burrow more than three times in twelve years, that's all it was! Maybe she had her own reasons. . . . She didn't want to lose anything. . . . She wasn't going to tell *us* though, who wouldn't have been wise enough to understand her, anyway.

Her daughter harked back to her scheme of getting the old lady shut up. "Don't you think that she is mad, Doctor? We can't get her to go out. . . . And yet that would do her good occasionally. . . . Yes, Grandma, it would do you good, really it would. . . . Don't say that it wouldn't! I assure you it would do you good." The old woman shook her head, firmly, obstinately, angrily, when she was spoken to like that.

"She won't let us look after her properly. . . . The shed's in a filthy mess. It's cold in there and she hasn't a fire. . . . Really, we can't have her going on living like that. We can't, can we, Doctor?"

I pretended not to understand. As for Henrouille, he had stayed behind by the stove; he preferred not to know exactly what we were all up to, his wife, his mother and me.

Then the old lady became angry again.

"Give me back all my belongings and I tell you I'll go away from here! I have enough to live on! You need never hear of me again! And we'll have done with all this once and for all."

"Enough to live on? But, Grandma, you'd never be able to get along on your three thousand francs a year, Grandma! Living has become much more expensive since the last time you went out. Wouldn't it be ever so much better, Doctor, if she were to go and live with the Sisters, as we tell her she should? The Sisters would look after her well. . . . They're so sweet and good."

But the prospect of St. Vincent's horrified her.

"Me go to the Sisters? The Sisters?" she rejoined at once. "I've never been to them yet. . . . Why shouldn't I go to the curé while you're about it? Eh? If I haven't enough money, as you say, well then, I'll go to work again!"

"Work? Why, Grandmamma! Where will you work? Ah, Doctor, just listen to that! Work — at her age! When she's nearly eighty! That's madness, Doctor. Who would dream of taking her? You're mad, Grandma!"

"Mad! Nonsense! Not at all! But *you're* certainly wrong somewhere, you dirty little beast!"

"Listen to her, Doctor — raving and insulting me! How do you expect us to keep her here?"

Then the old lady turned to me, against me, her new danger.

"How does that man know whether I am mad or not? Is *he* inside my head? Or inside yours? Would he have to be to know? Clear out, both of you! Go away, leave my house! You are wickeder than a hell full of devils, the way you bully me! Why don't you go and see my son, instead of standing here, jabbering drivel among the weeds. . . . He needs a doctor far more than I do. He hasn't any teeth left, that son of mine, and he used to have such beautiful teeth when I looked after him. Go on, go on, get out, I tell you, the two of you!" And she banged the door in our faces.

She peered out at us from behind her lamp, watching us go away up the court. When we had crossed it, when we were far enough away, she began to laugh. She had defended herself well.

On our return from this unpleasant expedition, Henrouille was still standing by the stove, with his back turned to us. But his wife went on harrying me with questions, all of them with a single meaning. . . . She had a little round, dark head. She kept her elbows glued to her sides while she talked, making no gestures of any sort. But she was very keen that this visit of the doctor's should not be wasted, that it should serve some purpose. . . . The cost of living was going up every day. . . . The mother-in-law's contribution was no longer enough. . . . After all, they too were growing old. . . . They could not always live in fear of the old lady dying without proper care, as they had in the past. . . . Of her setting fire to the place, for example. . . . Of her dying amid fleas and filth like that. Instead of going to a nice, proper asylum, where they would look after her well. . . .

As I looked as if I agreed with them, they became even more amiable, both of them. . . . They promised to say a lot of nice things about me in the neighbourhood. . . . If I would only help them, take pity on them. Rid them of the old woman. . . . She must be so unhappy herself in the surroundings she so obstinately insisted on living in.

"And we might be able to let her cottage," the husband suggested, suddenly waking up. . . . A *faux pas*, talking like that in front of me. His wife trod on his foot under the table. He couldn't understand why.

While they wrangled, I thought of the thousand franc note I could so easily pocket just by signing that certificate of madness for them. They seemed to want it frightfully badly. . . . Bébert's aunt had probably told them all about me and explained that there wasn't another doctor in all Rancy in such miserable straits. . . . That I could be had for the asking. . . . Frolichon

they wouldn't have offered a job like that to. Frolichon was
straight, a virtuous man.

I was quite absorbed in these reflections when the old woman
burst into the room where we sat plotting. You'd have said she
had guessed as much. What a surprise! She had caught up her
full skirts against her stomach and here she was, like that, suddenly letting fly at us and at me in particular. She had come
from the bottom of her courtyard just for this.

"Blackguard!" she yelled straight at me. "You can go now,
I've told you so already — get out! There's no point in your
staying here. I'm not going to any madhouse, I tell you, and I
won't go to the convent either! You can talk and lie as much
as you like — you won't get *me*, you rascal! These rogues will
go before me, these fleecers of an old woman! And you too,
you scum, you'll go to gaol, let me tell you, and pretty damn
quick!"

I was out of luck all right. Just when there was a thousand
francs going begging at one fell swoop! I left at once.

When I was back in the street she leaned out over a little
balcony to shout after me, far in the darkness that was hiding
me. "You cad! You swine!" she yelled. The echoes rang with it.
Damn the rain. I ran from one lamp-post to the next as far as
the public convenience on the Place des Fêtes — the first shelter
there was.

IN THE COMFORT STALL, LEG-HIGH, I FOUND BÉBERT. HE TOO HAD gone in there looking for shelter. He had seen me running when I left the Henrouilles. "Have you come from their place?" he asked. "They want you now on the fifth floor at home, to see the daughter. . . ." I knew this girl he spoke of well, with her broad hips, her long downy thighs, and something yielding and tender about her, that graceful precision of movement which completes women who are well-balanced sexually. She had come to see me several times since something had gone wrong with her stomach. In her twenty-fifth year, after her third miscarriage, she was suffering from complications, which her family called anæmia.

She was wonderfully well-built and solid, with a liking for copulation such as few females have. She was discreet in her mode of life, careful in speech and behaviour. Not in the least hysterical. But a gifted, well-nourished, balanced creature; a real champion in her own class, that's all. A beautiful athlete in pursuit of pleasure. There's nothing wrong with that. She only went with married men. And they were all of them people she knew well, men capable of recognizing and appreciating a fine natural success, men who don't take any vicious little bit for a real affair. No, her creamy skin, her charming smile, her walk and the noble proportions and swing of her hips won for her the genuine and just admiration of certain business men who knew what they were about.

Only of course these business men couldn't just divorce their wives on that account. On the contrary, it was a good reason for remaining happily married. So each time she was three months gone with child — it never failed — she went round to see the midwife. When you've a certain amount of spirit and you haven't a cuckold in hand, life is no laughing matter all of the time.

Her mother half-opened the landing door for me as cautiously as if I might have been going to assassinate her. She was whispering, but she whispered so loudly, so excitedly, that it was worse than if she had cursed me.

"Heavens above, what can I have done, Doctor, to have deserved such a daughter? Oh, but you won't tell anybody in the district, will you, Doctor? I rely on you . . ." She went on and on, flapping with fright and moaning about what the neighbours might think. She was in an hypnotic state of nervous imbecility. Such states go on for quite a time.

She let me get used to the dim light in the corridor, to the smell of leeks for the soup, to the wall paper and the idiotic mutterings and her own strangled voice. Finally, amid much senseless talk and exclamations, we came to her daughter's bedside; there lay the patient, utterly prostrate. I attempted to examine her, but she was losing blood so freely, there was such a mass of blood, that I couldn't examine her properly. Clots of it. It was spluttering between her legs as from the decapitated colonel's neck in the war. I simply put back the great wad of cotton and pulled up the coverlet.

The mother could see nothing, she could only hear herself talking. "I shall die, Doctor, I shall die of shame!" she wailed. I didn't attempt to dissuade her. I did not know what to do. In the little dining room next door we could see the father pacing up and down. He did not seem to have been able to make up his mind what attitude to take in the circumstances. Perhaps he was waiting for things to take some definite turn before choosing a point of view. He remained in an entirely vague state of mind. People move from one piece of play-acting to the next. While the stage isn't set, they cannot envisage its form or what their proper part is, so they stand there, doing nothing, in the face of whatever's happened, their impulses hanging loose like an unrolled umbrella, wavering incoherently, reduced to their simple selves, reduced to nothing. Lost sheep.

But the mother now, she had the leading part, as intermediary between her daughter and myself. She didn't give a damn what happened to the play; it was all set and she was having a wonderful time.

I had only myself to count on to break this disgusting charm.

I hazarded the suggestion that the girl should be removed at once to the hospital to be operated on immediately.

Alas, what a mistake! I had played straight into her hands, providing her with the perfect answer, the one she had been hoping for.

"What a disgrace! To the hospital, Doctor! What a disgrace for us! That is all that was needed — the last straw!"

There was nothing more I could say. I sat down and listened to the mother carrying on more noisily than ever, wailing her tragic absurdities. Too great a humiliation, too much trouble leads to absolute inertia. The world is too heavy a burden for you to lift. You give up. While she invoked heaven and hell, howling with misery, I hung my head and discovered a little pool of blood forming under the girl's bed and a trickle threading slowly along the wall towards the door. A drop fell regularly from the mattress. Plop. Plop. The towels were scarlet now between her legs. All the same I did ask, timidly, whether the placenta had come away entirely yet. The girl's pale hands, bluish at the tips, hung down loose on each side of the bed. My question was answered by the mother with a further flood of awful lamentations. But to pull myself together was really more than I could do.

I had been so long overcome by depression myself, I'd been sleeping so badly, that in this chaos I was no longer in the least interested as to whether any one thing happened before anything else. I only reflected that it was easier to be listening to this mother's wailings sitting down than standing up. It doesn't take much to give you satisfaction when you have become really resigned. Besides, what strength of will would have been necessary to interrupt this wild creature just when she "didn't know how she was going to save her family honour!" What a game! And how she yelled! After each abortion, I knew from experience, she behaved in the same way, trying of course to improve on herself each time. She would go on like this as long as she felt like it. . . . To-day she seemed to me ready to quadruple her efforts.

She too, I thought, as I looked at her, must have been a beautiful, a juicy piece in her time; but more talkative, I should say;

wasteful of her energies, more demonstrative than the daughter whose quiet, concentrated intimacy was a truly admirable achievement of Nature's. These things have not yet been studied in the marvellous way they deserve. The girl's mother guessed her daughter's animal superiority over her and jealously disapproved by instinct of her gift for tremendous delights, for enjoyment to her innermost depths.

Anyway, the theatrical side of this disaster absolutely thrilled her. Her mournful tremolos filled our little shrunken world, in which we were all merely mucking about, thanks to her. And one couldn't dream of getting her away from it. Still, I ought to have tried, of course. Tried to do something. It was my duty to, as they say. But I was too comfortable sitting down and too uncomfortable standing up.

It was a bit pleasanter at their place than at the Henrouilles; just as ugly but more comfortable. Quite cosy, really. Not sinister like the other hole, only just plain ugly.

Dazed and tired, my eyes wandered round the things in the room. Little valueless bits and pieces which had always been in the family; particularly the mantelpiece cover with pink velvet bobbles which you no longer find in shops now, and the Neapolitan porcelain, and a work table with a bevelled mirror, probably from an aunt in the provinces who'd had two of them. I didn't tell the mother about the pool of blood which I could see forming under the bed nor about the regular dripping which was still going on — she would only have shouted the louder and wouldn't have listened to me. She was never going to stop complaining and waxing indignant. No, she was committed to it.

As well hold one's peace and look out through the window at the grey velvet of evening beginning to cover the street opposite, house by house, — first the little ones and then the others; the tallest at last are taken too, and people scurry about among them, more and more slowly, doubtful and dim, hesitating across from one side of the street to the other before going off into the darkness.

Further away, far beyond the town walls, strings and clusters of little lights were dotted about the shadows like nails fastening forgetfulness across the town, and other little lights there were twinkling among the green ones, — spangles of red light, as if lots and lots of boats, a whole fleet come from far, were waiting there all of a shimmer for the great gates of the Night to open before them.

If this woman had only stopped for a second to breathe, if only there had been a great moment of silence, one could at least have let oneself renounce everything; one could have tried to forget the need to live. But she was on my tracks the whole time.

"Perhaps if I were to wash her, Doctor? What d'you think?" I answered neither yes nor no, but as I had the chance to speak, I again advised immediate removal to the hospital. More yelping, sharper still, more strident, more determined, in answer. Hopeless.

I went slowly towards the door, treading softly.

The shadows now separated us from the bed.

I could barely see the girl's hands now against the sheet, they looked so much the same in colour.

I went back and felt her pulse. Its beats were weaker, more fleeting than before. Her breath came only in snatches. I still could hear the blood dripping to the floor like the ticking of a watch going slower and slower, becoming more and more feeble. There was nothing to be done. The mother went before me to the door.

"Above all, Doctor," she urged me breathlessly, "promise me that you won't say a word about this to any one?" She implored me. "Swear you won't?"

I promised anything, everything. I held out my hand. Twenty francs. She shut the door after me, little by little.

Bébert's aunt was waiting for me downstairs with the proper grave expression on her face. "How's it going then? Badly?" she asked me. I realized that she had been waiting for me down there for the last half-hour to get her usual commission: two francs. I wasn't going to be allowed to dodge that. "And how did it go with the Henrouilles?" she enquired. She expected her *pourboire* on that too. "They did not pay me," I answered. Perfectly true. Her smile disappeared and her expression changed. She suspected me.

"It's an unfortunate thing not to be able to get people to pay you, though, Doctor. How do you expect people to respect you? Bills are either paid right away or they don't get paid at all." Perfectly true, too. I went away. I had put my beans on to boil before I went out. Now was the time, after dusk, to go and buy the milk. In the daytime people smiled when they met me in the street, carrying my bottle of milk. Naturally. No maid.

And then the winter dragged on, spreading out over months and weeks. There was no way out of the rain and the fog in which we were sunk.

There were plenty of patients now, but few of them could or would pay my fees. The medical is an invidious profession. When one's practice is among the rich, one looks like a lackey; when it's among the poor, like a thief. Fees! What a business it is! The people who're ill haven't enough money to buy food and go to the cinema with — and then are you going to take what money they have to make up your fees? Just when they are having a particularly thin time of it, too? It's not very pleasant. You let it go. You become kindly. And you go to bits.

When January's rent became due, I started by selling my sideboard — to make more room, as I told people, and be able to give physical culture classes in my dining room. Who believed me? In February, to pay my income tax, I sold my bicycle and the gramophone Molly had given me as a parting present. It played "No More Worries." The tune has stuck in my head to this day. And it's all I have left. Bézin had my records around in his shop a long time, and then finally they too were sold.

So as to give an impression of even greater prosperity, I announced that I was going to buy myself a motor car when the good weather came, and that was why I was selling off a few things first. I wasn't really hard-boiled enough to be able to go in for doctoring seriously. When people came back with me to the door, after I had told the family what to do and had written out my prescription, I would launch out on a whole series of general remarks, just to put off a little longer the moment for being paid. I didn't know my own business. Most of my patients were so wretchedly poor, so dingy, and also so morose, that I always wondered where they were going to find twenty francs to give me, and if they might not kill me in revenge. Yet I needed those twenty francs very badly myself. What humiliation! I shall blush for it for the rest of my life.

And my colleagues go on blithely talking about "fees"! As if the word were enough in itself and explained everything. . . . I could not help crying "Shame!" myself, and there was no way out of that. Everything can be explained away, I realize that. But it does not alter the fact that the man who has taken five francs from poor, disgruntled wretches is a scoundrel for the rest of his days. In fact, it was from this time on that I have known myself to be as dirty a blackguard as any. It's not that I lived wildly and wickedly on their five and ten-franc payments. No, indeed. Because the landlord got most of it, anyway. But even so, that's no excuse. One would like it to be an excuse, but it isn't quite. The landlord's lower than dirt, of course; that's all there is to that.

Through getting all upset in this way and walking about in the icy winter rain, I began to look like a tubercular case myself. Naturally. That's what happens when one has to give up all pleasures. From time to time I would buy myself a couple of eggs somewhere, but my actual diet was really only plain vegetables. They take a long time to cook. I spent hours in the kitchen after consulting time, watching them simmer, and as I lived on the first floor, I got a beautiful view from there of the whole of the back yard. Back yards are the dungeons to a row of apartment houses. I had lots of time to look down into my own, and particularly to listen to it.

Shouts and calls from a score of houses round sail in and clatter and echo there, and even the concierges' little birds chirrup after a spring they will never see again, languishing in their cages near the waterclosets, which are all grouped together in the shadowy depths at the end yonder, with their doors always battered and swinging loose. A hundred drunkards, male and female, inhabit this structure and fill the air with their puffed-up quarrelling and confused, exuberant oaths, especially on Saturdays after lunch. That's the big moment in family life. First there is a lot

of shouting and defiance, when the wine has gone to their heads,
and Father wields a chair, my God, as if it were a battle-axe, while
Mother flourishes a stick of firewood like a sabre. Then the weak
may look to themselves! The littlest one gets it in the neck. A
family scrap flattens everything that cannot retaliate and defend
itself against the wall: children, dogs and cats. After the third
glass of wine, the worst and blackest, it's the dog's turn to suffer;
some one treads heavily on his paw. That will teach him to be
hungry when human beings are hungry too. There's a great laugh
when he runs howling under the bed, like a soul in torment. That's
the signal. Nothing rouses a tipsy woman as much as an animal
in pain and bulls are not always to hand. The argument begins
again vindictively, and as aggressive as an evil dream; the female
sets the pace, shrilly calling her mate to battle. The mêlée ensues
at once, and breakable objects fly in bits. The courtyard is filled
with the fracas, echoing round in the shadows. The children
squeak with terror. They are finding out what Daddy and
Mummy are really like. Their wailings draw the wrath upon
themselves.

I waited several days to hear what sometimes occurred after
these family scenes.

It used to happen opposite my window on the third floor of
the house across the way.

I could not see anything, but I heard well enough.

There is an end to everything. It is not always death, it's often
something else and a good deal worse, particularly in the case
of children.

That's where they lived, these people, above the courtyard, just
where its shadows thinned out a bit. When the mother and father
were alone together, on the days when this thing happened, they
argued at first at length and then a long silence followed. The
thing was brewing. The little girl was needed first; they called
her in. She knew. She started whimpering at once. She knew
what was going to happen to her. Judging by her voice, she must
have been about ten years old. After a good few times I came to
understand what it was the two of them did to her.

First they tied her up; that took a long time; it was like

preparing for an operation. That excited them. "Little beast!" he said. "You filthy little brat!" the mother exclaimed. "You're going to get such a licking!" they both of them cried, while they scolded her for all sorts of things, things which probably they made up. They must have been tying her to the bedposts. All this time the child was whimpering like a mouse in a trap. "Oh, no, you won't escape, I tell you. You won't escape!" the woman went on, and a stream of imprecations followed, as if she were talking to a horse. She was terribly excited. "Be quiet, Mamma!" the little girl answered softly. "Be quiet, Mamma! Whack me — but don't talk like that, Mamma!" She did not escape; she was given a tremendous thrashing. . . . I listened to the end, to be quite certain that that's what was happening. I could not have eaten my beans while that was going on. I could not shut my window either. I wasn't any use at all. I couldn't do anything. I simply stood there and listened as always, as I did everywhere. Still, I think I somehow gained strength listening to this thing, strength to go on further, an odd sort of strength, and next time, I felt, why, next time I would be able to go deeper, and hear other cries that I had not heard yet or which I had not been able to understand before, because there seem always to be some cries beyond those which one has heard, cries which one has not yet heard or understood.

When they had thrashed their daughter until she could not yell any longer, she still cried a bit each time she breathed, a little sobbing cry.

I would hear the man say then, at that point: "Now come on, woman! Quick — now!" Happy as anything.

It was the mother he was saying that to, and then the door into the other room would bang behind them. One day it was she I heard say to him: "Oh, I adore you, Jules, you complete beast! The filthier you were, the more I should love you."

That's how they went together, their concierge told me, against the sink in the kitchen. Any other way they couldn't manage it.

All that I learned about them bit by bit. When I met them in the street, all three together, there was nothing odd about them. They went out for a walk like any ordinary family. The father I also used to see when I passed his shop on the corner of the Boulevard Poincaré, where it said "Shoes For Sensitive Feet" and he was first salesman.

Most of the time our back yard offered nothing but a spectacle of unrelieved hideousness, especially in summer, when it rumbled with the echoes of threats and blows and falls and confused cursing. The sun never reached to the bottom. The yard was seemingly painted with thick blue shadows, deepest in the corners. There were the concierges' little huts, like so many hives. Their husbands peed at night against the dustbins, and that made a noise like thunder in the court.

Washing tried to dry, strung up from one window to another.

After supper the talk in the evening was mostly of horses and racing when there was no brutality going on. But often these discussions on sport also ended pretty badly and there were brawls, and always behind at least one of the windows, for one reason or for another, blows were come to in the end.

In summer too everything smelt strongly. There was no air left in the back yard, only smells. The smell of cauliflower has it, easily, over all other smells. One cauliflower equals ten water-closets, even if they're running over. Every one knows that. The ones on the second floor were often out of order. Madame Cézanne, the concierge from Number 8, would come along then with her forked stick. I used to watch her, battling away. That's how we eventually got into conversation. "Personally," she advised me, "if I were in your place, I'd get pregnant women out of their difficulties. . . . On the quiet like. There are some women in this neighbourhood who live — you've no idea what a life they live! And there is nothing they'd like better than to give you work. . . . It's a fact. There's more to that than attending to tuppenny-ha'penny little clerks with varicose veins. . . . Especially as it means good pay."

Old Cézanne had a tremendous aristocratic scorn, though I don't know where she had got it from, for people who worked.

"Tenants are never happy; you'd think they were prisoners in gaol the way they make things difficult for everybody! . . . Either it's their lavatories are stopped up. . . . Or they've a gas escape somewhere. . . . Or somebody's been opening their letters. . . . There's always some complaint! Always making a damn nuisance of themselves! The other day one of them actually spat into his rent envelope! What do you think of that?"

She even had to give up trying to clear the lavatories sometimes, it was so difficult. "I don't know what they can have put down them, but they might at least not wait till it's dry. . . . I know them! They always let you know when it's too late. They do it on purpose, of course. Where I was before once they had to crack open a drainpipe it was so hard. . . . I don't know what they eat! Cement, I'd say."

NOBODY WILL GET IT OUT OF MY HEAD THAT IT WAS CHIEFLY DUE to Robinson if things were getting me down again. At first I didn't take much notice of this uneasy feeling. I was jogging along more or less all right from one sick bed to the next, but I had grown more restless now than I was before, increasingly so, like in New York, and I had begun to sleep less well than usual, too.

The idea of meeting Robinson again had come to me with a shock; it was like a sort of illness getting hold of me again.

With that whining, worried mug of his, it was as if he was bringing back some kind of bad dream to me, one I hadn't managed to shake off through too many years already. It was putting me right off my stroke.

He had landed back there in front of me. I should never see the end of him. I was sure he must have been looking out for me hereabouts. I certainly hadn't been going out of my way to find him. . . . And he'd be along here for sure, and I would have to get all mixed up in his affairs again. As it was, everything now brought his dirty presence back into my mind. Even the people I could see through my window, who looked so ordinary walking about in the street like that, even they made me think of him, standing there in doorways talking, cuddling each other. . . . Oh, I knew perfectly well what they were after, what they were hiding under that nothing-in-particular look of theirs. To kill others and to kill themselves, that's what they wanted; not right off, of course, but bit by bit, like Robinson, with anything that came to hand,—old sorrows, fresh griefs, still nameless hatreds. . . . Unless there is a war on, a war in full blast, and then the job takes only half the time.

I did not even dare to go out for fear of meeting him.

They had to call me two or three times over before I could

make up my mind to go and see patients. So most often when I got there they had already fetched in some one else. My wits were a jumble, like Life itself. The Rue Saint-Vincent I had only been in once before when they called for me to go and see the people on the third floor at Number 12. They even brought a cab round for me. I recognized the old grandfather at once. He spoke in a whisper and spent a long time wiping his feet on my doormat. A furtive old creature, grey and bent; he wanted me to hurry because his little grandson was ill.

I also remembered his daughter quite well; another fine lassie, now fallen off in looks, yet solid and silent, who had come home more than once to be aborted. Nobody blamed her for it. They only wished to heaven she'd go and get married and have done with it. Especially as she already had a little boy of two who lived at home with his grandparents.

Any little thing made this child ill and when that happened his grandmother, his grandfather and his mother all blubbered together copiously, in chorus, chiefly because he hadn't a real father. It is at such moments that family lapses are most felt. The old people believed, though they did not altogether admit it, that natural-born children are more delicate and more often ill than other children.

In any case the father, the fellow who it was supposed was the father, that is, had gone away, disappeared for good and all. He'd heard such a lot of talk about marriage, this young man, that in the end he had got bored. He must have been quite a way off by now, if he was still running. Nobody had been able to make out why he had deserted her like that, particularly not the girl herself. After all, he had always seemed to get a great deal of fun out of sleeping with her.

So now that the bird had flown, they all three stood round and gazed at the infant and wept. And there you were. She had given herself to this man, she said, "body and soul." It was bound to happen, and according to her, that explained everything. The baby had been born from her body suddenly, leaving it wrinkled and old. The spirit will put up with phrases, but the body is different; it's not so easy to please, it must have muscle.

A body is always something that is true; that is why it's nearly always sad and repulsive to look at. It's true also that I have seldom seen any maternity remove so much youth at one stroke. All that this mother had left, you might say, were her feelings and the breath in her body. Nobody had any further use for her.

Before the arrival of this illegitimate child, the family had lived in a most respectable, church-going quarter of the town; had been living there for years. They didn't all go into exile at Rancy for the fun of it, but to hide away, to disappear in a bunch, to be forgotten. As soon as it was no longer possible to keep the pregnancy a secret from their neighbours, they decided to quit their part of Paris and avoid "talk." Transplantation for the sake of Honour.

At Rancy it did not matter what your neighbours thought; in the first place, they weren't known there and, besides, the local council held the most abominable political beliefs; downright anarchists they were as a matter of fact, the talk of all France, a positive disgrace to the country. In this rapscallion milieu, other people's judgments wouldn't count.

The family had spontaneously punished itself, breaking away from all its relations and its old friends. A thoroughgoing drama, if ever there was one. They had nothing further to lose, they said. They had already lost caste. When you want to lower yourself in your own estimation, you turn to the People.

They didn't complain. They merely tried to comprehend, in fits and starts of weak revolt, what Providence could conceivably have drunk the day it played such a lousy trick on them — of all people.

For the daughter there was only one consolation about life in Rancy — but it was a very great consolation: that of being able to talk freely now to all and sundry about her "new responsibilities." Her lover's desertion of her had awakened a certain longing in a breast aching to be heroic and different. Once assured for the rest of her days of never having exactly the same fate as other women of her class and standing, and with the romance of a life devastated by a first love to fall back on, she accepted with delight the great sorrow which had been meted out to her, and the ravages of Fate became, as a matter of fact, a dramatic godsend to her. She squirmed with unmarried motherhood.

When her father and I entered the dining room, you could barely catch sight of their faces in the dim, economical light; so many splodges reiterating remarks which hung about in shadows heavy with that ancient cruet smell which all old family furniture gives off.

The child in the middle of the table, on its back among its swaddling clothes, let itself be felt. I pressed, to start with, on the wall of its stomach, very carefully and gradually, from the navel downwards, and then, still very gravely, I proceeded to auscultate.

Its heart beat like a kitten's, sharp and fast. Then, suddenly, the child had enough of my fiddling and probing and began to yell, as only one can at that age, incredibly. It was too much. Since Robinson's reappearance, I had been feeling very strange in mind and body, and the screams of this little innocent made a ghastly impression on me. What screams, my God, what screams! I couldn't bear it another second.

No doubt something else too made me behave in that stupid way. I was so furious I couldn't help expressing, out loud, the rancour and the disgust I had been feeling, too long, inside myself.

"Hey," I said to this little screamer, "don't you be in such a hurry, you little fool! There'll be plenty of time yet for you to yell. There'll be time, don't you worry, you little donkey! Pull yourself together. There'll be unhappiness enough later on to make you cry your eyes out and weep yourself silly, if you don't look out!"

"What do you say, Doctor?" the grandmother asked, with a start. I simply answered, "There'll be plenty!"

"What? Plenty of what?" she enquired in a horrified tone.

"You should understand," I told her. "You really should! You're always having things explained to you. Far too often. That's just what's wrong. *Try* to understand. Make an effort!"

"There'll be plenty of what left? What's he saying?" they all three asked each other, and the young woman of the "responsibilities" pulled a devilishly odd face, and then she set to herself and let off a series of stupendous howls. She'd lighted on the most marvellous possible opportunity for a breakdown. And she wasn't letting it slip. What pandemonium! What a havoc and hulla-baloo! What shudderings, and squintings, and chokings! Mar-vellous! I'd certainly torn it.

"He's mad, Mamma," she spluttered and sobbed. "The Doctor's gone mad! Take my little one from him, Mamma!" She was Saving Her Child.

I cannot think why, but she was so overcome she began to speak with a Basque accent. "He's saying frightful things, Mother! Mother, he's mad!"

The child was snatched from my hands exactly as if it were being snatched from the flames. Grandpapa, who had been so timid only a moment before, now took down from the wall an enormous mahogony barometer, like a mace, and accompanied me to the door, which he slammed behind me, kicking it to with his foot.

Of course, they took this as an excuse not to pay me my fee.

When I got back into the street, I wasn't very proud of what had happened to me. Not so much on account of my reputation in the neighbourhood, which couldn't very well be worse than people had already made it — quite of their own accord, mark you, without my having to give them any help — but still because of Robinson, whom I had hoped to shake off with an orgy of plain speaking, finding enough resolution in a wilfully created scene never to have anything more to do with him, by staging some sort of fierce altercation with myself.

This is how I had figured it out: I'll discover by way of ex-periment, just how much of a flare-up you can start with yourself if you try. But the thing is you're never through with a to-do and an excitement; you never know quite how far you'll have to go if you start being really outspoken. Or what people are still hiding from you. . . . Or what they'll show you yet . . . if you live long enough, if you look far enough into their sillinesses. It all had to be begun all over again.

I was in a hurry to go off and hide myself for the time being. I set off towards home down the Impasse Gibet at first, and then I went along the Rue des Valentines. It's a goodish way. You've time to change your mind. I was going in the direction of the sky signs. On the Place Transitoire I met old Péridon, the lamplighter. We exchanged a few commonplace remarks. "You going to the cinema, Doctor?" he asked. He put the idea into my head. It seemed a good one.

The bus took me there quicker than the Métro would have. After that shameful incident, I should certainly have left Rancy for good, if I'd been able to.

As you stay on in a given place, things and people go to pieces round you; they rot and start to stink for your own special benefit.

ALL THE SAME, I DID WELL TO GO BACK TO RANCY NEXT DAY, BECAUSE of Bébert, who fell ill at just that very time. Colleague Frolichon was away on holiday; Bébert's aunt hesitated for a while and then she asked me to take charge of the patient, I suppose because I was the least expensive of the doctors she knew.

It happened after Easter. The weather was improving. The first southern breezes were coming to Rancy and wafting factory soot onto our windowpanes.

Bébert's illness lasted for weeks. I used to go to see him twice a day. The people round would wait for me by the lodge, without seeming to be waiting, and all the neighbours came out on to their doorsteps. It gave them something to do. People came from quite a way to find out whether he was any better or not. The sunlight, threading its way through too many things, reached the street only as an autumnal glow, clouded and regretful.

I was given plenty of advice with regard to Bébert. As a matter of fact, the whole neighbourhood took an interest in his case. A great deal was said first in favour of, and then against my intelligence. When I entered the lodge, a critical and somewhat hostile silence fell, a ponderously stupid silence chiefly. The lodge was always full of old cronies, friends of the aunt's, so it smelt strongly of petticoats and rabbit's pee. Every one had his own favourite doctor, who was cleverer and more able than any one else. Indeed there was only one thing to be said in my favour and that, of course, was the one thing for which you are not easily forgiven: I was dirt cheap. Which looks bad for the patient and the patient's family, however poor they may be.

Bébert wasn't delirious yet, he merely had not the least desire to move. He began to lose weight daily. A little yellow, flabby flesh still clung to his bones and shook each time his heart beat. His heart seemed to be everywhere in his body, he'd got so thin in just over a month's illness. He smiled at me pleasantly when I came to see him. And in this gentle way his temperature rose to over 100° and then 102°, and there he stayed for days and weeks, looking thoughtful.

Bébert's aunt had finally shut up and left us alone. She had said all she knew, whereupon she went and wept, disconsolate, in all the corners of the lodge, one after another. Misery had come to her, in fact, when her words came to an end; she seemed not to know what to do with it; she tried to wipe it away with her handkerchief, but it came back into her throat, and tears came too, and she began all over again. She dropped tears all over herself and so came to look a little more dirty than usual, and she was astonished by it all. "Oh, dear; oh, dear," she kept saying. But that's all. She had cried herself to the end of her resources, her arms fell limp by her side and she stood there facing me, completely overcome.

And then even so her misery would come back to her with a jolt and she'd make up her mind again and go off sobbing. This went on for weeks, these comings and goings in her unhappiness. It couldn't help looking as if this illness was going to turn out badly. It was a sort of malignant typhoid, against which nothing that I tried was any good — baths, serums, dry diet, injections. . . . Nothing was any use. Do what I might, my efforts were in vain. Bébert was slipping, being taken irresistibly away, smiling. There he was, way up in his fever, in equipoise, with me scrabbling about below. Of course almost everybody urgently advised the aunt to send me packing there and then and get in another better and more experienced doctor at once.

The incident of the girl with the "responsibilities" had made its mark in the neighbourhood and been tremendously commented on. You could almost hear them gargling with it.

But as the other doctors were aware of the nature of Bébert's case and dodged away, in the end I stayed. Seeing that he'd fallen to my lot, I might as well carry on; that was the way my colleagues looked at it, as a matter of fact.

There was nothing more I could think to do, except go round to the *bistrot* and telephone now and again to one or two medical men I knew more or less well, in various hospitals up in Paris, asking them, who were so wise and so well-known, what they would do if faced with a case of typhoid like the one that was bothering me. They all of them gave me excellent advice, excellent advice that wasn't any use, but all the same I liked hearing them take trouble like that, and for nothing too, on behalf of the little unknown boy I had taken charge of. In the end, you are pleased by quite a little thing, by the slender consolations life's good enough to leave you.

While I was subtilizing my feelings like this, Bébert's aunt dissolved into floods of tears among her chairs and staircases: she only emerged from her bewilderment to eat her meals. It's true that she never forgot a single mealtime. She wouldn't have been allowed to forget them in any case. Her neighbours watched over her. They stuffed her up between sobs. "You've got to keep your strength up," they said. She even began to put on weight.

The smell of Brussels sprouts, when Bébert was at his worst, was absolutely rampant in the lodge. It was the season for them and every one sent her presents of Brussels sprouts, already cooked and beautifully hot. "They keep me going, you know," she readily admitted. "And they have such an excellent effect on the bowels!"

Before nightfall, on account of the ringing of the bell, so as to sleep lightly and hear the first ring, she filled herself up with coffee; then people didn't wake Bébert up, trying to get in and ringing two or three times. When I passed by the house in the evening, I used to go in to see if it wasn't all over at last. "Don't you think it may have been the camomile tea and rum he *would* drink at the fruiterer's that day of the bicycle races which has made him ill?" That idea had worried her from the start. Fool!

"Camomile!" Bébert murmured feebly, like an echo, far away in his fever. Why bother to argue with her? Once more I would go through the two or three little professional gestures which were expected of me and off I went into the night, not at all proud of myself, because like my mother I never felt quite innocent of any misfortunes which came along.

After more than a fortnight of this, though, I decided I had better go along to the Bioduret Joseph Institute and see what they thought of a case of typhoid like this, and ask them at the same time if they couldn't give me a little advice and perhaps let me have some vaccine or other to try. If I did that, I should have done and tried everything I could, even the most out-of-the-way things; and if after all Bébert died, well, perhaps I wouldn't be to blame for it. I got to the Institute, yonder at the other end of Paris, behind the Villete, around eleven one morning. They let me wander through laboratory after laboratory, first of all, looking for a wise man. There wasn't anybody in these laboratories yet, either wise or not. Just a litter of things in no sort of order, carcasses of little animals cut open, cigarette ends, twisted gas brackets, boxes and glass jars with mice inside quietly suffocating, retorts, a jumble of kidneys, broken stools, books and dust, still more cigarette ends—they were everywhere—and the smell of them, and of latrines, predominating. As I was in such good time, I thought while I was there I would go along to the tomb of that great savant Bioduret Joseph, which was down in the basement amid all the golds and marbles. A bourgeois-Byzantine fantasia of the purest inspiration. You paid on your way out, and the keeper was grumbling because some one had slipped him a Belgian coin. It is due to this Bioduret that numbers of young men in the last fifty years have decided to take up science. As many duds have been turned out in this way as ever was produced by the Conservatoire. They all become very much alike too, after a certain number of years of not being a success. In the general rout, an M.D. is as good as a "Prix de Rome." A question of catching the bus at a slightly different time. That's all.

I had a long time still to wait in the gardens of the Institute, a mixture of prison yard and public square, with flower beds carefully aligned along walls adorned with malice aforethought.

At last some of the young men on the staff came along. They were the first to arrive, and several already carried bags full of provisions from the near-by market, and looked very down at heel. Then the sages themselves appeared, mooching in through the gates more slowly and more reserved than their humble assistants, in little, unshaven, whispering groups. They branched off up the different corridors, scraping the paint off the walls. Old, grey-haired schoolboys coming into school, carrying umbrellas, weighed down by the pettiness of the routine and the desperate tedium of their experiments, vowed, for a paltry salary and in middle age, to these little microbe kitchens where they spent their days warming up endless concoctions of vegetables, asphyxiated guinea pigs and other nameless messes.

When all is said and done, they themselves were nothing more than old servants, ruminating and overcoated and absurd. Greatness in our day is to the rich alone, whether they be wise or not. These underlings of the Research Institute could only count as a means of livelihood on their own fear of losing their allotted places in this stuffy, famous, departmental dustbin. It was their titles of official pundits that they clung to above all else. Thanks to which title the chemists in town accorded a certain confidence still to their analyses (of course meagrely paid) of clients' urine and phlegm. Pangloss' unsavoury perquisite.

As soon as he got there, each methodical expert performed the rite of gazing for a while at the rotting, bilious entrails of last week's rabbit, which was stuck up on show in a corner of the room, an obscene little altar to science. When the smell of it became absolutely unbearable, another rabbit was offered up in sacrifice, but not before, because of the economy being practiced at that time with fanatical zeal by Professor Jaunisset, Secretary to the Institute.

In this way certain decaying carcasses underwent, for economy's sake, the most incredible permutations and protractions. It's all a question of getting used to things. Some of the more hardened laboratory boys could very easily have cooked their meals in a coffin crawling with life, they had got so used to the stench of decomposing flesh. In fact, these humble collaborators in the great enterprise of science sometimes surpassed even Jaunisset himself in thriftiness, beating him at his own game in spite of his almost incredible meanness, and making use of the Institute's gas to cook themselves stews and many other dubious, leisurely concoctions.

When the pedants had finished dully examining the entrails of the ritual rabbit or guinea pig, they had gently come to the second act of their scientific daily lives: the lighting of a cigarette. An attempt to neutralize the prevailing stench and boredom with tobacco smoke. And so from stub to stub, at last these wise men came to the end of their day around five o'clock. Then the various putrefactions were quietly put back to warm in the dilapidated stove. Octave, the lab. boy, concealed his boiled beans in a newspaper, so as to get them safely past the concierge; deceitful little beast, he was taking his supper home to the suburbs already cooked. His master was just writing a little line of something or other in some corner of his experiment notebook, timidly, doubtfully, with a view to that bore of a report he would have to make up his mind to prepare one of these days, to justify his presence at the Institute — and the meagre emoluments that entailed — before some infinitely impartial and disinterested Body of Academicians.

A real pedagogue will be twenty years on an average making the one great discovery, which consists in realizing the fact that one man's folly is very far from being another man's pleasure, and that every one here below finds his neighbour's vagaries distressing.

The madness of the scientist, which is wiser and more reasonable than any other, is even so the most intolerable of all. But when one has learnt the knack of living in a given spot, with the help of certain gestures, even though it may not be very comfortably, obviously one has got to carry on in the same way or resign oneself to a guinea pig's death. Habits are acquired quicker than courage, and especially the habit of having something to eat.

And so I went on looking for my old friend Parapine throughout the Institute, because that is just what I had come all the way from Rancy for. I must persevere in my attempt to find him. It wasn't awfully easy. I wandered around a long time, hesitating among so many passages and doors.

This old boy Parapine never breakfasted at all, and only had supper at most two or three times a week, but when he did, he ate prodigiously, after the fashion of Russian students, all of whose fantastic habits he still retained.

In his own particular subject, Parapine was considered to be a foremost authority. He knew everything there was to know about typhoid, either in animals or in human beings. His reputation had first been established some twenty years before this, when certain German authors once claimed to have isolated Eberthian bacteria in the vaginal excretions of an eighteen-months-old baby girl. That caused a tremendous rumpus in the realms of Truth. Parapine delightedly retorted, with as little delay as possible, and in the name of the National Institute instantly surpassed this presumptuous Teuton by himself cultivating the same germ, only in its purest form, in the sperm of an old invalid of seventy-two. Famous at once, all he had to do to keep himself to the fore in the world of science, was to fill a few unreadable columns every so often in various professional monthlies. And this he did, with ease, from that bold and lucky day till his death.

Everybody now who had a serious interest in science accepted and believed in him. Which means that nobody seriously interested in science needed to bother to read him. If this public were to become critical all of a sudden, further advance in medicine would be impossible. A year would be wasted over every printed page.

When I reached the door of his little cell, Serge Parapine was busy spitting fluently and continuously into all four corners of his laboratory, with an expression of such deep disgust on his face that it gave one pause. Parapine shaved from time to time but there was always enough hair on his lopsided cheeks to make him look like an escaped convict. He shivered without stopping, or at any rate seemed to be shivering, though he never removed his overcoat, an overcoat which consisted chiefly of a variety of stains and a mass of scurf which he neatly picked off and flicked away all round him, while a lock dangled down over his forehead to his pink and greenish nose.

While I was studying the practical part of my course at the Faculty, Parapine had given me a few microscope lessons and had on several occasions shown me genuine kindness. I hoped he would not have entirely forgotten me since those now distant days and that he would be able perhaps to give me some extremely valuable piece of medical advice in the matter of Bébert's illness, which was really upsetting me very much indeed.

I was actually finding myself much more keen on preventing Bébert from dying than I should have been on saving an adult. One never minds very much if an adult goes; that's always one sod less in the world, one thinks to oneself, whereas in the case of a child, the thing's not quite so certain. There's always the future, there's some chance . . .

When Parapine learned my difficulties, he asked nothing better than to help me and put me on the right track in my treatment of Bébert, but he had learnt so many things in twenty years, so many different and often contradictory facts about typhoid, that it had become very difficult for him now — one might almost say impossible for him — to make any definite or concrete pronouncement on the subject of this very ordinary malady and its cure.

"In the first place, do you, my dear colleague, do you yourself believe in serums?" he asked me for a start. "Eh? What do you think about them? And what about vaccines? Indeed, what is your impression? Many excellent brains nowadays have no use for vaccines at all. It's a bold line to take, of course . . . I think so too. But after all? Eh? Why not? Don't you feel there is a great deal to be said for this negative viewpoint? What do you think yourself?"

His sentences bounded one after another from his mouth in awe-inspiring leaps, amid an avalanche of enormous R's.

While he was roaming and roaring like a lion among these forlorn and passionate theories of his, the famous Jaunisset, Secretary to the Institute, who at that time was still alive, passed by beneath our window, intent and haughty.

Parapine at the sight of him turned paler, if that were possible, than he was already, and nervously changed the conversation in his eagerness to tell me at once how much it disgusted him to have to see the universally admired Jaunisset every day of his life. In a second or two he had described that famous man to me as a trickster and a most dangerous type of maniac, and had charged him with more monstrous, unheard-of, secret crimes than would have sufficed to fill a penal settlement for a century.

I could not prevent him from giving me a hundred and one hateful details of the grotesque calling which he was obliged to follow in order to feed himself: a hatred more exact, more scientific indeed, than that of other men similarly placed in offices and shops.

He talked about all this in a very loud voice and I was amazed at his outspokenness. His lab. boy could overhear what was being said. He had done his own little bit of cooking and now, for the sake of form, was still fussing about among the Bunsen burners and test tubes; but he had grown so accustomed to hearing Parapine deliver his almost daily tirade that, however extravagant his remarks might be, they now seemed to him entirely academic and insignificant. Certain small private experiments, which he very gravely conducted himself in one corner of the laboratory, struck him, by contrast to Parapine's outbursts, as marvellously instructive and exciting. Parapine's observations did not distract his attention in the least. Before leaving, he shut the door of the stove on his own personal microbes, carefully and religiously, as if it were a tabernacle.

"Did you notice that lab. boy, my friend? Did you notice that old imbecile?" Parapine asked me, as soon as he had left. "Well, for nearly thirty years now, clearing up my messes after me, he's heard nothing but scientific talk all round him, and plenty of it and thoroughgoing scientific talk at that. . . . Yet far from being put off by it, he, and he alone, is now the only person in this place who believes in that stuff! He's mucked about with my experiments until he's come to think them marvellous. He's thrilled to death about them! My smallest piece of scientific foolery enchants him. But isn't that always the way with all religions? Hasn't the parson long ago given up thinking about his Maker and doesn't the layman believe in him still? Heart and soul? Really, it's enough to make one vomit. Isn't my idiot of a lab. boy ridiculous enough to ape the great Bioduret Joseph in everything, down to his way of dressing and his goatee beard?

Did you notice that? Between ourselves, the great Bioduret was not so very different from my lab. boy, except that he had a world-wide reputation and his whims were more intense. . . . He's always seemed to me monstrously vulgar, that immense analytic genius, with his mania for rinsing out bottles with meticulous care and observing from a fantastically close range the birth and growth of moths. . . . Take away from the great Bioduret a little of his prodigious domestic niggardliness and what that is admirable remains, may I ask? I beg you, tell me. A crafty, scowling, disagreeable old concierge — nothing more. Besides, he showed very clearly at the Academy what a horrible old creature he really was during those twenty years he spent there, loathed by almost everybody, quarrelling with damn nearly every soul in the place, quarrelling the whole confounded time. . . . An ingenious megalomaniac. That's all he was."

Parapine in his turn was gently preparing to leave. I helped him to wind a sort of scarf round his neck and over all that invariable scurf, a kind of mantilla. Then it suddenly occurred to him that I had called to see him on a definite and very urgent matter. "There now," he said, "boring you with my own little affairs, I was forgetting about your patient! Forgive me, my friend; let us lose no time in returning to the real subject of our conversation. But what can I tell you, after all, that you don't know already? Amid so many unstable theories, so much contradictory data, the reasonable thing, when it comes down to it, is to make no definite choice. Do the best you can, my friend! Since you have got to do something, do what you can! As far as I am concerned, I may as well tell you, speaking between ourselves, that the typhoid germ has come to disgust me beyond words, beyond all belief, in fact! When as a young man I first took up typhoid, there were only a few of us engaged in this field of research; I mean to say, we knew exactly how many of us there were at the game, we could each of us help to establish the other man's reputation. . . . Whereas nowadays, it's a very different thing. They're pouring in from Lapland, my good sir, from Peru! More and more turn up every day! There are droves of investigators! Japan produces them in tens at a time! In the course of the last few years I've watched the world become absolutely flooded with preposterous specialist publications on this same monotonously recurrent topic. In order to stand my ground and hold down my job as best I may, I have to produce and reproduce my same little article from one international congress, from one review, to the next, just simply at the end of each season making a few nice, insignificant, purely marginal alterations to it. . . . But all the same, believe me, my friend, typhoid these days is as outworn as banjo or mandolin playing. It's a terrible mess, I can assure you. Every one has his own little tune to play and his own way of playing it. No, I may as well confess to you that I don't feel up to bothering my head about it any longer; what I want for the end of my days is to find some quiet little corner in research work, where I sha'n't have any enemies or disciples but just that unexciting distinction without jealousies, which is all I wish for and which I badly need. Among other trifling topics, I have thought of studying the comparative influence of central heating on hæmorrhoids in northern and southern countries. What do you think? Hygiene? Diet? It's the sort of bunk that's in fashion, surely? An investigation of that sort, properly conducted and drawn out, I'm sure would put me in the Academy's good books, as most of the Academicians are old men to whom these problems of heating and hæmorrhoids must prove of the keenest interest. Think what they've done against cancer, which so closely concerns them! Then, if the Academy were to honour me with one of its Hygiene medals . . . Um? Ten thousand francs? Why not? Why, that would pay for a trip to Venice. . . . Oh, yes, you know, I went to Venice once when I was young. . . . Yes, indeed. You can die of starvation there just as well as you can anywhere else, my dear Bardamu. . . . But you inhale the most sumptuous smell of death there, which you're never likely to forget."

When we got into the street we had to hurry back to fetch his goloshes, which he'd forgotten. That made us late. Then we rushed along as fast as we could to some place, he didn't say where.

We went the whole way up the Rue Vaugirard, with its litter of vegetables and rubble, and came to the edge of a square full of chestnut trees and policemen. We sneaked into the back parlour of a little café where Parapine perched himself behind a screen opposite the window.

"Too late!" he fretfully remarked. "They've left already!"

"Who have?"

"The little girls from the Lycée. . . . Some of them are so sweet. . . . I know their legs by heart, my friend. That's all I ask at the end of the day. . . . Let's go. It'll have to be some other time. . . ."

We parted the best of friends.

I SHOULD HAVE BEEN GLAD NEVER TO HAVE HAD TO GO BACK TO Rancy. Ever since that morning when I left the place, I had almost forgotten my ordinary cares; they were so deeply rooted there that they hadn't followed me around. Perhaps they might have died of neglect, like Bébert, if I hadn't gone back. They were suburban cares. Still, when I got to the Rue Bonaparte, I began to ponder again, unhappily. Yet it's a street you would say would please the passer-by, normally speaking. Few streets are as benign and graceful as the Rue Bonaparte. Nevertheless, as I got down towards the river, I began to feel frightened. I wandered up and down. I couldn't make up my mind to cross the Seine. We're not all of us Cæsars! Over there on the other bank was where my worries began. I decided to wait on this left side until nightfall. At any rate, that's a few hours of sunlight saved, I told myself.

The water lapped against the side where there were some fellows fishing and I sat down to watch them at it. I wasn't in any hurry, either, as a matter of fact; just like them. I felt rather as if I had reached the point, the age, I suppose, when one knows what one is losing with every hour that slips by. But one hasn't yet grown strong enough in wisdom to be able to stop oneself short on the road of time, and anyway, if one stopped, one wouldn't know what to do either, without that mad desire to rush forward which one has had since youth and so admired. You are already rather less proud of this youth of yours, you don't yet dare to announce in public that perhaps that is all youth is — a hurry to grow old.

The whole of one's ridiculous past is actually so choked with absurdities and false values and gullibility, that one might be quite pleased to stop being young all of a sudden, to wait and let youth slip away from you, standing back and watching it outdistance you and run on and be lost, seeing how utterly vain it is, passing a hand through its emptiness, taking one last look at it and then pushing off on one's own, sure of its really having disappeared, and calmly walking round by oneself to the other side of Time, to get a glimpse of what people and things really are like.

The men fishing on the edge of the embankment did not seem to have caught anything. They didn't even look really as if they particularly wanted to catch anything. The fish probably knew all about them. They were all just pretending. The last delightful rays of the sunlight were still making it pleasant and warm where we were. Reflections of gold and blue bobbed on the surface of the water. There was a wind, a nice fresh wind from the other side, coming through the trees, in smiling gusts coming through the branches. It was very pleasant. We stayed there two full hours, taking nothing, not doing anything. And then the Seine had darkened and a corner of the bridge went all red with the sunset. People going along by the river had forgotten all about us as we sat there between the city and the water.

Night came up out of the arches and climbed up across the whole of the Louvre, taking the façade and all the windows one after the other as they flamed out against the gathering dusk. Finally the windows too went out.

Once more the time had come to be leaving.

The second-hand booksellers along by the river were shutting up for the night. "Are you coming?" a woman called across the parapet to her husband by me, who was gathering up his tackle, his camp stool and the worms. He grumbled, and all the other fishermen grumbled after him, and we went up, me too, all of us grumbling, up above to where the people were walking. I spoke to his wife, just to say something pleasant to her before night came completely. She immediately tried to sell me a book. It was one she had forgotten to shut up in the box with the others, she said. "So I'd let you have it cheaper, almost for nothing . . ." A little old Montaigne, a real genuine one for a franc. I was quite ready to make the woman happy so inexpensively. I took the Montaigne.

The waters under the bridge looked thick now. I hadn't the least wish to go on. On the boulevards I had some coffee and opened the old book she had sold me. I opened it just at the page where Montaigne is writing a letter to his wife on the occasion of the death of a son of theirs. The passage interested me at once, probably because I immediately connected it in my mind with Bébert. "Ah!" Montaigne was saying to his wife, more or less like this, "don't be upset, my dear. Console yourself. You must get over it. . . . It'll be all right, you'll find. Why, only yesterday," he went on, "among some old papers of a friend of mine I came across a letter Plutarch wrote to his wife in circumstances exactly similar to ours. . . . And I thought his letter so excellent and so right, that I'm sending it along to you. It's a lovely letter. I wanted you to have it right away, I want you not to be unhappy any more, dear wife. I'm sending you this fine letter. It hits the nail on the head pretty well, this letter of Plutarch's, doesn't it, my love? You won't have got the most out of it at once. No, you must read it very carefully. Delve into it. Show it to other people. And reread it. I feel much better now; I'm sure it will put you all right again. . . . Your loving husband, Michael." There's a real work of art for you, I told myself. His wife must have been proud to have a cheerful husband like her Michael. Well, of course, that was their own affair. Perhaps one always makes mistakes when it's a question of judging other people's feelings. May they not have been genuinely unhappy perhaps? Unhappy in the style of the period?

But as far as Bébert was concerned, I was having a rotten day of it. I hadn't any luck with Bébert, alive or dead. It seemed to me there wasn't anything for Bébert to find in life, even in Montaigne. Perhaps it's always the same thing anyway for everybody, if you begin to get down to it — nothing at all. There it was, I'd been away from Rancy all day, I had to be getting back now, and I hadn't anything to show for it. I had absolutely nothing to offer, either to him or his aunt.

I took a little stroll round the Place Blanche before going back. I saw a lot of people in the Rue Lepic, more people than usual. So I went up too, to see what was happening. There was a crowd outside a butcher's shop. You had to squeeze your way into the circle to see what was going on. It was a pig, a large, an enormous pig. He was grunting away in the middle of the circle like a man who's been disturbed, grunting like hell. He was being damnably treated all the time. People were tweaking his ears to make him squeal. He twisted and turned, trying to escape, tugging at the rope which held him; other people teased him and he squealed all the louder in pain. And every one laughed all the more.

The fat old beast didn't know how to hide himself in the little straw he'd been given and, grunting and snorting, he kept scattering it all the time. He didn't know how to get away from these humans. He realized that. He piddled at the same time as much as he could, but that didn't do any good, either. Grunting and squealing did no good. There *was* no way out. Every one laughed a lot. The butcher behind in his shop made signs and jokes to his customers and waved a great knife in the air.

He was as pleased as Punch, himself. He had bought the pig and tied it up out there as an advertisement. He couldn't have enjoyed himself more at his daughter's wedding.

More and more people kept arriving in front of the shop to see the pig wallowing in great pink folds of flesh each time he tried to get away. But that wasn't enough. They put a small, excitable little dog on his back and made it skip about and snap at the pig's exuberant mound of flesh. That was so extremely funny that now you couldn't get through the crowd. The police arrived and moved people on.

When at that time of the evening you come out on to the Pont Caulaincourt you can see the first lights of Rancy beyond the great lake of night which covers the cemetery. Rancy's on the other side. You have to go all the way round to get there. It's the devil of a long way. You'd say you were walking all round night itself, it takes such a time, and so much walking round the cemetery, to reach the outer walls of the town.

And then when you get to the gates, you pass by the damp toll office where the little green official sits. Then you're quite close. The dogs of the neighbourhood are all at their posts, barking. There are some flowers in the gaslight though, on the stall of a flower seller who is always sitting there, waiting for the dead to come by from day to day, from hour to hour. The cemetery, another cemetery, comes next and then the Boulevard de la Révolte. It goes off broad and straight into the night with all its lamps. You keep up it on the left. That was my street. You never met any one in it. All the same, I should have liked to be somewhere else, a long way off. I should also have liked to have had felt soles, so that nobody would hear me at all getting in. There was no point in my being there anyway, if Bébert didn't get any better. I had done my best. I hadn't anything to reproach myself for. It wasn't my fault if there wasn't anything one could do in cases like that. I reached his door, I thought without having been seen. And then, when I had gone upstairs, I looked through the slits of the shutters to see if there were still people talking round Bébert's bed. Some visitors to the house were still leaving but they didn't look the same as they had looked yesterday. One, a charwoman of the district whom I knew well, was crying as she went out. "It looks quite definitely as if there's been a turn for the worse," I said to myself. "In any case, things certainly aren't going any better. . . . Perhaps the end has come already," I said to myself, "since already there is somebody crying there." The day was over.

I wondered really whether I counted at all in all this. It was cold and silent in my place, like a small night on its own in one corner of the greater night, for me alone.

From time to time echoes and the sound of footsteps came up into my room, growing louder and louder, humming and fading away again. . . . Silence. I looked again to see if anything was happening outside, across the way. It was only inside me that things were happening, as I went on and on asking myself the same question.

I fell asleep in the end on that same question, in my own private night like a coffin; I was so tired from walking so far and finding nothing.

ONE MIGHT AS WELL MAKE NO MISTAKE ABOUT IT, HUMAN BEINGS have nothing to say to each other; they only tell each other their own personal troubles and that's a fact. Each for himself, the world for all men. They try to shift their own unhappiness off onto somebody else when they make love, but it doesn't come off and, do what they will, they have to stick to the whole lot themselves; so then they begin again and try to palm it off once more. "You're a very pretty girl," they say. And life takes a hold on them again, until the next time they try the same little trick. "You're *such* a pretty girl . . ."

And between whiles you boast of having managed to be rid of your unhappiness, but every one knows, don't they, that you've not done any such thing but are just as miserable as you well can be. As you grow uglier and uglier and more repulsive, playing this game as you grow old, you can't even conceal your unhappiness any longer, your failure; and in the end your face has become only an ugly expression which takes twenty, thirty or more years to come up from your stomach onto your face. That is what a man will achieve, that and that alone, — an ugly expression which he has spent a lifetime making and often even then hasn't managed to finish off properly, because of how difficult and complicated an expression it would have to be to reflect his real soul without missing anything out.

At the time, I was engaged in delicately moulding mine with the bills I wasn't able to pay, though they weren't big, my rent which was out of the question, my much too light overcoat, considering the weather, and the grocer who grinned to himself when he saw me counting my coppers, hesitating in front of his Brie cheese and blushing when grapes went out of season and up in price. And then my patients helped too, always making a fuss about something or other. Bébert's having died didn't do me any good in the neighbourhood either. Still, his aunt hadn't changed towards me. One certainly could not say that she had behaved badly on this occasion. No, it was rather from the Henrouille quarter and that little house of theirs, that suddenly a whole heap of worries began to come my way and give me cause for alarm.

One day old Mother Henrouille, out of the blue, left her shack at the end of the garden, her son and her daughter-in-law, and came to call on me. She knew what she was doing. And then after that she often came to see me, to ask if I really did believe she was mad. It was a sort of amusement for the old lady to come over especially to ask me questions. She used to wait for me in what I called my waiting room: three chairs and a little three-legged table.

That evening, when I got back, I found her in the waiting room, consoling Bébert's aunt by telling her all the relations she, the old Henrouille, had lost by the way in the course of a long life: nieces by the dozen, an uncle here and an uncle there, a father way back in the past, halfway through the last century, a whole lot of aunts and daughters of theirs, who had disappeared here, there and everywhere, she didn't really remember quite where or how; her own daughters who had become so vague, so indistinct that she almost had to make them up in her mind now, with the greatest difficulty, if she wanted to talk to anybody about them. They weren't really even memories any longer, these children of hers. A whole procession of little, ancient deaths trailed in the wake of her old carcass, shadows long since silent, imperceptible sorrows which she was trying, with great difficulty, to stir alive again in any case for the consolation, when I arrived, of Bébert's aunt.

Then, in his turn, Robinson came to see me. Every one was introduced: and made friends.

It was from that time on, as I have remembered since, that Robinson took to meeting old Mother Henrouille, always in my waiting room. They used to talk together. On the day before Bébert was to be buried, the aunt was asking every one she met, "Are you going? I should so like it if you did."

"Certainly I shall go," the old lady said. "It's nice to have people about one on occasions like that." You couldn't keep her in her hutch nowadays. She'd become quite a gadabout.

"Oh, that's very nice then, if you say you'll come," the aunt thanked her. "And what about you, Monsieur; will you come too?" she asked Robinson.

"Madam, I'm afraid of funerals; you mustn't take it wrongly," he said, wishing to get out of it.

Whereupon each of them went on to talk for quite a time — on their own, of course — almost fiercely; and even the old, old Henrouille joined in the conversation. They talked much too loud, all of them, like mad people do.

So then I fetched the old woman and took her into my consulting room next door.

I hadn't much to say to her. It was she who asked me things. I promised not to keep on with the certificate business. We went back into the other room and sat down with Robinson and the aunt, and we all talked for a full hour about the case of the unfortunate Bébert. Every one in the neighbourhood agreed that I had gone to a lot of trouble to try and save little Bébert, that it was just something that was fated to happen, that altogether I hadn't behaved too badly, and that was rather a surprise to every one. When Mother Henrouille was told the child's age, seven years, she seemed to feel better and altogether relieved. The death of such a very young child struck her as an absolute accident merely, not like an ordinary death which might give her something to think about.

And Robinson once again started to tell us how the acids he had to handle burnt the inside of his stomach and lungs, stifled him and made him spit up quite black phlegm. But old Mrs. Henrouille didn't have to spit, she didn't work in acids, so what Robinson had to say on that subject didn't interest her in the least. She had only come to make up her mind exactly about me. She watched me out of the corner of her eye as I talked, a quick little vivacious blue eye; and Robinson did not miss one jot of all this latent uneasiness existing between us. It was dark in my waiting room, the large house across the street was going pale all over before succumbing to the night. After that, there was nothing but our voices between us and everything that voices always seem just about to say and never do.

As soon as I was alone with Robinson, I tried to make him understand that I did not at all want to see him again, but he came back just the same towards the end of the month and then he came every evening. It's true he wasn't very well; he had chest trouble.

"Mr. Robinson asked for you again, to-day," my concierge, who took an interest in him, would tell me. "Will he get over it, d' you think?" she went on. "He was coughing quite badly still when he came. . . ." She knew perfectly well that it annoyed me to have her talk to me about him.

It's true that he coughed a lot. "It's no good," he himself said, "I'll never get rid of it. . . ."

"You wait till next summer! Have patience. You'll see. It'll go away on its own. . . ."

The things one does say in such cases, in fact. I couldn't cure him myself while he was in this acid trade. But I tried to cheer him up all the same.

"I shall get all right all by myself, shall I?" he said then. "Listen to the man! You'd think it was easy to breathe the way I do. . . . I'd like to see you have a bloody thing like I've got on your chest. . . . You pass right out with a thing like I've got on my chest. . . . I'm telling you. . . ."

"You're depressed, you're not having too good a time of it at the moment . . . But when you begin to feel better, even just a bit better, you'll see . . ."

"Just a bit better? I'll be stiff by the time I'm a bit better! I should have done much better to have passed out in the war, that's what really would have been much better! It's all right for you to have come back, you've nothing to complain of!"

A man sticks to his own dirty memories, to all his own misfortunes, and you can't get him to see different. It's something to keep his soul busy over. He revenges himself on the injustice of the present by smearing filth over the future in his innermost heart. Exacting and cowardly at bottom. It's the nature of the beast.

I didn't answer him. And he was angry with me. "You see? You obviously think the same as I do."

For the sake of peace I went and fetched him some medicine or other for his cough. His neighbours complained, apparently, of not being able to get to sleep, he coughed so continuously. While I filled up the bottle for him, he wondered where he could have caught this chronic cough. At the same time, he was asking me to give him injections: gold-leaf injections.

"If I died of them, you know, it wouldn't signify. . . ."

But naturally I refused to undertake any sort of heroic method. I just wanted him to go away more than anything.

I myself had become thoroughly depressed, just seeing him around my place. I already had all the difficulty in the world not to let my own dejection overcome me completely, not to succumb to my desire to close down once and for all; and twenty times a day I asked myself, "What's the good?" So that to listen to his lamentations as well was really more than I could bear.

"You've no guts, Robinson," I told him finally. "You ought to get married; that might give you an interest in life." If he had taken a wife, he'd have let me alone more. That finally annoyed him and he left. He didn't like the advice I gave him, particularly not that advice. He didn't even answer me on this question of marriage. It was of course, it's true, a very absurd piece of advice to give him.

One Sunday when I wasn't on duty we went out together. We sat on the Boulevard Magnanime and had a little glass of *cassis* each. We didn't talk much, we hadn't anything much to say to each other. What is the use of words anyway, when one knows just where one stands? Only to slang one another. Not many buses pass on Sunday. It's almost a pleasure from the café terrace to see the boulevard empty and quite quiet in front of one. There was the gramophone of the place going on behind.

"Do you hear that?" said Robinson. "It's playing American tunes. I recognize those tunes; they're the ones they used to play at Molly's, in Detroit. . . ."

During the two years he had spent over there he hadn't got very far into American ways; still, he'd been rather charmed by their attempt at music, whereby they too try to ease themselves of accustomed burdens and the crushing sadness of having always to do the same thing every day; it helps them to shuffle around with a world that has no meaning, while it's playing. Lumbering bears there, the same as here.

He left his *cassis* untouched while he thought about all that. A little dust whirled up everywhere. Grubby pot-bellied children were playing round the plane trees, also attracted by the gramophone. Nobody is proof against music, really. There isn't anything else to do with one's heart, one willingly surrenders it. Behind all music one ought to try and catch that noiseless tune that's made for us, the melody of death.

Some shops were open on Sunday out of obstinacy; the old woman who sells slippers goes out for a walk and parades all her kilos of varicose veins from one shop front to the next, gossiping hard.

On a kiosk the morning's papers hang idiotically, looking already a little yellow, like a great artichoke of news that's beginning to go bad. A little dog pees on them quick, the vendor's asleep.

An empty bus rushes up towards where we're sitting. Ideas have their Sunday too in the long run; one's more than usually stunned. One sits there, empty, agape. Quite happy. There isn't anything to say, because after all nothing is happening to you any more, you're too feeble; perhaps one has disgusted Fate? That would be quite a reasonable supposition.

"Can't you think of any way for me to get out of this job that's killing me?"

He had reached the outcome of his train of thought.

"What I want is to break out of my job, see? I'm through with doing myself in, working like a mule. . . . I too want to get around a bit. . . . You don't know any one who needs a chauffeur, do you, by any chance? You know a lot of people though, don't you?"

They were Sunday ideas taking hold of him, gentlemanly ideas.

I didn't dare to dissuade him, to hint that with a beggarly, murderous mug like his no one would ever think of entrusting their motor car to him, that he'd always have too queer a look, in livery or out of it.

"You're not very encouraging, are you, in fact?" he concluded. "So you think I'll never get out of this show then, do you? And it's not even worth my while to try? In America I was too slow, you said. In Africa the heat was too much for me. . . . Here I'm not intelligent enough. . . . So there's always something everywhere I've too much or too little of. But I realize all that's just so much blah. Ah, if only I had some money! Then everybody would like me *so* much here, there—everywhere. Even in America. Isn't it true what I'm saying? And what about you? What we need is to own a house with half a dozen good, paying tenants in it. . . ."

"That's perfectly true," I replied.

He couldn't get over having come to this major conclusion all on his own. And he looked at me in the most extraordinary way, as if he'd suddenly discovered something unsuspectedly caddish about me.

"You're all right, when I come to think of it; you're in clover. You sell your nonsense to a lot of croaking invalids, and that's all you care. . . . You aren't under any one's orders, or anything. You come and go as you please, you're absolutely free. . . . You look a decent sort of cove, but you're really a pretty good swine underneath!"

"That's unfair, Robinson!"

"Well, find something for me to do then, man!"

He was dead set on this idea of giving up his work in the acids trade for others to do.

We went back down little side streets. Towards evening you'd take Rancy for a village still. The great farmlike house gates are half open. The courtyard is empty. And the dog's kennel is empty too. On some such evening as this, a long time ago now, the peasants left their homes, chased away by the great city approaching from Paris. One or two properties of that time remain, unsaleable and damp, a prey already to the limp creepers drooping down over brightly postered walls. The harrow hanging up between two gutter spouts has rusted almost right away. Here is a past which no one tampers with any longer. It is passing away on its own. The present inhabitants are far too tired to do anything about the outside of the house when they come home in the evening. They just flop by families into what remains of the common rooms, and drink. The ceiling is still marked with rings of smoke from the swaying oil lamps of that period. The whole district shakes to the unceasing rumble of the new works, but doesn't complain. Mossy tiles crash down on to cobblestones such as now only exist at Versailles and in ancient prisons.

Robinson accompanied me as far as the little municipal park, surrounded by warehouses, where on the scrubby grass between the workhouse, a slap and tickle and the sand heap, all the flotsam of the neighbourhood comes out to play and pee.

We drifted back to one thing and another. "You know, what I'd like is to be able to stand taking a drink." That's what he said to me. "When I drink, I get the most frightful cramps in the stomach, it's unbearable. It's more than that!" And he immediately proved to me that he'd not been able to stand even the little drop of *cassis* we'd taken that afternoon, by bringing it up there and then. "You see? That's what I mean."

At his door he left me. "The Palace of Draughts," he remarked, and disappeared from my sight. I didn't think I should see him again so soon.

My affairs looked as if they might be picking up a bit, that same night, it seemed.

There were two different urgent calls for me from the house where Police Headquarters were. On Sunday sighs are freer, feelings stronger, impatience greater. Pride is at the helm on that day, and has had a drop or two to drink. After a whole twelve hours of alcoholic freedom, there is a certain stirring among the slaves; it's not so easy to keep them quiet; they scuffle, and scrape the dirt off themselves, and clank their chains.

Two dramas were in full swing at the same time in the house where Police Headquarters were. On the first floor a man was dying of cancer, while on the third floor there was a miscarriage which the midwife wasn't being able to cope with. The good woman was saying a whole lot of absurd things to every one round while she washed out napkins, one after the other. Then she'd put in an injection upstairs and slip off to give the patient downstairs another injection — at ten francs the phial of camphorated oil, if you please. It was quite a big day for her.

All the inmates of the house had spent the day in their dressing gowns and shirt sleeves, facing up to everything that was going on, and well sustained with spicy food. The smell of garlic and other odder smells hung about the corridors and stairs. Dogs romped about on the staircase right up to the sixth floor. The concierge was busy looking after everything and everybody. She drank only white wine herself, because she found red wine so lowering.

The vast blousy midwife was acting as producer to both dramas, on the first floor and on the third floor, rushing about, pouring with sweat, overjoyed and vindictive. She was fed up by my arrival on the scene. The audience had been hers all day; it was her limelight.

Try as I might to manage her, to make myself as small as possible, to approve of everything (although really she had accomplished nothing but a series of damnable mistakes), my coming, and what I had to say, instantly infuriated her. And that was that. A midwife one has to keep an eye on is about as amiable as a cobra. You don't know where to put her so that she shall do you as little harm as possible. Each lot of tenants overflowed from the kitchen on to the landing, mixing with all the sick people's relations. And, my, what a lot of relations they had! Some fat, some skinny, they hung about in somnolent groups in the gaslight. It was getting late, and some of them had come up from the country, where bedtime's earlier than it is in Paris, and they were fed up. Everything I said to those connected with the drama downstairs and also to those connected with the drama upstairs, was ill received.

Death came soon on the first floor. So much the better and so much the worse. Just as the patient's last breath was rattling in his throat, his own doctor, Doctor Omanon, came along to see if he had died, and more or less started cursing me for being there. So I explained to Omanon that I was on Sunday duty, and that therefore my presence was only to be expected — and betook myself, with some dignity, upstairs.

The woman on the third floor was still bleeding profusely. For two pins she'd be dying too, before very long. I gave her an injection and went straight down again to Omanon's creature. That was all over and done with. Omanon had left. But he'd pocketed my twenty francs before he went, damn him. I'd drawn another blank. I didn't want to lose the job I'd got upstairs. So I dashed back there again.

I explained one or two things to the family while the bleeding went on. The midwife evidently did not agree with me. You'd almost have thought she earned her pay contradicting me. But there I was, worse luck; who gave a damn whether she liked it or not? There was going to be no nonsense. At least a hundred francs would be coming my way, if I could dig myself in and stay put! Just a little patience, and some science, for God's sake. It's hard work standing up to remarks and questions reeking of white wine, which mercilessly batter at your innocent head; it's no joke.

The family speaks its mind amid sighs and hiccups. The midwife stands by, waiting for me to put my foot in it, clear off, and leave her the hundred francs. But the midwife can go to hell! What about my rent? Who's going to pay that? These labour pains have been going on all day, I know that. There's a lot of blood, I know that too; but it's not over yet; one must hang on.

Now that the other fellow, the cancer case, had died downstairs, his deathbed audience slunk up to the third floor. While you're having a thoroughly bad night of it anyway, and have given up all idea of sleep, you may as well make the best of whatever there is to look at. The downstairs family had come to see if this business up here was going to end as badly as theirs had. Two deaths the same night, in the same house, why, that really would be the excitement of a lifetime! I should say so indeed! All the dogs of the place could be heard scampering up and down the staircase; careering around with bells on their collars. They came along too, to watch. People who had come from a long way off crowded in, whispering. Young girls suddenly "found out about life," as their mothers put it: and adopted a tender, knowing expression in the face of tragedy. That's the consoling instinct of the female. A cousin of theirs, who had been eying them all day, is tremendously fetched by it. He doesn't leave their side from that moment on. Tired as he is, it's a revelation to him. Everybody is worn out. The cousin will marry one or the other of them, but he'd like to have a look at their legs too, while he's about it, so as to be able to choose better.

Delivery of the fœtus makes no headway: the passage must be dry; it won't come away, it just bleeds. This would have been her sixth child. Where is the husband? I ask for him.

The husband had to be found, if I was going to be able to send the woman to the hospital. One of her relations had suggested that she should be sent to the hospital. A mother of a family she was, who wanted to get off to bed, on account of the children. But now, when the hospital was put up for discussion, no two of them would agree. Some were in favour of this step being taken, others were against it because it wasn't respectable. They didn't want it even mentioned. It got to such a pitch that some hard words were exchanged between relations which would never afterwards be forgotten; they would have passed into the family. The midwife despised everybody. But it was the husband I personally wanted to find, so as to be able to consult him, so that the thing should be finally decided one way or the other. He came forward at last out of a group of relations, looking vaguer than any of the others. Still, it was up to him to decide. Was it to be the hospital? Or not the hospital? What did he want done? He didn't know. He just wanted to look. So he looked. I showed him his wife's anatomy, her blood seeping, gushing, his whole wife bleeding away entirely before his eyes. She moaned, too, like a large dog that's been run over by a car. He didn't really know what he wanted done. They gave him a glass of white wine to steady him. He sat down.

Even so, no solution occurred to him. He is a man who works hard all day. He is well known on the market place and at the station, where he has carried sacks of vegetables, not small loads either, great big sacks of vegetables, for the last fifteen years. Everybody knows him. He wears vast, vague trousers, and his shirt is like that too. They remain on him but he doesn't seem to bother that much about his shirt and these pants of his. He seems only to be considering the ground and how to stand upright on it on his own two feet, set apart, as if at any moment the earth might start to quake under him. Pierre, his name is. We wait for him to speak.

"What do you yourself think, Pierre?" every one stands round in a circle and asks. Pierre scratches himself and goes and sits by the head of the bed, as if he found it difficult to recognize this woman who is always bringing sorrow into the world, and then he sheds some sort of a tear and stands up. I have started to write out a note of admission into the hospital. "Think, Pierre, man!" every one exhorts him. "Think a little!" He's trying all right, but he makes a sign to say it won't come. He gets up and goes off unsteadily into the kitchen, taking his glass with him. Why wait any longer for him? His conjugal indecision may last all night, everybody round realises that. One might just as well be moving on.

There was a hundred francs I'd lost, that's all. But I should have had trouble with this midwife in any case. . . . The whole thing was a foregone conclusion. Besides which, I wasn't going to try my hand operating at all, in front of all these people and feeling as tired as I was. "Well, there it is," I said to myself. "Let's go. Better luck next time, maybe. Accept the thing as it, is — let Nature alone, the bitch."

I'd hardly got on to the landing before they all wanted me back, and he came running out after me. "Hey, Doctor," he called. "Don't go, Doctor!"

"What do you expect me to do?" I asked him.

"Wait a moment, I'll come with you, Doctor. D' you mind, sir?"

"All right," I said, and I let him come down with me. When we got down to the first floor though, I went in and said good-bye to the dead man's family. Pierre went in with me, and we came out again at once. In the street he fell into step with me. It was fresh out of doors. We came across a little dog who was learning to answer the other dogs of the neighbourhood with long howls. He was obstinate and very plaintive. He already knew how to howl properly. Soon he would be a real grown-up dog.

"Why, if it isn't 'Yolk,' the laundryman's dog!" the husband remarked, delighted to have recognized him and to change the conversation. "His daughters fed him as a puppy with a baby's bottle. Do you know the laundryman's daughters? They live in the Rue des Gonesses."

I told him I did.

While we walked he began to tell me how, if you wanted to, you could bring a dog up on milk without its coming out too expensive. But all the time behind these remarks he was searching for an idea about his wife.

There was an *estaminet* still open near the gates.

"Coming in, Doctor? Let me stand you a drink. . . ."

I wasn't going to upset him. "Come on, then," I said. "Two coffees." I took the opportunity to bring up the subject of his wife again. He listened very seriously to all I had to say, but yet I couldn't get him to make up his mind. There was a great bouquet of flowers on the counter. It was the Matrodin's birthday, apparently. "The children gave it me," he informed us. So we stood him a vermouth and drank his health. There was the Intoxicants Act still hanging above the counter and a framed Board School Certificate. As soon as he saw it, the husband insisted on Martrodin's reciting the Subprefectures of Loir-et-Cher to him, because he himself had had to learn them once and knew them still. Then he claimed that it wasn't the café-keeper's name that appeared on the certificate, but some quite different name, and they both got annoyed, and he came back and sat down by me. His dilemma had taken a complete hold on him again. He didn't even see me leave; it worried him so.

I never saw him again. All the things that had happened that Sunday had depressed me a lot and tired me out as well.

I hadn't gone another hundred yards before I met Robinson coming my way, loaded with all sorts of planks, large and small.

I recognized him in spite of the dark. He was very annoyed to see me, and tried to walk on, but I stopped him.

"How is it you aren't in bed?" I asked him.

"Not so loud!" he answered. "I've been working . . ."

"What are you going to do with all that wood? Is that work too? Building a coffin or something? You've stolen it, I suppose?"

"No, it's a rabbit hutch."

"You breeding rabbits now?"

"No, it's for the Henrouilles."

"The Henrouilles? Do they keep rabbits?"

"Yes, they've got three of them, and they're going to keep them in the yard, you know, where the old woman lives. . . ."

"So you're going to build a hutch at this time of night, are you? It's an odd time to choose. . . ."

"It's Madame Henrouille's idea. . . ."

"A very extraordinary idea! What does she think she's going to do with the rabbits? Sell them? Top hats?"

"You can ask her when you see her; she is going to pay me a hundred francs, and that's all I know. . . ."

All the same, this business of a rabbit hutch struck me as very odd, and at night like that. . . . I kept on about it.

With that he altered the conversation.

"But how did you come to know them?" I went on. "You usen't to know the Henrouilles, used you?"

"The old woman took me to see them, I tell you, that day I met her at your place. . . . She's a talkative old thing sometimes. . . . You've no idea. You can't stop her talking. . . . She sort of made friends with me and they did too. . . . *Some* people like me, you know!"

"You'd never told me anything about all that. . . . Still, if you go to their house, you probably know whether they're going to get the old girl into an asylum or not?"

"No, they tell me they haven't been able to. . . ."

The whole conversation displeased him, I saw that; he didn't know how to shake me off. But the more he avoided me, the more I kept on. . . .

"Life's hard, though, isn't it? You've got to use your wits, eh?" he murmured vaguely. But I dragged him back to the point. I was determined to find out more about it. . . .

"People say the Henrouilles have more money than you'd think. Would you say that was true, now that you go to see them?"

"Yes, maybe they have. . . . But in any case, they'd be very pleased to get rid of the old woman. . . ."

He'd never been much good at deception, friend Robinson.

"They'd like to get her off their hands because the cost of living's going up so. They told me you wouldn't certify her mad. Is that true?"

And, leaving it at that, he asked me with some interest which way I was going.

"Been seeing a patient, have you?"

I told him something of my experiences with the husband I'd just lost by the way. That made him laugh a lot — but at the same time it made him cough too.

He huddled himself up so much as he coughed, that I could hardly see him standing next to me in the darkness; I could only vaguely see his hands clutching at his mouth like some pale flower fluttering in the dark. He went on and on. "It's the draughts," he gasped at last, when he'd finished coughing, just as we had come to the door of his house.

"God, there are a lot of draughts where I live — and fleas too! Have you got fleas at your place?"

I had. "Sure," I told him. "I catch them off my patients."

"Sick people smell of piss, don't you find?" he asked me.

"Yes, and of sweat too."

"All the same," he slowly remarked, after a moment's careful thought, "I should like to have been a hospital assistant."

"Why?"

"Because, you know, when people are well, there's no getting away from it, they're rather frightening. . . . Especially since the war. . . . I know what they're thinking. . . . They don't always realise it themselves. But I know. When they can stand up, they're thinking of killing you. Whereas when they're ill, there's no doubt about it, they're less dangerous. You've got to be prepared for them to do any damned thing while they're well — isn't that so?"

"It's very true," I had to admit.

"What about you; isn't that why you became a doctor?" he asked me.

I wondered, and then I realised that perhaps Robinson was right. But he began at once to cough again, like mad.

"You've gone and got your feet wet. You'll die of pleurisy going for strolls like this at night. . . . Go indoors," I advised him. "Go to bed!"

Coughing like that, bout after bout, wore him out.

"Old Mother H. is the one who's going to catch her death of cold!" he wheezed and chuckled into my ear.

"How's that?"

"You'll see," he told me.

"What's this they've thought out?"

"I can't tell you any more. You'll see . . ."

"Tell me about it, Robinson. Come on, you old sod, you know I never repeat anything I hear. . . ."

And now, suddenly, the wish came to him to tell me all about it; perhaps partly to show me that he wasn't to be taken for the resigned, dejected fool he looked.

"Go ahead," I urged him, almost in a whisper. "You know perfectly well I never talk. . . ."

That was the excuse he needed, to confide in me.

"Yes, that's right enough, you do keep your mouth decently shut," he admitted. And without another murmur he weighed straight into it. We were quite alone at that hour of night, on the Boulevard Coutumance.

"Do you remember the story of the carrot merchant?" he began.

But at first I didn't remember any story about a carrot merchant.

"You know. Surely you do? It was you who told it me. . . ."

"Oh, yes." I did remember it all of a sudden. "That railwayman chap who lived in the Rue Brumaire? Who had a bomb go off in his parts when he was trying to steal some rabbits?"

"Yes, that's right, at the grocer's on the Quai d'Argenteuil . . ."

"Of course, yes. Now I know," I said. "What then?" Because

I still didn't see the connection between this old story and Mme. Henrouille, Senior.

He proceeded at once to put me wise.

"Don't you see?"

"No," I said. . . . And very soon after that I didn't dare see.

"Well, damn it, you're pretty slow. . . ."

"You seem to me to have got rather off the track. You're not really going to start murdering the old Henrouille just to please her daughter-in-law, are you?"

"Oh, all I'm doing is I'm making them the hutch they've asked me for. . . . The bomb's their business—if they see fit . . ."

"How much are they giving you for all this?"

"A hundred francs for the wood, and two hundred and fifty for making it, and one thousand just for the story itself. . . . You see? And that's only a beginning. . . . It's a story, if one's any good at telling it, that's worth a regular fortune. . . . Eh, my boy; now do you realise?"

I realised, and I wasn't very surprised. Just rather more sad than before, that's all. Anything that one can say to try and dissuade people in a case like that amounts to very little. It's not as if life treats them well, is it, now? For whom and for what should they be sorry? Why try? Do unto others . . . ? Has any one ever been known to go down into hell and take somebody else's place there? Never. You see him send other people down there, that's all.

The impulse to murder which had suddenly come over Robinson seems to me to be more in some way an improvement on what I'd noticed till then, in other people, who were always half hating, half kindly, always irritating, in the indecisiveness of their attitude. Decidedly, through having followed Robinson in the dark as far as this, I had learned a number of things. . . .

But there was one danger: the Law. "The Law is dangerous, you know," I pointed out. "If you're caught you wouldn't escape with your health. . . . You wouldn't ever come out again alive. Being in prison would do you in. . . ."

"Well then, let it," he said. "I'm fed up with the ordinary business of living like everybody else does. One's old, one keeps on waiting for one's time to come to have some fun, and when it does. . . . You've been damned patient waiting for it if it does. . . . You've been dead and buried long before that. What they call honest toil is a mug's game. . . . You know that as well as I do. . . ."

"Possibly. But every one would try their hand at the other thing, the risky business, if it weren't for the fact that it *is* dangerous. . . . And the police aren't fools, you know. . . . There are pros and cons." We examined his position.

"I don't say you're not right," he said, "but you can understand that working as I work, in the condition I 'm in, not sleeping, coughing, doing jobs that would be too hard on a horse, there couldn't be anything worse for me now. That's my opinion. Nothing could be worse. . . ."

I didn't like to tell him that really and truly he was right, because afterwards he might have blamed me for it if this scheme didn't come off.

He tried to cheer me up by giving me several good reasons for not bothering about the old woman, who hadn't much longer to live anyway, whatever happened; she was much too old as it was. He'd just be arranging for her departure in fact, and that's all.

All the same, as dirty businesses go, it really was a very dirty business. Everything had already been arranged between him and the Henrouille couple. Now that the old girl had started going out again recently, one fine evening they'd send her to feed the rabbits. The bomb would be there ready. . . . It would go off slap in her face when she touched the door of the hutch. . . . The very same thing as had happened at the grocer's. She was looked upon as mad in the neighbourhood already. The accident would surprise no one. . . . The Henrouilles would say she'd been told over and over again never to go near the rabbits. . . . She had disobeyed orders. And at her age she'd certainly not survive an explosion like the one they were going to let her have. . . . Slap in the middle of the face like that. . . .

There were no two ways about it, that was the hell of a story I'd gone and told Robinson.

AND MUSIC CAME BACK WITH THE FAIR, MUSIC WHICH YOU HEAR AS far back as you can remember, in the days when you were small, the kind which goes on all the time here and there, in odd corners of the town, in little country places, wherever poor people go at the end of the week to sit down and wonder what they have become. "Paradise," they're told: and music is played for them, now here, now there, tinkling, pounding out the strains to which the rich danced the year before. Mechanical music which is the accompaniment to wooden horses and motor cars which aren't really motor cars and not at all scenic railways; it's heard in the Strong Man's tent (who hasn't any biceps and doesn't come from Marseilles); and where there's a woman who isn't bearded at all, a magician who's a cuckold, an organ that isn't even gilt, behind a shooting alley whose eggs are only shells. It's the fair for duping people over the week-end.

So we go along and drink that beer with no head on it. But as for the man who serves the beer, his breath genuinely reeks. And the change he gives you has some very strange coins in it, so strange that one goes on looking at them for weeks afterwards and gets rid of them again with enormous difficulty, and by giving them to a beggar. Dammit, it's the Fair. You've got to get your laughs while you can, midway between hunger and gaol; you must take things the way they come. You've something to sit on, so don't go complaining. That's always something. I've seen that International Stand again, the same one, the one Lola found that time many years ago now, in the park at Saint-Cloud. You come across everything once again at fairs; fairs are the bringing up of past pleasures. The main avenue at Saint-Cloud must long ago have filled again with strolling people. Parading up and down. The war was over long ago. And does the same fellow still run the shooting gallery, I wonder — if he came back from the war? All that interests us. I recognized the targets, but now you shoot at æroplanes. That's something new. An improvement. The latest thing. The wedding party's still there, and the soldiers and the Town Hall with its flag. All of it, in fact. Plus even more things to shoot at than there were before.

But people get much more fun out of electric cars, a recent invention, because of the pseudo-accidents you keep having in them and the terrific jolts they give your head and your insides. More yelling cretins came pouring up every minute to crash into each other and be flung about, making mincemeat of their kidneys. Nothing would stop them. They never gave in, never seemed to have been happy enough. . . . Some of them actually raved. They had to be dragged away from this destruction. You could have thrown death in as well for their franc, they'd have hurled themselves on this thing just the same. At four the Municipal Band was to give a concert in the middle of the fair ground. Collecting the band together was the very devil, because of the drinking places round about which absorbed all the musicians in turn. There was always a last one missing. They waited for him. They went to look for him. While waiting, and before everybody was back, there was time to get thirsty again and two more would disappear. . . . Then you had to begin all over again.

On the stalls spice bread made in the shape of pigs went bad with dust, and began to look like reliquaries in a church and endowed people who'd won prizes with a frightful thirst.

Families wait for the fireworks before going off home to bed. Waiting's part of the fun too. Under the tables a thousand empties clink in the shadows. Feet slide to signify consent or refusal. One hardly hears the music, one knows the tunes so well, nor the motors in motion behind the booths, making things work which you have to go and pay two francs to see. Your own heart, when you're a little tipsy with fatigue, taps away in your temples. It makes a thudding noise against the sort of velvet drawn tight round your head and inside your ears. That's the way one day it will come to burst. Let it! One day when the inner rhythm rejoins the outside one and all your ideas spill out and run away at last to play with the stars.

There was a lot of crying going on all over the fair ground because of all the children who kept getting crushed by mistake between chairs and the ones who were being taught to overcome their own desires and forego such immense petty pleasures as another ride on the merry-go-round. The fair must be used to help build character. It's never too soon to start. The little dears don't yet know that everything has to be paid for. They think it's out of kindness that the grown-ups behind these brightly lit counters urge people to take a look at the marvellous things they collect, control, and harbour with their shouts and smiles. They don't yet know the nature of things, these children. Their parents will slap them and teach them, and protect them against Pleasure.

There's no real fair except for those whose business it is, and with them it's deep and secret. It's in the evening that these people rejoice, when all the fool fair-goers, profitable animals, have gone away, silence has come back to the lines of tents, and the coconut stall has suffered the last little dog's last drop of pee. Then accounts can start. It's the time to make a census of the fair's attractions and its victims.

On the Sunday evening, the last day of the fair, Martrodin's barmaid sliced her hand rather badly, cutting sausage. Towards the end of that same evening everything round me became pretty clear, as if things had been indistinct long enough and now were all about to fall into place and speak clearly to me. But you mustn't trust people and things at such moments. You think they're going to speak, and then they say nothing at all, and are swallowed up again in darkness without your being able to tell what it was they had to impart to you. That, at any rate, has been my experience.

Anyway, what happened was that I saw Robinson again that evening at Martrodin's place, when I was going to start bandaging the barmaid's hand. I remember exactly how it was. Next to us some Arabs sat dozing, huddled together on a bench, half asleep. They seemed to take not the slightest interest in what was happening around them. In my conversation with Robinson I avoided touching again on the subject of that talk we'd had the other evening, when I discovered him carrying those planks. The barmaid's wound was difficult to stitch, and I couldn't see very well at the back of the shop. That prevented me from talking, having to pay attention to what I was doing. When I'd finished, Robinson called me over into a corner, and let me know himself that the affair was all set, and going to come off soon. I was annoyed at being taken into his confidence in this way; I had no wish to be told about it.

"Coming off soon? What's coming off soon?"

"Why, you know . . ."

"What, that thing still?"

"Guess how much they're going to give me now?" I didn't wish to guess.

"Ten thousand! Just so as I keep my mouth shut!"

"It's a lot of money."

"Why, yes, it's the very thing," he added. "It's those ten thousand francs I've been needing all this time. The *first* ten thousand francs, eh? You get me? I've never really had a job, but now, with ten thousand francs . . ."

He must have started squeezing them already.

He let me go ahead and reckon up all the things he would undertake and do with ten thousand francs. . . . He gave me time to think about it, lolling back against the wall, in the shadow. A new world. Ten thousand francs!

All the same, thinking about this business of his, I wondered whether I wasn't running some personal risk, if I hadn't drifted into some kind of complicity by not seeming to show immediate disapproval of what he was doing. I ought even to have denounced him to the police. I don't care a hoot about human morality myself, — just like every one else. What can I do about it? But there are all the dirty little stories, those dirty snippets Justice unearths when a crime has been committed, just to titivate the taxpayer, vicious brute. It's difficult to get away then. I'd seen it happen. Misery for misery, I preferred the noiseless kind to the sort that's all spread out in the newspapers.

I was, in fact, intrigued and sickened at the same time. Having got as far as this, once again I hadn't the courage to get really to the bottom of things. Now that it was a question of opening one's eyes in the dark, I was almost just as glad to keep them shut. But Robinson seemed determined that I should open them, that I should realize.

By way of a change, I turned the conversation on to the subject of women. Robinson didn't care for women much.

"As a matter of fact," he said, "I can get along all right without women — with their fat thighs, their Cupid's-bow lips and those stomachs of theirs which always have something growing in them, either a baby or a disease. . . . Their smiles won't pay your rent for you. Will they? Even me in my attic, if I had a wife, it wouldn't be much good my showing the landlord her buttocks on the fifteenth of the month; that wouldn't make him reduce the rent!"

Independence was Robinson's one wish in the world. He told me so himself. But Martrodin, the owner, had had enough of our little asides and plottings in corners.

"Robinson, Good God, the glasses!" he shouted. "D'you want *me* to wash them up for you?" Robinson sprang to his feet.

"I do a little extra work here, you see," he explained to me.

It was the fair, I expect. Martrodin was finding it extremely difficult to reckon up the takings; that annoyed him; the Arabs had left, except for two who were still dozing by the door.

"What are those fellows waiting for?"

"The barmaid," Martrodin informed me.

"How's trade?" I asked, for something to say.

"So-so . . . But it isn't easy. You see, Doctor, I bought this property for sixty banknotes down before the depression. I've got to get at least two hundred out of it. . . . See what I mean? It's true I get plenty of custom but a good many of them are Arabs. And they don't drink. They haven't got into the way of it yet. What I need is Poles. . . . Now Poles, Doctor, Poles drink like the devil. Where I was before in the Ardennes I used to have Poles from the enamel furnaces. That warmed them up, that did — them furnaces! And that's what we need: thirst! On Saturday they blew the whole lot. . . . Christ! There was something doing in those days. . . . Their whole week's pay — bang! But these here *bicots*, they ain't interested in drink; what they fancy is something far worse. . . . Drinking isn't allowed in their religion apparently, whereas this other thing is."

Martrodin had no use for them at all. "They're dirty hounds, damn it. It seems they treat my barmaid the same way. . . . Madmen, eh, don't you agree? It's a pretty awful set of ideas to have, Doctor, wouldn't you say? I mean, I *ask* you!"

The café keeper pressed his stubby fingers on the pouches under his eyes. "How go the kidneys?" I asked him, seeing him do this. I attended him for his kidney trouble. "You have at least given up the salt, I suppose?"

"Traces of albumen still, Doctor. The chemist analysed it for me the day before yesterday. Oh, I don't much mind if I die," he added, "either from albumen or from anything else — what gets me is having to work as hard as I do for such small profits."

The girl had finished with the crockery but her bandage had got so soiled with the bits left on the plates that it had to be done again. She offered me a five-franc note. I didn't want to take her five francs but she insisted on giving them to me. Séverine was her name.

"You've cut your hair, haven't you, Séverine?" I asked her.

"Oh, yes, I had to. It's the fashion," she told me. "Besides, long hair in this place collects all the smells of the kitchen."

"There's another part of you that smells far worse!" Martrodin broke in, disturbed in his accounts by our chatter.

"Yes, but that's not at all the same thing," Séverine retorted, very much incensed. "There are smells and smells. And as for you, Mr. Martrodin, shall I tell you how you smell? Not just one part of you — but all over!"

She was really very angry. But Martrodin wouldn't listen to any more. He growled and went on with his damned accounts.

Séverine couldn't manage to get her slippers off and put her walking shoes on, her feet had swollen so after a whole day's work in the bar.

"Well, then, I'll sleep with them on!" she exclaimed in the end, rather loudly.

"Come on now, run and put the light out at the back," Martrodin told her. "Any one can see you don't pay my electric-light bill."

"I can sleep all right in them," Séverine groaned, getting up.

Martrodin wasn't ever going to be through with those accounts of his. He had taken off first his apron and then his waistcoat so as to count better. He was having the devil of a tussle with them. From somewhere at the back of the bar came the clink of glasses: Robinson and the other washer-up at work. Martrodin drew large childish numbers with a blue pencil which he held crushed in his great assassin's paw. The barmaid was sprawling on a chair in front of us, half asleep. From time to time she started out of her somnolence. "Oh, oh, my feet!" she cried and then went on dozing.

But Martrodin woke her up with a yell. "Hey, there, Séverine! Take your Arabs out of here. I'm sick of the sight of them. Get out, all of you. It's time you went."

The Arabs, as a matter of fact, seemed to be in no hurry, although it was so late. Séverine woke herself up at last. "Yes, it really is time I went," she agreed. "Thank you, Mr. Martrodin." She took the two Arabs off with her. They had joined forces so as to be able to afford her.

"I'm coping with both of them to-night," she explained to me, as she went out. "Because I can't next Sunday, as I'm going to Achères to see my kid. You see next Saturday is his nurse's day off."

The Arabs got up to follow her. They didn't look at all vicious. Séverine regarded them rather coldly however; she was very tired. "Personally I don't at all agree with the owner, I prefer these Arabs myself. They're not as brutal as Poles are, but they're degenerate. There's no denying that, they certainly are degenerate. . . . Well, they can do whatever they damn well please, I don't suppose that'll stop me getting to sleep. Come along," she called to them. "Off we go, boys!"

And all three of them went off together, Séverine a little in advance of the others. They could be seen crossing the cold square littered with the débris of the fair; the gas lamp at the end lit their little group; for a second they showed white and then the darkness swallowed them. You could still hear their voices vaguely, and after that nothing at all. They had gone.

I left the café myself after that without speaking again to Robinson. Martrodin wished me a pleasant good night. A policeman was pacing along the boulevard. We stirred the silence as we passed each other. It made one jump occasionally to see a tradesman here and there poring aggressively over his figures like a dog gnawing a bone. A family on the spree was strung across the street at the corner of the Place Jean-Jaurès, yelling. They weren't making any headway, they were hesitating at the entrance of a side street like a fishing fleet in a gale. The father swayed across from one pavement to the other, peeing continuously.

The night had come into her own.

THERE IS ANOTHER EVENING I REMEMBER, ABOUT THAT TIME, because of what happened. First of all, soon after supper time I heard a tremendous rattling of dustpans being shifted by somebody. People often clanked dustpans about on my staircase. Then a woman started to moan and cry out. I opened my door onto the landing slightly, but stayed where I was.

If I'd gone out on my own when there was an accident, I should probably have been regarded simply as a neighbour and my medical aid would have been taken free. If I was needed, all they had to do was to ask for me in the ordinary way and that would mean twenty francs. Poverty takes the most merciless and cunning advantage of the altruism of others and the kindest impulses of the heart are ruthlessly punished. So I waited for whoever it was to ring my bell, but no one came. Money saved, no doubt.

Anyway, I had almost finished waiting, when a little girl stopped in front of my door, trying to read the names on the different bells. It turned out it was me she was looking for. Madame Henrouille had sent her.

"Who is ill at their house?" I asked her.

"There's a gentleman hurt himself there."

"A gentleman?" I immediately thought of Henrouille himself. "The master of the house? M. Henrouille?"

"No, they want you for a friend who is there."

"Do you know who he is?"

"No." She had never seen this friend of theirs.

It was cold outside, the child trotted along, I walked fast.

"How did it happen?"

"I don't know."

We walked past a little park. Once upon a time it had been a corner of a wood, now it was railed in and the slow, soft mists of

winter met at night amid its trees. Then a series of little streets.
Soon we came to their house. The little girl said good-bye. She
was afraid to go any nearer. The younger Mrs. Henrouille was
standing out on the doorstep, waiting for me. Her oil lamp
flickered in the wind.

"This way, Doctor," she cried, "this way!"

I asked at once, "Is it your husband who's hurt?"

"Come on in!" she said rather roughly, without even giving me
time to think. And I ran straight into the old mother-in-law in
the passage, who rushed at me and began to bellow. It was hell.

"Ah, the dirty swine! The blackguards! Doctor, they tried to
kill me!"

So it had gone wrong then.

"Kill you?" said I, as if greatly surprised. "Why should they
try to do that?"

"Because I wouldn't die off quickly enough, confound you!
That's why. God in Heaven! I'm damned if I'll die. . . ."

"Mother, my dear mother!" the daughter-in-law broke in.
"You're out of your mind; you're saying the most awful things,
Mother!"

"I'm saying awful things, am I? Well, really you've a frantic
nerve, you slut! Out of my mind, eh? I'm still sane enough to
get you all hanged, let me tell you!"

"But who's hurt? Where is he?"

"Oh, you'll see," the old girl said. "He's upstairs in bed, the
murderer! And he's made a pretty good mess of the bed; hasn't
he, you slut, you? He's messed up your dirty mattress with his
rotten blood — and not with mine! His blood must be the
filthiest muck — you'll never get that mattress clean again!
It'll stink for many a long day, that murderer's blood, d' you
hear? Ah, some people go to a theatre for excitement — but this
is where they'd find it! This is where the melodrama is. It's upstairs! Real, genuine melodrama! Not just a sham. Don't lose
your seat for the show. Hurry on up. The dirty sod may have
died by the time you get there — and you won't have seen anything!"

The daughter-in-law was afraid she might be heard in the

street and told her to shut up. In spite of what had happened, the daughter-in-law didn't seem to be particularly disconcerted, merely very annoyed that things had gone all wrong; but she stuck to her idea. She seemed quite certain that she'd been right.

"Listen to her, Doctor! Isn't it terrible to hear her talk like that? When actually I have always tried to make life pleasanter for her. You know that, don't you? I was always urging her to go and live with the Sisters. . . ."

It was too much for the old lady to hear her mention the Sisters again.

"Paradise—that's where you all wanted to send me, you bitch! Yes, you harridan! And that's why you and that husband of yours got that cutthroat upstairs to come here! To kill me, and not to send me to the Sisters! He messed it, you can be sure of that—it was damn badly worked out! Go on, Doctor, go and see the state that bastard's in up there—and he did it himself! Let's only hope he dies as a result of it. Go on, Doctor; go and see him while there's still time."

If the daughter-in-law did not seem to be in despair after what had happened, the old woman was even less so. She had had a very narrow escape, but she wasn't really as outraged as she made out. It was put on. This unsuccessful attempt on her life had really rather thrilled her, brought her out of the dim tomb she had been shut up in all these years at the end of that damp garden. At her age, now an exciting sense of vitality had returned and taken possession of her. She gloated over her victory and with joy at having a means of going for her beastly daughter-in-law as long as she lived. She'd got that now. She wanted me to be told every detail of this abortive attempt at murder and of how it had all taken place.

"And another thing, Doctor," she went on in the same excited tone, speaking to me, "it was at your house I met the murderer. It was in your consulting room, Doctor. . . . I didn't trust him, you know! Oh, no, I didn't trust him at all. . . . Do you know what he first suggested to me? That he should bump off my daughter-in-law. Yes, you, my dear daughter! And for quite a moderate fee too, I assure you. He suggests the same thing to everybody, of course; we all know that. So you see, my dear, I know what your man does for a living! I know *all* about it! Robinson his name is! Isn't that his name? Tell me it isn't his name. As soon as I saw him come nosing around here, I smelt a rat at once. . . . And I was quite right! If I hadn't been so suspicious, where should I be now?"

The old woman went on and on, telling me how it had all taken place. A rabbit had moved while he was fixing the bomb behind the hutch door. She herself had been watching him all this time from her hovel — "from a front row of the stalls", as she put it. And the thing had gone off in his face while he was fixing the trap. Right into his eyes. "One's a bit nervous when engaged on a murder. Naturally," she concluded.

In fact, the whole thing had been very clumsily mishandled and mismanaged.

"That's what men are like nowadays. That's exactly it. They get into the habit," the old lady went on. "They have to kill to eat these days! It's no longer enough for them just to *steal* their daily bread. And to kill old women too! That's never been heard of before. Never! I don't know what the world's coming to. . . . There's nothing but wickedness in their minds. But all of you are mixed up in this deviltry now! And now the fellow's blind. You'll have him on your hands for always. What about that? You haven't begun to know all the harm he can do."

The daughter-in-law breathed not a word, but she must have worked out her plan of salvation. She was a hard-headed villain. While we stood and thought about it all, the old woman started to look for her son in each of the different rooms.

"And, you know, Doctor, I've got a son somewhere! Where has he got to? What can he be up to still?"

She staggered up the passage, laughing uproariously.

For an old person to laugh as much as that is something that doesn't happen outside an asylum. You wonder what's up when you hear a thing like that. But she was determined to find her son. He had slipped out into the street. "Never mind then; let him hide and let him live a long time more! I don't suppose he would have chosen to have to live with that other fellow who's upstairs, who will never see again, the two of them together! Looking after him, feeding him! The bomb went off in his face. I saw it. I saw it all. Bang! Just like that. *I* saw it. And it wasn't a rabbit, I promise you. Hell and damnation! Where is my son, Doctor; where has he got to? Haven't you seen him? He was a dirty swine too, who has always been even more of a rogue than that other one — but now this devilish business has brought him out of himself, which is a good thing! Oh, it takes a long time to be brought out of so foul a nature as his is. But when it does happen, you're rotten through and through. There's no denying, Doctor, it's a good thing. It mustn't be spoilt!" She was enjoying herself enormously. She wished to astonish me by her superiority to what had happened, to confound the whole lot of us, to humiliate us, in fact.

She had seized on a profitable rôle which she found extremely exciting. That's a thing we're always pleased about. One is never quite happy while there's still a part left to play. The bitter grumbling of the old, all that she had had to be content with for the past twenty years, wasn't enough for the old Henrouille any longer. The virulent, unexpected new rôle that had come her way was going to be hers now forever. To be old is to have no ardent part to play, to slip into an insipid retirement and wait only for death. The wish to live came back to her old carcass, quite suddenly, together with an exciting rôle of revenge. She didn't want to die now, she didn't ever want to die. She radiated this eagerness to survive, this reaffirmation of herself. She'd found warmth, colour and excitement in the drama.

She was kindled by it, she didn't want ever to give up this new fire, or let us go. For some time she had ceased to believe in it. She had got to the point of not knowing what she could do not just to go on and let death come at the end of her mouldy garden, and then here suddenly was a flood of hard, revivifying facts.

"My death!" she yelled now. "I'd like to see *me* dying! D' you hear? I've eyes to see it, d' you hear? I've still got the use of *my* eyes. I want to see it clearly!"

She wasn't going to let herself die, ever. That was definite. She no longer believed she would die.

ONE KNOWS THAT THESE THINGS ARE ALWAYS DIFFICULT TO GLOSS over and that glossing them over costs money. No one knew what to do with Robinson, to start with. Send him to a hospital? That would obviously be likely to start a lot of talk and tittle-tattle. Send him back home? That wasn't to be considered, with his face in the state it was. So whether they wanted to or not, the Henrouilles were obliged to let him stay where he was.

He lay in their bed upstairs in an abject state of mind. He was overcome with an absolute terror of being kicked out and prosecuted. It was understandable. Really it was the sort of story that has to be kept very quiet. They kept the shutters in his room well closed but neighbours and people began to walk past the house more often than usual, just to look up at the shut windows and to ask how he was. They were told how he was, they were told all sorts of stories. But how could you stop them from wondering and talking? They added a good deal to the story. How could you prevent them from jumping to conclusions? Fortunately, the law hadn't yet become definitely suspicious. That at least was something. As far as his face was concerned, I was managing about that. Infection did not set in, in spite of the fact that a lot of damage had been done and the wound had been extremely dirty. For a long time I expected his eyes, even the cornea of his eyes, to have been so badly gashed that the light would only just manage to filter through them, if it ever did enter them again.

We would find some way of fixing up his eyesight for him, to some extent, if there was anything left to fix. For the moment, what we had to do was to patch up the wound as best we could and see to it that the old woman didn't compromise us all with her damned blabbing to the neighbours and any inquisitive person who might come along. It was all very well her being thought mad; that isn't always an adequate explanation.

If the police actually started to look into the matter, it was going to be the devil of a business dealing with them. It was already a delicate game preventing the old lady from making an obstreperous nuisance of herself in her little courtyard. Each of us, one after the other, would try to calm her down. You had to be careful not to cross her at all roughly but gentleness didn't always work either. She was feeling vindictive at the moment; she had got us on the run, and that's all there was to it.

I went round to see Robinson at least twice a day. He lay there all bandaged up and started groaning as soon as he heard my step on the stairs. He was in great pain, it's true, but not in quite as much pain as he tried to make me think. He would have reason enough to moan, and moan a damn sight more, I reckoned, when he found out exactly what had happened to his eyes. . . . I avoided making any forecasts for the future. His eyelids stung badly. He thought it was this stinging which prevented his seeing anything.

The Henrouilles had set themselves to look after him very carefully, according to my instructions. No difficulties in that direction.

The attempt was never spoken of now. The future wasn't mentioned either. When I was leaving in the evening, we all stood and looked at each other every time so insistently that we always seemed to me to be on the verge of doing away with one another, once and for all. Such a conclusion to our thoughts struck me as both logical and sensible. It's difficult to imagine what the nights in that house were like. Still, I would meet them again in the morning and we would together take up with people and things again as we had left them the night before. Madame Henrouille and I would wash the wound with permanganate and bandage it afresh and open the shutters a little, by way of a test. It was never any good. Robinson didn't even realize that the shutters had been opened a bit. . . .

That's the way the world goes, spinning in a night of peril and silence.

The son met me every morning with some little remark about the weather. "Ah, there you are, Doctor. . . . A bit frostier to-day," he'd say, looking up at the sky above his doorstep. As if it mattered what the weather was like! His wife went off to parley with the old lady through her barricaded door but only managed to increase her fury.

While in his bandaged state, Robinson told me about his early life. He had started in a shop. His parents had made him an apprentice to a high-class milliner. One day when he was delivering some goods, a lady-customer invited him to taste of a pleasure he had previously experienced only in the imagination. He had never gone back to his employer, he was so dreadfully ashamed of what he had done. To go to bed with a customer was certainly still in those days an unpardonable thing. The lady's crêpe-de-chine chemise had had an extraordinary effect on him. Twenty years later he could still remember that chemise exactly. The rosy scented limbs of that frolicsome young woman in an apartment full of cushions and fringed curtains had provided Robinson with grounds for endless depressing comparisons for the rest of his life.

Many things had happened since, though. He had been all over the world, he had gone through whole wars, but he never properly got over this vision. It amused him to think back on it, to tell me about this sort of youthful moment he had shared with the lady-customer. "Having your eyes shut like this makes you think better," he remarked. "Things slip by. . . . It's as if you had a cinema inside your block." I still didn't dare tell him that he'd have plenty of time to get bored with that little cinema of his. All ideas lead the way to death and the time would come when he wouldn't see anything but that and his own image in his cinema.

Next door to the Henrouilles' house now there was an engine working in a little factory. Their house shook with it from morning till night. And then there were other works further off, thumping away without pause, never stopping, even at night. "When the roof falls in, we sha'n't be here," Henrouille would say as a joke, but he was a little bit anxious all the same. "It's bound to come down sometime." Certainly little particles were already falling from the ceiling onto the floor. It was no good for an architect to tell them it was all right; as soon as you stopped and listened to the outside world you felt their house as if you were on board a ship, some kind of ship that was sailing from one fear to the next. We were passengers shut up in the hold, spending our time making plans that were sadder than life itself and trying to save money and distrusting the light as well as the darkness.

Henrouille went up to the bedroom after lunch to read to Robinson for a little while, as I had suggested he should. The days went by. He told the story of that marvellous young woman he had slept with when he was an apprentice to Henrouille as well. The story became a household joke in the end. That is what becomes of one's intimate secrets when they are brought into the open and made public. There is nothing frightful in us and on earth and perhaps in heaven above except what has not yet been said. We shall never be at peace until everything has been said, once and for all time; then there will be silence and one will no longer be afraid of being silent. It will be all right then.

During the weeks that his eyelids took to heal, I was able to feed him awful lies about his eyes and what was going to happen. Sometimes we pretended that the window was shut when really it was wide open; at others that it was very dark and gloomy outside.

However, one day when my back was turned, he went over to the window himself to make certain on his own and before I could stop him, he had removed the strips of cloth from his eyes. He stood there hesitating a good while. He felt the window posts to the right and left; he wouldn't believe it at first and then all the same he had to believe it. There was nothing else for it; he had to.

"Bardamu!" he shouted behind me, "Bardamu! It's open! The window's wide open, I tell you!" I didn't know what to answer; I stood there like a fool. He had his arms sticking straight out of the window, into the open air. He could not see anything, of course, but he smelt the fresh air. Then he stretched out his arms farther into the darkness, as far as he could, as if to touch the other side of it. He didn't want to believe it was true. His own private darkness. I pushed him back into bed and I said a lot of things to try and console him, but now he wouldn't believe what I said. He was crying. He himself had come to the end of things. There wasn't anything you could tell him now. There is a moment when you are all alone by yourself and have come to the end of all that can happen to you. It's the end of the world. Unhappiness itself, your own misery, won't answer you now and you have to go back, among men, no matter where. One isn't difficult at moments like that, for even to weep you've got to get back to where everything starts, to where the others are.

"And what will you do with him when he's better?" I asked the daughter-in-law at lunch after this scene. They had invited me to stay to lunch with them in the kitchen. At bottom, neither of them really knew how to get out of the situation they were in. The cost of supporting him terrified them both, especially her who was better informed than he was as regards the expense of arrangements for invalids. She had already gone so far as to see what she could do in the way of getting assistance from public bodies. But I wasn't told anything about these steps.

One evening after my second visit Robinson tried as hard as he could to get me to stay by him a little while longer. He went on and on reminiscing about all that he could remember of places we'd been and the things we'd done together, even things we had never tried to recall before. In his retirement, what we had seen of the world seemed to come back to him with all the cries, the kindnesses, the things one had worn, and the friends one had left behind, an absolute bazaar of outgrown feelings which he set up in his sightless head.

"I shall kill myself!" he warned me, when his suffering seemed to him too great to bear. But then he would manage to stagger on under it a little further, as under some burden that was far too heavy for him, an infinitely pointless suffering which he could find no one to talk to about on the road, it was so vast and many-sided. He wouldn't have been able to explain to me what he was feeling; it was beyond his powers of comprehension and expression.

He was a coward, by nature, as I knew, and he did too, always hoping that he would be saved from the truth. But on the other hand, I was beginning to wonder whether true cowards really do exist anywhere. . . . It would seem that you can always find

for any single man one set of things on whose behalf he is prepared to die and to die at once and to die quite happily. Only the
chance of dying prettily, as he would like, doesn't always come
along; he doesn't care for the chance he gets. So he goes off somewhere to die as best he may. . . . The man sticks around on earth
and every one takes him for a scullion and a coward, but really he
is simply not convinced. It only looks as if he were a coward.

Robinson was not prepared to die, now the chance was being
given him to die. Perhaps if it had come to him some other way, he
would have liked to quite a lot.

Death in fact is a little bit like marriage.

This particular death he didn't like at all, so there it was.
No getting round that.

He would therefore have to resign himself to accept inertia
and suffering. But for the time being he was still frantically busy
plastering his soul, in the most disgusting way, with his misery and
his distress. Later on, he would be putting some order into his
unhappiness and then a real new life could begin. It would have to.

"You may not believe it," he said to me that evening, stirring
up tag-ends of memories after dinner, "but although I'm really
not at all good at languages, I got to know enough English towards
the end of my time at Detroit to be able to carry on some sort of
little conversation. . . . Yet now I've forgotten almost all of it
except one phrase. . . . Just two words. . . . They're often come
back to me since I've had this thing wrong with my eyes: 'Gentlemen First!' It's almost the only thing I can say in English now,
I don't know why. Of course, it's an easy thing to remember —
Gentlemen First!" And so, to try and keep his mind off things, we
amused ourselves by talking English again together. We went
on saying Gentlemen First!; we said it on every and any occasion
like a couple of idiots. It was our private little joke. Finally, when
Henrouille came up to see how we were getting on, we taught him
how to say it too.

As we stirred up old memories, one wondered what could
possibly still exist of all that, of the things we had both known.
One wondered what could have happened to Molly, our sweet
Molly. . . . Lola I wasn't eager to remember, but still I should

have liked to have had news of them all, even of little Musyne, come to that. . . . She couldn't be very far away these days, living somewhere in Paris. Next door, in fact. But it would really have been a sort of expedition trying to get news of her again. . . . There were so many people whose names, habits and addresses I had forgotten, whose pleasant ways, whose smiles, after so many years of worrying and feeling hungry, would have gone stale like an old cheese and turned into the saddest of grimaces. Memories themselves are young at one time. . . . As soon as they are allowed to go a little mouldy, they turn into the most repulsive ghosts, oozing selfishness, vanity and lies. They rot like apples. We were talking of our youth, tasting it and retasting it. We didn't entirely trust it. By the same token I haven't gone to see my mother either for a long time. Going to see her did my nerves no good. . . . She was worse than I was as far as being unhappy was concerned. She always seemed to have been gathering round her in her little shop as many disappointments as possible throughout the years. When I went to see her, she would say, "Did you know that Aunt Hortense died two months ago at Coutances? Could you have gone to the funeral? And little Clémentin, you remember Clémentin? The floor polisher who used to play with you when you were small? Well, he was picked up dead in the Rue Aboukir the day before yesterday. . . . He hadn't eaten for three days."

Robinson's own childhood was something he couldn't bear to bring himself to think about, it had been so very far from enjoyable. After the business of the lady-customer he could remember nothing, even in odd corners of it, that didn't dishearten and sicken him, like a house full of smelly horrible things, old brooms, old washtubs, fussing women, and clouts over the head. Henrouille had nothing to tell us about his childhood up to the time of his military service, when he had had his photograph taken in full gala uniform; and this photograph was still to be seen hanging above the chest of drawers.

When Henrouille had gone back downstairs, Robinson unbosomed himself to me about how he was very much afraid he would now never see anything of the ten thousand francs that had been promised him. "No, I shouldn't count on them too much," I myself advised him. I thought it best to prepare him for this further disappointment.

Little lead pellets, what remained of the exploded bomb, were working their way to the edges of his wound. I removed them bit by bit, abstracting several every day. It used to hurt him a great deal when I probed just above the conjunctiva.

It was no good our being terribly careful, people in the neighbourhood had begun to talk just the same, making out all sorts of things. Robinson did not know about this, fortunately; it would have made him much worse if he had. There's no two ways about it, we were surrounded by suspicion. Madame Henrouille made less and less noise moving about the house in her bedroom slippers. You weren't expecting her and there she'd be by your side.

Right among the reefs as we were, the slightest hesitation would wreck the lot of us. Everything would split asunder, crack, be shattered, sink and be washed ashore. Robinson, the old lady, the bomb, the rabbits, his eyes, the incredible son, the cutthroat daughter-in-law, we would all be washed up there amid all our wickedness and our secrets under the gaze of thrilled, inquisitive people. Not that I had committed any actual crime. I hadn't. But I felt myself to be guilty, nevertheless. I was guilty, at any rate, of being willing in my heart of hearts that this should go on. And of not now seeing any reason why we shouldn't all go wandering off together, deeper and deeper into the night.

In any case, there wasn't any need to want the thing; it was moving along on its own. And it was moving damned fast.

THE RICH DON'T NEED TO KILL TO EAT. THEY GIVE EMPLOYMENT to people, as the saying goes. They don't do the hurt themselves. They just fork out. Everything is done to please them and every one's perfectly happy. Whereas their women are beautiful, the poor man's wife is a sight. It's the result of centuries — quite apart from their dressing well. Beautiful creatures, well-fed, well-washed. Life has been going on a long time and that is all it's arrived at.

It's no good the rest of us striving: we slip, stumble, over-balance into the alcohol which preserves both the living and the dead, we get nowhere. It's been proved. And that after centuries of watching our domestic animals being born, struggling and dying before our eyes without anything of any moment having happened to them, either, but just picking up the same miserable thread of life where other animals had left it. We really might have cottoned on to what was happening. Endless waves of trifling human beings come drifting down from the beginning of the ages to die all the time under our very noses and yet we persist in hoping for certain things. One isn't even capable of understanding death.

The wives of the rich, fed and flattered and rested, become pretty. That is true. After all, maybe that in itself is sufficient. You can't tell. It would at any rate be a reason for existing.

"Don't you think the women in America were better-looking than the ones over here?" That's the sort of thing Robinson would say to me now that he had started recalling his travels. His mind had taken an inquiring turn; he had even begun to talk about women.

I was going to see him a little less often these days because it was about that time that I was appointed to take charge of a small dispensing clinic for tubercular cases in the neighbourhood.

One may as well give things their right names: it brought me in eight hundred francs a month. The patients I had were people of the locality, of this semi-village never quite freed of its mud, sunk in refuse and bordered by lanes of palings, where over-developed, morbid little girls, playing truant from school, picked up from some old beast a couple of francs, potato chips and gonorrhea. A highbrow film setting, with dirty linen poisoning the trees and cabbage patches stinking of piss on Saturday evenings. I did not, in my own domain, accomplish any great miracle during those several months of specialized doctoring. But my patients did not want me to accomplish miracles; on the contrary, they were counting on their t.b. to remove them from the state of absolute penury they had always lived in to the merely relative poverty of life on a minute government pension. They had carried their more or less positive disease around, from one clinic to the next, since the war. They grew thin due to fever kept up by eating very little, vomiting a lot, drinking a great deal of wine and working too at the same time — one day out of three, as a matter of fact.

Their hope of a government pension possessed them body and soul. Like grace, their pension would come to them one day if they had the strength to wait a while before dying outright. You do not know what coming back and waiting for a thing is, until you have seen how completely the poor in hope of a gov-ernment grant can hang about and wait. They spent whole after-noons and weeks, while outside the rain came down, waiting on the threshold and in the entrance to my wretched dispensary, working out hoped-for percentages, longing for the definite, tested presence of bacillæ in their sputum, for real hundred-per-cent tubercular spittle. Relief from their illness lagged far behind the government pension in their hopes: it is true, of course, that they did hope to be cured — but they only just hoped for it, whereas their desire for a regular income, however tiny, dazzled them completely. There was no room in them for anything except little secondary ambitions, aside from this relentless, ultimate craving, and even dying for them became by comparison a fairly marginal fact, at most a sporting risk. After all, death is only a matter of a few hours, perhaps a few minutes even—whereas an income, like poverty, lasts a lifetime. The rich are inebriate in another way and cannot contrive to grasp these frenzied longings for security. To be rich is another form of intoxication: it spells forgetfulness. In fact, that is what one wants riches for: to forget.

I eventually got over my bad habit of promising health to my patients. It could not be much pleasure to them to be given the prospect of getting well. After all, to be well is only better than nothing at all. You're able to work when you're well, but what after that? Whereas a state pension, however infinitesimal, is simply and absolutely something divine.

When you've no money to offer the poor, you might as well shut up. If you start talking to them about anything else besides money, you are almost invariably tricking them, lying to them. The rich can be easily amused—mirrors, for instance, in which they can see themselves, will do, for there is nothing better to look at in the world than the rich. Every ten years to keep them happy the rich can be hitched up one pip in the Legion of Honour—like a sagging breast—and they're all right after that for another ten years. That's all. My charges, on the other hand, were poor and self-seeking; they were materialists entirely cooped up in their lousy plans to retire on the strength of having spat blood really positively. Nothing else concerned them in the least and for them it did not matter whether it was spring, summer, autumn or winter; they didn't notice anything like that; all they cared about was whatever had to do with coughing and ill health—for instance, that one catches cold much more frequently in winter than in summer, but that on the other hand it is easy to spit blood in the spring, and that in the very hot weather you can lose as much as three kilos a week. . . . Sometimes I would overhear them talking among themselves when they did not know I was there, as they sat awaiting their turn. They said the most awful things about me and told lies about me that absolutely made one gasp. It obviously braced them up a lot to go for me in this way; it gave them some mysterious courage which they needed so as to be really pitiless and tough and swinish, so as to keep going, and last out. Yet I had done my best to make myself pleasant to them in every way; I espoused their cause, I tried to help them; I gave them plenty of iodine to try and make them expectorate their filthy infections — and yet none of all this sufficed to neutralise their animosity.

They stood there smiling like servants when I spoke to them, but they hadn't any use for me at all; in the first place because I did them good, and secondly because I wasn't well off myself, and being treated by me meant being treated almost for nothing, which is never very flattering to a sick person, even while waiting for a government allowance. There wasn't any low-down story they would not have spread about me behind my back. Like most of the doctors in the district I hadn't a car, and it also seemed to them a weakness on my part that I should have to walk. Once you got them going — and my colleagues never missed a chance — you'd have said they revenged themselves for all my kindness, for my being so helpful and devoted to them. All of which is perfectly usual. And time slipped by just the same.

One evening, when my waiting room was almost empty, a priest came in to talk to me. I didn't know the fellow by sight and was on the point of showing him out. I didn't like priests, I had my reasons for disliking them, especially after that trick that was played on me by shipping me off from Santa Tapeta. But I attempted in vain to place this particular one, so as to be able to curse him with some degree of accuracy — I had never set eyes on the man before. Still, he must have been about at night in Rancy like myself, since hereabouts was where he lived. Perhaps he had avoided meeting me when he went out? I wondered. No doubt they had told him I didn't like clergymen. It seemed like it from the greasy way he embarked on his discourse. It was odd now that we hadn't come across each other by the same sick beds. He had officiated at a church just next door for the last twenty years, he told me. Plenty of people attended his church but very few of them did he get any money out of. He was something of a beggar himself, in fact. We had that much in common. The soutane he wore struck me as an extremely inconvenient garment for wandering about this suburban slush in. I pointed this out to him. In fact, I laid great stress on the weird unsuitability of such an attire.

"One gets used to it," he informed me.

The impertinence of my remark did not choke him off, he was even more amiable still. There was obviously something he wanted of me. His voice never rose above a certain confidential monotony, which derived — at least, so I suspected — from his calling. While he talked on in cautious preamble, I tried to imagine to myself all the things that this priest had to accomplish on his daily round so as to provide himself with nourishment; a heap of grimaces and promises much like my own. . . . And then I pictured him, for fun, naked before his altar. . . . That is the way you have to get used to: transposing from the very outset the people who come to call; you understand them much more rapidly after that, you glimpse at once, in no matter what personality, the underlying great hungry worm it really is. An excellent gambit of the imagination. Their nasty prestige weakens, evaporates. Entirely naked, all you have in front of you is really only a wretched, pretentious beggar swollen with conceit, with difficulty getting out its inane babble in one style or another. Nothing stands up to this test. You are on your feet again that way in an instant. Ideas are all that's left and ideas never alarm. Everything's safe with them, it all works out all right. Whereas occasionally it is difficult to bear the authoritative manner of a man in his clothes. Damnable smells and mysteries he retains in his clothes.

He had shocking bad teeth, this Abbé — decayed, dirty teeth, incrusted with greenish tartar, a fine alveolar pyorrhea, in fact. I was going to talk to him about his pyorrhea, but he was far too busy telling me things. The things he was telling me never stopped pouring out against the stumps of his teeth under the impulse of a tongue whose every movement I discerned. The bleeding edges of his tongue were cut at a number of little places.

It was a habit and, as a matter of fact, a pleasure of mine to observe small intimate details like this. When you consider, for instance, the way in which words are formed and uttered, human speech fails to stand up to the test of all these appalling trappings of spittle. The mechanical effort we make in speaking is more complicated and arduous than defecation. The mouth, that corolla of puffed flesh, which convulses when it whistles; sucks in breath, and labours, and ejects all sorts of viscous sounds past a barrier of dental decay — what a punishment it is! Yet this is what we are urged to consider ideal. It isn't easy. Since we are nothing but packages of warm and rotten tripes, we shall always have difficulty with sentiment. To love is nothing, it's hanging together that's so hard. Muck, on the other hand, makes no attempt either to endure or to increase. In this particular matter we are far more wretched than filth itself, with our frantic desire to last out as we are which constitutes such infinite torture.

Decidedly we worship nothing more divine than our own effluvium. All our unhappiness is due to having to remain Tom, Dick and Harry, cost what it may, throughout a whole series of years. The bodies we possess, a fancy dress of twitching, trivial molecules, revolt unceasingly against this frightful farce of managing to last. They want to be off, these molecules of ours, and lose themselves, as quick as they can, in the universe at large: little beauties! They hate just being "us", mere cuckolds of the Infinite! We'd burst to smithereens if we'd the guts, from one day to the next we only just fail to. Our darling agony is there, in atoms, enclosed within our hides, along with our pride.

As I was silent, appalled by my realization of biological ignominy, the Abbé thought he had got me and indeed began to take up a very friendly, even familiar, attitude towards me. Clearly he had found out all about me beforehand. With infinite precautions he broached the delicate subject of my medical reputation in the district. It might have been rather better than it was, he would have me understand, if I had borne myself very differently at the outset, in the first few months of my practice at Rancy.

"The sick, my dear Doctor, we ought not to lose sight of the fact, are conservative in outlook. . . . One can well understand that they are fearful lest Heaven and earth should fail them. . . ."

So that, according to him, I ought from the start to have turned toward the Church. That was the conclusion he came to — on spiritual as well as on practical grounds. Not a bad idea. I was careful not to interrupt him, but I was waiting, patiently, for him to come to the point of his visit.

For gloomy, confidential weather you couldn't have done better than the weather outside. You would have thought, so foul was it and so icily, insistently foul, that when you went out you would never see the rest of the world again, it would all have melted away in disgust.

My nurse had at last managed to put her files in order, all of them, right up to the very last one. She now had no conceivable excuse for staying behind to overhear us. So she departed, angrily, and slamming the door behind her, through a savage gust of rain.

IN THE COURSE OF THIS CONVERSATION THE PRIEST TOLD ME HIS name. The Abbé Protiste, he was called. He informed me in an exceedingly roundabout way that he and Madame Henrouille had for some time been trying to see if they could get the old woman and Robinson, both of them together, into some not too expensive religious institution. They were still looking round for one.

Looking at him carefully, the Abbé Protiste might have passed for a window dresser; he looked as most of them look; perhaps even for the head salesman of a department, sallow, dapper and dried up. He was truly plebeian in the meekness of his insinuations. And in his breath too. I never mistake a person's breath. This man ate too fast and drank white wine.

Madame Henrouille, Junior, he told me to start with, had looked him up at the presbytery itself, soon after the attempt on the old lady's life, to see if he could get them out of the dirty mess they had run themselves into. He seemed in telling me this to be trying to find some excuse, some explanation; he was some- how ashamed of being involved in this way. There was really no need, where I was concerned, to stand on ceremony like that. One understands how things are. He had come to join us in the dark, that's all. So much the worse for him then. A nasty kind of audacity had come over him too, bit by bit, as money changed hands. But that was his lookout. As a deep silence reigned in my dispensary and night had settled on the neighbourhood, he lowered his voice to a whisper, so as to confide in me alone. But it wasn't any good his murmuring like that; what he was telling me struck me as overbearing and intolerable, no doubt be- cause of the quiet around us, which seemed to be full of echoes. Perhaps they were only inside my own head. "Sssh!" I wanted to say to him all the time, whenever his voice was silent for a

moment. Even my lips were trembling a little with fear, and between sentences one stopped thinking altogether.

Now that he was joining us in our difficulties, this priest, he
didn't properly know what to do to follow after us four in the
darkness. We were a little band. He wanted to know how many
of us were already involved. And where were we heading for? So
that he too could hold hands with his new friends and advance
towards the goal we should all of us have to reach together or not
reach at all. We were all going the same way now. He would learn
how to get along in the dark, he said, like the rest of us. He still
wasn't very certain of his ground. He wanted to know how to
avoid tripping up. Well, he didn't have to come if he was scared.
. . . We'd all get somewhere together in the end and then we'd find
out what it was we'd been looking for in this whole business. That
is what life boils down to, a light going out in the darkness.

And besides, perhaps we never should know after all; we might
not find anything. Then we should have found death.

The thing at the moment was to creep ahead very cautiously.
We had started anyway, we couldn't go back. We hadn't any
choice. Their damnable Justice was there, with the law lurking
around every corner. Madame Henrouille, Junior, was holding
the old lady's hand, and her son and I held hers, and Robinson
held mine. All of us linked up together. That was how it was.
I explained all this to the Abbé at once. And he understood.

Whether we liked it or not, as I explained to this priest, it
would be a very bad thing, placed as we were at present, to let
ourselves be caught and exposed by any passer-by, and I laid
great emphasis on this. If we met any one, the thing was to
behave quite casually and pretend we were just out taking a walk.
That was the idea. Be as natural as possible. So now the priest
knew it all, understood it all. He shook me hard by the hand. He
was very frightened himself too, naturally. He was only just
starting. He hesitated and floundered about like a tyro. There was
no track and no guiding light where we were, just a certain
caution which we communicated to each other but didn't really
very much believe in ourselves. The words you say to reassure
each other on occasions like that get nowhere. No echo replies,

one has left human society behind. Fear says neither yes nor no. It absorbs everything you say, everything you are afraid of, the whole thing.

It's no good straining your eyes to see in the dark, either. The horror of being lost is all there is. It has swallowed up the night itself and your attempts to see through it. It empties you out. You've got to hang on though to the other fellow's hand, or down you'll go. The people who are out in the daylight can't understand you now. You are shut off from them by fear, which goes on crushing you until this thing comes to an end one way or another and you can join all the other rogues either in this world or the next.

All the Abbé had to do was to help us at the moment, and set to and learn his part; that was his job. Besides, that's all he had come to do, sweat away to find some home for the old lady to start with, and as soon as ever he could, and for Robinson too at the same time, at some convent place or other in the country. It seemed to him a possible scheme this, and to me too, of course. Only we'd have to wait several months for there to be room, and we couldn't wait. That was no good.

The daughter-in-law was right; the sooner the thing was arranged the better. Get them away. Get rid of them. Father Protiste had another scheme in mind. Rather an amazing scheme, I had to admit. Besides, he had an idea we ought both to get a commission on it, him and me. It ought to be put into execution straight away and I was to play my small part too. My part was to persuade Robinson to go south; I was to give him this advice in an ordinary, friendly way, of course, but at the same time I was strongly to urge him to go.

Not really knowing what was at the bottom of or behind this scheme of the Abbé's I ought perhaps to have made certain conditions or asked for some sort of guarantee on my friend's behalf maybe. . . . Because really, when you came to think of it, it was an extraordinary scheme this Abbé Protiste was proposing. But we were all so harassed by circumstances that the essential thing at the moment was that no time should be lost. I promised whatever was asked of me, to help and to keep my mouth shut. Old Protiste seemed to be quite accustomed to delicate dealings of this kind and I felt that he was going to make a number of things much easier for me.

How should we start? A discreet departure for the South of France had to be organized. What would Robinson say to that? And then going with the old lady too, whom he'd so nearly blown up! I'd be insistent. Yes, there wasn't anything else for it. . . . It was necessary that he should agree — for all sorts of reasons, not all of them good, — but powerful, every one of them.

As strange jobs go, it was a really remarkable one they'd found for Robinson and the old lady down South. At Toulouse it was. It's a fine place, Toulouse. We should, of course, see the town. We would go down to see them there. It was understood that I should go down to Toulouse when they were safely installed in their house and settled into the job and all.

And when I thought about it, it rather annoyed me that Robinson should be going away so soon and then at the same time it pleased me a lot, especially as for once I was to get a real little something out of it. They'd give me a thousand francs. That was agreed upon too. I only had to incline Robinson towards the idea of going south, assuring him that it was the best possible climate for eye wounds, that he'd be perfectly well off down there, in fact, that he was very lucky to have things turn out like this. That was the way to get him to fall in with the scheme.

After five minutes' thought along these lines, I was full of conviction myself and quite ready for a decisive interview. Strike while the iron is hot, that's what I say. After all, he'd be no worse off there than here. Protiste's idea, when one thought it over once more, seemed really eminently sensible. These priests know how to cover up the nastiest scandals for you, one must admit.

Robinson and the old woman were being offered a business which, after all, was as good as any other. A vault with mummies in it was what it was, if I wasn't mistaken. It was under a church and people came to see it and paid a fee. Tourists. A lucrative business, Protiste assured me. I almost believed him and felt slightly envious. You can't often make any profit by employing dead men.

I locked up the dispensary and we started out for the Henrouilles' together, the Abbé and I, through the slush, with our minds entirely made up. This was something new indeed. A thousand francs to look forward to! I'd changed my mind about old Protiste. When we got to the Henrouilles, we found them both with Robinson in the bedroom on the second floor. But what a state Robinson was in!

"There you are!" he called out excitedly, as he heard me coming up the stairs. "I'm sure something's up. . . . It is, isn't it?" he asked me breathlessly.

And he started wailing again before I could get a word in. The other two, the Henrouilles, made signs while he called out to me to help him. "What a hell of a mess!" I thought. "They've been in much too much of a hurry. Damn fools! D' you mean to say they've gone and broken the thing to him already, flat out? Without working up to it? Without waiting for me?"

Fortunately, I was able to get the whole thing going right, as you might say, by using other tactics. Robinson, after all, wanted nothing better than to be given another view of the same situation. That was sufficient. The Abbé was outside, not daring to come in. He lurked anxiously in the corridor.

"Come on in!" Madame Henrouille urged him at last. "Don't stay out there! You're not the least in the way, Monsieur l'Abbé. . . . Here you have us, a family stricken with grief, that is all . . . Doctor and priest! Is it not always thus in moments of misfortune?"

She was waxing devilish eloquent. The hope of extricating herself from this shady mess at last was making the old bitch lyrical after her own filthy fashion.

The helpless priest had lost his head and stood there bleating some yards from the sick man's bed. His nervous babbling set Robinson off again: "They're tricking me! You're all of you tricking me!" he yelled.

Fuss and nonsense, confound it, there wasn't any sense in all this. Getting all worked up. The same old thing. But it put me on my mettle; it started me going. I took the Henrouille woman into a corner and I put the thing to her clearly, because it was obvious to me that the only person present capable of handling this business was yours truly, come to that. "Let's get this settled," I said to her. "You'd better fix up with me right away!" When you've no trust left in a person, there's no offence to be taken, as they say. She got my point and shoved a thousand-franc note into my hand and added another, just to make quite sure. I had been firm about it. Whereupon I got down to making up Robinson's mind for him while I was on the job. We simply had to get him to decide to go south.

It's easy enough to say I was double-crossing. Even so, it's a question of when and how. Double-crossing is like opening a window in a prison. Every one wants to, but it isn't often you get the chance.

ONCE ROBINSON HAD LEFT RANCY, I REALLY THOUGHT LIFE WOULD get a move on and there'd be a few more sick people may be. But there weren't. In the first place, a slump occurred in the neighbourhood and a lot of people were thrown out of work, which is always very bad. And then, although it was winter, the weather turned dry and mild, when it's the wet and the cold that our profession needs. There were no epidemics either — in fact, it was a wretched season and quite useless.

I even saw certain of my colleagues going to visit their patients on foot, which just shows; smiling as they walked along, though really they found it most provoking and were only trying to economise by not using their cars. Personally, I only had a mackintosh to go out in. Was that why I caught such a dreadful cold? Or was it because I had got into the way of eating really much too little? God knows. Perhaps it was my old friend, the fever, getting a hold on me again. Anyway, the fact remains that one cold spell just before the spring I started to cough all the time and felt extremely ill. It was damned annoying. Then one morning I simply couldn't get out of bed. Bébert's aunt was passing my door at that moment. I called out to her. She came in. I sent her off at once to collect a small bill I was still owed in the neighbourhood. My last and only one. I got half of it, which kept me going for ten days, — ten days in bed.

You've time to think, lying on your back that long. As soon as I was better, I would go away from Rancy, that's what I decided. Rent two months in arrears. . . . So farewell, my four sticks of furniture! Without saying a word to any one, of course, I'd slip quietly away and never be seen more in Garenne-Rancy. I'd depart, leaving no trace and no address. When the stinking demon of poverty's after you, why argue? To say not a word and be getting along is the wiser part.

With my certificate, of course, I could set up wherever I liked in practice. But anywhere else it would be no pleasanter, no worse. A little better at first, obviously, because a certain time is needed for people to get to know you and get going and find out the way to do you some harm. While they're still searching for the spot where it's easiest to hurt you, you get some peace; but as soon as they have found that joint, it becomes much the same thing in every place. In fact, it's during the little interval when you aren't known in a new place that life's most bearable. After that, the same old bloody-mindedness begins all over again. They're like that. The thing is not to wait too long and let them all cotton on to your weak points. A bedbug has to be squashed before it gets back to its crack. Aren't I right?

As to the sick, the patients, I was under no illusions as far as they were concerned. They'd be no less mean or obstinate or craven in any other quarter of town than they were here. Just the same booze, movies, sports talk, the same happy acquiescence to natural needs, at either end, making up as here the same cloddish, dung-smeared, credulous crowd, always blathering, bargaining, malevolent and, between one panic and the next, aggressive.

But just as the sick man is allowed to roll over in bed and in life, so have we a perfect right to flop over, too, onto the other side: it's the only thing one can do and the only defence that's been found against Destiny. It's no good expecting to drop one's misfortune anywhere *en route*. It's as if one's misfortune were some ghastly-looking female, and somehow one had married her. Maybe it's better to end up by loving her a little than to wear oneself out beating her all one's life. Since you're not going to be able to suppress her anyway.

Well, I did slip quietly away from my second-floor flat in Rancy. They were sitting round a bottle of wine and chestnuts in my concierge's lodge when I walked past it for the last time. No one saw me or noticed me. She was scratching herself and he, leaning over the stove, bemused by the heat, had already drunk enough red wine not to be able to keep his eyes open.

Where those people were concerned I was sliding into the unknown as into a great tunnel with no end to it. It makes you feel fine that,—three fewer people to spy on you and harm you, three people who won't even know what has become of you. Fine! Three, because I count the daughter in too, their child Thérèse, who broke out in running sores, she was so badly bitten by fleas and bugs and couldn't leave the bites alone. It's a fact that one was so bitten at the concierge's that entering their lodge was like walking into a hairbrush.

The light of the naked and screeching gas jet in the hall fell on people passing by along the pavement and turned them at once into haggard, solid ghosts framed darkly in the doorway. They passed on, these people, and collected to themselves a little colour here and there at other windows and street lamps and then lost themselves, like me, in the night, black soft shadows.

There wasn't any need to recognize these passers-by. Still, it would have pleased me to stop them on their aimless stroll for just one second, just long enough to tell them, definitely, that I was getting the hell out of here, going away, a long way away, and I didn't give a tinker's damn for any of them and they couldn't do anything to me now, it wasn't any use their trying.

When I got to the Boulevard de la Liberté, the vegetable carts were rumbling up towards town. I went along with them. In fact, I was now almost out of Rancy altogether. It wasn't warm, either. So, wanting to get warm, I went round out of my way a bit to Bébert's aunt's place. Her lamp was a speck of light at the end of the corridor. "So as to end off properly," I said to myself, "I must go and say 'au revoir' to his aunt."

She was sitting there as usual amid all the smells of the lodge, and there was the little stove warming it all up, and that old face of hers always on the verge of tears, now that Bébert was dead; and on the wall above her workbasket a large schoolboy photograph of Bébert in a school suit and a béret and holding a cross. It was an enlargement paid for with the coffee firm's coupons. I woke her up.

"Good morning, Doctor!" She gave a jump. I remember quite well what she said.

"You don't look at all well!" she exclaimed. "Sit down, won't you? I'm not feeling too well myself. . . ."

"I've just been out for a little walk," I said, by way of explanation.

"It's very late to be going out for little walks," she answered, "especially if you're going in the Place Clichy direction. . . . It's bitter on the avenue at this time."

She got up and tottered around, making me a warm drink, talking all the time about everything and about the Henrouilles and about Bébert, of course.

There was no way of stopping her talking about Bébert and yet it hurt her and wasn't good for her to talk about him, and she knew that too. I sat and listened to her without saying a word; I was sort of dazed. She was trying to recall all Bébert's good qualities and she made a kind of window display of them — with a great deal of difficulty; yet she mustn't forget a single one of them, and she'd start all over again; and then it was all right and she had told me all the details of his being fed out of a bottle as an infant; but then she'd find yet another little quality of Bébert's which had to go with the others, whereupon she would begin the whole story again at the beginning and she'd forget a bit just the same, and in the end she was reduced to weeping a little out of sheer impotence. Her mind wandered, she was so tired. She fell asleep between sobs. It was a long time now since she had been able to recall to mind the memory of little Bébert, whom she had been very fond of. Limbo was near her now and rather hovered over her these days. A drop of grog and feeling tired and there it was; she'd fall asleep snoring like a little æroplane flying far away amid the clouds. She had nobody now in the world.

While she sat there in this collapse, amid the various smells, I reflected that I was going away and that I should no doubt never see Bébert's aunt again, that he, Bébert, had gone too, quietly and for good, and that she herself would be following after him before very long. Her heart was weak and old. Blood it pumped as best it could into her arteries; it had to struggle its way into her veins. She would be going off to the large cemetery round the corner, where the dead are like a waiting crowd. That is where she used to take Bébert to play before he fell ill, to that cemetery. And then it would all be over. They'd come and lay a fresh coat of paint on her lodge and then we should all have been picked up and put away, like balls which topple on the edge of a hole and take their time to drop in and have done with it.

They fly off, swish, at great speed, but they don't really ever get anywhere. Neither do we, and the purpose of the world is to collect them all again at the end. And the end wasn't far now for Bébert's aunt; she hadn't much driving force left. You cannot find yourself while you are in the midst of life. There are too many colours distracting your attention and too many people moving about round you. You only find yourself in silence, when it is too late, like dead men. There was I, still having to move around and go on somewhere else. It was no good my doing anything, no good my realizing . . . I couldn't stay on there with the boy's aunt any longer.

My degree made a bulge in my pocket, a bigger bulge than my money or my passport and my papers. Outside the police station the constable on duty was waiting to be relieved at midnight and spat the while as hard as he could. We said good night to each other.

Beyond the oil pumps on the corner of the boulevard was the toll gate with its two officials in their glass cage. The trams had stopped. It was just the moment to talk to these officials about life—which is always becoming harder and more expensive. They were a young and an old man, with scurf on their shoulders, bending over enormous ledgers. Through the glass you could see the great shadowy fortifications of the town advancing like breakwaters high in the night, waiting for ships from so far away, and such fine ships that no one would ever see ships like that. But I know I'm right. They're expected sometime.

We chatted for a while, the officials and I, and even had a cup of the coffee that was warming on the range. They asked me if I wasn't going off on my holidays, trying to be funny, me with my little bundle under my arm in the dark like that. "You're quite right," I replied. No good talking to these fellows about anything that wasn't entirely ordinary. They couldn't help me to understand. I was a little annoyed by their remark and felt I wanted to say something interesting, surprise them a bit, in fact. So I started in right away to talk about the smaller details of the campaign of 1816, in which the Cossacks, in pursuit of the great Napoleon, reached the very spot where we were standing — the fortifications of Paris.

I expounded all this to them with some brilliance, of course, and not a little ease. Having in a few words convinced them of my superior culture and startling erudition, I started off again up the avenue towards the Place Clichy, feeling much better.

You will have noticed that there are always two prostitutes waiting at the corner of the Rue des Dames. Theirs are the empty hours between the middle of the night and early dawn. It is thanks to them that life spans this gap of darkness. They serve as its liaison officers, with their handbags full of prescriptions, handkerchiefs that can be used for any purpose, and snapshots of kids in the country. When you go up to them in the dark, look out, because they hardly exist at all, these women, they're so specialised, just sufficiently alive to reply to the two or three queries which sum up all that you can get out of them. They're bugs in button boots.

Say nothing to them, don't go too near them. They're dangerous. I had plenty of room. I started to run along the tramway lines. And it's a very long street.

Right at the end is Marshal Moncey's statue. He's been defending the Place Clichy since 1816 against remembrance and forgetfulness, against nothing at all, decked with a coronet of pretty cheap pearls. I came along abreast of him one hundred and twelve years too late, running up the very empty avenue. There weren't any Russians now or any battles or Cossacks or soldiers or anything at all in the square, except a ledge of the pedestal one could sit on under the coronet. And a little workman's fire, round which three fellows sat shivering, with its filthy smoke making them squint. It didn't look too comfortable.

An occasional motor car dashed across and out of the square as fast as it could.

In a case of need you remember the main boulevards as being not so cold as other places. My brain only worked when I forced it to, because I was feeling so ill. With the aunt's grog inside me

I chased down there before the wind, which isn't so cold when you get it in the back. An old dame in a bonnet by the Saint-Georges Métro station was weeping for her little granddaughter, who was ill in a hospital, with meningitis, she told me. She begged from me with that excuse. She was out of luck.

I let her have a few words instead. I, in my turn, talked to her; I told her about young Bébert and about a little girl I'd attended in town once, when I was a student, who'd also died of meningitis. She had taken three weeks to die, as a matter of fact, and her mother in a bed by her side couldn't sleep it was so frightful; so she masturbated all the time, all those three weeks, and then afterwards, when it was all over, she went on doing it and they couldn't stop her.

Which proves that one can't live even for a moment without pleasures and that it's extremely difficult to be really miserable. Life is like that.

The old lady and I parted in front of the Galeries. She had to go and unload carrots in the Halles. She'd been following the vegetable route, the same as me.

But the Tarapout attracted me. It's a cinema situated there on the boulevard like a great, glowing cake. And from all sides people come scurrying to it like mites. They come out of the surrounding night with eyes staring wide, ready to fill them with visions of light. The ecstasy goes on all the time. They're the same people who crowd into the Métro in the morning. But here in front of the Tarapout they are happy; as in New York, they burrow down into their clothes and grub out a little money and then with minds made up, they rush joyfully into the glare of the entrances. The light almost undressed you, pouring down as it did on each person and movement and every thing, all the garlands of lamps. You couldn't have discussed any private matter in that hall, it was the exact opposite of the night outside.

I was pretty dazzled myself, so I went and sat down in a little near-by café. At the next table, I looked, and there was my old friend Professor Parapine having a beer, and as scurfy as ever. An unexpected meeting. Delightful. Great changes had come about in his life, he told me. No sort of joke. Professor Jaunisset of the

Institute had become so unpleasant, had treated him so badly, that Parapine had had to leave, resign and give up his laboratory; besides, there'd been the mothers of the little girls at the Lycée who had come and waited for him at the gates of the Institute and set upon him. A great to-do. Enquiries. Trouble.

At the last moment, through an ambiguous advertisement in a medical journal, he had managed to scrape hold of another small means of livelihood. Nothing much, of course, but still not too tiring a game and quite within his scope. It concerned the intelligent putting into practice of Professor Baryton's recent theories on the development of cretin children by cinematic processes. A tremendous step forward in the realm of subconscious. Everybody in town was talking about it. It was absolutely the up-to-date thing.

Parapine accompanied these special charges of his to the up-to-date Tarapout. He went and collected them at Baryton's up-to-date nursing home in the suburbs and took them back after the show, mowing, bloated with the visions they had seen, happy, and released, and much more up-to-date than before. That's all. As soon as they'd been set down in front of the screen there wasn't any more need to bother about them. A marvellous audience. They were delighted; the same film shown ten times over enchanted them. They had no memory. They were continually joyfully surprised. Their families couldn't have been more pleased. Nor could Parapine. Nor I either. We laughed at our ease and drank bock after bock to celebrate this reinstitution of Parapine on up-to-date lines. We would stay still two in the morning, after the last performance at the Tarapout, we agreed, and then collect his cretins and rush them back by car to Doctor Baryton's place at Vigny-sur-Seine. Great fun.

As we were both so pleased to see each other again, we began to talk about all sorts of things and to tell about the travels we'd been on and finally we spoke of Napoleon, who came into the conversation via Marshal Moncey and the Place Clichy. Everything's a pleasure when one's only object is to get on nicely and have a good time with some one, because then you really feel you are free. You forget about ordinary life, that is to say, about money.

Passing on from one thing to another, we even found a few humorous remarks to make about Napoleon. Parapine knew the story of Napoleon well. He had been extremely interested in it, he told me, in the old days in Poland when he was a student. He had been well educated, Parapine, unlike me.

So it was that talking about these things, he told me of how Napoleon's generals, during the retreat from Moscow, had had the hell of a time trying to prevent him from going to Warsaw to have a last supreme fling with the Polish mistress of his heart. That's what you have Napoleon up to, even in the midst of his greatest reverses and misfortunes. Really, it was a bit too much. He, the Eagle, the Emperor, with his Josephine at home and all! When you feel frisky that way, there's nothing'll stop you. It's no use once you're set on making whoopee — and we all are. That is what is so depressing. It's all one thinks about — in one's cradle, at the café, on a throne, in the W.C., every damned where! Cock-a-doodle-ooo! Napoleon or any one else! Wise man and fool alike! Fun first and foremost! To hell with the four thousand hoodwinked heroes in scarlet and gold (thought Genius in defeat) — so long as old Boney gets his slap and tickle! What a scamp the fellow was! Well, damn it all . . . that's life. That's the way it all ends. Just too bad. The tyrant tires of the part he's playing long before the spectators. He rushes off to bed with some one as soon as he stops storing up his excitements in the public service. It's all up with him then! Destiny drops him cold in the twinkle of an eye. Wholesale massacre is not what his fans object to. Oh, no. That's nothing. Rather not. But to have become a bore all of a sudden — that is what they won't forgive him. Tolerance of any reasonable action is all bluff. Epidemics come to an end only when the microbes are bored with their own toxins. Robespierre was guillotined because he kept repeating the same thing over and over again, and as far as Napoleon was concerned, he failed to survive two years of an inflation of Legions of Honour. It was the tragedy of this madman that he was obliged to furnish half sedentary Europe with a longing for adventure. An impossible task. It killed him.

Whereas the cinema, that new little clerk of our dreams, can be bought, hired for an hour or two, like a whore.

Besides, artistes are stuck about everywhere these days, as a safety measure, with a view to our not being too bored. You have them all over every building now, overflowing with thrills, their passionate revelations trickling from floor to floor. Every door a peephole. Which of them can wriggle most, and be more blatant, more soulful, more intensely abandoned than his neighbour? Nowadays public lavatories go in for *décor*, and so does the slaughterhouse and the pawnshop too — just to keep you amused and distract you, and let you forget your fate.

Living, just by itself — what a dirge that is! Life is a classroom and Boredom's the usher, there all the time to spy on you; whatever happens, you've got to look as if you were awfully busy all the time doing something that's terribly exciting — or he'll come along and nibble your brain. A day that is nothing but a mere round of the twenty-four hours isn't to be borne. It has to be one long, almost unbearable thrill, a twenty-four-hour copulation, willy-nilly.

You get the most deplorable ideas of this sort when you're needy and dazed and when every second of your life a desire for a thousand other places and things is crushed within you.

Robinson was another fellow who was, in his own way, harassed by infinite longings — or had been, before his accident happened to him; but now his account was settled. At least, I imagined so.

Seeing that now we were peacefully seated at a café, I in my turn told Parapine all that had happened to me since last we met. He understood things, you know; he understood about me, and I confessed to him that I had just wrecked my medical career by decamping from Rancy in the most unheard-of fashion. That's the way you put these things. Really, it was no joke. I couldn't dream of going back there, in the circumstances. Parapine quite agreed.

While we were pleasantly conversing in this way, and I was

unburdening myself to him, there was an interval at the Tarapout and the musicians of the cinema orchestra came over *en bloc* for a drink. We all had one together. Parapine knew these musician fellows well.

One thing leading to another, I learnt from them that as a matter of fact a pasha was wanted for the stage show. A silent rôle. The previous "Pasha" had gone off, without a word. It was a well-paid part though, in an act between films. Nothing strenuous. Surrounded furthermore, it shouldn't be forgotten, by a magnificent flight of English dancing girls — thousands of rippling, attractive muscles. Just my cup o' tea and one I badly needed.

I made myself pleasant at once and angled for an offer of the part from the manager. I put myself forward, in fact. As it was late, and they hadn't time to go and fetch somebody else for it as far as the Porte Saint-Martin, the manager was quite pleased to take me on. It saved him trouble. Me too. He barely looked me over. I'd do, in fact, straight away. I was engaged. So long as I didn't limp, that was all that mattered.

I made my way into the beautiful, upholstered underground precincts of the Tarapout movie palace: an absolute scented hive of little dressing rooms where the English girls, waiting for the show to start, pranced curiously about and swore. Overjoyed at having lighted on my bread and butter again, I instantly made the acquaintance of these care-free young colleagues of mine. They welcomed me into their circle really most charmingly. Angelic they were. Discreetly angelic. It's pleasing, too, not to be catechised or despised: England all over.

There was a lot on at the Tarapout. In the wings it was all luxury, ease, thighs, lights, soap, sandwiches. The scene of the divertissement in which we appeared was laid, I believe, in Turkestan. It was an excuse for choreographic convolutions and musical wrigglings and volleys of tambourine delights.

My rôle was essential, though summary. Loaded with raiment of silver and gold, I experienced some difficulty at first in installing myself amid so many properties and flimsy-looking lamps, but I got the hang of it and once I was set, beautifully in evidence, all I had to do was to sit there day-dreaming under the opaline spotlights.

For a good quarter of an hour twenty Cockney odalisques flung themselves melodiously about in bacchanalian frenzy, apparently in an attempt to convince me of the reality of their charms. They could have spared themselves the trouble: and I reflected that really to repeat all this five times a day was a lot for a woman to do, as they did, untiringly, time and time again, waggling buttocks unceasingly with that rather tiresome energy of their race, that pitiless obstinacy of ocean-bound tramp steamers endlessly ploughing away across infinite high seas.

THERE IS NO POINT IN STRUGGLING; WAITING IS ENOUGH, SINCE everything in the end will have to turn out into the street. It's the street which counts in the long run. There's no escape. It lies in wait for us. We will have to make up our minds, we will have to pass out into the street, not one or two or a few of us, but everybody. We hover about on the brink and make a great fuss, but it will come to that.

Everything is rotten indoors. As soon as a door closes behind a man he begins to smell at once, and everything that is his smells with him. He becomes outworn in body and soul. He goes bad. And if mankind stinks in this way, it's meant for us to notice. We ought to take steps about it. We ought to dig people out, expel them, expose them. All the nasty little human tricks are indoors, putting on finery, but they stink just the same.

Talking about people *en masse*, I know a chemist on the Avenue Saint-Ouen who has a lovely notice in his window: Three Francs the Bottle — a Dose for the Whole Family. The very thing. A communal rumble. The family takes its medicine like a man — like one man. Every one hates every one else like hell, that's the real family circle, but nobody complains because anyway it's cheaper than going to live at an hotel.

The hotel, now, an hotel is more alive and restless; it's not as smug as an apartment; you don't feel so guilty at an hotel. The human race is never at peace and obviously at an hotel one's readier for the last judgment, which will take place in the open street. As soon as the trumpeting angels come around, we shall be the first to get there, running down and out from the hotel.

You try not to attract too much attention to yourself at an hotel. But it's no good. As soon as you raise your voice too loud or squabble too often, dammit, you're discovered. In the end you don't dare use the jerry in your room, everything's so audible from one room to the next. Eventually you acquire perfect manners, as if you were in the navy. The world can rock from floor to ceiling at any moment; you are ready, you don't mind, you're so used to "forgiving" everybody twenty times a day, through just meeting them in the corridor, at an hotel.

You might as well learn to recognize each stable companion's smell when you go to the lavatory; it's a useful talent. Reality is pretty stark at a boarding house. Guests aren't cocky. They travel softly through life from day to day, not thrusting themselves forward, like passengers on some rather rotten old ship which is full of holes, and they know it.

The one I went and stayed at was mostly full of students from the provinces. It smelt of cigarette ends and breakfast coffee from right down at the bottom of the staircase. You were guided back to it at night by the dim light over the doorway and the gilt letters strung across the balcony like a set of ancient, enormous false teeth. A monster of a lodging house made abject by questionable goings-on.

One paid visits to one's neighbours from room to room. After years of grubbing about in the world of practical things, of living my life, as the saying goes, I now came up against undergraduates again.

Their desires were still the same, raw and clear-cut, no more and no less futile than before, when I had known them in the old days. The boys were different but the ideas were the same. They all went, now as always, at more or less regular times, to nibble a little medicine, bits of chemistry, hunks of law, and a mass of zoölogy, yonder at the University. The war had swept over their kind without altering anything at all about them, and when you mixed yourself up in their dreams, out of sympathy, they took you straight along with them to their own age of forty years. They gave themselves twenty years ahead, two hundred and forty months of carefully counted pence in which to achieve happiness in life.

A vision of the narrow path was their idea of happiness, their model of success, but it was all to be very gradual and according to plan. They pictured themselves, when they had "won through", surrounded by a small but quite entrancing family. Yet they would never, so to speak, have taken a good look at that family of theirs. Why bother? A family's fine but you don't need really to consider what it's like. Why, it's a father's joy and privilege to kiss his family without taking any real notice of it; it's his dream come true.

By way of adventure, they would have gone to Nice with their bride and her dowry, and maybe have taken to a cheque book in dealings with the bank. In the matter of wild oats, no doubt they'd have taken that same wife to some moderately low haunt one night. Nothing more than that. Everything else you find shut away in the daily papers and in charge of the police.

Staying at this lousy hotel made my young friends rather shame-faced and easily irritated. The bourgeois youth as an under-graduate at an hotel, considers himself in purgatory and, as it is understood that he cannot yet be saving money, he is determined to be Bohemian by way of relief, damned Bohemian: desperation in terms of *café crème*.

About the beginning of the month we went through a short but violent phase of erotic fever; the whole hotel fairly hummed with it. Feet were washed. An amourous expedition was got up. The arrival of money orders from the country made our minds up definitely. I could probably have provided myself with the same enjoyments on my own at the Tarapout with my English dancing ladies — and for nothing too — but, thinking it over, I renounced such easy conquests because of the talk there might be and the wretched, envious, pimpish little friends who always hang around the wings with an eye on dancers.

As we read a lot of dirty papers in our hotel, we knew plenty of tricks and addresses for having a good time in Paris. One must admit addresses are rather fun. You let yourself get inter-ested, even when, like me, you've gone the round of Bérésinas alley and travelled a good bit and learnt all sorts of odd gambits at that game; the attraction of hearing all about it from some one never seems entirely to fail. There is always a little bit of extra curiosity left in you somewhere for anything to do with smut. You think to yourself that you have nothing more to learn along that line, that you really can't waste any more time over it, and then all the same you begin again, just once more, just to make quite certain that you've lost all interest in that sort of thing; and damned if you don't find out something new and that is enough to start you off feeling optimistic again.

You wake up, you think more clearly than you did before, and you begin to hope for things you had entirely given up hoping for: inevitably turning back to look for the same old kick. Indeed, the female animal teaches you something at every stage of life. So (to get on with the story) one afternoon three of us from the hotel set off on a quest for inexpensive dalliance. It was easily come by, thanks to the good offices of Pomone, who ran an agency, and could fix you up any conceivable kind of carnal affair or transaction over there in his part of the world, Les Batignolles. Pomone's books were full of offers at all prices; he carried on his functions, this providential little man, at the bottom of a courtyard, with no days off, in a ill-lit cubbyhole in which you had to tread as delicately and cautiously as in an unfamiliar, pitch-dark public lavatory. You had to push nervously past several hangings before you reached the pander himself, invariably seated in dim confessional atmosphere.

Due to this gloom I never, truth to tell, really properly saw Pomone, and although we frequently conversed at length together and even collaborated at one time, and he has often suggested things to me and dangerously confided in me, I should certainly not be able to recognize him now if I met him in hell.

All I remember is that the furtive applicants who sat in his anteroom awaiting their turn to be interviewed, were always beautifully behaved and didn't speak to each other but showed great reserve, as if on a visit to some dentist who intensely disliked any noise — and wasn't much fond of light, either.

It was through a medical student that I got to know Pomone. He used to see a lot of him and earn himself a little easy pocket money, as he could boast, the lucky devil, of a fantastic muscular development. He used to be summoned to make little intimate parties go, in the suburbs, with an exhibition of Nature's gift. Ladies particularly, who wouldn't have believed it could be "as big as that", used to make a tremendous fuss over him. He was great fun for these arrested flappers. He appeared in the police records, this student of ours, under the awe-inspiring nickname of John Thomas!

Waiting clients very seldom struck up a conversation. Sorrow seeks a listener, whereas joy and the urgent impulses of nature are shamefaced.

It's a sin, whatever you may say, to be lecherous and poor. When Pomone learned about me and heard that I had been a doctor, he immediately unbosomed himself to me about the torment of his life. A vice was wearing him away. I believe too his lower bowels were constantly inflamed by a wicked fever in his lungs. Anyway, tuberculosis carried him off a few years later. He was also worn out, in a different way, by the unceasing chatter of conceited lady clients always making up all sorts of absurd nonsense, spinning incredible tales about nothing on earth or about their intimate charms, the like of which, to hear them talk, you'd think couldn't be found under any other mortal skirt in the world.

For the men, what you mostly had to find was amenable and admiring partners to fit in with their salacious whims. There were as many of these idiosyncrasies as there were men seeking love for hire, the same as at Madame Herote's. A morning's mail at Pomone's office brought in enough unsatisfied love to stop all the wars in the world for ever. Yet all this flood of sentiment never went beyond certain definite portions of the human anatomy. That was the pity of it.

His desk was snowed under with this disgusting cartload of commonplace passions. I wished to know about all this and decided to assist for a time in classifying this mass of sulphurous writings. You went about it, he explained to me, grouping them in various types, like ties or diseases, the quite mad ones on one side, masochists and fetichists on another, then flagellants and the domineering sort somewhere else — and so on throughout the lot. Pleasure pretty soon becomes hard work. There's no doubt about our having been turned out of Eden, that's certain. Pomone thought so too, with his sweating hands and interminable weakness which caused him both pleasure and remorse. After a month or two, I knew enough about him and his trade. I gave up going to see him so often.

At the Tarapout I was still considered a reserved, respectable and punctual performer but after a few weeks of this regular life, misfortune descended on me once more from an unsuspected quarter and I was forced brusquely again to give up my stage job and take to the dirty road once more.

When I look back on them now, those days at the Tarapout were in point of fact only a sort of crafty and unseemly hiatus. I was always finely dressed during those four months, I will say; sometimes a prince, twice a Roman centurion, an aviator after that, and always well and regularly paid. I ate enough at the Tarapout to last me for years. A capitalist's existence without capital. Treachery! Disaster! One evening they altered our number for I don't know what reason. The scene of our new act was the Embankment in London. I felt a bit doubtful at once; our little Britishers were going to sing on these false banks of the Thames, at night, and I was to be a policeman. An entirely silent rôle, I trod up and down by the river. All of a sudden, when I had given up thinking about it, their song became louder than life itself and inclined everything towards misfortune. And as they sang, I could no longer think of anything but all the sadness of the world and my own; damn them, their song turned my heart sour within me. I had imagined I had digested and outlived the worst of it! But this was the worst of all — it was a gay song, theirs, which wasn't gay. And there they were, these girls, swaying as they sang, trying to make it come off. My God, really I must say it was awful; it was as if we were spreading ourselves in unhappiness and sadness. . . . That's it. Roaming around in the fog in lamentation. It quivered in their wailing song, they made one older every minute. It seemed to trickle from the scene itself: in panic. Yet they went on and on, my little companions. They did not appear to understand what an awful evil effect their song was having on us all. . . . They mourned their whole life, twirling away there, grinning, beautifully in time. . . . When the thing comes to you like that, so distinctly, from such a distance, you can't be making a mistake, you can't resist.

Unhappiness was everywhere, in spite of the comfort of the stalls; it was on us, on the blackcloth; it was drenching the whole world round us. They were artists, oh, yes, they were complete artists. An utterly sordid misery surged up from their song and dance without their wishing to prevent it or even understand it. Only their eyes were sad. Eyes are not enough. They were singing the defeat of life and they didn't see it. They thought it was only love, nothing but love; they hadn't been taught the rest of it, little dears. . . . A little bit of the blues was what they were meant to be singing! That's what they thought it was! When you are young and don't know, you think it's all only unhappiness in love. . . .

> *Where I go, where I look . . .*
> *It's only for you . . . ou . . .*
> *Only for you . . . ou . . .*

That's what they sang.

It's the mania of the young to think of all humanity in terms of one body, the only one, a hallowed dream, a frenzy of love. They would find out later, maybe, where the end of all that was, when they were rosy no longer, when the pitiless grime of their own foul country had enveloped them all again, all sixteen of them, with their great horsey thighs, their little bobbing breasts. . . . The sordidness already had them by the neck, the little darlings; it was twined round their waists, they wouldn't escape. It had them already by the guts, by the breath in their throats, by every note of their shrill false voices too.

It was within. No costume, no painted scene, no lights, no smile to deceive, to impress this thing of misery; it knows its own; wherever they may hide, it roots them out; it merely takes its pleasures, allowing them to sing till their turn comes, allowing them all the absurdities of hope. Unhappiness is whetted, soothed, excited that way.

Our real misery, the ultimate misery, entertains us thus.

So much the worse, then, for who sings songs of love! Love is that same thing and nothing else, unhappiness again, now lying in our teeth, villainously — and that is all. It's everywhere, brute beast, don't wake it—even in bluff, out of bravado. It doesn't work, it doesn't stand for it. Yet, nevertheless, my English girls went through with this thing three times a day, with that Embankment scene and accordion music. It was bound of course to turn out very badly.

I let them carry on, but I may say I saw it coming.

First one of the little creatures fell ill. Death to little dears who irritate Misfortune! May they die and so much the better! By the same token one should be careful not to linger at street corners behind an accordion — that's often where the harm is done, where Truth will catch you. So a Polish girl came to take the invalid's place in their little rout. The Pole coughed badly too, between whiles. A tall, pallid, well-built girl she was. We made friends at once. In a couple of hours I knew all about her soul; I waited a bit longer, where her body was concerned. This Pole's form of madness was to mutilate her nervous system with impossible longings. Naturally she slipped straight into the English girls' filthy little song like a knife into butter, mournfulness and all. It began, their song, very prettily, in that guileless way dance tunes do, and then after a while your heart sagged within you as you listened to it, you felt so sad; and you felt that hearing it you were going to lose all your joy in life because it really is so true that everything comes to an end, youth and everything; and you were doubled up as they sang the words and after the words had gone by and the melody had drifted far away into the distance to its home, its real and only one, a bed in earth when all is at an end. Twice round the chorus came and by then you almost longed for that dear land of death, for a country of gentleness and sudden forgetfulness like a fog. Their voices were just like that, voices heard in a fog.

Every one came in on the chorus, joining in that plaintive burden of reproach against all those who are still wandering about in life, waiting on the quay sides, on all the embankments of the world, for life to have passed by at last, and all the time mucking about, selling things, oranges and false coins and junk, to the other phantoms; and all the police, the degenerates, the sorrows and the yarns they spin in that endless fog through which they grub in patience, day after day. . . .

Tania was the name of my new Polish friend. At the moment she was distracted, I learned, on account of a little bank clerk of forty whom she'd known in Berlin. She wanted to go back to Berlin and love him, whatever befell, cost what it might. There wasn't anything she would not have done as long as she could get back there and find him.

She chased around after theatrical agents, who might promise her a job, up grimy winding stairs to dirty offices. The scum, they pinched her thighs while waiting for answers to their letters which never came. But she hardly noticed what they did with their hands, she was so entirely taken up with her distant love. A week of this sort of thing had not gone by before a tremendous catastrophe occurred. She had stuffed Providence with temptations for weeks and months, like a cannon's mouth.

An attack of flu removed her marvellous young man. We heard the fearful news one Saturday afternoon. At once she dragged me off, dishevelled and haggard, to try the Gare du Nord. That was all right but at the *guichet* in her frenzy she clamoured to get to Berlin in time for the funeral. It took two station masters to stop her, to make her understand that it really was too late.

In the state she was in, it was quite impossible to leave her alone. She was entirely wrapped up in her tragedy, of course, and particularly wanted me to see that she was off her head. What a gift of an opportunity! Love thwarted by poverty and distance is like the love of a sailor; there can be no doubt about it and it works beautifully. In the first place, when you don't get a chance of seeing each other often, you can't quarrel and that's a great deal to start off with. As life is nothing but a delirium full of lies, the further away you are, the more lies you can put into it and the happier you are; that's obvious and quite reasonable. Truth is what's inedible.

Once we had thoroughly convinced Tania that there wasn't any possible train for Berlin, we fell back on the telegraph office. We wrote out a very long telegram, but when it came to sending it, that again was difficult, as we couldn't think whom to send it to. We knew nobody in Berlin except the dead man. There was nothing for us to talk about after that, except about his having died. Talking about that helped us to wander round the block two or three times and then, as we really had to do something to lull Tania's suffering anyway, we walked slowly up towards Montmartre, murmuring sorrowful remarks.

When you get to the Rue Lepic, you begin to come across people on their way up to the heights of the town, in search of amusement. They hurry along. And when they search the Sacré Cœur they look down into the night below, which is a great dark hollow heaped with houses at the bottom.

In the little square there, we went into the café which looked to us the cheapest. Tania, by way of consolation and out of gratitude, let me kiss her as much as I liked. She was also quite fond of drink. On the benches round merrymakers were already asleep, half-drunk. The clock above the little church began to chime one hour after another and never stop. We had come to the end of the world; that was becoming more and more obvious. You couldn't go any further, because beyond that were the dead people.

There, close at hand on the Place du Tertre, was where the dead began. We had a good place to see them from. They were passing over Dufayel's, that is to say, to the east of us.

All the same, you have to know how to see them — from inside and almost closing your eyes — because the great draughts of light from the electric signs make it awfully difficult to see them, even through the clouds. I realized at once that the dead would have taken Bébert to themselves; we even made a little sign to each other, Bébert and I, and then, quite close to him, we signalled to the very pale girl from Rancy who had had her miscarriage at last and was there now, all empty inside.

There were lots of old patients of mine here and there, and women patients whom I had long since forgotten about and many others, — the Negro on a white cloud, all by himself, who was the fellow they had thrashed rather too thoroughly, over there, I remembered him from Topo — and old Grappa too, that old soldier himself from the wilds! I had thought of them from time to time, I'd certainly thought of Lieutenant Grappa and the flayed Negro and my Spaniard, the priest; he too had come along with the dead that evening to pray in heaven, and there was his gold crucifix getting in his way as he hopped from cloud to cloud. He got caught up with his crucifix in all the dirtiest, yellow clouds, and all the time I recognized many more of the departed, more and more of them. . . . So many that one really is ashamed of not having had time to see them while they were living here by one's side year after year. . . .

You never have the time, it's a fact, except to think of yourself.

So all these blighters had turned into angels, without my knowing anything about it! There were clouds and clouds full of angels now, very odd-looking ones and disreputable ones in all directions. Jaunting around, high up over the town! I looked for Molly among them; now was my chance, my dear, my only friend Molly — but she hadn't come with them. She probably had a little heaven all to herself, close to the Lord God; she'd always been so kind, my Molly. . . . I was happy not to find her with all that riff-raff — because that's what these dead men were, scamps, just a lot of scapegrace ghosts that had been gathered together this evening over the town. They came in particular from the cemetery next door; more and more of them came, not decent ghosts at all. It's a small cemetery, where the Commune rioters who were executed are buried, and these were bloody ghosts who had their mouths wide open, trying to yell, but couldn't. . . . They were waiting, this lot, alongside the others for La Pérouse, La Pérouse of the Islands, who had ordered them all to reassemble that night on parade. . . . He wasn't ready himself, it took him such a time with that wooden leg of his which kept getting stuck the wrong way . . . he always had difficulty with it and besides he had to find his famous eyeglass.

He wouldn't come out onto the clouds without his eyeglass round his neck; it was a whim of his, that marvellous lorgnette for epic deeds; the devil of a wheeze, it made you see people and things from a long way off, always farther and farther away, and so of course nice to look upon however close up to them you went.

Near the Moulin La Galette some Cossacks who had run away were trying to hoist themselves out of their graves. They were struggling frightfully but they had often tried before. . . . They always fell back to the bottom of their tombs; they had been drunk ever since 1820.

Yet suddenly the rain shifted them out too, sobered by the cold shower, and up they shot high above the town. They spread out across the crowds, roistering around in the darkness. . . . It looked as if the Opéra most attracted the dead; its light signs blazing away in the middle, they splashed about in them and then went bounding off again to the other end of the sky; they skipped about so and there were so many of them, they made you quite dizzy. La Pérouse, ready at last, wanted them to hoist him up onto the last stroke of four o'clock; they held him up, fixed him into the saddle. Once installed and astride, he went on gesticulating and haranguing just the same as before. The stroke of four nearly shook him off as he was buttoning up his tunic. Behind La Pérouse is the main thoroughfare of heaven. There's a hideous mess-up: phantoms come twirling up from all four corners of the sky, the dead of every human epic. . . . They pursue and defy and charge each other, century against century. For a long time the North is cluttered with their foul mêlée. The horizon breaks away and becomes blue as the day at last begins to creep up through the great hole they have cracked open in the night as they take flight.

After that it becomes very difficult to find them again. You have to know how to get outside Time.

You find them again over England, if you manage it, but in that direction the mist is so compact and thick that it is like so many veils wafting up, one in front of the other, from the earth to highest heaven and for all time. With practice and with care, you can contrive to catch sight of them again even so, but not for long, because the wind is always blowing fresh squalls and fog in from the open sea.

The great female who sits there, guarding the Island, is the last of all. Her head is infinitely higher than the highest mists. There is no other nearly living thing in the Island except her now. Her red hair, far above everything else, still slightly gilds the clouds, and that is all that is left of the sun.

She is trying to make herself a cup of tea, so they say.

She may just as well try, since there she'll be throughout eternity. She'll never get her tea to boil because of the fog which has become much too thick and all-pervading. She uses a ship's hull for a teapot, the hull of the biggest and most beautiful ship, the latest she can find in Southampton Dock, and she warms her tea in it, oceans and oceans of tea. She stirs, she stirs it all with an enormous oar. . . . That gives her something to do.

She takes no notice of anything else, sitting there forever serious, forever busied with her tea.

The phantom hosts passed directly over her head, but she didn't even move, she is accustomed to all these Continental ghosts coming flying over and getting lost. . . . It is all over now.

With her fingers she pokes the live coals that are there under the ashes between two forests of dead trees. That's enough for her. She tries to get it to burn properly, everything is hers now, but her kettle will never boil again.

There's no life left in the fire.

There's no life left in the world for anybody, except just a little for her and it is all very nearly over now. . . .

TANIA WOKE ME IN THE ROOM WHERE WE HAD EVENTUALLY GONE to bed. It was ten o'clock in the morning. So as to get rid of her, I told her that I wasn't feeling very well and would stay in bed a while longer.

Life was beginning again. She pretended to believe me. When she had gone downstairs, I started out myself. I had something to do, as a matter of fact. That jaunt of the night before had left me with an odd feeling of remorse. The thought of Robinson came back to plague me. The fact was that I had, actually, left the fellow to his fate — worse still, to the tender mercies of Abbé Protiste. Which was saying a good deal. Admittedly I had heard that everything was going on well down at Toulouse and that actually the old Henrouille had become quite friendly towards him. But the thing is that under certain circumstances one only hears, doesn't one, what one wishes to hear and what suits one best. . . . These vague reports proved nothing definite, really.

Disturbed and curious in my mind, I now set out for Rancy in search of more definite, precise information. To get there, you had to go through the Rue des Batignolles, where Pomone lived. It was on my way. As I neared his place, I was much surprised to see Pomone in person at the corner of his street, apparently shadowing a little man pretty close. Pomone never went out, so it must mean that something of real importance was afoot. I also recognized the fellow he was following — it was a customer of his, "the Cid" he styled himself in correspondence. But we had discovered by roundabout means that this "Cid" creature had a job in the post office.

For years he had been badgering Pomone to find him a nicely brought-up little lady friend: that was his dream. But the young ladies he was introduced to were never refined enough for his taste. They committed *faux pas,* so he claimed. So it never worked.

When you come to think of it, there are two great categories of lady friend, — the "broad-minded" type and the ones who have been well brought up in "most respectable" homes. They're the two ways poor girls have of feeling superior, the two ways of exciting nervous and unappeased males, the "modest violet" type and the "modern miss."

All the "Cid's" savings, month after month, had been swallowed up by this quest. Now he had come to the end of his resources with Pomone and also to the end of all hope. Later I learned that he had committed suicide that same evening in some out-of-the-way spot. Anyway, as soon as I saw Pomone leave his house, I knew for certain that something curious was up. So I followed them for quite a time through this quarter, whose streets straggle on, losing their shops one after the other and finally its colours too, until suddenly it ends up among uncertain *bistrots* on the outskirts of the toll. When you're in no great hurry, you can easily lose yourself along those streets, drifting as one does at once, because it's all so sad and too casual a spot. If one had any money, one would take a taxi and escape, one gets so bored. The people you meet are so loaded with cares that you feel embarrassed on their account. Behind the window curtains you are almost convinced that the people who live there have left the gas on. There's nothing you can do to cope with it. "Christ!" you say — which isn't much.

Besides, there isn't even a bench to sit on, either. On all sides everything is brown and grey. When it rains, it rains from all sides too, into your face and from both flanks, and the street glistens like the back of a fish with a streak of rain down the middle. You cannot even say that it's a mess — it's more like a prison, almost a well-kept prison, a prison that doesn't need to be locked.

Slouching around like this, after a while I lost Pomone and his suicide, soon after the Rue des Vinaigriers. I had arrived so close to Garenne-Rancy that I couldn't help going and casting an eye over the fortifications.

Seen from far off, Garenne-Rancy is attractive enough, there's no denying it, because of the trees in the big cemetery. It wouldn't take much for you to make a mistake and imagine it was the Bois de Boulogne.

If you really want news of some one, why you've just got to go and ask somebody who knows. After all, I told myself then, I haven't much to lose by paying the Henrouilles a little visit. They must know what's happening down at Toulouse. And that is where I was committing a great imprudence. One's too trusting. You don't realize how far you have gone, yet you're there already, well into the regions of the night. Something has at once gone very wrong. Any little thing does it, and anyway, one ought not to attempt to see certain people again, especially not that sort. You never get yourself clear again after that.

Eventually, by walking round and round in circles, I found myself as if by habit only a few steps away from the Henrouilles' *maisonette*. I couldn't get over seeing it there in the same place. It began to rain. No one in the street except me, who didn't dare go any nearer. In fact, I was just going to turn back and let the matter drop, when the door of the house opened, a little, just enough for the younger Henrouille woman to beckon me across. Really she missed nothing. She had seen me waiting in distress on the pavement opposite. I had no wish at all, even so, to go over, but she was determined I should. She called me by name.

"Oh, Doctor — come quickly!"

She called me across like that, imperatively. I was afraid of being seen. So I hurried up onto her doorstep, and met the little corridor with the stove in it again, and once more faced the decoration inside that house. It gave me a very odd feeling of uneasiness, all the same. Whereupon she began to tell me that her husband hadn't been at all well for two months now and that, as a matter of fact, he was going from bad to worse.

At once, of course, I felt distrustful.

"And what about Robinson?" I asked hurriedly.

At first she eluded my question. Finally she faced it. "They're getting along all right, both of them. . . . Their business at Toulouse is going very satisfactorily . . ." she did in the end answer, but rapidly, just like that. And at once she started off again on the subject of her husband's illness. She wanted me to go and look after him right away, without losing another moment. I was so kind . . . I knew her husband so well . . . And so on and so on . . . He wouldn't trust any one but me . . . He had refused to see any other doctor . . . They had not known my address . . . Gabble, in fact.

Personally I had good reasons to fear that this illness of her husband's might have come about in some very curious way. I knew a bit too much about the good lady herself and the habits of the house. Yet some devilish curiosity made me go up to his room.

He was lying in the same bed where I had attended to Robinson, following his accident, some months before.

A few months will change a room — even if you haven't moved anything in it. However old and worn objects may be, they will still find, God knows how, some way of aging. Around us everything had changed. Not the furniture itself, of course, but things themselves, deep down. Things are different when you come across them again; they seem to have increased power to enter one's soul more sadly, deeper still, more softly than before, melting into that sort of death that is gently accumulating inside one, day by day, in underhand fashion, making you each day defend yourself a little less than you did the previous day. Occasionally you see life wilting, wrinkling, within you — and things and beings with it which, when you left them, were ordinary or important or dangerous in their day. The fear of drawing to a close has marked all that with wrinkles, while one trotted around town after one's pleasure or one's daily bread.

Soon there will only be harmless, pitiful, disarmed things and people round one's past — merely mistakes that have lapsed into silence.

The woman left us alone with her husband. He was in a fine way. He hadn't much circulation left. It was his heart that was the matter.

I had really the devil's own luck for coming up against this sort of case. I listened to his heartbeats, so as to do something in the matter, to produce the one or two expected gestures. His

heart ran on, his sick heart behind his ribs, ah, yes, you could
hear it running on, leaping after life — but it hopped in vain, it
wouldn't ever catch up with life. The game was through. Soon
it would lurch on and over, falling headlong into rottenness, all
juicy and red and pulp, like a crushed pomegranate. That's how
his frail old heart would look, against the marble, slit open by
a knife at the autopsy in a few days' time. For it would all end
in a fine magistrate's post-mortem. I foresaw as much, since every
one in the neighbourhood would have a lot of spicy comments to
make about this demise, which wouldn't be considered at all ordinary after that other affair.

They were lying in wait for his wife in the neighbourhood,
with all the collected gossip that was still in circulation about
the previous incident. That would come a bit later. For the
moment, old Henrouille did not know what to do or how to die.
He seemed already a little outside life, but still he couldn't escape
his lungs. He chased away breath, and breath came back to him.
He would have liked to let himself slip, but he had to go on living just the same, till the end. It was a really appalling job, and
it was breaking him.

"I can't feel my feet any more," he groaned. "I'm cold up to
my knees." He tried to touch his feet; he couldn't.

He couldn't drink, either. It was almost all over. I gave him a
brew which his wife had prepared for him and, as I did so, wondered what she mightn't have put in it. It didn't smell too good,
but you can't go by smell — valerian itself has a very nasty odour.
And besides, if you were gasping for breath as old Henrouille
was gasping, it didn't matter much whether there was anything
slightly odd about the stuff, or not. Yet he was struggling tremendously, working frightfully hard with all that was left of
the muscles under his skin to manage to suffer on and pant still
more. He was battling as much against life as against death. It
would be right to be allowed to burst at moments like that. When
Nature takes it into its head not to give another damn, really
there seem to be no limits. On the other side of the door that
woman was listening to what I said, attending to him, but I knew
all about her. Softly I went across to catch her at it. "Tweet,

tweet!" I said to her. She wasn't in the least annoyed but came and whispered into my ear.

"What you ought to do," she murmured, "is to get him to remove his plate. It must get in the way of his breathing." Well, yes, I was perfectly willing for him to remove his plate.

"But why not tell him so yourself?" I advised. It was a delicate thing to be asked to do, in the state he was in.

"No, no. It would be much better if you did!" she insisted. "It oughtn't to come from me; he wouldn't like it if I knew . . ."

"Oh" — I was greatly surprised — "why?"

"Thirty years he's worn one and he's never mentioned it to me. . . ."

"Couldn't one let him keep it then?" I suggested. "Seeing that he's so used to breathing with it. . . ."

"Oh, no! I shouldn't forgive myself," she answered with a certain particular warmth in her voice.

I went back then quietly into the room. The husband heard me come back near him. He was pleased to have me there. Between gasps he still spoke to me, even trying to say something nice to me. He asked after my affairs and if I had found a new practice. "Yes, oh, yes," I answered to all these questions. It would have taken too long and been too complicated to give him details. This wasn't the moment. Hidden by the door, his wife made signs to me to go on and ask him to remove his plate. So I leant over next to his ear and asked the man in a low voice to take it out. I dropped a brick. "I've thrown it down the lavatory," he said, with eyes more frightened than ever. Coquettish of him, in fact. And after that he rattled a good bit.

A man's an artist with whatever come handy. He, throughout his life, had concerned himself æsthetically about a dental plate.

The moment had come for him to bare his heart. I should have liked him now to give me his views on what had happened about his mother. But he couldn't any longer. He was retreating. He began to dribble very badly. This was the end. Impossible for him now to get a word out. I wiped his mouth for him and went downstairs. His wife below in the corridor wasn't at all pleased;

she almost went for me about that plate, as if it had been my fault.

"It was a gold plate, Doctor! I know. I know how much he paid for it. You can't get them anything like as good as that now. . . ." Quite a song and dance about it. "All right then," I said. "I'm perfectly ready to go on up and try asking him again," I was so annoyed. But only if she'd come with me.

That time her husband hardly recognized us. Just a bit he did. His rattling was a little less when we were close by him, as if he wished to hear everything that we were saying to each other, his wife and I. . . .

I didn't go to the funeral. There wasn't any inquest, as I had rather dreaded there would be. The whole thing passed off quietly. But that did not prevent our falling out permanently, — Widow Henrouille and I, on account of the old man's dental plate.

THE YOUNG ARE ALWAYS IN SUCH A HURRY TO GO OFF AND MAKE love, they're so hasty in seizing for their amusement on everything that's given to them to believe, that where sensation's concerned they never think twice. Rather like the people one sees travelling who gulp down everything that is put before them at the station buffet, while the whistle's going to blow. As long as you let the young have two or three odd lines that'll do to get a conversation shaping well for bed, that's all they want, they're as happy as can be. Youth is very easily pleased, physical joys are its own for the asking, of course.

The whole of young life lolls on a lovely beach down by the sea, where women at last appear free, where they are so beautiful that they no longer depend on the lies of our illusions.

But then, to be sure, when winter's come, one hates to come back, to tell oneself that that's all over, to admit it inwardly. You'd like to stay on in spite of everything, aged and chilled; you go on hoping. That's understandable. One's unworthy, it's no good blaming any one for it. Happiness and the pleasures of love before all else. That's what I say. And then too, when you begin to hide from people it's a sign that you are frightened of having a good time in their company. That's a malady in itself. It would be good to know why it is that one is never quite cured of loneliness. Another chap that I met during the war, in hospital, a corporal, once said something to me about such feelings. Pity I never saw the lad again. "The earth's dead," he instructed me, "and we're only worms on its ruddy great carcass, eating its entrails all the time, only eating its poisons. . . . There's nothing you can do with us. We're rotten from birth. That's how it is."

Though it didn't stop this philosopher having to be hurried off one evening to the bastions — which proves that at least he'd do to face a firing squad. There were two cops came to fetch him,

I remember, one large, the other small. An anarchist was what they said of him at the court-martial.

Years later, when you come to remember them, you'd very much like to bring back the words that certain people spoke and the people themselves, to ask them what it was they meant to say. But they're gone. One wasn't wise enough to get what they said. One would so like to know whether they have not changed their minds since then perhaps. . . . But it's altogether too late. All that's over. Nobody knows anything about them now. So you have got to go on your way alone through the night. You've lost your real companions. You didn't even ask them the question, the true, great question, when there was time. When you were along with them, you didn't understand. Man overboard. One's always behindhand, that's what it is. All of which are vain regrets that won't butter your bread for you.

In the end, thank heaven, anyway, Father Protiste came and looked me up one fine morning to share with me the bit we'd made on the business of old Ma Henrouille's vault. I had given up counting on the curé. It was just as if he'd lighted down from heaven. One thousand five hundred francs each! At the same time too he brought good news of Robinson. His eyes were apparently very much better. The lid wounds had stopped suppurating now. And they all of them down there wanted me to go down and see them. After all, I had promised I would. Protiste himself urged me to.

From what he told me, furthermore, I gathered that Robinson was shortly going to marry the daughter of the woman who sold candles for the church next door to the vault, which was the church the old lady's mummies belonged to. The wedding and everything had been arranged.

Inevitably all that led us to talk about the death of M. Henrouille, but we didn't keep on about it, and the conversation came back more pleasantly to Robinson's future and to the town of Toulouse itself, which I didn't know at all and which Grappa had talked to me about in the old days, and then to the sort of little business the two of them were running down there, Robinson and the old lady, and to the girl he was going to marry. In

fact, we chatted about everything and on all topics a little. . . .
One thousand five hundred francs! They were making me feel
indulgent, not to say optimistic. I considered all the suggestions
he made about Robinson eminently wise, sensible, judicious and
most apposite in the circumstances. . . . It would all be all right.
At least, so I thought. And we began to discuss ages, the curé
and I. Both of us were well past the thirties. The time when we
had been in our thirties was slipping way back into the past —
cruel, meagrely regretted shores. It wasn't even worth while turning to look back on those shores. We hadn't missed much by
growing old. "After all, one would have to be a very poor creature,"
I concluded, "to regret this or that particular year more than the
rest. We can go right ahead and grow old with a will, my dear
Curé. Was yesterday such fun? And the year before that? What
did you think about it? What is there to regret? I ask you . . .
Youth? We never had any . . .

"Really the poor get younger inside as they go on, rather than
otherwise, and towards the end, as long as they have tried to rid
themselves on the way of all the lies and timidity and unworthy
eagerness to obey which they were given at birth, actually they're
less unpleasant than when they started. The rest of what exists on
earth is not for them! It's no concern of theirs. Their job, their
only job, is to overcome that feeling of obedience, to spew it out.
If they can manage that before they're altogether dead, then they
can boast of not having lived in vain."

Clearly I was in excellent form. Those fifteen hundred francs
had braced me up like hell. I went on: "Youth consists, my dear
Curé, real youth consists in loving the whole world without distinction; that is the only thing that's young and new. And can
you say that you know many young people who are sound enough
to do that? I don't know any, personally. I see only scabrous old
stupidities breaking out on every side in bodies that are more or
less recent, and the more such sordidness breaks out afresh, the
more the young are teased by it and the more they swear they're
colossally young! But that's not true, it's all my bleeding eye.
. . . They're only young in the way furuncles are young, because
of the pus that hurts them inside and swells them up."

It annoyed Protiste to have me talk to him like this. . . . So as not to go on irritating him any longer, I changed the conversation. Especially as he had just been very nice to me, a downright windfall. . . . It's awfully difficult to avoid coming back on to some subject which is as much on your mind as that subject was on mine. The whole business of your life overwhelms you when you live alone. One's stupefied by it. To get rid of it you try to daub some of it off on to people who come to see you, and they hate that. To be alone trains one for death. "One ought not to die" — I went on and told him — "merely as a dog dies: one ought to take minute after minute to die, and every minute should be something new all the time, bordered with all the agony that would be needed to make you forget a thousand times over all the joy you might have had in a thousand years of lechery before that day. . . . Happiness on earth would consist of dying with pleasure, in the midst of pleasure. . . . The rest amounts to nothing at all, it's a fear one daren't confess to, it's just so much Art."

Protiste, hearing me discoursing after this fashion, came to the conclusion that I must surely have fallen ill again. Maybe he was quite right and maybe I really was entirely wrong about everything. Living on my own like that, looking for some retribution to fit the selfishness of the world, I had been inflaming my brain, rushing into a vacuum in search of that retribution. You make whoopee any way you can, when you don't often get a chance of going out because there isn't much money, and can even less often manage to get outside yourself and have a woman.

I admit it was a little wrong of me to go on at Protiste with my ideas, which went against his religious convictions — but at the same time it must be owned that there was a nasty little air of superiority about his whole person which must have got on many people's nerves. According to his view of things, all we humans were in a sort of antechamber to eternity, waiting with our numbers. His, of course, was an exceptionally good number for Paradise. Anything else left him quite cold.

Convictions of that sort are intolerable. On the other hand, when he offered, that same evening, to advance me the sum needed for my trip to Toulouse, I stopped badgering him and contradicting him. My anxiety not to have to meet Tania and her phantom at the Tarapout again made me accept his suggestion without further argument. A week or two of a comfortable existence at any rate, said I to myself. The devil has every trump to tempt you with. Never will one get to know them all. Even if one lived long enough, one would never know just where to turn to start on a new happiness. One would have left aborted happinesses about everywhere; there they'd be stinking in all the corners of the earth and one wouldn't be able to breathe even. The ones that are in museums, real abortions, make some people feel ill and likely to be sick, just to look at them. And so too are our bloodsome little attempts to be happy enough to make one ill a good while before actually dying altogether, they are so mangled and bad.

We would wither away entirely if we didn't forget about them. Not counting the trouble we've taken to get to where we now are, to lend excitement to our hopes, our rubbishy joys, our thrills, our lies. . . . All over, bar the shouting! Then what about our money? And all our little tricks with it too, and our eternities galore? And the things we make each other swear, and do swear to ourselves, and believe that the other person has never said before, or promised that before it filled our own mouths and hearts, and the fragrance and the fondling, and all the mimicry, —everything in fact that is meant in the end to conceal all that from us as much as possible, so as to avoid talking about it any more, for fear and shame of its all coming back to us like vomit? So it's not tenacity we lack; no, it's rather that we're not on the right road that leads to a tranquil death.

To go to Toulouse was again a foolish thing to do. Thinking it over, I realized as much. But by dint of following after Robinson in his adventures like this, I had developed a taste for this shadiness racket. Even back in New York that time, when I wasn't sleeping well, I had begun worrying whether I couldn't go along a bit further with Robinson, and further yet. You delve deeper into the night at first and start to panic, but you want to *know* all the same, and after that you don't come out of the

depths of the darkness. But there are too many things to understand at one fell swoop. Life's much too short. You don't want
to do any one an injustice. You have your scruples, you don't
want to jump to conclusions, and above all you are afraid of
having to die before you have done hesitating, because then you
would have come into the world for no purpose whatsoever. And
that really would be hell.

You've got to hurry, you mustn't spoil death for yourself. Or
waste the illness, the wretchedness which scatters away your hours
and days, the sleeplessness which makes a grey smudge of whole
weeks and years, and the cancer which may already be mounting
up inside you from behind, meticulous and gory.

One will never have the time, one tells oneself! Not counting
war, which too is always ready to rise up from the caverns im-
prisoning the poor. Are enough poor people murdered? One can't
really say. . . . It's a moot point. Perhaps the thing would be
to slit the throats of all those who don't catch on, d' you think?
And let more of them, more of the poor, be born — and so on
until some lot came along who understood the joke, the whole of
the joke. . . . As you go on mowing a lawn until the grass is
really good and lush.

When I got off at Toulouse, I found myself outside the station,
not knowing quite what to do. Half a pint at the station buffet
and there I was, strolling off down the streets. Unknown towns
are fun. That's when and where it's possible to imagine that
everybody you meet is nice. They're dreamy moments. You can
take advantage of your dreaming to go and waste a bit of time
in the public gardens. Nevertheless, after a certain age, unless
you've the very best family reasons for being there, you appear,
like Parapine, to be following little girls in a park, if you're not
very careful. The confectioner's just outside the entrance is better;
that lovely shop on the corner all twiddly-decorated like a music
hall with a lot of little painted birds dotted about on big, bevelled
mirrors. There you discover yourself, eating hundreds of buns,
reflectively. A refuge for seraphim. The young ladies who serve
there surreptitiously babble about their heart affairs, as follows:

"So I told him he could come and take me out Sunday. . . .

My aunt, who heard me, made an awful fuss about it because of Father . . ."

"But hasn't your father married again?"

"What has his getting married again got to do with it? Surely he's got a perfect right to know whom his daughter's going out with, even so?"

The other young serving lady thought so too, absolutely. Hence arose an enthralled discussion by the whole lot of them. In vain did I in my corner, so as not to disturb them, stuff myself, never interrupting once, with éclairs and jam tarts, in the hope that they would the sooner manage to resolve these delicate problems of family interference — they stayed up in the air. Nothing came of it. Their speculative impotence reduced them to hating in an entirely muddled way. They choked with illogicality, vanity and ignorance, these good young women, drooling their pretty little insults among themselves.

However, I couldn't help being fascinated by their labouring futility. I attacked the rum babas. I didn't keep count of the rum babas I ate. Nor did they. I really did hope not to have to leave before they had come to some conclusion. . . . But they were deaf with excitement and soon dumb too, as they stood there next to me.

Tart and contorted with malice, they waited pent in their lair behind the cake counter, each of them undefeated, tight-lipped and pinched, ruminating how to pay the other girl back even more spikily and swiftly next time, how to throw up any livid, hurtful idiocies she might happen to know about her little pal. A next time which wouldn't take long to come; she'd see to it that it did. . . . Tag-ends of arguments aimed at nothing at all. In the end I sat down so that they should the better bewilder me with their ceaseless din of words, their attempts at thought like a seashore of small, passionate, unending waves never straightening themselves out.

One listens, waits, hopes, here and over there, in trains and cafés, on the street, in the drawing-room, at the concierge's; one listens and waits for malice to put itself on an organized footing, as in war time, but it merely shudders and shakes; it never gets going, ever, either with these poor young ladies or with any one else. No one comes to our aid. A vast confused muttering, monotonous and grey, hangs over life, a foully discouraging mirage. Two ladies came into the shop and their entry broke the greasy charm of the ineffectual conversation spread between the young women and myself. The pressing attention of the whole staff was immediately focussed on these two ladies. Every one dashed to do their bidding and anticipate their slightest wish. They chose, here and there, and pecked at various pastries and *petits fours* to take away. When they came to pay, both politely squirmed and each insisted on offering the other little tidbits to eat then and there.

One of them prettily and fussily refused, explaining at great length and in confidence to the other ladies, who were tremendously interested, that her doctor had forbidden her all saccharines from now on, that he was a really marvellous man, her doctor, and that he had already effected the most wonderful cures in cases of constipation both here in Toulouse and elsewhere, and that, among others, he was at present curing her of an occlusion she had suffered from for over ten years, thanks to an altogether special treatment of his own, a marvellous method known to no other doctor in the world. The other ladies weren't going to be so easily beaten in this particular matter of constipation. They suffered from constipation worse than anybody. They vied with each other, demanding proofs. Thus doubted, our sufferer gave it them in fullest detail; she discoursed on the tearing pains she experienced now as a happy result of the treatment in question, adding that it was a veritable firework display when she went to the lavatory. . . . There was no gainsaying her superior claims.

Assuaged in this way, these voluble dames left the *pâtisserie*, Petits Oiseaux, being escorted over the threshold by a battery of the sweetest smiles in the place.

The public garden opposite struck me as ideal for a few moments' rest and recuperation; I waited there just long enough to get ready again before setting out to look for my friend Robinson.

Provincial park benches are almost always empty on weekday

mornings, by their clumps of cannas and daisies. Close to the rockery, on the strictly captive waters of a pond, a little zinc boat, floating cinders encircling it, was moored to the shore by a sodden rope. This skiff put out to sea on Sundays, so it said on the notice board, and the price of "once round the lake" was written up too: Two francs.

How many years? And young men? How many phantoms?

In every corner of a public garden you find, lying forgotten, any number of tombstones to dreams like that; bosky nooks echoing lovers' vows and handkerchiefs full of everything on earth. All quite absurd.

All the same, no more day dreaming! On your way, said I to myself; you've got to find Robinson and that church of his, Saint Éponime, and the vault in which he and the old lady have mummies on show. That's what I had come for; I might as well get going. . . .

So in a cab we started to thread our way at an odd little trot, delving among the shadowy streets of that old town, with the sunlight caught up there between the roofs. A great clatter of wheels we were making behind that hoofy horse over bridges and gutters. It's a long time now since these towns in the South were burnt down. They've never been so old as they are now. Wars no longer pass their way.

We reached Saint Éponime's church as it was striking noon. The vault was a little farther on, under a mound surmounted by a cross. They showed me where it was, right in the middle of a little dried-up garden. You went down into this crypt through a sort of barricaded hole. From some distance off I saw the crypt attendant, a young girl. I asked her right away for news of Robinson. She was at that moment locking the door. The young girl gave me a charming, friendly smile in answer to my question and at once told me news of Robinson, good news.

In the noonday sun there in that place everything about us went pink and the worn stonework of the church rose up to heaven, ready too with the rest to dissolve in air.

About twenty years old Robinson's little friend must have been, with legs straight and solid, a quite enchanting little bosom, a small, well-shaped, neat head on top of that, eyes a little too alert and dark perhaps for my taste. Not the dreamer type at all. It was she who wrote Robinson's letters for him, the ones I got. She walked ahead of me to the crypt, neatly stepping, trim of foot and ankle. Short, hard hands, firm-holding hands, the hands of a capable worker. A neat, swift turn of the key in the lock. The heat danced round us, shimmering above the flags. We talked about various things and then, once the door was opened again, she decided anyway to show me the vault, although it was lunch time. I began to feel rather more gay again now. We struck into the growing cool, she ahead with the lantern. It felt very good. I made as if to stumble over a step in the ladder so as to steady myself by catching hold of her arm; that went quite well, we laughed, and on reaching the beaten earth floor below, I kissed her a little on the neck. She protested at first, but not too much.

After a moment of friendliness, I slithered up against her body. It was fine with the lantern on the ground, because you could watch at the same time the shifting reliefs of the light on her legs. Ah! Nothing must be missed of moments like that! One's cock-eyed with excitement. It's worth it every time. What a fillip, what sudden good humour overtakes you! Conversation began again on a new note of understanding and easiness. We were friends. We had just economized ten long years.

"Do you get a lot of people coming to see the crypt?" I asked, short of breath and tactlessly. But I switched off that at once: "Your mother supplies candles for the church next door, doesn't she? Father Protiste also mentioned her."

"I only take Madame Henrouille's place over the lunch hour," she replied. "In the afternoon I work in a dress shop. In Theatre Street. Did you come past the theatre on your way here?"

Once again she put my mind at rest with regard to Robinson; he was ever so much better; even the eye specialist had thought he would soon see enough to be able to go out alone. He'd had a shot at it yesterday. It all augured excellently well. Old Mother Henrouille too was thoroughly pleased with the vault arrangement. She was doing good business and saving money. There was only one drawback: in the house where they lived, bugs prevented them all from getting any sleep, especially on stormy nights. So they burned sulphur in the house. It seems that Robinson often spoke of me and, what is more, said nice things about me. One thing led to another and soon we were talking about their engagement and how it had come about.

Actually with all this talk, I hadn't yet asked her her name. Madelon her name was. She had been born during the war. After all their intention of getting married suited me very well. Madelon was an easy name to remember. Presumably she knew what she was about, marrying Robinson. . . . Of course, however much better he might get, he'd always be an invalid. . . . She also believed that it was only his eyes that were wrong. . . . But he had the nerves of a sick man, and a sick man's outlook on life and everything else. I was almost on the point of telling her, of putting her on her guard. . . . Conversations about marriage have always had me guessing; I've never known how to make them go right or what to say.

By way of changing the subject, I took a sudden and keen interest in the things in the crypt; since I'd come a very long way to see the crypt, now was the time to take notice of it.

She with her little lantern, Madelon and I, we then brought the corpses out of the shadows, out of the wall, one by one. It must have given tourists something to think about, this place! Stuck up against the wall, as if sentenced to be shot, the long-since dead. . . . They were no longer made of skin exactly, or bone, nor wearing clothes. There was just a bit of each of these about them, that's all. In a very awful state, and full of holes everywhere. Time, which had been after their hides for centuries, still hadn't given them up. . . . It tore away little bits of their faces here and there, even now. It widened the holes in them and still found long strips of skin which Death, after their gristle, had forgotten. Their stomachs had been entirely emptied out, but that gave them a sort of little cradle of shade in place of a navel.

Madelon explained to me that these dead had waited for more than five hundred years in a quicklime pit before they reached their present state. You couldn't have called them dead bodies,

They had been dead bodies long ago. They had come, very quietly, to the borderlands of dust.

There were twenty-six of them in this crypt in all, large and small, each one wanting nothing better than to enter into Eternity. They weren't being allowed in yet. There were women with bonnets perched on the tops of their skulls, a hunchback, a giant, and even a baby, he quite finished too, with a little sort of lace bib, if you please, round his weeny, dessicated neck, and a tag-end of layette.

A lot of money Ma Henrouille made out of these centuries-old rakings. When I think that I had known her as near as anything to these ghostly creatures . . . So we slowly passed them all back in review, Madelon and I. One by one their so-called heads stood out in silence in the sharp light of the lamp. It's not exactly the darkness of night that they have in those sockets, it's almost a look, but it's much softer, like the look of people who know and understand. What one might object to is more their smell of dust, which catches you at the end of the nose.

Old Mrs. Henrouille never missed a single visit with the tourists. She made the dead work like a circus. They brought her in a hundred francs a day at the height of the good season.

"They don't look unhappy, do you think?" Madelon asked me. It was part of the ritual, that remark.

Death meant nothing to this little charmer. She was born in the war time, when death was cheap. But I knew well how people die. I've learnt that. It hurts like hell. You can tell tourists that these dead men are happy. They have nothing they can say to that. Ma Henrouille used even to tap them on the stomach when they had parchment enough left on them, and it would go "boom" dully. But that is no proof either that all's well.

Then in the end Madelon and I talked again about our own affairs. It was apparently really true that Robinson was better. That's all I wanted to know. She seemed genuinely keen on this idea of marriage, the little dear. She must be awfully bored stuck down in Toulouse. It wasn't often that one met a boy who had travelled around as much as Robinson had. There were a lot of interesting things he could tell of. Some were true and some weren't so true, either. Anyhow, he had already told them all about America and the Tropics. So what could be nicer?

I too had been to America and seen the Tropics. I knew a thing or two myself. I decided I'd tell them a few too. Why, it was just because we had done a bit of travelling about together, Robinson and I, that we had become friends. The lamp went out. We lit it ten times over while we sized up the future with the past. She kept her breasts from me, because they were much too sensitive.

Nevertheless, as Ma Henrouille would be coming back from lunch any moment now, we had to go out into the daylight again, up the sharp, ricketty stairs which were as bad as a stepladder. I noticed that.

THE LITTLE STAIRCASE WAS SO FLIMSY AND TREACHEROUS THAT Robinson did not often go down into the crypt where the mummies were. As a matter of fact, he usually stayed in front of the door, exchanging pleasantries with the tourists, and also getting accustomed to letting a little fresh light filter in places through his eyelashes.

Meanwhile old Ma Henrouille kept things going in the depths below. She really toiled like a nigger over these mummies. The visiting tourists she regaled with a little speech about these parchment-clad corpses of hers.

"There is nothing offensive about them, ladies and gentlemen; they've been preserved in quicklime, just as you see them now, for over five centuries. Ours is a unique collection. . . . The flesh has clearly entirely disappeared: only their skin remains, and that has turned much darker in colour. . . . They are naked, but not indecent. . . . You will observe that a baby child was buried along with his mother. . . . His little corpse is wonderfully preserved. . . . And this strapping fellow still retains his shirt, which has some lace left on it, even now. None of his teeth are missing. . . . You will notice — " She rapped each one on the chest by way of bringing her peroration to a close, and it sounded like a drum — "Look, ladies; look, gentlemen; this one has only one eye left . . . dried up, you see . . . and so's his tongue — quite leathery, like the rest of him." She tugged at it. "He's putting out his tongue but that doesn't make him at all repulsive. . . . You may give what you please, ladies and gentlemen, on your way out, but the usual thing is two francs a head, children half price. . . . You may touch them before you leave . . . And see for yourselves . . . But do not, I beg you, handle them too roughly . . . They're extremely fragile. . . ."

As soon as she arrived down here, old Ma Henrouille had

thought of raising her prices: it was a point that had to be referred to the Bishop to decide. But there was a certain amount of difficulty in this, because the vicar of Saint Éponime wanted one third of the takings to accrue to him personally, and also because Robinson was continually complaining as he said she didn't give him a large enough share of the receipts.

"I've been done," he concluded, "properly done. . . . And it's not the first time, either. . . . I really have the most bloody awful luck! And it's a paying show, you know, this crypt of the old girl's. You can take it from me she makes a damned good thing out of it, the old hag."

"But you didn't put up any of the cash, man!" I objected, to calm him down a bit and make him see reason. "And you're well fed: you're decently looked after. . . ."

But Robinson was as obstinate as a mule — a real case of persecution mania, that's what was the matter with him. He refused to understand; he would *not* be resigned.

"When all's said and done, you're pretty well out of a damned ugly bit of business, if you ask me! You can't complain. You were heading dead straight for Cayenne, if we hadn't switched the points. . . . And here you are grumbling! Quite apart from having found little Madelon, who's so good to you and has such a soft spot for you . . . Although you're ill and all . . . So what have you got to complain about? Especially now that your eyes are so much better."

"One would say you thought I didn't know damn well what I've got to complain about, wouldn't one?" That's the way he answered me. "But I just feel I've got to complain. . . . That's how it is . . . It's all I have left . . . Listen to me, will you? It's the only thing they'll let me do . . . No one need listen if you don't want . . ."

And there it was; as soon as we were alone together, he never stopped bewailing everything. I'd come to the point when I dreaded these confidential moments of his. I watched those eyes which blinked as I looked at them and still oozed a bit in the sun, and I came to the conclusion that really he wasn't a very attractive person, Robinson. There are some animals so made that it isn't any good their being simple and unfortunate and all; one's aware of it, but one just can't bear them all the same. They've something lacking.

"You could have pegged out in a cell . . ." I started off again, wanting to get him to think it over a bit more.

"But I've been to prison, I tell you . . . it's no worse than this . . . you're on quite the wrong track."

He had never told me that about having been in prison. It must have happened before we met, before the war. He stressed the point, and ended up, "There's only one kind of liberty, let me tell you, only one: and that's first of all to have your eyesight, and secondly to have your pockets full of dough — the rest's all hooey!"

"Well, what are you trying to get at, then, in the end?" I asked him. When you made him have to take a decision like that, forced him to declare himself and really speak his mind, he went all to pieces. Yet it was just what it would have been interesting to know.

While Madelon was away, during the day, at her workroom and old Ma Henrouille was showing her bits and pieces to people, we two went to a café under the trees. This café under the trees was a spot Robinson liked very much. Probably because of the noise the birds made overhead. What masses of them there were! Especially about five o'clock, when they were returning to their nests, thrilled at its being summer. They settled down onto the square then, like a thunder-storm. It was even said about these birds that there was a hairdresser whose shop was close by the garden, who'd gone mad, merely through hearing them all twittering away together for years. Certainly you could not hear yourself speak. But it was nice all the same, Robinson thought.

"If only she'd give me a regular four sous per visitor, I wouldn't say . . ."

Once in every fifteen minutes or so he harked back to this worry of his. Between whiles though, the memory of days gone by seemed to come back to him, and anecdotes too, anecdotes about the Pordurière Company in Africa, among others which, come to think of it, we'd both of us known, and some of them hair-raising stories which he had never yet told me. Not dared to, perhaps. He was a pretty reserved, even secretive, chap at bottom.

As regards the past, it was chiefly Molly I remembered clearly, when I was feeling good, like the echo of an hour that has struck far in the distance; whenever I thought of anything that was nice, at once I thought of her.

In the end, when selfishness loosens some of its hold on one, when the time has come to be through with all that, the only memory one has kept in one's heart is that of women who really did love men a little, not just one man, even if it was you, but all men.

When we came back from the café in the evening, we had done nothing, like retired non-commissioned officers on half pay.

During the season there were endless streams of tourists. They hung about in the crypt and Mother Henrouille contrived to make them laugh. The vicar kept an eye cocked at these goings-on, but as he was nabbing more than his share, he lay low; besides, smutty stories were a bit beyond him. A fine sight, and worth hearing, was Ma Henrouille, surrounded by these cadavers of hers. She'd gaze right into their faces for you — she wasn't afraid of death, and yet so wrinkled, so puckered herself that she was like one of them — sidling up with her lantern to blather away right in their apologies for faces.

When we got back to the house and had collected for dinner, we would go on arguing, about the food, and then Ma Henrouille used to call me her "little Doctor Jackal" because of the differences of opinion there'd been between us at Rancy. But only in a facetious way, of course. Madelon bustled about in the kitchen. These premises we lived in got only a very feeble light, they were an annex to the sacristy, and extremely narrow, cluttered with beams and dust-filled corners. "All the same," the old lady used to point out, "although, as you might say, it's always nighttime in this place, you can at least always find your way to your bed, your mouth and your pocket — and that's really all that matters."

She hadn't mourned long, after the death of her son. "He always was delicate," she told me confidentially one evening, "and here am I, seventy-six years old, and I never in my life complained of being ill. . . . He was always complaining and saying he wasn't well; it was part of his character, just like that Robinson of yours, to give you an example. . . . For instance, that's a difficult little staircase down into the vault, isn't it? You know it, don't you? . . . I find it tiring, I admit, but there are days when it brings me in two francs for each step. . . . I worked it out. . . . Well, if that's what I was getting, I'd climb right up to the sky if you suggested it. . . ."

Madelon used to put a lot of spices into our food and plenty of tomato. It was grand. And light red wine too. Even Robinson had taken to drinking wine after living in the South. Robinson had already told me everything that had happened since he arrived down here. I no longer listened to him. To tell the truth, he disappointed and rather disgusted me. "You're respectable middle class," I came to the conclusion (for at that time that, to my mind, was the most insulting thing you could say to any one). "You really have no thought for anything beyond money . . . by the time you get your eyesight back, you'll have become nastier than the rest of them. . . ."

Swearing at him didn't put him out in the least. You'd have said, on the contrary, that it rather pulled him together. He knew it was true, anyway. The young man's quite out, I felt; there's no use bothering any more about him. There's no doubt about it. A young woman with a certain amount of guts and a certain amount of vice in her system will transform a man for you so completely that you won't know the result. . . . Here's Robinson, I reflected, whom I once took for an adventurous sort of bloke, and he's really only a poor fish, cuckold or no, blind or not. . . . So there it was.

On top of which the old Henrouille had at once contaminated him with her passion for saving money, and Madelon had too, with her desire for marriage. That just about covered everything. He was pretty well up the spout. Especially as he'd soon be taking a liking to the kid — I know what it's like, all right! It would be a lie, anyway, to pretend I wasn't just a bit jealous; it wouldn't be fair. Madelon and I got together from time to time for a minute or two before dinner, in her bedroom. But these interviews weren't easy to fix. We didn't breathe a word. We were as discreet as discreet could be.

You mustn't think because of that that she didn't love her Robinson. That hadn't anything to do with it. Only he was merely playing at being engaged, so of course she too merely played at being faithful. They were just fond of each other. In these matters it's all a question of knowing what to expect. He was going to wait till he was married before he laid a hand on her, he told me. That was his plan. Well, he was welcome to eternity; mine was the immediate moment. Anyway, he'd spoken to me about another project he had of setting up a small restaurant with her, and giving old Henrouille the go-by. It was all going to be perfectly straightforward. "She's nice, customers will like her," he foresaw in his best moments. "Besides, you've sampled her cooking. She's in a class of her own with a frying pan."

He thought he might even wheedle a little initial capital out of Ma Henrouille. Yes, I thought that was O.K., but I foresaw he'd have a good bit of difficulty bringing her up to scratch. "You see everything through rose-coloured spectacles," I said to him, meaning just to calm him down and make him think things over a bit more. Right away he began to cry and say I was horribly unkind. Obviously one mustn't discourage people and I agreed at once that I'd been wrong and that really it was my moroseness that had always been my undoing. Robinson's line had been copper engraving before the war, but he wouldn't have anything to do with it now at any price. That was for him to decide. "With my lungs as they are, what I need is open air; get me? And besides, my eyes will never be what they were." He was quite right too, in a way. I had no answer to make. When we went along the crowded streets together, people turned round and were sorry for the poor blind man. There's pity in people for the blind and infirm; they really have got love in reserve. I'd often felt the presence of this love in reserve. There's any amount of it. No good saying there isn't. Only it's a pity people should still be such sods, with so much love in reserve. It stays where it is, that's what. It's stuck away inside and it doesn't come out, doesn't do them any good. They die of love — inside.

Madelon used to sit with him after dinner, looking after her little Léon, as she called him. She read the paper to him. At the moment he was mad about politics and the Midi papers are festered with politics, of a really lively kind.

Around us at evening the house sank into the dilapidation of ages. That's just the time, after dinner, when the bugs have their little chat, the time too for trying out on these bugs the effect of a corrosive solution that I wanted later to surrender to some chemist for a small sum. A bit of a side line. The idea rather took the old girl's fancy; she used to help me with my experiments. We walked round together from nest to nest, looking at every crack and cranny, and squirting swarms of them with my bug poison. They staggered and passed out in the beams of a candle carefully held for me by old Mme. Henrouille.

While we worked, we talked of Rancy. Just to think of the place gave me a pain; I'd have stayed at Toulouse for the rest of my days. I could ask nothing better, when all's said and done — a regular crust and some time to myself. The happy life, dammit. However, I had to be thinking of getting back to work. Time was passing, and so was the curate's bonus, and my savings.

I wanted, before leaving, to give Madelon a few further pieces of instruction and advice. Undoubtedly it's better to give people cash when one can afford to, and would like to be helpful. But it's also some use to a person to be forewarned and know exactly what they may expect and, above all, just what they are risking by jumping into bed with people to right and left. That's what I said to myself, especially as Madelon really rather frightened me where disease was concerned. She was a bright girl, true enough, but when it came to microbes, just as ignorant as they're made. So I embarked on fully detailed explanations of what she ought to pay particular attention to before saying "yes" when some one was nice to her. Points about colour . . . and moisture . . . In fact, the classical things that one ought to know, that are so eminently practical, worth knowing . . . When she had listened to what I had to say, and had heard me out in full, she protested for the sake of form. In fact, she treated me to a sort of scene about it. "A perfectly respectable" girl she was . . . I ought to be ashamed of myself . . . I had got a shockingly wrong impression of her . . . And just because with me she had, she didn't make a practice . . . I must have a very poor opinion of her . . . "Men were all such beasts."

In fact, what every lady always says on such occasions. I could have seen it coming. A smoke screen. But all that interested me was that she had heard what I'd said and seemed to have taken in the more essential points. . . . The rest didn't signify a bit. Having heard me well, what was really making her feel sad at heart was to think that you could catch all these things I'd told her about simply through being tender and having fun. It didn't matter that it was really Nature; she considered me just as disgusting as Nature herself, and that's what was such an insult to her. I didn't stress the point further, except just to comment slightly on certain precautions which are really so convenient. In the end, we played the psychologist and tried to do a little analysing of Robinson's character. "He isn't exactly jealous," she told me at this point. "But he has his difficult moments."

"All right, all right!" I said, and I set out to define Robinson's temperament, as if I myself really knew what he was like, but I realized immediately that I didn't know Robinson at all — aside from one or two rough indications of his character. No more than that.

It's astonishing how difficult it is to conceive of what will make one human being either more or less likeable to others. . . . Yet one wants to help him, to stick up for him — and one just babbles. . . . You open your mouth, and it's pitiful. . . . You're absolutely lost.

It isn't easy in our day to play the La Bruyère. The whole subconscious mind slinks away from you as you approach.

JUST WHEN I WAS GOING TO GO AND BUY MY TICKET, THEY MADE me stay — for another week, was the idea. The point being to show me the country round Toulouse, the banks of the fine cool river, which I'd heard so much about, and above all those lovely vineyards, about which every one in town seemed so proud and pleased, as if they all owned land themselves. I mustn't leave without having seen anything except Madame Henrouille's mummies. They couldn't allow that. Fuss, in fact . . .

I was silent in the face of such polite overtures. I didn't dare to seem eager to stay, because of my intimacy with Madelon, an intimacy which was getting to be rather risky. The old lady was beginning to suspect that there was something between us. A bit of a business.

But the old lady wasn't coming with us on this expedition. For one thing, she didn't intend to shut the vault, even for a single day. So I agreed to stay on and we went off one fine Sunday morning into the country. We supported Robinson between us, each taking him by an arm. We went down to the station and took Seconds. The compartments smelt of sausage, though, just like Third. We got off at a place called Saint-Jean. Madelon seemed very well acquainted with this part of the world; she kept meeting people she knew from all over the place. It looked like being a fine summer day, a really grand day. Robinson had to be told about everything we saw all the time as we went along. "There's a garden just here. . . . Now we're coming to a bridge, with a man sitting on it fishing. . . . He isn't catching anything, though. . . . Look out, here's a bicycle coming . . ." The smell of chips, for instance, gave him a sense of direction at once. It was he, in fact, who led us along to a place where they were selling them at half a franc a portion. I'd always known Robinson to be fond of chips, as I am too. It's very Parisian, this liking for potato chips. Madelon preferred vermouth, dry and by itself.

Rivers don't have an easy time of it in the South. They seem not to be getting on too well; they're always on the point of drying up. Hills and the sun, fishermen, fish, boats, ditches, washhouses, vines, weeping willows, they all want some, all clamour for it. It's asked to give up far too much water and there isn't much left in the riverbed. In some places you'd say it was more like a badly flooded road than a real river. As we'd all come out to enjoy ourselves, obviously we'd got to set about it at once. As soon as we'd finished the chips, we came to the conclusion that a little excursion in a boat, before lunch, would be fun; me rowing, of course, and they two sitting opposite me, hand in hand, Robinson and Madelon.

So we slip off downstream, as they say, scraping the bottom every now and then, she squealing, he not too happy either. Flies and still more flies. Dragonflies too, surveying the surface of the water, all a pair of bulging great eyes, and with little fearful flicks of their tails. Astonishing heat everywhere, hazing the water. We glide across it from those long flat swirls over there to an encounter with rotten branches over here. . . . Close to the broiling banks we pass, in search of gusts of shade which we grasp as best we can under trees not too stricken by the sun. Talking makes you hotter still, if that's possible. Still you don't like to say you're not enjoying it much.

Robinson, naturally enough, was the first to have had enough of this boat business. So I suggested we go and sit outside a restaurant. We weren't the only ones to have had the same little idea. All the anglers on that stretch had already installed themselves at the café before us, eager for a drink before lunch, entrenched behind syphons. Robinson didn't like to ask me whether it was an expensive café I'd chosen but I spared him this worry at once by assuring him that all the prices were marked and all very reasonable; which was true. He still held on to Madelon's hand.

I can say now that we paid in this restaurant as though we'd eaten, but we had really only attempted to eat. It's better not to talk about the dishes we were served. They're still there.

Then after that, fixing up about some fishing for Robinson and me, so as to while away the afternoon, was far too complicated a business, and it would only have made him miserable because he wouldn't even have been able to see his float. But as for more rowing, as an alternative, I was already far too done in after just the morning's effort. That had been quite enough. I'd lost the form I once had on the African rivers. I had grown old that way too, just as in everything else.

But to change our form of exercise anyway, I suggested that a little walk, a little simple walk on foot along the banks, would do us a whole heap of good — at any rate, as far as the long grass we could see less than three quarters of a mile away by a row of poplars. So we started off again, Robinson and I walking arm in arm, Madelon a few yards ahead of us. It was easier that way, walking through the grass. As we rounded a bend in the river, we heard some one playing an accordion. The sound came from a sloop, a beautiful sloop moored at this spot in the river. The music made Robinson stop short. Being blind, it was quite understandable that it should, and besides, he'd always had a great fondness for music. So, pleased at having found something to entertain him, we settled ourselves down right there on the grass where it was less dusty than on the steep bank near by. You could see that it wasn't just an ordinary sloop. Very spick and ornamental it was, a yacht just for living in, not for carrying cargo, all decorated with flowers up above and even a very smart little kennel for the dog. We described the yacht to Robinson. He wanted to know every detail.

"I should like to live in a fine clean boat like that myself," he remarked. "Wouldn't you, Madelon?" turning to her.

"I know what you mean, dear," she answered. "But it's a rather expensive idea you've had, Léon! It would cost a good deal more to buy, I'm sure, than a tenement house."

At that we all three began to wonder what a yacht like that could possibly cost, and lost ourselves in endless estimates. . . . Each held to his own figure. It was that habit that people like ourselves have of always calculating about everything out loud.

The strains of the accordion came over to us very coaxingly all this time and we could even catch the words of a song they were singing to it. . . . In the end, we all came to the conclusion that anyway a sloop like that must cost at least a hundred thousand francs. . . . That gave you something to think about!

> *Ferme tes jolis yeux, car les heures sont brèves . . .*
> *Au pays merveilleux, au doux pays du rê-ê-êve.*

That's what they sang inside the cabin, mingled voices of men and women, a little out of tune but pleasant all the same because of the setting. It fitted in with the hot sun and the fields and the afternoon hour and the river.

Robinson insisted on making it thousands and thousands. He was sure, such as we had described the yacht to him, that it must have cost considerably more than we'd said. It had a piece of glass on top so as to let more light in, and bits of brass everywhere; luxurious it was . . .

"You're tiring yourself out, Léon," Madelon tried to quiet him. "Why don't you lie back on the grass; it's nice and thick, and you'll feel rested. . . . Whether it's five thousand or five hundred thousand, you and I haven't got that much, have we? So it's really not worth getting all worked up about."

But he lay on his back and went on worrying all the same about the cost of the thing, and he wanted frightfully to know all about it and try to see a yacht like that, that cost such a lot to build.

"Has it a motor?" he asked. *We* didn't know.

I went and had a look at the back of it, as he was so keen about it, just to please him, to see if I could see the exhaust of any little motor.

> *Ferme tes jolis yeux, car la vie n'est qu'un songe . . .*
> *L'amour n'est qu'un menson-on-on-ge . . .*
> *Ferme tes jolis yeuuuuuuuux! —*

The people inside the boat went on singing like that. At last we began to feel awfully drowsy. . . . They were putting us to sleep.

Then all of a sudden the spaniel inside the little kennel came leaping out and dashed on to the gangway and started barking in our direction. He woke us up with a start and we yelled angrily at the spaniel. Robinson was much alarmed.

At that a fellow who looked as if he might be the owner of the yacht came out on deck through the little hatch place. He said we weren't to yell at his dog and we had a word or two with him about that. But when he realized that Robinson was, so to speak, blind, the man calmed down all of a sudden and was really rather put out. He changed his mind about telling us to go to hell and even went so far as to take the line that he'd made a bit of a fool of himself, so as to put things right again. By way of making it up, he invited us to come and have coffee with him on board his yacht, because it was his birthday, he added. He couldn't have us all staying out there in the sun, we'd roast. . . . And so on. And so forth. Besides, it would be just right, because they were thirteen at table. . . . He was a young man, this proprietor fellow, rather an eccentric. He was fond of boats, he went on to say. We could see that. But his wife was nervous of the sea, so they lay up in this place, on the pebbles, as you might say. His friends on board seemed quite pleased to see us. And so was his wife quite pleased; a beautiful creature who played the accordion like an angel. And really it was very nice of them to have asked us, anyway; we might have been Heaven knows what. It was nice and trusting of them. . . . We realized at once that it wouldn't be right to let our charming hosts down. Especially not in front of their guests. . . . Robinson had many faults, but he was, normally, quite decently sensitive. Inwardly he realized, just by the sound of their voices, that we'd got to behave now and not say anything vulgar or anything. Our clothes weren't good, admittedly, but at any rate they were clean and decent. I took a closer look at the owner of the yacht; he must have been thirtyish, with a handsome head of poetic brown hair and a pretty suit like a sailor's but more ornate. And, as it happened, his lovely wife had real "velvety" eyes.

They'd just finished lunch. A lot had been left over. We wouldn't refuse just a taste of the sweet — no, indeed we would not. And a glass of port to wash it down? It was a long time since I had heard such well-bred voices myself. Educated people have a certain way of talking which intimidates you and, as for me, downright frightens me, especially their women — though it's really only absurdly turned, pretentious phrases, but as polished as old furniture. It's an alarming kind of talk they have, although lifeless in itself; you're afraid of tripping up on it just answering what they say. And even when they put on coarse accents, when for fun they sing the songs of the poor, they still retain this polished tone which fills you with distrust and dislike, a voice which has a sort of little whip in it always, as that's what you always need for talking to servants with. It's rather thrilling, but at the same time it makes you want to put those women of theirs on their backs, just to see their dignity, as they call it, melt away.

I explained quietly to Robinson how the whole place was furnished; with nothing but antiques. It reminded me rather of my mother's shop, but it was cleaner, of course, and better arranged. My mother's place had always smelt of old pepper.

And hung on the walls all round were paintings by the owner. He was an artist. It was his wife who told me this, making a very pretty fuss about it. His wife was in love with her husband, you could see that. Her husband was an artist, a fine figure of a man, with lovely hair and a lovely income — everything that's needed to make a woman happy; and on top of that you had the accordion, friends, dreamy days afloat on a beautiful stream which went eddying past you as you lay there, content never to leave your moorings. . . . All these things were theirs to enjoy; and with it a whole, sweet, precious world of freshness, created between them by a screen against the wind and the breath of a ventilator, and divine security.

Now that we'd come in and joined them, we had to be put at our ease. Iced drinks and strawberries and cream, my favourite sweet. Madelon squirmed for a second helping. She had become all pretty-mannered too, now. The men thought her charming, especially the father-in-law, very well to do; he seemed delighted to have Madelon by his side and took tremendous trouble to be nice to her. The whole table had to be ransacked to find titbits for her to eat, and she even had cream on the tip of her nose. From what one could gather, the old man was a widower. No doubt he'd forgotten it. Quite soon, with the liqueurs, Madelon was a little bit squiffy. The suit Robinson had on, and mine too, bore evidence of fatigue, and a year's continual use and several years' continual use, but in this sheltered light that couldn't be noticed. All the same, I felt rather abashed among all these people with their every comfort, clean as Americans, so well washed, so well got up, as though ready for an elegance contest.

Madelon, now that she'd livened up, was no longer behaving quite so well. Tilting her perky little profile towards the pictures, she began to say silly things; our hostess rather realized this and picked up the accordion again to smooth things over, while everybody sang — and quietly we sang too, but not in tune and not very cheerfully — the same song that we had heard outside a little while ago, and then another.

Robinson had managed to enter into a conversation with one old gentleman who seemed to know everything there was to know about cocoa. A good topic. Colonial meeting colonial. "When I was out in Africa," to my great surprise I heard Robinson remark, " — I was at that time forestry surveyor to the Pordurière Company — I used to put the whole population of a village on to harvesting . . ." et cetera. He couldn't see me, so he let himself go, hand over fist. He didn't mind what he said . . . Remembering all sorts of things that never happened . . . Filling the old gent up with it . . . But, good God, it was all *lies!* Anything he could think of to put himself on a level with the old gentleman, who was a cocoa expert himself. Robinson, who'd always been so circumspect in his remarks! It annoyed and distressed me to hear him hold forth like this.

He'd been given the place of honour in the angle of a broad and scented settee, a glass of old brandy clasped in his right hand, while with the other he described in sweeping gestures the majesty of untamed jungles, the furies of an equatorial storm. He was well away, definitely well away. . . . How Alcide would have guffawed if he too could have seen him, sitting there in his little corner. Poor Alcide. . . .

Well, yes, of course it certainly was beautifully comfortable on board their yacht. Especially now that there was a slight river breeze beginning to rise and, framed in the ship's windows, the ample folds of the curtains fluttered like dainty, gay little flags.

Another round of ices after that again, and then champagne as well. It was the owner's birthday; hadn't he told us so at least a hundred times? He intended making every one happy on this occasion, even passers-by; meaning us, on this occasion. In an hour, or two, or three maybe, we'd all be friends under his roof, his old friends and the others and even strangers, even us three, picked up off the bank, the best he could do; so not to be thirteen at table. I was just going to let off my little chant of happiness but then I thought better of it, feeling proud all of a sudden, seeing the point. And so I saw fit to tell them, in order to justify their invitation, which I had badly on the brain, that in asking me onto their boat, they were entertaining one of the most distinguished medical men of Paris. They could hardly doubt it, of course, from my attitude. Or from the insignificance of my two friends, either! But as soon as they knew what an important person I was, they declared themselves delighted and flattered and one by one lost no time in revealing to me their own little personal aches and pains; I took advantage of this state of affairs to get better acquainted with the daughter of a shipowner, a sturdy young cousin of my host's, who as a matter of fact, suffered from nettle rash and said the least thing gave her flatulent acidity.

When you're not used to comfort and good things to eat, you're intoxicated by them in no time. Truth's only too pleased to leave you. Very little's ever needed for Truth to let go of you. And after all, you're not really very keen to keep hold of it. In this sudden abundance of ease, a marvellous megalomania is all over you before you know it. I began to make a speech myself, while I talked of nettle rash to the little cousin. You strive to leave daily humiliations behind you by attempting, like Robinson, to put yourself on a like footing with the rich, by proffering lies, which are a poor man's coins. We're all ashamed of our unprepossessing flesh, our own deficient frames. I couldn't bear to show them my own reality; it was as unworthy of them as my behind would have been. At all costs, I had to make a good impression. I began to answer fancifully the questions they asked me, just as Robinson had with the old gentleman. I, in my turn, was swamped with pride. My vast clientèle . . . Overwork . . . My friend Robinson, the engineer . . . Who had offered me the hospitality of his cottage in the country . . . Near Toulouse . . .

And anyway, when he has eaten and drunk well, the other fellow is easily convinced. Anything will do. So fortunate. Robinson had preceded me in the furtive delight of spinning a yarn straight out of your head; to follow needed but slight initial effort.

As he wore smoked glasses, people couldn't very well make out what state Robinson's eyes were in. We generously ascribed this infirmity of his to the war. From then on, we were properly settled and raised, first socially and next patriotically, to a level with our hosts in general; in the beginning, they had been slightly surprised by this caprice of the husband's, who, being a fashionable painter, was liable from time to time to do such very odd things. . . .

Our fellow guests had begun to find all three of us *most* charming — and really ever so interesting. . . . Considering that she was Robinson's fiancée, Madelon was perhaps not behaving quite as she should have; she flirted with everybody, including the women — so much so that I wondered if the whole thing wasn't going to degenerate into an all-in necking party. But it didn't. Remarks died away bit by bit, thwarted by the awkward strain of going beyond words. Nothing came of it.

We lay there, clinging to our last words and the cushions, completely dazed by our joint efforts to make each other happy, more deeply, more warmly happy, and even yet a little happier still, body replete, in spirit only, doing absolutely all we could to pack into the present moment all the possible contentment of this world, all the marvellous things that one knew in one's heart, and about everything in general, so that one's next-door neighbour should profit by it too and might confess that that was exactly the admirable mystery he himself had been looking for, and lacking, these many years, in order to be perfectly happy himself, at last and forever after. One would have managed to reveal to him one's own real reason for existing. And he, then, would have had to tell the world at large that he too had found the key to his existence. And we'd have had just one more drink together to celebrate this delectable discovery and it would stay forever thus. Never again to lose this charm. . . . And, most of all, never to return to that dreary time before this miracle, before we met, before so marvellously encountering each other. . . . All of us together forever more! At last! And always!

The owner of the yacht could not refrain from breaking the spell.

He had a weakness for telling us about his painting; he chattered about his pictures, which really obsessed him much too much, now, later on and all the time. And so, through his obstinate folly, tight though we were, banality came crushing back on us. I'd thrown my hand in, went and delivered myself of a few well-turned, fine-sounding compliments to the captain, the sort of sweetness in words artists adore to hear. That's what he had badly needed. As soon as he had heard my eulogies, it affected him like successful copulation. He sank onto one of those bulbous sofas he had on his boat and almost immediately fell asleep, very gently, in obvious bliss. The other guests, meanwhile, gazed into each other's faces with dulled and mutually fascinated scrutiny — hesitating between almost irresistible drowsiness and the ecstasy of divine digestion.

I saved up this longing for sleep myself and kept it for the night to come. Day's surviving fears too often scare away sleep and when you've the luck to build up for yourself, while you can, a small supply of bliss, you need to be an awful fool to squander it in pointless preliminary siestas. Keep all that for the nighttime. That's my motto. Always remember there's the darkness to follow. Besides, we'd been asked to stay on to dinner; now was the time to work up a fresh appetite. . . .

We took advantage of the prevailing stupor to slink out. We all three made an exquisitely neat get-away, skirting the somnolent guests attractively littered round our hostess's accordion. That lady's eyes, softened by music, fluttered in search of the shadows. "See you later," she said, as we passed her by; and her smile finished in a dream.

We did not go far, the three of us, only to a place I had noticed where there was a bend in the river, between two rows of poplars, big pointed poplars. From there you could see the whole of the valley, and in the distance the little town in its hollow, clustered round the church tower, which jutted like a nail into the red glow of the sky.

"When have we a train back?" asked Madelon, suddenly anxious.

"Don't worry," he reassured her. "They'll be taking us back by car. . . . The fellow said so. They've got one."

Madelon said no more. She was dreamy with contentment. It had been a really good day.

"What about your eyes, Léon; how are they now?" she asked him.

"They're much better. I didn't want to say anything to you about it, because I wasn't sure, but I really think I'm beginning to be able to count the bottles on a table even — especially with my left eye. I had quite a bit to drink, did you notice? And wasn't it good stuff!"

"Left is the side of your heart," Madelon remarked happily. She was delighted, naturally, at his eyes being better.

"Kiss me and let me kiss you!" she said to him. I began to feel in the way, with them carrying on so effusively. But I found it hard to clear out, because there was nowhere much I could go. I made as if to retire behind a tree a little way off, and waited there until they should recover themselves. It was sweet, the things they were saying to each other. I could hear all of it. The dullest love talk is always pretty amusing when one knows the people concerned. And I had never heard them say this sort of thing before.

"You really do love me?" she was asking him. He answered, "I love you as much as my eyes."

"Oh, Léon, that's a marvellous thing to say! But you haven't seen me yet, have you, Léon? Perhaps when you've seen me with your own eyes, not only with other people's, you won't love me so much any more? When you do, you'll see other women too and maybe you will start to love them all. Like some of your friends. . . ."

That remark, made in a low voice, was meant for me. There was no mistaking it. She thought I was a good way off and couldn't hear. So she let me have that nasty knock. She wasn't losing any time about it. He, my friend, started to protest. "Good Lord!" he said. That wasn't fair, it was a slanderous accusation. . . .

"What, me, Madelon? Not a bit of it," he said, shielding himself. "I'm not his sort at all. What makes you think I am the same as he is? When you've been so sweet to me always . . . I'm not the chap to fool around. I'm in earnest, I tell you. I never go back on my word. You're pretty, I know that already; but you'll be prettier still once I've seen you . . . There! Are you happy now? You're not crying any longer? After all, I can't say more, can I?"

"That's lovely, Léon," she answered, pressing herself against him. They were swearing everlasting love to each other; nothing could stop them now, the whole of heaven was not large enough for them.

"I want you to be always happy with me," he said very softly, after a while. "I want you to have nothing to do all day and yet have enough of everything you want."

"Oh, you're wonderful, darling Léon. You're nicer than I thought even — you're sweet and true and everything that's lovely!"

"It's because I adore you, my precious . . ."

And they clung together more passionately, holding each other still closer in their arms. Then, as if to keep me as far removed as possible from their own intense happiness, they again turned nastily on me. She said, "Your friend, the doctor, is a nice man, isn't he?" Off she went again, as if she simply couldn't get over the thought of me.

"Yes, he's nice. I don't want to say anything against him, since he is a friend of yours. . . . But he's the sort of man, I should think, who treats women very badly. . . . I wouldn't say unpleasant things about him, because I believe he is really attached to you. . . . But he's not my sort, I must confess. You see, I — you won't be angry if I tell you something, will you?" No, nothing was going to annoy our Léon. "Well, it seems to me that, if anything, our doctor's a bit too fond of the women. . . . You know . . . Rather like an animal. Don't you think so? As if he was all the time ready to pounce on them, you might say. Just doing all the harm he can and then going on his way. Don't you think he's like that?"

He thought so indeed, the dirty dog; he thought whatever she wanted him to; in fact, her remarks struck him as extremely true and amusing. Yes, terribly funny. He encouraged her to go on, helpless with laughter.

"That's quite right what you say about him, Madelon. Ferdinand's not a bad fellow, but you'd hardly say that he behaves particularly well and no one could say he was faithful. . . . I'm sure of that."

"You must have known him to have plenty of mistresses, haven't you, Léon?" She was out to get the low-down, the little bitch.

"Well, maybe I have," he retorted, evenly enough. "But you know — In the first place he — It isn't difficult . . ."

Some meaning had to be extracted from these remarks and Madelon proceeded to do so.

"All doctors are beasts, of course, most of the time. Every one knows that. But I should imagine he's what you might call weakness itself."

"You're absolutely right," my good, my gallant friend agreed. "In fact, I've often thought he must take drugs; sex has such a hold on him. . . . Then too, he's more than normally constructed. . . . If you were to see him without his clothes! It's not natural!"

"Oh," said Madelon, perplexed at this and trying to remember what I did look like without my clothes. "Do you think he may be diseased then? Eh? Tell me." She was suddenly very worried; these intimate revelations upset her.

"That I can't say," he was forced to admit regretfully. "I couldn't be certain . . . But there's every chance of it with the life he leads."

"All the same, you're most likely right; no doubt he does take drugs. That's probably why he's so odd sometimes."

Madelon's little brain was very busy all of a sudden. She added, "In future, we'd better be slightly on our guard against him."

"You're not frightened of him though, are you?" he asked her. "Surely he's nothing to you? He's never made advances to you, has he?"

"Oh, no, of course not that! I wouldn't have allowed it! But there's no knowing what mightn't come into his head. . . . Just think if he had a fit or something! That can easily happen to you if you take drugs. . . . Anyway, I certainly wouldn't have him to attend to *me* if I were ill!"

"Nor would I, if it comes to that," Robinson agreed. Whereupon more kissing and sweet speeches followed.

"Darling, darling," she said, rocking him in her arms.

"My precious, my adorable," he answered. Then between whiles there was silence, broken every so often by sudden storms of kisses.

"Tell me quickly, as often as you can, that you love me, while I kiss you as far as your shoulder. . . ." It was a little kissing game, beginning at her neck and throat.

"Oh, I'm all red in the face," she gasped. "You're smothering me! Let me breathe!" But he didn't let her breathe. He began all over again. I, in the grass near by, tried to see what was about to take place. His lips were at her breast, caressing her. A pretty pastime, to be sure. It was making me very red in the face too, thanks to quite a number of emotions all at once—on top of which I was also experiencing complete astonishment at my own indiscretion.

"We will be very happy, we two, won't we, Léon? Tell me you are sure that we will be happy."

That was during an interval. It was followed by still more plans for the future, a future which was to last forever and plans enough to remake the world anew — a world to hold only the pair of them, of course. Certainly I wasn't to have any place in it. It seemed as if they could never finish ridding themselves of me, or sufficiently erasing the dirty memory of me from their intimacy with each other.

"Tell me, have you been friends long with Ferdinand?" The idea was very irritating to her.

"Yes, quite a time . . . in various places," he answered. "We met at first by chance when travelling. . . . He's a chap who likes getting about and seeing things. . . . So am I, in a way. And so we've sort of travelled along together for some time now. See?" He was making ours appear a casual acquaintance.

"Well, listen, you'll have to stop being such friends with him, my dear! And you'd better begin right away," she said, very definitely and tartly. "It's going to be put a stop to. It is, isn't it, honey? And from now on, you won't be having any other fellow traveller but me, see? Isn't that so, honey?"

"Why, you're not jealous of him, are you?" he asked. He was rather put out by her remarks, the bastard.

"No, I'm not jealous of him but I love you too much, don't you see, Léon? I want to have you all to myself; I don't want to share you with any one. And in any case, he's not the right sort of person for you to be mixing with, now that I am in love with you, Léon dear. He's too vicious. You understand, don't you? Tell me you love me a lot, Léon! And that you understand me."

"I adore you."

"Good."

WE ALL WENT BACK TO TOULOUSE IN THE EVENING.

Two days later the accident happened. The time had finally come for me to leave and I had nearly finished packing my bag, when I heard some one shouting something outside the house. I listened. They were telling me to come down quick to the vault. I couldn't see who was calling me like this — but from the tone of their voice, it was clear that something desperate was the matter. They seemed to be in a hell of a hurry.

"Right you are; half a minute, though! Is it that urgent?" I answered, thinking to myself, "Not so fast!" It must have been about seven o'clock, just before supper time. We were going to say good-bye at the station. That had been agreed upon, as it suited everybody; the old lady would not be home until later. On that particular day, she was expecting the visit of pilgrims to the vault.

"Come quick, Doctor!" they called from the street. "Madame Henrouille has had an accident."

"All right, all right," I said. "Coming at once. I'll be straight down."

But then, after a moment's thought, I added, "You go on ahead and tell them I'll be along as fast as I can. Just let me get my trousers on. . . ."

"But there's no time to be lost!" they went on, clamouring from below. "She's lost consciousness, I tell you! It looks as if she's broken a bone in her head! She fell down the steps into the vault . . . right down to the bottom."

"Is that so?" I said to myself, when I heard this pretty story. I didn't have to think much longer. I cleared out straight to the station. That was that.

I caught the seven-fifteen all right, but only just.

No good-byes were said, after all.

THE FIRST THING THAT STRUCK PARAPINE WHEN HE SAW ME AGAIN was that I wasn't looking at all well.

"You must have been tiring yourself out down there," he remarked, suspicious as ever.

Well, of course, I had had an exciting time of it in Toulouse, but after all, why complain? I had come off pretty lightly and escaped serious trouble; at least, I hoped so, sneaking off at the critical moment like that.

So I explained the whole story to him in detail and confided my suspicions to Parapine. But he didn't feel that I had acted particularly adroitly in this affair. . . . However, we hadn't time to go into the matter at any length, because the problem of finding a job for me had gotten so pressing during the interval that I had to be getting a move on. There was no time to be lost, therefore, arguing it all out. . . . I had a bare hundred and fifty francs in hand now and I really didn't know at all where to turn to get settled again. To the Tarapout? There were no jobs going there these days. The slump was on. Should I go back to Garenne-Rancy then? And try sounding my old practice again? I did think of doing that at one moment, even so, but only as a very last resort and much against my will. Nothing dies out so quick as a sacred flame.

In the end it was Parapine himself who put me on to something, thank God, in the shape of a small post he found for me, as it happened, on the staff of the asylum where he himself had been employed for several months now.

Things were going pretty well. Parapine was not only in charge at this place of the cinema class among the lunatics, but he also looked after the electric-treatment racket. At a given time, twice a week, he let off magnetic storms above the heads of the melancholy inmates assembled for this particular purpose in a very dark and air-tight room. A sort of cerebral sport, in fact, the putting into practice of his boss Professor Baryton's brain wave. And it was he, this canny colleague of ours, who took me on at an extremely small salary but with a contract as long as your arm, full of clauses all of which were, naturally enough, to his own advantage. A real employer, in fact.

Our emoluments at this asylum were exceedingly small, it's true, but we weren't badly fed and we were certainly very well housed. You could take the nurses to bed with you. That was allowed and tacitly understood. The Chief raised no objection to such diversions on our part and was actually aware that these erotic facilities attached his staff to the place. He was no fool, no martinet.

Besides, it was hardly the moment to catechize or to make terms, considering I had just been offered a little bit of bread and butter which was more than heaven-sent. Thinking it over, I couldn't quite understand why Parapine had shown me such active kindness. His doing this for me puzzled me completely. To put it down to brotherly feelings on his, on Parapine's part —well, no, that was really too beautiful. It must be something rather more complicated than that. Still, you never know . . .

We had our midday meal together — that was the arrangement — at Baryton's table, seated round this distinguished alienist with his pointed beard, his short fat thighs; a nice little man, apart from any consideration of his own pocket, on which point he was really utterly sickening whenever there was half a chance of the subject coming up.

I must say he spoilt us with macaroni and harsh Bordeaux claret. An entire vineyard had been left him in somebody's will, he explained. Which was pretty tough on us. It was no sort of a vintage, I declare.

His asylum at Vigny-sur-Seine was always crowded. It was billed as a "Sanatorium," because it had a big garden round it, in which our lunatics went for walks when the weather was fine. They strolled about in it with their heads balanced very oddly and, it seemed, precariously on their shoulders, as if in constant fear of spilling everything they contained on the ground, if they stumbled. They had all sorts of outlandish things skipping about inside, of which they were horribly fond.

The lunatics never talked to us about the precious things they had stored up in their minds without a whole series of terrified contortions or very condescending, high-and-mighty airs in the manner of tremendously powerful and punctilious officials. Nothing, not even a gold mine, could coax these creatures to venture outside their minds. All that makes a lunatic is the ordinary ideas of mankind shut up very tight inside a man's head. The outer world held well at bay and that's enough. Then the mind gets like a lake without an outlet; it's a head bolted and barred, infected, stagnant.

Baryton got his macaroni and vegetables wholesale from Paris. So that tradespeople of Vigny-sur-Seine were not at all fond of us. In fact, to put it bluntly, they loathed us like hell. But this animosity didn't spoil our appetites. When I first went there, Baryton used regularly at meal times to elaborate philosophical dissertations and conclusions out of our desultory remarks. But having spent a lifetime in the company of the insane, having made his daily bread out of them, sharing meals with them, counteracting their insanities as best he might, nothing was more irksome to him than to have to go on discussing their foibles at our meal times. "They shouldn't enter into the conversation of normal people," he would insist peremptorily and on the defensive. He personally was strict in his observance of this mental hygiene.

Baryton was very fond of conversation, almost nervously addicted to it; but he liked it to be amusing, reassuring and full of good sense. "Loonies" were a subject he did not care to dwell on. An instinctive antipathy towards them was as much as he ever intended feeling for them. On the other hand, it enchanted him to listen to our talk of travels and adventure. He could never have enough of that. Parapine had been partially freed from his verbosity since my arrival on the scene. I was just what was needed to keep the Chief amused during meals. For his benefit, all my travels were passed in review at table and recounted at great length, suitably arranged, of course, and decked out in the proper literary trappings. Baryton made a great deal of noise with his mouth and tongue when he ate. His daughter always sat on his right. Although she was only ten, his daughter Aimée already seemed faded. There was something inanimate about Aimée; a sort of greyish tinge was stamped on her face, as if continual unhealthy little clouds were passing forever before her eyes.

There was a certain amount of friction between Parapine and Baryton. Yet Baryton never bore any one any malice so long as they did not interfere in any way with the profits he made out of his establishment. His accounts had long been the one sacred thing in his life.

One day, at the time when he still spoke to Baryton, Parapine quite suddenly told him straight out at table that he lacked ethics. At first, this remark displeased Baryton. But afterwards all was well again. You can't go quarrelling over a little thing like that. Baryton derived, from listening to the accounts of my travels, not only a romantic pleasure but also delight at the thought of having saved money. "Hearing you talk, Ferdinand, one feels there is no need to go and see these places for oneself, you describe it all so well, Ferdinand." There was no prettier compliment he could have thought to pay me. Into this asylum we only admitted lunatics who were easy to manage, never maniacs of dangerous or definitely homicidal tendencies. It wasn't by any means a sinister spot. Very few bars and only one or two cells. Perhaps among them all the most disquieting case was that of his own little daughter Aimée. She wasn't numbered among the afflicted, but obviously the child was haunted by her environment.

From time to time a shriek or two would reach us in the dining room, but the cause of these screams was always pretty trivial. They didn't last long, anyway. Occasionally one would observe sudden and prolonged outbursts of frenzy coming over some group of inmates during their ceaseless prowlings to and fro, between the beds of begonias, the pump, and the clumps of trees. That was all put right without much trouble or alarms by giving them tepid baths and flagons of Thébaïque syrup.

Sometimes the lunatics would come to the few refectory windows which gave on to the street, to scream and cause a commotion in the neighbourhood, but usually they kept their horror to themselves. They took great pains to husband their private horror against our scientific onslaughts; they adored putting up a resistance against us in this way.

When I think nowadays of all the lunatics I got to know at old Baryton's, I cannot help being doubtful whether there are any other true manifestations of the inner working of our souls besides war and disease, those two nightmares of infinite duration.

The great weariness of life is maybe nothing but the vast trouble we take to remain always for twenty or forty or more years at a time reasonable beings — so as not to be merely and profoundly oneself, that is to say, obscene, ghastly, and absurd. It's the nightmare of having to present to the world from morning till night as a superman, our universal petty ideal, the grovelling sub-man we really are.

We had all kinds and conditions of patients in the asylum, at a variety of prices. The wealthier ones had strongly upholstered rooms in the Louis XV style. To these Baryton paid his little daily visit, for which a heavy charge was made. They waited for it. From time to time he would be received with a couple of hellishly good clouts across the face, really terrific and long premeditated. Instantly he'd enter this on the bill as "Item. Special Treatment."

Parapine maintained an attitude of reserve at table, not because my successful anecdotes, which pleased Baryton, in the least annoyed him. Quite the reverse. He seemed less preoccupied than in his old microbe days, definitely almost happier. The fact was that he had been very badly frightened over the business of his escapade with the minors. He was somewhat disconcerted now in matters of sex. In his free time, he used to amble about the grounds of the asylum himself, exactly like one of the inmates, and when I chanced to run into him, he would give me a little passing smile but such indistinct, pale smiles they were that you'd have taken them for farewells.

By engaging both of us on his technical staff, Baryton had made a good acquisition, for we not only at all times gave him our entire devotion, but we also entertained him with the echoes of the adventures which he liked so much, and was frozen and hungry for. At times he would take a delight in showing us how pleased he was. But nevertheless towards Parapine he always evidenced a certain reserve.

He had never been entirely at his ease with Parapine. "Parapine . . . you know," he said to me one day in confidence, "Parapine's a Russian!" The fact of being Russian, to Baryton, was something as descriptive, morphological, and irreparable, as being a "diabetic" or a "blackamoor." Once launched on this subject, which had been on his mind for many months, he set his brain working like mad in my presence and for my particular benefit. I hardly recognised the man as the same Baryton. We were walking down together to the local tobacconist's to get some cigarettes.

"Parapine, of course I quite realise, Ferdinand, is extremely intelligent, yet his is an absolutely arbitrary kind of intelligence, all the same. . . . Don't you agree with me, really, Ferdinand? . . . Besides, he's a fellow who simply will not adapt himself to things. . . . You'll notice that about him at once. Why, he isn't even at home in his job. He isn't at home in the world . . . Isn't that so? And he's wrong . . . quite wrong . . . Because he isn't happy. That proves it. Whereas, look at me, Ferdinand. I know how to adapt myself." (He thumped his chest.) "If to-morrow the earth were to start spinning the wrong way round, for example what should I do? Why, I should adapt myself at once! And do you know how I should do that, Ferdinand? I would sleep the clock round and then it would be O.K. Nothing more to it than that! I should be readjusted! But can you guess what your Parapine would do in like circumstances? He would be worrying it all out, puzzling and being bitter about it, for the next hundred years. I'm positive that's what he would do . . . Isn't that so? If the earth were to turn the other way round, he'd never sleep again. . . . He would discover God knows what special injustice in the whole thing, some intolerable injustice. That's his pet mania, by the way; he used to talk to me a hell of a lot about things being unfair in the days when he still did deign to speak to me. . . . And do you think now he would be content just to whine about it? That in itself wouldn't be so bad! . . . But not a bit of it! He would work out some scheme for blowing the Earth to bits. . . . In revenge, Ferdinand! And the worst of it all, I'll tell you what really would be the worst of it all — but now this, of course, is entirely between ourselves — He'd find a way of doing it! I promise you he would, he'd find one! See here, Ferdinand, and try and remember what I'm going to explain to you — there are just ordinary madmen and there are madmen who're in agony over the set form of our civilization. . . . It is horrible to me to think of Parapine having to be included in this class. . . . Do you know what he once said to me?"

"No, sir, I don't."

"Well, he said: 'Nothing exists, Mr. Baryton, between the penis and mathematics. Nothing at all! It's a vacuum.' And wait now, listen to this — do you know what he's waiting for, before he speaks to me again?"

"No, Mr. Baryton, I have no idea. . . ."

"Hasn't he told you?"

"No, not so far . . ."

"Well, but he has told me . . . He's waiting for the arrival of an Age of Mathematics! That's what he's waiting for. He's made up his mind. What do you think of such impertinent behaviour towards me — his senior? His chief?"

I really had to have a good laugh and make light of this outrageous fancy, so as to try and pass it off between the two of us. But Baryton didn't in the least regard it as just a joke. He even found grounds to be indignant over lots of other things. . . .

"Ah, Ferdinand, I see that all this seems to you a merely trifling matter! An innocent jest, an idle conceit, one remark among many. . . . That is what you would seem to imply, is it not? Merely that . . . Oh, unwise Ferdinand! On the contrary, let me take good care to put you on your guard against such slips, which so falsely appear insignificant. I assure you, you are wrong — absolutely and entirely wrong! A thousand times mistaken, if the truth be known. . . . In the course of my career, you will surely give me credit for having heard, one way and another, pretty nearly everything there is to hear as to every conceivable kind of raving! I've known them all. . . . You will admit that much, will you not, Ferdinand? And you will furthermore have noticed, I imagine, Ferdinand, that I do not give the impression of being one who is subject to tribulation of mind or emotional exaggerations? That's so, isn't it? My judgments aren't biased in the least by a word or several words or even by the force of several sentences or of an entire speech. Fairly simple, both by birth and by nature, you must surely concede that I am one of those largely inhibited people whom words do not frighten. Well now, Ferdinand, where Parapine is concerned, I have, after conscientiously summing him up, felt obliged to be on my guard — to formulate very definite mental reservations. . . . His particular form of peculiarity is totally unlike any of the more usual and harmless ones. . . . It seems to me to belong to one of the rare and dangerous types of originality, to a species of extremely contagious manias: to put it briefly, the social and overweening type. . . . Perhaps it's not yet actual madness exactly that we've to deal with in your friend's case . . . Maybe not. It's probably as yet only overconviction. . . . But I know what I'm talking about in this matter of contagious dementiæ. . . . There is nothing more perilous than overconviction. . . . I myself, as I stand here talking to you, Ferdinand, have known a goodly number of these men with fixed ideas — due to very various causes. Those who prattle about justice have always struck me as definitely the most deranged. . . . At first these seekers after justice used rather to interest me, I admit. . . . But now these maniacs annoy and irritate me beyond words. . . . Don't you agree? One discovers in men a certain remarkable facility for transmitting this kind of thing, which I find appalling — and all men have it. D'you hear, Ferdinand? Take note of this, Ferdinand: they *all* have it. Just as for liquor or for lechery. . . . The same predisposition. . . . The same fatal urge . . . infinitely widespread . . . Do you laugh, Ferdinand? Then you too alarm me, Ferdinand. Weak . . . vulnerable . . . inconsistent . . . dangerous Ferdinand! And here was I imagining you to be a sound and serious-minded person! Remember that I, who am old, Ferdinand, could afford to snap my fingers at whatever the future may hold in store! *I* may do that. But you — !"

In principle, I always and in all cases thought the same as my Chief. Practically speaking, I had not advanced far in the course of a very chequered career but nevertheless I had learnt the etiquette of a proper deportment in the service of other people. I had at once got on with Baryton; thanks to this knowledge, we became quite good companions in the end; I wasn't difficult, I didn't eat much at meals. I was really quite a decent sort of assistant, in fact: cheap to employ, not in the least ambitious, not likely to be troublesome at all.

VIGNY-SUR-SEINE STANDS BETWEEN TWO LOCKS, BETWEEN TWO BARE rises. It's a village that is being transformed into a suburb. Paris is about to swallow it up.

It loses a garden a month. You enter it and find posters bedizening it like a Russian ballet. The bailiff's daughter knows how to shake cocktails. The tramcar, which seems likely to become a part of history, is the only thing which won't disappear without a revolution. People don't like it at all, children haven't the same accent as their parents any more. One feels almost embarrassed to be still part of Seine-et-Oise. The miracle's taking place already. The last nook of garden has disappeared with Laval's rise to power and charwomen charge twenty centimes more an hour since the summer recess. A bookmaker's arrival is advertised. The postmistress buys pederastic novels and imagines much more realistic ones in her own mind. For two pins the *curé* says "Hell" and, if you're awfully good, gives you tips on the exchange. The Seine has killed all its fish and is being Americanized 'twixt a double row of cutter-sweeper-tractor machines which give it frightful false teeth of rubbish and old tin cans. Three real-estate men have been clapped into gaol. We're getting on. This local transformation of the land did not escape Baryton's notice. He regretted very much not having had the gumption, twenty years ago, to buy more land on the other side of the valley at a time when they begged you to take it for twopence the yard, like rather stale tart. Those were the good days. Happily his psychotherapeutic asylum still held its own very nicely. Not, however, without certain difficulty. Patients' insatiable families never ceased demanding, nay, insisted on having, the most up-to-date cures, more electrical, more full of mystery, more everything else. . . . The latest mechanical contrivances, above all, appliances even more showy was what they wanted, and at once. And so as not to be outdone by competition, he was obliged to buckle down to it. He mustn't be beaten by similar institutions hidden away in the neighbouring woods of Asnières, Passy, and Montretout, lying in wait for any luxury "loon."

Baryton, aided by Parapine, hastened to fall into line with modern tastes, as inexpensively as possible, of course, buying at a discount, or secondhand, or at sale prices, but without failing to appear, thanks to the acquisition of new electric, pneumatic and hydraulic gadgets, better equipped than ever to pander to the fancies of his captious, monied little inmates. He groaned at having all this useless apparatus forced upon him, at being obliged to conciliate the good graces of the deranged themselves. . . .

"I opened my asylum, Ferdinand," he confided in me one day, pouring out his regrets, "just before the Exhibition, the big Exhibition. . . . There was only a handful of us alienists about in those days, and we were far less depraved and strange than we are to-day, believe me! Not one among us at that time ever tried to be as mad as his patient. . . . It was not yet the fashion to rave, oneself, on the pretext of bigger and better cures, an indecent fashion, I would beg you to note, as is almost everything which comes to us from abroad. . . . When I first went into practice, Ferdinand, the French medical profession still had some self-respect left. . . . Doctors didn't consider it incumbent on themselves to go off their heads at the same time as the sick people committed to their charge. The idea being to achieve perfect harmony with them, I suppose? I give it up. . . . To please, to humour them? Where will all this lead us? I ask you. . . . By being more astute, more morbid and more perverse than the most crack-brained of our asylum inmates, by wallowing with a sort of muddy pride in all the various insanities they parade before us, where will that lead us? Are you in a position to reassure me, Ferdinand, as to the fate of our human reason? Or even of mere common sense? At this rate, how much common sense shall we have left? None. . . . It's clear to be seen. . . . None at all! I can promise you that. It is perfectly obvious. . . .

"Ferdinand, is it not true that in the face of a truly modern intelligence, everything in the end assumes equal importance? Nothing's white . . . nor black either. . . . It's all unravelled. That's the new system! It's the fashion! Then why not, for a start, go mad ourselves? Right now? And boast of it to boot? Make one great parrot house of it, and ourselves advertise our madness! Who can stop us? Answer me that, Ferdinand. . . . One or two supreme, superfluous human scruples? A few sickly misgivings? You know, Ferdinand, sometimes when I listen to certain of our confrères — and I'm referring to the most highly esteemed and most sought after, both by patients and the academies — I ask myself where they are leading us. Honestly, it's diabolical! These lunatics stagger, appall, and infuriate me, and above all, they revolt me! To hear them report at one of their modern conferences the result of their personal researches makes me blanch with terror; my mind boggles as I listen to them. Possessed, malignant, captious and cunning, these favourite exponents of modern psychiatry, by dint of superconscious analyses, are thrusting us down into the abyss! Down to the nethermost depths, I tell you! Some day, Ferdinand, if you of the younger generation do not react against all this, the fatal slip will have occurred — understand me, the fatal slip! For we are overreaching ourselves, sublimating ourselves, bludgeoning our brains, and we shall have crossed the border line of intelligence, to the other side, the fearful side from which there is no return. . . . Why, one would think that these supercrooks were already confined in the regions of the damned, so fiercely do they fiddle with their powers of judgment day and night!

"Day and night I say truly, Ferdinand, for you know that even at night they don't stop fornicating throughout their dreams, the dirty scum! Delving into, dilating, inflaming their brains! And that about sums it up. It is a disgusting medley of worn-out organisms, a hotchpotch of bubbling, delirious symptoms which ooze and leak from them at every pore. . . . We have our hands full of the remnants of our human understanding, sticky with them, grotesque, contemptible, putrid. . . . Everything will crumble, Ferdinand; everything is crumbling. I predict it, I, Baryton, an old man, and it won't be long now, either! You will live to see this tremendous rout, for you are still young. You will live to see it! Ah, and I promise you you will have some fun. . . . You will all join in aberration, in one vast burst of madness! One too many! Go ahead — be mad! You will be released, as you put it. You have been tempted, longing for it to happen, for too long! Audacity — it certainly will be that, I can tell you! But once you are there amongst the madmen, you won't return, mark my words!

"Remember this well, Ferdinand, that the beginning of the end is the loss of a sense of proportion. I am in a position to tell you, Ferdinand, how the grand confusion started. It began with a wild lack of moderation! Foreign frenzies! An outworn sense of fitness, an end to strength! It was written. . . . Chaos for all then? Why not? For every one? It is agreed. We are not going in that direction, we are rushing there. . . . It's a real rout. I've seen the soul, Ferdinand, give way bit by bit, lose its balance and dissolve in the vast welter of apocalyptic ambitions. It began in 1900. That's the date! From that time onwards the world in general and psychiatry in particular frantically raced to see who could be most perverse, salacious, original, more disgusting, more creative, as they say, then his little next-door neighbour. A first-class scramble! Each strove to see who could immolate himself the soonest to the monster of no heart and no restraint. . . . The monster will scrunch us all, Ferdinand, that's how it is, and rightly so. . . . What is this monster? A great brute tumbling along wherever it listeth! Its wars and its droolings flood in towards us already from all sides. We shall be swept away on this tide — yes, swept away. The conscious mind was a bore, apparently. . . . We sha'n't be bored any longer! We've begun to give Sodom a chance and from that moment we've started having 'impressions' and 'intuitions'. . . . Just like women!

"Is it really necessary, at the point we have now arrived at, to encumber ourselves with dangerous words of logic? Certainly not! Logic would only be a kind of restraint in the presence of infinitely subtle psychological savants such as our own day produces, genuine progressives. . . . Don't imagine me to be saying, Ferdinand, that I despise women. By no means! You know that.

But I dislike their intuitions. I am a testicled animal myself, Ferdinand, and when I've got hold of a fact, it is hard to shake me off it. . . . Only the other day a very curious thing happened to me, speaking of all this. . . . I was asked to admit a writer into my asylum. . . . The fellow was nuts, all right. Do you know what he had been shouting for the last month? "We micturate! We micturate!" That's what he went yelping through the house. He'd got it badly, there was no question of that. He'd crossed the border line of intelligence, but the point was, actually, that he had the very greatest difficulty in making water. . . . An old stricture of the kidney was poisoning him, blocking up his bladder. . . . I passed probe after probe into him, rid him of it drop by drop. . . . The family would have it that it was due to his being a genius. It was no use my trying to explain to them that really what was wrong was his bladder; they wouldn't hear of it. . . . In their view, he had succumbed to a flash of excessive brilliance and that was that. . . . In the end, I was forced to fall in with their opinion. You know, don't you, what families are; it's impossible to make a family see that a man, whether he's a relation of theirs or not, is nothing but arrested putrescence. No family would pay for the upkeep of arrested putrescence."

For over twenty years, Baryton had never succeeded in satisfying the ticklish vanity of his lunatics' families. They made life hell for him. Patient and well balanced as I knew him to be, he nevertheless retained in his heart an old residue of rancid hate against the families of his patients. . . . At the time when I was living in contact with him, he had become exasperated and in secret was obstinately seeking to free himself once and for all from this family tyranny, by one means or another. . . . Every one has his own reasons for wishing to escape his personal misery and every one of us, in order to manage it, coaxes some ingenious method out of circumstances. Blessed are they for whom mere whoring does the trick!

Parapine, for his part, seemed content to have chosen the way of silence. As to Baryton, he, though I only realized it later, often asked himself in his heart if he would ever contrive to escape from these families, and their hold over him, and the thousand beastly commonplaces of alimental psychiatry—from his whole situation, in fact. He had so great a longing for absolutely new and different things that at bottom he was ripe for evasion and flight; whence, no doubt, these critical tirades. . . . His ego was being choked by routine. There was nothing left for him to sublimate; he just wanted to go away, to take his body somewhere else. There was no harmony in him, so that to be through with it all he had to upturn everything like a bear.

He, who considered himself so reasonable, cut himself loose by means of an altogether most regrettable scandal. I shall endeavour later on, at my leisure, to explain how all this came about.

As far as I myself was concerned, for the moment there seemed to me to be nothing wrong with my job as his assistant. The routine work of treatment was not at all strenuous, although indeed from time to time a certain uneasiness seized me, when, for instance, I had conversed at too great a length with the inmates; a sort of vertigo used then to take hold of me, as if these people had led me far from my usual haunts, without seeming to do so, from one ordinary little remark to the next, by innocent phrases, right into the very middle of their own delirium. For a second I would wonder how to get out, or whether by any chance I had not been shut up once and for all with their madness, not realizing it.

I hovered on the dangerous outskirts of the mad, on their border line, so to speak, always being pleasant-spoken with them —which it was my nature to be. I wasn't tottering but all the time I felt I was in danger, as if they were artfully luring me into the purlieus of their unknown city. A city whose streets became softer and softer as you advanced between their slimy houses, the windows melting away, that would not shut, midst dubious rumours. The doors, the ground slipping, and still you were seized by the desire to go a little further, so as to know if you would have the strength even so to recover your reason. . . . Among the ruins, reason soon turns to vice, like good humour and sleepiness with neurasthenics. You can think of nothing besides your reason. Nothing counts after that. Laughter's over.

Thus everything was progressing from doubt to doubt when we came to May 4th. A notable occasion, that Fourth of May. It happened on that day that I was feeling so extremely well that it felt rather as if it was a miracle. Pulse 78. As though after a good lunch. Then suddenly everything began to spin round. I gripped on tight. It all turned sour. People took on the queerest look. They seemed to me as sharp as lemons and even more malevolent than before. No doubt from having climbed too high, too giddily, to a high crest of health, I had come crashing down before the mirror, to gaze with passionate interest at myself growing old.

You no longer count your cares when these vile days come crowding in between your nose and eyes — there's room enough there alone for all the summed-up years of many men. Far too much for one man.

By and large I suddenly found I would have preferred to go back that very instant to the Tarapout. Especially as Parapine had also given up talking to me too. But the Tarapout was out, as far as I was concerned. It's hard lines to have no one but your boss to turn to for every material and spiritual comfort, especially when he's an alienist, and one's not too sure now about one's own head. One's got to stick it and not say a word. There were still women for us to talk about, a benign topic, and one on which I could still hope to make him laugh from time to time. On this subject he used indeed to accord me a certain credit for experience, a minor disgusting competence.

It wasn't at all a bad thing that Baryton should look with some disdain upon me as a whole. An employer is always somewhat reassured by the ignominiousness of his staff. At all costs the slave should be slightly, even much, to be despised. A mass of little chronic blemishes, moral and physical, are a justification of the fate which is overwhelming him. The world gets along better that way, because then each man stands in it in the place he deserves.

A being who is useful to you should be low, flat, prone to weakness; that is what's comforting; especially as Baryton paid us really very badly. In cases of acute avarice like this, employers are always a bit suspicious and uneasy. A failure, a debauchee, a black sheep, a devoted black sheep, all that made sense, justified things, fitted in, in fact. Baryton would have been on the whole rather pleased if I had been slightly wanted by the police. That always makes for real devotion.

I had, of course, long ago given up every kind of self-esteem. Such feelings had always seemed to me much above my position in life, a thousand times too extravagant for my resources. I was perfectly comfortable, having made that sacrifice for good and all.

At present all I needed was to keep myself tolerably well balanced as far as food and physical condition went. The rest no longer mattered to me in the very least. But all the same, I found it very hard to live through certain nights, especially when the memory of what had happened at Toulouse came to keep me wakeful for hours on end.

At such times I imagined, I couldn't help myself, all sorts of dramatic consequences to Mother Henrouille's header into her cellarful of mummies, and fear crept up within me from my entrails, fear seized my heart and held it, thumping, till it made me bound right out of the sheets to pace across my room, first one way, then the other, into its deepest shadows and into the morning light. During these attacks I came to despair of achieving for myself sufficient peace of mind ever to sleep again. Never believe straight off in a man's unhappiness. Ask him if he can still sleep. If the answer's "yes", all's well. That is enough.

But I should never again be able to sleep to the full. I had, as it were, lost the habit of confidence, the confidence it's essential you should have — and truly vast it needs to be — to sleep soundly among men. I should have required at least an illness, a temperature, a definite desperate climax to get back some of this indifference, and neutralize my personal anxiety, and so retrieve foolish, divine tranquillity. The only bearable days I can remember in the course of many years were the few days of a sultry feverish attack of influenza.

Baryton never questioned me about my health nor did he

bother about his own. "Science and life make the most disastrous mixture, Ferdinand. Always avoid taking care of your health, believe me. . . . Every question you put to your body becomes a wedge-end of anxiety, of obsession. . . ." These were his simplified and pet biological principles. "Cunning old bird!" he wanted me to think. "The obvious is enough for me," he'd often say too, hoping to make me blink with surprise.

He never spoke to me about money, but that was only so as to think of it the more himself, more intimately.

All this mix-up of Robinson's with the Henrouille family remained, still only partly understood, on my conscience, and I often tried to tell bits and episodes of it to Baryton. But it didn't interest him in the least. He much preferred my African experiences, especially those which referred to members of our own profession whom I had met in all sorts of odd places and the weird or dubious medical methods of these most unusual colleagues of ours.

From time to time we at the asylum would pass through a period of alarm on account of his little daughter Aimée. Of a sudden, at dinner time, she would be found to be missing from her room and not in the garden. Personally, I always expected to come across her dismembered body behind some bush one fine evening. With our lunatics wandering about all over the shop, the worst might happen to her. As it was, she had already had several very narrow escapes from rape. When this occurred, a hell of a lot of squeals and douches and explanations ensued. It was no good telling her not to go up certain too sheltered paths; the child was invincibly attracted back each time to these dark corners. Her father never failed on each of these occasions to thrash her more than vigorously. It did no good. I believe the whole thing rather appealed to her.

We on the staff had to be somewhat on our guard when we encountered or passed lunatics in the corridors. Madmen have a greater facility for murder than ordinary mortals. So it had become a sort of habit with us to turn our backs to the wall when we met them, prepared always to welcome them with a good hefty kick in the pit of the stomach if they made the slightest move.

They watched you closely and passed on. Aside from madness, we understood each other beautifully.

Baryton deplored the fact that none of us knew how to play chess. I had to start learning the game just to please him.

During the day Baryton was remarkable for an irritating and detailed activity which made life all round him exceedingly trying. A new little idea of some flatly practical kind would blossom in his mind each morning. In order to replace the rolls of lavatory paper by packets of loose sheets, we were obliged to ponder for a whole week, which we wasted in contradictory determinations. Finally it was decided that we should wait for the sales and then go the round of the shops. Following that, another tedious problem presented itself; viz., flannel chest protectors. . . . Should they be worn over one's shirt or under it? And what was the best way of administering sulphate of soda? . . . Parapine withdrew himself in stubborn silence from these sub-intellectual wrangles.

Egged on by boredom, I had finished up by telling Baryton many more adventures than had ever really taken place in the course of my travels; I ran dry. After which it was his turn to monopolize the entire conversation with his suggestions and petty reticences. There was no way out. He had won by wearing me down. And I had no such complete indifference with which to defend myself as Parapine had. On the contrary, I had to answer him, despite myself. I couldn't now prevent myself. I could no longer avoid arguing futilely with him on the comparative merits of cocoa and *café crème*. . . . He was casting a spell of stupidity over me.

We burbled at each other about everything and nothing under the sun, about elastic stockings for varicose veins, optimum faradic currents, cures for cellulitis of the elbow. . . . I had come to the point of blathering, exactly in accordance with his hints and likings, about everything and nothing, like a master at the game. He would accompany me and run on ahead of me in this infinitely wasteful promenade. He saturated me with conversation to last me forever and a day. Parapine laughed like hell in his beard, hearing us wander off on quibbles as tortuous as the macaroni, and spattered the boss's claret all over the tablecloth.

Still, God rest the soul of this old bastard Baryton. In the end, I made him disappear, even so. But it needed tremendous cleverness to do it.

Among the patients entrusted to my special care, the more slobbery females led me the hell of a dance. . . . Always having to attend to them with douches and catheters. . . . Their little pranks and smacks in the eye; their gaping imperfections to be kept clean all the time. . . . One young bedlamite frequently earned me the Chief's reproval. She wrecked the garden by pulling up all the flowers; that was her mania, and I didn't like the Chief having anything to say. . . .

"The Bride" they called her, an Argentine; physically speaking not at all bad, but her mind was just one single idea — that of marrying her father. One by one she picked all the flowers in the garden and stuck them into the great white veil which she wore everywhere, night and day. The case was one of which her fanatically religious family was horribly ashamed. They hid their daughter away from the world, and her idea with her. Baryton's theory was that she had succumbed to the consequences of too rigid and severe an upbringing, to an obdurate morality which had, so to speak, exploded inside her brain.

At dusk, all our creatures were brought in, after long calls, and we went the round of the various rooms, above all to prevent the more excitable ones from abusing themselves too frequently before going to sleep. Saturday evenings it was particularly important to hold them in check and pay special attention to this sort of thing, because on Sunday, when their relations visit them, it's bad for the reputation of the place for them to find the patients pale and fagged out.

All this reminded me of that time with Bébert and the syrup I had prescribed for him. At Vigny I gave quantities of this marvellous syrup. I had kept the prescription. I ended up by believing in it myself.

The doorkeeper of the asylum used to run a sweet little business with her husband, — a real hefty guy whom we had to call on now and again when some job needed tough handling.

Thus things went on, and months slid by, fairly well on the whole, and we would not have had much to complain of if Baryton had not suddenly hit on another of his grand new ideas. No doubt he had for some time been wondering if he could not maybe get rather more out of me for the same money. Finally he hit on just the thing.

One day after lunch he trotted out his scheme. First of all, he had had us served a bowl brimful of my favourite sweet — strawberries and cream. That struck me at once as damned suspicious. Sure enough, I had hardly despatched the last of his strawberries before he turned sharply in my direction.

"Ferdinand," he said, just like that, "I have been wondering if you would be willing to give my little Aimée a few English lessons. . . . What do you say to that? I know you have an excellent accent — and in English a good accent's half the battle, isn't it? Also, Ferdinand, without wishing to flatter you, may I say that you have always been kindness itself?"

Taken aback, "Certainly, Monsieur Baryton," I said.

And it was agreed, without further ado, that I should give Aimée her first lesson in English the very next morning. And others followed, in due course, for weeks and weeks. . . .

We entered with these English lessons on a period of the gravest unrest and misgiving, during which time events followed each other in a rhythm which wasn't at all that of normal life.

Baryton insisted on being present at his daughter's lessons. In spite of all my care and trouble, poor little Aimée couldn't make head or tail of this English. Really not the first thing, to tell the truth. She did not care one little bit what all these strange new words could conceivably mean. She just wondered why we should all of us want to keep on so, in this malicious way, trying to make her remember what they meant. . . . She didn't cry, but she came very near to crying. Aimée would have preferred to be left quietly alone to muddle along with the small amount of French she knew already, whose difficulties and facilities amply sufficed to keep her busy all her life.

But her father did not look upon it at all in this light. "You've got to grow up into an up-to-date young woman, Aimée dear," he would urge, trying all the time to make her feel better about it. "I, your father, have lost a great deal through not knowing enough English to be able to get along properly with foreign patients. . . . There, there. . . . Don't cry, precious! Just listen to Monsieur Bardamu who's so patient with you, so kind. . . . And when you've learnt to pronounce the 'thes' with your tongue, as he shows you, I'll give you a lovely shiny bi-cy-cle. . . ."

But Aimée had no wish to achieve these "thes" and "enoughs." It was her father who said them for her instead, the "thes" and "boughs," and quite a lot more things, in spite of his Bordeaux accent, and his mania for logic, which is such a damned nuisance in English. One month, then another, of this sort of thing went by. As her father grew more and more passionately keen to master English, Aimée had less and less often to do battle with these vowels. Baryton took up all my time. He monopolized me, never let go of me, he pumped my English out of me. As our rooms were next to each other, I used to be able to hear him first thing in the morning while he dressed, turning his everyday life into English. "The coffee is black . . . My shirt is white . . . The garden is green . . . How are you to-day, Bardamu?" he yelled through the partition. He quite soon acquired a liking for the most elliptical forms of the language.

This perversion of his was bound to drag us quite a way. As soon as he came into contact with great literature, it was impossible for us to pull up. . . . After eight months of abnormal progress of this sort, he was practically prepared to readjust himself entirely, on Anglo-Saxon lines. And so it was that he contrived to make me utterly disgusted with him, twice over.

By degrees we had reached the point where little Aimée was left entirely outside our conversations and more and more to her own devices. She retired once again, peaceably, into her private clouds, with no intention of asking for anything that was left over. She simply was not having to learn English any longer, and that was that. Baryton could have the whole lot.

Winter came round again. It was Christmas time. Travel

agencies were advertising cheap return tickets to England. I noticed their posters on the boulevards, going to the cinema with Parapine. . . . I even went in to find out about the prices.

Then at table later, talking about other things, I let fall a couple of words on the subject to Baryton. At first, my information did not seem to interest him at all. He let the remark pass. I even thought he had forgotten all about it, when one night he himself referred to it again and asked me to bring him along a prospectus some time.

Between our sessions of English literature, we'd often play Japanese billiards and *"bouchon"* in one of the isolation wards, this one being well provided with solid iron bars, just above the porter's lodge.

Baryton excelled at games of skill. Parapine regularly played him for drinks and as regularly lost. We spent whole evenings in this little improvised billiard room, especially in winter when it rained, so as not to muck up the chief's best reception rooms. Sometimes we would have a troublesome maniac under observation in there with us, but that wasn't at all usual.

While Parapine and the boss rivalled each other in skill on the carpet or floor, I would amuse myself, if one can call it that, by trying to experience the same sensations as a prisoner in his cell. That was something I had missed. If you try hard enough, you can achieve quite a liking for the queer people who pass by in these suburban streets. At the end of the day, you can almost feel pity for the little bustling movement that the tram creates as it brings home from Paris subdued, submissive bunches of men who have been at work throughout the day. Round that first bend beyond the grocer's their defeat comes to an end. They pour quite silently back into the night. One has hardly had time to count how many of them there were. But Baryton very rarely let me muse at my leisure. He'd break off in the middle of a game of billiards to pester me with some absurd question.

"How do you say 'impossible' in English, Ferdinand?"

In short, he never tired of making great strides in his English. With the utmost stupidity of which he was capable, he strove for perfection. He would not hear of half measures or of anything being "more or less" right. Luckily a crisis was to deliver me from him. Not a moment too soon.

By degrees, as we forged ahead in our reading of English history, I noticed him losing some of his assurance and finally the better part of his optimism. When we got to the Elizabethan poets, profound, undefinable changes seemed to come over his mind and spirit. I was reluctant at first to let myself be convinced of this, but finally I was forced, with the rest of us, to accept Baryton for what he'd become, truly a lamentable specimen. His attention, formerly so keen and so precise, now floated away towards vague and interminable digressions. And little by little it was he who took to sitting there for hours on end in his own home, before our very eyes, lost in reverie, already far removed. . . . And although I had been profoundly and thoroughly disgruntled with Baryton for some time past, I nevertheless felt a certain remorse as I watched him go to pieces like this. . . . I considered myself somehow responsible for this débâcle. The chaos of his mind was not entirely inexplicable to me. So much so that one day I suggested that we should call a halt for a time in our studies of literature, with the excuse that a break would do us both good and leisure would give us an opportunity to look out new material. . . . He wasn't in the least taken in by my feeble ruse and refused on the spot, quite kindly but firmly. He intended to proceed without slackening on our joint spiritual discovery of England. . . . Just the same as he'd begun. . . . I had no answer to that. . . . I capitulated. He was actually afraid he might not have enough hours left to live to accomplish this task completely. . . . And though I feared the worst, there was nothing for it but to pursue with him, willy-nilly, this desolate and purely academic quest.

Truly Baryton was no longer himself. Things and persons round about us, slowed down and fanciful, were already losing their importance, and even the colours we'd known them have before assumed an entirely equivocal and dreamlike sweetness. . . .

Baryton now showed only a gradually languishing interest in the details of running his establishment, although after all it was his own creation, the work of his own hands, in which he had been intensely engrossed literally for more than thirty years. He left the entire management of the place to Parapine. The gathering disorder of his brain, which in public he bashfully strove to hide, soon became utterly obvious to us, irrefutable, a physical thing.

Gustave Mandamour, the policeman we knew at Vigny, whom we employed at times when there was some big job on hand, and certainly the most unobservant being it has ever been my lot to meet among others of his sort, asked me one day, about that time, if maybe the boss hadn't heard some very bad news. . . . I reassured him as best I could, but hardly with conviction.

Baryton was no longer interested in tittle-tattle. His one wish was not to be disturbed on any pretext whatsoever. At the beginning of our studies we had, for his liking too rapidly, run through Macaulay's "History of England," an exhaustive treatise in six volumes. At his command we perused the whole of this great work again — and that under altogether alarming mental conditions — chapter by chapter.

Baryton seemed to me more and more perilously affected by meditation. When we came to that utterly implacable passage in which Monmouth the Pretender has just landed on the uncertain shores of Kent . . . Just at the moment when his adventure begins to revolve in nothingness . . . When Monmouth the Pretender no longer quite knows what it is he pretends . . . What he wants to do. What he's come here to do. When he begins to feel that he'd be glad to go away but no longer knows whither or how to escape . . . When defeat rises up in front of him . . . In the pallor of morning . . . As his last ships are borne away seawards . . . When Monmouth, for the first time, starts to think . . . Then Baryton himself felt sick at heart, powerless to forge his own decisions. . . . He read and reread the paragraph, muttering it over to himself . . . Exhausted, he shut the book and flung himself down beside me.

From memory, with eyes half shut, he repeated the passage many times; and in that English accent which was the best of the many Bordeaux twangs I had given him to choose from, again and again he recited it to us.

Confronted by this adventure of Monmouth's, in which all the pitiable absurdity of our puerile and tragic natures is exposed, so to speak, in the face of eternity, Baryton himself went dizzy and as he was holding to our common fate merely by a thread, he let go completely. . . . From that moment I can truthfully say he was no longer one of us . . . he had come to the end of his tether.

Towards the close of that same evening, he asked me to go to him in his private office. I certainly expected, at the stage we'd now reached, that he would inform me of some big resolution he had taken, such as, for instance, to sack me on the spot. . . . No, that wasn't it at all. . . . On the contrary, the decision he had arrived at was entirely favourable to me. But it so rarely fell to my lot to be surprised by some piece of good fortune that I could not help a tear or two welling up into my eyes. Baryton graciously took this sign of emotion to mean regret on my part and felt called upon to console me.

"You will surely not go so far as to doubt my word, Ferdinand, when I assure you I have needed something more and much greater than courage to resolve to leave this house? You know my sedentary habits. I am getting on now, and my whole career has been one long, careful and detailed proof of a steadfast hardness of heart, either immediate or delayed. How can it be possible for me to have come, in the course of a few short months, to abjure all this? Yet here I am, mentally and physically in this condition of self-detachment and benevolence. Ferdinand: Hurrah! —as you would say in English. Truly my past means nothing to me now. I am going to be born again, Ferdinand! Yes, born again! I am going away. Ah, your tears, kind friend, could never lessen the definite disgust I feel for everything that has kept me here throughout so many empty years. It's been too much. . . . I'm through, Ferdinand! I tell you I am leaving. Cutting loose! Escaping! I am tearing myself up by the roots. I know it. I bleed! I can see all that. Yet not for anything in the world, Ferdinand, could you make me alter my decision; no, for nothing in this world . . . D' you understand? Even if I had dropped an eye out in this mud, I would not turn back to look for it. Can I say more than that? And now do you doubt the sincerity of my determination?"

I didn't doubt it at all. Baryton was evidently capable of anything. What's more, I believe it would have been fatal to his reason if I had crossed him in the state he had worked himself up into. I let him have a bit of a rest and then, all the same, I did try to sway him a wee bit; I risked making a last supreme effort to bring him back to us. By means of slightly sideways arguments; I was pleasantly oblique. . . .

"I beg you, Ferdinand, to abandon all thought of making me alter my decision. It's irrevocable, I assure you, and I should be very grateful if you would not speak of it again. Would you, for the last time, like to do me that favour? At my age, after all, sudden impulses are extremely rare. That is true. But when they come, they're irresistible."

Those were his words, almost the last he spoke. I merely record them.

"Perhaps, dear Monsieur Baryton," I dared in any case to interrupt him, "perhaps this impromptu holiday which you think of taking may prove in point of fact merely a romantic break, a welcome diversion, a bright interlude in the austere course of your career? Perhaps after you have tried another mode of life . . . more pleasureful, less dully methodical, than the life you lead here . . . Maybe then you will come back to us, happy to have been away, unattracted by the thought of further novelties. . . . You would thereupon automatically and easily resume your place at the head of affairs here . . . Proud of your recent experiences . . . Renewed, refreshed, in fact, and no doubt thenceforth completely reconciled to the day-by-day monotony of our working round . . . Grown old, in a word—if you will allow me, Monsieur Baryton, so to express myself?"

"Ah, age, what a flatterer he is, this Ferdinand! He knows how to touch the weak spot of my uncovered masculine pride, sensitive and imperious still, in spite of so much weariness and so many trials in the past. . . . No, Ferdinand, all the ingenuity you may employ cannot soften the profound hostility and disillusion in my heart. . . . No, no, Ferdinand, the time to hesitate and retrace my steps is over now! I am, I admit, Ferdinand, empty! Crushed! Overcome! That is what forty years of shrewd trivialities have done for me. It is infinitely more than I can bear. . . . What do I aim to do? Do you wish to know! I can tell you, and only you, my greatest friend, you who have been willing in your admirable disinterestedness to share an old man's sufferings and defeat. . . . I want, Ferdinand, to try to go and do away with my soul, as one goes and does away with a mangy old dog — a pet who stinks and sickens you — so as to be alone. Quite alone at last . . . Before the end comes . . . Calm . . . And one's own self."

"But, my dear Monsieur Baryton, I had never received from your speech or manner any indication of the violent despair whose intractable stress you now disclose. . . . I am dumbfounded. Quite to the contrary, your ordinary conversation has appeared to me to this very day eminently sane and to the point. Your abundant lively initiative . . . The methodical and judicious exercise of your medical skill . . . In vain might I have sought for the least sign in your daily life of any breakdown or collapse . . . In truth, I notice no such thing."

But for the first time since I had known him, Baryton took no pleasure in my complimentary remarks. In fact, he gently asked me to desist from continuing the conversation in this laudatory vein. "No, my dear Ferdinand, I assure you . . . This evidence of your friendship for me to some extent tends to sweeten in an unexpected way my last moments here, but not all your solicitude can render even tolerable for me the memory with which this place is impregnated, of a past which entirely overwhelms me. . . . I wish, at all costs, you understand, and in whatever circumstances, to leave all this in my wake."

"But what about the house itself, Monsieur Baryton; what are we to do about that? Have you considered that?"

"Of course I have, Ferdinand. . . . You will take over the management during all the time I am away; that's quite simple. Have you not always been on the best of terms with our clients? They will therefore be only too pleased to accept you as Director.

It will all be perfectly all right, you'll see, Ferdinand. As to Parapine, since he cannot endure conversation, he shall take charge of the mechanical side, the apparati and laboratory. . . . That's his strong suit. So everything's settled for the best. . . . Besides, I no longer believe in people being indispensable. There, even in that, you see, my friend, I have changed."

Indeed, there was no doubt. He was unrecognisable.

"But, Monsieur Baryton, aren't you afraid that your departure may be most spitefully misconstrued by your professional friends in the neighbourhood? In Passy, for instance? And Montretout? And Gargan Livry? By all around? Spying on us . . . By our indefatigably malicious confrères . . . What construction will they put on your voluntary disappearance? What motives will they impute to it? Flight? What otherwise? A prank? Fiasco? Bankruptcy? Who knows?"

This eventuality had no doubt given him long and painful pause. He was worried at this point, and turned pale before my eyes as he thought of it. . . .

His daughter Aimée, our feeble-witted Aimée, was going to have a pretty rough time of it as a result of all this. He was entrusting her to the care of an aunt of hers who lived in the country, a stranger really. Thus, with his private affairs arranged, it only remained for Parapine and me to look after his interests and run the place for him to the best of our ability. Heigh-ho, for a ship without a captain!

I felt justified, since he had given me his confidence, in asking him in what direction he felt this new adventure would take him. . . .

Without the flicker of an eyelid, "England, Ferdinand!" he replied.

All this had overtaken us in so short a space of time, to me it seemed difficult to assimilate, but just the same we had to get used to this new fate with alacrity.

Next day, Parapine and I helped to fix him up some luggage. The passport, with all its little pages and visas, amazed him rather. He had never had a passport before. While he was about it, he would have liked to have had several, so as to be able to change occasionally. We were able to convince him it wasn't possible.

Once again, he wavered over the question of the hard or soft collars he ought to take and how many of each sort. This problem, barely solved, brought us very nearly up to the time of the train. The three of us jumped on to the last tram for Paris. Baryton was taking only a small suit case with him, as he meant, wherever he went and in all circumstances, to travel light and be perfectly mobile.

At the station, the imposing height of the international trains impressed him mightily. He hesitated to mount such majestic steps. He stood back from the coaches as if gazing up from the foot of a monument. We helped him a little. Having taken a second, he smilingly addressed to us a comparison of a practical nature. "The firsts aren't *any* better," he said. We shook him by the hand. The time had come. The whistle blew for the train to start, which it did with a shudder and a clashing of steel, on the tick of the minute. Thus our adieus were brutally curtailed. "Au revoir, my friends!" he barely had time to shout, and his hand appeared, uplifted towards ours. . . .

His hand moved yonder in the smoke, waving through the noise, snatched by the night further and further into the distance across the rails, still gleaming white. . . .

ON THE ONE HAND WE DIDN'T REGRET HIS GOING, BUT ALL THE same his departure made the house seem damnably empty.

In the first place, the way in which he had gone off made us rather sad — in spite of ourselves, you might say. It wasn't natural, the way he had left. We wondered what mightn't happen to us after a move like that.

But I didn't have much time to wonder or even to feel bored either. Only a few days after we had taken him down to the station, there was a visitor to see me at the office, to see me personally. The Abbé Protiste.

I had quite a bit of news to tell him — very exciting news. Above all the incredible way in which Baryton had given us all the slip and gone rambling off north. . . . Old Protiste couldn't get over this when I told him, and when he at last understood what I was saying, he could see nothing in the new development but the advantages for me of such a situation.

"That your Director should have placed such trust in you strikes me as a most flattering preferment for you," he kept on droning at me.

I did my best to calm the man down, but he was well into his stride and nothing in the world would shake him from this set idea of his; he kept on prophesying the most magnificent future for me, "a brilliant medical career," as he put it. I couldn't get a word in edgeways. Even so with a great deal of difficulty he did eventually revert to serious topics, and in particular Toulouse, whence he himself had returned the night before.

Of course I let him in his turn tell me everything he knew. I even showed surprise and stupefaction when he informed me of the accident which had befallen the old lady.

"What? How's that?" I broke in. "She's dead? I say, but when did that happen?"

So bit by bit he had to spill it all out. Without exactly telling me that it was Robinson who had tripped the old girl up on her little staircase, he anyway didn't prevent me from suspecting as much. She hadn't had time to say "Ouch!" We understood each other well enough. Very prettily done, very neat. . . . The second time he'd had a shot at it, he hadn't bogged it at all. This time he'd put it over swell.

It was lucky that Robinson was supposed by the neighbors in Toulouse to be still entirely blind. As it was, no one had looked for more than an accident in all this, a very tragic accident, to be sure, but in any case understandable enough when you came to consider everything, the circumstances and all, the old person's age and how it had happened at the end of the day, when she was tired. . . . Personally, I had no wish to know more for the present; as it was, I had quite enough to go on with. But it was devilishly hard to get the Abbé to change the conversation. He'd gotten the whole thing on the brain. He returned to it again and again, always, no doubt, in the hope of making me slip up and say something compromising; or so it seemed. . . . But there wasn't anything doing. . . . He could go ahead and try. . . . Still, he did give up eventually and contented himself merely with telling me about Robinson and Robinson's health. . . . About his eyes. . . . Much better they were, apparently. But with him it was the moral side that had always been weak. Definitely a washout now, I gathered. And this in spite of the kindness, the affection those two women continued to shower on him. . . . In return, he never stopped grumbling about his hard lot and the life he led. . . .

It didn't surprise me, didn't at all surprise me, to hear all this from the Curé. I knew what old Robinson was like. An ungrateful disposition he had. But I distrusted the Abbé even more. . . . I was as mum as a mouse while he talked to me. He had to do all the confiding. . . .

"Despite the fact, Doctor, that, quite apart from the happy prospect of an approaching marriage, life has now been made both pleasant and easy for him, your friend, I must confess, disappoints all our hopes. . . . Is he not once more a prey to that fatal love of dubious adventures, that taste for going off the rails, which you recognised in him of old? What do you make of these tendencies of his, Doctor?"

Robinson's one idea down there in fact, if I undertsood aright, was to chuck up the whole thing. The girl and her mother were very put out about it, of course, and as upset as may be imagined. That's what the Abbé Protiste had come here to tell me. It was all not a little perturbing, to be sure, and for my part I was definitely determined to hold my tongue and not intervene any further in the little affairs of this family. . . . Our conversation was inconclusive and we parted, the Abbé and I, at a tram stop — rather coolly, if the truth be known. As I went back to the asylum, I didn't feel at all easy in my mind.

Very soon after this visit our first news of Baryton reached us from England. A few post cards. He hoped we were all well and wished us "good luck." He dropped us a further line or two from several odd places. A card with no wording on it showed us that he had gone across to Norway. And a few weeks later a telegram arrived to reassure us slightly: "Calm crossing," from Copenhagen. . . .

Just as we had foreseen, the chief's absence was most maliciously commented on in Vigny itself and in the country round. It would be better for the Institute's reputation if in the future we were to give no more than the fewest possible explanations as to the motives prompting this absence, either to our patients or to our colleagues in the neighborhood.

Months passed, extremely cautious months, silent and unrelieved. In the end, we came entirely to avoid any evocation of Baryton's memory. Actually his memory really rather made us feel a little ashamed. . . .

Then summer came again. We couldn't stay in the garden, keeping an eye on the lunatics all the time. To prove to ourselves that we did have some slight liberty anyhow, in spite of it all, we'd venture as far as the banks of the Seine, just to get out a bit.

Beyond the mound of the other bank is where the great Gennevilliers plain begins, a lovely long stretch of grey and white, with its factory chimneys standing gently out through a haze of dust and mists. Right by the towpath there's the bargees' *bistral*, guarding the entrance to the canal. The yellow stream comes pushing in against the lock.

We used to gaze down on it for hours on end, and to one side too, over a kind of broad marsh, whose smell wafted stealthily up on to the road with its motor cars. You got accustomed to it. It had no colour left, this mud, so old was it and so worn out by the risings of the canal. On summer evenings sometimes, the slime would look kind of gentle and nice, with the sky gone pink and sentimental. We'd come down there on to the bridge to listen to them playing accordions on the sailing boats, waiting before the lock gates for the night to be over so as to pass through to the river. The ones that come down from Belgium are the most musical. They've colour everywhere, green and yellow, and clothes hanging up to dry full of tapes, and strawberry-pink combinations too, which balloon out as the wind leaps into them, in gusts.

I'd often go quite alone to this café on the marsh, after lunch when time hangs heavy and still, and the publican's cat is at peace within four walls, as if enclosed in a little heaven of blue linoleum, all by himself.

There I'd too be drowsy in that early afternoon hour, out of sight and out of mind, as I thought, waiting for time to pass.

I saw some one come along up this road from way off. It didn't take me long to guess. He'd hardly got to the bridge before I knew who it was. My old friend Robinson! Impossible to make a mistake. "He's come along here looking for me!" I said to myself, right away. . . . "The curé must have given him my address. . . . I'll have to get rid of him as soon as I can."

Just then, I thought it was hell to have to be bothered with him, just when I was beginning to fix up a good, new little peace of mind for myself. You don't trust what comes to you up a long road, and you're quite right. So here he was now, nearing the café. I came out. He seemed surprised to see me. "Where've you come from now?" I asked, not very pleasantly. "Garenne," he said. "Oh," I said, "all right. Have you eaten?" He didn't much look as if he'd eaten, but he didn't care to appear all empty-bellied on arrival. "Hiking around still, are you, eh?" I went on. Because I may say I wasn't at all pleased to see him again. I didn't like it a bit.

Parapine was also coming up from the canal side, to look for me. That was a good thing. Parapine was tired of being on duty so often at the asylum. . . . . It is true too that I was taking things fairly lightly. In any case, both he and I would have given a good deal to know just when Baryton was thinking of returning. We hoped he'd stop roaming about moderately soon and come back to take over his darn madhouse and run it himself. It was more than we could cope with. We weren't ambitious, either of us, and didn't give a damn for any prospects in the future. Which was wrong of us, of course.

There's another thing to be said in Parapine's favour: he never asked any questions about the financial management of the asylum or my methods of dealing with our clientele; however, I told him just the same, against his will, you might say, and when I did, I talked alone. In the case of Robinson, it was important to tell him what was happening.

"I've often mentioned Robinson to you, haven't I?" I asked him by way of introduction. "You know. . . . The man I made friends with during the war. You remember, don't you?"

He had heard me tell all those war stories and stories of Africa a hundred times over and in a hundred quite different ways. It was a habit of mine.

"Well, here's the very man himself," I went on, "come all the way from Toulouse to see us. . . . We're all going to have supper together at the house." As a matter of fact, coming forward in this way in the name of the house, I felt a little uncomfortable. It was, in a way, an indiscreet thing to have done. The situation required a smooth, ingratiating air of authority on my part, which I was very far from possessing. And Robinson wasn't helping matters at all. On the way home, he already showed signs of curiosity and uneasiness as regards to Parapine, whose long pale face beside us greatly intrigued him. He thought at first that Parapine was a lunatic too. Since he had found out where we lived in Vigny, he was seeing madmen everywhere. I told him it was all right and not to worry.

"And what about you?" I said. "At least, you've found some sort of a job since you got back?"

"I'm going to start looking for one," was as much as he'd say in reply.

"But your eyes are all right again? You can see now, can't you?"

"Yes, I see almost as well as before."

"So you're quite content then?" I said.

No, he wasn't. Not at all content. He had something better to do than be content. I refrained from mentioning Madelon to him as yet. That was a subject which it was still too delicate for us two to touch on. We got on quite nicely over a drink before dinner and I took that opportunity to tell him a lot of things about the asylum and plenty of other details besides. I've never been able to prevent myself from prattling indiscriminately. Not so very different from Baryton really, at bottom. By the end of dinner, the atmosphere had grown cordial. After it was over, I couldn't very well send Léon Robinson away again, just like that. I decided there and then that for the present they should rig up a little camp bed for him in the dining room. Parapine continued to express no opinion. "There, Léon," said I. "That'll be somewhere for you to stay, while you're still looking for a job." "Thanks," he answered simply, and every morning after that he took the tram into Paris to look for a commercial-travelling job, so he said.

He was fed up with factory work, he said; he wanted to "travel." Of course, he may have gone to some trouble trying to get a job as a traveller, one must be fair, but anyhow the fact remains he didn't find one.

One evening he was back from Paris earlier than usual. I was still in the garden, keeping watch near the big pond. He came to look for me there, wishing to have a couple of words with me.

"Listen," he began.

"I'm listening," I said.

"Couldn't you give me something to do right here? . . . I can't land a job anywhere else."

"Have you tried hard?"

"Yes, I've tried hard."

"You want a job in the asylum? But what doing? Do you mean you can't find yourself some little job in Paris? Would you like me to talk to Parapine about it and see if we know any one who could help?"

My offering to take a hand in trying to get him a job annoyed him.

"It's not that you absolutely can't find anything," he then went on. "One might find something . . . some small job. . . . That's possible, of course. . . . But you've got to understand how it is . . . I'll tell you. . . . It's simply got to seem as if I was a bit wrong in the head. . . . It's important and it's essential that I should seem to be a bit wrong in the head."

"All right," I said at that point. "You don't need to tell me any more. . . ."

"Yes, but listen, I must tell you, Ferdinand; there's a whole heap more I've got to tell you," he insisted. "You've just got to understand what I'm driving at. . . . And, anyway, I know you —I know how long you take to understand things and make up your mind."

"Go ahead, then," I said, resigned to it. "Go ahead, tell me."

"Listen, if I don't seem to be nuts, it's going to be just too bad. . . . Things'll be in a hell of a mess, I can promise you that. She's capable of having me arrested. . . . Now d'you get me?"

"Madelon, are you talking about?"

"Why, sure it's Madelon."

"That's pretty!"

"You've said it, Ferdinand."

"Is it all off between you two then?"

"I guess so."

"Come this way, if you're going to tell me more about all this," I broke in at that point, and I led him off to one side. "It'll be safer . . . with these lunatics about . . . they understand things too, you know, and can be pretty awkward about repeating what they hear when they like, even if they are mad."

We went up to one of the isolation rooms and once we got there, he didn't take long to give me the whole affair, especially as I already knew very well what Robinson was capable of and anyway the Abbé Protiste had let me guess a good deal of it. At his second attempt, he hadn't made a mess of it. No one could say that he'd slipped up again this time. Oh, no. Not a bit of it. That had been that, all right.

"You see, the old girl kept getting my goat worse and worse. . . . Especially after my eyes began to heal. . . . When I was beginning to get around in the street on my own, I mean. From then on, I was seeing things all right again. . . . And I saw the old bird too. . . . Couldn't see anything else, damn it. . . . I had her there in front of my eyes all the time. It was as if she was stopping up existence for me. . . . I think she did it on purpose. Just to sour things for me. . . . I can't explain it otherwise. . . . And besides, in that house we all lived in — you know what it's like, don't you — it wasn't easy not to get sore with each other. . . . You know how small it was. You were all on top of one another. . . . No one could deny that."

"And the steps down to the vault weren't too good either. Were they?" I had myself noticed how dangerous that staircase was when I went over the place for the first time with Madelon, — how the steps were shaky, even then.

"No, that didn't need much doing to it," he admitted, with perfect frankness.

"And how about the folk down there?" I questioned him further. "The neighbours, the church people, the reporters. . . . Didn't they have any little remarks to make, what, when all this happened?"

"No, you know, they didn't. . . . Anyway, they didn't believe me capable of such a thing. They looked on me as a poor, washed-out creature. . . . A blind man. Get me?"

"So that as far as that goes, you can consider yourself lucky — because otherwise, eh? But Madelon? What part did she play in all this? Was she in it too?"

"Not exactly. . . . But up to a point she was, of course, all the same, because the crypt, you know, was to be ours entirely when the old girl passed out. . . . That's the agreement that had been come to. We two were going to take over between us."

"Then why couldn't you hit it off together after that?"

"Well, you know, that's rather complicated to explain."

"Madelon didn't care for you any more?"

"Why yes, quite the reverse; she cared for me a lot, and she was certainly dead keen on the marriage business. . . . Her mother was set on it too, much more than before. She wanted it to take place right away, on account of old Ma Henrouille's mummies which were our property now, and enough for all three of us to live on comfortably in the future."

"What happened to break it up between you, then?"

"Oh, you know, I wanted them to leave me alone. . . . That's all it was. The mother and the daughter both."

"Listen, Léon!" I pulled him up when I heard him say that. . . . "Listen to me. That isn't on the level, you know, even at that. Put yourself in their place, Madelon's and her mother's — would you have been pleased, if you'd been them? Would you, though? When you first went down there, you'd barely a shirt on your back, you'd no job, nothing; you kept on all day about how the old woman was pocketing your dough and one thing and another. . . . Then she's out of the way — you put her out of the way, rather. . . . And you start pulling faces again just the same, the way you do. . . . Put yourself in the place of those two women; try doing that! It's intolerable, man! I'd pretty soon have told you what you could do with yourself, and damn fast too, I would. . . . That's what you certainly deserved, that they should kick you clean and hard in the pants. . . . And you may just as well know it."

That's the way I spoke to Robinson.

"Possibly," he answered me back at once, "and you may be a doctor and an educated man and all the rest of it, but you don't understand my make-up one little bit."

"Shut up, Léon!" I had to say to him; really it was too much. "Shut up, you little misery, you and your precious make-up!

You talk like a sick man. It's a damned pity Baryton's gone haring off, Christ knows where, or *he'd* have taken you in hand all right! And that's the best thing that could happen to you, anyway. You ought to be locked up, for a start! D' you hear? Locked up! Baryton would have looked after your make-up for you!"

"If you'd had what I've had and been through what I've been through," he retorted, when he heard me say that, "I've no doubt you'd be a sick man yourself. You bet your life you would. And worse than me too, maybe. . . . A weak-kneed sissy like you!" And then he started to curse me up hill and down dale, just as if he'd a perfect right to.

I had a good long look at him while he bawled me out. . . . I was accustomed to being called names like that by the lunatics. It had longed ceased to bother me.

He'd grown thinner since Toulouse and something too, which I hadn't ever known in him before, had come over his face, like a portrait, I thought, superimposed on his features, — a sort of already forgottenness, with silence all round it.

Mixed up in all this Toulouse business there was something else, something far less serious, of course, which he hadn't been able to get over, and which, when he thought of it, nauseated him again like bile. And that was having been forced to grease the palms of a whole host of middlemen for nothing. He couldn't stomach having had to hand out commissions right and left, when they'd taken over the crypt, — to the priest, the woman who let the chairs, the Town Hall, the Church Council and a whole lot of others; and all to no purpose, when you come down to it. It knocked him right up, the very thought of it. Robbery was what he called that sort of thing.

"Well, and are you married at last, after all this?" I wound up by asking him.

"No, I'm telling you. I wasn't having any after that."

"But little Madelon was a pretty cute piece though, surely? You wouldn't deny that?"

"That's not the point. . . ."

"But, damn it, of course it's the point. You've told me you

were free, haven't you? If you were so set on leaving Toulouse, you could have perfectly well have let her mother run the crypt for a time . . . You could have gone back there later on. . . ."

"As far as being physically attractive's concerned," he continued, "you're quite right. She really was charming, I admit; you hadn't misled me, and that's a fact, especially as just imagine —when I saw things again for the first time, as if it had happened on purpose, the first thing I saw was her, in a mirror. . . . You can imagine it, can't you? In the light! It was almost two months after the old woman had had her fall. . . . I was trying to see Madelon's face and sight returned to my eyes suddenly, while they were on her. . . . A flash of light, in fact. . . . Do you get me?"

"Wasn't that nice?"

"Yes, it was nice. . . . But that isn't everything."

"You cleared out just the same."

"Sure—and I'll explain, as you seem to want to understand. . . . It was she in the first place who began to think me odd. Said I'd lost interest in life. . . . Wasn't nice to her any more. . . . A lot of silly nonsense of that sort."

"Maybe it was your conscience that was troubling you."

"Conscience?"

"Well, how should I know?"

"You can call it what you like, but I wasn't feeling too good. That's all I know about it. . . . All the same, I don't think it can have been conscience. . . ."

"Are you ill then?"

"Yes, I should say that's it, ill . . . Anyhow, that's what I've been trying to get you to see for the last hour. . . . You'll admit you're pretty slow on the uptake."

"Oh, all right," I answered. "We'll say you're ill, if you think that would be the safest plan."

"You'd do well to," he insisted, "because I can't guarantee anything where that little girl's concerned. . . . She's capable of squealing to the cops any minute."

It was as if it were a piece of advice he was giving me, and I didn't want any advice from him, thank you. I didn't like this

kind of thing at all, because of the complications that were starting all over again.

"D'you think yourself that she'd squeal?" I asked him further, to make quite certain. "But she's something of an accomplice of yours, though, isn't she? That ought to make her think
twice, say, before starting to blab."

"Think twice!" he leapt when he heard me say that. "Any
one can see you don't know her." It made him laugh to hear me
talk that way. "Why, she won't hesitate a second! Honestly,
man. . . . If you'd seen as much of her as I have, you'd have no
doubt of it. She's in love, I keep telling you. . . . Haven't you
yourself ever had any dealings with women in love? When she's
in love, she's mad, that's all there is to it. Mad! And it's me she's
in love with and me she's mad about! It's perfectly simple. That
doesn't stop her. Quite the reverse."

I couldn't tell him it really rather amazed me that Madelon
should have reached such a pitch of excitement in the space of
only a few months; after all, I had had some slight experience
of her myself, come to that. I knew what I thought about her,
but I couldn't tell him.

From the way she had behaved in Toulouse and as I had
heard her when I was behind the poplar that day of the yacht,
it was difficult for me to suppose that her nature could have
changed so completely in such a short space of time. . . . She'd
appeared to me quick-witted rather than tragical, to have a
pleasantly open mind and to be quite ready to get fixed up by
means of bluff and little tricks, wherever there was a chance
of their catching on. But at the present juncture I had no further
remark to make. The only thing to do was to let it go. "Right.
All right," I said. "What about her mother, though? She must have
set up a bit of a holler when she realized you were slipping out
on them for good?"

"Say—didn't she, though? She jabbered all day long about
my having the instincts of a swine and that, mark you, just
when what I badly needed was just the opposite—to be treated
particularly nicely! What a game it was! It couldn't go on like
that, with the mother either, you know, so in the end I suggested

to Madelon that I would leave the crypt to the two of them, while I went off on my own for a bit; I'd go travel about alone a piece, see something of the world again. . . .

" 'You'll take me with you,' she protested. 'I'm engaged to you, aren't I? Léon, either you take me with you or you don't go at all! . . . And what's more,' she insisted, 'you aren't well enough yet, anyway.'

" 'Hell, I'm all right. And I'll go alone,' I told her. So there we were, stuck.

" 'A wife goes everywhere with her husband,' her mother said. 'Why don't you get married?' She backed her up just to make me really sore.

"Listening to all this rot made me feel like hell. You know me. As if I had needed a woman to go to the war with. Or to come out of it again! And I didn't have any women with me in Africa, did I? And you didn't find me having women around in the States, did you? Anyway, to hear them arguing away like this, hour after hour, gave me a pain in the stomach. Gripes, man! I know what women are good for. You do too, I expect? Damn it all. I've been around in my time, too. In the end one evening, when they'd made me lose all patience with their yowling, I let out finally and told the mother exactly what I thought of her. 'You old cow,' I said to her. I said: 'You're even more of a B.F. than Ma Henrouille was. . . . If you'd known a few more people and been around a bit more, as I have, you wouldn't be in such a hurry to go about giving every one advice. And just mucking about with tag-ends of tow in a corner of that god-forsaken old church of yours, you won't be getting to know any more about life, see? It would do you good to get out a bit more. . . . Why don't you go out for a walk sometimes, you old skunk? Maybe that'd freshen you up. You'd not have so much time for saying prayers; you wouldn't look such a blistering idiot!'

"That's what I said to that mother of hers. For a hell of a time I'd had it on my mind to have a whack at her, honestly I had — and she badly needed it, anyway. . . . But, all in all, it was me it did good to mostly. . . . But you know, you'd have thought that was all the old scab was waiting for, me spreading myself like that, to let fly at me in her turn and call me every kind of bastard she could think of! She flared up all right — said really more than she need, as a matter of fact. 'You felon! You cad!' she squealed. 'Why, you don't even work for your living! I've been feeding you for nearly a year now, I and my daughter — you good-for-nothing pimp!' You can imagine what it was like. A slap-up family scene. . . . She sort of thought for quite a time and then she said it under her breath, but you know she had let it out then and she really meant it: 'Murderer! You murderer!' she called me. I felt a bit queer when she said that.

"The daughter, hearing her mother speak that way, seemed afraid I might knock her down on the spot. She flung herself between us. She shut her mother's mouth with her hand. Quite right. So they are in league against me, both of them, I thought to myself. It was obvious. . . . In the end, I let it go. It wasn't the moment to be violent. . . . And anyway, what did I care whether they were in league together or not? Maybe you think that now that they'd let off steam, they'd let me alone for a time? You'd say so, wouldn't you? But oh, no! That wouldn't have been like them at all. The daughter began all over again. . . . She was all hot in the head and hot somewhere else too. . . . She went to it again, harder than ever:

" 'I love you, Léon, you know how much I love you, Léon. . . .' That's all she knew, — that 'I love you' of hers. As if it was an answer to everything.

" 'You still love him?' her mother broke in, when she heard her say that. 'But can't you see he's nothing better than a tramp? Lower than dirt? Now that he's got his eyesight back, thanks to the care we've taken of him, he's going to do you wrong, my daughter! Listen to your mother, my darling — she knows.'

"Every one wept in the end, even I wept too, because in spite of everything I didn't want to put myself too much in the wrong with these two bitches, or to quarrel with them more than I need.

"So I pushed off, but too many things had been said for this situation to be left very long as it was between us. It dragged on anyway for weeks, with us snapping at each other every other moment and keeping a watch on each other all day and above all, at night.

"We couldn't decide to part but our hearts weren't in it. It was still mostly certain fears we had in common which kept us together.

" 'You don't love another, do you?' Madelon asked me sometimes.

" 'No, of course not,' I'd try to reassure her. 'Sure I don't. But it was obvious she didn't believe me. To her way of thinking you had to love somebody in life and we couldn't get beyond that.

" 'Tell me,' I'd say to her, 'what should I be wanting with another woman?' But she'd got love on the brain. I couldn't think what to say to calm her down. She went to lengths I'd never dreamt of before. I never would have believed she could have things like that in her head.

" 'You've stolen my heart away, Léon,' she'd accuse me, and she seriously meant it. 'You want to leave me,' she'd threaten, 'Well—go then! But I warn you I shall die of a broken heart if you do, Léon!' Now why should she be going to die because of me? What sense did that make, eh? I ask you. . . . 'No, no, look here, you're not going to die,' I'd say. 'I haven't done a thing to you, anyway! I haven't given you a child or anything, have I now? Just think! You haven't caught any infection off me, have you? Well, then? I just want to go away, that's all. Go off on holiday, as you might say. There's nothing strange about that, after all. . . . Try to be reasonable.' Yet the more I tried to make her understand my point of view, the less it appealed to her. In fact we just couldn't come to an understanding. She went sort of crazy at the thought that I might really feel the way I said I did, that it was nothing but the truth, entirely straightforward and sincere.

"She also believed it was you who were urging me to clear out. . . . So then, seeing that she couldn't hold me back by making me ashamed of my attitude, she tried to keep me another way.

" 'Don't imagine, Léon,' she said, 'that I wish to keep you because of the crypt or anything. . . . You know money doesn't really mean anything to me, fundamentally. . . . What I want,

Léon, is to be with you. . . . To be happy. That's all. It's natural enough. I don't want you to leave me. . . . It's wrong to separate when one has loved as we two have loved. . . . Swear to me at least, Léon, that you won't be gone long?'

"And this sort of thing went on for weeks and weeks. . . . She certainly was in love and a hell of a nuisance. . . . Every evening she harped back to this love-madness of hers. Finally she was willing at all events to leave the vault for her mother to look after, on condition that we should both go off together to hunt for a job in Paris. . . . It was always 'together' though. What a game! She'd fall in with any scheme except my going my way and she hers. . . . Nothing doing, so far as that went. . . . But the more she seemed stuck on that, the iller she made me feel, of course.

"It wasn't worth trying to make her see reason. I was beginning to be made to see myself that it was really so much time wasted and that her mind was made up and that everything I said only made her madder still. So I simply had to set to and think out some scheme to rid myself of her love, as she called it. That's how I hit on the idea of putting her off by telling her, casual like, that from time to time I went a bit queer in the head. . . . That I was taken that way sometimes. . . . Never knew when it was coming. . . . She gave me a dirty look, a very odd look. She wasn't too sure it wasn't just another yarn of mine. . . . But then, anyway, what with all the things I had told her had happened to me before, and the war having affected me, and especially that last business of the old lady and also my strangely altered attitude towards her, all of a sudden, it did give her something to think about all the same.

"And she thought about it for more than a week, letting me alone all that time. . . . She must have whispered a word or two to her mother about my being subject to these fits. . . . Anyway, they no longer made quite such a fuss about keeping me, after that. 'It is all right,' I said to myself, 'It's going to work. . . . I'm free at last.' I saw myself quietly on my way to Paris, with no bones broken. . . . Not so fast, though! I began to play the game a little too well. . . . I went in for fancy work. I thought

I'd hit on the perfect scheme for proving to them once and for all that it really was the truth. . . . That I really did go cuckoo at times. . . . 'Feel that!' I said to Madelon one evening. 'Feel this bump on the back of my head. Can you feel the scar on it and that great bump I've got, eh?'

"But when she'd properly felt the bump on the back of my head, I can't tell you how thrilled she was. It gave her a whole lot more of a kick, it did indeed; it didn't disgust her at all! 'That's where I was wounded in Flanders. That's where they trepanned me,' I kept on.

"'Oh Léon!' she exclaimed as she felt the bump, 'I'm terribly, terribly sorry, darling Léon! . . . I've doubted you up to now, but from the depths of my heart I beg you to forgive me! I realize now I've been horrid to you. Yes, oh, yes, Léon dear, I've been dreadfully unkind. . . . I'll never be unkind to you again! I promise. Oh, but I want to make amends, Léon! At once. You *will* let me make amends, won't you? I'll make you happy again! I'll look after you from now on, I'll always be patient with you. I'll be so sweet to you. You'll see, Léon. I'll understand you so well that you won't be able to get on without me. . . . I give you back my whole heart; I belong to you. All of me, Léon. My whole life I give to you, Léon. But tell me at least that you forgive me; you do, don't you, Léon?'

"I hadn't said a word of all that myself, not a thing. She'd said it all, and so it was easy enough for her to answer herself on her own. . . . Then, what in hell *would* make her stop?

"Touching that scar and that bump of mine had, you might say, sort of made her quite drunk with love all of a sudden. She awfully wanted to take my head in her hands, never let it go again, and make me happy to my dying day, whether I liked it or not. And after that her mother was never allowed to yell at me any more. Madelon wouldn't let her mother speak. You wouldn't have recognised the girl; she wanted to protect me from every least little thing.

"A stop just had to be put to all this. I'd have preferred us to part good friends. . . . But that wasn't even worth trying for. . . . She was sick with love now and all of a heap. One morning when they were out shopping, she and her mother, I did what you did, I made up my little bundle and quietly pushed off. . . . You surely can't say after all this that I wasn't patient enough? Only I promise you there wasn't anything to be done. . . . Now you know all about it. And when I tell you there's nothing that girl isn't capable of and that she may come here any minute to have another crack at me, you needn't come and tell me I'm imagining things! I know what I'm talking about. I know what she's like, all right. And we'd be much easier in our minds, I think, if she were to find me already by way of being shut up with a lot of madmen, see? Like that, it'd be less difficult for me to make out I didn't understand any more. . . . With her, that's what you need to do. . . . Just not understand a thing."

Two or three months previously, all these things Robinson had just told me would still have interested me a lot, but I'd grown sort of old all of a sudden.

At heart, I had grown more and more like Baryton; I didn't care a damn. This whole Toulousian escapade of Robinson's was no longer a really vivid danger to me; I tried to wax excited over the situation he was in, but it just seemed stale. Whatever people may care to make out, life leaves you high and dry long before you're really through.

The things you used to set most store by, you one fine day decide to take less and less notice of, and it's an effort when you absolutely have to. You're sick of always hearing yourself talk. . . . You abbreviate. You renounce. Thirty years you've been at it, talking, talking . . . You don't mind now about being right. You lose even the desire to hang on to the little place you've reserved for yourself among the pleasures of life. . . . You're fed up. From now on, it's enough just to eat a little, to get a bit of warmth, and to sleep as much as you can on the road to nothing at all. In order to get interested again, you would have to find new faces to pull for the benefit of the other people. But now you haven't the strength to renew your repertoire. You stammer over your words. You still, of course, go on looking for gambits and excuses for staying on with the boys, but death's there with you too, stinking alongside all the time now, less mysterious than a game of cribbage. The only things that still mean anything very much to you are the little regrets, like never having found time to get round and see your old uncle at Bois-Colombes, whose little song died away forever one February evening. That's all one's retained of life, this little very horrible regret; the rest one has more or less successfully vomited up along the road, with a good many retchings and a great deal of unhappiness. One's come to be nothing but an aged lamppost of fitful memories at the corner of a street along which almost no one passes now.

If you're to be bored, the least wearisome way is to keep absolutely regular habits. I made a point of seeing that everyone was in bed in the house by ten o'clock. It was I who put out the lights. And the business ran itself.

Anyway, we didn't trouble to think up anything new. The Baryton System of Cinematic Cures for Cretins was quite enough to keep us going. The establishment had given up economizing much. Wasteful expenditure, we calculated, might make the Chief come home, since it was such torture to him.

We'd bought an accordion for Robinson to give his charges something to dance to in the garden in summertime. It was difficult to keep the lunatics occupied at Vigny day after day and night after night. You couldn't send them to church all the time; they got too bored.

We got no further news from Toulouse and the Abbé Protiste never came back to see me again, either. Life in the asylum became settled and furtively monotonous. Morally speaking, our consciences weren't entirely easy. There were too many ghosts, one way and another.

Still more months passed. Robinson began to look better in health. At Easter, the lunatics became somewhat restless; women in light dresses were passing back and forth before our garden railings. Burgeoning spring. We prescribed bromide.

Since I had worked at the Tarapout, the casts had been changed there several times. The little English girls were far away now, they told me, in Australia. We shouldn't be seeing *them* again. . . .

I wasn't allowed back stage, after my Tania episode. I didn't press the point.

We started writing letters to one place after another, chiefly to the consulates in the northern countries, hoping to get some inkling of Baryton's possible movements. We got no answer of any interest from any of them.

All the while Parapine discharged his technical duties deliberately and in silence. In the last two years he had certainly not uttered more than a score of remarks in all. It came to my having to decide the small practical and administrative details and everyday requirements of the place almost on my own. I slipped up once or twice, but Parapine never blamed me in any way. We got on together by dint of sheer indifference. In any case, an adequate influx of new patients kept the place financially on its feet. When we'd paid the tradespeople and the rent, we had still quite enough left over to live on ourselves, after regularly making Aimée's allowance over to her aunt, of course.

Robinson, I thought, was much less jumpy now than he had been on his first arrival. He was looking better and had put on three *kilos*. In fact, it seemed that as long as there was any insanity left in people's families, they would be delighted to turn to us, admirably placed as we were, within easy reach of town. Our garden alone was worth the trip out. People came all the way from Paris to admire our baskets and our clumps of roses on fine days in summer.

It was on one of these June days that I first thought I recognized Madelon, in the middle of a strolling group of people. She stood quite still for a moment or two just at our gate. Right at first I didn't want to let Robinson know anything about this apparition, so as not to frighten him, but then, after all, when I'd thought about it carefully, a few days later, I advised him not to stir far from the house in future, at any rate for a time, on those aimless strolls round the neighbourhood which he'd got into the habit of taking. This advice of mine he found disquieting. He did not, however, make any attempt to know more.

Towards the end of July, we got several post cards from Baryton, from Finland this time. We were glad to get them but still there was no word about returning home; he merely once again wished us "Good Luck" with a whole lot of other pleasant messages besides.

Two months passed into the distance, and others followed them. . . . The dust of summer clad the roads again. One of our madmen, on All Saints' Day, caused a bit of a hullabaloo in front of the Institute. Up to now a quite peaceful, well-behaved patient, the funereal exaltation of All Saints' Day disagreed with him. We weren't quick enough to stop him screeching from his window that he never wanted to die. More and more passers-by kept finding him deliciously droll. It was in the midst of this flare-up that again, and this time much more distinctly than before, I received the very disagreeable impression of thinking I recognized Madelon standing in the front row of a group of onlookers, in exactly the same place, opposite our gateway.

Later, during that night, I woke in an agony of mind; I tried to forget what I'd seen, but all my efforts to forget were vain. It was no good trying to get any more sleep.

I hadn't been back to Rancy for a long time now. As soon as be haunted by my nightmare, I wondered whether I mightn't just as well go and have a look-see in that direction, whence all misfortunes came, sooner or later. . . . Down yonder, I had left nightmares behind me too. . . . An attempt to forestall them might pass at a pinch for some sort of precaution. The shortest road to Rancy from the Vigny direction lies along the embankment as far as the bridge at Gennevilliers — that flat one, stretched out across the Seine. The slow river mists are torn apart at the water's edge, curl, hasten, sail up, tremble and sink down over the other side of the parapet round the bitter, flaring light of the ancient oil lamps. There on the left, the squat great works, where tractors are made, hides in a slab of darkness. Its windows are open to the mournful fire which is burning it away inside and never gets put out. Once past the factory, you're alone on the riverside. . . . But you can't lose your way. . . . You realize more or less when you've arrived by how tired you are feeling.

Then all you have to do is to turn left up the Rue des Bournaires and it's not very far after that. It isn't hard to know where you are, because of the red and green signals at the level crossing, which always show a light.

In the pitchest-black night I could have gone to the Henrouilles' little house with my eyes shut.

I'd been there often enough, at one time. . . .

Yet that night, when I reached their door, I stopped to ponder instead of going forward.

She was living alone in the house now, I reflected. . . . They were all dead, all the others were dead. . . . She must have known, or at least she must have surmised, how that old mother-in-law of hers had met her end down there in Toulouse. . . . What had she felt about it, I wondered. . . .

The lamp-post on the pavement shone white on their little glass portico, as if there was snow on the step. I stayed there, at the corner of the street, just looking, a long while. I could just as well have gone on and rung the bell. She would certainly have opened to me. After all, we hadn't really quarrelled as badly as all that. It was icy-cold standing there where I had stopped. . . .

The street still ended in a quagmire, as in my time. The authorities had promised to do something about it; nothing had been done. No one came by that way.

It's not that I was afraid of her, afraid of Madame Henrouille, Junior. No. That wasn't it. But all of a sudden, as I stood there, I no longer had any desire to see her again. I'd made a mistake, setting out to visit her again. There, in front of her house, I realized in a flash that there wasn't anything now she could tell me. . . . It would now be even a bore to have her talk to me; that is all. That's what we had come to mean for one another.

I had gone further ahead into the night than she had, even further than the older Henrouille woman, and she was dead. . . . We weren't together any more. . . . We had parted for good. . . . Separated not only by death, but by life too. . . . It had happened that way by force of circumstances. Each for himself! said I inwardly. . . . And I went off again on my own road towards Vigny.

She hadn't enough education to follow me now, the younger Henrouille woman. . . . Character she had, certainly she had

that. . . . But no education. That was the snag. No wisdom!
That's what's essential — knowledge! So she couldn't understand
me now, nor understand what went on around us, however obstinate and bloody she might be. . . . That's not enough. . . .
You need a heart and understanding to go further than the rest
of the people. . . . It was along the Rue des Sanzillons that I
went to get back to the river and then down the Impasse Vassou.
My troubles were settled . . . I was feeling almost good! Pleased
because I could realize that there was no longer any point in
bothering any more about the daughter-in-law Henrouille, I had
ended up by losing her *en route*, the creature! What an episode
that had been. We'd got on well together, after our own fashion.
. . . We'd understood each other well enough at one time, the
Henrouille woman and I. . . . Quite a while that had lasted. . . .
But now she wasn't low enough down for me, she couldn't get
down. . . . Didn't know how to join me. . . . She hadn't the
brains or the strength. You don't climb upwards in life; you go
down. She couldn't get down there to me, where I was . . . There
was too much of the night covering me. . . .

Passing in front of the tenement building where Bébert's aunt
had been concierge, I almost thought of going in, just to see the
people who now occupied her lodge, in which I had looked after
Bébert, the place from which he had slipped away. . . . Perhaps
there was still that schoolboy picture of him over the bed. . . .
But it was too late to wake people. I passed on without making
myself known to them.

A little further on, on the Faubourg de la Liberté, I came again
to Bézin's junk shop, with the light still burning. . . . I wasn't
expecting that. . . . But it was only just a gas jet over the goods
in his window. Bézin knew all the gossip and the low-down on the
whole neighbourhood, through hanging about the cafés; so familiar
a sight all the way from the Foire aux Puces to the Porte Maillot.

He could have told me a thing or two if he'd been awake. I
pushed his door. The bell rang all right, but no one answered.
I knew that he slept at the back of the shop, in the room he ate
in, as a matter of fact. . . . That's where he was, too, all in
darkness, with his head on the table between his arms, sitting

sideways over the cold supper awaiting him — a plate of lentils. He had not started to eat it. Sleep had seized him as soon as he'd got in. He was snoring hard. It's true he'd been drinking too, of course. I remember the day well. It was Thursday, the day of the Lilas junk market. He had a bundle open on the floor at his feet, full of cheap bargains.

Myself, I'd always thought Bézin a good sort, as decent a bloke as most. He was all right. Easy-going, not tiresome at all. I wouldn't wake him up out of curiosity, just to ask him my little questions. . . . So I pushed off again, putting his light out for him before I went.

He found it hard to make ends meet, of course, in this sort of little business he carried on. But he at least had no difficulty in sleeping.

I turned back towards Vigny again, feeling sad as I thought of all these people, these houses, these dim and dirty things which now no longer spoke to me at all, straight to the heart as they had spoken once, and I, too, though I might seem all cock-a-hoop, had maybe not enough strength left either now, I felt sure, to go on a long way further by myself, like that, alone.

WE KEPT TO THE SAME ARRANGEMENT FOR MEALS AT VIGNY AS WE had in Baryton's time; that is to say, we all sat down to them together, but for preference we now ate in the billiard room over the porter's lodge. It was less formal than the real dining room, which was still reminiscent of those most unhumorous English conversations. Besides, there was too much fine furniture in the dining room for our liking — genuine 1900 pieces, with opal-tinted window panes.

From the billiard room you could see everything that happened in the street. There might always be something to that. We spent all day Sundays in this room. Occasionally we'd have guests — some local doctor we'd invited to supper — but our most usual companion was Gustave, the traffic cop. He, indeed, was a regular visitor. We had struck up an acquaintanceship through the window, as we watched him on Sundays at his post on the crossroads which marked the entrance to Vigny. He used to get into difficulties with the cars. It started with some casual remark from us, and after several Sundays we had come to know one another quite well. I had happened to attend both his sons at one time in town; first one with measles and then the other with mumps. He was our faithful friend, Gustave Mandamour — that was his name — and he hailed from the Cantal. In conversation he was a little trying, as he had difficulty with his words. He could find them all right but he couldn't pronounce them; they just stayed somewhere at the back of his mouth, rumbling.

One evening — I believe it was for a joke — Robinson casually invited him in to billiards, but it was his nature always to persevere with everything, so after that he came every evening at the same time: eight o'clock. He liked being with us, he preferred it to going to the café, as he told us himself, because of the political discussions which frequently grew heated between the habitués there. Whereas we never talked politics. For Gustave, in his position, politics were a somewhat delicate topic. He had had a certain amount of trouble on that score already. In the first place, he ought not to have talked politics, especially not when he'd had a few drinks, and that's what did happen. In fact, he was known to booze a good deal; it was his weakness. But at our place he felt himself secure on all scores. He himself admitted as much. We didn't drink. It was all right for him to come to our house, no ill effects could come of it. He came to us in perfect trust.

When Parapine and I considered the situation we had once been in and the one we had chanced on at Baryton's, we didn't feel like complaining, it would have been quite wrong of us if we had; because really, as a matter of fact, we had had the most miraculous kind of luck and were well provided with everything we needed, both in the way of consideration and material comforts.

Still, personally, I'd always had my doubts about this miracle lasting. I had a sticky past and already it was catching me up again, like a hang-over of Fate. Just starting in Vigny as I was then, I had already received three anonymous letters which had seemed to me as nasty and threatening as they well could be. And then, following that, several more utterly spiteful missives. It's true, of course, that we often had anonymous letters sent to us at Vigny and normally we didn't pay any particular attention to them. Most of them came from former patients whose persecutions had started harassing them again at home.

But these particular letters did worry me rather; they were not like the others; they were more definite in their accusations, which invariably referred only to Robinson and myself. To tell the truth, they accused us of living together. It was a dastardly aspersion. I didn't like to mention the matter to him at first, but eventually I did bring myself to, as I kept getting more and more letters on the same lines. Then we tried to make out whom they might be from. We worked over a list of all the possibles among our mutual acquaintances. We couldn't make out who it could be. Anyhow, it was a futile sort of thing to accuse us of. Inversion was not in my line and Robinson didn't care a damn about sex, of either one kind or another. If there was anything on his mind, it certainly wasn't connected with any urges of that sort. No one but a jealous woman could have thought out such disgusting nonsense.

All told, we knew of nobody except Madelon who would be capable of making a set at us here in Vigny with disgusting fabrications of this sort. I didn't mind if she went on writing us all this muck or not, but the danger was that, furious at getting no reply, one of these days she might come after us in person and treat us to a public scene in the Institute. We could expect the worst.

We lived through several weeks of this sort of thing, jumping every time we heard the bell. I was expecting a visit from Madelon or, worse still, the police.

Every time that Gustave Mandamour came round for his game rather earlier than usual, I wondered if he wasn't bringing a warrant in his belt, but at that time he was still as friendly and soothing as could be. It was only later that he too began, most noticeably to change. At that period he was still losing almost every day, at every game he played, with the utmost serenity. If his attitude towards us changed, it was certainly our own fault.

One evening, just to know, I asked him why he didn't ever happen to win at cards; I had no real reason for asking Mandamour that; it was just my passion for always knowing the wherefore and the how of things, especially as we didn't play for stakes anyway. Then, as we discussed the bad luck he had, I went closer to him and, looking at him more carefully, noticed that he suffered quite badly from short sight. Actually, in the light we had in that room, he could only with difficulty distinguish spades from clubs. One couldn't have that.

I put his infirmity right for him, giving him a nice pair of spectacles. At first he was very happy just having them on, but that didn't last. Now that he was playing better, thanks to the glasses, he lost less often than before and took it into his head in future never to lose at all. And as that was impossible, he started to cheat. And when he happened to lose in spite of cheating, we would have him sulking on our hands for hours at a time. In short, he became impossible.

It was damned annoying; the least little thing put him out of temper, and what's more, he would now try in his turn to vex us, to give us something to worry and fret about. When he lost a game, he revenged himself in his own way. And yet I repeat we weren't playing for money, but just for the fun and kudos of the game. All the same, he was furious. . . .

And so one evening, when he had had bad luck, he turned on us before he left. "Gentlemen," he said, "I am going to warn you to look to yourselves. . . . Considering the type of people you're acquainted with, if I were you, I'd watch my step. . . . There's one dark girl in particular who has been walking past your house quite regularly of late. . . . Much too regularly, if you ask me. . . . She probably has her reasons. . . . And if she were after having a word with one or other of you gentlemen, I shouldn't be too surprised . . ."

That's how Mandamour threw this pernicious thing in our teeth as he went out. Oh, yes, he got his little effect all right. But I pulled my wits about me in an instant. "Ah, thank you, Gustave," I answered, perfectly calmly. . . . "I can't think who this dark girl you mention can be. None of our female patients has so far, to my knowledge, ever had cause to complain of our care of her. . . . No doubt it's some poor madwoman. . . . We shall discover her again in time. Still, you are quite right; it's always best to know. . . . Thank you yet again, Gustave, for having thought to warn us. . . . And *good* night."

Robinson at that couldn't get up from his chair. When the policeman had gone, we examined this piece of information he had given us from all angles. It might perhaps not be Madelon after all. . . . There were plenty of other women who did come roaming around under the asylum windows. But all the same, there was a grave likelihood of it being her and this surmise was enough to petrify us. . . . If it were she, what was she planning to do next? And anyway, what could she have had to live on all these months in Paris? If she were going to come here herself and raise Cain in the place, we'd have to bestir ourselves and make plans, right away.

So, "Listen here, Robinson," I said at that point; "make up your mind; now's the time; decide now and don't go back on it. . . . What are you going to do? Do you want to go back to Toulouse with her?"

"No, I tell you — no. No. No. No!" That was the answer he gave me. So now I knew.

"All right," I said. "All right. But if that's the case, if you really don't care to go back down there with her, the best thing, I think, would be for you to go and earn your living abroad somewhere, for a time at least. Like that, you'd be sure of giving her the slip. She couldn't very well follow you that far, could she? . . . You're young still. You're strong again. . . . You're rested. . . . We'll give you a little ready cash: then — so long! That's what I think. And anyway, you realize, don't you, that there's no place for you here. . . . It can't last indefinitely, you know. . . ."

If he had only really listened to me, if he had gone away at that juncture, that would have suited me down to the ground; it would have been fine. But he didn't go away.

"You're kicking me out, Ferdinand!" he protested. "That's not kind, at my age. . . . Take a good look at me. After all. . . ." He didn't want to go away. He was, in fact, tired of moving around. "I don't want to go beyond where I am," he insisted. "You can talk as much as you like . . . do what you like . . . I won't go."

That is how he responded to my friendly gesture. All the same, I kept on.

"And what if she were to give you in charge for the murder of old Madame Henrouille, let's suppose she did that. . . . You said yourself she was perfectly capable of doing it."

"So much the worse, then," he replied. "She can do what she likes."

That was something new, a remark like that, coming from him; up to now fatalism hadn't been much in his line.

"At least, go and get yourself some little job hereabouts, in a factory—then you wouldn't have to be here with us all the time. . . . If they came for you, there'd be time to let you know."

Parapine entirely agreed with me on that point and even went so far in this contingency as to address a few words to us again. So that clearly this thing that was happening among us must have struck him as extremely serious and important. What we needed to do was to think out some way of fixing Robinson up, of camouflaging him somehow. Among our business connections we numbered one local employer, a coach builder, who owed us some slight gratitude for certain extremely delicate little services we had done him at critical moments. He was quite ready to give Robinson a trial at hand painting. It was a pleasant job, not hard work, and decently paid.

"Léon," he was told, the day he took up the job, "don't ball it all up now; don't go and get into trouble with those deplorable ideas of yours. . . . Get there in time. . . . Don't leave before the others. . . . Say 'Good morning' to everybody when you arrive. . . . Mind your p's and q's, in fact. You're in a respectable workshop now and you're there on our recommendation."

But then all the same he went and got himself spotted at once —and it wasn't his fault either—for making use of the head's private washroom, and a snooper in the next workshop split on him. . . . And that did the trick. He was hauled up. There was an argument. He was fired.

So here was Robinson back on our hands again, out of a job, after only a few days. As bad luck would have it.

And on top of that, he started in to cough again, almost the same day. We overhauled him and discovered a complete series of wheezes up the whole of his right lung. There was nothing for him to do but to keep to his room.

This happened one Saturday evening just before supper and some one was asking for me, waiting to see me, in the reception room.

A woman, they said.

It was she, with a little three-cornered hat on, and wearing gloves. I remember quite well. No need to beat about the bush; she had come at just the right moment. I let her have it straight from the shoulder.

"Madelon," I forestalled her, "if it's Léon you're looking for, I don't mind telling you at once that there's no point in your keeping on about it; you might as well go home again. He's wrong in the lungs and the head. Pretty seriously wrong. . . . You can't see him. . . . In any case, he hasn't anything to say to you."

"Not even to me?" she urged.

"No, not even to you. . . . Particularly not to you. . . ." I added.

I thought she would burst out at that. She didn't. She only stood there before me, shaking her head from side to side, her lips tight shut, and with her eyes she tried to discover me in the place where she had left me in her memory. I was there no longer. I had moved, I too had shifted in her memory of me. In our present circumstances, I should have been afraid of a man, of some tough lout, but with her I had nothing to fear. She was weaker than I was, as the saying goes. As long as I can remember, I had always wanted to clout a face possessed by anger, as hers was, just to see what happens to an angry face if you do. That, or a fat cheque, is what you need so as to see an instant change come over all the passions which dodge around in a person's head. It's as lovely to watch as a sailing ship going "about" on a high-running tide. The whole mind answers to the new shift in the wind. That's what I wanted to see.

For twenty years at least I had been pursued by this desire. On the street, in cafés, in all the places where people, with greater or less aggressiveness, fretful and bragging, fly at each other's throats. But I had never dared, for fear of being slugged myself, and above all for fear of the shame which follows coming to blows. But here was the opportunity for once, magnificent.

"Are you going to get out?" I asked her, just to make her angrier still, to bring her to the proper pitch.

She no longer knew who I was when I talked to her like that. She started to smile, abhorrently, as if she were finding me very ridiculous and negligible. . . . Biff! Bang! I landed two slaps across her face which would have been enough to shake a house.

She tottered and fell flat across the broad pink divan on the opposite side of the room, against the wall, her head in her hands. Her breath came in little gasps; she moaned like a little dog that's been too thoroughly thrashed. Then after that she seemed to think a while and suddenly she jumped up, lithe and supple, and was out of the door without even turning her head. I had seen nothing. It hadn't been any good.

BUT WE WERE NO MATCH FOR HER; SHE WAS CRAFTIER THAN THE whole lot of us put together. And the proof of it is that she got to see her Robinson again — and saw him, what's more, exactly as and how she wished. The first to spot them together was Parapine. They were sitting outside a café opposite the Gare de l'Est.

I had already suspected that they were seeing each other again but I didn't wish to appear in the least interested in their relationship. It was none of my business, anyhow. He did his job at the asylum, not altogether too badly — a beastly job, if ever there was one — looking after the paralytic cases: tidying them up, washing them, changing their linen for them, making them slaver. We had no call to ask more from him than that.

If he arranged to see Madelon on the afternoons I sent him up to Paris to shop for us, that was his affair. The fact remains that we ourselves never saw anything more of her at Vigny after the face-slapping episode. But I guessed she must have had some pretty unpleasant things to tell him about me after that.

I didn't even mention Toulouse to him now, as if none of all that had ever happened.

Six months passed in this way, whether we liked it or not, and then of a sudden a vacancy occurred on our staff; we had immediate and urgent need of a nurse with plenty of experience of massage work. Ours had gone off and left us without warning to get married.

A goodly number of fine-looking girls put in for the post and as it turned out, we only had the difficulty of choosing among so many well-built creatures of all nationalities who flocked down to Vigny-sur-Seine as soon as our advertisement appeared. In the end we picked on a Slovak of the name of Sophie, whose complexion, whose easy and at the same time gracious bearing and divinely healthy appearance we found, I must admit, irresistible.

This Sophie child of ours spoke only a few words of French, but I took it on myself — it was, in all politeness, the least I could do — to give her lessons in the language at once. I experienced, forsooth, on coming into contact with such freshness, a renewal of my interest in teaching, though Baryton had done everything to put me off it. But I was impenitent. My hat, though, what exquisite youthfulness! What spirit! What muscles! What an excuse! Elastic! Rippling! Perfectly astonishing. Loveliness too, unhampered by any of the false or genuine prudishness which so gets in the way of ordinary, too occidental conversations. Personally, and to be quite frank, I admired her to distraction. I proceeded from one set of muscles to the next, by anatomical groups. . . . By muscular slopes, by sections. . . . Vigour at once so well coördinated and so easy-flowing, lodged in sheaves of muscle now resilient, now yielding to the touch — I could never tire in its pursuit . . . beneath that velvety, taut, untaught, miraculous epidermis . . .

The era of living delights of the great, incontrovertible physiological harmonies is yet to come. The body of a godhead mauled by my unworthy hands . . . the hands of an honourable man, that unknown parish priest. . . . First must come Death and Words. . . . What loathsome claptrap. It's smeared from head to foot with a thick coating of symbolism and quilted top to toe with such a foul artiness that your man of culture tries his luck in bed. . . . Let who can manage it then! A swell, a dandy racket! A saving, after all, not getting a thrill except out of looking back. We've got that all right, we've got reminiscences; you can buy reminiscences, and jolly fine ones, lovely ones to look back on, to your heart's content once and for all. . . . Ah, but life's more complicated, above all the life of the human form. . . . A desperate task . . . There's none more difficult, hazardous. Compared to this vice of seeking after perfection in shapes, cocaine's nothing but a hobby for stationmasters.

But let us get back to our darling Sophie! Her mere presence seemed a stroke of daring in the sulky, sombre, timorous atmosphere of our house. After we had lived under the same roof with her a little while, we were, it's true, still charmed to have her on our nursing staff, but even so we couldn't help fearing that, some time or other, she would disorganize the sum total of all our infinite cautiousness or merely one fine day come suddenly to realize the pitiful griminess of our condition. . . . Poor Sophie, she was not yet aware of the extent of our cringing surrender. A set of hopeless failures. . . . We admired her aliveness by our side, if she merely rose and came to our table or walked away again. . . . She enchanted us. And each time she performed these simple gestures, we were overcome with joy — and surprise. In some way, we seemed to gain in poetry just in admiring her being so utterly beautiful, so much more unselfconscious than we were. . . . The rhythm of her life was drawn from other sources than ours. Ours were jangling rhythms, sickly and sad. . . . This happy impulsation, at once precise and gentle, which animated her from the waves of her hair to her ankles, troubled us; it charmed us but it made us uneasy, that is the word — uneasy.

Our cross-grained knowledge of the things of this world rather resented, even if instinct did not, the fresh delight of this creature — knowledge ever present, fundamentally afraid, taking refuge in life's depths, accustomed to accept the worst, self-enured to it.

Sophie had that winged, supple and balanced carriage which one so often finds in the women of America, the bearing of a people of the future, whom life carries ambitiously and lightly towards new forms of enterprise. . . . A brigantine of tender gaiety headed for the Infinite.

Parapine, who wasn't, you'd have said, at all given himself to any particular lyricism over matters of attraction, would smile to himself as soon as she went out of the room. . . . The simple fact of contemplating her did your soul good. . . . Especially mine, in justice be it said, which longed for it so much.

In order to catch her out, to make her lose a little of this pride, this sort of power and hold she had over me, in short, to render her slightly more human to fit our own paltry proportions, I used to enter her room while she slept.

And then was Sophie quite another sight to see — this a familiar one, yet all the same surprising, and also reassuring, as without show or circumstance, almost without bedclothes, lying across her bed, thighs anyhow, limbs glistening and relaxed, she tussled with fatigue. Deep within herself, she worried sleep and growled upon it. Only at such moments was she within my reach. No witchcraft or enchantments here. No mere facetiousness. Dead serious, this. She laboured on the further side of existence, squeezing still more vitality from it yet. Greedy she seemed at such times, drunk with gulping all she could of it. She was worth seeing too, after these bursts of snoring, all swollen with them still, and beneath her rosy skin her lungs and windpipe filled with ecstasy. She was droll then, and as ridiculous as any one else. She trembled with happiness several minutes more and then all daylight descended on her again and, as if after the passing of too ominous a cloud, glorious and delivered, she gathered up once more the impetus of her life.

All that can be embraced. It's nice to touch the precise moment when matter becomes life. You soar up to the infinite plains which stretch out before mankind. "Ooo!" you say: and "Ooo!" As much as you can you enjoy riding that moment and it's like great wide desert sands.

Of our number, her friends rather than her employers, I was, I believe, her most intimate friend. It's perfectly true, of course, that she deceived me regularly with the male nurse in charge of the agitated cases ward, an ex-fireman; for my good, as she explained, so as not to tire me out with the mental strain I had to make in all the work I had to do, which suited the outbursts of her own unruly nature not too well. Entirely for my own good. She cuckolded me for hygienic reasons. There was nothing to be said in answer to that.

All this state of affairs would have brought me really nothing but pleasure had it not been that the Madelon business still preyed on my mind. One fine day I ended up by telling Sophie all about it, to see what she'd say. It helped me rather, telling her my troubles. I had had enough of the endless wranglings and bitterness that this unfortunate love affair of theirs had caused, and that's a fact. Sophie entirely agreed with me.

As Robinson and I had been such friends in the past, Sophie thought we all ought to make it up — just make it up quite nicely and as soon as possible. This advice came from a good heart. They have many good hearts like that in Central Europe. The thing is, she wasn't really wise to the characters and reactions of our own people; with the best intentions in the world, she was giving me entirely the wrong advice. I realized that she had made a mistake, but I only realized it too late.

"You ought to see Madelon again," she suggested. "She must be a very nice girl at heart, from what you tell me. . . . Only, of course, you provoked her and have been thoroughly brutal and horrid to her! . . . You owe her an apology and ought even to give her a lovely present to make her forget about it all. . . ." That's the way they did things in her country. What she advised was, in fact, extremely courteous. But not a bit practical.

I followed her suggestion as much as anything because I glimpsed the possibility, beyond all these bowings and diplomatic how-d'you-do's and scrapings of a little foursome which would be utterly delightful if it came off — and revitalizing too. Under the pressure of circumstances and passing years, my friendly feelings were taking, I am sorry to observe, a surreptitiously erotic turn. Treachery! And Sophie, without meaning to, was now abetting me in this betrayal. Sophie was a little too curious by nature not to be attracted by risks. An admirable character with never any complaint to make and not anxious in any way to minimize life's occasions, distrustful on principle only. Just my kind. And she went a great deal further than that. She understood how necessary it is to change and change about in one's diversions between the sheets. An adventurous disposition, hopelessly infrequent in women, you'll have to admit. Definitely we'd both chosen well.

She would have liked me to give her — and that I can quite understand — some description of what Madelon was (made) like. She was afraid of appearing clumsy in the presence, in any intimacy, of a Frenchwoman — especially in view of the great reputation for particular artistry in this line with which the Frenchwoman's name has been associated abroad. As for having to put up with Robinson as well, it was only to do me a pleasure that she would consent to such a thing. The idea of Robinson didn't appeal to her in the least, she told me, but be that as it may, we were agreed. And that was what mattered. Very well then.

I waited a little while for a good opportunity to come along of dropping a word or two to Robinson about my scheme for a general reconciliation. One day, when he was in bursar's office, copying out medical reports in the big ledger, the moment struck me as opportune to broach my idea. So I interposed and quite simply asked him how he thought it would be if I approached Madelon with the suggestion that all the recent unpleasantness between us should be forgotten. . . . And might I not at the same time introduce her to my new-found friend, Sophie? And whether indeed he did not himself feel that the time had come for us all finally to make it up and be friends again.

At first, I noticed, he faltered a little and then he replied, but without much enthusiasm, that he didn't see why not. . . . Actually, I believe Madelon must have told him that I would pretty soon be making some attempt to see her again, on one pretext or another. About having slapped her that day she came to Vigny, I breathed not a word.

I wasn't going to risk getting myself sworn at in this place and be called a cad by him in public, because after all, even though we might be old friends, in this house he had to take his orders from me. Before all else, my authority had to be preserved.

It would do quite well to fix up this next step for January sometime. We arranged, because that was easiest, all to meet in Paris one Sunday; and then we could go to the movies together and maybe take a short turn round the Batignolles fair for a start, if it wasn't too cold. He had promised to take her to Batignolles in fair time. Madelon was crazy about travelling fairs, he told me. Well now, that was fine! Meeting again for the first time like that, it would be as well to choose a fête for the occasion.

MY, BUT THE FAIR WAS SOMETHING TO GET AN EYEFUL OF, THOUGH! And a head-full of, too! Crash and bang — and bang again! I spin you round here . . . And carry you off there! And I shake you up too! So there were we all in the mêlée, under the lights, in the hubbub, in the thick of it all. Walk up, walk up — this way for showing your skill and taking a chance and howling with laughter. Whoops! Every one tried in his overcoat to look his best, to appear gay and wide-awake; though a little distant all the same, just to show people that ordinarily one went elsewhere for one's amusement, to much smarter, more "expensive" places, as the English say.

Witty, light-hearted merrymaker was what you pretended to be, despite the cold north wind which also helped to humiliate you and that depressing fear of making too free with all these diversions and having to regret it next day and maybe for a whole week following.

A great regurgitation of music splutters up inside the roundabout. The roundabout can't quite throw up its waltz from "Faust", but it tries the best it can. Deep down it goes, that waltz, and then mounts up again, swirling against the round top overhead, which revolves like a great cake sprinkled with electric lights. The organ's not comfortable; it has a musical pain in its pipes, in its stomach. "Like some nougat? Or would you prefer a box of chocolates? Whichever you'd rather. . . ."

Of us, the four of us, at the shooting alley, it was Madelon, with her hat pushed back off her forehead, who showed most skill. "Look," she said to Robinson. "My hand's absolutely steady. And yet we had quite a lot to drink." That's to give you an idea of what the talk was like. We'd just come out of a restaurant. "One more go!" Madelon won it, Madelon won the bottle of champagne. Ting — Tiiiing! Whiz! Then I bet her something;

I bet her she wouldn't catch me in a dodge-em-car. "Oh, won't I?" she says gaily. "All aboard — we'll take one each!" Right. Come on, then. I was glad she'd accepted, it was a way of making friends with her again. Sophie wasn't jealous. She knew it was all right.

So Robinson gets in behind with Madelon in one car and I leap into another with Sophie and we have a grand series of collisions. Wallop — take that! Oh, you would, would you? But soon I realize that Madelon doesn't like it, doesn't enjoy being jolted about like this. Nor does Léon, either; he hates it. Obviously he's not at his ease with us. As we clutch at the barrier to get out, some little sailor boys come banging into us, men and women alike, and make us various offers. We swerve. We hit back. We laugh. More and more bruisers bear down on us from all sides amid the music and the excitement; you get such frightful dunches in these sorts of barrels on wheels that each time you bang into some one your eyes start out of your head. Whoopee! Violence and jollity — the whole gamut of the pleasures. I'd like to get in right with Madelon again before we leave the fair. I try awfully hard to, but she no longer responds to my advances. Positively not. She even sulks at me. She holds me at a distance. I'm baffled by this. In one of her moods again. . . . I had hoped for something better. Even physically she's changed; everything about her has changed. I notice that by comparison with Sophie she loses, she lacks lustre. Being friendly suited her better but you'd say now she feels above all this. That gets on my nerves. I'd gladly slap her again, to see if that would bring her to her senses; let her tell *me* what's made her so superior, tell *me* that to my face. Oh, but smile, damn you, smile! We're at a fête, you can't go moping around like this. Put some life into it!

She's found work with an aunt of hers, she tells Sophie after that, as we walk along. In the Rue du Rocher, with an aunt who makes corsets. Well, I suppose that's true.

From then on it wasn't hard to see that as a reconciliation the whole thing was a wash-out and my little idea, too, was all spoilt. Really a crashing failure.

We had made a mistake planning to see each other again.

Sophie hadn't properly understood what the situation was. She didn't see that we had only complicated things by meeting again. . . . Robinson ought to have told me; he ought to have warned me that she was through to this extent. . . . A great shame . . . Oh, well, there it was . . . Ting-a-ling . . . a-ling. Keep it up even so, and all the time . . . This way, this way for the "Caterpillar", as they call it. I suggest it; it's me who pays— I'm again trying to get back into Madelon's good books. But she continually gives me the slip, she avoids me; she manages, in the crowd, to get onto another seat in front with Robinson; I'm stymied. Waves of eddying darkness daze us. Nothing to be done, I conclude to myself quietly. And Sophie has come to agree with me. She realizes that in all this I've once more fallen a victim to my dirty mind. "You see? She's vexed. I think it would be better to leave them alone now. . . . We two might go and take a look round the Chabanais before going back. . . ."

That was an idea which greatly appealed to Sophie; back in Prague she'd often heard people talk about the Chabanais and there was nothing she would like better now than to see it with her own eyes so as to be able to judge for herself. But when we considered the money we had on us we worked out that it would cost too much. So there was nothing for it but to take a renewed interest in the fête again.

While we were in the Caterpillar, Robinson must have had a row with Madelon. Both of them got down off it, altogether loathing the whole fair. It certainly was unsafe to go near her to-night. To calm her and smooth things over, I suggested an all-absorbing form of entertainment — a competition fishing with rings for the necks of bottles. Madelon took to it with a bad grace. All the same, she easily beat the lot of us at it. She got her hoop just above the cork in the bottle and slipped it over before you could say knife. So. Click: and there it was! The showman couldn't get over it. He handed her out a demi Grand Duc de Malvoison as a prize. That shows you how clever she was at it. But still she wasn't satisfied. She at once announced she wouldn't drink it. "It's lousy stuff," she said. So then Robinson immediately uncorked it and drank it. Hup! And at one swig too. A funny thing for him to do, seeing that really as a rule, he didn't drink.

We came to an "Aunt Sally" after that — a zinc backdrop and a wedding group of dolls. Clang! Clang! We all had at it, with hard balls. . . . It's depressing how bad I always am at these things. I congratulate Robinson. He too can beat me at whatever game we try. But skill at games doesn't make him smile, either. Really, you'd have said both of them were being forced to some awful labour. There was no way to liven them up, to remove those frowns. "We're at a fair, d' you realize?" I yelled; really for once I was at my wits' end.

But it was all the same to them what I did to cheer them up, what I kept saying into their ears. "What's the matter with you?" I asked them. "How about the young ones? What are they going to do about it? . . . Isn't youth going to have its fling? I don't take it lying down, do I? And I'm ten pips older than the rest of you. Eh, honey?"

They looked at me then, Madelon and he, as though they were in the presence of some jibbering, glassy-eyed, foam-flecked idiot and it wouldn't be even worth while answering what I said. . . . As if there wasn't any use now in even trying to talk to me, for I certainly shouldn't understand what it was they tried to tell me. . . . Not one single word about anything. . . . "D' you think maybe they're right?" I asked myself and looked round very anxiously at all the other people round us.

But they were doing all the right things to be amused, these other people; they weren't just brandishing their little sorrows about like us. . . . Not at all. *They* were taking their share of the fun. A franc's worth here! Fifty centimes' worth there! Wise-cracks to laugh at, tunes to hear, sweets to suck. . . . They buzzed around like flies, even holding their little larvæ in their arms, livid, pasty-faced babies, so pale in the too great light they were almost on the point of disappearing. One little spot of pink these babies had left, that's all, about their noses, the place for catching colds and being kissed.

Among all the various booths, how well I recognized the "Stand of All Nations", as just then I passed it by — that brought back memories. But I said nothing to the others. Fifteen years, I said to myself, for only me to hear — there's fifteen years have gone by . . . A good long stretch. And one's lost a buddy or two on the way. . . . I wouldn't have thought they'd ever have shifted that "Stand of All Nations" out of the mud it was sunk in, back there at Saint-Cloud. . . . But it had been all nicely done up, almost as good as new, it was these days, and with music now and all . . . . Well . . . there it was. People were shooting away at it, thirteen to the dozen. A shooting alley always pays. There was the egg back again, like me; in the middle, on top of almost nothing, bobbing up and down. Two francs it cost to shoot. We passed on; it was too cold to have a go, better to keep on walking. But not because we hadn't enough money, there was plenty in our pockets still, money jingling, playing a little tune of the pocket.

I'd certainly have tried any darn thing at that moment to get some different idea into the heads of these people, but no one helped at all. If Parapine had been with us, no doubt it would have been even worse, considering how lugubrious he always was when there were people around. Fortunately, he'd stayed behind to look after the asylum. As far as I myself was concerned, I was sorry to have come. . . . Then, even so, Madelon began to laugh; but it was no fun hearing her. Robinson by her side sniggered so as not to be out of the picture. Then Sophie at that point suddenly started trying to be funny. That made the whole thing complete.

As we went past the photographer's stall, the fellow caught sight of us hesitating. We didn't want to go in and be photographed, any of us — except possibly Sophie. But there we soon were, facing up to the camera, thanks to hovering about so much in front of his entrance. We gave way to his drawled injunctions and stood there on the three-ply bridge of what purported to be a ship — he must have built it himself — *La Belle France*. The name was on the fake life belts. There we stayed a good long time, gazing straight ahead of us, defying the future. Other customers waited impatiently for us to come down off the bridge and they were already taking it out on us for having to wait by regarding us as frightful sights; and what's more, they told us so, and in no uncertain manner.

They were taking advantage of our not being allowed to move. But Madelon, she didn't care, she swore back at them with a good, full-flavoured Southern accent. She was beautifully audible. It was a wow of a retort.

Magnesium flare. We all snarl. A snap each. We're uglier than we were before. The rain comes through the canvas roof. The soles of our feet are sore — with fatigue and as cold as ice. The wind had found holes all over us as we posed, so that now our overcoats seem barely to exist.

We've got to start wandering around again among the booths. I don't dare suggest going back to Vigny. It's still too early for that. Now that one's chattering with cold, that mawkish music from the roundabout seizes the opportunity to jangle on one's nerves just a little bit more. The collapse of the whole world — it's that the confounded thing's giggling about. It screeches a message of defeat through all its silver-painted pipes. The tune sails off to fade into the near-by darkness across the smelly streets which run down from Les Buttes.

The little servant girls from Brittany cough far more this winter, of course, than they did last, when they hadn't been in Paris long. Their thighs, streaked blue and green, decorate as best they may the saddle girths of the wooden horses. The young men from the Auvergne, who pay for rides for them, careful little post-office officials, take careful precautions when they go to bed with them, as every one knows. They're not going to catch it a second time. The servant girls rock themselves to the revoltingly melodious racket of the roundabout and wait for love. They're not entirely happy about it, but they'll pose even when it's 10° below zero, because this is the supreme moment, the moment to try out their youthful charms on that permanent lover who may, perhaps, be somewhere here, already smitten, hidden among all the other saps in this chilled crowd. As yet, Love doesn't dare. . . . Everything comes to you in the end, though, as it does in the films, and along comes happiness as well. Let the son of the proprietor love you but one single day and he will nevermore leave your side. . . . That's what happens, that's all it needs. . . . Of course he's lovely, and of course he's handsome, and of course he's rich.

Near by in the kiosk next to the Métro, the old woman who keeps it doesn't care a cuss about the future; she's got conjunctivitis and she scratches her eyes with her fingernails and gradually makes them fester. It's a pleasure, after all, of a kind, an obscure pleasure costing nothing. Six years those eyes of hers have lasted her and they're itching better and better.

Groups of fair-goers, bunched against this death of cold, make haste to huddle round the tombola. They can't quite get there. Buttocks as warming-pans. So then they trot quickly across the leap for warmth into that knot of people opposite, outside the calf with two heads.

Hidden behind the public lavatory, a little fellow who's on the verge of unemployment is naming a figure to a couple up from the country, who blush with excitement. The morality cop's wise to their little game but the devil he cares; his meat for the moment is the exit of the Café Miseux. The whole of this week he's been watching the Café Miseux. Must be at the tobacconist's or in the back parlour of the dirty bookshop next door that this thing's going on. Anyhow, it's been reported for some time now. One of the pair, so information goes, procures girls under age, who appear to be merely selling flowers. Anonymous letters again. The chestnut merchant at the corner, he's also tipped the wink on his own. He had to, anyway. Everything that's on the pavement belongs to the police.

That sort of machine gun you hear going crazy in mid-air yonder, in short, sharp bursts of sound, that's only the motor bike of the chap in the "Wheel of Death." An escaped convict, so they say, but you can't be sure. At all events, he's already crashed through that tent of his twice in this same place, and then again two years ago at Toulouse. Would to God he'd smash the whole machine sometime and have done with it! Why can't he smash his face and his vertebral column once and for all, and then that would be enough said about *him*. Makes you mad to listen to him. . . . Take the tram too, with its bell and all — it's already killed two Bicêtre pensioners over there by the barracks, in less than a month. The bus, on the other hand, is a decent sort. It takes all the care in the world drawing up on the Place Pigalle, really rather irresolutely, blowing its horn, all out of breath, with four passengers in it who get down very carefully and slowly, like kids coming out of the choir.

Passing on from trays of trinkets to presses of people, from roundabouts to swings, we had come out at the other end of the fair ground, where there's a great empty, quite black, void for families to pee into. . . . About face, therefore! Retracing our steps on our way back, we ate some chestnuts to get a thirst up. A nasty taste in the mouth we got, but no such thing as a thirst. A worm too, in one chestnut, a dear little weeny one. Madelon hit on it. Of course; it would be her. Actually, it was from that moment onwards that everything began to go really wrong between us. Till then, we had kept ourselves more or less in check, but this incident of the maggot made Madelon absolutely furious. Just when she stepped aside to a gutter to spit the thing out, Léon went and said something to her, as if to prevent her. I don't know what it was he said nor what had come over him, but this turning aside to spit he suddenly didn't approve of at all. He asked her, pretty idiotically, had she found a pip in it? . . . It wasn't the thing to say, I admit. . . . And now Sophie managed to get mixed up in the argument; she didn't know what they were quarreling about. . . . She wished to know.

Then that annoyed them all the more, having Sophie, a foreigner, interfere — naturally it did. And at that point, a party of rowdies pushed between us and we got separated. They were young people out for a pick-up actually, but gesticulating, blowing whistles and letting off a whole series of terrified squeals. When we were able to join up again, Robinson and she were still fighting.

"Now's the time to go home," I thought. "If they're left here a moment or two longer in each other's company, they'll make a scene right in the middle of the fair. . . . That'll be enough for to-day." There it was; it was all a washout. "Shall we leave?" I suggested. He looked at me in a sort of surprised way. Still, that seemed to me the most reasonable and appropriate decision to make. "Well, haven't you really had enough of this fair?" I added. He signed to me that it would be better if I asked Madelon first what she thought about it. I didn't at all mind asking Madelon what she thought about it, but I didn't think it a particularly wise move.

"But we'll be taking Madelon along with us," I finally exclaimed.

"Taking her along? Where? Where d' you want us to take her to?" he said.

"Why, to Vigny, of course," I answered.

That tore it! I'd put my foot in it again. But I couldn't unsay it; I'd already spoken.

"Well, we've got an empty room for her at Vigny," I continued. "After all, it's not as if we hadn't plenty of rooms. . . . We could all have a little bite of supper together before going to bed. . . . Wouldn't that be much more amusing than staying here, freezing to death as we have been these last two hours. It'll be easy enough . . ." Madelon made no comment on my proposals. She didn't even look at me while I was speaking, but all the same she had missed not a word of what I'd just said. . . . Well, there it was, I *had* said it and that was that.

When I happened to stray a little to one side, she quietly came up to me and asked me whether I wasn't trying to put something over on her, inviting her to Vigny like this. I said nothing. You can't reason with a jealous woman like she was; it would only have meant a hell of a lot more flapping and fussing. Besides, I didn't quite know who and what she was jealous of. It's often difficult to distinguish all these emotions that are prompted by jealousy. Jealous of everything, I suppose she was, as one always is.

Sophie didn't quite know now what line to take, but she still tried hard to be pleasant. She had even taken Madelon's arm in fact, but Madelon was far too incensed and far too delighted at being incensed to be put off by any friendly gestures of that sort. With the very greatest difficulty, we threaded our way through the crowd towards the trams on the Place Clichy. Just when we were going to catch the tram, a cloud burst over the square and the rain came down in torrents. The heavens poured themselves down on us.

In a second, every car had been rushed and taken. "You're not going to affront me in public like this, are you, Léon?" I heard Madelon asking him as they stood there beside us. "You've seen enough of me, have you? Why not say so, then — *say* that you've had enough of me?" she went on. "Say it. Though you don't see me often. But you'd rather be alone with the other two, eh, would you? . . . You all go to bed together, I'll bet, when I'm not there . . . Tell me that you'd rather be with them than with me . . . Say it, so that I may hear you." And then, after that, she said nothing for a time, her face closed in a pout round her nose which stuck up in the air and dragged on her mouth. We were waiting on the pavement. "You see how I'm treated by your friends? Can't you *see*, Léon?" she began again.

But as for Léon — one must do him that amount of justice — he didn't answer her back, he didn't say anything to upset her, he stared across the square at the houses on the other side, at the boulevard and the traffic.

All the same, he could be a tough nut too when he wanted to be. When she saw that these attempted threats didn't work, she tried another tack and thought she'd put it over on him with tenderness while we still waited. "I love you a lot; listen to me, d' you hear that I love you a lot? . . . Do you realize at least how much I've done for you? Maybe it was just a pity I came to-day? You do love me a little though, don't you, Léon? You couldn't not love me at all . . . You have got a heart; speak, Léon, you do care a wee bit, don't you? Then why do you scorn my love? . . . We've had such lovely times together . . . But how cruel you are to me, Léon! You've shattered my dream, Léon. You've soiled it! You may well say that you've shattered all my illusions! Do you want me not to believe in love any more, eh, do you? And now are you wanting me to go away for good? Is that what you want?" All this she kept asking him while the rain came through the café awning.

It dripped down among all the people. Really she was just as he'd warned me she was. He hadn't made any of it up; that was what she really was like. I wouldn't have believed they could have come so quickly to such a pitch of emotional tension. But it was so.

As the cars and all the traffic made a great deal of noise all round us, I managed in any case to whisper a quiet word into Robinson's ear about the state of affairs, to see if we couldn't get away from her now and have done with it all as quickly as possible, seeing it was all such a failure; just give her the slip on the q.t. before everything went really wrong and there was some really bitter and deadly quarrel . . . I feared that might happen. "Do you want me to find some excuse?" I whispered. "And we all go back on our own?" "No, for heaven's sake not," he said. "Don't do that! She'd be quite capable of throwing a complete fit on the spot, and then we would never be able to stop her." I didn't press the point.

After all, perhaps he, Robinson, enjoyed having himself sworn at like this in public. Anyway, he knew the girl better than I did. As the downpour came to an end, we got a taxi. We dashed at it and there we all were, huddled up together inside it. At first no one spoke. Things were strained between us and I for my part had dropped quite enough bricks for the moment. It wouldn't do me any harm to wait a little while before I began again.

Léon and I took the folding seats in front and the two women sat in the back. On evenings when there's a fair on, the road to Argenteuil's very crowded, especially as far as the Gate. After that, it's a good hour's run down to Vigny, on account of the traffic. It's not much fun sitting for an hour opposite each other not saying anything, just looking at one another, especially when it's dark outside and you've got a rather anxious feeling about the people you're with.

Yet all the same, if we had stayed like that, angry, but each one angry within himself, nothing would have come of it. That's still my opinion to-day, when I think back on it.

When all's said and done, though, it was through me that we did start to talk again and then the quarrel resumed, fiercer than ever. One can never be sufficiently defiant with words; words don't seem to be saying anything much; they don't seem dangerous certainly, just little puffs of air, little clicks in the mouth, neither one thing nor the other, and as soon as they reach the ear easily apprehended by one's great soft grey lump of a brain. One's unsuspicious about words . . . and some misfortune ensues.

Among them, there are some hidden away under all the others, like pebbles. You don't particularly notice them and then suddenly they've made all the life there is in you tremble, all of it entirely, both in its weaknesses and in its strength. . . . And you're terrified . . . The thing's an avalanche . . . You swing in the air above a torrent of emotion like a hanged man . . . A hurricane has come up and passed on, and it's been much too strong for you, so violent that you'd never have believed it could be as violent as that and yet be made up of nothing but just feelings. . . . So one's never distrustful enough of words, that's the conclusion I've come to. . . . But let me first tell things in their order: the taxi was gently following along behind a tram as half the road was up. "Prrrr . . . Prrrr . . ." it went. A sewer every eighty yards. Only I didn't feel that was good enough, having that tram in the light . . . In my usual garrulous, childish way, I grew impatient. Really it was insufferable, such a small, funereal pace and such lack of decision everywhere. I hastened to break the silence, asking the tram what the hell was the matter with it. I watched, or rather — for you could hardly see now at all — tried to watch Madelon in her corner on the left at the back of the taxi. She kept her face turned towards the outside, towards the scenery, towards the night, to tell the truth. I was annoyed to notice that she was still as obstinate as ever. Damned tiresome I was in any case, I'll admit. I said something to her just to make her turn her head in my direction.

"Well now, Madelon," I asked her, "maybe you've some suggestion to make as to how we could all amuse ourselves, and yet don't like to put it forward? Would you like us to stop in somewhere before we get back? Let's have it."

"Amuse ourselves! Amuse ourselves!" she retorted, as if I'd insulted her. "That's all you people ever think about — being amused!" And then and there she heaved a whole series of sighs, deep sighs and so touching I've seldom heard their like.

"Well, I'm doing my best," I said. "It's Sunday to-day, you know."

"And what about you, Léon?" she turned to him. "Are you doing your best too, eh?" It was straight enough.

"Sure I am," he said.

I looked at them both as we passed the street lamps. Angry they were. Then Madelon leant forward as if to kiss him. It was obvious that not one chance of dropping a brick would be missed that evening.

The taxi was going very slowly again, because now there were strings of lorries every few yards along the road. Being kissed annoyed him and he pushed her away — rather roughly, I must admit. There's no doubt it wasn't at all a nice thing to do, especially not with other people present.

When we got to the end of the Avenue de Clichy, by the gate, it was already quite dark, the shops were lighting up. Even under the railway bridge, which always echoes so loudly, I heard her voice saying, "Don't you want to kiss me, Léon?" She was keeping on about it. He didn't answer. Whereupon she turned on me and apostrophised me directly. "What have you done to Léon to make him so horrid to me? Do you mind telling me that — at once? What awful things have you been putting into his head?" That's the way she went for me.

"Why, nothing, not a thing!" I told her. "I haven't said a word to him! I don't meddle in your quarrels."

And the best of it is that it was perfectly true; I hadn't said anything at all to Léon about her. He was free to do what he liked; it was his lookout whether he stayed with her or left her. It was none of my business. But there was no point in trying to convince her of this, she was no longer in her right mind, and we fell back into silence as we sat opposite each other in the taxi — but the atmosphere was so charged with an impending scene that this couldn't last long. She had taken to addressing me in one of those sharp tones of voice which I'd never known her use before, a voice as monotonous too as a person whose mind is quite made up. Huddled back as she was in her corner of the taxi, I could now hardly see her expression at all and that put me out a good deal.

Sophie had been holding my hand all this while. She didn't know what to do with herself now that things had taken this turn, poor child.

We were just beyond Saint-Ouen when Madelon again began on a full and frenzied inventory of the grudges she had against Léon, again asking him endless questions, at the top of her voice now, about his fondness for her and his fidelity. For us two, for Sophie and me, nothing could have been more embarrassing. But she was so overwrought that she didn't mind a bit that we were there to hear her, quite the reverse. Clearly too, it hadn't been very clever of me to shut her up in this box with all of us; it echoed and, with a temperament like hers, it made her want to treat us to a first-class scene. There again, this had been a master-stroke of mine, this taxi.

Léon gave no sign of life. In the first place, he was tired after the evening we'd just been spending together, and then, too, he lacked sleep; that was always his trouble.

"See here, calm down now!" I managed, even so, to get in edge-ways. "You can quarrel as much as you like, both of you, when we get home. You'll have plenty of time then."

"Get home?" she said then, in really an indescribable tone. "Get home? We'll never get home, I tell you. . . . And, anyway, I've had enough of all your revolting little tricks," she went on. "I'm a decent girl. I'm better than the whole lot of you put together. You set of pigs. . . . It's no good your trying to get the better of me. . . . You're not worthy of understanding me. . . . You're too rotten, all of you, at that, to understand me. . . . You're beyond all hope of understanding anything clean and beautiful."

In fact, she was attacking us in our self-respect, and there was a good deal more in this strain and it was just no good my keeping very much to myself on my folding seat and behaving as well as I could and not making a sound so as not to excite her any more; every time the taxi changed gear she went off again on a fresh tirade. The least little thing at such moments lets loose hell, and it was as if she was overjoyed at making us miserable; she couldn't help following up her instincts to the limit.

"And don't imagine that you'll get away with this," she continued to threaten us. "And that you're going to get rid of the little girl nice and quietly! Oh, no, you won't. You may as well know that, at once. No, it's not going to go as you'd like it to. You're disgusting, all of you. . . . You've caused my unhappiness. I'll wake you up, you dirty swine."

Then suddenly she leant over to Robinson and seized him by the overcoat and began to shake him for all she was worth. He made no attempt to extricate himself. I wasn't going to intervene. You'd even have thought Léon liked seeing her getting a little more excited still, because of him. He grinned; it wasn't natural; he shook like a puppet on the seat, while she yelled at him, eyes downcast, head dangling.

Just when, even so, I was going to make some little gesture of remonstrance to interrupt all this unmannerliness, she turned back and blazed out at me, blazed out what she had long been harbouring in her heart. Now it was my turn, with a vengeance. . . . There, in front of everybody.

"You be quiet, you dirty beast!" she said—just like that. "It's none of your business what happens between Léon and me! I'll have no further affronts from you,—d' you hear me? Eh? I won't have it. If you ever even raise a hand towards me again, I, Madelon, will teach you how to behave! Bah—cuckolding your friends and then striking their girl friends. . . . What a bloody nerve the bastard's got! Aren't you ashamed?" As for Léon, when he heard these truths uttered, he sort of woke up a bit. He wasn't grinning now. I wondered for a second whether there wasn't going to be a flurry and a fight, whether we weren't going to come to blows, but there wasn't room in the taxi to hit out, anyhow, with all four of us in it. That reassured me. It was too narrow.

Especially as we were now going fairly fast over the cobbles of the boulevards by the Seine and the taxi jolted too much even to move.

"Come, Léon," she ordered him then. "Come away; I'm asking you for the last time to come away with me! D' you hear me? Let them go to the devil. Do you hear what I'm saying to you?" A complete comedy!

"Stop it! Stop the taxi, Léon! Stop it, or I will myself."

But Léon didn't budge from his seat. He was all done in.

"You don't want to come then?" she began again. "You won't come?"

She had already warned me that, as far as I was concerned, the best thing I could do was to keep my mouth shut. That settled me. "Aren't you coming?" she kept repeating. The taxi was still speeding ahead, the road was clear now and we bounced about more than ever. We were being flung about all over the shop like luggage.

"Right," she concluded, as he made no answer. "All right. Very well! You'll have brought it on yourself. . . . To-morrow — do you hear me? — not a moment later than to-morrow, I'll go to the police station and I'll explain to them there at the police station just how Mother Henrouille fell down those stairs! Now d' you hear me, Léon? . . . Now are you happy? You've stopped pretending to be deaf? Either you come with me at once — or else, to-morrow morning, I go and tell them about it. . . . Well, are you coming or aren't you? Speak up." The threat was direct enough.

Then, at that point, he did decide to give her some sort of answer.

"But you're in it too, you know," he said to her. "You can't talk."

She didn't calm down at all when she heard him answer like that; quite the reverse. "What the hell do I care," she said, "whether I'm in it or not! You mean that we'd both go to prison? . . . That I was your accomplice? Is that what you mean? Well, there's nothing I'd like better."

And she began to squeal with laughter suddenly, as if in hysterics, as if she'd never known anything half as funny as that.

"But there's nothing I'd like better, I tell you. I like the idea of prison, d' you hear? Don't go and imagine you can scare me with this prison of yours! I'll go to prison as much as you like — but you'll go too, my good swine! At least, you won't not care a hoot about me much longer, see? I'm yours, all right, but you're mine too. All you needed to do was stay and not leave me back there in Toulouse. I can only love once — and once for good and all! I'm not a whore."

She was challenging us as well, Sophie and me, when she said that. She meant it in regard for faithfulness and for respect.

In spite of all this, we were still bowling along and he still made no move to stop the taxi.

"You're not coming then? You'd prefer to go to prison? Right! You don't care whether I denounce you or not? Or whether I love you or not? You don't give a damn for that, either? Nor for what will become of me? You don't care a damn about any of it, any-way, do you? Why not say so?"

"Yes, in a sense you're right," he replied. "But it's not you any more than any one else that I don't give a damn about. . . . And above all, don't go and take that as an insult! You're really quite sweet, if it comes to that. . . . But I've no longer any wish to be loved . . . I hate the thought of it."

She hardly expected to have a thing like that said to her, right there, to her face, and so much did it surprise her that she no longer quite knew how to carry on with the tirade she'd begun. She was considerably disconcerted, but somehow she managed to get going again. "Oh! So you hate the thought of it, do you? How do you mean, you hate the thought of it? Explain yourself, you ungrateful cad."

"Madelon, it's not you; it's all of it disgusts me," he answered her. "I've no wish for it. You mustn't blame me for that."

"What? What's that you say? Tell me again. . . . Me and all of it?" She tried to understand. "Me and all of it? Explain that, will you? What does it mean? Don't talk Chink to me — tell me in French, in front of the others, why now I disgust you. Don't you get the same kick out of making love as every one else, you great brute? You get excited then, don't you? Dare to say — in front of every one — that you don't get sexually excited?"

Despite her fury, there was something rather comic about the way she stuck up for herself with her remarks. But I didn't have time to laugh long, for she returned to the attack. "And what about him; he enjoys it well enough, whenever he happens to catch me in some dark corner! The dirty beast . . . with his dirty paws! . . . Let him dare to tell me it isn't so. . . . But why don't you all admit that you just want a change? Confess it. . . . That something new is what you're after. Some really no-limit party! Then why don't you get a virgin? You bunch of degenerates! You herd of dirty swine! Why do you bother with pretexts? You've tried everything and you're bored, that's all it is! Only now you've not even got the courage of your vices. Your own vices frighten you."

And then it was Robinson who took it on himself to reply. He'd lost his temper too, in the end, and he swore as loudly as she did.

"Oh, yes, I have!" he exclaimed. "I've plenty of courage and I daresay quite as much as you have! Only—if you really want to know the whole of it . . . why, it's every darn thing that repels me and disgusts me now. Not only you! Everything! . . . Love especially. . . . Your love along with every one else's. . . . All this sentimental monkey-business you're so fond of—d' you want me to tell how that strikes me? It seems to me like making love in a lavatory! Now do you understand? . . . And all this sentiment you rout out to keep me glued to you affects me like an insult, if you'd like to know. . . . And on top of that, you don't even suspect as much because it's you who 're such a numbskull because you don't realize things at all. . . . And you don't even guess that you make one sick. . . . It's enough for you· just to repeat all the drivel people talk. . . . You think that's quite all right. . . . That's quite enough, you think, because other people have told you there's nothing greater than love and that it would always work with every one and that it lasts for ever. . . . Well, as far as I'm concerned, you know what they can do with their love. . . . D' you hear me? It doesn't catch on with me, my good girl, that stinking love of theirs! . . . You're out of luck! You're too late! It no longer works with me, that's all! And that's what you go getting into such tempers about. Do you *have* to make love in the middle of all that's going on? And seeing the things one sees? Or maybe you don't notice anything? No, I think it's that you just don't care. . . . You play at being sentimental when really you're as tough a little animal as any one. . . . You don't mind eating rotten meat? Helping it down with that Love sauce of yours? That's good enough, is it? Not for me, it isn't. If you don't notice anything, you're lucky. That's because your nose is blocked up! You need to be as thick-skulled as you are, all of you, not to be sickened by it. . . . D' you want to know what there is between you and me? I'll tell you — there's the whole of life between us. . . . But maybe that isn't enough for you?"

"But I've a perfectly clean home," she retorted. "You can be poor and be clean all the same, can't you? When have you seen the place not clean back at home? Is that what you mean when you insult me like this? . . . And I'm clean in my person, too, let me tell you, sir! You may not be able to say the same yourself. And maybe your feet couldn't, either!"

"But, Madelon, I never said that. I never said anything like that. That it's not clean at your place? Can't you see you don't understand?" That's all the answer he could think of making, to calm her down.

"So you say you haven't said anything? Not *said* anything? Hark at him now, making me out to be lower than dirt and then pretending he hasn't said anything! You'd have to kill him to stop him telling any more lies. . . . There's not enough space on earth for such scum! The filthy, rotten pimp! Oh, no, there's not enough . . . The scaffold's what he needs!"

She wouldn't be quieted now. You could no longer get what they were saying in the taxi. You could only catch certain great words in the noise of the motor and the whir of the wheels in the wind and the rain which came flapping against the doors in squalls. Threats — the space between us was full of them. "It's vile of you . . ." she kept repeating. She couldn't now talk of anything else. "It's vile of you!" And then she flung down her last card. "*Are* you coming?" she asked him. "Are you, Léon? One . . . Are you going to come? Two . . ." She waited. "Three . . . You're not coming, then?" "No," he said, not stirring an inch. "And you can do what you like about it," he even added. . . . There was her answer for her.

She probably edged back in her seat, right back. She must have held the revolver with both hands, because when the flash came, it seemed to be straight from her stomach and then almost at once two more shots, one after the other. . . . Then we had the taxi full of acrid smoke.

The taxi didn't stop though. Robinson fell on to me, on his side, jerkedly, and he was burbling. "Hep! Hep!" He didn't stop grunting "Hep! Hep!" The driver must have heard.

He slowed up a bit at first, to make certain. Eventually he came altogether to a standstill, by a gas lamp.

As soon as he opened the door, Madelon pushed him back violently and then she jumped out. She clambered over the parapet and flopped. She bolted into the darkness across the fields, splashing straight through the mud. I called to her, but it wasn't any use; she was already a long way off.

I found it difficult to know what to do with the wounded man. To take him back to Paris was probably the most practical course. . . . But we weren't far now from our house. The local people wouldn't know what the whole thing meant. . . . We wrapped him up, Sophie and I, in overcoats and settled him in the same corner where Madelon had sat and had shot. "Go gently," I said to the driver. But he still went much too fast; he was in a hurry. The bumps made Robinson groan all the more.

When we got to the house, the driver wouldn't even give us his name; he was anxious because of the trouble it was going to get him into with the police, being a witness and so on.

He even said he was sure there were bloodstains on the cushions. . . . He wanted to get away at once without waiting. But I took his number.

Two bullets had hit Robinson in the stomach; maybe all three had; I still wasn't quite certain how many there'd been.

She had shot straight in front of her, I'd seen that. There was no blood from the wounds. Although, between the two of us, we held him up carefully, he stumbled a lot all the same and his head rolled. He spoke but it was difficult to understand what he said. He was already delirious. "Hep! Hep!" in a singsong voice. He had time enough to die before we got him in.

Our street had been recently repaired. As soon as we got to the gate, I sent the concierge flying off to fetch Parapine from his room. He came down at once, so with his help and a male nurse's, we managed to get Léon upstairs and into bed. Then, when we'd undressed him, we were able to feel and examine the walls of his stomach. They had already stretched a good deal to the touch and were now quite soft in certain places. Two holes, one above the other, I found, but not the third; one of the bullets must have missed.

For myself, if I'd been in Léon's shoes, I should have preferred an internal hæmorrhage; it floods your stomach and is over quick. The peritoneum fills up and that's the end of that. Whereas, with peritonitis, there's just infection to look forward to; it's a long business.

You could wonder, too, how he was going to set about having done with it all. His stomach was swelling, he was looking at us, already quite fixedly; he moaned — not too much, though. There was a sort of calm. I had already seen him when he was very ill and in many different places, but this time here was a case in which everything was unlike what it had ever been before, his gasping, his eyes, everything. We couldn't hold him now; you'd have said he was slipping away from minute to minute. He was sweating such large drops of sweat that it was as if the whole of his face had wept. At such moments it's a little embarrassing to have become as poor and as hard as one has. One lacks almost everything that might be of use in helping some one to die. One has nothing left inside one but things that serve the purposes of everyday life, — a life of comfort, one's own life, a damned insensibility. On the way you've lost confidence in things. You've chased and harried all the pity you had left in you carefully, right to the back of your system, a dirty little ball. You've pushed pity to the lower end of your bowels, with the rest of the refuse. That's the best place for it, you tell yourself.

There was I, standing by Léon's side so as to be of help to him, and never have I felt so awkward. I couldn't manage it. . . . And he couldn't find me. . . . He tried to and he just gaped. . . . He must have been looking for some other Ferdinand, one of course much greater than me, so as to die, or rather, for me to help him to die, more quietly. He made efforts to discover whether there hadn't been perhaps some improvement in the world. He was going over it all, poor wretch, in his mind, wondering whether men hadn't changed just a bit for the better while he had been alive; whether he hadn't sometimes, without meaning to, been unjust toward them. But there was nobody but me, really me, just me, by his side, — a quite real Ferdinand who lacked what might make a man greater than his own trivial life, a love for the life of others. I hadn't any of that, or truly so little of it that it wasn't worth showing what I had. I wasn't death's equal. I was far too small for it. I had no great conception of humanity. I would even, I believe, have more easily felt sorry for a dog dying than for Robinson, because a dog's not sly; whereas, whatever one may say, Léon was just a bit sly. I was sly too; we were all sly. . . . All the rest of it had fallen by the wayside and even those facial expressions, which are still some use by a death-bed, I'd lost as well. I had indeed lost everything along the road, I couldn't find anything of what you need when you're pegging out, only maliciousness. My feelings were like a house you only keep for the holidays. They were barely habitable. Besides which, too, a man wants a lot when he's in his death agony. A death agony in itself's not enough. You've to get a good kick out of dying, your last hiccups for breath must be made to provide a thrill as you sink below life itself and urea fouls your bloodstream.

Dying men go on whimpering still because they can't now get as much of a thrill as they want. . . . They clamour . . . and complain. . . . That's just the fuss misery kicks up as it slips out of life into death itself.

He came to slightly, after Parapine had given him an injection of morphine. He spoke to us then about this thing that had just happened. "It's better that it should end like that," he said, and then: "It doesn't hurt as badly as I'd have thought." When Parapine asked him where exactly he felt the pain, it was clear that he had already partly gone but also, in spite of everything, that he was keen to tell us something more. He hadn't the strength or the means to tell us. He wept, he suffocated and directly after-

wards he laughed. He wasn't like an ordinary ill man, you didn't
know what attitude to take towards him.

It was as if now he were trying to assist us to live. As if he
had sought out pleasant things for us to stay on for. He held onto
each of us by a hand. I kissed him. That is all there is that one
can do in such cases, without going wrong. We waited. He said
nothing now. A little later, an hour perhaps, not more, the
hæmorrhage did come, in an abundant, an internal, an overpower-
ing flood. It carried him off.

His heart began to beat faster and faster and then very fast
indeed. It was racing after the worn-out blood, thin and far away
in his arteries, tingling at his finger tips. The pallor spread up
from his neck and covered his whole face. The end came, choking.
He went, as if he had taken a spring, and gripping onto both of
us with both his arms.

Then almost at once there he was back again before our eyes,
his face strained, already beginning to take on his dead man's
weight.

We stood up and we disengaged ourselves from his hands. They
stayed up in mid-air, his hands, quite stiff, and blue and dis-
coloured in the light of the lamp.

Now, in that room, it was as if Robinson were a foreigner
who'd come from a frightful land, whom no one would dare
speak to.

PARAPINE KEPT HIS HEAD. HE SENT SOMEBODY OVER TO THE POLICE station to fetch a cop. It turned out to be Gustave, our Gustave, who had been on point duty and now was "on" late at the station.

"What a dreadful thing to have happened!" Gustave said, when he came into the room and saw Robinson. After that he sat down to puff and blow a bit, and also to have a drink at the nurses' table, which hadn't yet been cleared away. "Seeing as how it's a crime," he remarked, "it'd be best to take him along to the headquarters," and then he said: "He was a good chap, Robinson; he'd never have hurt a fly. I don't understand why she should have killed him." He drank some more. He shouldn't have. Drink went to his head. But he was fond of the bottle. It was a weakness with him.

We went and got a stretcher down from upstairs with him from the storeroom. It was far too late now to be disturbing the staff; we decided to carry round the body to the police station ourselves. The police station is a long way off, at the other end of the town, beyond the level crossing, the last house you come to.

So we set out, — Parapine holding the front end of the stretcher, Gustave Mandamour bringing up the rear. Only they didn't walk very straight, either of them. Sophie even had to guide them a little down the narrow stairs. I noticed at this point that she didn't seem particularly moved. Yet the thing had happened at her side and really so close that she might have been hit by one of the bullets while that maniac was firing. But Sophie, as I had already noticed on other occasions, needed time before she could get worked up enough to feel things. It wasn't that she was cold, she could be tempestuously the reverse, but she had to take her time about it.

I thought I'd follow them and the body a bit of the way, so as to feel quite certain it was really all over. But instead of following properly after them and their stretcher, as I should have, as a matter of fact I strayed across from side to side the whole length of the road and finally, once I'd passed those great school buildings that are next to the level crossing, I slipped off down a little road which leads at first between hedgerows and then plunges straight down towards the Seine.

Over the top of the railings I saw them make off with the stretcher into the distance, and they looked as if they would suffocate with the scarves of thick mist slowly wrapping round behind them. Down by the river the current pressed strongly against the barges wedged tight together against the lock. Off the Gennevilliers flats, the mist came in cold puffs, lolling across the eddying surface of the water, making it glisten under the arches.

That way, far in the distance, lay the sea. But at present there was nothing I could wish to feel about the sea. I had something else to do. Try as I might to lose my way, so as not to find myself face to face with my own life, I kept coming up against it everywhere. I met myself at every turn. My aimless pilgrimage was over now. Let others carry on the game! The world had closed in. We had come to the end. . . . As we had at the fair! . . . Being sorrowful isn't all; there ought to be some way of starting up the music again, of discovering a further poignancy. . . . But not for me; let others carry on. One's asking to have youth back again without seeming to ask for it. Impudence! But I wasn't ready to go on any longer now either! And yet I hadn't gone as far in life as Robinson had . . . I hadn't made a success of it; that much was certain. I hadn't acquired one single good solid idea, like the one he'd had to get himself severely manhandled like that. An idea as large as my own clumsy, great head, greater than all the fear that was in it, a beautiful idea, some splendid, some really comfortable one to die with . . . How many lives should I have had to live to get myself an idea stronger than anything else in all the world? There was no way of telling! It was all no good! My own idea, the ideas I had, roamed loose in my mind with plenty of gaps in between them; they were like little tapers, flickering and feeble, shuddering all through life in the midst of a truly appalling, awful world.

Perhaps it was going a bit better now than it had twenty years ago; it couldn't be said I hadn't made some little progress, but even so there was never any chance of my managing, like Robinson, to fill my head with a single idea, some really superb idea that was definitely stronger than death, nor of my ending up, just because of my idea, exuding joy and insouciance and courage—a lush demigod!

Then all of me would be full of courage. It would drip from every part of me and life would be nothing itself but the perfect pattern of courage, so that everything would run smoothly, all things and men from earth up to heaven. And so much love would one have, too, thrown in, that Death would be imprisoned in love along with joy, and so comfortable would it be inside there, so warm, that Death, the bitch, would be given some sensation at last and would end up by having as much fun with love as every one else. Wouldn't that be pretty? Ah, wouldn't that be fine? I laughed about it, standing there alone on the river bank, as I thought of all the dodges and all the tricks I'd have to pull off to stuff myself like that full of all-powerful resolves. . . . A toad swollen out with ideals! The fever had come, after all.

For the last hour, my friends had been looking for me. Especially as they had seen pretty clearly that when I left them I wasn't in particularly good shape. Gustave Mandamour was the first to catch sight of me under my lamp post. "Hey—Doctor!" he called. He certainly had an awful voice. "Come along. This way, Doctor. You're wanted at headquarters to make your statement. You know, Doctor," he added, but this he whispered in my ear, "you know, you're not looking at all well!" He came along with me. As a matter of fact, he lent me a helping hand. Gustave was very attached to me. I never reproached him about the drink business. I understood everything. Whereas Parapine was a little severe on him. He sometimes made him feel ashamed of himself about the drink. Gustave would have done a great deal for me. Why, he admired me! He told me so. He couldn't tell why. Nor could I. But the fact remains, he admired me. He was the only one.

We walked up two or three streets together until we caught sight of the lamp outside the police station. You couldn't miss your way now. It's the report he'd have to write which was worrying Gustave. Though he didn't like to tell me so. He had already made every one sign it at the bottom but even at that there were a lot of things which weren't in his report yet.

Gustave had a large head, my style of head; in fact, I could wear his kèpi, which just shows; but he was very forgetful about details. The ideas didn't come easily; he laboured when he talked and it was a good deal worse when he tried to write. Parapine would certainly have helped him to prepare his report but then Parapine hadn't seen any of it happen. He'd have had to invent things. And the Inspector didn't want any inventiveness in reports; he wanted just the truth, he said.

I was shivering as we climbed the little staircase at police headquarters. I couldn't tell the Inspector anything very much. I really wasn't well.

Robinson's body had been laid out there, in front of the prefecture's great rows of dossiers. Printed forms lay everywhere around the benches, together with cigarette stubs. On the walls scrawled insults to the police only half rubbed out.

"Did you lose your way, Doctor?" the Inspector asked me, at any rate quite cordially, when I did at last put in an appearance. We were all so very tired that we all rather burbled at each other in turn.

Finally between us we settled the times and the trajectories of the bullets, one of them being still embedded in the spinal column. It hadn't been found. He would be buried with it. They were hunting for the other bullets. The other bullets were somewhere in the taxi. It was a powerful revolver.

Sophie came to join us there. She had fetched me my overcoat. She kissed me and held me tight against her, as if I was going to die too or fly away. "But look, I'm not leaving you." I told her several times, doing my best to make her understand. "I'm not going away, Sophie." She wouldn't be reassured.

Standing around the stretcher, we embarked on a long discussion with the Inspector, who had in his time, as he pointed out, seen a great many crimes and not-crimes committed and catastrophes occur, and wanted to tell us about his various experiences all at once. We didn't like to leave for fear of hurting his feelings. He was really much too kind. He enjoyed having a chance to talk with educated people for once, instead of just ordinary toughs. So that to keep him happy, we dawdled on in his precious station.

Parapine hadn't a mackintosh. Listening to us lulled Gustave's mind. His mouth hung open as he listened and his thick neck stuck forward, as if he were dragging a cart. I hadn't heard Parapine employ so many words in conversation for many years now, not in fact since my student days. The whole of what had happened on this day had gone to his head. We decided to go home now, at last.

We took Mandamour along with us and Sophie too, who still from time to time caught me to her, her whole body strong with the strength of her concern for me and tenderness and a heart full also and overflowing and lovely. I felt the directness of it myself, the directness of her tender strength. It put me off my stroke; it wasn't my strength, and it was my own strength I needed to go off and croak superbly some day, like Léon had done. I hadn't any time to waste making faces. "On with the job!" I said to myself. But no idea came.

She wouldn't even let me turn back to go and have another look at the corpse. So I left without having another look. "Close the Door" it had written up. And now Parapine was thirsty. Thirsty from talking, I suppose. From talking too much, by his standards. When we got to the *estaminet* by the canal, we banged on the shutters for the space of a minute or so. Doing that reminded me of the road to Noirceur that time in the war. The same little light showed above the door, ready to go out any moment. Finally, the owner came in person to open to us. This fellow didn't know. We told him all about it and how such a dramatic thing had happened, a dramatic piece of news. "A love tragedy," was how Gustave described it.

This bar on the canal was opened just before dawn for the benefit of the bargees. Towards the end of the night the lock gates begin slowly to open. After that the whole countryside comes to life again slowly and starts to work. The banks of the river come apart from it very gently. They leave, they lift themselves up from the water between. The day's work steals out of the shadows. You begin to see everything again, all very simply, all hard. Winches close by, fences, timber yards yonder, and far away on the road men, too, returning from still further distances, coming towards us. They straggle into the grey light in little chilly groups. To start the day, they splash their faces with the morning light as they walk up past the dawn. They go on. All you can truly see of them is their pale, simple faces; the rest of them's still in the night. They'll all of them have to die too, some day. How will they take it?

They plod on up towards the bridge. Beyond it, little by little, they're lost in the flatness of the land and still more of them follow after these have gone, — more men, paler each time as the day rises up all round. And what are they thinking?

The man who ran the *estaminet* wanted to hear all about the drama and the details of it; he wanted to be told everything. Vaudescal his name was. A lad from the North; and scrupulously clean.

Gustave told him as much and more.

He made an endless rigmarole of the incident; all the things Gustave kept saying weren't the point at all; again we were getting lost among words, and as he was a little drunk, he would begin all over again. Only, of course, there actually wasn't anything to say about it, nothing at all. I wouldn't have minded listening to him, anyhow for a time, quite quietly, like a sleep, but the others wouldn't; they disagreed with him and that made him extremely angry.

In a rage he went and lashed out at a little stove. The whole thing came crashing down; the chimney flue, the grill, the red-hot coals. He was as strong as ten men.

And on top of that, he thought he wanted to show us how the Fire Dance really should be danced. Taking off his shoes and leaping among the glowing coals . . .

Gustave and the fellow who owned the place had had a row at one time over a slot-machine which wasn't licensed. Vaudescal was a crafty creature; he wasn't to be trusted very far. Those shirts of his always were too clean for him to be really honest.

He was a snooper and a sneak. The riverside's stiff with them.

Parapine suspected that Mandamour, now that he was drunk, was aiming to get him turned out. It was he who prevented him from doing his Fire Dance; and he made him feel ashamed of himself. We pushed Mandamour back to the other end of the table. There eventually he crumpled up and behaved himself, and amid smells and immense sighs, fell asleep.

Far away, the tugboat hooted; calling across the bridge, the arches one by one, a lock, another bridge, further, further away. . . . It was calling to itself every boat on the river, every one, the whole town, and the sky and the country and us, all of it being called away, and the Seine too, everything, — let's hear no more of all of this.